PRAISE FOR

Monica Ferris's Needlecraft Mysteries

"Ferris's characterizations are top-notch, and the action moves along at a crisp pace." —*Booklist*

"A comfortable fit for mystery readers who want to spend an enjoyable time with interesting characters." —*St. Paul Pioneer Press*

"Delightful . . . Monica Ferris is a talented writer who knows how to keep the attention of her fans." —*Midwest Book Review*

"Filled with great small town characters . . . A great time . . . Fans of Jessica Fletcher will devour this." —*Rendezvous*

"Another treat from Monica Ferris." —*Mysterious Galaxy*

"A fun read that baffles the reader with mystery and delights with . . . romance." —*Romantic Times*

"Fans of Margaret Yorke will relate to Betsy's growth and eventual maturity . . . You need not be a needlecrafter to enjoy this . . . Delightful." —*Mystery Times*

Sew Far, So Good

Monica Ferris

BERKLEY PRIME CRIME, NEW YORK

THE BERKLEY PUBLISHING GROUP
Published by the Penguin Group
Penguin Group (USA) Inc.
375 Hudson Street, New York, New York 10014, USA
Penguin Group (Canada), 90 Eglinton Avenue East, Suite 700, Toronto, Ontario M4P 2Y3, Canada
(a division of Pearson Penguin Canada Inc.)
Penguin Books Ltd., 80 Strand, London WC2R 0RL, England
Penguin Group Ireland, 25 St. Stephen's Green, Dublin 2, Ireland (a division of Penguin Books Ltd.)
Penguin Group (Australia), 250 Camberwell Road, Camberwell, Victoria 3124, Australia
(a division of Pearson Australia Group Pty. Ltd.)
Penguin Books India Pvt. Ltd., 11 Community Centre, Panchsheel Park, New Delhi—110 017, India
Penguin Group (NZ), 67 Apollo Drive, Rosedale, North Shore 0632, New Zealand
(a division of Pearson New Zealand Ltd.)
Penguin Books (South Africa) (Pty.) Ltd., 24 Sturdee Avenue, Rosebank, Johannesburg 2196,
South Africa

Penguin Books Ltd., Registered Offices: 80 Strand, London WC2R 0RL, England

This is a work of fiction. Names, characters, places, and incidents either are the product of the author's imagination or are used fictitiously, and any resemblance to actual persons, living or dead, business establishments, events, or locales is entirely coincidental. The publisher does not have any control over and does not assume any responsibility for author or third-party websites or their content.

PRINTING HISTORY
Berkley Prime Crime trade paperback edition / December 2009

Library of Congress Cataloging-in-Publication Data

Ferris, Monica.
  Sew far, so good / Monica Ferris. — Berkley Prime Crime trade pbk. ed.
    p. cm.
  ISBN 978-0-425-23275-0 (trade pbk.)
  1. Devonshire, Betsy (Fictitious character)—Fiction.   2. Needleworkers—Fiction.
3. Murder—Investigation—Fiction.   4. Minnesota—Fiction.   I. Ferris, Monica.
Unraveled sleeve.   II. Ferris, Monica. Murderous yarn.   III. Ferris, Monica. Hanging
by a thread.   IV. Title.
  PS3566.U47S48 2009
  813'.54—dc22
                                                                    2009035351

PRINTED IN THE UNITED STATES OF AMERICA

10 9 8 7 6 5 4 3 2 1

CONTENTS

Sew Far, So Good

Unraveled Sleeve

Acknowledgments

There really is a Naniboujou Lodge, and I wish to thank the owners and staff for allowing me to set this mystery there. And without the aid of Joan Marie Verba, the details, symptoms, and treatment of severe allergies would not have been so realistic. The many members of RCTN, an Internet newsgroup, have again proved themselves invaluable in keeping me on track with the esoterica of needlework. I would also, and again, like to thank my editor, Gail Fortune, for finding cracks in the original plot of this novel and making me mend them.

One

Through a ring of uniformed police officers, Betsy glimpsed the body of a very fat man. A ruby ring twinkled on the hand that loosely gripped a matte black gun. A beautiful young blonde draped in furs stood nearby, looking at Betsy slantwise through narrowed eyes. Beside her was an unshaven man in old-fashioned prison stripes. Next to him was an elegantly dressed man with a gray goatee, and clinging to the elegant man's arm was a bosomy woman in a white silk blouse unbuttoned nearly to the navel.

Officer Jill Cross, Detective Mike Malloy, and Godwin DuLac appeared suddenly, apparently from behind the circle of policemen. Mike barked, "All right, Betsy, who did it?"

Godwin said cheerfully, "Come on, Betsy, you're so *clever! Tell* him!"

Betsy looked at the suspects, but nothing clever occurred to her.

Jill said, "Mike needs to shoot the murderer. It's important." She began to shout, "Let's go, tell Mike who did it, so we can all go home! It's cold, Betsy, and we want to go home!"

Everyone began shivering. Except Betsy—and the corpse. Betsy looked between the cops' elbows, hoping the corpse would start shivering, which would mean he wasn't really dead. Then she could tell them it was a joke. That would be clever. But he didn't move. Betsy wanted to go home, too, but she had to answer them first. Who killed the man?

In a rising panic, she realized she had no idea.

"Maybe it's you, Betsy," said Godwin.

Jill and Mike exchanged surprised looks that turned suspicious and then gratified.

"I knew it, I knew it!" said Mike.

"No!" said Betsy. "No, no!"

"Why sure," said Mike, and added something incomprehensible that convinced Jill and Godwin.

"Wait, wait—" said Betsy, trying to think.

"Now *I'm* the clever one," said Godwin.

Jill came to take Betsy by the arm. "I'll hold her while you shoot her, Mike."

Mike drew a snub-nosed revolver and pointed it at Betsy, who couldn't think of something clever to say to save her life.

Just as the gun went off, Betsy sat up in bed with a gasp. Her heart was thumping painfully against her ribs. She was suddenly wide awake and breathing hard.

It was a sunny March morning, the temperature already approaching thirty. Betsy went down the stairs from her second-floor apartment, through an obscure back door beside the stairs, and down a short hall that led to facing doors, one to the parking lot and the other into the back room of her shop. She unlocked the shop door and Sophie slipped through.

"Goooooood morning!" chirruped a light tenor voice. "On time this morning, aren't we?"

"In body, if not in spirit," said Betsy.

"Are you awake enough to give me an opinion?" Godwin, a slim young man in a clingy cocoa brown sweater and black wool slacks, was striking a pose in front of the checkout desk. "What do you think?" he asked, doing a model's turn.

Betsy gathered her wits for a look at the sweater. Godwin had knit it himself of silk yarn. It had a barely raised pattern of diamonds across the middle of his chest that continued across his back, and the drape of the thin, soft material on his gently buffed arms and shoulders was exquisite.

"It's beautiful," said Betsy honestly, "and the fit couldn't be better."

"John says if I gain three ounces, it will show."

"That's why I would never own a sweater like that," said Betsy, who was sure she could lose five pounds without it showing.

"You're slimmer than you were back in December," said Godwin, giving her a judicious look. "You're dressing fatter than you are. You'll be surprised when you buy that new wardrobe."

"You think so?" Even the thought of shopping for an entire new wardrobe could not brighten Betsy's face.

Godwin had two remedies for gloom. If Betsy's spirits couldn't be raised by shopping, then, "You need a change. Take a trip to a nice, warm place, get a tan, meet some fun new people."

"Yes, well, I've got to finish up some things here, first."

Betsy's sister's estate had finally been closed. As of nine days ago, Betsy was officially wealthy. She hadn't done anything with the money yet except pay some overdue bills and take a few baby steps toward closing on the building her needlework shop and apartment were in. The current owner was a careful man, anxious not to give away anything more or sooner than necessary, so buying property from him was a slow process.

Betsy had never been rich before, but she had heard of people who won a big lottery prize only to be worse than broke a year later. She was determined not to make that mistake herself. But in her current state of chronic exhaustion, she was in no condition to make wise choices.

When her sister died, Betsy had found herself sole proprietor of Crewel World, and had been struggling with the two steep learning curves of needlework and owning her own business. But she found she enjoyed the challenges, and especially liked being her own boss. So far, the shop had stayed in the black. But now there was the added burden—a surprise to find it was actually a burden—of being sole inheritor of three million dollars. It would be so wonderful to just close everything down for a month, get really far away, think about what she wanted to do, where she wanted to go.

Or would she go anywhere? She liked Crewel World. Her customers were such nice people, most of them, loyal and patient. Besides, while needlework wasn't what Betsy would have chosen as a hobby, much less a career, it was surprisingly engrossing and created such beauty that she was no longer sorry it had been thrust upon her.

She looked around the shop. It had a big front window, splashed with counted cross-stitch patterns and needlepoint canvases—mostly in green because St. Patrick's Day was near, but also tulips and other spring flowers, and Easter-themed projects and patterns. Back here it might have been dim, but well-placed track lighting put light everywhere it was needed. A dividing set of shelves cut off the rear portion and disguised the long, narrow shape of the shop.

Then she noticed the warm smell of coffee. Betsy went to pour herself a cup. "Did you put up the canvases that came in yesterday?" she asked, and was surprised at how slow the words came out. She was tired. Actually, more than tired, she was exhausted.

"Not yet. Look, why don't you take the morning off? Go back upstairs and sleep some more."

She shuddered. "No, I don't want more sleep. The problem is not getting to sleep, it's the nightmares." She went to the big desk that was the shop's checkout counter.

"Pretty bad?"

"Awful," she said frankly. "Terrifying. I might have known this would happen; I'm not cut out for murder investigations. Twice now, people I knew and liked have turned out to be murderers. And another one tried three times to murder me. I don't want to do this anymore—" Betsy turned away from Godwin's look of compassion. It wasn't sympathy she was after. She thrust her fingers into her hair. "Have you vacuumed yet?"

"In a minute. I'm sorry sleuthing is making you so miserable, because I *love* it when you prove you're so much more clever than everyone else, even the police. And I love it that you're so good about telling me first. In a gossipy town like Excelsior, that makes me Queen."

Betsy couldn't help smiling. "You mean King, don't you?"

"No, honey, *you're* the King. Queen is my place, and *much* more my style." He winked at her and strolled to the back room to get out the Hoover.

Still smiling, Betsy took the deadlock key from a desk drawer, went to the front door to unlock it and turn the needlepointed sign around so OPEN showed through the window. She paused at the white-painted old dresser just inside the door. Ads for stitching retreats, classes, and conventions were tucked into the frame of its dim mirror. One was for a stitch-in to be held in Fort Myers, Florida. *Don't I wish, she thought.*

Thrust out from the opposite wall was an old, white, glass-fronted counter. On top were three sample sweaters with patterns next to them, and a plastic chest with little transparent drawers filled with beads of every size, shape, and color, along with threadlike beading needles. There were two books on beading leaning against it, but the woman who had loaned Betsy her beaded purse had picked it up on Friday and Betsy hadn't managed to borrow another beading project to replace it. She was not remotely skilled enough to do beadwork worthy of inspiring a customer.

However, that forest green sweater was hers. One of her customers, Rosemary, was an excellent teacher, and Betsy was especially proud of the cable stitching. Betsy gave it a little rearranging tug as she went by. The glass-fronted cabinets held back issues of stitchery magazines, the more expensive and fragile wools that couldn't bear the repeated touch of fiber fondlers, and unperused needlework books for customers who insisted on extra-fresh editions.

Betsy went back to the checkout desk to put the key away and place the forty dollars opening-up money in the cash register.

The shop's front door opened with an electronic *bing* and Betsy turned to her first customer of the day. It was Mrs. Savage, who hoped to match a tomato red shade of needlepoint wool. Betsy directed her to the triple row of wooden pegs on the long wall, hanging with loosely knotted skeins in what only seemed like every possible color.

Betsy took a thin stack of painted needlepoint canvases from the desk to the rack of fabric doors hanging on a wall and began to attach the canvases with drawing pins.

Bing went the door again and Betsy turned to see a hearty-looking man with an outsize attaché case grinning at her. "Ms. Devonshire?" he said, and when she nodded faintly, he came forward, hand extended. "I am very, very glad to meet you!" he said in a deep, rich voice that ran up the scale to *glad* and then back down again, shaking her hand with a grip that stopped just short of painful.

He swung the case up onto the desk and opened it. Inside were eight-by-ten color photographs of houses. Big houses. "I'm sure you must be thinking about moving out of that small apartment of yours into something much more suitable for a person of your income," he began.

"No, I'm not," said Betsy.

His surprised chuckle started high and ran steeply down the scale, and Betsy smiled, not because she liked it, but because it reminded her of Throgmorton P. Gildersleeve—old-time radio's most famous pompous ass. "Very nice, you have an interesting sense of humor," he said. "I almost believed you there for a second. Now, I have a house—not too large, but a beautiful house, built just over a year ago, right on Lake Minnetonka, not ten minutes from—"

"I am not interested in buying a house. I like living over my shop."

"You can't possibly mean that."

"Why not? My sister lived upstairs, and the money I inherited came from her."

The woman seeking tomato red wool came over to the desk. "What do you think, Betsy? Is this a match? Or is this one closer?"

"I beg your pardon, but Ms. Devonshire and I are discussing—"

But Betsy interrupted him, saying to her customer, "Let's go stand by the window, Mrs. Savage. We can tell better in natural light." She said over her shoulder to the salesman, "Please go away, can't you see I'm busy?" Anger put steel in her tone, and by the time she and Mrs. Savage agreed that one of the skeins was a near perfect match to the sample Mrs. Savage had brought in, the salesman had gone.

"He must be new to the real-estate business, quitting that easy," remarked Godwin after Mrs. Savage had also left. "I thought that fellow on Saturday was going to set up camp."

The phone rang, and Betsy answered it. The caller mispronounced Betsy's name ("Devon-shyre" instead of "Devon-sheer"), and wanted Betsy to know that another American Family would become homeless every minute they talked, and would Betsy care to make a substantial contribution to an organization whose goal was to build a tent city on the grounds of Minnesota's state capitol building—

Betsy kept a lot of American Families in their homes by hanging up at that point.

By noon the shop, while crowded, had exactly two paying customers. The other people were there to sell Betsy a Lincoln, a Chrysler, land in Arkansas, Florida, and Mexico; to collect for crippled children, blind adults, homeless horses, and women whose emphysema was caused by secondhand smoke; to double Betsy's inheritance in six months or six weeks; to reminisce about how she and Betsy had been best friends in grade school, where they had promised that if one ever got rich she would share it with the other; and to sign Betsy up for cellular phone service, cable television, satellite television, and a professional interior decoration of the new house this gentleman with him wanted to build to Betsy's specifications on land he was also prepared to sell her.

Staring around wildly, Betsy began to cry, which caused Godwin to lose his temper and chase them out with a steel knitting needle.

"That decorator I think I could've taken," Godwin said with a snort when the shop was empty of all but the woman walking her fingers through the counted cross-stitch patterns in the half-price box. Betsy's tears turned to laughter at that, but the laughter died instantly when she heard that infernal *bing* that meant someone else was coming in. She turned a stony face to the front door.

Shelly Donohue was standing there, looking startled. "Wow, something's got your underwear in a knot," she said, a half-formed smile fading.

Shelly was a medium-sized woman who worked in the shop part-time. She was about thirty-five, with long hair pulled into an untidy bun at the nape of her neck. She wore a full-length, down-filled coat and boots that looked suitable for walking on the moon. In honor of the sunshine, the coat was open.

"It's all right for me to be here," she said, because school was in session and she taught fourth grade. "My students are on a field trip to the Minneapolis Art Museum this afternoon. What's wrong, anyway? You don't look well."

"I'm just tired," said Betsy, shoving her fingers into her hair, a gesture she was afraid might become habitual.

"And every sales rep on the planet is on the phone or here in person, trying to cut himself a slice of Betsy's inheritance," said Godwin. "I've been telling her all morning she should go to Cancún for a week, get away from all this. She could soak up some rays by day and party by starlight. Enough strawberry margaritas will scare away the nightmares while she gets a break from the money mongers."

"Nightmares?" echoed Shelly, coming to put a hand on Betsy's arm. "How awful! I just hate it when I have a nightmare." A smile with a trace of envy in it appeared. "What are you dreaming, the IRS is after your money?"

Godwin said, "This is serious! She's dreaming about death and corpses—"

"Oh, ish!"

"Hush, Goddy," said Betsy, adding to Shelly, "They're about what you'd expect after what I've been through lately. Kind of a delayed reaction to December, I guess." Around Christmas, someone had tried to murder Betsy. "I'll be all right pretty soon. I'd take Godwin's advice, but we're shorthanded as it is, and Joe is being difficult about selling me this building, and anyway I've got some ideas for changes I want to make in the shop, so I need to talk to an architect or—" Shelly and Godwin exchanged swift glances of dismay. "What?"

"What kind of changes?" asked Shelly.

"Nothing drastic," said Betsy. "I was thinking of replacing that dresser up by the front door—"

"No, no, you can't do that!" said Godwin.

"Why not?" asked Betsy. "The drawers don't go back far enough to hold the bigger canvases, some are curled up in there. And the veneer on the top is lifting."

Godwin said, "Honey, there are people who, if they walk in here and don't see that dresser, will think they've come to the wrong place."

"Okay, we can find a carpenter who will build us a dresser just like the current one, only two inches deeper front to back."

Shelly turned and walked to the dresser. "But don't you see? If you push out two inches into the walk space here, then you'll have to cut two inches off the counter." She turned and put a hand on the counter. "You can't do that; I just love this old counter."

"So do several antique dealers who have offered me enough to pay for both a new counter and a new dresser."

"Oh, Betsy, please don't sell this counter! Don't change anything! This place is perfect as it is!"

"I agree," said Godwin, nodding sincerely.

Tired as she was, Betsy understood what was really going on. Betsy's sister Margot had founded Crewel World, had brought in the counter and the dresser, had put the wooden pegs on the wall and the curious set of canvas doors. She had been a compassionate but driving force in this town, with countless friends. So long as these things remained, Margot was, in a way, still here.

Shelly looked a little ashamed. "I know, don't say it, we don't have the right to make demands like this. Crewel World is yours now, so you get to do whatever you want with it." She looked around, her smile upside down. "At least you didn't close it."

"For which there are a lot of grateful people," added Godwin. "But you shouldn't make any decisions about changes right now. You should go away for a week, even a couple of weeks, then you'll see the place with new eyes, and be better able to decide what you really want to do."

"But don't go anywhere Godwin suggests," said Shelly. "His favorite places are like Animal House every night. In fact, go farther away than Mexico. Have you ever been to Spain?"

"No, just England and France."

"Well, I went to the Costa del Sol one winter, and it was marvelous. It's warm and sunny, it has sleepy little towns with winding narrow streets, and there's the Mediterranean Sea to bask beside. Barcelona is nearby, with a cathedral you have to see to believe, and there's a castle called Montserrat—"

"Spain's too far!" objected Godwin.

"But that's the attraction," replied Shelly. "It's far from here, way over on the other side of the Atlantic. And the Costa del Sol has these lovely little shops, nothing like here at home. I bought an alabaster statue of a medieval saint for about twenty dollars, very crudely done, but powerful, his eyes just glower at you—"

Godwin said, "Yes, the very thing for someone haunted by bad dreams. Cancún is just as warm and it's lively and never boring. Their beaches are really nice, and there are dolphins who will come and play with you." He sighed. "Wish I could go there now myself."

"But Spain's so exotic, and full of history, with—"

The conversation, which was bordering on argument, cut off when the door sounded, marking the arrival of three members of the Monday Bunch. A group of women stitchers who met every week at Crewel World to work on projects, the Monday Bunch gave advice and support to one another, and indulged in Excelsior's favorite pastime, gossip.

Within a few minutes two more arrived, making six, counting Shelly. Stout Kate McMahon, with her graying red hair and broad smile, was finishing up a hardanger project. Betsy had thought to take up hardanger, and so she came to stand behind Kate and watch.

"What is that, a satin stitch?" she asked.

"Not exactly. I push the needle in here, coming up here, four threads up. You have to watch carefully, because this square has to match exactly the square across from it, and also line up with this square and this square. See, here or here is wrong."

Betsy leaned closer and felt her eyes cross. She couldn't quite see what the difference was. "I think I need to be more nearsighted to do hardanger."

Kate laughed. "Yes, I take my glasses off when I do this."

Betsy went back to her chair and took out the needlepoint project she was working on, a pillow with rows of geese in various poses alternating with the heads of daisies. If it went on as well as it had begun, she planned to display it in her shop.

Godwin, working on a lush and colorful counted cross-stitch pattern of a medieval castle, said, "Betsy's thinking of taking a vacation. March in Minnesota is the pits, don't you agree?"

Alice Skoglund, a broad-shouldered woman with a strong chin and a tendency to verbal faux pas, agreed. "I hate early spring. That's when the snow starts to melt and uncovers all the little animals that died during winter."

"Mercy, Alice!" exclaimed Martha Winters.

"Well," she said, only a little abashed, "it is."

Bing! went the door to the shop.

"That's why I like to fly away to Cancún," said Godwin, consulting his pattern and grimacing at the number of half stitches in the section he was working. "I've suggested Cancún to Betsy." He glanced up toward the door. "Oh, hi, Jill. We're talking about a getaway for Betsy. She really needs one. Can you join us for a while?"

They all looked at Officer Jill Cross standing just inside the door, big in her uniform, her smooth pale face looking back placidly. "For half an hour," she said, lifting a bulging plastic bag with the Crewel World logo on it.

"I think Betsy should go to romantic Spain," said Shelly.

"Too far," said Godwin. "Go to Mexico—you don't have to worry about your internal clock getting all wonky."

"I think she should go to Hawaii," said Kate. "It's tropical, but it's also America."

"There are Minnesotans who winter in Mexico," noted Martha, around the end of a piece of floss she was moistening in her mouth. "You might find yourself in the middle of Old Home Week down there. That would be nice."

Betsy frowned at the thought of Minnesota sales reps on a vacation won by never missing an opportunity. Suddenly distant Spain seemed more attractive.

Shelly spoiled that by saying, "Liz and Isobel are going to Spain. Actually, so is Father Rettger—but I think he's going to Compostella, not Costa del Sol."

Godwin, seeking to change the subject, said, "Martha, some people think it's *not nice* to lick your floss."

Martha, complacently relicking her floss before threading her needle, said, "Some people should find more important things to worry about."

Jill came to the table with a small sheet of paper in her other hand. "Here," she said, putting it in front of Betsy.

Betsy picked up the sheet of paper. It was an announcement for a stitchers' retreat. "Where did you get this?"

"Off the mirror on your dresser." Jill gestured with a minimal nod of her head toward the front of the store. "I saw it when Godwin put it up there a couple of weeks ago, but it got covered up by that announcement about CATS." CATS was a big convention for stitchers coming to Minneapolis in November.

"May I see that?" asked Kate, and Betsy handed her the flier. "Oh, Naniboujou! I've heard of that place." She twisted around to look up at Jill. "But it's way up on the North Shore, isn't it? Practically on the Canadian border."

"Brrrr!" Godwin shivered dramatically. "It's still the dead of winter up there!"

"It's still the dead of winter down here," said Betsy, surprised.

"No, it isn't," said several women, equally surprised. Pat said, "Why it's only March and there's bare spots on the ground already, and if you look at the branches of the trees, you can see the buds are swelling. I'm expecting a crocus any day now."

"I've been to Naniboujou," said Martha Winters, working her needle under some finished stitches on the back of her linen before starting to stitch—she might be a floss licker but she would never tie a knot at the end of her floss. "Only in the summer, of course. But it's a beautiful place, a lodge with a big dining room that serves wonderful food, right across from a state park with miles of hiking trails. Lake Superior is right outside your window, and they have these old-fashioned Adirondack chairs down on the shore, so you can sit with a glass of iced-tea and watch the waves."

"Just the thing to do in March on the North Shore," said Shelly. "Wade a mile or two through six feet of snow in a state park, and rest afterward on the lakeshore with a glass of iced tea while watching the next blizzard blow in from Canada."

Even Martha laughed at that.

"Did they have a band on Saturday night?" asked Godwin.

"No band, no bar, no television," said Martha. "Not even a phone in your room."

Kate handed the flier back to Betsy. "The application is still on this. Which isn't surprising, nobody we know would want to head north this time of year, would they?"

There was a murmur of agreement.

Betsy looked up at Jill. She was a tall woman, strongly built—though most of her bulk was from the bulletproof vest under a heavy shirt and winter-weight jacket. She had ash blond hair and equally pale eyebrows on a face that rarely showed what she was thinking. She was looking at Betsy now with that calm, unreadable face.

The calm transmitted itself to Betsy. *Nobody I know, no television, and no phones, no phones, no phones*, thought Betsy. "If the stitch-in is this weekend, can we still get a room?" she asked.

"I called in my reservation six weeks ago," said Jill. "And got the last room. I had to take one of the expensive ones, with a fireplace. It's also a double. The stitch-in is just for the weekend, so you can move into your own room on Monday. I'm staying a week; I had to take some vacation or lose it, and I thought I'd get in some cross-country skiing." Jill was made for Minnesota; Betsy was sure she considered summer to be a sad break from winter sports.

Betsy looked again at the brochure. The room had knotty pine walls, the bed looked comfortable. One whole week. She looked at Godwin. "Can we get enough part-timers for you to manage a whole week?" she asked.

Godwin sighed dramatically—but he did everything dramatically. "Well, I don't know if I should try to help you, if you won't take my advice and go someplace warm and fun." Then he smiled and said, only a little less dramatically, "All right, Cancún won't go broke because you don't go there this year. And of course we'll manage. Didn't two of our part-timers complain last week that they weren't getting enough hours? We'll manage just fine."

Two

They left early Friday morning. Betsy, still wan and heavy-eyed, was also helplessly annoyed as she walked to Jill's car. She was being followed by a tall, redheaded woman in a chartreuse coat who wanted Betsy to buy a portfolio of Internet stocks. The woman had a fistful of documents as vividly colored as she was, and was talking very rapidly about e-this and dot-that.

Jill, though not in uniform, got out of the driver's side of the car and said, "Eh-hrrrum!" The woman glanced at her, stopped in her tracks for a second look, then turned and hurried away.

"How do you do that?" asked Betsy, putting her two suitcases down. "I actually snarled at her, but she kept on talking. All you did was clear your throat."

"I look at them like I think they may resist arrest," replied Jill placidly. She went to the trunk of her car, opened it, and put Betsy's suitcases in beside her own.

There were other things in the trunk: a Dazor light, a sewing frame, a box marked WINTER SURVIVAL KIT, snowshoes.

Betsy pointed to the snowshoes. "What are they, antiques?"

Jill smiled. "Well, I did make them back when I was sixteen."

"What, you liked to make reproductions of old things?"

Jill frowned very slightly. "No, people still use them. When you want to walk over deep snow, there's nothing as good as snowshoes." She closed the trunk. "That state forest right across the road from Naniboujou has an interesting waterfall. I thought I might walk back in to see it."

"What's so interesting about it?"

"Half of it disappears into a rock."

Betsy couldn't think what to ask about that, so she looked at the cross-country skis fastened to the rack on top of Jill's car. There were two pairs, she noticed. Jill said, just a little too casually, "Grand Marais has some very easy cross-country ski trails."

Betsy let her face reflect her thought: *As if.* She went to get in the passenger side of the big old Buick. She'd tried cross-country skiing with Jill and been surprised and disappointed at the exertion required. Like her cat, Betsy was not keen on exercise.

The wide, comfortable seat of the car welcomed her. Betsy fastened her seat belt and relaxed with an audible sigh as Jill pulled away from the curb. "Say, Jill," she said, "would you consider being my bodyguard when we get back? Easy job, you'd just stand behind me clearing your throat at all those dreadful people who insist on a share of my money."

"You don't need a bodyguard. Going off for a week to an unannounced destination will discourage most of them. When you're not there to hound, they'll go hound someone else. You're going to have to be firm and persistent with the rest. Which I've seen you being, when you're in your detective mode."

Betsy grimaced. "I hope you got a good look, because those are going to be mere memories from now on. I'm resigning my commission and turning in my badge. Neither of which I was ever issued, by the way."

Jill gave Betsy a faintly surprised look. "I thought you liked detecting."

"No, not at all. I certainly didn't go looking for cases, they just sort of happened. And I didn't know what I was doing. Clues more or less fell out of the air right in front of me."

"Huh," remarked Jill, then went wordlessly back to driving.

They went past the beautiful Victorian Christopher Inn, then over the bridge and onto Highway Seven, heading toward Minneapolis. Betsy looked out the window at trees and houses passing by. The road was clear and dry, white with dried salt—whiter than the crunchy honeycombed snow pulling its filthy skirts away from the verge. The sky was a light, cloudless blue.

"But that only means you're a natural," said Jill, suddenly picking up the topic again.

"Yes, but I'd have to harden my heart too much to keep doing it, dealing with crime and criminals, and I wouldn't even want to know how to do that."

"Do you think my heart is hard?"

That surprised Betsy. "No, of course not! But you—you're—" Betsy had to think for a moment. "You don't let things hurt you. You have this . . . I don't know, a kind of imperviousness. You don't get angry or scared."

"I was raised to—not to let things get to me," said Jill, and from the way that was wrenched out of her, however cleanly, Betsy knew it was a confession. Jill was as reticent about her upbringing as about her feelings. "But just because I don't break into tears or fall into a rage every time I'm sad or angry doesn't mean I don't feel those emotions."

Betsy, embarrassed, had to think a few moments before she could reply. "How do you deal with the ugliness you face every day?"

"It's not every day—this is Excelsior, after all, not Chicago or DC. And what I do is, I don't take it personally. I think of myself as a street sweeper or garbage collector, taking the crud off the streets. The rotten egg isn't stinking just to annoy me. And somebody has to clean it up."

Betsy nodded. "I'm glad you can do it. The world would be impossible without police. But with me, it's different. I get involved at a personal level, because it involves people I know. And I can't do that anymore. Not when I dream all night about friends who turn out to be murderers."

"Not all of us do."

"But in a recent dream you were at the front of the pack, shouting at me to tell you whodunit. And I had no idea." Betsy frowned. "That was probably the oddest part, you shouting. You have never shouted at me, ever. In fact, I don't think I've ever heard you shout at anyone." She smiled. "But you clear your throat real good."

Jill chuckled softly, then said, "See how unreal the dream was? In your dream you couldn't solve it, but in real life you can."

"Please. I'm absolutely sure that next time I'm faced with a case, it will be just like what I dreamed: I won't have the first clue."

"I take it you never solved a mystery before you came here and figured out who murdered your sister?"

"Absolutely."

Jill fell silent. Betsy sighed and closed her eyes. The car was warm, the seat comfortable, Jill the kind of driver who inspires confidence. Before she realized it, she dozed off.

She was on a train at night, looking out the window into utter darkness. Suddenly a man wearing a Richard Nixon mask slammed through the door into the car, and shot the woman in the first seat with a silenced gun. The woman slumped sideways, and the man ran away, but everyone else in the car immediately turned to Betsy. One said, "Who was that masked man?" in a serious voice, which at first terrified Betsy because she had no idea, then amused her so much she started to giggle, which woke her up.

"What?" asked Jill.

"Stupid dream. Tried to be a nightmare, didn't quite make it." Betsy yawned and looked out the car window. They were on a section of freeway lined with concrete walls, some striated, some smooth. The marked sections had remnants of vines clinging to them, demonstrating the purpose of the striation. "Where are we?" she asked.

"Six-ninety-four East, about to cross the Mississippi. Not even out of the Cities yet."

"How do we get to the North Shore?" asked Betsy. "Follow the Mississippi? It originates in Lake Superior, doesn't it?"

"No, it starts as a brook you can step across in the upper central part of the state. But the North Shore does refer to Lake Superior. We drive about a hundred miles north to Duluth, then follow the Superior shoreline northeast to Grand Marais, then sixteen more miles to Naniboujou."

"Grand Marais," repeated Betsy. "That's a beautiful name. Is it a big city?"

"It's sometimes called the Scandinavian Riviera." Jill smiled, as if at a joke.

"What?" asked Betsy.

"You'll see."

"What happens at a stitch-in?" asked Betsy.

"It's like the Monday Bunch, only it goes on for two days. There's usually a class on some aspect of needlework, a time for show-and-tell, lots of friendly advice from people sitting near you, and plenty of time to make some real progress on a project."

Betsy looked out the window. The land was nearly level, the pastures outlined with trees and shrubs, with shaggy farmhouses and newer suburban models tucked among more trees, their chimneys smoking faintly.

After a while she slept again. No dreams this time, or when, after a period of looking out the window, she dozed off. Again she woke, this time to a land-scape only a little whiter than near the Cities, with small, well-kept houses, their chimneys steaming, set back among crowds of naked gray trees. She yawned. Was she never going to stop feeling sleepy?

Jill said, "It must be frightening to find that sleuthing is the talent God gave you, rather than one for counted cross-stitch or finding a good man. And you can choose to bury this talent if you like. But I'm not sure that will give you the peace you're looking for."

Betsy, annoyed at Jill for nagging but too tired to argue, watched a long row of billboards approaching, advertising a casino. "Where are we?"

"Hinckley. About halfway to Duluth."

She closed her eyes—really, this seat was almost too comfortable—and immediately fell back into a dream-troubled doze.

With a start, she asked, "Are we nearly there?" and was dismayed at the whiny-child tone of her voice.

"No, we're still half an hour out of Duluth," said Jill.

They were passing a lake dotted with what looked like old-fashioned out-houses. Ice fishermen, she knew, were huddled inside them, poised over a hole chopped in the ice, holding a miniature fishing rod. "Do ice houses ever fall through?" she asked.

"Once in a while. They're supposed to take them off the ice pretty soon—they're already off down in the Cities." Jill glanced over at the lake. "I see they've ordered the cars and trucks off up here."

Betsy said, "I remember somewhere in Wisconsin they used to put an old car out on a frozen lake and you could enter a raffle to bet when it would fall through."

"They used to do that up here, too. Look, I was thinking while you were asleep, and I think I understand why you feel you shouldn't feed the dream-maker any more real-life crime. And I'll support you if you choose to do that. It's a shame, though; I've met exactly one other person with your talent for solving criminal cases."

"Was he another cop?"

Jill nodded. "She, actually. A Saint Paul detective. But she wasn't like you, she's one of those people who operate at a whole different level than us humans. Another cop told me once that all she has to do is walk into a room and the perp will start sweating, and pretty soon the truth comes out of his pores, too. You're not like her because you're amiable, and because you solve these things like it's a game. But like her you're seriously good."

"If this were a game, I wouldn't mind going on with it, because I wouldn't mind losing once in a while. But murder is serious, peoples' lives are at stake. If I accuse someone falsely—" She sighed and put her head back, closing her eyes. "I could not bear that."

After a minute or two of silence, Jill said quietly, "All right, I promise I won't ask you to go sleuthing again, and I'll discourage others from coming to you."

"Thank you," Betsy murmured. Having received the support she felt she badly needed, Betsy relaxed—and suddenly didn't feel quite as exhausted.

Jill said, "Did I tell you Lars is selling his hobby farm?"

Lars was Jill's boyfriend, a fellow police officer and a workaholic. That he'd give up a source of hours of backbreaking labor surprised her. "No, you didn't. What's he going to do with the money, invest in something that's even more work?"

Jill laughed, and Betsy asked, "Does he ever take a vacation?"

"Not since I've known him. Oh, he takes time off, but it's just so he can concentrate on some major project, like refinishing every floor in the house that went with the farm he's about to sell."

They were coming into Duluth, a city set on a broad and high terraced hill overlooking a magnificent harbor. I-35 swooped in a big curve down the hill, then ran near the lake. The overpasses had silhouettes of Viking ships carved into them.

North of the city, bluffs stood with their feet in the icy water of Lake Superior. I-35 ended and they picked up Highway 61, which ran through tunnels in the bluffs. Then the land opened out again, though now Betsy noticed something stressed about it, something very opposite from the lush farmland farther south. The snow cover was deeper, but Betsy sensed the soil under it was thin, as if bedrock were just a few inches below that. Naked granite poked up here and there, dark brown or rust red, ancient stuff, worn smooth between the creases. Trees, fewer in variety, looked to be struggling. Betsy told herself not to be foolish; for all she knew, the trees were young, the soil rich.

But knowing that in Mississippi and Georgia the azaleas were blooming, and in Maryland the tulips were nearly finished, while here one could still go ice fishing, troubled her adopted California soul. She was not bred to be ice-bound despite her youth in Wisconsin.

The towns north of Duluth were small and looked as stressed as the land. Small houses, some merely cabins, shabby bars, and unkempt gas stations lined the road. Here were nothing approaching the beautiful mansions in the northern suburbs of Duluth. Of course, these buildings weren't flimsy, like the shacks Betsy had seen on a trip through the Deep South years ago. Up here, a person couldn't live in a house with thin walls or broken windows.

How did the people manage to survive in Minnesota before insulation and storm windows? Betsy wondered. And what on earth did the pre-Columbian Indians do when winter set in?

But she didn't ask Jill; she only gazed out at the tall pines and clusters of aspen—or were they birch? She didn't know. The trees thinned out and there was Lake Superior on her right, a beautiful, restless slate blue. *DMC 824,* thought Betsy, absently comparing the color to a floss number. *Wait a minute,* she thought, *the lake ice is out already. I guess there are signs of spring up here after all.* That thought occupied her happily the rest of the journey.

Three

Look for the entrance sign for Judge Magney State Park," Jill said, so Betsy looked.

They had gone through Grand Marais a few miles back and Betsy had seen why Jill smiled when she called it the Scandinavian Riviera—it was a pretty little town, especially in contrast to the hardscrabble villages they had gone through. Like Duluth, it was on a steep hill that stepped down to Lake Superior, but just as this hill was much more modest, Grand Marais couldn't hold a candle to Duluth, much less the Riviera. And therein lay the joke: Scandinavians, who dominated Minnesota culture, were presumed to be an unassuming people who would find this modest little town just their speed.

Highway 61 ran alongside the lake. The trees were mostly pine, with the occasional cluster of birch. The snow cover was deep and fresh, and by the plumes of exhaust coming from other cars, the bright sun hadn't managed to raise the temperature anywhere near freezing.

The sign was easy to spot; it was one of those green billboards the federal government puts up. A dozen yards past it was a commercial billboard with an American Indian feather headdress on it, announcing the entrance to Naniboujou.

Jill slowed, signal blinking, and made a right turn onto a narrow, snow-packed lane. A hundred yards away was a two-story rustic building covered with black wooden shingles under a gray roof. A scatter of trees marked the broad lawns beside and behind the lodge. A shingled tower marked the front of the building, and all along the wall beside it were tall, many-paned windows rising to peaks, framed in red.

The car crunched to a halt in the parking area, and Jill shut off the engine. "All out," she said. Betsy, very stiff, stood a moment outside the car and took a deep breath of the still, bitter-cold air.

As they walked to the lobby door—which wasn't in the tower, but alongside it—Betsy saw the restless surface of Lake Superior barely twenty yards away. No beach was visible, just a shallow drop-off at the edge of the lawn to blue water. She could hear little waves shushing.

"Come on," said Jill, and Betsy saw her standing beside an open door.

The lobby was very small and strangely shaped. Shelves between the door and a single double-hung window were full of sweatshirts in various colors. A shelf under the window held collectibles and books, a theme that continued on more shelves. The rest of the room was mostly a check-in counter, with a wooden staircase and a door marked PRIVATE beyond it, amid a whole collection of odd angles.

The dark-haired man behind the counter greeted Jill warmly by name, and Betsy wondered how often Jill had been here. Betsy glanced to her right, through an open doorway, and her eye was startled by a large open space painted in primary colors. She went for a look, stepping into a room forty feet long and two stories high, full but not crowded with tables draped in midnight blue. There was a man in a brown uniform sitting alone at one of the blue tables, lingering over a cup of coffee.

There was a huge cobblestone fireplace at the far end, with a small fire burning brightly. A pair of cranberry couches faced one another in front of it. A row of French doors marched down each side of the room. One row looked out over the parking lot, the other looked into a sunlit lounge.

Betsy took another step into the room. Every inch of wall and ceiling was painted from the smallest box of Crayolas in unshaded blue, yellow, red, green, and orange. Squiggly lines, jagged lines, and rows of the pattern called Greek keys covered every surface—except between the French windows, where there were big faces, with Aztec noses and tombstone teeth and half moon ears. It was startling, bold, amusing, wonderful.

"Come on, we'll drive around back," said Jill.

"What?"

"Our room's easier to get to through the back door."

"Oh. Okay." Betsy, trying to look at the room and follow Jill at the same time, stumbled, and Jill caught her by the arm. "Who painted that room?" Betsy asked as they went out into the cold again.

"Antoine Goufee, a Frenchman. It was back in the twenties, and I hear they haven't so much as touched it up since."

"What was he smoking, I wonder?"

Jill laughed. "It is interesting, isn't it?" She started the engine. They drove around the side of the building, which stood at a more-than-ninety-degree angle to the front portion. Jill pulled up at the far end. There were four other cars already there, like their own, crusted with road salt. "Let's unload."

The back door was unlocked. It let into a plain wooden stairwell that smelled faintly of age. At the top was a landing with a couple of foldaway beds. Through a door there was a richly carpeted hallway paneled in golden knotty pine. Prints of nineteenth-century Native Americans punctuated the walls.

Their room was at the other end of the hallway, through a door set at an angle. *This place is just full of angles*, thought Betsy.

It took two trips to bring up the luggage and needleworking equipment. The room was small, and seemed smaller because its walls and ceiling were also paneled with planks of knotty pine. The bed was a four-poster, its cover forest green, and the two windows had narrow blinds behind forest green drapes. There was a fireplace with a dark metal surround flush against the wall, a small desk, a closet. The bathroom was little, too.

"See?" said Jill. "No phone, no TV."

"Uh-huh," said Betsy, looking at the one bed. It was queen-sized, but she had not shared a bed with another female since she was nine. Still, the bed looked as inviting as it had in the brochure. Despite all her dozing in the car, she craved a nap.

Then she looked at her two big suitcases. Oh, why had she brought so much? The task of unpacking seemed overwhelming.

Jill said, "You look all tired out. Care to trust me to unpack? You take your knitting and go down to the lounge. It's really pretty down there."

"No, I couldn't, really . . ." Betsy began to sigh, then stopped. If she couldn't nap, not having to unpack was a very pleasant second choice. "Well, thanks," she said. She picked up her canvas bag and went out. There was a staircase right across the hall, and Betsy went down it to find herself in a short passageway that led to that amazing dining room. This time she was at the fireplace end. The big smooth stones, she saw, were matte ovals of granite, probably taken from local rivers. The small fire was still burning cheerfully, and the cranberry couches looked very inviting. The room was empty; the man in the brown uniform had gone away. On the far wall, a large Indian's head was thrown back in laughter.

Betsy went for a look into the sunlit lounge. It ran the length of the dining room, but its ceiling was low and it was painted a soft, warm cream. Six pairs of windows lined the room, and groups of couches and chairs with deep cushions and wicker arms invited one to come in and be comfortable. Sunlight picked out the polished surfaces of low tables and deep windowsills, the narrow green and blue stripes of the cushions, and the fuzziness of the leaves on the potted geraniums.

Betsy picked a couch about halfway down, angled so she could lift her eyes and see the lake. She had grown up in Milwaukee, on the shore of Lake Michigan, and had lived many years in San Diego. She found views of big expanses of water homey and comforting. The clean white snow had only a pair of ski tracks across it. A dead birch, its trunk black and white, its limbs lopped short, stood near the shore. A quartet of birds, too far out to be identified, wheeled and turned over the water, which had gone from DMC 824 to a pale blue-gray—DMC 799, perhaps—scattered with golden coins of sunlight. The lawn outside the window wasn't very broad, and edged with the brown and red stems of leafless bushes. Beyond was a mix of evergreen and birch trees, here and there a narrow pine thrusting itself high above the other trees. There had been a vogue for narrow artificial Christmas trees, but Betsy hadn't realized there actually was such a variety. She wondered what it was, and a phrase from an old book with a Canadian setting came to her: lodgepole pines. Were these lodgepole pines, so tall and straight?

She opened the canvas bag of needlework. Though she called it her knitting bag, it actually held counted cross-stitch and needlepoint projects, too. But when she was tired she liked the soothing rhythm of knitting. She took out the sweater she was making. She was doing the cuff of one sleeve, and she liked deep cuffs. Knit one, purl one, across and back again, nice and easy. She was doing the sweater in a heather mix of blue wool on number seven needles.

Across and back, across . . . and back. The room was warm and quiet. Betsy wasn't a lazy person, but she was physically worn out as well as sleepy. She caught herself nodding and shook her head. Knit, purl, knit, purl, knit . . . Perhaps she should have changed out of her sweatshirt, she was getting very warm. She looked out the window at the immaculate blue sky, the gray branches of the trees.

Something large floated into view over the trees. A hawk? No, look at that, it was an eagle—and its head was snow white, it was a real, live bald-headed eagle! As if responding to her wish, it curved toward her in its flight and glided down, lower and lower, until it was crossing the lawn nearly at ground level, scarcely six yards from the window and startlingly large. It rose abruptly near the lakeshore to land on top of the dead birch, settle its wings, and look out over the water. In that moment it seemed to become part of the tree; she might never have realized it was there if she had not seen it land. She watched it awhile, but it sat still, so she returned to her knitting.

Knit, purl, knit, purl, then turn the needles around and do more of the same back across. Knit, purl . . . knit . . . purl . . . Her head was heavy, her eyes closed of their own accord. She laid her head back for just a minute . . .

"Hello?" said a soft voice.

Betsy opened her eyes and saw a woman had come to sit across from her. The woman was very fair, dangerously thin, with short, pale blond curls. The sunlight made them gleam like a halo. She was wearing a powder blue and white Norwegian sweater with elaborate pewter fastenings, the cords and voice box of her neck prominent above it. She had her own canvas bag with her, a light blue one with dark blue wooden handles, and had brought out a counted cross-stitch pattern of a Victorian doll wearing a lace-trimmed dress. Her fingers were very slender, separating two threads from a cut length of lavender floss with tender delicacy. Betsy was sure she didn't know her, yet the woman looked vaguely familiar. "Hi," Betsy said.

"Are you here for the stitch-in?" asked the woman. She opened a Ziploc plastic bag and took out a damp blue sponge, bent it in the middle until it resembled an open mouth, then closed it on a section of floss—some women declared that floss was less liable to knot or tangle if dampened.

"Uh-huh," said Betsy. "I'm from Excelsior."

"That's down near the Twin Cities, isn't it? But I hear we've got people coming from as far away as Chicago. I'm only from Duluth."

Since she didn't introduce herself, perhaps Betsy was supposed to know her. Seeking a clue, Betsy said, "This is my first time at a stitch-in."

"Really?" The woman put the tip of the dampened floss in her mouth— Betsy smiled; here was another floss licker, and never mind that she'd already moistened her floss. "This is the first time I've come to one at Naniboujou," she continued, deftly threading her needle, "though I've been to lots of others. And of course I've been here many times. I just love this place, even though they make us stand outside to smoke nowadays. Maybe it will help me quit."

Betsy nodded, remembering how she had decided to quit the day she found herself standing outside in a chill downpour, damp and shivering, shackled to Mistress Nicotine. How much worse it would be in this frigid climate! But she did not say what a friend always said, "Smokers of the world, unite! Throw off your chains!" Because it was no laughing matter and teasing only made things worse.

So instead, Betsy said, "I can't get over that dining room."

"Yes, it's just amazing, isn't it?" The woman picked up her fabric—a cotton evenweave, Betsy noted. "I first came here twenty-seven years ago, on my honeymoon—" She bridled just a little, obviously thinking Betsy would be surprised to learn she was old enough to have been married twenty-seven years ago.

So Betsy politely said, "You don't look old enough to have been married twenty-seven years," though that was not true. Sunlight can be cruel, and it clearly showed the tiny lines of a woman in her midforties, at least. Face-lifted, too, Betsy thought, noting the oddly placed creases in the woman's cheeks when she smiled. Though very thin people's faces creased differently when they smiled.

"Oh, yes, I have two grown-up children. My daughter still lives at home, but my son is out of college now and looking to work in environmental protection. Do you have children?"

"No," said Betsy. "We tried, but it turned out I couldn't get pregnant."

"How sad. They do give you a link to the future, I think. What are you working on?"

"A sweater. I've learned to like all kinds of needlework, but knitting I find most soothing."

"I like counted cross-stitch best for relaxation. It takes my mind away from my troubles."

As if reminded, the woman stopped stitching to look a little downcast. Impulsively Betsy asked, "Is it something you want to talk about?"

"Well, people will see us together, I suppose. And wonder. You see, my husband and I are divorced, but we're trying to get back together. Since we honeymooned here . . ." She blushed and looked away, out the window. Betsy smiled; that someone less than eighty years old could actually blush when mentioning her honeymoon was as charming as it was silly. "I wonder . . ." The woman paused again. "This is just too stupid," she said, drawing a deep breath. She put her stitching away with swift efficiency as she murmured very quietly to herself, "I must go get Eddie, then." And she stood and strode out.

Betsy frowned after her. Who was Eddie? Oh, of course, her ex-husband. And Betsy thought she recognized the lure of a nicotine fix, too. Probably wants to borrow a cigarette from him, or ask him to join her in one. *Poor thing,* Betsy thought, remembering her own struggle against the habit. Maybe that's how she stays so thin. Though the woman didn't look just fashionably slender, she looked emaciated. Perhaps she was ill. Maybe this attempt to reconcile was triggered by a serious illness, perhaps something caused by smoking. Betsy tried to think who she knew, or should know, who was ill with cancer or emphysema. But no name came to her, perhaps because she was still a little sleepy.

She looked down at her knitting and picked up her needles. Was the next stitch knit or purl? Knit. She set off again on the cuff, but the cozy silence made it difficult to concentrate. Not that it was hard, or anything, just knit one, purl one, knit one, purl . . . No good. Yawning, she let her hands descend into her lap.

This lounge was so beautiful. Beams rising between the pairs of windows leaned gently inward, leading the eyes up, to where the ceiling beams were painted the same color as the walls. So long as her head was already leaning back, she let it fall against the back of the couch. Her eyes closed . . .

She struggled awake. She'd been having a dream about a sinister blond woman who wanted her to have a cigarette, and for a moment or two she wasn't sure she was awake yet. The couch was unfamiliar. She was in a long room full of odd shadows.

The dream about the thin blond woman had been set in a long room full of sunlight. Or had there really been a woman? The dream had been in two parts, she thought, and only in the second was the woman sinister.

And she actually was in a long room. But she was alone, and it was dusk outside. Was this part three of the dream?

Her nose twitched. No, the room was real, she was at Naniboujou Lodge, and there were some very delicious smells coming from the dining room, accompanied by the sound of quiet talk and the clinking of silverware on porcelain.

She shoved her knitting into her bag, but left the bag on the floor. Was Jill eating dinner without her? She got clumsily to her feet and went to the door at the end of the room, walked into the dining room, and paused to look around. There was a small crowd of perhaps thirty or thirty-five women and three men seated at the tables, eating, talking, laughing. The stitchers-in had arrived. But none was Jill.

Betsy turned, went past a long and broad counter, behind which was an old-fashioned circular red velvet couch with a red velvet pillar sticking up out of its middle, and into the lobby.

There was no one at the check-in desk. A wooden staircase, not wide, with a carpet runner, stood ahead of her. A stylized bird, a crow or an eagle, was carved on its finial post. She remembered that bird from when she had come down last time. Betsy went up. Her room, she remembered, was at the end of the corridor near the staircase, its door set at an angle. She came to the top of the stairs and paused. The stairs turned completely around, going up, emptying into a short hallway, and she had to wait till her head turned itself back around again. Through there was the corridor, and there was the angled door.

Her key was in her pocket, right? Right. Funny Jill hadn't come down, if it was dinnertime. This was one of these package deals, the meals included in the price of the weekend, so missing a meal wouldn't save her any money. Maybe she was taking a nap.

The dumb key wouldn't turn in the lock. Betsy pulled it out and turned the knob—and the door opened. There was no light on in the room, but there seemed to be someone on the bed. "Jill?" said Betsy, but softly, in case Jill was asleep.

Betsy found the light switch, and a lamp came on. There was, in fact, some-one on top of the comforter, but it was the thin blond woman. Her complexion was blotchy and her lips were blue. And she didn't seem to be breathing.

The room was small. In three steps, Betsy was beside the bed. She looked around. The suitcases had been put away, though something dark was draped across a chair. There was no one in the room.

Except for the woman on the bed. Betsy reached out to touch her.

No pulse, no breath, skin eerily cool. This was too dreadful, this was nightmarish.

Betsy turned and blundered out, yanking the door closed behind her. She more stumbled than ran down the twisting stairs. There was still no one behind the counter in the lobby. What kind of place was this, where the front desk was unmanned and people came to die on other people's beds?

The feeling of unreality was so strong that Betsy didn't want to run into the dining room, yelling about a dead woman. A dark-haired man in a white shirt and navy trousers was standing at a lectern halfway down the room. He looked a lot like the friendly clerk who had been behind the check-in counter earlier. Betsy hurried to him to say in an urgent undertone, "There is the body of a dead woman on the bed in my room."

He stared at her for a long moment, then said, "Are you sure?"

"Yes."

"Who is she?"

"I don't know. I talked to her earlier, but I don't think she told me her name. She's here for the stitch-in, I know that."

"What room are you in?"

Betsy couldn't remember, but thought of her key. She brought it out. "Twenty," she said, reading the number off it.

The man said, "Come with me," looked around, and started toward the fireplace end of the room. There, he took the elbow of a young wait person with braids wrapped around her head and a coffeepot in each hand and said in a low voice, "Billie, I have to go with this woman to her room. Take over for me?"

"Sure."

Since they were at the fireplace end, he went out the door that let onto a short passageway, and up the back stairs she suddenly remembered she had come down originally. He didn't ask for her key, but used a passkey of his own to open the door. Betsy, unwilling to see that still face again, hung back.

"Hello?" said the man.

And Betsy heard a sleepy reply, "Hello?"

Betsy peered around the man's elbow to see a figure sitting up on the bed. It was Jill.

Four

Jill struggled to awaken. Recognizing the man's voice, she asked, "What's wrong, James?"

His voice was strained. "I—I'm not sure, Ms. Cross. Your friend said—"

"Betsy?" Jill said sharply. "Where is she?" She realized it was dark out. "Say, what time is it?"

"Seven thirty-five," said James.

"I'm right here," came Betsy's voice from behind James. "But, I don't understand. I came up here just two minutes ago and there was a dead woman on the bed."

"What?" Jill sat the rest of the way up. "Come in, come in. What happened?"

James went to the fireplace to give Betsy room to come in. He turned and looked with Jill at Betsy for an explanation.

But Betsy didn't have one. Not a coherent one, anyway. "I was in the lounge knitting, and this woman came in and sat down across from me. She was very pretty but very thin. Blond hair, curly, cut short. She had a blue and white sweater, one of those Scandinavian sweaters." She gestured at her shoulders, describing the starburst pattern with her fingers.

Standing just inside the doorway, Betsy looked bewildered. She was wearing what she'd worn on the trip up, an old blue sweatshirt one size too large; and leggings, unflattering on her short, plump figure. Betsy looked anything but commanding normally, and now she looked ruffled and scared.

But she didn't lie.

Jill said, "Go on."

"I don't know what's going on. I was asleep, you see, then I came up here to find you, because it's dinnertime, and instead I saw her, on this bed, and she was dead. So I ran back downstairs to tell someone, and James came up with me, only it was you on the bed."

Jill looked over at James to see if he could shed more light on Betsy's story.

He shook his head. "No one matching that description has checked in while I was on the desk—and I'm the only one on the desk this weekend." Trying to be helpful, he asked, "What time did you see her in the lounge, Ms. Devonshire?"

Betsy shrugged helplessly. "I'm not sure. I came down there right after we got our luggage up to our room—"

"That was a little after three," Jill put in.

Betsy continued. "I brought my knitting down, but I dozed off, and this woman spoke to me, woke me up. It was still daylight, the sun was shining on her hair, I remember how it shone in the sun. We talked just a little while. She said she was here for the stitch-in and to reconcile with her ex-husband. Then she said she wanted to meet him for a cigarette and went out, and I went back to sleep, and when I woke up it was dark."

"You fell back asleep?"

Betsy nodded. "I had a dream about her, then I woke up again, and I wondered if you'd come down to eat without finding me. You weren't in the dining room, so I went up to our room. Only when I opened the door there she was, that same thin woman, dead."

"Are you sure it wasn't me you saw? It was dark after all," said Jill.

"Oh, yes. I turned the light on, and I touched her. Her lips were blue, and she wasn't breathing at all, and I couldn't find a pulse. I didn't know what to do, I couldn't think what she was doing in our room, or where you'd gotten to. I came right down and got you"—Betsy nodded toward James—"and you brought me up, only it was Jill asleep on the bed."

Betsy looked as if she didn't expect to be believed, as if she wasn't sure of her story herself.

"So this woman appeared to you between naps," said Jill.

"Yes," agreed Betsy reluctantly. "But it wasn't a dream, Jill. I mean, dreams are kind of vague, and this woman wasn't vague, not the first time. The pattern of that sweater, one of those starburst kind, I could draw it for you, you know how I'm getting about knitting patterns. And the sweater had fancy pewter fasteners, not buttons. You don't dream details like that."

"No, I guess not." Jill scooted to the edge of the bed and hung her legs over. She rubbed her eyes with her fingertips, trying to pull her thoughts together. She said, "You're sure you didn't go to some other room by mistake?"

"No—well, there's only one room right at the top of the stairs, at an angle, not flat along the wall, right? With a fireplace?"

"That's right," said James. "But here we are, in your room, and there's no dead body in here, thank God. I don't know what else to say. Except that I've got to get back. You'd better come down soon, if you want to eat."

"We'll be right down," said Jill. "Just let me wash my face."

A dash of cold water helped. Jill came out of the bathroom to find Betsy, looking half ashamed, waiting by the window.

"Lighten up on yourself, Betsy," Jill said. "Everyone has dreams that seem real. I've done it myself. And this is just another one of the kind of dreams you've been telling me about. More realistic than the others, but your unconscious had to get it right at least once, right? Come on, let's see if a hot meal makes you feel better."

Betsy said, as they went out the door, "Is James related to the check-in clerk? They look a lot alike."

Jill laughed. "They are the same person. He's James Ramsey. He and his wife Ramona own this place. Very fine people."

Most of the other guests had either finished or were eating dessert by the time they got down, so they sat alone at one of the small tables along the outside wall. Heavy sheets of clear plastic were hung on the French doors to keep out the cold.

"The idea was," said Jill, "to open these doors and set up tables under an awning along this wall and serve food and drinks out there—in the summer, of course."

"But they never did that?" asked Betsy.

"I don't think so. Well, maybe the original owners did. This place began life as a very large and exclusive private club. People like Ring Lardner and Babe Ruth signed up as members. It opened in July 1929." Jill paused, one pale eyebrow raised just a bit.

Betsy frowned at her, then said, "Oh! Of course, October 1929, the Crash, followed by the Depression."

Jill nodded. "Naniboujou never really got off the ground as a private club. This building was supposed to be bigger, there were supposed to be tennis courts on that lawn between here and the lake, all sorts of things never happened. Most of the land was sold—some of it became the state park across the road—and the lodge kept changing hands. It was even a nightclub for a while, and a Christian retreat. Now the Ramseys run it as a public lodge. But they refuse to apply for a liquor license."

"They don't need a liquor license if this is the usual kind of food they serve," observed Betsy, lifting her fork.

The salad had been mixed greens with purple onion slices, strawberries, some kind of soft cheese—brie, Betsy thought—with a dressing made of raspberry vinegar and poppy seed. It was followed by a spinach lasagna so light it was apparently made with eggs as well as cheese. With the lasagna came carrots glazed with brown sugar, orange juice, and ginger. The bread was fresh-baked sourdough. Jill, sighing happily, said the food was always wonderful. Dessert was lemon-flavored ice cream with tiny, chocolate-coated chocolate cookies.

Over coffee, Jill said, "Tell me some more about the woman you dreamed you saw."

"Why? I'm starting to agree with you, it was probably a dream," she said. "I was so tired, I'm still tired, I've been tired for weeks." But Jill only waited, so Betsy said, "Okay, the woman was like an angel, kind of. Inhumanly thin, like something that lives on manna or ambrosia, not spinach lasagna and ice cream. A golden angel—except she didn't have a message for me. Don't angels generally come with messages?"

Jill didn't reply, but kept her face still, waiting.

So Betsy continued. "After she left, I went back to sleep. Or the dream ended. And I had another dream, where the thin woman wanted to do something wicked, I don't remember what, but she kept whispering about it. And she wanted me to smoke a cigarette with her. Then I woke up again and smelled delicious food and it was getting dark, and you hadn't come down, so I decided to come up and get you. I went through the lobby—Why do they have two staircases going up to the second floor?"

"Because it's easier to get luggage up to the second floor the back way," said Jill. "They don't want guests dragging luggage through the dining room."

"No, not the back door, I mean two staircases up to the front of the hallway, one off the lobby and the other off the dining room." She frowned. "How come I only saw one staircase when I came down?"

Jill said, "The staircase off the lobby goes to the wing that faces the lake. The staircase off the dining room goes to our wing."

"There are two wings?"

"Sure, didn't you know that? We've got the wing that overlooks the west lawn, it's got the knotty pine paneling. The other wing has painted walls."

Betsy half closed her eyes, remembering something. "Uh-oh," she said. "The stairs off the lobby go to the wing without the paneling, right? The stairs off the dining room go to the wing with knotty pine—our wing?"

"Yes."

"Well, it's the room at the top of the lobby stairs where the body is, because I went up those stairs."

"Are you sure?"

"I'm sure I went up the lobby stairs. And if there's a door up there set at an angle, and there's a fireplace in that room, too, then yes."

Jill put her cup down. "Wait here," she said. She went out to the lobby, where James was checking in a late-arriving couple.

When he'd finished and the couple went up the hallway beside the staircase, she said, "The room at the top of the stairs from here has a fireplace, right?"

"Yes, why?"

"Is it painted green?"

"Yes."

"Who's in there?"

James checked his register and said, "Frank Owen."

"By himself?"

"Yes."

"Come with me a minute," she said, unconsciously using her cop voice, and started back into the dining room. James, frowning, hustled to catch up.

"What's this about?" he asked, and she explained Betsy's mistake.

When they got back to their table, Jill said to Betsy, "The fireplace room in the east wing has been reserved by a man as a single. No wife or significant other along."

James said, "Mr. Owen used to be married to a woman who might match the description Ms. Devonshire gave, but—"

Betsy interrupted, "They came here on their honeymoon."

James's eyebrows lifted in surprise. "Yes, that's right. That was before we bought Naniboujou, but they told me about it, said they were glad we could take it over and keep it open."

"This woman I saw was his ex-wife. She's here, or she was here. She said they were going to try for a reconciliation. She's the woman I saw dead."

"But he didn't reserve for two," James said.

"Maybe she came to surprise him here," said Betsy.

Jill asked, "How did she know he was here to surprise?"

"How should I know?" demanded Betsy, exasperated. Heads at nearby tables turned toward them, and Betsy said, more quietly, "Maybe he always comes here this time of year."

They both looked at James, who shrugged and said, "He comes up two or three times a year, usually in the summer, but yes, also in winter. They used to do a lot of cross-country skiing, until his wife got sick. I think he's taking it up again, in fact."

"Sick?" echoed Betsy, and Jill remembered Betsy's description of a very thin woman.

"She's got a lot of allergies," said James. "It started with something she came in contact with as a nurse, and it kind of spread in every direction. She's allergic to pollen, dog dander, pork, dairy products, wheat, and I don't know what all else. She had to give up all her sports. And he gave up doing them, too, to take care of her. But eventually they divorced, and so now he's going back to skiing, at least."

Jill said to Betsy, "But didn't you say she went out for a cigarette? Isn't smoke one of the big things people with allergies stay away from?"

"Yes, that's right," conceded Betsy.

"Mrs. Owen smokes, or used to," said James. "We're smoke-free, and she used to complain about having to stand outside to have her cigarettes."

"Yes, she said that," said Betsy.

James continued. "I don't know if she still smokes; after their divorce she stopped coming; she hasn't been here in years."

Jill had nothing else to ask, so he went away. Betsy said, "Maybe we should go ask Mr. Owen what he did with his wife's body."

Jill studied Betsy, her tired face with its frightened eyes. "He'll say he hasn't seen her, of course. If he's murdered her, he's not going to admit it. And if she never was here—"

"No, she was here. Too many things fit. His room is where I saw her, and the description matches, according to Mr. Ramsey. Unless I'm psychic, and I don't think I am. Maybe if we talk to him he'll say of course she was here, he found her ill in his room and took her to the hospital. I'd like that; I can stop worrying that I'm going crazy." Betsy looked around the dining room. "Maybe he's here, having dinner." Among the two-dozen or so women were three or four men.

"No, I asked James to point him out, and he said Mr. Owen wasn't in the dining room."

"What does he look like?" asked Betsy.

"Beats me, I didn't think to ask. All right, let's go."

They went out into the small lobby, and feeling James's eyes on them all the way to the first landing, went up the narrow wooden stairs to the second floor.

Again there was that feeling of funny angles as they went around a not-ninety-degree turn and across the oddly shaped landing and came into the painted hallway. There, an echo of their own hallway, was the door set at yet another angle. After a moment, Betsy became aware of Jill's questioning regard, so she nodded. This was, in fact, the hallway she had entered, thinking it led to her and Jill's room.

Jill walked to the angled door and knocked brusquely.

A man's voice inside said, "Come in."

Jill turned the knob—the door was not locked—and opened the door. She felt Betsy close behind as they went in.

The room was painted a medium green. The windows and four-poster bed were the same as in their own room, down to the paisley pattern on the comforter.

There was nobody on the bed. A slim man with thick, coarse graying blond hair and a heavy mustache was sitting at the little desk, a half-eaten slice of pizza in one hand. The room was redolent of cheese, sausage, and spiced tomato. "It's from Sven and Ole's in Grand Marais," he said, lifting the slice a little. "I always get one of their pizzas when I'm up here. May I ask why you're here?"

"Where's your wife?" asked Betsy.

"I don't have a wife," he replied.

"Are you Frank Owen?" asked Jill.

Betsy said, "Eddie Owen, you mean."

The man said, "My name is Frank Owen. Who are you?"

"My name's Jill Cross and I'm with the Excelsior Police Department."

"Kind of a long way from home, aren't you?" Owen's voice was quiet and warm, with no hint of tension and only a little puzzlement.

"I talked with your wife earlier today," said Betsy—and was disappointed when there was no guilty start, only a mildly surprised look—"and she told me she was here with you in hope of a reconciliation."

Owen's mustache shifted just a little, in either a grimace or a little smile. "She's not here, I haven't seen her."

"Has she talked to you about reconciling?" asked Jill.

He nodded. "We've tried it, several times. It never works. It took me a long time to realize it was never going to work. Are you two friends of hers?"

Betsy shook her head and Jill said, "So you did at least talk to her."

"Not today." Owen shook his head and put down his slice of pizza, accepting that he wasn't going to finish eating it anytime soon. "I wouldn't dream of telling Sharon I was coming up here, and I certainly didn't invite her to stay with me. She did call a couple of weeks ago, hinting she wanted to see me, but I wouldn't agree to that." His voice was firm, his blue eyes almost too guileless.

"Where were you this afternoon?" asked Jill.

He looked at her for somewhat longer than it should have taken him to remember his whereabouts that recently. But there was no annoyance in his face and voice when he replied patiently, "I got here around noon and had lunch in the dining room. I came up to my room and unpacked, then lay down for something over half an hour, maybe an hour. Then I got up and drove to Grand Marais. I did a little shopping—my daughter collects Inuit art, and there's a gift shop in town that sells it—but I didn't buy anything. I shopped for a new set of ski poles and then took a nice run on one of the Pincushion trails, came back to town, bought this pizza, came back here, and was having a quiet little supper when you two knocked on my door." He looked at Betsy. "Who's she, by the way?"

"She's with me," Jill said, and hoped Betsy wouldn't add anything.

Betsy didn't, but Owen asked her, "What else did she say?"

Betsy shrugged. "Not much. Does she smoke?"

Owen grimaced. "Yeah. She keeps trying to stop, her doctor's all over her about it. She's allergic to damn near everything else, you'd think she'd be allergic to tobacco."

"Are her allergies serious?" asked Jill.

Owen nodded and sighed. "She lives on lamb and a special diet supplement without soy or dairy in it, she can only wear silk or cotton, and despite being very careful she's in the hospital two or three damn times a year—" He cut himself off, having grown heated and abruptly realizing it. "It's a damn shame," he said, more quietly. "When we first got married we used to go rock climbing, cross-country skiing, adventuring, and run marathons. She was great, I had trouble keeping up with her. Then she got this latex allergy—she's a nurse, it was the gloves she had to wear—and it was like dominos falling. I tried to be helpful, I tried to keep up with all the new rules, but she got to be such a witch about it—" He blew lengthily through his mustache, cooling his temper again. "It was at least partly my fault, I just couldn't go along with the constant changes in the rules." He looked longingly at his pizza. "At least now I can have things like this in the house again." He smiled up at Jill and Betsy. "And peanut butter. You wouldn't believe how much I missed peanut butter."

Betsy asked, "Does your ex-wife have a black or dark blue coat, kind of shiny? And a big black purse?"

"I have no idea."

A few minutes later, on their way up to their room, Jill said, "What's this about a shiny coat?"

"I suddenly remember seeing a shiny coat, a full-length one, draped across a chair when I came up and found Sharon's body. It was some dark color." Betsy was frowning, trying to remember. She hadn't of course, been really looking at anything but the body. "Or maybe it was the black lining I saw, like it was turned or folded so the lining was showing. And there was something else, a big black purse, I think. Both of them were on the chair Frank Owen was sitting in this time. What do you think about Mr. Owen?"

"He's mad at her, which is understandable. He married an athlete and wound up with an invalid. Tough bounce for both of them."

"I wonder how long ago they divorced. When I talked to Mrs. Owen, it sounded as if it hadn't been long, but I got the feeling from him that it's been a while."

Jill asked, because Betsy had an uncanny feel for such things, "So what do you think? Did he murder her?"

"I don't know. I don't know if it's Sharon Owen's body I saw—though whose else could it be? Did you notice he didn't slip once?"

"Slip on what?"

"He always referred to her in the present tense."

Five

The bed was big, so each woman had enough room to spread a little without danger of encountering a leg or something even more intimate. Nevertheless, Betsy lay on her side close to the edge and told herself firmly not to sprawl.

She composed herself to sleep, but it wouldn't come. The napping in the car, and the nap in the lounge, combined to make her wakeful. Plus there was the uncomfortable thought that she might wake in the night, become aware of someone else in the bed, and think it was Hal, her ex-husband. And forgetting all that had happened the last few months—no, that was ridiculous. Still, it had been a long time . . . Whoa! Where that might lead had her very wide awake indeed.

Jill, on the other hand, was already asleep. *Must have a clear conscience*, thought Betsy with a wry smile. She slipped carefully out of bed, but stood a moment, unwilling to turn on a light. It was dark in the room, and there was no noise out in the hall. Betsy thought, *I'll get my knitting bag and go into the bathroom—Oops*. She'd left the bag down in the lounge.

She pressed the button on the side of her Indiglo watch. It was ten-thirty, not very late. On the other hand, things were scheduled to begin early tomorrow morning. Perhaps everyone had gone to bed. She stepped carefully across the room, feeling her way with hands and toes. Finding the door, she leaned against it, listening. Silence.

She felt her way back to the bed and the robe at the foot of it. She loved her robe, a real antique of gray flannel with broad maroon stripes. It was much too big for her, covering her ankles and crossing deeply in front. She liked to think it had once belonged to Oliver Hardy. She tied it on, pushed her feet into her felt slippers, then went on noiseless feet to the door again, and out.

The hallway was dimly lit, the stairs down to the dining room a little brighter. The dining room itself was an immense dim cavern, its sole source of light the lounge, which was brightly lit. There were about twenty stitchers at work in there. Betsy paused outside the doorway. The stitchers were all dressed, and here she was in nightclothes.

No, wait, there was a woman in a velour nightgown. And there, another woman in a lovely peignoir. So now Betsy felt frumpish.

And then she felt annoyed. She wanted her knitting, it was in that room, she wasn't naked, so why shouldn't she go get it? She straightened her spine and walked in.

Some of the women smiled at Betsy, but most just gave her an incurious glance and continued with their work and talk. "I call them CASITAs, Can't Stand IT Anymore," one woman with flashing blue eyes was saying. "You know, an acre of blue or sixteen yards of backstitch. I keep them in a big drawer."

The woman she was talking to laughed. "CASITAs, I like that, Melly! I keep mine at the bottom of the pile of UFOs, hoping I'll never work my way down to them."

Betsy found her bag sitting on one of the coffee tables. She retrieved it and made her escape.

Back upstairs, she opened the door to the room as quietly as she could, and found the light on and Jill sitting up with a magazine. "If you weren't back in another two minutes, I was going to come looking for you," she said.

"I'm sorry," apologized Betsy. "I didn't mean to wake you."

"You couldn't have helped it, I'm a light sleeper," said Jill. "What's up?"

"I couldn't sleep, and then I remembered I left my knitting downstairs. I was going to sit up awhile in the lounge, but there's a whole group holding a session."

"Well, this *is* a stitch-in. There are women in attendance who will get maybe an hour of sleep a night. James will probably lose money just on the coffee. But I'm glad you're back, I want to show you something." Jill closed the magazine and handed it to Betsy. "Here, look at the cover."

It was *American Needlework Magazine,* and the cover featured a piece of linen with a bouquet of cross-stitched pansies surrounded by hardanger squares. "I brought it because I've been thinking of trying hardanger," Betsy said. "Kate does it, you know."

"Yes, but that's not what I mean. Look at the designer, her picture is up in the corner."

There was an inset in the upper left corner of the cover, a head-and-shoulders photo of a painfully slender blond woman wearing a blue and white Scandinavian sweater with silver fastenings. The cover announced an interview with Kaye of Escapade Design, and an original pattern designed by her for the magazine's readers.

"Oh, my," said Betsy.

"She's even wearing the same sweater you described, down to the pewter fasteners."

"Yes, I see that," said Betsy. She opened the magazine and found the interview with Kaye and skimmed the first few paragraphs. A larger photo of Ms. Kaye in a sunlit room accompanied the article—the cover shot had been cropped from this photo. Betsy said, "I read this article. When I read about the mystery teacher, I remembered Kaye lives in Duluth and was hoping it would be her." The literature had announced a class but, hoping to stir up interest, said the nature of the class and its teacher would be revealed at the stitch-in.

"See? You were hoping she'd be here, and so you dreamed she was. And because you've been having bad dreams, you dreamed she was murdered."

Betsy sighed and closed the magazine. "Now I do feel like an idiot. Poor Mr. Owen, what he must have thought of us! I'm sorry, Jill, dragging you into this—but it seemed so real!"

"I'm sure it did. Well, don't worry about it. I'm going back to sleep. You?"

"Yes, all of a sudden I'm tired."

And this time, despite her concerns, despite the naps, despite a fear of nightmares, she'd barely closed her eyes before she was asleep.

But no matter how many times she fled up the stairs, she always found herself in the lobby. James was behind the counter, his friendly eyes gone cold and his smile evil. Betsy would make some feeble excuse and flee up the stairs, only to step back into the lobby at the top. She knew she'd been going up these stairs for a while. And she knew that one of these times he was going to bring out a great big knife and stab her with it.

But there was nothing else she could do but run despairingly up the stairs.

Here she was again—and there was James, and this time he had a Crocodile Dundee knife in his hand. He put it crosswise in his mouth, like a pirate, so he could use both hands to climb over the counter. She turned toward the stairs. But her legs were moving slowly, as if mired in molasses.

She yelled and struggled, but he was beside her, saying her name.

He grabbed her by the arm, she struggled to pull free—and someone had taken her by the shoulder and was saying her name.

"No! Help, no, leggo!" Betsy said, or shouted.

"Betsy, Betsy, wake up, wake up!"

Jill's voice.

It was all right, it was Jill.

"Oh! Oh, my goodness, wow! Gosh, what a nightmare! Thank you, Jill!" Betsy sat up. Her hands were trembling, her heart was racing. "I thought . . . I thought James was going to get me that time."

"James?"

"Yes, he was behind the counter in the lobby, and the lobby was at the top of the stairs, or the bottom, it didn't seem to matter."

"I see." Jill's tone was very dry.

Betsy shook her head. "Well, I guess you had to be there." She lay back down. "Whew!" she said. Then, "Sorry about that. Was I very loud?"

"More thrashing than noisy. You mentioned stairs, so I guess that's what it was, climbing stairs."

"Yes, lots and lots of stairs, but none of them got me away."

"That's the way it is, sometimes," Jill said. In a firm tone Betsy thought of as her "cop voice," Jill said, "But now you'll go back to sleep and dream only slow, quiet, pleasant dreams."

"Yes, ma'am," she said obediently—and to her surprise, she not only went right back to sleep, she slept the rest of the night in peace.

She was wakened the next morning by a pleasant alto rendition of "Let the Punishment Fit the Crime." She thought for a moment she was in her own bedroom, listening to KSJN's zany *Morning Show*, then realized the tuner wasn't a little off station. The hiss was the rush of a shower.

No need to drag herself out of bed to get down to the shop. Today she would sit among stitchers and get some real work done.

The thought startled Betsy. She hadn't felt her growing interest in needlework was anything other than an honest attempt to learn enough to be an intelligent help to her customers. She had inherited the shop. At first, she kept it open because there were customers waiting to give her money for things already in the shop, and she needed to support herself while the money portion of her inheritance worked its way through probate. She had good employees already on board, and running a needlework shop with them seemed more interesting than any temporary job she might otherwise have found.

But she had come to like needlework for its own sake—and why not? It was beautiful stuff. There were counted cross-stitch patterns as exquisitely detailed as any painting. It took patience, and an eye for detail, to make one of those big pieces. And if they were challenging to work, what an eye it must take to design the patterns! Betsy vowed one day to go to a needlework show and meet some of these amazing people.

Betsy's own natural talent seemed to be in the area of needlepoint, where a couple of mistakes didn't screw up the whole doggone piece, and where you could get creative with stitches, fibers, and colors.

The shower and voice cut off together. Betsy, not wanting to be caught lazing in bed, hastily climbed out. She went to the closet and found her clothes in something like the order she would have chosen herself, if Jill hadn't done it for her. She settled on a brown wool skirt and an ivory sweater.

Jill came out of the bathroom wrapped in a thick terry robe, her pale hair only slightly darkened by being wet. "Good morning," she said. "Did you sleep all right?"

"The second time, yes, thank you. Where'd you put my underwear?"

"Bottom drawer, on the left."

Drying off after her own shower, Betsy's stomach growled. Wow, she was hungry. She hadn't been really hungry since back in December, when a dose of arsenic had ruined her digestion for what she feared was forever. But here she was, wondering if breakfast would be as good as last night's dinner.

It was: waffles with a delectable orange-rum syrup, and the bacon just smoky enough. There was a side dish of peeled grapefruit sections that had never seen the inside of a jar.

Jill didn't mention the too-real dreams Betsy had been having, for which Betsy was grateful.

They were savoring second cups of coffee—robust without being bitter— when a tall, heavyset woman with a very short haircut walked to stand in front of the fireplace. She wore an unflattering purple knit dress.

"Good morning!" she called, with laughter in her voice, and called it several more times, until the room quieted down. Betsy looked around. She thought at first that here was a nice cross section of young, old, slim, fat, tall, short, and everything in between—even a woman in a wheelchair—then she realized everyone looked prosperous. Of course, nobody poor would spend three hundred dollars for a weekend of stitching.

Including Betsy.

Betsy felt a little guilty about that, but only for a moment. After all, not everybody could be poor.

The woman said, "Good morning," one last time, then went on. "As most of you know, I am Isabel Thrift, treasurer of the Grand Marais Needlework Guild. Welcome to the First Annual Naniboujou Stitch-In. I am so pleased at this wonderful turnout for this first time. But . . ." Her tone was suddenly very sober, and a soft, portentous groan went around the room. Obviously rumors were about to be confirmed. "But, as some of you know, the organizer of this event hasn't been feeling well lately. Two days ago the doctor diagnosed walking pneumonia, and going to her car after leaving his office, she fell and broke her leg. The pneumonia isn't the walking kind anymore; she's at St. Luke's in Duluth. But the hard work is done, and the stitch-in goes on. Charlotte Porter is, of course, also president of the Grand Marais Needlework Guild. And she's the one who arranged for our mystery guest, who, I'm pleased to announce, is going to teach two classes, one on hardanger and a beginner's class on designing counted cross-stitch patterns." There was a pleased murmur. "Charlotte wouldn't tell me the teacher's name; she was very mysterious about it." Isabel's tone was again humorous and the ladies laughed.

Betsy sat up straighter. Wow, she was going to get an actual glimpse of how designing was done!

Isabel continued. "So, will our mysterious instructor please stand up and introduce herself? Or himself?"

There was a rustle as everyone looked around. But no one stood up.

"Maybe it was Charlotte herself who was going to teach the class," someone suggested.

But another said, "No, Charlotte doesn't do hardanger well enough to teach it."

Isabel forced a smile and said, "Well, this *is* mysterious!"

There was brief, uncomfortable laughter, then a quiet murmur moved around the room as Isabel frowned and tried to think what to say next. A slim woman with a deep tan at the next table said, "Who?" to the table beyond hers, and repeated the name to the others. "Kaye of Escapade Design."

Betsy said to Jill, "I see I wasn't the only one thinking it might be her."

Isabel said, "Well, maybe she's not here yet. While we wait for her, let's get started. Come on into the lounge."

The room filled with pleased, anticipatory murmurs as the guests began to stand and move.

Jill and Betsy returned to their room to load up with the paraphernalia of needlework. Betsy took a moment to tuck the magazine into her knitting bag.

Back downstairs, the women—and two of the men—had just about filled the sunlit lounge. There was a sign-in sheet on a clipboard displayed on a table; Jill and Betsy signed it.

Jill said, "I see two seats there," nodding toward the middle of the room. As they moved toward them, Betsy glanced out the big windows and halted in amazement. The lake steamed as if it were coming to a boil. A light breeze bent the steam this way and that, uncovering small areas of dark blue water and quickly covering them again.

"Oh, pretty!" said Betsy.

"Yes," Jill said, "the air is colder than the lake. As soon as it warms up a little, the steam will quit."

Jill followed Betsy to a pair of facing couches. Isabel was sitting on one, the strong sunlight putting lavender highlights on her purple dress, and on the other was the tanned woman who had repeated the name "Kaye of Escapade Design."

Isabel said, "Sit down, sit down! I'd introduce you to Carla, but I don't know your names."

"I'm Jill Cross," Jill said, sitting next to Carla, "and this is my friend Betsy Devonshire. We're from Excelsior, where Betsy owns a needlework shop."

Betsy sat next to Isabel, smiled, and said, "Hello."

Carla, whose short hair was salt and pepper, smiled back and said, "I'm Carla Prakesh, from Duluth and Fort Myers, Florida. What kind of needlework do you sell?"

Betsy said, "Needlepoint and counted cross-stitch, knitting yarn, and patterns, some crochet supplies. I carry only a few Penelope canvases, as not many people care to do both petit point and needlepoint on the same piece." She mentioned that because the brown canvas Carla was working on was called Penelope.

"And isn't that a shame?" drawled Carla. "I mean, trame is the original, isn't it? This is how the medieval noblewoman applied her needle. Cross-stitch was done by the peasants."

Betsy didn't know what to say. While she really liked needlepoint herself, she didn't think it was because she carried the genes of a medieval noblewoman.

Isabel had made a sound in her throat, and Betsy glanced over to see she was working on a cross-stitch pattern of roses.

"Where do you find your trame canvases?" asked Betsy. Only a few months ago she would have pronounced it "trame." Now she knew it was pronounced "trah-*may*." In trame, the pattern is first painted onto the canvas, then floss is basted horizontally across the pattern in colors to match, and the result sold to a stitcher who stitches over the basting. It is an expensive form of needlework, but allows complex and beautiful patterns, often based on medieval and Renaissance patterns or the paintings of old masters.

"I buy them from a sweet little shop in Fort Myers," Carla replied, with an archness that encouraged her listeners to deduce that "sweet little" meant very upscale. "Perhaps you've heard of it? C. Chapell is the name."

"No, but I'm new to the business," said Betsy. "I inherited the shop from my sister, and I still have a great deal to learn about it."

Carla drew a deep breath to expound further, but Isabel had simultaneously drawn a shallower breath and so got in ahead of her with, "What are you working on this weekend, Jill?"

Jill had set up her project, a large painted canvas of an elegant tiger sitting on a green silk pillow, looking over his shoulder at the viewer in a grand and aloof way. She had a set of stretcher bars and was preparing to stitch the needlepoint canvas onto the bars.

"I love the way he sits alone in all this space," said Jill, "and I'm tempted to just fill the background with basketweave stitch."

"Oh, I think it would be boring to do that much basketweave," Carla said. "Don't you, Isabel? Well, maybe not you; you do all your pictures with lots and lots of little x's."

Isabel's roses were highly detailed, in at least six shades of pink and six of green on very fine, snow white linen. "I don't find counted boring at all," she said with hardly any rancor.

"But with just plain basketweave and all in the same color, the slightest flaw would just jump out at you, Jill," remarked Betsy, the voice of experience.

"Now if it were trame," pounced Carla, "there would probably be a pattern of jungle leaves and flowers in fifteen or twenty colors all around that tiger. Very lovely and elegant."

"But leaves and flowers wouldn't look as good as this vast plain," said Jill, smiling at her subtle pun. "Maybe I won't even stitch over it, just have it finished with a white backing. Or maybe a lighter shade of green than that pillow he's sitting on." She held it out at arm's length by the top stretcher bar, her head cocked a little.

Jill was rarely forthcoming like this, especially among strangers. Betsy sat back, watching, sure Jill was up to something.

Jill said, "I wonder what our mystery instructor would suggest."

"Who can guess? No one knows who she was supposed to be," said Isabel, making a single cross-stitch in a deep shade of pink on a rose petal.

Jill said, "But didn't Carla here say it was Kaye of Escapade Design?"

Carla said, "No, I heard someone else say that. I don't know for a fact who it was supposed to be."

Betsy said, "Do you know Kaye?"

"Yes. She's from Duluth, as am I. So naturally our paths have crossed a few times."

"Is she a good teacher? I'm thinking about hardanger, and it might be helpful to take a class."

Carla grew thoughtful. "Well, she's all right, I suppose. Of course, her specialty is counted." The drawl was very apparent. But apparently realizing she'd gone a little too far, she amended, "Now she is a very talented needlewoman, she really is. Her hardanger is amazing. And with beginners she can be sweet. But if anyone comes to her with an idea of their own, she's not . . . sympathetic. Not actually rude, just not . . . sympathetic." She looked at Isabel for confirmation.

And, reluctantly, Isabel nodded. "But we don't know that she was supposed to be the mystery teacher."

"Who was the first person to suggest it was Ms. Kaye?" asked Jill.

Isabel said, "Oh, it was probably several people getting the same idea at the same time. She was the obvious choice."

Carla said, "I don't even know who it was I heard saying it was her, but as soon as I heard the name, I thought that was probably who it must be. She and Charlotte have been friends forever."

Isabel looked up from the paper pattern clipped to the edge of her hoops and nodded. "I think that's why her name was suggested. She only recently started selling her designs, but I know she's been designing for several years. Charlotte's the one who encouraged her to submit her designs to catalogs and teach classes. Her designs are good, and some are very clever."

"And they're selling well," acknowledged Carla, with what Betsy was sure was as much envy as fair judgment.

"Do you design?" Betsy asked her.

"Goodness no. I prefer the classic models and am quite happy in my humble place as faithful stitcher." She smoothed a section of her work over her lap. It was of a medieval woman standing outside a pavilion set up under stylized trees. Betsy was sure she had seen that same design in a book on medieval and Renaissance tapestries.

Betsy was reaching into her knitting bag for her own project when James called her name. "Ms. Devonshire?"

Betsy raised a hand. "I'm over here."

James came to her and said quietly, "Ordinarily I wouldn't do this, and if you like, I will say I was unable to find you. But there's a phone call for you in the office, from someone named Godwin. He says he's sorry, but it's very urgent."

"All right, I'll come." Godwin had a tendency to panic, but he knew how much she needed this break. It probably really was important.

James led her to a door in the far end of the lobby, which he had to unlock. Behind it was a tiny, cluttered office. He handed her a heavy black receiver from a very old telephone. "Hello?" said Betsy.

Godwin said breathlessly, "Oh, thank God they found you! I'm *so* sorry to take you away from your weekend, but this is an *emergency*! You won't believe what's happening here, it's just *awful*!"

"Take it easy, Godwin, slow down, what's the matter?"

"There's water coming through the *ceiling*! It's ruining *everything*!"

"Water? What, is it raining there?" That was a silly question; there were apartments over the shop, rain would have to leak through the roof, the upstairs ceiling and then the floor of Betsy's apartment.

"No, it's *not* raining! That's the *point*! It's *not* raining!"

"Then where is the water coming from?"

"That's what I'm *talking* about! It's coming through the *ceiling*! It's not dripping, it's *dribbling*! And it's ruining *everything*!"

James made an excuse-me gesture at Betsy and left, closing the door behind him. "Where is it coming from?"

"The *ceiling*!"

"For heaven's sake, Godwin, make sense!"

"I *am* making sense! There is water, *water* simply *pouring* through the ceiling of the shop, and it's getting *all over* everything! There's a *huge* puddle right in the middle of the floor!"

"Where is it—no, never mind, it's coming from my apartment, obviously."

"Oh," said Godwin, "is *that* what you were asking?" He giggled. "Silly me! Yes, it *must* be coming from your apartment, mustn't it? Did you leave the water in your *bathtub* running?"

"No." Betsy thought. "And I didn't leave the water in the kitchen running, either." She thought some more, trying to picture various possibilities and a cure for each. She said, "How bad is the water damage in the shop?"

Godwin sounded calmer now. "It's coming through in *two* places, actually, one where the library table is, where it seems to have *killed* the cordless phone and wet down the basket of loaner tools. And it just *soaked* the spinner rack of perle cotton floss; it's standing in a puddle, a *big* puddle, you could go *splashing* in it. And the *ceiling* is kind of *bulging down*, like it's going to *crack open*—"

His voice was starting to sound panicky again, and Betsy said hastily, "All right, all right, something needs to be done immediately. You're there, you know where I keep the spare key to my apartment, you go up and see what's going on. Shut off the water supply to whatever's running over, if that's the problem. Then fix it—or get it fixed, whichever. I'll reimburse you when I get back. Or, if you're maxed out, use the shop's credit card. Then contact our insurance agent, who is going to have a cow." Back in December Betsy had made a claim for smoke damage.

There was a brief silence, then Godwin said without any italics, "You're so good in an emergency, Betsy! I suddenly feel much better. All right, I'll summon a plumber or a roofer or whatever, as soon as I find out what the problem is. Then I'll call Mr. Reynolds. Are you going to start back now? How many hours are you from here?"

"No, I'm not coming back. Why should I? You're a trustworthy, competent person, you've steered me through enough problems in the shop for me to know that. Of course, if you get upstairs and find there's a gaping hole in the roof that's pouring melting snow into my apartment, then maybe you should call me again."

Godwin's laugh this time had more assurance in it. "Yes, all right, but I don't think *that* will be the problem. And you're right, I can take care of it otherwise myself. Now I think about it, we had a waterpipe break one time, it made an even worse mess, but there were no fatalities, so I don't suppose there will be any this time, either. But let me add, Joe Mickels was landlord then, too, and he was a real stinker about it. But I suppose, since you've started dating him, he'll be much sweeter."

Betsy said, "But I'm not dating him anymore. Didn't I tell you? He thought because I was so clever about maneuvering him into selling the building to me that I was his kind of person, a little too interested in making money. We went out three times, and every time, all he wanted to talk about was all the clever ways there are to make money, and hinting that no one knows how rich he really is. Which makes it all the more ridiculous that he's the cheapest date I've been out with in my life."

Godwin laughed. "I can believe that. He made an ass of himself at an all-you-can-eat buffet once, eating till he waddled, and insisting on a doggie bag. But I wish you'd strung him along for a while. It would make this problem a lot easier to deal with."

"No, friendly doesn't work on Joe. Better he still thinks I'm too clever for him, so when you call him, tell him I've already been notified. That may keep him from trying to get cute. Whew, I'm glad we haven't signed the final papers yet." Betsy had been going round and round with Joe about the sale, trying to bring him to the closing, but he was apparently determined to hang on to those rents as long as possible.

"All right. Are you having fun up there? Is that why you don't want to come home?"

"Not yet. But soon, I think."

"Well, get lots of rest. Take at least one nap a day. 'Sleep knits up the raveled sleeve of care,' you know. That's Shakespeare."

"Yes, I know. And I think you're right. Now, go show me my confidence in you is not misplaced."

"Yes, ma'am. And, Betsy . . . thanks."

Betsy hung up. But not wanting to return to the lounge, where Carla waited, she sat for a bit, looking around. The office was not only tiny, it was oddly shaped and without a window. A computer took up most of the desk space, but it sat on a very old desk, possibly original to the building. The walls were papered with cheery yellow roses, one section almost hidden behind Post-it memos, lists, and other reminders. The door was old and ill-fitting—another reason to think the office was a retrofit. Light could be seen at the bottom where there was an inch or more of space.

How wonderful to be the owner of Naniboujou, with its beautiful lounge and magnificent dining room, but how sad to spend the wakeful hours in here, struggling with maintenance, heating, insurance, the wait staff, the kitchen, without even a window to look out of at the lake. Of course, what with changing bed linen, serving meals, chopping wood for that fireplace, and coping with guests who complained of dead bodies in their rooms, perhaps the owner didn't spend all that much time in here.

Betsy was reminded of a sign she'd needlepointed back in February: THE ONLY THING MORE OVERRATED THAN NATURAL CHILDBIRTH IS OWNING YOUR OWN BUSINESS.

But at least she wasn't going to be the one shelling out big bucks to do the repairs back home. The thought of Joe's greed doubling back to bite him in the butt made her smile suddenly, and she lolled back in the chair, tipping ash off an imaginary plutocrat's cigar. But the chair, an executive model, dropped backward so sharply she thought it was going over. She threw herself forward and the chair slammed upright, throwing her onto the dark hardwood floor.

"Ouch, dammit!"

After a second, she rolled onto her backside, and sat quietly for a minute, gently rubbing her left knee, squeezing her eyes shut to keep tears from flowing.

As the ache subsided, she took a deep breath and dared to look for injuries. The knee, while painful, didn't have broken bones poking out. It didn't look bruised. In fact, there wasn't even a run in her panty hose. She brushed at her skirt, which wasn't very dusty, and leaned forward to start getting up. Her eye was caught by something grayish white on the floor near the back of the knee well of the old wooden desk. It looked like one of those fat markers for a whiteboard, or maybe a highlighter, probably dropped and kicked out of sight.

Awkwardly, favoring the painful knee, she crawled forward to retrieve it.

It wasn't a marker. It was a translucent tube with black and yellow printing on it, filled with a colorless liquid. And clearly labeled: EPIPEN.

Betsy reached up to grab the front edge of the desk with her free hand and got her feet under her. She pulled the chair forward and sat down. There was liquid inside the object and what looked like a very big-bore needle. Instructions printed boldly on it said to remove the gray safety cap, with an arrow pointing to the other end. The cap was a flat thing, with a gripping edge like the milling on the rim of a quarter. The instructions continued that one was to put the needle end against the thigh, and "using a quick motion," push "until injector functions." *Ouch*, thought Betsy.

Smaller printing described the pen as an auto-injector which would deliver a "0.3 milligram intramuscular dose of epinephrine," and noted it was "for allergic emergencies (anaphylaxis)."

Did the owner of this place suffer from allergies? If so, he would be pleased to know where this device had gotten to. She put it in the center of the desk, and would have reported finding it, but the lobby was unmanned, so she returned to the lounge.

"What's up?" asked Jill.

"Godwin says there's water leaking into the shop from the ceiling. I told him to handle it."

Jill raised her pale eyebrows in surprise.

"What?" said Betsy.

"You think the boy is up to it?"

"Sure, don't you?"

"I'd rather it was Shelly working this weekend. She's calmer in an emergency."

"Oh, Godwin's already over the vapors. He'll be fine." Betsy rummaged in her knitting bag for her own project, a counted cross-stitch pattern of a rose window, to be stitched on black Aida cloth. She found the round plastic box in which she kept her floss, the Aida cloth, and spare needles. She unfolded the cloth on her lap, and her eye was caught by a finished section of Carla's trame. "You do really excellent work," she said, trying to keep the note of surprise out of her voice. People as rudely opinionated as Carla were often less than talented.

Jill leaned forward for a look. "You did the faces in petit point," she noted. "Nice." Petit point stitches are half the size of needlepoint ones, and enable the stitcher to get lots of detail on faces and hands. That's why there was Penelope canvas, which was double woven to make both petit point and needlepoint stitches possible on the same canvas.

Betsy said, "How long does it take you to complete a project this large?"

"About four months, if I get to work on it steadily," said Carla. "Of course, that rarely happens. One is so busy nowadays, with travel and committees and all." She heaved an overburdened little sigh.

Betsy noticed a tiny movement and glanced at Isabel, who was heaving a sigh of her own and rolling her eyes at Carla. Betsy barely suppressed a giggle, and bent over her canvas bag to look for her scissors and the paper pattern, lifting and moving her knitting aside, hiding a grin. But honestly, the way things curled down and out of sight in this thing—*The American Needleworker* magazine she had tucked in was lifted with her knitting and fell out.

"Oh, did your *Needleworker* come already?" asked Isabel. "Mine's probably in my mailbox then, waiting for me to come home."

Betsy pulled out the pattern, handed the magazine to Isabel, and continued to root in her bag for her scissors. "I pay extra for first-class delivery, because it's so annoying when a customer comes in with a question about something she saw in a needlework magazine or catalog, and I haven't read it yet."

Isabel didn't answer. Betsy found her scissors in their little case on the bottom, hung them around her neck on a braided cord, and looked over to see Isabel staring at the cover of the magazine as if she'd never seen a counted cross-stitch pattern of pansies before.

"What?" asked Betsy.

"Well, look who's on the cover!"

"Who?" asked Carla.

"It's Sharon Owen."

Betsy frowned and said, "No, that's Kaye of Escapade Design."

"Well, sure, Sharon Owen and Kaye of Escapade are the same person. No way for you to know that, I suppose, but Sharon Kaye Owen is her full name." Her sigh this time was authentic. "I really was hoping she'd be our surprise instructor. We do like to support local talent." She saw Betsy was staring at her and said, "Is something wrong?"

Six

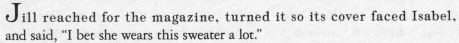

Jill reached for the magazine, turned it so its cover faced Isabel, and said, "I bet she wears this sweater a lot."

Isabel said, "She does. It's knitted of silk, because she's allergic to wool, so it's unique. But how did you know that?"

Jill said, "Because she was wearing it when Betsy saw her here yesterday."

"You mean she *is* here? Why haven't we seen her?"

Betsy said, "Yesterday afternoon Sharon Owen sat down across from me right in this lounge. We talked a little bit about how great Naniboujou is; she said she's always loved it, and that she had come up here on her honeymoon. She also said she was here to meet her husband—"

Carla interrupted, "She's not married."

Betsy said, "You're right, *ex*-husband. She said she was here to try to reconcile with him."

"Never happen! She's been divorced from Frank for eleven years."

Betsy said, "Is Frank also called Eddie?"

Isabel replied, "No, of course not. Why?"

"I thought she said at one point she was going to meet Eddie."

Jill said, "None of the three men here are named Eddie?"

Isabel shook her head. "No."

Betsy said, "Maybe he's an employee here."

Carla said dryly, "Maybe it's Eddie she wants to reconcile with."

"What do you mean?" asked Betsy.

"Now, Carla," warned Isabel.

But Carla said, "She's always running off with some boyfriend or other." She frowned and added with a faux air of thoughtful frankness, "Well, actually, she never tries to reconcile with the boyfriend once she leaves him, at least as far as I know. She just dumps him forever when she decides to give Frank another try. But of course she can't stick with Frank, either."

Isabel, frowning at Carla, said, "It's kind of sad, really. One of those cases of can't live with him, can't live without him."

But Carla said, "That's strictly on her part. He's done with her, no chance in the world he'll take her back. He finally realized she's one of those people who make promises they have no intention of keeping. All she ever did was get the children excited and hopeful, then she'd abandon them again. He should never have let her come back after she left the first time, because then and every time after, she'd be nice to everyone for about a month, then get bored and unhappy and be out the door, on to bigger and better things."

"That might have been true once about the children getting hopeful," said Isabel, "but they aren't exactly children anymore. Beth must be twenty-two or -three, and Douglas is what, twenty months younger than she is?"

"Eighteen," Carla said, adding with an air of quoting an authority, "It doesn't matter how old the children are, they still suffer when there's a bad divorce. Besides, Beth never really left home, she just took over the mothering chores from Sharon Kaye. Frank's done all he can, more than he should, really, but Sharon is a perfect witch with a capital B."

Isabel said firmly, "This is all very interesting, but wandering off the point. The point is, was Sharon Kaye actually here? Ms.—Devonshire, is it?—"

"Betsy," said Betsy.

"Betsy seems to think so. And as I said, it would make sense if Sharon Kaye was the mystery teacher. She does beautiful pulled thread and cutwork. And her latest cross-stitch pattern is amazing. Even that very first one in her series, the 'When I Grow Up' teddy bears, is adorable. I've been stitching them on an afghan for my granddaughter. I know she can be impatient with people—"

Carla sniffed pointedly.

"But, I'd give her a chance, if it were up to me. And Charlotte is, after all, her friend. If she was here yesterday, why isn't she here now?" Isabel stood and put her project on the cushion where she'd been sitting. "I'm going to ask if anyone else has seen her."

As Isabel stood and began working her way from group to group down the room, Carla said to Betsy, "What's that you're working on?"

Betsy's pattern was a counted cross-stitch pattern from a booklet called *Rose Windows,* by Sue Lentz. She had taken the book to Kinko's and after a copyright discussion with the man behind the counter paid for an enlargement of the pattern labeled "Traditional." Like the others, the pattern was a circle cut into rows of wedges around a central medallion. Because the cover showed it stitched on black, she'd cut a length of sixteen-count Aida from her shop's supply, added a spool of Kreinik Confetti blending filament, and selected antique DMC colors. Though the pattern wasn't for a beginner, Betsy had gotten used to color changes, doing a set of Christmas tree ornaments, and had surprised herself by working a snowflake pattern that called for careful counting. She'd heard black was difficult to stitch on, but sixteen-count wasn't tiny. And these glowing colors would look especially nice on the matte black of Aida. If it came out well, she'd frame it and hang it as a model in her shop.

Betsy unrolled the black cloth and said, "I'm better at needlepoint than I am at counted, but my shop sells both, so I thought I'd better at least try something more advanced." She showed the pattern to Jill. "Not that this is really advanced."

Jill snorted faintly.

Betsy said, "What, Miss I Only Do Needlepoint?"

"That's not as easy as it looks. You have to really pay attention to your counting on circular patterns."

It was Betsy's turn to snort. "You have to really pay attention to any counted. Isn't that the point?" She ran her fingers down the ribbon pinned to the fabric to where her needle threader was attached. "Anyway, all I brought to work on besides this is my knitting."

Knitting was Betsy's therapy. It freed her mind to ponder, to wonder, to connect things. But Betsy didn't want to think—not about finding a woman's dead body on a bed, or worse, that her bad dreams had become so realistic she could no longer tell them from reality.

She found the center of the fabric. The one-inch medallion in the center was old gold, and she threaded her needle and set to work. "Count twice, stitch once," was the advice given by counted cross-stitchers, and Betsy was careful to obey. Still, Isabel was gone long enough that she came back only as Betsy was putting in the last three stitches. "No one else has seen Sharon Kaye," she reported.

"Perhaps we should call Charlotte in the hospital," suggested Jill. "Ask her if Sharon Kaye is, in fact, the surprise guest."

"Why?" asked Carla. "It isn't important, is it? Sharon isn't here now, and

neither is our mystery teacher. That is, unless Isabel takes my earlier suggestion. What do you think, Isabel?"

Isabel said, "I don't think so, Carla. For one thing, hardly anyone here is
interested in trame, and for another, you don't have enough supplies with you
to give everyone a chance to try it. Merely talking about it won't satisfy."

Carla tried to take that in good grace, but there was a snappish emphasis
to the next few stitches she took on her canvas.

Betsy kept her eyes on her work, threading her needle with the soft pink
of the first wedge and counting carefully before taking the first two stitches.
But when the silence went on and on, she glanced up to see Carla, her embarrassed cheeks overriding her artificial blush, smiling apologetically at Isabel.
"I'm afraid I do ride my hobbyhorse hard," she said.

"It's all right," said Isabel stiffly.

Betsy smiled, too, relieved the tension was not because of her and her strange
story. "There seems to be something obsessive about needlework. I don't know
if it draws the kind of person inclined to obsess, or if doing the work brings out
the obsession. I have customers who seem to suffer withdrawal if they have to
stop stitching for as long as a week." Betsy's smile deepened a bit. "Such a delicate, dainty art, needlework," she continued, her own needle flashing. "Created
with fibers twisted tight, and sharpened, highly polished steel."

Carla's eyebrows lifted in surprise, then she laughed. "I like that!"

Isabel said, "I don't feel obsessed. When I pick up my needle, I remember
my mother doing needlework by lamplight, and my grandmother, and I can
sense her grandmother under an oil lamp, and hers, and hers, and so on, until
we are back sitting by the fire, trying a new pattern on doeskin and keeping an
eye out for the sabertooth that took a neighbor's child last night."

Jill remarked, "We are bloody-minded today. I wonder why."

Carla said, "I think we're disappointed and angry. All that hinting, and no
surprise."

Isabel said, "I think the idea of a mystery teacher was always a bad one.
Everyone had a secret wish for what the class should be on or who the teacher
should be, each one different, so most of us were doomed to disappointment
even if the instructor showed up."

"That's true," said Carla.

Isabel said, "Who would you have liked it to be, Betsy? I mean, if it could
have been anyone at all."

"Anyone? Joyce Williams. I'd love to sit and watch how she knits those
Latvian sweater patterns. Or Kaffe Fasset. I hear he's a wonderful teacher. How
about you, Jill?"

Jill said, "Susan Porta, maybe. Or Jean Hilton. They both do exotic fibers,
and that's what I like to use in needlepoint."

Isabel said, "I'd like Charley Harper to come by. Not because I think he'd have something to teach me, but because, judging by his designs, he has a terrific sense of humor." She added, more darkly, "And I'd like to have a word with him about the way he designs his patterns."

Betsy said, "I like Charley Harper, too. I especially love the one of the brown pelican sitting on a brown piling in silver rain. The pattern's in my stash, along with the cobblestone Aida cloth and floss. I picked a thin silver braid for the rain, and the Aida is a nice big fourteen-count . . ." Her voice drifted off as she began to think about the project. Then she laughed. "I already have more projects than I can finish in a year. Now that I have a little money, it's going to be really hard not to buy lots more."

Jill said, "When you no longer resist temptation, you will know you are officially a stitcher."

Isabel said, "I have a T-shirt that says, WHOEVER DIES WITH THE BIGGEST STASH WINS. I'm definitely in the running."

Betsy said, "I sell a T-shirt that says, WHOEVER DIES WITH THE BIGGEST STASH IS DEAD. WHEN'S THE ESTATE SALE?"

The women laughed. Carla said, "I don't think I've heard of Charley Harper."

Jill said, "Counted cross-stitch," and Betsy looked for and saw the very slight raising of Carla's upper lip.

Honestly, she thought, *why there has to be this split between the counted cross-stitch and needlepoint communities, I cannot understand. It's worse than dog people versus cat people.*

Betsy and her sister Margot had had both cats and dogs, often simultaneously, while growing up. So it was no surprise that Crewel World carried cross-stitch, knitting, and needlepoint supplies.

There was a period of silence while everyone settled into their projects. Betsy finished her first wedge in DMC, then got out the Kreinik metallic filament and snipped off a foot of it. It changed colors every couple of inches from gold to blue to green to silver. She consulted the pattern and began the first stitch. Pulling it through, the ultra-fine stuff, twisted and crinkled around a very thin thread, caught on the cloth, and slipped out the eye of her needle.

"That should look very pretty," noted Isabel.

"Yes. This will be my first try at a blending filament." Betsy took another stitch, holding the filament in the eye with her fingers, and this time the filament knotted without warning, and when she tugged experimentally, it broke.

She glanced at Jill, who was smirking subtly. Betsy stuck her tongue out at her, teased the filament loose, cut off the knotted portion, rethreaded her needle, and set off again. But with almost every stitch, when the filament didn't twist and knot, it slipped out of the needle or snagged and broke. It was impossible for Betsy to lose herself in a stitching pattern when the thread was being difficult. Despite herself, thoughts of Sharon Kaye began to intrude. At last she growled, stuck her needle in the fabric, and asked, "What hospital did you say Charlotte Porter is in?"

Isabel said, "What a good idea! I think it would be a nice thing if we bought a get-well card and everyone signed it. She's at St. Luke's in Duluth."

But Betsy wasn't thinking about a get-well card. She stood and said, "Excuse me, I'll be back in a few minutes." Then she remembered: No phones in the rooms.

Jill murmured something and Betsy bent to hear it said again. "Pay phone in the lobby."

She nodded and went out into the lobby, where she found James on duty and got him to break a five-dollar bill into coins. She sat down in a dark corner near the office where the pay phone lurked. In a few minutes, the heap of coins considerably diminished, she sat frowning.

Charlotte Porter was feeling quite, quite comfortable, thank you, and thanks so very, very much for the sympathy expressed by the stitch-in people, weren't they nice, and she was sooooo sorry she couldn't be there. She had her stitching with her and had thought perhaps to join the stitchers in spirit, but the pain medication was making it sooooo hard to work on her Celtic Christmas angel. Mystery guest? Oh, wasn't she there? How strange, Charlotte had talked to her day before yesterday and she had assured Charlotte she'd be there. Her name? "Kaye of Escapade Design. Sharon Kaye Owen, yes, yes, yes, you know her? Wonderful lady, terrific friend, good teacher. I can't believe she's not there yet. She's going to teach an advanced class on what-is-it, hard-anger, and a beginner's class on designing a counted stitch pattern, cross-stitch. She was sooooo excited about it."

"Did she say anything to you about her ex-husband being here?"

"Oh, is Frank there? Let me think, she does go on about him, doesn't she? She thinks she's still in love with him, though of course she isn't, she just can't bear thinking that someone else might get him. Though she hasn't got him anymore, I've told her that lots of times. I shouldn't be talking like this about her, she's a very good friend and a very, very fine woman, talented and very, very, very patient with beginners especially. That's why I agreed when she volunteered to teach at Naniboujou. Isn't that a lovely, lovely name? Some people call it Nanny-*boo*-zhou, but it's pronounced Nanny-boo-*zhou*. So Frank is there? He and she used to go up there all the time, until the divorce. Which was all her fault, I suspect. The divorce was. I shouldn't say that, either, should I? It's the pain medication, I suppose. It makes me feel sooooo very nice, but a bit talkative. Do you suppose they gave me truth serum?" The idea amused Charlotte, and she giggled in a slow, strange way.

"I believe some truth serums are actually pain medications," said Betsy.

"Oh, my dear, you mustn't take what I'm saying as the truth," said Charlotte, giggling some more. "I'm just saying whatever comes into my head, speculating out loud." She lowered her voice to a whisper. "Gossiping."

"I understand," said Betsy. "But I think you've talked enough for now, and I should let you get some rest."

Since it was nearby, Betsy made use of the restroom and then went back to the lounge, where, in a pretense of looking at Jill's project, she murmured that Sharon Kaye Owen was, in fact, the mystery teacher and had talked with Charlotte about teaching at the stitch-in as recently as Thursday.

Betsy sat down and took up her needle, but after about ten minutes, Jill said, "I want a cup of coffee," and looked pointedly at Betsy, who obediently said she'd like one, too.

Carla said, "They leave a pot out, but it's probably awfully strong by now."

Jill said, "Maybe we can get them to make a fresh pot. Come on, Betsy."

Betsy followed her across the chromatic dining room to a pair of doors on the other side of the fireplace. Jill pushed through the one with the marks of people shoving on it, Betsy on her heels, and they were in the kitchen.

"Hi, Amos!" Jill called, and a trim, gray-haired man looked up from a big pot he was stirring on an eight-burner stove.

"Hi, Jill!" he said. "Arrested anyone lately?"

"No, but that doesn't mean there isn't someone who needs arresting." She walked to the big stove at which he stood.

Amos laughed, then saw something in Jill's face and said, "What's wrong?"

"We're not sure." She turned slightly and said, "This is my friend Betsy Devonshire, who owns a needlework shop in Excelsior. Betsy, this is Amos Greenfeather, chef here at Naniboujou for the past six years."

He had the broad face and black eyes of a Native American, but not the usual impassivity Betsy had come to expect. He made a little French-style bow in her direction, and Betsy said, "Your meals are delicious."

"Thank you." He smiled broadly.

Jill said, "Would you know Sharon Kaye Owen if you saw her?"

"Never heard of her. Is it important? Maybe the wait staff would."

"Are they around?"

"Most of them." He turned the heat down under his pot and went to the back of the long, narrow kitchen. Like all places not frequented by paying customers, it was a little shabby. The big stove was elderly, the stainless steel pot on it was scratched from countless scrubbings, and ceiling tiles over it were warped by heat and steam. But everything was spanking clean, and the only smells were the fabulous ones of bread baking and stew stewing.

Amos came back with four women and a fresh-faced young man. All wore clean white shirts. The women were in dark skirts well below the knee and comfortable shoes, the young man in navy twill trousers. No multiple piercings, no Kool-Aid-red hair. How quaint, thought Betsy. How refreshing.

"Would any of you recognize Sharon Kaye Owen if you saw her?" asked Jill.

"I would," said a woman with short, dark brown hair and beautiful light brown eyes. She looked a little older than the others, and she spoke with the authority that marked her as their senior in rank, too. "She used to be a frequent guest at the lodge."

"I don't think I ever saw her," said the young man, and the other women also shrugged.

"She's a little taller than I am," said Betsy, "very thin, with blue eyes and very light blond hair, short and curly. She was wearing one of those Norwegian sweaters, blue and white with a starburst pattern around the neck, and pewter fastenings."

"Did any of you see her today?" asked Jill.

Shrugs and negative shakes of heads.

"Yesterday?"

Same response.

"I saw her yesterday afternoon," said Betsy. "I came downstairs from our room and went into the lounge. She came in and sat down across from me. We talked for a bit and then she said she wanted to go see Eddie, and I think, to have a cigarette." Betsy looked at the young man. "Is your name Eddie?"

Looking slightly alarmed, he shook his head. "No."

Betsy asked, "Is anyone working here named Eddie?"

The senior woman said, "No."

Betsy persisted, "Didn't any of you see her going out? Or standing outside smoking? This would have been after four o'clock."

"Not me," said a woman whose dark blond hair was in braids wrapped around her head.

"No," said the young man. The other two shook their heads.

"We were pretty much on break from the dining room," offered the woman in braids. "Around three, everything's cleaned up from lunch, and dinner is a ways off."

"But suppose someone comes in and wants a meal?" asked Betsy.

"Too bad," said the young man with a regretful smile. "The kitchen's closed except at mealtimes."

"But I saw someone in the dining room yesterday afternoon about three," said Betsy. "He was wearing a brown uniform."

The wait people all looked at one another, then at Betsy. "We don't serve meals except between eight and nine-thirty in the morning, eleven and one-thirty in the afternoon, and six-thirty and eight in the evening," the young man explained patiently.

"Well, there's generally coffee," said the senior woman, the one with the light brown eyes. "Guests can come and serve themselves as long as it lasts."

"Yes, but by three o'clock that stuff's pretty rancid," remarked the woman with braids.

"Coffee's coffee to people who need a caffeine fix," said the chef.

"So you don't remember seeing him, either?" asked Jill.

"Nope," said the third woman, and everyone agreed that they hadn't seen him.

Betsy's heart sank. Such a small, telling detail—and it was false, too? But Jill said, "I remember him, he was sitting at a table in the middle of the room."

Heartened, Betsy asked, "Does anyone know about a company hereabout whose employees wear brown uniforms? Chocolate brown, not tan."

The young man said, "Park rangers."

Jill said, "And there's a state park ranger station right across the road."

"But it's mostly closed in the winter," the woman in braids said.

"What does 'mostly' mean?" asked Betsy.

The young man said, "Well, a ranger comes by once in a while to see if the box they leave out for admittance fees needs emptying, and to fill up the tray with more maps of the trails. And they have this guy, he's not a real ranger, go back on a snowmobile once or twice a week to see if a hiker broke a leg and froze to death."

The wait staff sniffed quietly, whether at the lack of more frequent patrols or the silliness of winter hikers, Betsy couldn't tell.

"Does this man on a snowmobile wear a park ranger uniform?" asked Betsy.

"No," the senior woman said.

Betsy closed her eyes. She'd only glimpsed the man sitting at the table. Maybe he wasn't wearing a uniform, only a brown jacket and trousers. Why had she been so sure it was a uniform?

Her eyes opened again. "Do the park rangers have patches on their sleeves? White or maybe buff?" She sketched a good-sized triangle on her shoulder.

"Yes, they do." The older woman nodded. "Did the man you saw have a patch?"

"Yes."

There was nothing more volunteered from them, and there was an air of impatience as they waited to see if Betsy had more questions.

"Okay," said Jill, "let's understand this. There was a park ranger having coffee in the dining room yesterday afternoon. Betsy and I both saw him, but none of you did. So the fact that nobody else saw Sharon Kaye Owen, who sat across from Betsy in the lounge and said she was here to reconcile with her husband, doesn't mean she wasn't just as real. She was here."

Betsy said, "And she's dead."

Seven

There was a shocked silence. Then the senior woman said, "How do you know that?"

"Because I went up the stairs from the lobby instead of the dining room, and into Frank Owen's room, thinking it was mine. She was lying on the bed, and she was dead."

"Oh, you're the woman!" said the senior woman. "James told me about you. But there wasn't a body in either of the upstairs fireplace rooms, was there? So we decided it was some kind of . . . peculiar mistake." She was being polite to a guest.

"We're assuming somebody moved it, Ramona," said Jill. "There was plenty of time to do that between when Betsy first saw it, and when we figured out what room she had seen it in."

Ah, so this was James's wife, co-owner of the lodge. Ramona knew who, and what, Jill was; and Jill's acceptance of Betsy's story put a new complexion on things. *How incredibly valuable to have a police officer backing you up,* thought Betsy.

Ramona asked, "What do you want us to do?"

Betsy was surprised at the lack of rancor in her voice. Rather than jumping to a denial that such a thing could possibly happen in a quiet and happy place like Naniboujou, or expressing concern about Betsy's sanity (options very much on Betsy's own mind), Ramona wanted to know what the next correct step might be.

Jill said, "I think the police should be called at this point. Grand Marais Police are the controlling authority, right?"

Ramona said, "No, the person to call would be the sheriff. But what would be the good of that? There's nothing for him to investigate. All we have is the unsubstantiated word of a guest that a stranger no one else saw came and is now gone."

"There's some substantiation," said Jill. "The person Betsy saw was supposed to be here. She was the 'mystery teacher' Charlotte Porter invited, her name is Sharon Kaye Owen of Escapade Design. Isabel Thrift can confirm that."

"Sharon Kaye Owen? Is that who we're talking about? Oh, my, I know her! But she hasn't been here in years."

"Car!" exclaimed Betsy.

"Car?" echoed Ramona, looking slantwise at Betsy.

"She didn't ride up here with someone, so she must have driven herself. What kind of car does she drive?"

"I have no idea."

Betsy went out the swinging door into the dining room and crossed it to the lounge, to where Isabel was sitting.

"What kind of car does Sharon Kaye drive?" she asked.

"I don't remember."

Carla said, "It's blue, a Saab, I think." She frowned and reiterated, "I think."

Betsy straightened up and called for the room's attention, then asked, "Does anyone here know what kind of car Sharon Kaye drives?"

"A gray BMW," said someone.

"No, I think it's light green," disagreed someone else.

"It's blue," said Carla firmly. "Kind of a medium shade."

"Thank you, never mind," Betsy said.

She went back into the dining room, where Jill waited. Betsy said, "We need to get a list of what everyone's driving, so we can eliminate possibilities. Let's ask Isabel—"

Jill interrupted, "What makes you think the murderer left her car here?"

The excitement of the chase cut off as if someone twisted the faucet, hard. Betsy sat down. "That's right, that's right. In fact, he probably drove her away in her own car."

"Not far," said Jill. "If you're thinking he came back here afterward." She sat down across from Betsy.

"I am?"

"Well, Frank Owen's the one you suspect, isn't he? The obvious one."

"I suppose so."

"Well, who else could it be?"

"I'm not sure. Did you notice how Carla leapt to Frank's defense?"

"Carla?" Jill turned that over in her mind. "Okay, I think I did, on reflection."

"If there's something between Carla and Frank, and Sharon Kaye tried to put a stop to it . . . Or, it could be Eddie. Since he's not here, maybe he drove here with Sharon Kaye and drove off with her body."

"Who's Eddie?"

"That's a very good question. Let's go talk to Frank."

Frank Owen was dressing to go out, in wool knee pants, argyle stockings, and a forest green sweater with cable stitching, a cross-country ski outfit. He opened the door to his room with the sweater around his neck and down one arm, the rest of it gathered on his other shoulder. He frowned at Betsy, looked beyond her at Jill, then frowned back at Betsy again.

"What kind of car does your wife drive?" asked Betsy without preamble.

"Ex-wife."

"What kind of car does your ex-wife drive?"

"I have no idea." He shoved his other arm into the sweater and pulled it down.

"Have you tried to call her today?"

"No, why?"

"To find out if she's all right."

He twisted his shoulders impatiently. "Of course she's all right. She was never here, that's all."

"Well, she was supposed to be here, to teach a class to the stitch-in people."

He frowned at Betsy, then Jill, who nodded. He said slowly, "I suppose that does make a difference, doesn't it?"

"Do you have her home phone number?"

"Yes," he said, and got it from a big black notebook that zippered closed.

She started to turn away, but Jill said, "Wait a second. Just because she's not here doesn't mean she's at home." She asked Frank, "Do you know where else she might be?"

"I don't have her current boyfriend's number, if that's what you mean."

"Is his name Eddie?"

"No, Tony. Why?"

"Maybe she's at your place?"

"I very much doubt it, Liddy knows how I feel about Sharon. But my daughter sometimes goes to have lunch with her." He added, "Maybe Liddy knows where she is."

"Might your daughter know what she's driving?" asked Jill.

"I don't know. Possibly. Why, what's so important about her car?"

Jill said, "May we have Liddy's phone number? Is that your daughter's name, Liddy?"

"Yes, Elizabeth, called Liddy." He recited the phone number; Betsy wrote it under Sharon Kaye's home phone number.

"Well, thank you, Mr. Owen," said Jill.

He started to close the door, then opened it again. He said, his voice showing the same mild concern on his face, "I think I'll come down with you."

Down in the lobby, Betsy got out her quarters and dimes and dialed the number Frank had given her. After four rings an answering machine began, saying in a crisp, competent voice, "You have reached Escapade Design. At the tone, leave a message."

Betsy said, "Hello, I'm calling from Naniboujou Lodge. Are you there, Mrs. Owen? Please pick up if you are there." No one did, and Betsy hung up.

"Which doesn't prove anything," said Frank. "She's the only person I've ever known who can ignore a ringing phone."

Jill said, "But surely, if she heard the name Naniboujou Lodge, she'd be reminded she was supposed to be here and take the call."

Frank's mouth thinned. "Not if she doesn't want to hear a critical voice."

"Is your daughter at home?" asked Betsy.

Frank checked his watch. "Probably."

Betsy dialed the number. "Hello, is this Elizabeth Owen?" she asked when a woman answered.

"Yes?"

Betsy said, "I'm calling from Naniboujou Lodge. We're trying to locate your mother. She was supposed to teach a class at a stitch-in here."

Elizabeth said, "Oh, yes, I knew Mama was going to teach a class. Was that this weekend? Isn't she there?"

"No, and we're wondering if you know where she might be."

"Not at home?"

"No, we tried that."

"Then I'm sorry. I didn't know the class was this weekend, or I would have warned Daddy. He is there, isn't he?" A note of anxiety crept into this question, and she added, "Is he all right?"

"Yes, he's fine," said Betsy. "I'll let you talk to him if you like. But your mother seems to have gone missing."

"Missing? I don't understand. You mean she never arrived?"

"No, she was here, I talked with her yesterday. But she doesn't seem to be here now."

"How . . . peculiar. Well, maybe she left again. She's been known to do that."

"Do you know her boyfriend Tony?"

A note of wariness crept in. "Yes, why?"

"Could she be with him?"

"No, he's in Chicago for some kind of training, won't be back till next weekend."

"What kind of car is she driving?"

"A blue Volvo, brand-new. Vanity plates, of course, 'escapade' spelled S-K-P-A-Y-D. Among other things, that was a poke at our last name, Owen."

"Thank you, Ms. Owen. Here, your father wants to talk to you."

Betsy handed the receiver to Frank, then she and Jill hurried up to their room and put on coats, then went down the back stairs to the parking lot.

A sky blue Volvo with the vanity plates described was the third car from the end of the row, its fenders white with salt. Through a backseat window they could see a wicker basket with the lid fastened down.

"No," said Jill.

"No what?" said Betsy.

"That basket isn't nearly big enough."

"No," agree Betsy. Not even for an extremely thin woman, folded small.

The car was locked. They walked around to the back. Betsy said, "Could—could she be in the trunk?"

Jill said, "It's probably locked. Let me see." She fumbled with a mittened hand for the release under the edge of the trunk lid. She found it, pulled, and with a tiny creak, the lid lifted. There were two suitcases in the trunk, but no body.

"I was scared she'd be in there," said Betsy.

"I was afraid she wouldn't be," said Jill. She lowered the lid again, latching it. "I don't understand why this car is still here."

Betsy said, "Maybe because she's still around here somewhere, too."

They heard footsteps crunching and turned to see Frank approaching, hatless and pulling his fists up inside his sleeves like twin turtle heads. "This it?" he asked, his breath smoking in the cold air.

"Yes," said Betsy. "Are you sure she didn't come knocking on your door?"

"She might have. I was out most of the time. Actually, I don't see how she knew I was going to be here in the first place. I sure didn't tell her."

"Who did you tell?"

"My daughter and—" He paused, obviously struck by something. "A couple other people," he finished lamely, but added more strongly, "I don't think any of them would tell Sharon, they knew how I felt about her. My daughter says she didn't, and is sorry she didn't warn me Sharon was coming."

"If Sharon didn't know you were here, where did she think she was going to stay?" asked Jill.

"I don't know." said Frank. "I didn't know anything about her or her plans." The sun went behind a cloud and he shivered. "Look, it's too cold to be standing around talking. I'm going back inside." He set off for the front of the lodge. Betsy and Jill went with him. He said, "I still think there's some kind of logical explanation for all this. She's probably gone off with some friends."

"Is that like her to behave so irresponsibly?" asked Betsy.

"Oh, hell yes. Since her life got so limited by her allergies, she grabs at any kind of pleasure she can have, whenever she can, and damn any promises she made. It makes sense, I suppose, but it's frickin' annoying to anyone who thinks he can rely on her."

They followed him back inside, where he excused himself and went from the lobby into the dining room, and headed for the fireplace. Betsy, watching him go, asked Jill, "If he'd gone to his car instead of back in here, would you have arrested him?"

"For what? First, he's not standing there with a knife in his hand and Sharon Kaye's body at his feet; second, I'm out of my jurisdiction and not here on official business; and third, without a gun and handcuffs, I'm not sure I could have taken him. He looks pretty wiry." She was smiling faintly. "Why, is he back on your list of suspects?"

"He was never off. But anyway, we really can call the sheriff now, right?"

"Oh, yeah, with that car sitting there, I'm sure they can get a search warrant for both it and Mr. Owen's room."

The front desk was unmanned. But the door to the tiny office was open. James was sitting inside, and Betsy could see the ruled lines of a bookkeeping program on his computer monitor. As they headed that way, Betsy said thoughtfully, "I wonder who was the other person he told?"

"Beats me."

James agreed that the presence of Sharon's car was concrete proof that Sharon had been here, and that a thorough search of the building and grounds was the obvious next step. "I'll call Sheriff Goodman," he said.

Fifteen minutes later a salty, dirty white car with a five-pointed star on its door pulled up. Sheriff Gregory Goodman, a short, brisk man with slicked-back dark hair and a rough-edged voice, was more indignant on behalf of the lodge than its owners.

"I still can't believe what you're telling me!" he barked at Betsy when she told him her story of seeing Sharon dead in room 10 for the second time. "Things like this just don't happen to decent folk like the Ramseys!"

"Yes, they do," said Betsy sadly. "Not often, and it is terrible, but they happen."

Goodman frowned at her. "You sound like you been in a mess like this before."

"I have," said Betsy. "More than once. I came up here to get over the last one, and now I seem to be involved in another one. Of all the things in the world, this is what I wanted least."

Her sincere tone brought a sharp look from James, and the sheriff asked, "How do you know the person you saw on the bed is Sharon Kaye Owen? Have you ever met Mrs. Owen before?"

"No. But her appearance is striking, and her picture is on the cover of a magazine I subscribe to. That's why, for a little while, we thought perhaps I'd only dreamed I saw her. Because when I saw her, she was wearing the same sweater she's wearing in the photo."

"So how come you think now you didn't dream the whole thing?"

"I told you: Because her car is here. And she was supposed to be here to teach a needlework class." Betsy knew from previous encounters with law enforcement people that they made every witness tell his or her story at least twice, and then asked questions.

Goodman, frowning, went back a page in his notebook, read something, and nodded. "How sure are you that when you saw her on the bed she was dead?"

"I went close to her, and I could see she wasn't breathing. Her lips were blue, and her face was discolored in places. I pressed the carotid artery in her neck, but couldn't find a pulse." Betsy shivered. "I was sure she was dead."

"But you're not a doctor. Or a nurse."

"That's right."

"So it's possible she had passed out, then woke up after you left and walked out under her own steam."

"Yes, that's possible. The question is, since she didn't take her car, where did she go?"

Jill and the sheriff exchanged a look, and suddenly Betsy felt a chill. It would be horrible if she woke and, sick and confused, wandered out in the cold, perhaps into the surrounding woods, to become another body found too late by that part-time forest ranger.

Maybe, Betsy thought, *I should have stayed with the body. I could have opened the door and yelled for help, couldn't I?* She shook herself out of that thought, having learned long ago that "shoulda-woulda" regrets were the most useless.

"Show me the car," Goodman said, and Betsy and Jill walked out with him. He walked all around it, peering in the windows, but didn't touch the door handles. Betsy, noticing that, was glad she had refrained as well.

"The trunk was unlatched so we opened it," said Jill, and he gave her a disapproving glance.

"There's two suitcases in it," said Betsy. "But no dead body. We pushed it closed."

Goodman went back to his squad car to check the vanity plate, and when it proved to belong to Sharon Kaye Owen of Duluth, he asked a deputy to swear out a search warrant for the car and for a search of the lodge and its out-buildings. When Jill offered to assist, he told her to go stand guard on Frank Owen's room, allowing no one in. "Is he here?"

Betsy looked into the dining room. "He's over there, by the fireplace."

The sheriff looked as well. "Who's that with him?"

"Carla—what's her last name? Prakesh. One of the stitchers." Carla had left her Penelope canvas to sit on the couch opposite Frank, listening intently while he spoke to her.

The sheriff started across the room. Betsy watched to see if he would arrest Frank. When the two glanced toward him, Carla stood but Frank didn't. The sheriff said something, Carla replied and added something more to Frank, then went into the lounge. The Sheriff sat down and pulled out his notebook.

Betsy, feeling her work was done, decided to go into the lounge. She paused in the doorway, blinking, shifting gears from sleuth to stitcher. The sun poured full strength through the windows, its brilliance doubled by reflection off the snow-covered lawn. It came through the big windows like a barrage, ricocheting off the light-colored walls and ceiling. If it had been sound, it would have been deafening.

There were about thirty women and two men in the room. They were all busy. The sunlight flashed on the movement of needles, laying tools, embroidery hoops, the knobs on scroll bars. Wool, acrylic, silk, and cotton colors glowed, both on the stitchers and their work. It was so womanly a scene, the quiet, cheerful voices, the peaceful bent heads, the busy hands—and not Betsy's responsibility to supply their material or cope with their wants or complaints. And now, with law enforcement on hand, there was no pressure to do any sleuthing.

Betsy looked around, thinking to sit with or near Carla, but the woman had chosen the last open place in a cluster of upholstered chairs the stitchers had rearranged.

At first disappointed, Betsy told herself firmly she was relieved; after all, she wasn't going to sleuth anymore. She retrieved her needlework bag from beside Isabel, who was describing an encounter with a "pattern from hell" to a woman nodding sympathetically, and continued down to an empty wicker chair facing a sofa on which sat a plump woman totally involved in her stitching. Her indifference was welcome; Betsy didn't feel like talking to anyone right now. Anyone else, anyhow. She looked through the glass of a French door, where the sheriff, now standing, looked about to lead Frank out of the dining room.

Betsy again firmly quashed her curiosity, and got out her stitching.

She pulled her needle from its place on the border of the Aida cloth, consulted the Sue Lentz pattern, and took a couple of stitches.

"Oooh, the rose window patterns; I worked those a few months ago," said the woman sitting across from Betsy, not so totally involved in her own work after all. She was a tall, heavyset woman, her dark blond hair given golden highlights by the sun.

"Did you enjoy it?"

"Not the stitching." The woman chuckled. "But they were beautiful once they were finished. I see you're working the one on black."

"Yes, I haven't tried doing a pattern on black before, and I guess it's time. I'm Betsy Devonshire, I inherited a needlework shop in Excelsior and I've decided to keep it running. That means I have to get serious about needlework."

"I'm glad to hear you're keeping the shop open. We treasure our independents because of the special attention and the classes—though too often we buy our floss at Michael's or Wal Mart."

"I know." Betsy sighed and the woman chuckled again. Betsy leaned forward to see what she was working on. It was a rectangular needlepoint canvas, painted with grapevines top and bottom, and a beautiful uncial H leading off a William Morris quote: HAVE NOTHING IN YOUR HOUSES THAT YOU DO NOT KNOW TO BE USEFUL, OR BELIEVE TO BE BEAUTIFUL.

"I don't think I've seen that canvas before," said Betsy.

"It's a Beth Russell kit, I ordered it from England, by Internet. I'm Nan Hansen, by the way. Oops!" She had begun to reach out a hand to Betsy, but instead knocked over the bottle of water resting on the arm of the couch.

"Nice to meet you."

Nan picked up the bottle of water and put it on the coffee table. "Were you out for a walk? It's so lovely up here in the summer, but I've never been one for winter sports. Outdoor ones, anyway. You're a lot braver than I am."

Betsy was considering how to reply to this when a man's rough-edged voice called from the other end of the room, " 'Scuse me, ladies! May I have your attention!"

Betsy looked up to see Sheriff Goodman standing, hands on hips. "Who's in charge of this sewing shindig this weekend?"

Isabel stood. "Since the woman who organized it couldn't be here, I suppose I am."

"Will you come with me, please?" Goodman said, bending a turned-back forefinger at her.

They were no more than out the door when James Ramsey came in. The lodge owner said into the staring silence, "As most of you know, Sharon Kaye Owen was supposed to be here to teach a class. She was actually seen here yesterday, but not since, nor can she be located anywhere else. The reported circumstances of her disappearance are . . . disturbing, and the sheriff is here to begin an investigation. I'm sure he'll be asking all of you some questions." A brief murmur rose and quickly died as he continued. "Her car has been found in the parking lot, so a search will be conducted of the premises. I know this is an inconvenience and I apologize for it, but of course we are anxious to have this mystery solved."

A murmur of agreement rose, but one woman asked, "Are they going to search our rooms?"

"I can't imagine why," said James. "Can you?" There was uncomfortable laughter. "Now, if you will excuse me?" He bowed slightly, and left the lounge.

When he was gone, their voices rose in varied discussion of this turn of events. But in a couple of minutes, as work resumed, the noise quieted.

"You seem to have stirred up a mystery—maybe," Nan said to Betsy.

"Me?"

"Yes, that's what you were doing outside, looking for Sharon Kaye's car, isn't it? Of course it was, you were in here asking what kind of car Sharon Kaye drove. Are you a detective? I know that woman you were with is a police officer. What's going on, can you tell me?"

"There's hardly anything to tell," said Betsy. "Did you know Sharon Kaye?"

Nan nodded, and pulled a strand of cream-colored yarn through another basketweave stitch. "Yes, I did. A few years ago, she buckled down and got really good at counted cross-stitch, after years of just fooling with it. But then she couldn't do what she really loved anymore, which was climb mountains and swim oceans. She liked doing hard things, so I suppose we shouldn't have been surprised when she recently decided to challenge herself by designing."

"Were her designs any good?"

She took another stitch. "Well . . . not brilliant or breaking new ground. But competent, and getting better with every new one."

A woman across the way cleared her throat, and when they looked at her she said, "I'm doing the flower series she designed." She held up her project, a counted cross-stitch pattern of five daffodils in a glass vase. "I'm Linda Sava-reid, from Albert Lea. This is the first pattern of hers I've worked, and I love it. Her design is so easy to follow." Linda had streaky brown hair and the gentle, competent air of a grade school teacher Betsy had once loved.

Nan said, "Getting on the cover of *ANW* was a real coup for her. If she ever comes up with something really fresh, she could become one of the shining lights of counted design." She looked at Betsy over half-moon glasses. "Well, unless . . ." she said.

"Unless she's dead," said Linda.

"Yes."

Having broken the subject open, the women on the couch with its back to Betsy began talking about Sharon Kaye, and soon the women across from them joined in. Betsy shamelessly eavesdropped (and so she didn't realize for some while that she was making some mistakes in counting her stitches).

"I can't imagine her dead," said a woman with an interesting white streak in her russet hair. She had finished stitching a hardanger pattern of squares and was very carefully snipping out their centers. "She sort of took over any room she was in."

"I hope nothing bad has happened to her," said one young woman dressed in a red sweat suit. She was stitching the alphabet in bright silks on Quaker cloth. "She is so nice! When I was just starting out, she sat with me for half an hour and showed me how to grid and follow a pattern. She was so patient and so encouraging, it made me feel special."

"Well, good for you, Katy; she was rude to me every time we met," said a young woman with several earrings and a glint in her eye.

"Now, Anna," warned Nan.

"Humpf!" snorted Anna. "You know as well as I do, she could be damn rude when she felt like it, and what's worse, she always had to have her own way about everything or she'd walk out right in the middle of whatever we were doing."

"She wasn't well," said Nan.

"She was as well or as sick as she wanted to be," retorted Anna. "All that stuff about being allergic! I saw her shopping at a mall once, looking healthy as a horse, then she turned up the next morning at a stitch-in wearing a mask and whining that someone present had eaten peanut butter. She positively enjoyed making us all feel guilty for having a life. Poo!"

Linda Savareid turned in her seat to say, "I had a student in my seventh grade class who was allergic to peanuts—and believe me, it's not a guilt trip. A fellow student brought an assortment of cookies as a birthday treat one day. Some had peanut butter in them, but none of us knew it. The allergic child ate one and stopped breathing. If he hadn't had an EpiPen with him, he'd've been dead before the ambulance arrived."

"What's an EpiPen?" asked Nan.

"It's a medical device designed to be used by non-medical people," said Linda. "It delivers a big dose of epinephrine to someone having a severe allergic reaction, and can keep them alive until they get to a hospital."

Nan said, "Sharon Kaye has one."

"I didn't know she had allergies," said a young man stitching a Norman Rockwell painting of a fisherman in a small boat in the rain. "She came to our store and was a wonderful teacher. But she never said a thing about being allergic." He turned to the even younger woman sitting beside him. "Remember when she came to our store, Suzy?"

The young woman nodded, but kept her eyes on her knitting. She was making an argyle sweater in four colors of wool.

The young man continued. "Miss Kaye taught a class of six people just starting out in cross-stitch."

"When was this?" asked Betsy.

"Right after we opened, eighteen months ago. She drove all the way to Fergus Falls, and got us off to a good start. We're in our second year now, still doing pretty good." There was a note of pride in his voice, and his back straightened. "It was all Suzy's idea. I wanted to buy a farm. Right, Suz?" He nudged the woman beside him, who blushed becomingly and still didn't look up. She looked barely out of high school, and Betsy wondered at the audacity of such young people opening their own business. Betsy also wondered why such a shy woman would decide to go into a business that demanded constant customer contact.

"And you say she was a good teacher?"

"She was wonderful," murmured the young woman.

"How long did the class last, Mike?" asked another woman in somewhat absent tones. She was working on a canvas held firm with scroll bars. Rather than fasten it to a stand, she had made a big loop of ribbon, twisted it into a figure eight, ran it around her neck, and put a loop of the eight around each of the two top knobs of the scroll bar. The bottom of the frame was braced on her ample tummy, and she was using both hands, one to push the needle into the top and the other to pull it through. As a result, her bargello pattern—waves of various colors done in long, vertical stitches—was progressing very rapidly.

"All weekend," said the young man, "Saturday morning and Sunday after-noon, three hours each. Every student who signed up came to both sessions." He looked at Betsy, and she saw he had devastating green eyes.

"I'm surprised Sharon lasted the entire weekend," said Nan. Her voice was slightly squashed, as she was bent severely forward to poke around on the floor for a pair of dropped scissors. "Oof, there they are! It would be more like her to do what she did here, change her mind at the last minute. Or quit partway through. I've known her for years, and she's always been what she calls whimsi-cal. Whim of steel, if you ask me."

"Now be goot, Nan," said a woman wearing a deep yellow cardigan. Her project was a tiny bouquet of roses being worked with a single thread of silk on fine gauze. She wore a very large magnifying glass attached to a gray headband. Her eye, then her nose, then her ear in succession were hugely magnified as her face turned past Betsy toward Nan, a disconcerting effect. When she spoke, it was fluently, but with a German accent. "She is not here to defent herself, so be kind."

"Oh, there's no defense for what she does." Nan wove her needle into a cor-ner of her canvas so she could concentrate on this conversation. "In fact, there's generally some mischief in it. Haven't you ever noticed that, Ingrid? Charlotte's in the hospital, so here's her chance to make us all mad at Charlotte by walking out on her agreement to teach a class."

"But you're not mad at Charlotte," Betsy pointed out.

Nan replied, "You just watch, next month Sharon will come to our stitch-ers' meeting and be so contrite and sweet, and she'll have such a clever explana-tion, everyone, probably even me, will be glad to forgive her. Charlotte hasn't got that charm, and what they'll remember next year, when Charlotte tries to organize another stitch-in, is that she promised us a surprise guest teacher at this stitch-in and didn't deliver."

Betsy said, "And you think Sharon Kaye did that on purpose? To make the group mad at Charlotte?"

Nan backed down at this blunt restatement. "Well, probably not. She and Charlotte are friends, after all. It's just that's always how things turn out around her. If some project gets in trouble, no matter how thickly Sharon Kaye's involved in it, somehow she never gets any of the blame. Maybe it isn't malicious, it could be that she just does whatever she feels like doing without any thought to how it will affect others. I'm sure if she agreed to come up here and teach a class she really meant to teach it. But then she got another invita-tion that seemed like more fun, and it never occurred to her to say something. Or she got here and saw someone she doesn't like, and just went away without telling anyone about it."

Ingrid said, "I think it more likely she got here and something set off an allergic attack. She wouldn't haff time to tell somebody about it, she would just go, quick, off to the emergency room."

"Emergency room—are her allergies that serious?" asked Betsy. "I mean, her ex-husband told me she smokes, and I wouldn't think someone with serious allergies would smoke." Betsy was trying to pretend she wasn't really interested in the topic of Sharon Kaye's allergies by continuing to work on her cross-stitching. It was hard to see the openings in the weave of the black cloth when the background was her brown skirt, so she kept having to hold the fabric up toward the window to make the tiny openings in the weave visible.

"Oh, it's so *aw*-ful that she smokes!" Ingrid said. She had an expressive face and voice, eyebrows lifting, lip movement exaggerated, voice going up and down the scale, like the magnifying glass that caused the weave on her yellow sweater to swell then collapse again as the lens moved across it. "I haff told her over and over that she simply must quit, because she does have serious allergies that put her in the hospital sometimes, and smoking affects breathing, everyone knows that. And when she feels an attack coming on, it's important she get medical attention *immeeee*-dee-utly. I once saw her collapse from—what is the word? Some kind of shock."

"Anaphylactic," said Linda.

"That's right, anaphylactic. She has carried that device you were talking about that can inject medicine ever since that time she collapsed right in front of us, and nobody knew what to do. It was very frightening!"

Betsy said, "Did anyone ever see her use the pen? I should think if she carried it, she wasn't pretending to have allergies, because what would happen if she used that pen and wasn't really in anaphylactic shock?"

Linda said, "It's like a big dose of amphetamine, so surely it would be dangerous to use it if it wasn't a real emergency."

The EpiPen Betsy found in the lodge office had been full of medicine, unused. She said, "She didn't become ill while I talked with her, or at least she didn't seem ill. Could she tell when an attack was coming on? She just said she had to go meet someone, not that she was having an attack. I thought perhaps she was having a nicotine fit."

"Trust me," said Ingrid, "she would never mistake a nicotine, ah, what did you call it, 'fit' for one of these attacks. It was very important to her to keep track of those things, because first she turns red, then she turns blue, then poof! Collapse, and perhaps she is dead."

Betsy remembered the dead woman's blotchy face and blue lips. And the blush when she had mentioned her honeymoon. Maybe she was starting an allergic reaction then. *Now don't make too much of that blush*, she told herself. *Maybe she's the sensitive type. And maybe she just got bored and walked out. Anyway, if*

she did die here, they'll find her. And if not, be grateful. So don't think about it anymore.
She looked at her stitching: she'd gone over two threads instead of one. And
trying to unstitch it by going back through the same hole caused the floss to
snag and fray. This stupid Aida fabric! She unthreaded her needle and used its
tip to tease the floss out of the fabric. Trying not to think about Sharon Kaye
was making her head hurt.

Nan said, "Are you all right?"

Betsy squeezed her eyes shut and murmured, "Just a bit of a headache."
This part of her stitching was starting to look really wrong. She picked up the
pattern to do some recounting.

"Say, Anna, where's Parker?" asked Nan.

"Prying agates out of the ice on the beach," said Anna. "He's writing a
paper on the geology of the North Shore. We were here last summer and he
made me hike to the Devil's Kettle and back—those stairs!"

"Agates?" said Betsy, thinking of marbles.

"Beautiful stones you find along the shore of Lake Superior," said Anna.
"Dull brown on the outside, but slice them with a saw and they are magnificent
inside."

"Oh, I've seen them!" said Betsy. Glassy layers of delicate color, sometimes with
a hollow center, agate slices were for sale in gift shops down in the Cities. "I wondered why I saw three men in the dining room and only two here in the lounge."

The talk went on to vacations and tourists and hiking.

It was nearly an hour later that Jill came in.

Betsy looked up and said, "What did they find?"

Jill replied, "Nothing. No sign of Sharon Kaye." She spoke quietly, but
Nan overheard her and immediately turned and passed the word along, and in
a few seconds the room was abuzz with the news.

Betsy felt giddy, whether with relief or distress she didn't know. She said to
Jill, "So what are they going to do now?"

"Nothing. The sheriff and his crew have gone away."

"But—" Betsy rubbed a spot over her left eyebrow, where the headache was
really pounding. Why hadn't they found anything? Had they looked absolutely
everywhere? Was there something else she could have told the sheriff, some
other question she could have asked? No, no, no, stop it! This no longer involved
her. She had done her duty. But . . . She stood. Jill said, "What now?"

"I have to ask Isabel something." A dim notion had made its way out of
the thicket of pain. She stooped beside Isabel to ask, "If Sharon Kaye had an
allergic attack, she might have asked someone to take her to the hospital. Is
there someone who signed up for this event who isn't here?"

Isabel said, "That's what the sheriff asked me. I told him no. Everyone who
signed up is here."

So even that dim light was extinguished.

"Here," said Jill from behind her, "you're looking tired. I think you should lie down for a while. I'll get our things and walk you up to our room."

As they walked to the door beside the big stone fireplace, Betsy asked, "Did they do a really thorough search of Frank's room?"

"Yes, Goodman's crew was very professional."

Betsy said, "What I don't understand is why the door to Frank Owen's room was unlocked when I went up there the first time. If I had a dead body in my room, I'd sure lock the door until I got rid of it."

"So would I." Jill nodded.

"Maybe the murderer didn't have a key." They started up the stairs, Betsy leading.

Jill said, "So you're still thinking maybe Frank Owen wasn't responsible for the body? Then what was it doing in his room?"

"I don't know. Because the murderer needed somewhere to put it and that room wasn't locked?" She stopped and turned around on the stairs. "But that would be stupid, wouldn't it? Why carry her upstairs to hide her? Why not just take her out the back door? I thought he might have planted the body in Frank's room, but if that was his plan, why come back and move it? That wouldn't make sense—but nothing about this does." She turned away and started up again, dizzy from the pain in her head. "Am I going crazy? I don't want to investigate, so why can't I leave it alone? What's the matter with me? Is this what a nervous breakdown feels like?"

"I don't think you're having a nervous breakdown. I think there are obvious questions occurring to you, as they would to anyone who found a body. I also think you need to get a little distance from it for a while. A nap may help."

In their room, Betsy took a couple of aspirin, then removed her shoes and lay down on the bed. Jill shut the blinds and folded the quilted coverlet over her.

"Jill?"

"Yes?"

"I saw an EpiPen in the little office off the lobby. Could it be Sharon's?"

Jill came to look intently at Betsy. "Was it used?"

"No. I found it on the floor under the desk."

The intent look went away. "Did you ask James about it?"

"No, he wasn't in the lobby, so I just left it in the office."

"Maybe it belongs to someone who works here."

"Yes, of course." Betsy closed her eyes—she was so very tired!—and tried to block out the thoughts vying for her attention. But in they trooped, pushing and shouting and waving their arms. Her head felt squeezed in a vise.

"I'm allergic to cigarette smoke" was a common complaint, even among people not allergic to other things. Yet Sharon Kaye smoked.

Was she one of those people who claimed to be allergic just to gain sympathy? Then what about the collapse Ingrid had described? Suppose the EpiPen Betsy found was Sharon's. If Sharon had an allergic attack, why wasn't it used? What was it doing in the office? That office door was kept locked; Sharon couldn't have put it in there herself. Was James somehow culpably involved in all this?

Or was it possible Sharon hadn't been here at all, that this had been a dream after all? No, she must have been here, her car was here. The car made it real.

If Sharon had been here, why did she leave? Someone had suggested that Sharon had left because she saw someone she didn't like. Who didn't Sharon like? More important, who didn't like Sharon? Certainly some of the stitchers had been acid-tongued when speaking of her.

Was it a coincidence that Sharon's ex-husband chose this weekend to come here, the same weekend Sharon agreed to come and teach a class?

Maybe it was learning he was here that had sent Sharon away. Certainly Betsy would not stay in a hotel, especially in a remote location, if her ex-husband turned up.

What was Hal up to now? Thank God he'd stopped sending flowers. The pig.

Was her headache a little better?

What was the cause of that water leak in the shop? Was she right to trust Godwin to handle it?

Was Godwin taking good care of Sophie?

If he forgot to give Sophie water, could the cat perhaps turn on the faucet in the bathtub and refresh herself?

And, of course, not being able to turn it off, the water would run and run, and the tub would fill and overflow.

And Godwin was upstairs in her apartment, lifting buckets of water out of the tub and pouring them onto her living room carpet while shouting, "Get an ax, chop a hole in the floor before Sophie drowns!"

And the cat was swimming neck deep in water toward a toy motorboat whose engine was idling over by the window. Sophie was too big for the motorboat, she would tip it over and sink it if she tried to get aboard. Betsy didn't have an ax; she took a meat cleaver from the kitchen and stepped into the living room and sank in over her head, and swam down, down, reaching for the carpet, cleaver at the ready, holding her breath, but by the time she got down to the carpet, she was already in need of air, so she dropped the cleaver and started back up, kicking desperately for the surface, which was too far away, she needed to breathe, she couldn't hold her breath any longer, she would have to open her mouth and breathe water, she was going to drown.

Betsy sat up on the bed, gasping.

Then she fell back on the pillow, to inhale more deeply and less desperately while her heart slowed down.

Well, at least this bad dream wasn't about murder.

What time was it, anyway? She looked at her watch. Nearly noon. Half an hour's sleep, not enough.

But despite the brevity of the nap, and the bad dream, she felt better. Her headache was gone, anyway. Rather than try to sleep some more, she'd wash her face and comb her hair and go back downstairs to stitch some more.

She went down the stairs into cooking fragrances and found the dining room was being set up for a buffet lunch. The long, broad counter at the other end was being laden with a delectable array of salads, cold cuts, meatballs, chicken wings, marinated vegetables, and desserts. A line was forming, snaking down the long room, winding among the tables. Betsy inhaled deeply and went into the lounge to retrieve Jill, and found her almost alone and everyone else still there packing away their stitching.

They got into line. Betsy complained about her problems with the rose window pattern. Jill said, "If you put a white cloth on your lap, you can see the holes in the fabric a lot better."

"Well sure, I know that!" Betsy grimaced. "I just didn't think of it." This was certainly not one of her brighter days. Talking about the patterns painted on the walls and how they would make pretty and easy cross-stitch patterns, they chose the first table they came to with two seats available. It was already occupied by a man and a woman. It wasn't until they had put their plates down that Betsy realized the woman was Carla.

But it would have been very rude to walk away at that point, so they sat. Carla said, "Jill, Betsy, I've been having the most interesting discussion with Anna's husband Parker, here. He's been out looking for garnets—no, agates. He's a graduate student in geology, and full of the most amazing facts about this part of the state. Mr. Lundquist, this is Jill Cross and Betsy Devonshire, of Excelsior, who are here for the stitch-in."

"I took a course in geology several aeons ago," said Betsy, glad to discuss a topic that didn't involve either crime or trame. "I enjoyed it very much—especially the part about continental drift and earthquakes, since I was living in California. But if I remember correctly, this area is stable, geologically speaking. And therefore not terrifically interesting."

"Well, that's partly correct," said Parker, with the pedantic air of the becoming-learned. "The bedrock around here is of the Keweenawan Supergroup, intrusive rocks of dominantly mafic composition."

"Which means?" asked Carla with a little smile.

"Composed of something that looks like granite, but isn't, not really. There was once a rift in the earth's mantle here, and consequently lots of volcanos.

The bluffs around here are the lava flows, which were thousands of feet thick. If you walk up along the Brule River, you can see how the water has cut a slice in it. The soil that overlays it is glacial drift, left behind when the last glacier retreated about twelve thousand years ago. This area is the North Shore Volcanic Group, which formed approximately eleven hundred million years ago, although most of Minnesota is part of the Canadian Shield, Precambrian rock six hundred to thirty-six hundred million years old."

"Good Lord!" said Carla. "Older than—well, old."

"Is that what you're studying?" asked Betsy. "The Precambrian formations?"

Parker shook his head. "I've been studying the Brule River rhyolite flow, part of a very ancient mountain range, the Sawtooth Mountains. The hills around Grand Marais are a remnant of them."

Betsy said, "What about the Devil's Kettle?"

"What about it?"

"Jill told me the water goes into a rock and never comes out again. Has that got something to do with the rift? Can you explain where it goes?"

"I believe the water probably flows underground and empties into Lake Superior."

Jill said, "But they put dye into the kettle, and it never showed up in the lake or anywhere."

"Oh, it will, eventually. I'm trying to prove a theory that there's a large and very slow-moving aquifer deep underground, which is fed by the Devil's Kettle."

Betsy said, "Are you saying that one of these days someone will be fishing along the shore here, and suddenly yellow dye will show up in the water?"

"It's possible," said Parker. "Though if my theory is correct, none of the people involved in the original experiment will be alive to see it. I think the water presently going into the aquifer will spill into Lake Superior in seventy-five or a hundred years."

"Have you been to see the waterfall?" asked Jill.

"Oh, yes, I went there a dozen or more times last summer—in fact, I was there again last week."

"Isn't it frozen solid?" asked Betsy.

"No, the river has a cover of ice, but the waterfall is open. I took some photographs along the riverbank, and of the falls itself. There is an interesting mix of boralfs and udipsaments along the top there, though of course none of it visible because of the snow cover."

"Of course," said Carla dryly, and Betsy laughed.

"I hope you will excuse my language," said Parker, abashed.

"Oh, I wasn't just laughing at you," said Betsy. "I was thinking of how Carla loves to talk about her favorite kind of needlework in almost exactly the same tone of voice you use talking about geology."

Carla, surprised, laughed. "It's true, it's true!" she said. "I was wondering why I liked this man. It must be because I recognize a fellow spirit. When I get interested in something, I obsess."

Jill asked, "What else have you obsessed on besides needlework?"

Carla's laugh cut off as if she'd been slapped. "What do you mean by that?"

"Nothing," said Jill, surprised. "You made a general statement that you obsess about things, and I wondered what else you had obsessed over."

Carla blinked. "Oh. Of course." She smiled. "Well, cooking; I love to cook; I have over a hundred cookbooks and a kitchen that can cook an eight-course meal for twelve—though I don't do that often; I'm a widow and my one child lives in New Zealand. And I do a lot of volunteer work for the Humane Society. I am currently on four animal welfare committees."

Betsy said, "I'm interested in animal welfare, too—I used to do wild animal rescue for the San Diego Humane Society when I lived out there. I'm going to have to check into what's needed in Hennepin County now that Excelsior's my home."

"I specialize in bird rescue when I'm in Florida," said Carla. "I've raised I don't know how many baby birds blown out of their nests by hurricanes."

"When I was nine I raised two baby robins I found in our yard after a storm," said Jill.

"I once found an orphaned baby raccoon," said Parker, and the awkward moment was quickly forgotten as the four got into a discussion of the amusing and healthy ingratitude of rescued wild animals.

Eight

After lunch, Jill said, "Well, back to the lounge?"

Betsy replied, "Not yet. I want to see if James can help us figure out where Sharon Kaye thought she was going to stay if Frank wouldn't let her move in with him."

Jill said, "I'm glad you're not taking your own advice about this."

"What do you mean?"

"You said you weren't going to get involved in sleuthing anymore."

"This isn't sleuthing! I mean, the police did the sleuthing and didn't find anything, so I'm going to find something that will make them try harder."

Jill could hide an emotion better than a world-class poker player. Still, Betsy narrowed her eyes at her. But Jill only nodded and said, "Okay."

"I've already told you Sharon Kaye Owen didn't have a reservation," James said a minute later, from behind the counter in the lobby.

"But did anyone change their reservation from a single to a double?" asked Betsy.

"I'll check." He checked his registration file. "Yes, Charlotte Porter changed her reservation from a single to a double about four weeks ago, and prepaid for two people."

Jill asked, "Did Charlotte tell Sharon Kaye her ex-husband was going to be here?"

James made a "How-would-I-know?" face, and Betsy said, "Charlotte didn't mention it to me when I phoned her—but she was pretty drifty from pain medication."

Jill nodded. "So it's possible Sharon Kaye didn't know Frank was going to be here."

Betsy said, "I think she did. Otherwise, she would have claimed Charlotte's room—it was paid for, after all, and Charlotte meant to share it with her. But she didn't claim it, which probably means she was hoping Frank would ask her to join him. Frank said he didn't know she was here. If that's true—" Betsy cut herself off; this was coming dangerously close to real sleuthing.

Jill asked James, "Can anyone read your check-in list to see who else is here?"

James shook his head. "If someone asks specifically, we will tell them so-and-so has checked in. But as I already said, I never saw Mrs. Owen, I had no idea she was at the lodge. Nobody asked me about her before you two did. And I'm the only one on the desk."

Betsy said, "I'm more and more sure she knew he was going to be here. In fact, I think it was his being here that made her decide to come. Because don't you think, Jill, that it's too big a coincidence that she decides to teach at a stitch-in at a time and place her ex-husband, with whom she wants to reconcile, happens to be?"

Jill asked James, "How far in advance did Frank Owen register?"

James said, "I'll have to check. But I can tell you the Grand Marais Embroiderers Guild reserved a block of rooms back in October, and no one else had reserved a room for this weekend that far back." James turned again to his registration file. "Mr. Owen reserved his room five weeks and two days ago. I warned him about the stitch-in, but he said he didn't think they'd bother him."

Jill said, "Did he ask if Sharon Kaye was coming?"

"I don't think so. If he did, I would have said she wasn't, because I didn't have her name on the list of people coming."

Betsy said, "But that works, don't you see? Five weeks ago Frank decides to come up, and a week later Charlotte changes her reservation to a double. No, wait, if I was allergic to everything, I'd want a room of my own."

Jill said, "The room I reserved was the last of the stitch-in's block, and that was six weeks ago."

James said, "Yes, that's right. She couldn't have gotten a room of her own."

Betsy said to James, "So the lodge is full, right? Sharon Kaye had to share a room, because Jill got the last stitch-in room, and then Mr. Owen took the one room left over."

James said, "Yes, we didn't quite get the innkeeper's dream of every room but one taken."

Betsy frowned. "I should think you'd want them all taken."

"No, the rest of the dream is that a reporter for an important travel magazine has a car breakdown right outside your door and just falls in love with your place."

"So as of now you're full up?"

"No; since neither Charlotte Porter nor her roommate turned up, we've got an empty room." He smiled. "But there's no sign yet of the *New York Times* travel correspondent."

James went back to his bookkeeping and Jill said, "I just thought of another possibility to eliminate: Call the area hospitals. She might be in one of them, too sick to let anyone know where she is."

There were a surprising number of them in the phone book. After the fourth call, Jill went away. Betsy continued through a fortune in dimes and quarters, calling hospitals and medical clinics, none of which had admitted or treated a patient named Sharon Kaye Owen.

Finished at last, she went back to her room and got a white hand towel, brought it to the lounge, and stood just inside the door. A number of the stitchers looked at her the way people will look at the scene of a car accident, and she showed them her best customer-welcoming smile until they went back to their work. Jill declared her place in the room by raising the canvas tiger in its frame and indicated an empty place across a coffee table.

Betsy found her canvas bag and brought it to the empty place. She draped the towel across her lap and got out her rose window pattern. Amazing how having a gleaming white lap made the weave so much easier to see, but she hadn't even found her place when a woman in a wheelchair rolled up to them. She was about twenty-five, a streaky blond athletic type, with the too-bright, aggressive look of a hawk in her eye.

Betsy blinked at her, surprised. She had seen the woman in the dining room and, now on this closer look, recognized her as someone she'd seen wheeling around Excelsior. She'd had no idea she was a stitcher. Certainly the woman had never come into Betsy's shop. But there on her lap was an almost-finished cross-stitch pattern of butterflies.

"Hi!" she said brightly. "I'm Sadie Cartwright." She leaned forward a little and said in a lower voice, "It's interesting you're here, because if anyone here can solve the mystery of Sharon Kaye's disappearance, it's you, correct?"

"Why do you say that?" asked Betsy.

"Because Jill Cross may be a cop, but you're the one with a nose for solving mysteries!"

"I'd disagree with you, because I see mystery I can't solve right in front of me. How come I didn't know your name, but you appear to know all about me?"

Sadie laughed. "I order my stitching supplies from the Internet, that's why I never come into your store. And the reason I know about you is that I've come to Shelly Donohue's class a few times to talk about life in a wheelchair, and I usually have lunch with her after. She loves to talk about her part-time job in Crewel World, and she's always bragging how Betsy Devonshire is a regular Miss Marple. She says you go around pretending to be an ignorant amateur, then all of a sudden someone is on his way to jail and it's all your doing. Now you're up here and we've got a mysterious disappearance, and who's the first one to sniff it out? Betsy Devonshire, the Sherlock Holmes of the needlework set!"

"I'm not Sherlock Holmes," said Betsy, "nor am I Miss Marple. I don't have any special skills as a detective, I don't like getting mixed up with crime, and I have no intention of investigating what happened to Mrs. Owen."

"See?" crowed Sadie, forgetting to speak quietly, rolling her chair back and forward in a show of pleasure. "Just like she said you do! 'Oh, I don't have any idea what you're talking about, but if you want to know who did it, just watch who I dance with tonight,'" she quoted in a high, breathless voice, though Betsy had never said such a thing in her life. "Ha! Shelly introduced me to Irene Potter, who told me you're so good you should sell your needlework store and hang out your shingle as a private eye. So don't pretend with me. I bet you'll have this little case all wrapped up before we go home tomorrow afternoon." Laughing, Sadie turned her chair in a single deft movement, and started back up the room.

"Wait!" said Betsy, but Sadie didn't.

"Durn," said Jill, "she'll tell everyone."

"I didn't know Irene bragged about me," said Betsy. "I thought she didn't like me."

"She wasn't bragging, she was dreaming out loud. She knows that if you turn private eye, you'll sell Crewel World. And you already know that above all else in this world, Irene Potter wants to own Crewel World."

"She told you that I should be a private eye?"

"She told Shelly that, and Shelly told me and probably a lot of other people—you know what a gossip Shelly is."

"Yes, I just got a reminder of that." Betsy frowned at the far end of the room, where Sadie was leaning forward to talk to a pair of women, both of whom glanced toward Betsy with wide eyes.

Jill said, "Speaking of not sleuthing, what did you find out?"

"She not in any hospital in Duluth," said Betsy. "And we're sure she's not home, and she's not with her daughter."

"She's not here, either," said Jill.

"That's because murderers don't ordinarily leave their victims strewn around."

"Sure they do," said Jill. "Especially in a hotel, because who wants to get caught staggering down a hallway with a body in his arms?"

Betsy had no reply for that. She picked up her Aida cloth, and determinedly started in. The fourth wedge forming the circle around the center medallion was quickly done, now that she could see what she was doing. She got out the spool of Kreinik metallic and cut off twelve inches of it. It felt weightless in her hand, and though it looked like colored metal, it was thin as plastic film. Thinner. When she tried to put it through the eye of her needle, the metallic part immediately separated from the very fine brown thread it was wrapped around. Licking it didn't put it back together; she had to snip off the separated ends. On the third try she got both pieces through and began to stitch, trying to work slowly and gently so as not to snag or break the gossamer stuff.

Jill looked casually around the room, seemingly at no one in particular, then said, "Look, she's telling the whole room."

Betsy stretched, moving as if to work a kink out of her neck, and looked over her shoulder. Sadie was halfway up the room now, talking to three interested stitchers. Betsy asked Jill, "What do you think she's saying about me? Do you know her?"

"Not well. She's a good person, she won't be telling lies. She acts a little tough, that's all. Compensating, maybe. She's genuinely strong, though, runs that wheel-chair up the sidewalks like it's a souped-up truck."

One of the stitchers glanced up and saw Betsy looking, touched Sadie on the shoulder, and the two looked back at Betsy, Sadie with a big white grin.

But Betsy's ear was caught by a woman nearer, saying, not quietly enough, "I hear that when there's a murder, the police always look first at the person reporting it."

Betsy felt a dash of cold anger. But she didn't want to look around to see who said it, so she went back to her stitching. In her anger, she pulled hard at the Kreinik, which instantly broke. Sighing, she turned her fabric over and used her threader to work the broken end under other stitches on the back, rethreaded the broken-off strand, and tried again to work little x's around the wedge.

But her focus remained on the talk all around her. Nan's voice rose into audibility. "I say, if Sharon is dead, she probably did something to deserve it."

And someone replied with a laugh, "If they look for motives, that would mean a lot of us are suspects!"

Betsy suddenly flashed on seeing the dead woman on the bed, reliving her own reaction of terror, sorrow, and helplessness. How dreadful to dismiss a death so callously! This was too much, she took a breath and would have risen to relieve her feelings had not Jill forestalled her by saying gently, "The air in here is getting a little close. How about we take a walk?"

Betsy glanced at Jill and saw a reflection of her own anger on that normally enigmatic face. She said in a carrying voice, "Yes, I think a walk out in the fresh air is just what I need!"

They went upstairs to change into wool slacks (gray for Betsy, navy for Jill) and cotton turtlenecks (white for Betsy, cranberry for Jill), over which they put coats, scarves, hats, and mittens. They pulled on insulated boots, went down again through the dining room to the lobby, and out the door.

The air was dry, very cold, and smelled of woodsmoke.

Betsy looked across the parking area and saw a great wall of logs and cords of fireplace wood. "Is all that for the fireplace?" she asked.

"No, they heat the lodge and its water with wood. That shed over there houses the furnace and boiler. This being March, the wood supply is nowhere near what it was back in October."

Betsy started across the parking and turnaround area. Though the sun was brilliant and the air calm, the tamped-down snow creaked under their feet, and Betsy could feel the tingle of bitter cold inside her nose and through her mittens. "This feels much colder than Excelsior. I wonder that the temperature is?"

"About ten above, I think," replied Jill. "Not too bad with no wind."

The furnace shed was about ten by twenty feet, corrugated steel painted a dull green. A metal chimney spilled fragrant smoke into the still air. Though a path had been cut through the snow to its wooden door, it had snowed after the path was dug, and instead of shoveling again, people had simply trampled the new snow down. Consequently, the path was icy and uneven, full of heel-shaped depressions, their edges worn smooth.

"Treacherous footing," Betsy noted, stepping carefully and keeping her elbows out to improve her balance.

Snow had drifted three feet deep along one side of the shed, but the ground within a foot of the wall was bare, and Betsy could feel the air grow a little warmer as she approached the door.

"Where are we going?" asked Jill behind her.

"I want to see the furnace, to see if it's big enough."

"For what?" asked Jill. "Oh," she added.

"Did the sheriff look in here?"

"Yes. I kind of followed them around once I was released from guarding Mr. Owen's door. But he was only in the shed for a couple of minutes."

Nearly to the shed, there was a thick V in the snow heaped beside the path. It looked as if someone had fallen to his knees. Other marks indicated he'd dropped what he was carrying and picked it up piecemeal. Betsy bent over the marks, expecting to see bits of garbage or wastebasket detritus, but she couldn't see anything at all.

The ground right in front of the door was covered with a sheet of plywood on which was laid a rope doormat, both of them frost-covered and marred with sooty footprints. There was no trash or litter to be seen—wait. Betsy stooped and pried up something in the trodden snow beside the wood. It was a skein of DMC 208 cotton floss with one of its two black and gold wrappers still around it. "I see they've already burned trash from today," said Betsy. "I wonder who threw this away? It's hardly been used. Pretty color." It was one of the colors she was using in her pattern. It didn't look dirty. She shook off fragments of ice and put it in her pocket.

The shed was empty of everything but the furnace, which took up nearly all the space. It was old and large, swathed in what looked like plaster. Its door was black cast iron, opened by lifting it clear of a stubby hook—"Ouch!" Betsy yiped, snatching her hand back—and hot to the touch. She took her mitten off and folded it in half to use as a hot pad. The inside of the furnace was half full of white-hot coals on which very pale yellow flames danced.

Betsy looked around for a poker or a stick and didn't find one. There was nothing else in the shed, not even chunks of wood. "I don't suppose there'd be anything left by now anyhow," she said, bending for a closer look. The air pouring out of the furnace was enough to singe her eyebrows.

"Not so you could just look in and see it," agreed Jill. "Close the door."

Betsy obeyed, and Jill continued. "The maintenance man comes out here pretty often to put more wood into that furnace. It's not like coal or charcoal, wood burns fast, you've got to keep feeding it or the fire goes out."

Betsy said, "So if there'd been something in there that wasn't wood, very likely he'd've seen something left of it in there when he came out to feed the fire."

Jill said, "Plus, remember the smell of woodsmoke when we approached? That isn't what a burning body smells like. He'd've noticed that. It's a very distinctive odor."

Betsy felt a prickling in her throat. "Don't tell me things like that!" she said, swallowing.

"Hey, coming in here was your idea. Make up your mind, Betsy! Let's either go on investigating, or do what I suggested in the first place: Go for a walk."

"My mind *is* made up!" snapped Betsy. "Let's walk!" But outside the shed she said, "Hold up a minute. I'm sorry. It's turned into some kind of reflex, this snooping business. I sincerely do want to stop but I'm having trouble doing that. Please be patient with me."

"Sure."

"Thanks. Now, where did you want to walk to?"

Jill led Betsy back across the parking lot then across the lawn to the lakeshore. The snow on the lawn was well over a foot deep, with a thick, crunchy top that held their weight for a second or two, then let their feet break through to their knees. But cold as the air was, the lake was not frozen, not even along the pebble-strewn shore. It was a very dark blue and stretched out to the pale blue horizon. Toward the north—well, east, actually, Betsy told herself—the land rose to form dark bluffs. Lake Superior wasn't Lake Michigan, running north and south, or the Pacific Ocean, where from San Diego one looked west; here it was a fat finger pointing southwest, and they were on the northern shore, where Minnesota formed a long, narrow arrowhead between the lake and the Canadian border.

Jill looked up and down the beach. "Here's where they put the Adirondack chairs Martha was talking about. It's like meditation to just sit and watch the lake."

Watching big water was soothing, so they did that for a minute or two. Far out, the restless surface was growing swaths of dark lavender on its deep blue. The big patterns of color had smaller, more subtle changes included in them. The sun, still well south this time of year, made golden spangles here and great, molten-brass puddles there.

Betsy's attention shifted from aesthetic to artistic. How could you capture something like that in a needlework pattern? Uneven stitch, maybe, with silks and metallics?

There was a quiet, staccato gush of the waves on the narrow beach. The eagle appeared suddenly, flying low over the surface of the water, its wings wide, its high-pitched cry a surprise in so large a bird. Betsy watched as it went up along the shore, diminished to a silhouette, then soared without effort up the split face of the dark stone bluff. The bluff was topped with a mix of pine trees standing in snow against a bright blue sky, and the eagle rose higher than their highest tops, turning around, riding a breeze. Betsy had a sudden sense of privilege, of standing in a special place.

She turned to Jill who, reading her face, laughed and said, "I see you've met Naniboujou."

"What?"

"Naniboujou, the Cree god this place is named for. This is his country. He was their god of the outdoors, though if you read his legends you realize he was also a god of joy and pranks."

"I knew there had to be an explanation for the name of this place. Tell me about him."

"Well, let's see. Oh, I know: One time, when Naniboujou was young, he saw a large flock of geese resting on the water of Gitche Gumee, which we call Lake Superior. He loved goose dinner, but he was such a large god, one goose would not make even a snack for him. And if he shot a goose with his bow and arrow, the others would fly away. So he pulled a length of bark off a white pine tree and braided a long, long twine from the fibers inside it. Then he slipped under the water, swimming up to the geese, and there he began tying their feet one to another's. Now this happened long, long ago, when Naniboujou was young and greedy, and he could not stop at nine or twelve or twenty; he had to capture the whole flock, every single one. But when he was reaching for the left foot of the last goose, he couldn't hold his breath anymore and burst through the surface to take a breath. Well, of course, the geese all flapped up into the sky. Naniboujou had hold of the end of his twine and he didn't let go, thinking he could hold them. But there were so many geese tied to that twine that instead they lifted him up into the air with them. He considered that he was a very large god, and they would soon tire and come down, but he was the one who got tired, and at last he had to let go. Down, down he fell, right into a marsh—kersplut! Up to his elbows in muck. Wet and covered with duckweed, he had to go home hungry. But to this day, geese fly in a long skein, their feet still tied together with Naniboujou's twine."

Betsy was delighted. "Is that a real story from the Cree?"

Jill nodded. "Mr. Greenfeather told it to me."

Betsy said, "That painting of him laughing must be from before he fell into the swamp and went home wet and hungry."

"Not at all—he laughs because he loves pranks, even on himself. They say if you go hunting or fishing, you should give him a pinch of tobacco or he'll run the deer off and frighten the fish away." Jill looked out over the water again. "But he isn't just a prankster, he's a god of peace, too. There was never a war fought around here, between Indian tribes or the Indians and white people."

Betsy sobered. "That makes it all the more terrible, what's happened here now." They looked out over the water until Betsy's troubled spirit grew a little more calm, then she asked, "Do you go swimming when you come up here in summer?"

"Gosh, no," said Jill. "Lake Superior is never warm enough to swim in. It stores up cold all winter." She stepped off the snow-covered lawn onto the narrow, thickly pebbled beach. "Well, actually I suppose it might be warm enough for a short dip in September, after absorbing heat all summer. But by then the air is too chilly. Superior holds on to its summer heat so well it never freezes when winter comes again. At least this part of it doesn't. Further north cars can drive on the ice out to the islands. And of course Duluth Harbor freezes. They make a big deal of the ice finally going out in the harbor, so shipping can resume."

She stooped to pick up a stone, rub it with a mittened thumb to see if it was worth keeping, and throw it far out into the water. She threw like a man, putting her back into it, and the stone went surprisingly far. "The average life expectancy of someone falling off a boat into Lake Superior is eight minutes."

A great swath of lake began lightening into a sky blue. "Why do big bodies of water change colors like that?" asked Betsy.

"Beats me," said Jill. "But have you noticed how each one seems to have its own set of colors? The Gulf of Mexico has a light green you never see up here, and there's a shade of blue on Superior I haven't seen anywhere else."

"Yes, it's about a what, DMC 312?"

Jill laughed. "And you still think you're not a stitcher! And that's not all stitching has taught you, Miss Sharp Eyes. Come on, let's follow the shore this way." Jill walked south—well, west—okay, southwest—along the shore, past the snow-covered lawn to where naked, redstemmed brush choked the land, to where the gravelly beach widened. The brush thinned out and Betsy realized they were coming to the mouth of a river.

The river was frozen, its ice lumpish under the snow. At its mouth, Betsy could see water flowing from under the ragged edge of ice into the lake.

Jill said, "This is the Brule, and not quite a mile from where we're standing is the Devil's Kettle Falls."

Betsy looked up the river. "Have you seen them?"

"Oh, sure. It's a nice waterfall, all set in rocks and coming down in two stages. There's a trail up along this side of the river to it, but at the end you have to go down some stairs."

"It is a big waterfall?"

"Pretty big. Each stage is maybe fifteen feet high. A lot of water comes over it, thousands of gallons a minute."

Betsy stared at Jill. "How big is the hole in this rock the water goes into?"

"About ten feet across."

"A hole that big, and thousands of gallons a minute? Parker Lundquist must be thinking of an enormous aquifer! No, he's got to be wrong, the water has to be just pouring out somewhere, if not downstream, then somewhere else."

"I assure you, it doesn't. The Brule and its waterfall is in a state park visited by thousands of people who tramp over every square foot of the place, and none of them have ever reported finding a previously unknown spring or river that water could come out in."

"Maybe it feeds a lake, and the water flows in from the bottom, so the dye they put into it was never seen on the surface."

"There are no lakes in this area. None. Well"—she turned and looked out over Superior—"there is this one humongous one. Anyway, dye floats, so someone would have seen it coming out no matter where. No, the water just disappears down this big old hole, like a drainpipe into Hades."

Betsy walked a few yards up the shore of the river to look and listen some more. A ten-foot-wide hole that had no apparent bottom . . . Upriver, she could see a bridge that took the highway over the river, but not beyond that. Nor could she hear anything. "You said there's a trail? I don't see one."

"It starts on the other side of the highway, in the park. But it's no good for cross-country skis. Too narrow, with lots of low branches and underbrush."

"Who wants to ski up it? But we could walk up it, couldn't we?"

"You saw what it was like to walk across the lawn back there. You want to do that for a mile going in—and another mile back? No, we'd have to use snowshoes, and if you think cross-country skiing is a workout, just try snowshoes."

"Is there a road we can drive up?"

"No. Do you seriously want to go up there?"

"Yes, I think I do."

"Well, we can ski up the river."

Betsy looked at the uneven surface of the river and said, "Is it safe? I thought Parker said the falls aren't frozen."

"And they probably aren't. But you can see that the river is. I've done it before, the ice is safe. It's an easy trip, not so many ups and downs as the trail. We'll get off the river before the falls, climb up the bank, and look down into the kettle."

Betsy sighed surrender. "I knew you were going to find some way to get me on those skis," she groused.

Jill laughed like Naniboujou's portrait, head back and mouth open. "All right, let's go get the skis. And tell James where we're going."

"Why does he need to know?"

"Because if we fall and hurt ourselves, we don't want to lie there until that almost-a-ranger decides to come along and finds our frozen bodies."

Nine

Betsy went with Jill, back to the lodge then out to her car, where they donned light, narrow skis that fastened to their boots only at the toe. Each taking a pair of poles, they started back along the lawn toward the lake's edge. It was a lot easier skimming the surface of the snow than crunching through and having to lift one's feet high to take the next step, Betsy decided.

"What's this?" she asked, stopping beside some marks in the snow. They came from the distant highway across the lawn, swooping close to the back door, down nearly to the lake before turning around and going back the way it had come in. It was the ski trail she had seen earlier, but now she noticed a difference from the trails she and Jill were leaving. The skis that made this were wider, deeper, and set well apart. And the skier had apparently dragged something behind him that fit neatly between the skis.

"Snowmobile," said Jill. "There's a constant fight going on in the legislature about whether to expand or cut back on the snowmobile trails, especially in the state parks. Meanwhile they run everywhere, in the parks, across private property, and along the shoulders of roads. Snowmobiles are noisy and fun, but dangerous when the driver is a child or drunk. People either love 'em or hate 'em, nobody's neutral."

But Betsy thought perhaps she might be neutral. She understood the desire for a wilderness experience unbroken by the stink and snarl of engines. On the other hand, a snowmobile was a fast, easy, exciting way of getting far back into the woods. One could always shut the engine off to enjoy the silence after one arrived.

They went back to the mouth of the Brule, skied alongside it for a while, then edged gingerly onto the snow-covered ice. Up here were the tracks of several skiers who had done likewise, avoiding the thin ice near the lake. By the time they were as far as the highway, they were in a head-high rock canyon. The river narrowed as they went up it, but on the other side of the bridge it was still over twenty feet across.

"This is some of the oldest rock in the world," said Jill, nodding toward the rusty brown and black bluffs on either side of them. "Older than the dinosaurs. Parker can say it's not granite, but it's as hard as granite, so it took a long time for the river to carve this deep."

"Uh-huh," said Betsy, a little breathlessly, picking herself up. Again. The surface of the river was uneven, and the drape of the snow didn't always tell the truth about what was under it.

Out of sight of the highway, the canyon deepened to over thirty feet. "The riverbed is full of big rocks," said Jill conversationally, stopping yet again so Betsy could both regain her feet and catch her breath. "The water flows over the rocks and freezes unevenly. But down underneath, it's still flowing. If you listen you can hear it."

And standing in the deep silence of a forest in winter, Betsy listened. Sure enough, there was a faint gurgle underfoot. "Are you sure the ice is thick enough to hold us?" she asked, shifting her weight back onto her skis instead of leaning so much on the points of her poles.

"Oh, yes. But if you do go through, try to grab hold of the downstream edge of the ice with your arms so you don't get swept under. The current's pretty swift here, but it's a long way down to the lake. I don't know if you could hold your breath that long."

Betsy stared at Jill, who didn't seem to be kidding. She looked around. The snow-covered surface would give no hint of a crack. Despite the evidence that others had safely come before them, Betsy wondered if maybe they should walk along the shore—except that wasn't possible. The dark canyon walls rose vertically on either side. Here and there a bush or small evergreen clung, but too few and far apart to be much aid to a person trying to climb to the top. They had to continue on the river.

"Don't worry, it's never given way to me or anyone else that I know of." Jill started off again, pushing hard on her poles. "Come on, let's keep moving."

Betsy trailed behind awkwardly, legs and arms complaining at the unaccustomed exercise. Jill went into the long, graceful movements of the experienced cross-country skier. Betsy tried to emulate her, but soon she was breathless again. This was worse than the cross country trip Jill had taken her on back in December. She realized that going upstream meant they were going uphill. There wasn't any level place to just glide along, or any downhill place to slide.

The farther they went, the steeper the incline became. As she tired, there seemed to be ever more lumps and dips where the water had apparently frozen in the act of moving over boulders. Jill seemed to find dodging among the bumps no problem, but Betsy found that between her own awkwardness and the more difficult terrain she had to stop more and more often to rest. The river was distinctly narrower here, but the slope of the canyon was less vertical, and there were more trees and bushes. In fact, just up there was an opening to a slope that was barely a slope at all, set with mature trees—and beyond it, on more steeply rising ground: What was that?

Jill, probably missing Betsy's sonorous breathing, looked around, turned, and came back. She looked where Betsy was staring. "Oh, the stairs? They built them to keep hikers from breaking branches and young trees getting down to the riverbank—The falls are just ahead and they're pretty to look at from below, too."

Betsy remembered talk about the wooden stairs, and had expected to see them. But over there, in the middle of a wilderness, was a twisting wooden staircase twenty or more landings high, much higher than the really tall trees growing near the riverbank. Almost as amazing, there were footprints in the snow that lay on the steps.

"People actually use those?" she said.

"In the summer mostly," said Jill. "If they walk the trail to see the falls, they have to come down them. They come out over there to see the foot of the falls, and then climb a steep hill beyond those trees to see the top. I guess it's lack of oxygen or something because most summertime hikers just trundle down the stairs—forgetting that the only way home is back up again. In the winter sensible people come up the river, though you can see by the footprints some people don't have good sense."

"Unbelievable," said Betsy. "Whew!" she added, feeling her knees trembling, and taking a few steps to relieve the tension in them.

Jill said, "Let's take a real rest before the final push."

She led the way to a half-fallen tree that leaned obligingly out over the water. Betsy draped herself gratefully over it for a minute, then brushed snow off and jumped up to sit on it with a heartfelt sigh.

"How much farther?" she asked.

"Not far at all. If you listen, you can hear the waterfall."

Betsy cocked an ear and began to realize that not all the noise in the neighborhood was her harsh breathing. There was also the deep rush of a good-sized waterfall.

After too short a rest, Jill said, "Let's go. We don't want to start getting cold. I think we should travel along the riverbank now. The rocks along here are bigger, and the water's still excited from going over the falls, so the ice may be thinner."

The skiers who had come before them had also left the river at this point or a little beyond. Jill went to the left bank, where she took off her skis and stood them upright in the snow. Betsy followed suit, and they began to move both up and forward. It wasn't easy, the bank was steep, and her legs were still complaining about the skiing. Also, the deep snow was difficult to walk in, and what appeared to be drifts were sometimes low-growing bushes with surprising resistance in their branches. Snow leveled little hollows in the ground that ambushed their feet. Trying to keep up, Betsy brushed by spruce that sent a tumble of snow down her neck. Jill, a few yards ahead of Betsy, turned to see what the holdup was now and her feet went out from under her. She whooped in amusement as she fell. But instead of regaining her feet with her usual athletic ease, she started a half slide, half tumble backward that nearly knocked Betsy down as she came by. Betsy grabbed futilely at her, but then Jill reached and caught hold of the trunk of the snow-dumping spruce, brought herself to a halt, and stood up laughing.

"Are you all right?" called Betsy, nevertheless alarmed.

"You bet." Still chuckling, Jill dusted snow and pine needles off herself, climbed back up past Betsy, and they went on.

Soon after, Betsy felt her knees give way. She sat down in the snow. "Are we almost there?" she pleaded.

Jill did not answer. She was up and ahead of Betsy, looking downward, motionless. Betsy staggered to her feet to climb that last distance, then she, too, stood and stared.

The falls were even more impressive than Betsy expected, broader and thicker, set among huge boulders. The water was mostly white, and it split into two streams as it poured down the first step, divided by a thrusting thumb of rock. At the base, half the water swirled forward to cascade down again; the other half poured into an immense black rock split open on its flat top. The rock with its opening was half hidden under a thick coating of ice.

But the water was not flowing smoothly into the opening, as she expected. Instead the hole was throwing water outward and back up into the face of the waterfall, spurting like a full bottle held under a running faucet. Then even as they looked, the spurting stopped and water poured smoothly into the rock— only to suddenly start fountaining upward again, splashing onto the trees and rocks on the nearer shore. Everything within reach of the spatter was thickly coated with ice, the tree branches hanging heavy all around.

Betsy said, "Gosh, that's even more amazing than what you described!"

Jill said, "It's not supposed to be acting like this. Normally, the water just pours into that opening and vanishes. I've never seen it jump up and spill over like that." Jill started moving forward again. "Maybe a big rock broke loose and went in there, partly blocking it up somehow."

Betsy said, "No, no, Jill! Stop!"

"What's wrong?" Jill asked, pausing to look around.

"We're not the first ones here," Betsy said, pointing to numerous footprints near the falls, some of them ice-coated, too.

"Well, I told you, people come back here all the time."

"No, you don't understand. I don't think it's a rock blocking the inside of that kettle. Let's not go any nearer and spoil the footprints. Let's go report this right away."

Ten

The trip back down the river was difficult. Betsy was frightened, tired, and in a hurry, an inefficient combination that slowed progress and produced lots of tumbles.

"Go on, go ahead, tell them!" gasped Betsy at last, no longer struggling to rise.

"No, no, we're staying together," said Jill, coming back to pull Betsy to her feet by one arm.

After what seemed hours of effort, they arrived back at the lodge, unfastened their skis, and knocked the worst of the snow off themselves before hurrying in.

James was not in the lobby. Leaning on the counter to peel off her coat, Betsy said to Jill, "Will you call Sheriff Goodman? I'm too tired to make sense. Tell him to hurry."

She went into the dining room to drape her coat, hat, and mittens over the back of a chair and sit on one of the couches in front of the fire. She held out numb fingers to the flames.

He just has to believe us now, she thought. *How dreadful to put her in that kettle thing! Whoever did that thought she'd vanish forever, like a dead bug washed down the drain. Instead she's stuck inside the rock somehow, clogging it. And the water is beating down on her . . . They must come, someone has to get her out of there. He just has to believe Jill.* After a while there was the sound of china on china, and she looked up to see Frank Owen standing in front of her with a steaming cup on a saucer. As he bent to present it to her, the scent was of cocoa, not coffee.

"You looked like you could use this," he said.

"Oh . . ." Betsy's words stuck in her throat. "Th—thank you," she managed, and took it from him.

He sat down across from her. "You look cold. Did you stay out too long?" he asked.

"No," she said. "I mean, yes, I suppose so." She realized she was trembling, which he had taken for shivering. Though she was probably shivering, too. Here perhaps was the person who had put Sharon in that place, yet he was showing a casual compassion to the person who had found her. Or was he? Not very long ago, someone else tried to give her some arsenic-flavored nourishment. She took a tiny sip of the hot cocoa and said, "Ow, it's too hot."

"Sorry!" he said, and took the drink from her. "I didn't realize," he apologized.

"That's all right. Where did you get it? There's only coffee out, I thought."

"I asked the kitchen staff. You were looking very miserable, and I know how bad it can be to get really chilled. They always take good care of their guests here at Naniboujou." He pinched the cup between thumb and forefinger, testing its temperature. "I don't think it's all that hot, it's just that you're so cold. Come on, try it again. You need something to warm your inside."

"No, thank you," she said. "I—I'm not really cold."

"No? Then what's the matter?"

"I think we did too much. I'm . . . tired."

He sat back. "Where all did you go?"

He was uncomfortable asking that casual question, Betsy could tell. From their first meeting she realized he was probably like Jill, a careful guardian of his real thoughts and feelings, and therefore unwilling to pry into another's. But apparently genuine concern overrode his reticence.

Or a need to know.

Watching him closely, she said, "We went out to see the woodpile—I don't think I've ever seen so much firewood in one place before."

"Yes, they buy logs all summer, cut and split it themselves to the right size. Is that all you did? Walk around the woodpile?"

"No, then we walked along the shore, where we saw an eagle flying."

"Oh, that's The Old Codger. He's kind of a fixture around here. He doesn't fly south but stays here year-round. His favorite perch is on top of that broken birch down near the beach."

"Yes, I saw him land on it yesterday. He kind of vanishes into it, it's easy not to realize he's there. The Old Codger—has he been around for years, then?"

"Actually no. James says he turned up here three summers ago. Some guest took a photograph of him that he sold to a calendar company. It was labeled THE OLD CODGER. How far did you walk along the shore?"

Betsy said, watching for a reaction, "Not far, but then we skied up the river to the Devil's Kettle."

"Ah, that's why you're tired. Is it frozen over? A frozen waterfall is attractive, though attractiveness isn't the attraction of the Devil's Kettle." He smiled under the thick mustache. "If you know what I mean."

Either the man had nerves of steel or he knew nothing. Betsy replied, "Yes, it's the fact that half the water goes down to no one knows where. And no, it isn't frozen over."

"Any theories as to where the water goes?" he asked, again holding out the cocoa. "Are you sure you don't want this? I think it's cooled down enough to drink now."

"All right. Thank you." Betsy took it. "There's a geology grad student here studying it. He thinks there's a big, slow-moving aquifer deep underground, and that someday a fisherman will be amazed to see dye that was poured into the waterfall years ago at long last coming out into the lake."

"I'd like to be the person who sees that," said Frank, tickled at the idea. "But that aquifer must be down really deep; I understand we're sitting on top of a thousand feet of solid granite left by ancient volcanoes."

Betsy didn't want to get into a discussion of the difference between mafic rock and granite. She blew on the surface of the cocoa then took a cautious sip. It was rich and sweet, not at all too hot. "Well, the alternative theory is that the water goes down to hell, and I think I'd sooner believe in a deep aquifer than that hell is only a thousand feet down from here."

"If it were, you'd think the winters up here would be milder," he said, surprising Betsy into a chuckle.

He asked, "So if it's not because you're cold, and you weren't disappointed at the waterfall, what is it that's got you sitting here looking like a funeral?"

Betsy was at first struck speechless at this close brush with the truth, but then got angry—was he playing with her?—so she asked bluntly, "Mr. Owen, where is your wife?"

"Ex-wife," he corrected gently. "And I told you, I have no idea."

"Why did you divorce her? Because she was sick all the time?"

"I didn't divorce her, she divorced me. Not that I wasn't thinking about it. She wasn't one of those women who turn sweet in adversity."

"Why did she divorce you?"

"She said she found someone who was better at meeting her needs. His name was Eric Handel—"

"Not Eddie?" interrupted Betsy.

"No, Eric. Why?"

"Because when I talked to her, she said something about going to get Eddie. Or meet Eddie." It had been "get Eddie," hadn't it? That sounded more like a staff member than a boyfriend.

Frank was talking. " . . . it's possible the man presently meeting her needs is named Eddie. Eric was a long time ago, and they only stayed married a year."

"Was there someone else after Eric?"

"Oh, yes, several. You want names? Let's see if I can remember them all. She left Eric to come back to me, but she only stayed three months because I'd quit teaching chemistry to work in a chemistry lab, and I couldn't get clean enough for her. After that there was a fellow named . . . Jack, I think. Jack Mallow? Merrow? Merrill? He lived in San Francisco. The kids really liked him, they spent a summer out there with him and Sharon. I thought that one would last, but he didn't. Then there was Max, but after that . . . my memory fails me. There was another one or maybe two after Max, but I don't remember their names. One may have been an Eddie. But the only one she married was Eric."

"Is she seeing anyone now?"

"The last I heard, someone named Tony. She's pretty serious about him, though she's generally serious, and that can change at anytime." He cocked his head sideways at Betsy. "Maybe she's moved on to this Eddie—dammit, now you've got me believing you saw her. No, no, there's no Eddie."

"Are Sharon and Tony living together?"

"As I understand it, she would have moved in with him, but his condo association allows pets. He hasn't got one, of course, but other condo owners do, and just walking down a hallway where a dog has been could put Sharon in the hospital."

"Her allergies are that serious?"

"Oh, I'm afraid so. Used to be, we did a lot of challenging things, but now just walking outdoors in the spring is dangerous for Sharon. She built a house specially designed for the hyper-allergic, two kinds of air filters, sealed walls and floors, everything washed only with water, baking soda, and vinegar."

"What about your children? Do they have allergies, too?"

"No, thank God. Elizabeth and Douglas are both out of school, they both have jobs, and there's never been any sign of even hay fever."

Was he talking this openly to convince her of his innocence? Or because he still halfway believed her and was trying to talk himself out of it?

Betsy asked, "That house Sharon built. That must have cost you something."

He shrugged. "Not me, it was built with her money. She can afford to build whatever kind of house she wants. She could build one like it on every continent if she wanted to."

"Oh, I didn't realize—"

"Sharon's grandmother invented a couple of gadgets, one of which still turns up on every washing machine made. That started the family fortune, but it really took off when Sharon's father proved himself brilliant in surgical instruments and real estate. But Sharon and I signed a prenup—which was fine, I make a sufficient living, especially since I only have to support myself. Because she set up a trust fund for each of our children that has fed, housed, entertained, and educated them with no strain. When they turn thirty they'll be able to access the principal and they'll become very wealthy, too. But the rest of the money, and there's still a whole lot of it, is all hers."

"Who gets it when she dies?"

"I don't know. Not me."

Betsy said, "It seems kind of sad. She could buy anything, go anywhere, but she became allergic to everything she used to love."

"It is sad. And Sharon's angry about it, which is why she's often bad company."

"Was bad company, Mr. Owen. Sharon's dead."

He bristled, a little. "Why are you so sure she's dead?"

"Because when we skied up to the Devil's Kettle, it was acting very strange, as if someone had put something inside it, something big enough to partly plug it. I'm afraid that's where Sharon's body went when it was taken out of your room."

He stared at her. "The hell you say."

"Jill's calling the sheriff now."

"Did you see her inside the kettle?"

"No, but Sharon was here and then nobody could find her, and now the Devil's Kettle is plugged with something."

He stood. "And you think—? My God, why? It could be a chunk of ice, a tree limb, even a dead raccoon!"

"Jill says she's never heard of the falls being plugged up before."

"And so you leap to the conclusion it's my dead ex-wife? How did you convince this Jill person that you're right?"

"She's a friend. And she's a cop."

"What, a captain of detectives?"

"Well . . . she's a patrol officer—"

"In some dinky town somewhere south of here. So you got her to do your dirty work, call the sheriff for you, even though nobody but you thinks Sharon is dead in the first place. Is this how you do that famous detecting, going around to different places, finding meaningless 'clues' and scaring folks?"

Betsy wondered who told him she was an amateur sleuth. "I am not scaring people needlessly, Mr. Owen," she said. "I have investigated very real crimes, and though I dislike getting involved in yet another one, it seems I have no choice until I can convince the proper authorities to take appropriate action."

"And if the sheriff refuses to take action? Then what, you call the local TV station?"

"I'll do whatever I have to—"

"If you get this story into the papers or on television, I'll encourage James and Ramona to take legal action against you!"

"Why?"

"Because you would presume to damage the reputation of their lodge, thereby hurting them and their loyal employees and their faithful customers— for no good reason!" He cut himself off with an angry gesture, turned on his heel, and walked away.

Betsy, looking after him, thought, *What if he's right?* and then, *But what if I'm right?*

The cocoa was cold. She carried the cup to the sideboard outside the kitchen and put it down next to the nearly empty and acrid-smelling coffeepot. She walked up to the lobby, saw Jill just hanging up the phone, and waited for her.

"That took a long time. What did he say?"

"It was a hard sell. I don't think he believed the falls are acting like I described. He says he's never heard of the Devil's Kettle acting that way, so I said maybe he'd better have a look. Was that Frank Owen stomping through here just ahead of you?"

"Yes, he's angry with us for hurting the reputation of the Naniboujou Lodge and its loyal employees and customers by saying someone died in one of their rooms. Jill, what if I'm wrong?"

"I don't think you are. Sharon's car is here, she had an important role to play here, she was seen here, and she doesn't seem to be anywhere else. I've listened to a lot of sadly mistaken stories, and your story doesn't sound like one of them."

They walked back to the fire, which had burned down to a few weak flames among black and broken pieces of log. Betsy selected a birch log from the little stack in the holder and put it on the coals. The firebox was hot, flames immediately leaped up to crackle eagerly at the white, paperlike bark of the log. She added another log and they sat down to watch the progress of the burning in silence, each lost in her own thoughts.

So it was a while before they realized someone was standing near, waiting patiently to be noticed.

Betsy looked up and saw a tall, extremely attractive woman with dark red hair and a scatter of freckles across a queenly nose. "Hi, I'm Liddy Owen," she said in a low, pleasant voice. When Betsy didn't at once recognize the name, she added, "You called me to ask where my mother was."

"Oh, of course!" said Betsy, standing. She asked eagerly, "Did your mother get in touch with you?"

"No," said Liddy, adding, when Betsy's face fell, "and I take it you haven't found where she went, either."

Betsy hesitated but Jill said, "No. I assume you're here because you're worried about her?"

Liddy looked inquiringly at Jill and Betsy said, "Ms. Owen, this is Jill Cross, a friend of mine from Excelsior, where we both live."

"How do you do?" said Liddy, adding to them both, "Mama usually calls me when she's broken an engagement, once she thinks about it, in case someone else calls me looking for her. But she hasn't yet. I was at work all day Friday and at home until a couple of hours ago, so she could have gotten in touch if she wanted to." Liddy pulled off her right glove to begin unbuttoning her black woolen coat. "And I can't locate her." Under the coat she wore a finely knit cream dress embroidered with thistles around the neck. She let the coat slip off her arms and Betsy saw she had the slender figure it took to do the dress justice. She looked around the big room and said, "I haven't been up here since I was twelve, but it's just as amazing as I remember." She turned to look up at the laughing head of Naniboujou high on the far wall, surrounded by the brilliant colors of a sunrise. "I just love that painting. So happy—just like we were when we used to come up here, back when I was a little girl."

"Jill says that Naniboujou is a god of peace, the outdoors, and pranks. I should think that such a god might make a perfect summer realm for a child."

Liddy's big gray eyes searched Betsy's. "What a lovely thought! And you're right, we had such fun back before—" She turned and said, "Is there coffee?"

Jill said, "Only what's left over from lunch. It's probably pretty rank by now."

"Well, then, let's not have any. But can we sit awhile? I want to talk to you."

"Of course." All three sat down.

But Liddy apparently couldn't think how to start, so Betsy asked, "Are the other faces also Cree gods?"

"So I was told," said Liddy, looking at the wall over the French windows. "I understand one of the two at this end of the room is the god of Lake Superior." Her eyes moved over the gods painted on either side of the fireplace. "And another is the Cree god of death." Her fingers, clasped in her lap, tightened. "I hope Mama's all right."

"I hope she is, too," said Betsy.

Liddy made a wry face, one corner of her mouth pulled back, one eyebrow lifted. "Mama has never been very reliable, and I wouldn't have come, but she really did seem eager to be here, and when I found out she wasn't, I got worried."

"Could she have gone to Chicago to be with her boyfriend?" said Betsy.

"No. After we talked, I called down there to ask. But he hasn't heard from her since Thursday. Tony Campanelli is very nice, very reliable. He's younger than Mama, but Mama doesn't look her age. And she's good with Tony's children. He shares custody of his little boy and girl. They adore her, of course, just like Doogie and I did when we were their age." But she waved that away as irrelevant. "I saw Mama's car in the parking lot; I assume you did, too?"

"Yes." Betsy nodded. "The sheriff was here a while ago—" She looked at Jill. "Did they search her car?"

"Yes, but they wouldn't let me come near. They didn't take anything away; her luggage is still in it. Who's Doogie?"

"My brother, Douglas."

Betsy asked, "Where is he? Is it possible your mother is with him?"

"No, I called him, too. But she wouldn't have gone to stay with him. Doogie is playing forest ranger this year, and he's got some incredibly grubby cabin outside Grand Marais, where the kitchen is a hot plate and the toilet is at the end of a path. Mama likes her comforts. She considered staying here the moral equivalent of camping." She looked around the beautiful room and smiled. "And that was before she got all those terrible allergies. I'm so glad Doogie and I didn't inherit them."

"Yes, if you're allergic to a lot of things, you couldn't be a forest ranger." Betsy smiled.

"Oh, he's not a ranger, he's kind of an apprentice. He doesn't even get to wear a uniform. He does things at the station like sweeping up and answering the phone." She shrugged and did a brief reprise of the wry face again. "But he says he likes it, he may even go back to college in the fall to study forestry."

"Does he work at the ranger station across the road?" asked Jill.

"No, in Grand Marais. That station in the Judge Magney Park isn't open in the winter. At least wasn't when we used to come up here. God, those were happy times!" She said that devoutly, then realized she'd already said something like it, and gestured as if to erase the strong feeling in her words. "But that was a long time ago, it's old history, not important. What's important is, where on earth could Mama have gone?"

"You're from Duluth, is that right, Ms. Owen?" asked Jill.

"Yes, that's right. Call me Liddy. I probably shouldn't have come up, but it's not that long a drive, and I couldn't just sit at home waiting. You know how it is."

"I'm sorry you're being worried like this," said Betsy.

"Not your fault," said Liddy. "She probably got a call from friends going to sail around the British Virgin Islands and invited herself along for an impromptu vacation." She shook her head ruefully and asked, "Is my father still here?"

"Yes," said Betsy. "I was just talking with him before you came." She wished she hadn't said that; she could see Liddy was going to ask about that, and she didn't want to tell Liddy about her conversation about the waterfall.

She looked away and saw someone standing in the doorway to the dining room, wearing a dull orange goosedown jacket and gray denim trousers. He was a young man, tall and thin, with brown hair and a redhead's freckled complexion. His nose was slender and prominent, his mouth sensitive, his pose somehow defensive. Betsy had the curious feeling she'd seen him before.

Liddy called, "Doogie!" and stood. Of course, he looked very like her. He started for her, but Liddy gestured at him to wait, said "Excuse me" to Jill and Betsy, and hurried to meet him. She led him behind the long counter at the far end of the room and began an intense discussion.

Betsy asked, "How long do you think it will be before we hear if they found her at the falls?"

"I don't know, but it won't be right away. So let's go into the lounge."

They barely noticed the lifted heads or murmured remarks this time, so focused were their thoughts on what dreadful thing Sheriff Goodman might find in the Devil's Kettle.

Betsy got her Rose Window project out. The sun was low enough in the sky to make a strong, slanting light on the white towel she draped across her lap. But the pattern was full of pitfalls. Betsy finished another wedge in light olive and antique pink. The first wedge had been worked in horizontal and vertical stitches, the second in diagonal, then the third like the first and the fourth like the second. It seemed that just as she got used to thinking horizontally, she had to think diagonally. Betsy grumbled under her breath at the heedless cruelty of designers who made such unnecessary complications.

And each must be surrounded by the nasty, delicate Kreinik, slowly, carefully, accompanied by more grumbling.

But held at arm's length, Betsy's grumble melted into a pleased smile, as she saw how attractive the pattern was, its subtle complexities only adding to its beauty. Only, it looked a little off balance. Perhaps because the circle wasn't finished?

"Officer Jill Cross?" called a man's rough voice. Betsy looked around. Standing in the doorway was Sheriff Goodman in his fur-collared coat. His matching hat had earflaps and a gold badge pinned to it. He lifted his chin at them, his face full of grim news.

"Come with me," muttered Jill, but Betsy was already putting her needlework into her bag.

The two hurried toward Goodman, who turned and walked away, leaving them to follow him into the center of the dining room, where a deputy waited. Doogie and Liddy were gone.

"What have you found?" Jill asked the sheriff.

"There was the body of a woman inside that hole in the rock," said Goodman. "It was a hell of a fight to get it out, we've got a deputy with a broken arm and a ranger with a wrenched back."

"I'm sorry to hear that," said Jill, her voice shocked and sincere.

"Is it Sharon Kaye Owen?" asked Betsy, ruthless in her need to know.

"It could be. The body is a blonde, real skinny, wearing a blue and white sweater under a dark blue coat. The ME thinks it wasn't in there more than a day. But of course we need someone to give us a positive ID. Is Mr. Owen still here?"

"Yes, and Sharon's son and daughter are here, too," said Betsy.

Goodman's eyebrows lifted. "They are? When did they arrive?"

"A couple of hours ago."

"They're possibly up in their father's room," offered Jill. "They're adults."

"What are their names?" asked Goodman.

"Liddy and Doogie Owen," said Betsy.

" 'Liddy and Doogie'?"

"Nicknames for Elizabeth and Douglas," said Jill.

The sheriff looked at his deputy, a short, heavyset man who looked part Indian, and jerked his head toward the lobby. "Room at the top of the stairs. I want all three." The deputy departed unhurriedly.

"Are you going to arrest them all?" asked Betsy.

Goodman looked pained. "For what? Ma'am, we don't know that she was murdered. There were a lot of footprints in the area, some leading right across the ice to that waterfall; it's possible she went to see it up close, slipped, and fell in."

Betsy wanted to shout at him that Sharon Owen couldn't have gone to see the falls, she was taken up there dead, she'd died in an upstairs bedroom rented by her ex-husband. But as she drew an angry breath, Jill caught her eye and shook her head very slightly, and Betsy bit her tongue.

"Hello?" said Liddy's voice, and they looked around to see Liddy and Doogie approaching, their father behind them with the deputy bringing up the rear.

The sheriff immediately removed his furry hat, and his face went solemn.

"Oh, my God," Liddy said, the question she was about to ask dying on her lips. Her brother suddenly looked scared, and his mouth opened, but Liddy spoke first. "What is it?" she said. "Tell us what's happened."

"Are you Sharon Owen's daughter?"

"Yes, I'm Elizabeth Owen, and this is my father, Frank Owen, and my brother, Douglas. Please—"

"We found the body of a woman under the Devil's Kettle Falls up the Brule River. I'm very sorry to say it's possibly your mother. I'm going to ask you, Mr. Owen, to take a look at it, see if you can identify it." He was addressing Doogie, not Frank.

"Oh, no, no," said Doogie, his scared look becoming more pronounced, "I can't do that, please don't ask me to go look at her. My dad here, can't he go?"

"You are the immediate family, sir. Unless—How old are you?"

"Twenty-one." Just admitting to being of age seemed to put some backbone into the young man.

"You see," said the sheriff, "since your father and mother are divorced, he's not really next of kin."

"Oh. Well, I suppose—I mean, of course, I . . . understand. Where is . . . where is the body?"

"In Grand Marais. If you'll come with me?"

"Shall I come, too?" asked Liddy.

"No, ma'am, I don't think you'll want to see this."

"Perhaps I ought to—" began Frank.

"No sir, there's no need for you to come." His tone indicated dismissal.

"Very well." Frank touched Doogie on the arm. "We'll be waiting right here for you, son."

"Yessir." Doogie turned to Liddy. "I'll be back as soon as I can. And it'll be all right. I mean, maybe it's not her."

"That's true," said Liddy, grasping at straws. "Now you listen to the sheriff, don't do—don't make any decisions without talking to me first, understand? And Dad, too, of course."

"Yes, yes, all right," said Doogie. To the sheriff, "Let's go."

Liddy and Frank watched them leave, Frank with concern, Liddy with a painful intensity. When Liddy turned back, it was awkwardly, and her face was white.

Frank said, "Here, what's the matter?"

Jill said, pulling out a chair, "She needs to sit down. Can I get you something, Liddy? A glass of water?"

"Yes, water, thank you." Liddy put her long fingers on the table, palms hanging off the edge, and bowed her head, eyes closed.

"Now, hon, where's my brave little soldier?" Frank murmured, coming to stand behind her and put his hands on her shoulders. Without lifting her head she reached up to touch one of his hands, and her mouth firmed into a straight line.

Betsy sat down across from Liddy and said, "I'm so sorry."

She looked at her. "You think it's my mother they found, don't you?"

"Yes, I'm afraid I do."

"Why?" When Betsy didn't reply at once, Liddy demanded, "What do you know you're not telling me?" She looked at her father. "What do you know?"

Jill put a glass of water in front of Liddy and said to her, and Betsy, "Let's not borrow trouble, all right?"

And Liddy suddenly pulled herself together, shoulders squaring, chin lifting, displaying a stronger version of the backbone her brother had also found. "Yes, you're right. I'm sorry." She lifted the glass and took several small sips.

Betsy looked toward the row of French doors overlooking the parking lot, her eye caught by movement, and they all watched as Sheriff Goodman and his deputy put Doogie into the patrol car's backseat. It wasn't until the car's headlights came on that Betsy realized the swift purple twilight of winter had fallen.

Too awful how the world goes right on, thought Betsy, remembering how it continued after her sister was buried. Here, too, the sun had gone down. The delicious smell of roast beef had grown strong without her noticing. Soon the stitchers would be coming in to eat and drink and talk about silk and overdyed floss, and how seductive linen was to stitch on. Betsy felt cold and stiff, and wished she were home.

How much worse this must be for Liddy!

They stayed at the table they were sitting at as the stitchers came in. The waitress took Liddy's name and advised the kitchen they'd need an extra meal. The beef was prime rib, tender and medium rare, just the way Betsy liked it. But she couldn't do it justice, and Liddy ate only a few bites. Jill and Frank, on the other hand, conscientiously cleaned their plates, and kept the conversation firmly on cross-country skiing.

They had nearly finished dessert when Doogie came back. He looked badly shaken. "It's her," he said, pulling a chair away from a nearby table and sitting down hard.

"Oh, my God!" said Liddy. "Oh, no, oh, no!"

"Oh, yes," said Doogie flatly. "What's more, they asked some damn hard questions about where I was on Friday. I don't know why they talked to me like that. It's perfectly clear to anyone with a brain that she was glad to be visiting a place she loved, that because it was winter there were no allergens to keep her from taking a hike to the falls. They even agreed I could be right, that she got here and went for a hike in Judge Magney Park, and walked right to the edge of the falls from up on top, where the ice broke and she fell in. They said the opening in the top of the rock narrows inside, so she stopped it up instead of going on down." He locked eyes with Liddy and said, "It was horrible, having to see her like that. I couldn't even tell it was her at first, because she was so beat up from being inside the Devil's Kettle. Our mama was so beautiful, but this person I saw was all crooked and—"

Liddy made a faint sound of protest, swayed, and fell out of her chair.

"For God's sake, Douglas!" barked Frank, moving swiftly to kneel beside her. Doogie rose, looking stern rather than apologetic. Jill whipped around to kneel on the other side.

James appeared as if out of nowhere. "What's the problem?" he asked. "Shall I call an ambulance?"

"She fainted, that's all," said Doogie with a curious indifference. James backed off but hovered at a distance.

Jill was checking her for injuries, murmuring in a soothing voice. Frank lifted her limp hand to rub it gently while Doogie and Betsy watched.

At last Liddy muttered something and Frank lifted her back into her chair. He patted and stroked her hand some more. "Are you all right now, soldier?" he asked.

"Yes, yes, 'm all right," she said, her voice tired and cross, pulling her hand free. "Sorry, I'm sorry, making a spectacle of myself. Oh, Mama, Mama!" Frank knelt to offer a shoulder, and she wept on it.

James, satisfied the emergency was over, went away.

After a bit, Doogie said, "Take it easy, Liddy, take it easy." He gave a hard look at the the people at the nearby tables, who turned away, embarrassed.

"Is there anything we can do?" asked Betsy when Liddy's weeping slowed nearly to a halt.

"Oh, I think you've done enough," said Frank.

"What—what do you mean?" asked Liddy, lifting her head to look wildly at her brother, who shrugged, then back at her father.

"I'm not talking about your brother, but these two. Didn't they tell you? That one"—he pointed at Betsy—"says she saw your mother dead on my bed yesterday afternoon." His voice swelled with anger. "She and her friend here call the sheriff out and he searches my room, searches the whole damn lodge. Can't find hide nor hair of her, of course. Then she and her friend go on a hike up the Brule and come back saying they saw the waterfall acting strange and they get the sheriff and his deputies out there, and they find Sharon's body inside the Devil's Kettle.

"Now the sheriff is looking slantwise at us because of this one's story, but you two weren't even here on Friday, and I haven't seen Sharon in months! What's more, no one else saw Sharon here at Naniboujou. I told the sheriff that when he was here the first time, and I told the deputy when he came up to my room. When he says what do I think, I said to him what I say to you: Look at the ones who are telling all these strange stories, the ones who see Sharon when nobody else does, the ones who told the sheriff where to find Sharon's body. Look at these two!"

Eleven

Frank Owen's voice had been getting louder and louder, and more and more attention was being paid to him. By the end of his speech the whole room was looking their way. Without being aware of the attention, or not caring, Frank left the room.

The diners broke into murmurs. Liddy, casting angry looks at Jill, then Betsy, stood and hurried out after her father, Doogie close behind. Betsy heard Doogie murmur, "Isn't Dad brilliant?" to his sister's back.

A waitress, bearing down on Betsy's table with a fresh dinner, stared after Doogie, then shrugged and headed back for the kitchen.

Betsy turned her face to her plate to avoid her eyes being caught by anyone sitting nearby.

"Heck!" muttered Jill, the sincerity in her voice lending weight to the mildness of the epithet.

"What are we going to do?"

"Nothing!" said Jill, and raised her own voice. "You told me, you told the staff, you told the sheriff she was dead, and no one believed you. Now she turns up dead. All that means is you were right. The fact that the body was moved from where you saw it indicates foul play. Sharon Kaye told you she was here to see Frank, to try to get their relationship back on track. It was his room you saw the body in, but someone took it away. You had obviously never been to the Devil's Kettle before I took you there this afternoon, at which point Sharon's body had been inside it for hours." Betsy had looked at Jill when she started speaking and Jill never broke eye contact, but she was addressing the room. "The police don't suspect you. Why should they? You're not lying or hiding facts, you're the one reporting what you find. They're suspicious of the obvious person, the person who knew Sharon, the person Sharon was coming to see, the person in whose room she died!"

The room filled again with murmurs. Jill took a bite of apple crumble and said, much more quietly, "That'll fix 'em."

And indeed it did. Before leaving the dining room, perhaps half of the stitchers came by the table, casual and friendly (as if they hadn't made imputative remarks in the lounge earlier, or listened minutes ago with growing belief to Frank Owen's accusations).

Nan wanted to know if Jill had ever known another murderer who tried to get rid of a body in some strange way, and Linda Savareid remarked that of course it would have taken a strong man to carry a dead body through all that snow up to the Devil's Kettle.

Which was something that hadn't occurred to Betsy. There had been ski trails on the river and footprints on those remarkable wooden stairs. And all around the falls. Jill said it would be a very difficult walk up the snow along the river without snowshoes. How much more difficult while carrying a dead body. Who but someone in fine physical condition could do that, much less venture to climb that steep bank or come down those many icy steps?

Isabel came by to say, "I think this whole thing is so sad. Frank was disappointed and impatient with Sharon over her illness, but I will admit, Sharon treated Frank shamefully."

"Frank was as understanding and patient with Sharon as it is possible to get!" muttered Carla to Isabel as she brushed by her. She did not look at Jill or Betsy.

The last person to stop by was Sadie Cartwright, rolling up in her wheelchair. "Now that they've found the body just where you said it was, we'll see some action, right? Who do you think moved it? Not Frank, he's too obvious. It's always the least obvious one, isn't it? I think it's Doogie. Who would suspect a person with a silly name like that?"

And with another of her loud laughs, she whirled away.

Betsy said, "Gosh, she's annoying!" She turned back to Jill. "I wonder what time Carla checked in on Friday?"

"That may not matter," Jill pointed out. "I didn't need a key to open the back door to our wing, and I wouldn't need one to get into the other wing, either. Anyone who has been here before might know that." Jill sat back in her chair and looked hard at Betsy. "Decision time, girl."

"What do you mean?"

"I mean, when the autopsy shows Sharon Kaye Owen wasn't drowned, they are going to arrest Frank Owen, if only for attempting to hide a death. If that's okay with you, fine. On the other hand, if you don't think Frank is guilty of any crime, then you have to decide whether or not you're going to try to get to the bottom of this mess. Whatever you decide, I'll be with you. But this speculating and prying while claiming you don't want to damage your psyche with another investigation is getting old."

Betsy said angrily, "I am not—Well, so what if I try to figure out what happened? Everyone in this room was talking about it, you heard them!"

"They're going back to the lounge to stitch. What are you going to do?"

Betsy fell silent. What she had planned to do was go ask James if he could tell her who was checked in by 3 P.M. on Friday.

Jill said, "Face it, you have the biggest curiosity bump in Excelsior, which makes you probably the nosiest person in the state—if not the entire upper

Midwest. Plus, you have a gift for investigation. I know that combination has brought you all kinds of grief, but on the other hand, there are two murderers and one would-be murderer whose names would be unknown if it wasn't for that gift. Only you know if that's a fair exchange. But the question has to be answered, you can't keep whipsawing yourself like this."

Betsy sighed. Jill waited her out. At last Betsy said, "I appreciate your unwavering support of my wavering. I really, really don't want to get involved in murder anymore. The quiet life has never looked so attractive to me. On the other hand, I had a nice talk with Frank Owen earlier today, and I liked him. It's not just that he seemed nice—because he wasn't when he thought I might hurt some innocent people—his reactions to my questions were of a crystalline innocence I found convincing. I don't think he's guilty of murder."

Jill said, "And you're going to report all this to the sheriff, and let him investigate?"

"Yes. So okay, he can ask James about check-in times."

"So it's back to the lounge, right?"

"Yes, let's go see if Carla is in there. I'm wondering if her bad-mouthing Sharon has less to do with a dislike of Sharon than a liking for Frank."

Jill coughed, fist to mouth, and followed Betsy to the lounge. Carla was not there.

Jill said, "She'll probably be here in a minute. Meanwhile, Ginni Berringer promised to show me a project she's working in Schwalm embroidery. I know you used to do embroidery, so let's both go see it."

Ginni was a plump woman with dark eyes and dark hair pulled back into a little bun. The embroidery was done in white coton Broder on 32-count white linen, hearts and tulips in a design that made Betsy think of rosemaling, or the kind of artwork produced by the Pennsylvania Dutch. Ginni was an advanced embroiderer, Betsy used to embroider, so in another minute the pair were talking about coral knots, chain stitch, and buttonhole scallops. "I've pulled every fourth thread inside the heart," Ginni said, "and I'm about to start the eyelet filling."

"Very nice," said Betsy.

"I wouldn't want to try that," said Jill, who had never done embroidery. "But it's very handsome." She went off to do more work on her tiger.

In another minute Betsy said, "I think I'll quit bothering you with questions and join her."

Betsy got her canvas bag and pulled out the rose window pattern. Slowly and carefully, with only two errors found immediately and corrected, she finished the last wedge. She clipped a short length of the Kreinik, consulted the pattern, looked at the wedge—and saw she had started it a stitch farther over than the pattern called for. Growling softly, she frogged—rip it, rip it, rip it—the error out and started working it again. But after a dozen stitches she saw that while she had corrected its placement in relation to the previous wedge, now it didn't sit correctly in relation to the inner medallion. Or the first wedge, which was next to it. She looked back at the previous wedge, and saw it, too, didn't sit where it should in relation to the center.

Jill heard her groan of dismay and asked, "What's wrong?"

"I have messed up big-time. These last two wedges are wrong. It would break my heart to frog them. I know people find a way to work around an error, but I can't see how to do that here. Can you?"

Jill shook her head. "I'm sorry. Counted cross-stitch broke my heart years ago and I gave it up. Maybe you should talk to Nan or Sadie or someone else here who does counted."

But Betsy couldn't face the other questions that would come if she initiated a conversation.

"I'll ask them tomorrow. It's getting late, I think I'll just go up to bed."

She wasn't all that sleepy, just tired and discouraged. She brushed her teeth and discontentedly got into her pajamas. As she crawled between the sheets, she wondered if she should take some aspirin against the muscle soreness she would probably wake up with because of that strenuous trek up and back down the frozen Brule, but the thought was only half formed before she slid off a dark cliff into slumber.

Soon she was in a canoe floating down a fast-moving river. It was summertime. The banks were level, scattered with trees and flowers. But the water was a little rough, complicating her efforts to work on a counted cross-stitch pattern of a big barking basset hound.

Suddenly a roar ahead indicated she was coming to a waterfall, and she knew it was the Devil's Kettle. Unless she paddled for shore, she would dive, canoe and all, into that hollow black rock and never be seen again. She began stitching faster, because she could not put down the stitchery until it was finished. The water grew rougher, the canoe bouncing over the rapids, and it became difficult to get the needle through the right place from underneath. Fumbling with it, the needle slipped out of her fingers and came off the thread to fall into the bottom of the canoe. Somebody on the shore shouted at her to hurry, the water was cold. She bent over to look for the needle among the leaves and pine needles that covered the ribs on the bottom of the canoe, and noticed she was barefoot. The roar got louder, but bending over was all right, because she didn't want to watch the falls come closer and closer. As the person on shore shouted at her to stop, she felt the canoe tip over the falls, and woke with a start. She was alone in bed.

There was a conversation in distressed voices going on out in the hall. "I'm all right, please stop fussing!" someone was saying.

Betsy climbed out of bed and reached for her robe, holding it around her shoulders with one hand while she hurried to the door and opened it.

Jill was out there, wrapped in her thick terry robe, with auburn-haired Liddy in a lush, cream-colored, ankle-length silk nightgown trimmed in ecru lace, suntanned Carla in a pale green chiffon peignoir, and plump Isabel in a pink flannel nightgown stitched with her initials in elaborate script. Liddy was barefoot, tousled, her eyes wide and confused, tears streaking her cheeks.

"What's going on?" asked Betsy.

"Sleepwalking," said Jill.

"I'm fine, I'm awake now," said Liddy.

"She's staying in my room, and I heard her open the door on her way out," said Isabel. "I got up and called her name, then realized she was sleepwalking. They say not to wake them, but I followed because I was afraid she might fall down the stairs."

Carla said, "Isabel knocked on my door as they went by, and I came out, and I told her she should take Liddy gently by the hand and lead her back to bed."

Isabel continued. "But I didn't want to because what if she woke up, and just then your door opened and it was Jill. She said it's okay to wake sleepwalkers, if you do it gently. But by then Liddy was halfway down the stairs. I still thought we shouldn't touch her, but Jill insisted, so we let her go get her, and sure enough, as soon as she took her by the arm, Liddy woke up and started crying."

Jill said, "She's scared, that's all."

Liddy, who wasn't crying now, said, "I'm telling you, I'm all right."

Isabel said, "I told her, 'Hurry, let's get her back to bed before she catches her death of cold.' I mean look at her, barefoot on a night like this! But see how she's crying. I don't know if Jill did the right thing."

Jill said, "If we'd left her alone, she might have gone outside."

"I wouldn't have done that!" exclaimed Liddy. When she saw them looking at her, she went on, shamefaced. "I don't know what made me walk in my sleep. I haven't done that since I was a child. I'm sure I won't do it again."

"What were you dreaming about, do you remember?" asked Betsy.

"No. Actually, I don't think I was dreaming," said Liddy. She wiped her cheeks with the backs of her hands and sniffed hard. "I'm sorry for creating such a disturbance—again. It seems to be what I do up here, fall out of my chair, walk in my sleep, scare people."

"We're not in the least afraid, we all know you're upset about your mother," said Isabel, taking her by an elbow and leading her away. "Good night," she said firmly over her shoulder, a hint to the others to return to their rooms.

"Well!" said Betsy a few minutes later, climbing back into bed. "What do you think about that?"

"I think Isabel's right. Liddy is upset about her mother. It's sad when a parent dies, and Sharon died in an awful way. Liddy came up here because she was worried about her, remember. I wonder if it's true she wasn't dreaming? She was rubbing her fingers as if they were cold."

"I was having a bad one," said Betsy. "I dreamed that I was about to go over the falls in a canoe." She began squirming around and pulling at her too-big pajama bottoms to smooth away a fold. "Maybe you should go order her not to sleepwalk, like you told me not to have any more nightmares last night. It worked, you know."

Jill sighed, but gently, and said in a firm voice, "No more bad dreams. That's an order."

"Yes, ma'am," said Betsy, composing her mind to obedience.

And again, it worked.

"You should bottle that voice," Betsy said the next morning at the breakfast table. "Or, anyway, sell recordings of it."

Jill protested, "You are the one in control of your own head. Just listen when you order yourself not to have any more bad dreams. You don't need me to do that."

Betsy took her first bite of Wake Up Huevos—eggs scrambled with tomatoes, jalapenos, cilantro, scallions, and a hint of garlic, served over tortilla strips and topped with sour cream, grated cheddar, and salsa—and focused intently on that. "Wow," she murmured, and took a second bite to confirm it was as good as it had seemed. "Forget the cattle drive, let's come up here again in September," she said.

Off and on, Jill and Betsy talked about going on a late-summer cattle drive offered by a dude ranch. Jill said, "Speaking of that, I found a new place, not a dude ranch, that allows people who can ride to come along. It costs a thousand dollars for two weeks. They supply the horses, but you have to be able to ride and work cattle."

Betsy hadn't been on a horse since she started getting plump—or had she started getting plump when she gave up riding? Now she was wealthy enough to afford a health club membership and lose that weight, get back in shape. She put down her fork, immediately determined to at least not put on another pound.

Because she could just see herself rounding up strays while dust kicked up, and the cattle bawled, and the cowboys whistled at the herd to keep it moving. And maybe a cow with a sore back would need to be cut out to have it doctored. Savvy cow ponies did all the work of cutting a steer out of the herd; all a rider did was aim him at a cow and hang on.

Betsy had attended a horse show at which there was a cutting contest. A horse had to separate a steer from a small herd and keep it from returning. Betsy remembered how badly the cow had wanted to rejoin its fellows, and how that horse had jumped and dodged so nimbly it was a wonder the skilled rider wasn't flung off. She said, "Do you know someplace I can get some riding lessons? Now I think about it, I'm kind of rusty."

Jill said thickly, around a sticky pecan muffin, "I'll check into that. Have you ever ridden a quarter horse?"

"No, but I rode a mustang for a couple of years."

That began an animated discussion about horses. Betsy picked unconsciously at her *huevos* while they talked until she suddenly realized she was looking down at a clean plate. The food here was simply too good to resist.

They were having a final cup of coffee when Sheriff Goodman sat down at their table as abruptly as if he'd been teleported into the chair. "Where's Elizabeth Owen?" he asked without preamble.

Betsy and Jill both craned their necks, looking around. "I don't see her," Betsy said at last.

"Liddy had a bad night last night," said Jill. "I guess she's sleeping in this morning."

"She's staying here, then?"

"She was in Isabel's room last night," said Betsy. "I don't know about Doogie." She looked at the lawman. "You've got news?"

"Sharon Kaye Owen was dead before she was put in that hole in the rock. From the look of her lungs, the Cook County medical examiner thinks she was suffering a severe, possibly lethal, allergic reaction. He's asking the Mayo Clinic down at Rochester to do fancier tests than he can. But you see how that makes it more likely that what you told me about seeing her body in Mr. Owen's room Friday afternoon is true. You're sure it was Mr. Owen's room?"

"It was on the second floor, a room painted green, with a fireplace, and whose door is at an angle to the corridor. There is no other room on the second floor of the lodge with a fireplace except ours, and our room is paneled in knotty pine."

"You're sure you went up to the second floor?"

"Absolutely."

"But Mr. Owen wasn't in there when you went in?"

"No. I tried to use my key and it didn't work, but when I tried the door, it was unlocked."

Jill said, "It has occurred to us that it was very foolish of Mr. Owen to leave the body in an unlocked room, but the door wasn't locked when the two of us went to talk with him later, and it was unlocked when your crew arrived to search the room. He apparently doesn't lock his door when he stays here."

Goodman shrugged. "Hardly anyone locks their doors at the lodge." He looked around the room. "Have you seen Frank Owen this morning?"

"Wait a minute," said Betsy. "Are you going to arrest him?"

"No, I'm going to have a little talk with him." He looked around the room. "Is he here?"

Jill said, "He's over there," and nodded toward the big stone fireplace.

Betsy looked in that direction and saw him at one of the larger tables, where the geologist Parker Lundquist sat with Anna, Isabel, Carla, and three other women. When the sheriff stood, Owen glanced over, and his face became still. The others at the table looked where he was looking, and they, too, became still. It was like an infection, that stillness. By the time the sheriff reached the table, no one else in the room was moving or talking.

Goodman bent over and spoke very quietly to Frank, who nodded gravely and stood. "I'll see you later," he said, or something like it, to the others at his table, and they nodded confusedly at him, not sure whether to believe him, pretend they believed him, or openly doubt him.

As Goodman escorted Owen from the room, a wave of whispers followed behind them, which broke into speech the instant they reached the lobby.

"Did you see that?" seemed to be the gist. A few dared the scorn of their fellows by adding, "I knew it, I just knew it."

There was a high-pitched cry of rage from the lobby. Jill was on her way toward the sound before Betsy could stand, but she hurried to catch up.

In the lobby were Liddy and Doogie, a single suitcase between them. Liddy was in a hysterical rage, shouting at the sheriff. "He's done nothing, nothing! You can't take him! I'll have you fired if you don't let go of him!"

"Ma'am, ma'am," the sheriff kept saying, stepping back with one hand on Frank's arm, the other reaching to ward her off, "he's not under arrest. We just want to talk to him."

Doogie moved to stand between Liddy and the lawman, facing her. "Listen to me, soldier," he said very firmly. "You are behaving like a little girl, and we can't have that. This is a serious situation, and you need to pull yourself together."

"He's right, Liddy," said Frank, and to the sheriff, "May we go upstairs and get my coat and hat?"

"Yessir, no problem."

"But, Daddy, Daddy!" cried Liddy. "You can't leave me! Make them let you go, I want you to come home with me!"

"I can't do that right now, soldier. But I won't be long. You stay here until I get back."

"I can't! I can't!"

"Of course you can," he said. "I expect you to calm down right now."

And amazingly, she took a shuddering breath and fell silent.

"Here—" He pulled his room key from his pocket and gave it to the sheriff. "Let's go up."

Liddy, her eyes two blue wounds, stared after him. "I'll be brave," she whispered. "But I want to go home."

"We're not going home until we find out what's going to happen," said Doogie. "Dad might need us, and we both had better be on the spot, ready to do whatever needs doing." Liddy nodded, then closed her eyes and put her face on her brother's chest. After a moment, Doogie put a stiff arm around her and stood firm. This controlled young man was a striking change from the scared boy of yesterday.

Betsy caught a movement from the corner of her eye and turned to see Carla come into the lobby. "What's going on out here?" she demanded.

"The sheriff is taking my father away!" cried Liddy.

This confused Carla, as obviously the sheriff was following Frank upstairs.

Doogie said, "They're going to get his coat, then he's taking him into Grand Marais."

"I can't bear it, I can't bear it!" Liddy wept.

Carla stepped around Doogie to take Liddy from behind, saying gently, "Come up to my room, both of you."

"No," said Doogie. "The two of us are going up to Dad's room as soon as they leave."

"Please, will you come with us?" said Liddy, surprising Doogie.

Before he could object, Carla said, "Of course, baby, of course."

Betsy said, "If you don't mind, I would like—"

"Not now," said Carla. "Not now." Her voice continued, sweet and gentle, and already Liddy's anguished sobs were lessening as they vanished up the stairs, Doogie following close behind.

In another minute, Frank came back down with Sheriff Goodman, and they went out to the parking lot without either of them so much as nodding at Jill or Betsy. Through the window set into the door, they watched as the sheriff led Frank by the elbow to his patrol car and put him into the backseat. Beyond them, the lodge maintenance man came out of the furnace shed brushing bits of bark off his front. He halted and stared at the scene in front of him.

Jill said quietly, "Poor fellow—but no wonder Liddy likes Carla. When you're brokenhearted, you naturally prefer 'baby' to 'soldier.'"

Betsy started to reply, but turned it to a wordless exclamation, and ran out the door to the parking lot. Jill started to follow, but stopped on the little front deck to watch as Betsy, slipping and shouting and waving her arms, ran up the lane after the patrol car. Its brake lights came on, and Betsy, huddled against the cold, bent to speak to the sheriff. Then she went around to climb in the back, and the car's backup lights came on.

When the car stopped beside the door, Betsy climbed out and rushed in. "Where is it?" she said.

"What?" asked Jill.

"That floss I found out by the shed. Where is it?"

"How should I know? Last I saw it, you were putting it in your coat pocket."

Betsy fled into the dining room.

"I'll wait here," the sheriff said, and Jill stared at him uncomprehendingly.

Twelve

Betsy dodged among the tables as she dashed across the dining room, through the door, up the stairs, and into her room. She was back a minute later to hand the floss to the sheriff. "See if—it's pure cotton—or not," she gasped, all out of breath.

"Why, what's this about?"

"Murder. If this floss is—something other than pure cotton—If it's got peanut oil, pollen—dust, cat hair—wheat flour, dried milk—anything Mrs. Owen—was allergic to—this—this could be—the murder weapon."

Goodman looked at the slim lavender skein. "Where did you get this?"

"Out by the furnace shed. Dropped."

"And you probably didn't pick it up with tweezers or keep it in a plastic bag."

Betsy waved a finger at him. "You—there first—didn't find it at all." Jill cleared her throat, and Betsy flinched and then said more humbly, "No, I put it in my coat pocket."

"Uh-huh."

But Goodman put it in his shirt pocket, buttoned the flap down, and went away.

Betsy went into the dining room and sat wearily on the Victorian round couch with the pillar growing out of its center.

"All right, tell me what that was about," Jill said.

"I remember that Sharon Kaye put the end of her floss in her mouth to wet it before threading her needle. Stitchers who do that, do that habitually. Someone who knew Sharon was a floss licker might think to switch flosses, put something she was allergic to in place of her cotton floss, or dip the floss into something she was allergic to. Or spray the floss with something. But then the evidence had to be destroyed. Remember that place in the snow by the furnace shed, where it looked like someone fell?"

Jill nodded.

"Okay, that was him. Or her. The idea was to get rid of the body and everything of Sharon Kaye's he could get hold of, any proof she had been here at all.

He, or she, was in a hurry. He was carrying everything, including her project bag, out to the furnace, and he slipped and fell, and in his haste to pick everything up, he missed one little something. I think it's a very important thing."

"The lavender floss."

"Yes, I remember she was using lavender floss. And though I very cleverly found it, I didn't realize its significance and much less cleverly put it in my pocket and forgot all about it. I hope they don't delay the test, or have to send it away to get it tested."

"I can't imagine the lab test for fibers is all that elaborate. We'll probably know fairly soon."

"But that's not all. There is no Eddie. What she said was, 'I have to go get my EpiPen.'"

"Are you sure? Wait a second, why did she have to leave to get it? People who need them have them at hand. Why wasn't it right there with her?"

"Because it was in her purse, and she didn't have her purse with her. All she had was her canvas sewing bag. Maybe she went right up, as soon as she arrived. If Frank was out, she couldn't ask him if she could stay, so she didn't bring her luggage up to his room."

"So why didn't she bring the coat and purse down again?"

"Maybe she was pretty sure she could convince him to take her in. Or she did bring them down and left them—where?"

"In the ladies' room," said Jill. "There's a coatrack in there."

"Then her murderer is a woman," said Betsy. "Because she went in there to retrieve them and bring them up to Frank's room, where I saw them."

"That all fits. But why was her car still here, then? If the murderer had her purse, he had her keys."

Betsy blinked at Jill and felt the confident structure she'd been building sway dangerously.

From the other side of the counter came the sound of someone rapping on a table. Isabel's voice said, "Good morning, everyone!" with no trace of her usual good humor. Jill and Betsy stood to watch.

Isabel was standing in front of the fireplace, hands raised to command attention. She continued. "I'm sorry to be the bearer of bad news for those of you who haven't already heard—though I suspect that's very few of you. Sharon Kaye Owen of Escapade Design was found dead in Judge Magney State Park yesterday. And as you just saw, Cook County Sheriff Goodman took her ex-husband away for questioning. This is very sad and distressing for those of us who knew Sharon Kaye and Frank. Sharon was so vibrant, and Frank always seemed so very pleasant." She paused and showed her own distress by intertwining her fingers and squeezing them into painful configurations. After a few moments she said, "I am going to call for a vote. The stitch-in is going to end at three this afternoon in any case. Should we call a halt to it now, and quietly go home? Or should we continue? I'll ask for a show of hands. Everyone who thinks we should go home now, raise your hands."

Three women immediately raised their hands, saw they were a minority, and yanked them back down again. One shook her head to show she'd changed her mind.

Sadie, wheeling forward, raised her hand, but it was for permission to speak. "I didn't know Sharon Kaye or her husband, so maybe it's not right for me to have an opinion. But I came up here to meet some stitchers, learn new techniques, and—and just be around people who share my passion for needle-work. I don't want to go home till I have to."

Anna, who had been one of the trio to raise her hand to vote to go home, stood. She looked wretched, and her voice was uneven as she said, "I want to retract my vote to end the stitch-in. I think Sadie's right, I think we should stay. Some of us have fond memories of Sharon, and perhaps we can share them."

Betsy turned to Jill, but saw she was already thinking the same thing Betsy was: Anna had displayed no fondness for Sharon yesterday. Jill murmured, "The workings of conscience in the presence of death is a mysterious thing."

"I agree with Anna," said Nan, who looked equally distressed, and several others nodded and raised their hands as if to vote in favor of sharing fond memories.

"Very well," said Isabel, not sounding happy about it, "the stitch-in will continue. Let us adjourn to the lounge."

Jill and Betsy sat down again.

Betsy said, "Every time I think I understand what happened, there's always this odd piece sticking out. I probably ran after the sheriff for nothing, too. That floss will turn out to be totally innocent."

"Then how did it get out by the furnace?"

"It could have fallen out of someone's pocket. I doubt we're the only ones who have gone for walks."

Jill said, "All right, the floss is innocent. What does that mean? Sharon's death was an accident?"

Betsy thought a minute, frowning. "Suppose she did go see Frank, and he induced the allergic reaction accidentally. He said he was pleased to have things around that she was allergic to, like pizza and peanut butter; maybe she walked in on him enjoying a peanut butter sandwich."

"Then all she had to do was walk out again, probably. But all right, suppose she walks in, turns blue, collapses. If it was an innocent accident, why not just report it? In fact, suppose the reason you walked in and she was in there all alone was that he was downstairs trying to find someone to report it to. That would explain why he wasn't there when you walked in."

"But he didn't report it, or someone would have said something. And he told us he never saw her. So if he didn't go to report it, where did he go? No, if he was there when it happened, and he went out, it was to prepare to take her away. You know, go unlock his car."

Jill said, "Maybe he was in the bathroom when you came in, and didn't want to answer embarrassing questions. But we haven't answered two basic questions: If Frank isn't responsible for Sharon's death, what was she doing dead in his room? And why was she taken away?"

"You think they're going to arrest him?"

"I think they're going to hold him for twenty-four hours."

"I wish—" said Betsy, then cut herself off.

"You wish what?"

"Nothing." Betsy's smile was a little sour. What she wished was that Sheriff Goodman appeared a little more confidence-inspiring, but she didn't want to bad-mouth one law enforcement officer in front of another.

Jill said, "How about this: Frank deliberately had something in his room that would induce an allergic reaction, knowing Sharon was going to come and see him."

Betsy thought a moment. "And he could claim he didn't know she was going to walk in on him. But that puts us right back to your basic question: Why, if he was setting up an accident, ruin it by taking the body away?"

"Frank didn't do that, someone else did. Frank induces the reaction, somebody else sees the body and moves it."

"But who? Neither Liddy nor Doogie was here to do that."

"I bet Carla was. You said you think she's in love with Frank. Okay, maybe he's in love with her, too. Maybe he came up here to see Carla as well as get a little skiing in. But here comes Sharon Kaye, as usual, to spoil things. So Frank decides to murder her. He sets it up to look like an accident, but before he can finish things, Carla pops in for a little kissy-face, sees Sharon Kaye on the bed, and thinks, 'I must protect my man.'"

Betsy said, "I don't think Carla's capable of carrying a dead body up that trail."

"You'd be surprised what a person who is really scared can do."

"Well—maybe." But Betsy thought about those many flights of icy wooden stairs.

"All right, suppose you're right, someone doctored the floss. I vote for Liddy; she probably knows Sharon's needleworking habits better than anyone."

"Except Carla," said Betsy.

"But if Carla messed with the floss, then who—Oh, I see! Sharon Kaye staggers up the stairs into Frank's room, and he's the one who panics and hides the body!"

Betsy nodded. "That sounds more like it."

Jill said, "Still, I wish we could have gotten to Liddy before Carla took her away. She's gone all to pieces since they found Sharon's body, just about like you'd expect if she's the one responsible for this mess. If we talk to her, she'll probably confess, if she's guilty."

Betsy said, "She couldn't have done it. Sharon disappeared on Friday during working hours, and Liddy said she was at work all day. That's too easy to check, so I doubt Liddy would lie about that."

"Murderers as rattled as Liddy is tell stupid lies. She's acting very hinky."

" 'Hinky'?"

"It means suspiciously, in a criminal sense. Backing into a doorway when a squad car comes by is hinky."

"I see," said Betsy. "Motive?"

Jill said, "Money, probably. But also, from what we've been hearing, Sharon was a beautiful, charming, self-centered woman with a jealous, controlling streak. Probably Liddy has a lot of mixed feelings because her mother kept coming back and then abandoning her again. If it turns out the floss was exchanged or doctored, we'll get the sheriff to check her alibi. Because I think she's our best candidate for this."

"Doogie has the same motives as Liddy, money and abandonment."

Jill said, "But he's really risen to this terrible occasion. Before, he was an awful wuss. Anyhow, he was at work, too. Sweeping up the ranger station in Grand Marais."

"Maybe we should suggest the sheriff check his alibi, too. Did you see how Carla is suddenly acting like the surrogate mommy to those two? Her concern seems real. And they like it, especially Liddy."

Jill nodded. "Yeah, but I'll bet you a dollar she's got no alibi at all. Love can also be a powerful motive."

"All right, it would be hers. Along with anger that Sharon Kaye was trying to come between her and her man. Still . . . I wish I knew who gets Sharon Kaye's money. There's a whole lot of it. Frank doesn't get any, thanks to a prenuptial agreement he signed. He told me he doesn't know where the rest goes. The obvious answer is, to the children. Liddy and Doogie had large trust funds set up when they were born, and they can't access the principal till they're thirty. They're living comfortably off the income from the trusts, but I wonder if one or both of them uses drugs, or is a gambler."

Betsy looked up the stairs. She was sure that with Carla as a gatekeeper, they were not going to be able to question either of the Owen siblings until Carla chose the time. In the controlling arena, Carla shone as brightly as Sharon.

James walked into the dining room and stopped, looking around. He saw

Jill and Betsy and said, "There you are, Ms. Devonshire. I'm very sorry, but that young man is on the phone again. Mr. DuLac?"

"Oh, help." Betsy sighed. "All right, where?"

"In the office, like before. I left the door open for you." He headed off in the direction of the kitchen.

"I'll be in the lounge," said Jill.

Betsy picked up the heavy black telephone receiver in the office and said, "Okay, Godwin, what is it now?"

"A man just walked in here with a letter for you. Instead of a stamp, it has 'By Hand' typed in the corner, and he made me sign for it. The return address is 'Touhy and Howe, Attorneys, in the IDS Center, Minneapolis.' Betsy, do you know who they are?" He said that as if he knew, but wasn't sure Betsy would.

"Sure, Mr. Touhy is one of Joe Mickels' lawyers."

"I *knew* he would try something, I just *knew* it! There's probably a *summons* in here! He's taking you to *court*!"

"No, a summons has to go to the actual person, and it's never in an envelope. This probably has something to do with the sale of the building."

"Oh, then this is about the *water leak*! He thinks he's found a way to make *you* pay for it, I bet! But he can't *do that*, can he? I mean, the building *still* belongs to *him*, right?" Godwin in a panic put up italics like a porcupine erects its bristles.

"Calm down, Goddy! If you want to know what it's about, open the envelope."

"Can I? Is that legal?"

"Why not? You signed for it, didn't you? So you have legal custody. It's addressed to me, so I can give you permission. For heaven's sake, open it and see what kind of headache it contains."

The letter was a formal notification of a meeting two weeks hence in the office of Mr. Langston Touhy, Esquire, in the IDS Tower in Minneapolis, at which time and place papers concluding the sale of the building in which Betsy's apartment and shop were contained would be signed.

"Oh," said Godwin, considerably let down. "Well, why'd he send something this ordinary by courier?"

"Because he agreed to give me two weeks' notice of this signing, and the date is exactly fifteen days from today. I think you're right: He's trying to conclude the sale quickly now, in case there's more water damage that hasn't shown up yet."

"It's today's date on this thing. Getting an attorney to work on a Sunday isn't exactly cheap," Godwin pointed out.

"How much was the estimate for the water damage?" asked Betsy.

"Oh, my God, Betsy, wait till I *tell* you! The water is coming from the roof, it's been spilling down an opening in the side wall for days, running between the floor of your apartment and the ceiling of the shop, and pooling right in the center, where it finally soaked through! I asked for a ballpark figure on what it's going to cost to fix it, and he said *nine thousand*! I told them to put a temporary patch on the roof, which all by itself will cost about five hundred but that's only *temporary*! And that doesn't include the cost to repair the ceiling or replace the damaged goods!"

"And how often are ballpark estimates way under the actual cost?" asked Betsy, and answered herself: "Often. It's going to cost much more than nine thousand before we're through. What Joe will do is offer to deduct nine thousand from the price of the building. That's why the rush, he wants the deal done before we find out we need a whole new roof. I guess the bloom is off the rose."

"What does that mean?"

"In the face of spending real money, any chance at romance is dead, dead, dead."

"That evil, *sneaky* old man!" said Godwin, at length and not exactly in those words.

A few minutes later, Betsy hung up with a sigh. Maybe she shouldn't have gone away. What with troubles she wasn't allowed to leave behind in Excelsior and a mystery up here, she wasn't getting much of a rest.

She left the office, checking the door after she pulled it closed to make sure it locked. It was a fine old door, to judge by the solid thickness of the wood, but ill-fitted to the frame. At the hinge end she could fit the toe of her shoe under it.

Betsy stood a moment, frowning at the door, then went off on a search for James.

She found him in the kitchen, checking the blend of lettuces in a very large salad bowl. "Did you find an EpiPen on your desk yesterday?" she asked.

"EpiPen? Oh, that plastic thing for allergic reactions. Yes, I did. I wondered where it came from. Is it yours?"

"No. I found it on the floor of your office and left it on the desk. Are you sure it doesn't belong to an employee or someone who has access to that little office?"

"Yes, I'm sure. Anyone needing help as serious as that pen offers would be sure to warn us all about it." He shrugged. "Plus I asked."

"Then I think I know who it belongs to. May I have it back?"

"Of course. Come with me."

The device had been put in a drawer behind the lobby counter. Betsy took it and asked, "So long as you're back there, can you tell me when Carla Prakesh checked in?"

"All right." He checked his log and said, "She missed dinner on Friday, she didn't drive up to our door till almost nine. I remember because she asked for help unloading her car."

"Thanks." Betsy went into the dining room and sat on the circular couch with the pillar to take another look at the EpiPen. If Sharon hadn't dropped it, might it have saved her life? She held it up and jiggled it gently. The liquid inside was thin as water. The plastic was heavy, and formed a blunt point at the needle end. She gripped the safety cap and tried it. It would not move. She tried harder, but it was stuck fast.

Perhaps it had jammed when Sharon dropped it. She held it closer to her eyes. Was that something—? A thin trail of some clear substance ran around the cap. She prodded it with a fingernail, but it was as hard as plastic. No wonder it wouldn't turn, the cap was sealed to the body of the pen.

She had seen this same thin, unyielding seal before, on a favorite mug she had dropped, broken, and repaired. Impermeable, unbreakable, permanent. Superglue.

She had a sudden, sharp vision of Sharon, eyes red and tearing, skin flaming and itching, as she frantically twisted the cap, trying to get it off. As her throat began to swell shut, the one thing that could fend off death would not open for her use. Realizing that, she either dropped it as useless, or threw it down in frustration—and it had rolled under the door.

Where the person who had sabotaged it could not retrieve it, as he had retrieved the betraying canvas bag of stitchery and burned it.

Betsy put the EpiPen in her skirt pocket and went to the lounge. Jill had a group of five or six stitchers sitting or standing around her, watching as she stitched something on a piece of scrap canvas, talking quietly as she did so. "You can see how the arrowhead shape of the Amadeus stitch is formed," she was saying as Betsy approached. It appeared that the group was getting its surprise teacher after all—though it was likely Jill was as surprised as any of them.

Ingrid, sitting near Jill but working on her own project, looked up as Betsy came in, and her face filled with compassion. "More badt news?"

"Yes, I'm afraid so. Jill, may I see you alone for a minute?"

"Sure." Jill handed the canvas to Linda Savareid, seated beside her, and said, "Now I've got the second one started, you finish it and start another beside it. The rest of you watch, and kibitz to your hearts' content." She followed Betsy through the dining room, where James was supervising the lunch setup, and into the lobby, which was empty.

"Look at this," Betsy said, pulling the EpiPen out of her pocket.

Jill took it, read its printed instructions, noted that it was fully charged, and said, "Where did you find this?"

"Under the desk in the office, when I took that first call from Godwin. I thought it belonged to someone who worked here, so I left it on the desk. But it doesn't. James put it behind the check-in counter, waiting for a guest to ask about it, and no one has. It must be Sharon Kaye's. Look at it, the cap has been glued on."

Jill twisted the cap, gently then harder. Then she, too, pried at the thin line of glue around the cap. "Very nasty. How did it get into the office?"

"My guess is, it rolled under the gap in the door."

Jill walked to the office door, tried it, and found it locked, then fit the device to the space under it. Toward the hinge end, there was ample room.

Betsy said, "This is murder, Jill. Someone sabotaged her EpiPen, got her a long way from medical help, and triggered an allergic reaction somehow."

"Who?" asked Jill.

"I don't know. Someone who had access to her purse or whatever she kept her EpiPen in. And probably not too long before she came up here, in case she was in the habit of checking the thing. I checked on when Carla got here, and it was late Friday night. And I bet if you check, she'll have a solid alibi for the afternoon."

"Well, that eliminates her."

"Actually, it doesn't. If you think about it, that puts her on the list. It wasn't a case of getting Sharon Kaye up here and then triggering the attack. The attack was arranged somewhere else, then she was sent up here. I'm sure that when they test that floss, they'll find it exchanged or coated with something. This was set up by someone who wanted to be at a distance when Sharon Kaye had that allergic attack. So when they heard the news they could murmur sadly, 'How awful, how tragic,' and maybe produce a tear." Her mouth tightened. "How wicked."

Jill said, "So your original theory is right. The person who took the body away is the one sitting down with the sheriff right now. He came back to his room and found her and panicked. We've got two crimes, two different perps."

Betsy nodded. "Yes, I think that must be it. And as for the car, I think he missed his chance to move it. People were arriving, maybe he thought it had already been seen, or was afraid he'd be seen driving it away."

Jill said, "You should call Sheriff Goodman right now and tell him about the EpiPen."

"All right." But as Betsy got out her wallet to dig for change, she heard footsteps on the stairs and looked up to see Doogie coming down.

"Ah, nuts, I might've known I'd run right into you two," he said, half annoyed, half amused. "But I told Liddy that if I saw you I'd ask, so maybe you can tell me when they are going to release my father."

Betsy replied, "I have no way of telling that. I'm not connected with any law enforcement agency."

"How about your friend, the cop?"

Jill said, "I have no connection with local law enforcement."

Betsy said, twiddling her left eyebrow significantly, "Jill, why don't you call the sheriff and ask him? I think he'll be willing to talk to you, as a fellow law enforcement person. Ask him if and when he's going to release Frank. Meanwhile, I want to talk with Douglas." Betsy could not bring herself to call a murder suspect Doogie.

Faced with this offer of quid pro quo, Douglas could only nod. "Come up to our room, okay?" He looked into the dining room and led the way back up the stairs.

He gave two brisk knocks on the angled door to his father's room even as he turned the knob. Apparently his whole family wasn't big on locks.

Betsy followed him in. Liddy was lying on her stomach on the bed, propped up on elbows. Carla was sitting in a little upholstered chair by the fireplace, in which a small fire burned.

Douglas said, obviously in response to a request he go down and check, "They're still setting up lunch, so we'll have to wait awhile longer."

Liddy sighed and lay completely down.

"Well, it's your own fault," Douglas said. "You should have eaten last night, or come down this morning for breakfast."

Carla said, "Doogie, have a little sympathy for your sister."

"How little can I have?" Douglas made an amused wincing face and said, "Sorry. Oh, by the way, Ms. Devonshire here has asked her friend to find out Dad's status, so in return I said she could talk to us a little bit."

Carla stood. "I won't agree to that."

"Fine," said Douglas. "Why don't you go watch them setting up in the dining room and let us know when lunch is ready?" He walked to the door and opened it for her.

Carla sniffed and walked out.

Thirteen

Douglas went to the chair she'd vacated and gestured for Betsy to sit on the straight-backed chair near the door. She obeyed.

Liddy said, "We heard you're some kind of private eye."

"Oh, no. My friend Jill Cross is a police officer—a patrol officer, not an investigator. I don't have any official status at all. Except in my needlework shop, and even there one of my employees is the person to ask for real help." Betsy crossed her legs and leaned back with what she hoped was casual grace. "Do you do needlework, Liddy?" she asked.

Liddy eyed her suspiciously, but the question was innocuous, and Betsy kept her expression light. The young woman had changed into jeans and a cotton sweater, and she looked very young. She rolled over and up to sit cross-legged on the bed, hands on her knees. There were dark shadows under her red-rimmed eyes. "Yes, Mama taught me to crochet and do needlepoint when I was nine or ten, and then I counted cross-stitch when she started doing that several years later. After the divorce, actually. It was in San Francisco; we spent a whole summer out there, remember, Doogie? I love San Francisco, it's so beautiful and sophisticated. And we both liked Jack a whole lot. I hadn't been there before, and so I thought anyplace in California was warm and sunny and I packed swimsuits and shorts, but San Francisco is chilly and I hardly got to wear them at all. Instead, we shopped for new clothes for me and rode cable cars and explored Chinatown and Fisherman's Wharf, and when we went home at the end of a day, Mama taught me to do counted. I guess I was her first student."

"I've heard from several people that she was very patient with her students. Was she as patient with you?"

Liddy relaxed further, pleased to talk about her mother. "Oh yes. Very. Well, at first. It was all so wonderful in San Francisco until she and Jack started to fight. Things got very tense the last couple of weeks." Liddy frowned. "I wish she could have stayed with Jack. She would have been happy, and then so would we. But Mama was very fickle."

Douglas cleared his throat. She gave him a "What-did-I-say?" look and deliberately continued to Betsy, "I loved my mother." She had to stop and swallow before she could continue, in a higher, more wavery voice. "But my mother could be very difficult. I used to think she was indifferent to our needs. Now I think it was because of the allergies. She had to concentrate on not getting sick, on staying away from things that made her sick, and that took all her attention. Even so, there were times when she came home and was wonderful to us. But she always went away again." She folded her lips inward, and fell silent.

Betsy said, "Did the allergies start before she divorced your father?"

"Oh, yes." Liddy nodded. "We were eight and nine when it started. That's the same age Tony's children are now."

"Tony was her current boyfriend."

Douglas said, "But our parents were younger than Tony when we were that age. So it wasn't the same."

"No," said Liddy, "and it's not the same. They won't—" She put her hand over her mouth, and tears flowed over the fingers. In a moment they stopped and she said in a much firmer voice, "Nobody could possibly think my father murdered my mother!"

"Of course not, Liddy," said Douglas. "Once they talk to Dad, they'll see he couldn't possibly have anything to do with any of this any turn him loose." He looked at Betsy. "You don't think he's a murderer, do you?"

"No, I don't," replied Betsy, almost truthfully. "What's more, the sheriff didn't say a word to indicate he thought Sharon was murdered." Unless Jill was talking to him this minute. Which was extremely likely. "In fact, the sheriff told me your mother suffered a severe allergic attack before she died. Perhaps she was seeking a private place to use her EpiPen and went to your father's room. I saw her there, dead. She did have an EpiPen with her, of course."

"Liddy, don't talk to her about this!" ordered Douglas.

"Yes," said Liddy, ignoring him. "She had several, and never went anywhere without them. It saved her life once that I know of."

"So let's say she was having an attack. She would need to use the pen and then lie down, wouldn't she?"

"No, what she would need is to go to a hospital," said Douglas, not quite so belligerently.

"She would need to be driven to an emergency room," agreed Liddy. "The EpiPen only keeps her alive long enough to get to one, it doesn't stop the anaphylaxis."

Betsy nodded. "And if she had an attack here, then possibly there was no one in the lobby to ask for help to get to a hospital. The front desk isn't always manned, I've noticed. But she knew your father was here, she said to me that she came here to talk to him, to be reconciled with him. So let's suppose she went upstairs and knocked, and when there was no answer, she tried his door. It opened and she went in. She must have been very sick—climbing stairs has to be hard on someone having trouble breathing. So she used the pen and lay down to wait for it to go to work. But if you're right, the pen wasn't enough, she needed more drastic aid."

"Why didn't she use the phone?" asked Liddy.

"Because there aren't any phones in the rooms, didn't you know that?"

She looked around. "No, I didn't notice that. How odd. Weren't there phones when we came here years ago, Doogie?"

"I think so. I don't remember," he said.

Betsy took the reins of the narrative back. "There is a pay phone in the lobby, but it's off in a dim corner. Maybe she didn't notice it when she went into the lobby from the lounge. So she went up to your father's room, but he wasn't there. She didn't have the strength to go back downstairs. So she lay down on the bed and died. When I saw her, her lips were blue, and I thought she might have been smothered, you know, as if with a pillow."

Douglas made a sound of shock or distress but when Betsy looked at him, he looked away with a gesture for her to continue.

"When I found her, I was scared and ran to tell someone. If in the meantime your father came back and found her dead, he may have panicked. He had told people he would never take her back, and if he said it angrily, they might think he had something to do with her death. So he decided to get rid of the body. Do you know if they had quarreled recently?"

Douglas said, "I don't know. But what you said . . . that sounds plausible. They were always quarreling—"

"But not recently!" cried Liddy. "You know Dad hasn't talked to Mama in weeks, he hasn't seen her in months, so why would he panic? He hasn't got anything to do with this. Plus, he simply wouldn't hide a dead body, especially Mama's!"

"You don't—" began Douglas, turning on her. She stared him down. "Well, all right, you're right. He wouldn't. But then who?"

Liddy said, frowning, "I don't know. But now that they know it was an allergic reaction, the sheriff will know it was a natural occurrence, Dad didn't kill Mama—no one killed Mama."

Doogie said, "You're right, I agree, not murder, never murder. Maybe the autopsy report will show what she was having a reaction to." He asked Betsy, "Is that possible?"

Betsy said, "I don't know. We'll have to wait and see."

Douglas asked, "If they don't release Dad, who is responsible for taking care of my mother's body? I don't like the idea of her being stuck in a refrigerator somewhere until . . . well, until this is straightened out."

"They've done the autopsy, that's how they found out she didn't drown," said Liddy. "So they have to give her back, don't they?"

Betsy said, "I don't know. I think you need legal advice. It's a crime to hide a body, you know."

Douglas said, "I called Dad's attorney and he said he doesn't handle criminal cases—"

"Doogie!" cried Liddy. "I thought we agreed, Dad didn't do anything wrong!"

"We know that, but who knows what the sheriff will charge him with? We have to face facts, Liddy. Dad's in trouble with the law, and we have to act quickly. I asked Dad's attorney to recommend someone, and he did, and the new attorney said he'd go straight to Grand Marais. That was last night, so he's probably there with Dad now. I had to wire him a retainer before he would even phone Dad."

Douglas stood and came to a kind of attention, like the soldier Frank called on Liddy to be. Liddy, on the other hand, was drooping with woe.

"Do you have the money to make bail for your father?" asked Betsy.

Douglas nodded. "Yes. Unless it's hundreds of thousands, of course. That would take a few days to round up."

Liddy perked up at Betsy's look of surprise and said with a sly smile, "What, nobody told you my mother was rich?"

"Actually, yes. But it takes time for a will to be admitted to probate—even more time, if there isn't a will. Months." Betsy was speaking from experience.

"No, you still don't understand," said Liddy. "Our mother set up trust funds for each of us when we were born. That's all we get, that's our inheritance. But Mama's no piker; the income from those trusts has kept us in socks and school and sports cars all our lives. What, you thought Doogie works for the Forest Service because he needs the money? No, we work because—Why do we work, Doogie?" Her tone had turned dry and mocking, another abrupt mood change.

"What's the matter with you, Liddy?" he asked, half angry, half concerned. He said to Betsy, "Mother's estate goes to a private laboratory researching allergies. She told us that years ago."

Liddy continued as if he had not spoken. "We work because we want to make a difference, because we want fulfillment, because that's what's expected of healthy young people, because there's satisfaction in having money you earned yourself, because it's hard to fill the lonely hours with idle amusement. But as a happy homemaker, I fill the lonely hours just fine." She looked at Betsy with a strange little smile. "Are the dead lonely?" she asked.

"I think it depends on where your spirit goes after death," said Betsy.

" 'Heaven for the climate, hell for the company'!" quoted Liddy, the smile turning real. "Oh, my God!" she said and began to cry, with loud sobs this time.

Douglas gave Betsy a cold look and went to sit beside his sister on the bed, his hand on her bent back. "I think you should leave now," he said. "I hope you got what you wanted, and I hope you're satisfied. We'll see you at lunch for an answer to our question about our father."

Betsy left the room, and found Carla waiting out in the hall. "How dare you make that child suffer even more than she's already suffering?" she said with a hiss as she reached past Betsy for the doorknob.

"Wait!" Betsy said. "Please? May I talk with you for just a few minutes? It won't hurt, surely, for Liddy to have a bit of private time with her brother."

Carla stepped back to look with cold suspicion at Betsy. "What do you want to talk to me about?"

"About Sharon Kaye."

"I can't tell you more than I already have."

"I think you can. And you can tell me more about Frank as well as Douglas and Elizabeth. Maybe between us we can find the truth."

"Oh?" Carla still glared, but Betsy, remembering how Jill could calm a person with a calm look, accepted her glare, and Carla looked away first. "Oh, what does it matter? All right." The anger vanished into mere annoyance, Carla went past Betsy to the head of the stairs.

"Come on, I promised I'd let Liddy know as soon as lunch was served."

"Fine," said Betsy, following her down.

They went into the dining room and sat on the round couch with the pillar. The faded red fabric was scratchy, and the circle was small enough that it was impossible for them to look one another in the face without leaning forward, or hanging halfway off the seat.

Wait people were bringing dishes, flatware and glasses to the counter, further breaking any sense of intimacy.

Carla said, "Sadie told me you investigate crime, so you must know about things like what is going to happen to Frank?" Her interest was obvious, even desperate, though she was not looking at Betsy.

"I don't know what the penalty is for concealing a death, but it can't be as serious as even the least serious charge of homicide. The question is, why did Frank try to hide Sharon's body?"

"He didn't!" objected Carla sharply. "He doesn't know anything about Sharon dying in his room! He didn't know she'd even been there until you and Jill came knocking on his door."

"How do you know that?"

"Why . . . he told me," said Carla, and closed her eyes against Betsy's next question.

Betsy asked, "Did he come to Naniboujou to see you?"

Carla grimaced and opened her eyes. "Cut right to the chase, don't you?" Betsy held her tongue, and Carla said, "He came because he loves this place, and to do a little cross-country skiing—and yes, to see me."

"Did Sharon come here to try to break up the relationship between you and Frank?"

"I don't know. Perhaps. Yes, I think so." Carla paused a few moments, thinking before she spoke. "Sharon couldn't get along with Frank, but every time he started to look elsewhere for female companionship, she came back to him, saying she wanted to reconcile. I'd watched her do it once before, but I didn't recognize it for the game it was. Then she found out Frank and I were getting close and she started in again with talk of reconciliation. She was using exactly the same language as before, and I suddenly realized this was a pattern of behavior. I couldn't think what to do, but at last I spoke candidly to Frank about it—and to my utter surprise, it was like someone turned on a light in Frank's head. Poor man, he kind of stared at me and said, 'Do you know, I think you're right,' like he was surprised at my perspicacity." Carla gave a halfhearted chuckle, then leaned forward to confide, "You and I come from a generation that said the woman must never reveal her tricks to the man, nor speak of another woman's tricks. Just like we must never let on we're smarter or stronger than he is."

Betsy nodded. She had started adolescence at a time when women still held such notions, though some had started questioning them—and a few had even laughed at them. But some still took them seriously even now, in the twenty-first century. She said, "Were you really angry with her?"

Carla nodded. "At first, when I realized what she was up to. But I won, you see. Frank wasn't going to take her back. We talked about it, and he was quite firm on that." Chin up, she smiled in remembered triumph.

But Betsy thought of the confident way Sharon had spoken of a reconciliation. Carla might have won, but Sharon hadn't known it.

"How well did you know Sharon? Were you friends?"

Carla frowned at her. "No, of course not."

"Yet you seem to know her pretty well. Did you see much of her at needlework functions?"

"A fair amount. I never talked to her about Frank, of course. Or the children, except to ask her how they were. And she always said they were doing very well, as if she knew, or even cared. Her treatment of them was totally self-serving. Yanking them this way then that, saying she was coming home for good, then smashing their joy with an indifference that was shocking in its cold-bloodedness."

"Did you talk to Liddy and Douglas about this?"

Carla hesitated, then said, "Yes, I did, once they knew about Frank and me."

"Knew what?"

"What happened was, Frank and I were having dinner at his house and they walked in on us. That was last summer. We'd thought they were gone for the weekend, sailing on Lake Michigan, but they came back Saturday night because the weather had turned bad. It was embarrassing, but—" Carla smiled again, this time in a way that let Betsy understand it might have been even more embarrassing if the two had come in an hour later than they did.

"What did they say when you talked to them about Sharon?"

"That was a few weeks later, after they got over the shock of learning their father had a girlfriend." Carla laughed. "At first, they defended her to the uttermost, poor things. But I could tell they were hurting, her behavior was— what's the word? Whipsawing, that's it, whipsawing them."

Like I am doing to Jill, thought Betsy. "Are they close, the brother and sister?"

"Yes, very. Their mother's . . . 'inconstant love' is the term Frank used, and isn't that the most poignant thing you've heard in a while? Anyway, she'd been behaving like that for years, so Liddy had taken over parenting Doogie. Frank allowed that, which I think might have been a mistake. I think that's why she's still living at home, so Doogie can feel they'll both be there for him, his father and his sister. Of course Doogie's twenty-one, so it's past time Liddy started thinking of her own future. I'm doing what I can for him, and I consult with Liddy about what Doogie likes and needs, which makes both of them happy. I think I'll be as good for them as I am for Frank. At the very least, I can relieve Liddy of responsibility for Doogie."

"What do they think of the relationship between you and their father?"

"Oh, I'm sure they approve. Naturally they want their father to be happy."

But Betsy knew that children who "defend their mother to the uttermost" were not normally pleased to find another woman in her place. There could be all sorts of cruel angles here. Carla might be angrier than she had said she was about Sharon trying to come back to Frank, and not so sure as she had appeared to be that she had won the battle for Frank's heart. Douglas and Liddy might like Carla much better than their own inconstant mother—so much that they saw their mother as a threat to the stability Carla could bring. Or as a threat to their father's happiness. Or perhaps only Douglas hated his mother—how Freudian! Or, had their father at last come to hate her and, his eyes opened to her perfidy, try to hide her body because he had murdered her?

"You knew about Sharon's allergies, right?"

"Oh, yes; everyone knew."

"Yet she smoked."

"I know, and not some delicate, low-tar brand, but something extra long and dark, very exotic." Carla's lip curled slightly.

"I heard she was trying to quit."

"I know she still smoked. Well, she did cut back, but . . ." Carla shrugged.

"Did you also know she carried an EpiPen everywhere she went?"

"Yes, she showed several of us how to use it after that one time she had a severe reaction at a meeting and none of us knew what to do. She came to the next meeting with one in her purse and showed it to us and demonstrated how to use it. Not difficult, fortunately. And even more fortunately, we never had to."

"She carried it in her purse, or her sewing bag?"

"It was in a plastic bag in her purse. Easier to find than in a project bag.

You could dig for ten minutes in her project bag before you'd find something that size. And of course time is important when you need to use that thing."

"My bag hides things, too," said Betsy with a wry smile. She hadn't even owned a knitting bag—project bag, that was a better name for the thing!—as recently as September, and already hers was a jammed mess. She sold two kinds of needlework carriers in her shop, but it hadn't occurred to her to buy one for herself. "What do you use?"

"I'm not one of those ultra-organized fanatics. I roll my canvas up into a plastic tube, and I carry everything else in a big plastic box. I use ZipLoc bags for my silks, and the box has compartments for my scissors, needles, laying tool, dololly, and any other oddments. I had Frank hot-glue a magnet to the inside of it for my needles. The box itself is light, so it's easy to carry. I don't use a frame for any but the biggest projects, and I don't travel with those. Since I have two homes, I keep a Dazor light at both places, because I have projects I'm working on in both, too."

"You do a lot of needlework?"

"A great deal."

"After Sharon, isn't Frank a little leery of getting involved with someone else who does needlework?"

Carla said, with perfect seriousness, "Well, I hardly think someone who does trame is in the same class as someone who does counted, don't you think?"

Betsy got to hide her smile by turning her head at the sound of footsteps. It was Jill. "What did he say?" Betsy asked.

"He's on his way."

"Who?" asked Carla, eyes lighting up.

"Sheriff Goodman." The light went out. Jill explained, "Betsy found something and the sheriff wants a look at it."

Carla looked at Betsy. "What did you find?" she asked, and the fear was back in her voice, now colored by anger that Betsy hadn't said anything about a find.

"An EpiPen I think is Sharon's."

"Why does the sheriff want Sharon's EpiPen?" She seemed genuinely puzzled. "And how do you know it's Sharon's?"

"Do you know anyone here besides Sharon who carries one?"

"Well, no. But is finding her EpiPen important?"

"Maybe," said Jill.

Carla said, "Well, if you want to know who else might have one, ask Isabel. She's handling lost and found, she would know if someone is missing one."

"Yes, of course," said Betsy.

She went in and found Isabel, who was all but finished with her roses on linen pattern. Betsy watched her for a minute, as Isabel, caught up in the excitement of finishing a project, was stitching very rapidly. Her tongue was just showing between her lips, its tip moving a little in rhythm with her stitching.

"Ha!" Isabel said, an exclamation of triumph, and turned her work over to run the end of the floss under several stitches and snip the remainder off with a tiny pair of gold scissors. "Ahhhh," she said, relaxing and turning it back again to regard it happily. The pinks glowed against the snowy linen, and Betsy suddenly realized there were realistic drops of dew in the pattern of petals.

"Very nice," said Betsy, and Isabel, startled, looked up.

"Oh, hello, Betsy."

"Isabel, does anyone else here carry an EpiPen?"

Isabel blinked, changing gears from stitcher to person-in-charge. "Why, no, not that I know of. In fact, I think Sharon was the only person bothered by anything more serious than hay fever. Why?"

"Because I found an EpiPen and I wondered who might have lost it." Betsy showed it to Isabel.

Isabel took it and looked at it. "No one's asked about one of these," she said, and stood. "May I have everyone's attention for a moment?" she called, and slowly the lounge quieted as faces turned to her. "I have here an EpiPen," she continued, waving it over her head. "Did anyone here lose this?"

There was a silence, broken when Nan said, "It's Sharon's, of course. Where did you find it?"

Isabel said, "It was found here at the lodge," glancing at Betsy and getting a nod of confirmation. "So none of you claims it?"

No one did, though two women wanted to know if Jill was coming back to finish her lesson on the Amadeus stitch. Betsy said she didn't know.

Isabel sat down again, and Betsy took the EpiPen back from her. "Is there something significant about that thing?" asked Isabel.

"Yes, but I'm waiting for the sheriff to come, so I can tell him about it."

"Is it that it hasn't been used?"

"You noticed that?"

"Sharon showed us how to use it, so yes, I noticed that it's still full of whatever the medicine is called. I take it that means Sharon didn't have an allergic attack after all."

"Ladies?" said a man's voice. It was James, standing at the other end of the room. "And, gentlemen," he added with a little smile. "Lunch is served."

Everyone began to put things away, except those who just had to run out the last two inches of floss, or finish a row of stitches. The quiet murmur of the room grew a little louder with anticipation: Naniboujou's meals had been a delight so far.

The room had nearly emptied when Betsy, who had forgotten where she left her project bag, finally found it and was making sure everything she had with it was there. She heard, "Ms. Devonshire?" in a gruff voice. Betsy looked up to see Sheriff Goodman standing not far from her.

She followed him to the tiny lobby, where she quietly described finding the device and showed the sheriff where it had been sealed shut.

"This pen does not belong to anyone working at the lodge, or anyone here for the stitch-in, so it has to be Sharon's. And it could not have been sealed like this by accident. I believe it was done deliberately by someone hoping for just what we have: Sharon Kaye Owen dead of an acute allergic reaction."

"The first test on that string you gave me came back one hundred percent cotton."

"So it wasn't a blend substituted for the cotton. Then you'll find it's been sprayed or dipped in peanut oil or powdered latex or something equally lethal to Sharon. Because why sabotage the EpiPen unless you know she's going to need it?"

Goodman stared at her, seeming for the first time to take her seriously. He asked, "What time did you see the body in Mr. Owen's room?"

"I'm not sure. It was dark, and they were serving dinner in the dining room, which would make it after six but before seven-thirty."

The sheriff nodded once, sharply, and went to the lobby. James handed over the phone behind the desk and Goodman dialed. "Gimme the jail!" Goodman barked when someone answered. There was a pause, then: "I want you to put a hold on one Francis Arvid Owen till I get back there." Another, shorter pause. "What? Oh, hell! Oh, dammit to hell! Where'd he—yeah, yeah, yeah, damn all lawyers. Did you eyeball the car? Well, dammit—Yeah, yeah, I know, I know. Hell, he's probably taking him to the nearest airport! All right, put out an APB, wanted on probable cause murder. That's right, murder! I've got the evidence right here in my hand!"

Fourteen

The sheriff left. Betsy saw him barking orders into his radio as he fishtailed one-handed up the snow-packed lane to the highway. Remembering Frank Owen's mild manner, she thought Goodman's ferocious attitude a bit overdone.

On the other hand, whoever was responsible for that sealed EpiPen certainly deserved a bit of ferocity. Considering the blue-lipped woman lying cold and still on Frank Owen's bed, maybe a lot.

Betsy returned to the dining room. Liddy and Douglas were sitting with Jill and Carla. Liddy took one look at Betsy's face and stood. "What's happened? What's going on?" she demanded as Betsy approached.

Heads turned, so Betsy raised a hand to request silence and, on arriving, at their table said, "Let's go into the lounge."

Jill, Carla, and Douglas came, too. Betsy said, "I showed Sheriff Goodman an EpiPen I found in the office. It had been tampered with. I thought perhaps someone was using it as a prop in a first-aid class, but no one will claim it. So it's probably Sharon's."

"Tampered with?" echoed Carla. "How?"

"The cap was sealed shut. With superglue, I think. The sheriff called the jail, but Frank has already been released on bail, so he ordered an all-points bulletin for him. Have any of you any idea where he might go? I think someone should call and warn him about this."

"Yes!" Liddy exclaimed. "Let's call—"

But Jill interrupted, saying, "That's a very bad idea, Betsy. You don't help a wanted man get away."

"No, no, not to help him get away, to tell him to turn himself in. I don't want him to get shot by someone trying to apprehend him."

"Oh, my God!" said Liddy, lifting her arms as if in surrender. "Oh, no, Doogie, we have to do something! Call someone, tell them! Have that search called off!"

Douglas frowned at her. "I suppose we can try to contact Dad's lawyer—"

"That may take too long; there must be something—" Carla said, her voice high and frightened.

Liddy turned to Jill, arms forward now in appeal. "Please, you're with the police, for the love of God, stop them! Don't let them shoot my father!"

People in the dining room were falling silent, watching and listening through the French doors that separated the lounge from the dining room.

"Keep your voices down, please!" begged Betsy. "You'll have everyone asking questions."

Jill took Liddy's hands in her own. "Take it easy, your father is in no danger." She shot a cool glance at Betsy, then continued in the same soothing voice to Liddy, "No one is going to shoot anyone. Your father doesn't carry a gun, right? Answer me: Right? Or wrong?"

Liddy, trembling, tears spilling out of closed eyes and running down her cheeks, nodded. "R—right. Right."

"And when I talked to him, I thought that I have rarely encountered a more laid-back person—and I've lived in Minnesota, land of the staid, all my life."

Despite herself, Liddy smiled. "That's t—true."

"So when a police officer comes up to him and says, 'Mr. Owen, will you come with me?' what is your father likely to do?"

Liddy's eyes opened and she said with an odd, choked laugh, "He'll say, 'Sure, you bet.'"

Douglas said, "That's right, that's exactly right."

"See? No shooting."

"Yes, yes, no shooting." Liddy nodded again and Jill released her. Liddy collapsed onto a couch and put her hands over her face.

"Here now, what's all this?" said a quiet voice, and they all turned to see Frank Owen coming toward them. With his Sorel boots, down jacket, ashen hair, and thick, drooping mustache, he looked quintessentially Minnesotan. Walking behind him was a slender man of medium height in an exquisite gray suit, a gray overcoat hanging off his shoulders. He had an expensively shaped mane of salt-and-pepper hair, gold-rimmed eyeglasses, and an unlit cigar tucked into a corner of his mouth. All that, plus his extremely self-assured manner, announced that here was a high-priced attorney.

"Daddy!" shouted Liddy, jumping up to run over and hug Frank.

"Gosh, Dad, you don't know how glad we are to see you!" said Douglas, going to stand near him. His manner was both diffident and protective.

"Oh, I think we have a pretty good idea," said the lawyer, giving Liddy and Frank some room. "But once they found there was nothing funny about the cotton floss"—he cast a sharp look in Betsy's direction—"they decided they had to turn us loose."

"Sorry to disappoint you, sir," said Jill. "The sheriff left here just a couple of minutes ago. He's putting out a want on Mr. Owen, on a charge of murder."

"Murder?" echoed Frank, disentangling himself from his daughter's embrace. His shaggy eyebrows raised high, he said to Liddy, "Explain this to me."

"It's too awful, they're all so stupid, they won't listen!"

Douglas said, "This woman"—he gestured toward Betsy—"found Mother's EpiPen in the lodge office. Someone had superglued the cap on. Mother couldn't use the pen when she had an allergic reaction, and that's why she died."

Liddy interjected, "So the sheriff is charging you with murder. I know, I know, that doesn't make any sense! But that's what he's doing. And so—and so everyone is looking for you, and they have guns, so you'd better call them."

"Call who?"

The lawyer said smoothly, "The Cook County sheriff is the person to contact, since he put out the want. I'll call him, Mr. Owen. But we don't have to do that immediately. They aren't likely to let you out on bail on a charge of murder, so you'll need to make some arrangements about your job and your house. We can do that before I call Sheriff Goodman to arrange for your surrender.

But more than that, you and I need to talk. We'll need some privacy. Do you still have a room here?"

"The only phone for guest use at Naniboujou is a pay one in the lobby," warned Jill.

"That's why I have one in my pocket," said the lawyer, pulling out a tiny cell phone.

Frank had pulled one from his jacket pocket as well, Douglas was reaching into his shirt pocket, and Carla was reaching for her purse. There were smiles all around.

"We've been up in your room, so I suppose it's still yours," said Douglas.

Liddy said, "I think now I really ought to go home. The police will come there, and may break in if no one answers when they ring the doorbell." Her voice took on a note of pleading. "I can't bear staying here, especially in that room. Mama died in that room. I can do whatever you want done from home, make phone calls, arrange with work for you to get a leave of absence. Right? Doogie can do whatever needs doing here."

"Yessir, of course I can," said Douglas.

But Frank eyed him coolly. "You've got a job of your own to go to, son," he said. "Besides, when I really need someone I can rely on, Liddy has always come through."

Betsy exchanged a glance with Jill. Douglas was turning back into a little boy right in front of them under his father's remarks.

Frank said to Liddy, "You'll get a different room tonight, soldier. But since they'll keep me in Grand Marais, I need someone who is not a long-distance phone call away."

"Oh, God, please," said Liddy, and it was a prayer.

"Hey, now, hey now, who's my brave soldier?" he said, looking a little surprised at this display of weakness.

Carla said, "Honestly, Frank, if you could see how brave your son has been through all this, you'd be very pleased. He's the brave soldier, not Liddy."

Douglas spoiled it by whining, "Come on, Dad, I can call the station and tell them I need some time off. That job's nothing important, after all."

"Every job's important."

Liddy found a remnant of backbone somewhere and said tiredly, "It's all right, Doogie, I'll stay."

"Good girl," said Frank.

Carla said, "I don't think—"

The attorney interrupted, "We'd better get started, Mr. Owen."

But as they turned to go, Betsy said, "Douglas, Liddy, you don't by some chance have a set of keys to your mother's car, do you?"

Liddy stared blankly at Betsy. "No."

Douglas shook his head. "I don't even know what kind of car she was driving."

"Why do you ask?" asked the lawyer.

"There are some items missing—her coat, her purse, her project bag. They're not here in the lodge, and we can't see them through the windows of her car. We were wondering if they're in a wicker basket in the backseat."

The lawyer frowned. "Who are you?"

"My name is Betsy Devonshire. This is Officer Jill Cross. She's with me," Betsy said with the same authority Jill had used making the same explanation to Frank. The attorney nodded and led Frank away, Douglas and Liddy following.

Carla called, "Frank, is there anything I can do?"

Frank stopped, hesitated, then said, "Will you come sit with me while I make arrangements?"

She hadn't expected that. "All right."

Betsy watched them all go, then said to Jill, "Now what?"

Jill shrugged. "Is there anything left to do? You found the body, you found the EpiPen, you've got the authorities interested in conducting a serious investigation. Frank is in the hands of an attorney who will make arrangements for him to turn himself in. You've done your part, and you didn't have to accuse anyone of murder. Aren't you satisfied?"

Betsy looked at the group, which had stopped again to talk near the door to the lobby. "I suppose I should be." But she wasn't.

"Come on," said Jill, "let's get some lunch while there's still a selection."

Thus encouraged, Betsy tried again to break the binding cords of curiosity. She went with Jill to the dining room, where people were lining up for seconds. Jill was greeted by several women impatient to talk of their success—or lack of it—with the beautiful but difficult Amadeus stitch. Two of the women wanted Betsy to come and sit with them, too, obviously goggling with curiosity about what had gone on in the lounge.

But Betsy didn't want to talk anymore about the Sharon Kaye murder. She waved at the women to go ahead, filled a plate with salads, and found an unoccupied table near the kitchen door, where the constant passage of wait people bringing refills made it undesirable.

She sat down and began to pick at the cranberry–apple salad. She had barely gotten two bites when Sadie wheeled up. "So, who did they arrest for murder?" she asked cheerfully.

"Nobody," said Betsy repressively.

"Why not? Did they decide it was some kind of accident? She fell into the waterfall?"

"No, she was taken to the waterfall after she died. Mr. Owen was charged with moving her body and released on bail."

"Yes, I saw him come back. Did he say why he did it?"

"No."

"Do you think he murdered Sharon Kaye?"

"I don't know."

"Come on, you've been sleuthing, you must have an opinion. Are you seriously saying you don't know?"

"Yes, I am. I don't know. I really don't know."

So Sadie huffed—the exhalation could hardly be called a mere sigh—in disappointment and wheeled off.

Betsy finished her lunch in peace, then went back to the lounge.

Jill was sitting with the women she'd had lunch with. They were asking her about the cashmere stitch now, though when Betsy walked up, they all stopped to listen to what she might say.

Betsy said, "I'll be down at the other end of the room."

Jill nodded and immediately caught the attention of the women by saying, "Now here's the real catch to that stitch."

Betsy went first to find her project bag, and then to a place at the far end of the long room. The little love seat there was empty and facing a door to the parking lot. She sat down, her back to the room, a position which suited her mood very well.

She got out the black Aida cloth and tried to concentrate on the pattern. She checked and found the error in the previous wedge. She'd have to frog both wedges.

Wait, no she wouldn't. All she had to do was frog the last one she'd done, make a very slight adjustment in the pattern—leave out two stitches here, add a stitch there—and that last wedge would fit right in where it belonged. It wouldn't make a very noticeable change in the shape of the wedge. She smiled to herself. "Real" stitchers often spoke of adjusting patterns, changing colors, or even removing whole elements, and here Betsy was doing the same thing. Her smile broadened. She was catching on to this stuff!

With increasing confidence Betsy quickly undid and restitched the wedge, and held the hoop out to admire her work. The change she had worked in it was barely noticeable, not bad at all.

She outlined it with Kreinik and was well into the last wedge when a secondary shadow fell across her pattern, blocking the light from the door, rather than the still-brilliant windows. She looked up to see Linda Savareid bent over from a polite distance, trying to see what she was doing.

"Like it?" asked Betsy.

"Very nice. Kreinik gives such a pretty sparkly effect. And an unusual pattern, too, kind of asymmetric."

Betsy frowned at her black Aida cloth. "It's not asymmetric, it's a circle. See? It just looks crooked because I'm not finished with it." She handed the pattern to Linda, who turned it around for Betsy to look at. At this distance, it was easy to see the adjustment she had made did not disguise more serious errors in placement. Instead of a circle, the wedges outlined an egg shape. She bit her lip to keep from groaning out loud. Her anxious, placating brain said she could use that, make it an egg-shaped rose window; it would be pretty, all she had to do was continue making constant adjustments as she went along.

Which was not remotely possible. First of all, it looked ridiculous shaped like that. Secondly, if she'd botched the stitching with a pattern to guide her, how could she make adjustments to a pattern as she went along?

Linda, trying to keep from laughing, said, "So why should you be different from us mere mortal stitchers?"

"Mere mortal—! Look at the beautiful work everyone else is turning out! I make a little adjustment to the pattern because I didn't want to frog almost all of what I've done, but I only made it worse. I don't know whether to go ahead and frog, or just toss the thing away." She sighed. "Am I ever going to stop being a beginner?"

"Sweetie, we're all beginners somewhere in the needle arts. Each of us learns a little more over time, but only a very few master this craft. There's just too much to learn. How long have you been at it? A couple of years?"

"Four months."

Linda stared at Betsy. "Four months?"

"Yes. I inherited a needlework shop from my sister—"

"Crewel World! That's who you are! Margot Berglund's sister, right? I've heard about her—and you!"

"Sadie Cartwright talked to you, huh."

"No, no, this was before I came to this stitch-in. Anyway, I don't listen to Sadie, her tongue's dipped in acid."

"Unlike several other people I could name."

Linda laughed. "Guilty, at least as far as Sharon Kaye Owen, Ms. Escapade Design, goes. Now there was a witch!"

"Please—after all, she's dead."

"Why does that matter? I never did get that business about not speaking ill of the dead."

"There's a very old belief that the ghost of a dead person hangs around for a while, and making him angry by saying bad things about him causes him to wreak havoc."

"Good heavens! And you believe that?"

"No, of course not. But that's how it got started, not speaking ill of the dead."

"How do you know that?"

"My ex-husband was a history professor. Thanks to endless dinners and parties with his peers, I picked up scads of useless bits of information like that."

Linda laughed. "Has any of it helped solve mysteries?"

Betsy threaded her needle through the edge of her fabric and released it from the hoops. "No. If my ex-husband had been a science professor, I might have had something I could use."

"Like what, for example?"

"Well, like what kind of allergen is odorless and tasteless, and won't show up in a lab test, but that nevertheless causes a fatal allergic reaction."

Linda sat down. "I can't help you there. But is that what you think happened? Something was deliberately put on her floss?"

"Yes. Because when I first saw her, she was fine. She wet her floss before she threaded her needle, said something I now think was, 'I've got to go get my EpiPen,' and when I saw her again, she was dead."

"So it also has to be something that doesn't wash off easily."

"What do you mean?"

"You said she wet her floss. Did she wet her fingers and run it down the floss, or use a sponge, like I do?"

"She wet it with a sponge. But what I meant was, she stuck the end of it in her mouth. That's how she . . . ingested the allergen." Betsy sat back frowning.

"Oh, a floss licker." Linda nodded. "People who are making heirlooms don't do that; saliva eventually damages the floss."

"It does?"

"That's the argument against it I've heard. But I figure by the time my work is old enough to be a treasured heirloom, if it ever is, which I doubt, they'll have figured out a way to reverse saliva damage. Not that I've ever noticed any on my grandmother's work, and she licked every piece of floss that went through the eye of her needle."

Betsy laughed, Linda laughed and went away, and Betsy, after sighing for another minute over her spoiled pattern, decided it was definitely a CASITA, not to be stood anymore. She folded it, put it into her project bag, and got out her knitting.

Fifteen

When Betsy would sit down to rest, or watch television, or just think, her mind would prod her with lists of things she ought to be doing. But knitting was doing something. Knitting, especially a simple pattern, didn't take much brain power, so her mind was free to compare and ponder. And for the first time since she had come to Naniboujou, Betsy wanted to really think.

She went to work again on the sleeve of her sweater, working on the last rows of the cuff. But this was not like the last time she sat in this lounge, going knit, purl, knit, in the deep and sunny silence. Now, distractions abounded.

First, a monologue from Isabel caught her attention. "When Liddy broke her engagement to that nice man last Christmas, he was just devastated—and so was Frank. He was beginning to think she'd never move out, but Carla started encouraging her to try for that position at Nordstrom's as a buyer. Carla says Liddy has the most exquisite taste, and she should know, Carla's degree is in clothing design—it's been kind of a bond between the two of them. She's really very good for Liddy. And, of course, if Liddy gets the job, she'll be traveling constantly, and that will give Frank and Carla the opportunity they need to form their own bond."

"Only if one of them doesn't go to prison for murder," Ingrid said, lofting selected words for emphasis.

Betsy pulled her attention away, but it was caught by Nan saying, "She was a good person, so generous with her time." This was amusing, compared to the last time Sharon Kaye was the topic of discussion, but all that came back was someone else saying fervently, "Yes, yes, that's right."

Betsy pulled firmly on her attention as she began to concentrate on switching from the knit—purl of the cuff to the rice stitch of the sleeve. Here she had to add stitches to create fullness.

Who had the best alibi? she asked herself, knitting a stitch, but not taking it off the left needle. She knitted it again, adding a stitch to the total. Who had the most to gain from Sharon Kaye's death?

She went back and forth three times, doing the rice stitch, and then began the complication of a twist of cable that would run up to the shoulder.

Betsy had been surprised to discover that the cable stitch was formed by actually twisting the yarn where the two rows crossed one another. She had

been sure it was an illusion, like the one that looked like woven strips of knitting. She got out the short plastic needle with the hump in its middle and
knitted four stitches onto it, then moved the needle behind the sleeve while
she knitted four more, then picked up the little needle and knitted the four
back onto her big needles, then went back to the rice stitch. Four rows later, on
her way back across, she did the same thing, only this time she put the little
humpbacked needle in front while she knitted four stitches.

She remembered when she was learning the cable stitch, how extraordinarily satisfying it was to look down and see the twist of lines running up
the knitting. It wasn't hard to do, not once you knew how. You just had to
remember, this time in front, this time in back. Otherwise you had the curious
illusion of the cable on top somehow coming from below, even though it had
crossed on top last time, too. Like an Escher drawing. To look real, it had to be
two lines crossing under and over one another.

"Betsy," said a voice.

"Hm?" There, she had recaptured the hanging stitches.

"Betsy," it said, more firmly.

Betsy looked up. It was Jill.

"What's up?"

"The BCA is here to process a crime scene."

"What's 'BCA'?"

"Bureau of Criminal Apprehension, a state organization that investigates
crimes. Particularly useful to small local law enforcement agencies that can't
afford the expense of a first-rate crime lab. Wanna watch?"

Betsy bent down to put her knitting away. "Will they mind?"

"Not so long as we keep our distance. But that's not why I came for you.
Guess where they're going first?"

"Well, I dunno. Frank's room, I guess. Oh."

Jill's smile had a hint of malice in it. "I want to see that criminal attorney's
face. Come on."

There were four of them, two men and two women, none in uniform. They
were carrying black, heavy cases and mounted the stairs behind James with a
heavy, patient tread. Jill and Betsy braved the cold to run around the lodge
without coats, coming up the back stairs to enter the hall just as James was
knocking on the door to Frank's room.

The door was answered by the attorney, who managed to overcome his
stunned silence at the sight of their badges to say that he was that very minute
going to call Sheriff Goodman and arrange for Mr. Owen to surrender.

The lead investigator said, "Uh-huh."

Beside Betsy, Jill sniggered softly.

A deputy came out to collect Frank and his attorney, and the BCA crew went to work. They spent about an hour in Frank's room, and then went down the back stairs. Betsy and Jill had come closer, standing outside the room to wait for results, but the team refused to say anything. Still, they could not prevent them from observing at a distance, and when Betsy, standing on the landing, saw them pluck a tiny bit of something from the back door frame, Jill murmured, "Fibers, probably. With luck it's from her sweater, because that will be easy to compare."

They went out the back door and Betsy asked, "What are they going to look at next?"

"Her car, I'd guess."

"Can we watch that, too?"

"Too cold to stand out there long. Let's ask Amos if we can stand very small in his kitchen and look out a window."

The kitchen staff was busy clearing the counter and the tables, bringing things into the kitchen. Carla, Douglas, and Liddy were still sitting at a table, using the excuse of not-finished desserts to remain there.

In the kitchen, a dishwasher was making grinding noises. The aromas were of applesauce and roast pork; dinner preparations were already under way.

Through the window Betsy and Jill could see Sharon Kaye's sky blue Volvo with the team of four BCA investigators standing around it. They wore the heavy gear of people who spent a lot of time outdoors in a Minnesota winter. One had a video camera and was walking sideways around the car, camera to one eye. He went over every inch of the car, from door handles to license plates to tire tread to the splash of freeze-dried road slush on the roof.

When at last he was done, he said something to one of the women standing beside a very large black tool chest. She replied, nodded, and opened the chest.

She reached confidently in, then with a look of surprise looked inside, moving things around. Still squatting, she asked something of the man who wasn't videotaping. He turned from a conversation with the other woman to gesture at the box, and she looked again. When she still couldn't find it, she called to him again. He came over in that way men walk when they're exasperated. He stooped to reach into the box. The exact same surprised look crossed his face when he, too, couldn't put his hands on whatever they were looking for.

The two of them began taking things out of the box, little things that looked like dentist tools and tweezers in clear plastic holders, and big things like pry bars and hammers, and medium things like spatulas and little paint tins and small glass jars full of black or silver powder, and a throwaway camera. But not what they were looking for. The man, naturally, left the woman to put the things back in the tool chest. He went back to the other woman, who appeared angry, and he apologized and for some reason glared at the man with the video camera, though he wasn't doing anything at all right then.

"Wait here," said Jill.

"Uh-uh!" said Betsy. The two hurried up to their room, Jill moving with the swift grace of the athlete, Betsy panting behind. They grabbed their coats, went down the hall to the back stairs, and outside, Betsy still fumbling with her buttons.

"Need a shim?" asked Jill as she approached the quartet.

"How'd you know?" asked the woman who had been angry with the man. She was tall and dark, with suspicious eyes and a mouth thinned by authority.

"We were watching out the window." Jill gestured toward the kitchen, and the woman turned to look at the window set in the black shingles of the lodge as if she suspected it of larceny.

"You got one?" asked the man with the video camera.

"Yes, it's in my kit, in my trunk, right there." Jill pointed toward her big old Buick three cars away.

"What are you doing with a shim?" asked the other man in a voice with handcuffs in it.

"Opening doors of cars with the keys locked inside. I'm Officer Jill Cross, Excelsior PD."

"God, you guys still offering that service?" said the woman, finishing fitting things back inside the toolbox.

"Oh, it's sweet little Excelsior," said the man with the video camera. "What else are they gonna do to justify their existence?"

"You want the shim or not?" said Jill, and they all four looked at her. But her amazing poker face absorbed their looks like a desert floor sucks up water, leaving no trace behind.

"Yes, thanks," said the tall woman.

Jill went to her trunk and returned with a flat bar cut into the shape of a hook at either end. She handed it to the woman beside the box, who took it to the driver's side of the Volvo and worked it down behind the rubber seal on the bottom of the window. She moved it around experimentally, and finally hooked something, and on the second try, the door lock button lifted.

Betsy, careful not to catch the eye of any of the investigators, watched while the big wicker basket was searched. No coat, no purse, no project bag, just two smaller baskets. One held a collection of plastic containers of evenweave cloth, cardboard bobbins wound with varying colors of floss, and stapled sets of graph paper, some blank and some with simple patterns; the other a collection of sets of more coarsely woven cloth, small scissors, white cotton floss in two thicknesses and stapled sets of instructions. In the bottom of the basket was a large tablet of blank paper and a ZipLoc bag of markers. Sharon's materials for her two classes.

In the glove compartment were maps, a flashlight, and an EpiPen. *A spare, surely*, thought Betsy. Liddy had said she carried several.

The trunk was opened from inside the car. The matching canvas suitcases contained gray, navy, and black slacks woven of a material that was probably silk, half a dozen hand-knit sweaters, three cotton blouses, a nice silk dress, gorgeous silk underwear, an open carton of More cigarettes, and a large makeup case with a mirror that lit up. In the makeup case was another EpiPen.

Betsy waited until they were finished searching, then approached the woman not responsible for the big black tool chest—who was busy dusting for fingerprints inside the Volvo—to say, "May I make a suggestion?"

The woman turned. "Who are you?"

"My name is Betsy Devonshire, and I'm a friend of Officer Cross, who loaned you her shim. I'm the one who saw Sharon Kaye Owen's body here at the lodge, and it was Jill and I who discovered that the Devil's Kettle was blocked with Sharon's body. I also found the EpiPen in the lodge that was sealed shut with superglue, which I believe was a factor in Sharon's death. I see you found two more of the EpiPens. Are they also sabotaged?"

The woman went to the big paper bag into which she had been putting smaller paper bags marked with evidence tags. She found and ripped open two of the smaller bags with the authority of one who is allowed to do that sort of thing, and pulled out the EpiPens.

"Don't seem to be," she said. "How was it done on the first one?"

"The cap was superglued in place."

The woman tried the cap of one, and it started to turn. She screwed it back down. "Nope, this one is fine." The second one appeared to work properly as well. She went to the little stack of brown-paper evidence bags—which looked a lot like lunch bags—on top of the Volvo—and put each pen in one, stuck new Evidence labels on them, and said to Betsy, "Come over here," and led Betsy out of earshot.

She introduced herself as Investigator Michelle LaPere, and pulled out a notebook. "So you're the one who thought we'd find something on that floss that Ms. Owen was violently allergic to?"

"Yes, ma'am," said Betsy. "I saw her put an end of a piece of that floss into her mouth to thread her needle, and soon after that I believe she started to have an allergic reaction. I wonder how thorough the test was, because I really think that's what induced the attack."

"Well, I'm sorry to poke a hole in your balloon, but the floss is one hundred percent cotton and there appears to be no foreign material on it. That's two strikes against you, one on the floss and now this one on the pen."

"Okay, I struck out on the floss. But I'm sure that attack was induced somehow, deliberately, by someone who wanted it to look like an accident. I think that's why these EpiPens are in good working order, so people might conclude Sharon forgot to move one from her car to her purse. I've been told she carried several."

"I don't understand why they all weren't sabotaged."

"I think the one I found was supposed to be taken away, hidden, or destroyed. Someone carried some of her things to the furnace shed to burn them, and dropped that lavender floss. Her coat and purse, a canvas bag with her stitching in it are all gone. I think the sabotaged pen would have gone, too, but it rolled under a locked door and he couldn't get it back."

"He?"

"Or she. I don't know who yet."

A tiny smile quirked in the corner of the woman's thin mouth. "The floss you gave Sheriff Goodman. Was that the floss someone dropped out by the furnace?"

"Yes."

"And you think it was the murderer who did that."

"Yes."

A small, patient sigh escaped the BCA investigator. She asked, "So how was the attack induced, if not by the floss?"

"I don't know. Something on her needle, perhaps, or on something else she handled. In fact—" Betsy stopped, thinking.

"What?"

"I can't help but think there are two separate crimes involved here. Sharon Kaye died of a severe allergic attack. There's nothing suspicious about that, considering that she was allergic to just about everything. So why hide the body? And though some of her things are missing, her car is here. It's like—"

"Like what?"

"I don't know. But it's murder, it's got to be."

"There are so many odd things about this case that I'm inclined to agree something illegal was going on. How about you tell me what you know, from the start."

Betsy explained what she knew and what conclusions she had arrived at while LaPere listened carefully, asked sharp questions, and took a lot of notes. Before they were finished, Betsy was sure most of her toes were frostbitten, though not that she had convinced the investigator of anything. LaPere's face could give Jill lessons in impassivity. At last LaPere looked over at the man without the camera and said, "Bobby, go find out what they do with the wood ash from that furnace. Arrange to bring it to Grand Marais. I want it sifted for sewing needles."

Betsy thought to correct her—hardanger needles and counted cross-stitch needles were not the same as ordinary sewing needles—then thought better of it. It didn't matter. Steel needles wouldn't burn in a fire, and their presence in the ashes would prove what had become of Sharon Kaye's project bag.

LaPere dismissed her, and Betsy went back into the lodge, looking for the maintenance man. She found him taking thin birch logs out of a canvas carrier and stacking them neatly in the holders beside the fireplace.

His name, he said, was Dan—actually, what he said was, "I'm Dan, the maintenance man," accompanying the rhyme with a wry smile, having apparently discovered that using rhyme himself preempted others from doing so. He was a wiry young man with an open face and the restless air of someone who has a lot to do.

"That furnace out in the shed," said Betsy, "do you burn trash in it?"

His eyes rounded, as if he were being accused of some crime. "Oh, gosh, no! Only wood and paper. We never burn trash in the furnace."

"So if they find sewing materials in the ashes, it isn't because you emptied a wastepaper basket into the furnace."

"No, ma'am."

"Thank you," said another voice, and Betsy turned around to see Michelle LaPere waiting her turn to talk to Dan. "Doing my job for me, I see," she added.

"I apologize," said Betsy. "But while I was talking to you, I thought of that question and couldn't help asking it."

"How about I go get more wood while you two talk?" suggested Dan.

"Fine," said LaPere. "But don't be long."

When he was out of earshot, Betsy asked, "Do you think Frank Owen is guilty of this murder?"

"I came into the game too late to know that for myself. As I investigate further, I may come to that conclusion. Though I will tell you his alibi is pretty solid; he was in Grand Marais most of the afternoon, shopping and skiing, seen there by several people. On the other hand, the town is only sixteen miles away. Do you think he's guilty?"

"No. It's interesting, I think everyone involved is lying about something, but obviously they're not all guilty of murder."

"Do you have any idea which one is guilty?"

"Not a clear one. You might talk to Carla Prakesh. She and Frank were romantically involved, and Sharon was trying to break them up. And the children, Elizabeth and Douglas, need to be looked at closely. It's not for the money; their mother left a lot of money, but not to them. But Elizabeth's behavior especially is . . . hinky. Do you use that word, too?"

Again the tiny quirk. "Yes. May I ask why you've involved yourself in this?"

"Actually, I've been trying to stay out of it. But things keep nagging at me."

The lobby was full of suitcases, but the women were all back in the lounge. By checking out ahead of time, they could stitch uninterrupted until they were shooed out the door for home. Betsy wound her way through the luggage to the pay phone. She called the ranger station in Grand Marais and asked three questions.

Then she called Sheriff Goodman.

After talking with him she found Linda and asked to borrow the blue sponge she used to dampen floss to smooth its kinks and keep it manageable while doing cross-stitch.

Then she went to find Jill.

The two filled mugs with coffee and went to the table where Carla, Douglas, and Liddy still sat, looking sad.

"Do you mind if we join you?" asked Betsy.

Liddy and Carla looked about to mind very much, but while they tried to think of a less rude way of saying so, Douglas said, smiling, "No, not at all. Sit down. Maybe some cheerful company will cheer Liddy up."

Jill and Betsy sat and tasted their coffee while Betsy tried to think how to begin this conversation.

Carla threw etiquette aside and said directly, "I don't know how you have the nerve to sit here. After what you have done to me and these young people, taking their father and my dear friend away from us, to sit down and expect us to be polite is the sheerest gall I have ever encountered."

"I didn't arrest Frank Owen," returned Betsy. "I reported the finding of a dead woman to the police, and things followed from that. The sheriff is the one who decided Mr. Owen murdered her. As a matter of fact, I don't think he is guilty."

"You don't?"

"Oh, I'm so glad!" said Liddy, with a faint hint of sarcasm in her voice.

"Why not?" asked Douglas, tossing a frown of censure at Liddy.

"He has an alibi, for one thing. He was in Grand Marais and the Pincushion cross-country ski trail during the time the murder happened."

"I thought the sheriff had concluded it wasn't murder. I certainly don't think it was," said Douglas. "Our mother was extremely allergic to all kinds of things. She'd had serious reactions before, so it's no surprise that she had another. It was just horrible luck that she had one here at a time when there was no member of the staff around to help her. I'm sure she went upstairs to ask Father to call an ambulance, but he wasn't here, either."

"What about the EpiPen?" asked Jill. "That was no accident."

"Sure it was, in a way," said Douglas. "Factory defect, obviously. Or a demonstrator model that got shipped accidentally."

Liddy looked at Douglas as if seeing the light at the end of a dark, sad tunnel. "I hadn't thought of that!" she said. "But of course, that must be what happened."

"No," said Betsy. "Long ago I worked for a manufacturer and I assure you, demonstrator models are never mixed with working models, for exactly the reason you're talking about, a consumer might get hold of a nonworking model. No, someone deliberately sealed the cap onto that device. Just as some-one arranged for your mother to come up here, and then arranged for her to have a severe allergic reaction."

"Now wait just a minute," objected Carla. "Are you saying that *Charlotte Porter* is responsible for Sharon's death?"

"No, of course not," said Betsy, surprised. "Oh, I see what you mean. No, if you talk with Charlotte, you'll find that Sharon volunteered rather than that Charlotte asked her. Sharon found out Frank was going to be here, and decided she had to come. You told me how Sharon Kaye reacts to any woman getting close to her ex-husband, so I don't imagine you were the one who told her he was coming up here the same weekend you were."

"No, of course not. I told him about the stitch-in and he said he'd been wanting to come up and do some cross-country skiing, and now he could see me as well. I certainly didn't see any need to let Sharon know that her ex-husband was courting me."

"Who did you tell?" asked Jill.

"No one. Well, Liddy and Doogie, of course. I mean, I don't want them to think their father and I would do anything clandestine."

"Then Dad must have told her," said Douglas.

"No," said Betsy. "Because he also knew Sharon's pattern of breaking up any relationship he formed with another woman, so he would have been very careful not to let her know about Carla."

"That's right," said Liddy. "Mama still loved Daddy, in her own way. And she loved us, too. But she didn't want any other woman to take her place. So nobody told her. It was a coincidence, her coming up here."

"But why would it matter if she knew?" asked Jill. "Didn't she have her own boyfriend?"

"Oh, Tony Campanelli didn't matter," said Douglas. "She was always get-ting boyfriends, and then leaving them again."

"No, this one was more serious," said Jill. "I heard that Sharon and he had talked about getting married."

"That would never have happened," said Liddy. "Tony has two young chil-dren, and Mama's life is complicated enough without adding young children to the mix. I talked to Tony myself, and warned him not to get too serious, because Mama had an intricate medical problem with many foods and that might complicate things for the children."

Betsy said, "Yes, those poor children. Didn't you tell me that those young-sters are about the age you two were when Sharon Kaye left your father for another man? And that's what this was really all about, isn't it? Saving two small children the grief you and your brother suffered?" And Betsy reached into her lap for the small blue sponge, which she put on the table in front of her plate.

All the color left Liddy's face.

"No," said Douglas at once.

"Why did you do that?" asked Carla, staring at the sponge.

"Because I thought someone did something to Sharon's floss to induce an allergic attack, but she didn't. The floss is just fine, as pure as the day it was purchased. But somehow someone induced an allergic attack in Sharon Kaye. I was present at the start of it. It could have been put on the needles, but why, when there was something even easier at hand? The allergen was put on the sponge Sharon used to dampen each length of floss as it was cut, to make it more manageable. If that length she cut and dampened hadn't been burned, we could prove it."

"I didn't do any such thing," said Liddy, reaching for the sponge.

"They have some really amazing tests nowadays," Jill remarked, very deftly sliding the sponge out from under Liddy's fingers even as they began to close on it. "Finding even trace amounts of things like latex powder or milk solids." She held it under her nose and inhaled.

"No!" screamed Liddy, lunging across the table at Jill, sending silverware, food, and crockery flying.

"Stop it, stop it, stop it!" shouted Douglas, grabbing his sister by an arm and shoulder to pull her back. "Sit down, for God's sake! Can't you see she's bluffing? It's not possible that is Mother's!"

Jill, Douglas, and Carla picked up fallen chairs and the bigger pieces of crockery, and shoved the wet tablecloth around on the table to sop up spilled liquids.

Women filled the doorways and windows of the lounge, staring.

A wait person slammed out of the kitchen, but Jill waved her away.

"Why not?" asked Betsy, who had not moved, as if the incident had not happened.

Douglas gave his sister a final push to make her stay in her seat and sat down himself with a thump. "What?"

"Why can't it be her sponge? How do you know we didn't find your mother's purse and project bag in the trunk of her car?"

"She didn't keep them in the trunk," replied Douglas, never taking his eyes off Liddy, who was watching Jill put the sponge away in her purse.

"You don't know that," said Liddy, surprised, her head coming around. She said to Betsy, "He knows that isn't Mama's because he burned everything, the idiot. I told him to burn just the sponge and the EpiPen. Mama carried spare EpiPens, so who would miss one? And who would notice the sponge wasn't there? They'd notice if the floss was gone, or the needles, but not all stitchers use sponges. I had it all planned out, I told Mama about Dad going up to the lodge, and talked about him and Carla, and I brought a box of dried milk and sprinkled just a little on her damp sponge and put it back in the little poly bag. Mama's not allergic to polyethylene."

"When was this?"

"I had her over for brunch Friday morning, just before she left to come up here. I sealed her EpiPen, the one she keeps in her purse, when she went to the bathroom. There was plenty of time, she has to use the bathroom off the back bedroom, way upstairs, where there's no perfumes or shampoo, no potpourri, nothing that she's allergic to, and I got out the little hepa filter to run, like I always do when she visits." She sighed. "All those rules. We were always having to be so careful, changing our clothes when we came home from visiting a friend who had cats, never using fabric softener, or hair spray, or perfume. I know everything she's allergic to, there was a long list of things to choose from."

"Liddy! Elizabeth!" Douglas groaned, but she continued as if he hadn't spoken.

"I planned it all very carefully. I even arranged to be at work when it was going to happen. I asked her to phone me when she left so I could check to be sure she arrived, then I phoned Doogie that she was on her way."

"Oh, my dear child," said Carla, "do you realize what you are saying?"

"Of course she doesn't!" said Douglas. "She's having a nervous breakdown, anyone can see that. For heaven's sake, Liddy, stop making a fool of yourself!"

Liddy smiled at Carla. "But it wasn't because of you, dear Carla. I like you, and Dad likes you, and we all want Dad to be happy. Sharon made him so miserable, and she made Doogie's and my life a living hell, coming home to say she loved us, then walking out, over and over. We kept thinking it was our fault, but no matter how good we were, she'd just leave again. And Betsy is absolutely right, she was talking about marrying Tony, who has two young children. I like to think I got over Mama, but poor Doogie, he's never been a brave soldier like me, he's got a broken heart from Mama treating us like disposable diapers. I did what I could for Doogie, but after all, I'm only sixteen months older than he is, and I'm not really his mother." A sob escaped her, and she waved a hand in front of her face in apology.

"Please stop talking, Liddy!" groaned Douglas.

She went on. "Mama told me how Tony had introduced her to his children, and how they were two darlings, sweet and good, and I'm sure she was being so charming and nice and kind to them, just as she was to us. Over and over, every single time, she broke our hearts, until we didn't have real hearts anymore, just little bags of broken rocks. It wasn't fair. I couldn't bear it. All of us so messed up, Daddy, Doogie, me—and now she was starting in on Tony and poor little Benjamin and Annie. I couldn't let that happen, could I? Well, could I?"

Into the silence that followed, Betsy said, "I saw the snowmobile tracks on the lawn. I suppose skimping one grooming of the Pincushion mightn't be noticed, Douglas."

"What are you talking about?" he said.

"When I called the ranger station in Grand Marais, they told me you were assigned to groom the Pincushion cross-country ski trails last Friday. That's done on a snowmobile. They gave you the key to the shed where the snowmobiles are kept. You're familiar with the Pincushion and the trails through Judge Magney State Park, aren't you? You're the apprentice who goes through the park looking for stranded or injured tourists. So you noticed, didn't you, that it's the same key that opens the shed in Grand Marais and the shed across the highway. It even opens the station over there, too, where there was a spare uniform, which you borrowed. The ranger in Grand Marais says they always keep a couple of spare shirts and trousers and even a jacket there, because ranger work can be messy, and you can't meet the public in a messy uniform."

"No," agreed Douglas.

Betsy continued. "You put on the uniform, and you sat in the dining room and sipped that dreadful overcooked coffee until she arrived, didn't you? You watched while she sat down in the lounge to talk to me and work on her new design of a Victorian doll. And she had an allergic attack. What did you tell her, that Frank was in his room with a cell phone?"

Carla said, "What—Doogie, too?"

"Oh, yes," said Betsy. "It took both of them. It was Liddy's idea, and she used Douglas as her cat's paw."

Douglas said, "What cat's paw? I never was here, I never saw my mother until—until they made me come and, identify her body. I never touched my mother's body."

"Oh, Doogie, never mind, she knows everything." Liddy's eyes, huge and shadowed, turned to Betsy for confirmation.

But Betsy could not lie, not now, when truth was the most important thing. "I don't know everything. What I don't understand is why Douglas tried to hide the body. Sharon died of an allergic reaction, which anyone might think was an accident or even, for her, a natural death, to be expected since she was so violently allergic to so many things."

"Yes, you did it all wrong, Doogie," said Liddy. "Not like I told you at all. Why did you do it like that?"

Douglas turned on her ferociously. "Because, you silly bitch, she didn't die of that allergic reaction! I smothered her!"

The silence this time was electric, then Douglas exhaled noisily and pulled at the wet and rumpled tablecloth as if to straighten it, but quit after the one pull. "I know you said it couldn't go wrong, Liddy, but it did, big-time. First, when that doctored EpiPen got away. I watched it roll under the door and it scared me, but I thought maybe we could do it anyhow. I said I didn't have a quarter to call an ambulance, and she said she'd left her coat and purse up in Dad's room. I said his cell phone is probably up there, too, and I took her and her canvas stitchery bag up there, but of course Dad always has his phone with him, so I said I'd find someone to call an ambulance and get her spare EpiPen out of the car. I went down the back stairs and hung around outside for fifteen minutes, and no one saw me. But when I went back up there, she was still breathing. She was suffering—it was horrible, I had to end it for her, she was hurting . . . And anyhow I couldn't wait any longer. Dad might come back, or someone out in the hall might hear the noise she was making. So I put a pillow over her face and held it down for a really long time, till I was sure she was dead."

"Oh, my God, Doogie!" cried Liddy, horrified. "You poor thing!"

Jill and Carla looked at Liddy wide eyed. Betsy was sure she'd never heard anything more cold-blooded in her life.

Douglas said, "Well, I've read they can tell when someone's been suffocated, so the original plan to make it look like allergic reaction was shot to hell. I ran back up the lane and across the road to the shed and got the snowmobile and brought it around to the back door, not knowing Miss Nosypants had already walked in on Mama's body. I went up and put her coat on her, and got her purse and that canvas thing her sewing stuff goes into. The scariest part was taking her down that hall and down the stairs. I could hear women talking in the rooms. But no one came out and saw me. I was going to put everything down the kettle and come back to drive her car away, but by the time I got just out to the highway I had stopped three times to pick up the bag and the purse and coat, so I put the coat on her and hid the bag and purse in the ditch, and went up the long back trail in the near dark to the river, a ride from hell I assure you, and carried her down the falls and dropped her in. She went right down out of sight and I ran back to my snowmobile and drove it back to the ranger station. Then I had to walk up and down in the ditch for what seemed like an hour before I found the purse and bag, but be damned if I could find the car keys. I finally walked over to the shed, where there was a light, and I opened the door and dumped everything out of the bag and her purse, and they just weren't there."

"So you didn't fall," said Betsy.

"Fall?" he said, looking at her politely. "No, I didn't fall."

Liddy said, "You don't pay attention, Doogie. Her keys were in her coat pocket, she always puts her keys in her coat pocket, didn't you ever notice that?" She began to giggle, an eerie, high-pitched sound, and Douglas slammed his hand on the table to make her stop.

He continued. "So I picked up everything and put it in the furnace, went back to the station for my car, and drove like hell back to Grand Marais, where

I clocked out and went home scared to death." He sighed a long sigh and said quietly, "It started unraveling when the EpiPen rolled under the door. I should've known right then we were screwed. But I thought we might still get away with it when they said she died of an allergic reaction. I suppose being knocked around in that kettle covered up what happens to smothered people's eyes. But I was right after all, it was the EpiPen that tore it for us."

"What about the eyes?" asked Betsy.

Jill said, "He means petechial hemorrhages, tiny marks in the eyes of someone who's been smothered. But I suppose once they examined the lungs and saw such strong evidence of an allergic reaction they didn't look any further. Anyway, I suspect the symptoms of smothering might be hard to tell from someone dying of a severe allergic reaction, which also stops the breathing."

"You only had to be patient," said Liddy mildly. "She would have died by herself, if you'd just waited awhile."

He turned again on his sister. "And have this snoop walk in on me hovering like a buzzard over her? No way! But if you'd kept your crybaby mouth shut, we'd be going home about now anyhow!"

Liddy scolded him, "So what if somebody walked in, even Dad? They'd've just found you trying to help Mama. So it isn't my fault, it's yours, Doogie, it's all your fault!" Her tone was that of a big sister who has been found with little brother rooting around in the Christmas presents hidden in a closet, and it would have been funny if it hadn't been so wildly inappropriate to the occasion.

Betsy looked at Jill, who had the look of a cop being handed an extremely unlikely excuse for speeding. *Ah,* thought Betsy, *she's getting a head start on her defense.*

"Douglas Owen, Elizabeth Owen, I am placing both of you under arrest for murder," said a rough voice, and everyone looked up to see Sheriff Goodman, accompanied by the quartet from the BCA. "You have a right to remain silent," he continued, and everyone sat quietly until the ritual warning was completed. "Do you understand your rights as I have explained them?"

"Yessir," said Douglas, "and I wish to speak with Dad's attorney."

Goodman looked at Liddy, who, eyes very wide, whispered, "Yes."

Goodman asked Jill, "They say anything incriminating?"

"Oh, yes indeed," replied Jill. "I suppose you want us all to come by to fill out a report."

"That's right. Finish your . . . meal first." He frowned deeply at the wet rubble they were sitting in. "Well, anyhow, I'll be waiting for you." He included Carla in his sweeping glance, then had Liddy and Douglas stand while they were handcuffed and led away.

"My word," said Carla, after they'd gone. "I was going to marry their father."

"No reason why you shouldn't," said Jill, brushing a shard of coffee cup off her lap.

"Oh, no, it's impossible now. In a few years everyone will halfway forget who murdered whom, and I might find myself included on the wrong list. I can't believe they murdered their own mother—and not for the money, but to protect two little kids they didn't even know."

Betsy said, "Most children work their way through the pain and anger of divorce. It leaves a scar, of course, but most children recover and lead productive lives. But Sharon kept renewing the wound. Because she was a vicious, selfish person, they were never allowed to get over it. Liddy says she did it to save Tony's children, but I wonder if this might have been an attempt to reach back in time to save herself and her brother, doing what she wished someone had done for her all those years ago. I think she both loved and loathed her mother. And worse, she planted and nurtured that hatred in her brother."

"So you think Liddy was the prime mover in this," said Jill.

"Don't you?"

"Actually, I do. Though with a good lawyer and the lack of a money motive, there might be trouble proving it. Doogie, after all, was the person on the scene with the pillow. But of course there are the incriminating statements we just sat through. What an odd way for Douglas to behave! If he'd simply aborted the plan and just helped his mother, brought her the spare EpiPen out of the car, no one might have been the wiser, and they might have had another chance down the road to try it again. Or if he'd just walked away into the sunset, left his mother to die in Frank's room, who knows what trouble poor Frank Owen would still be in?"

"That's why I called him a cat's paw," said Betsy. "She told him what to do, and it never occurred to him not to struggle on through with the plan."

"How awful!" cried Carla. "And I would bet those two would have let their father go to prison for it, don't you think? Oh, poor Frank! Those were his children! Oh, what is he going to do?"

"Seek comfort from a woman who loves him?" suggested Betsy. "Who would promise to stand by him for better or worse?"

Carla looked at Betsy, and very slowly a little smile formed. "That would be generous and kind of me, wouldn't it? And I really do like him very much, you know."

Two wait people came to tidy up the floor and table, spreading a new cloth. "If you would like something to eat," said one—Billie, the woman with the braids wrapped around her young, freshly scrubbed face—"I'll see if the cook can make you an omelet."

"Thank you, no," said Carla, and Jill and Betsy shook their heads. They all stood. "I think I'll drive into Grand Marais alone," Carla said. "In case Frank wants me to run any errands." Her dark face pulled into a grimace. "Or bring the children something, I suppose."

Sixteen

Coming back from Grand Marais and the lengthy and tiresome completion of reports, statements, affidavits, and other paperwork, Betsy sighed and squirmed in the passenger seat.

"What's the matter?" asked Jill.

"I don't know. I just feel restless. It's late, I should be sleepy—God knows I tried, but I couldn't seem to get enough sleep; it must be the air up here or something—but now I feel like, oh, I don't know, like a long walk up the lakeshore, or even putting on those skis and heading up the river again. If I were home, I'd be cleaning out cabinets or scrubbing the bathroom tile."

Jill asked, "Are you pregnant?"

"For heaven's sake, why do you ask that?"

"Because I had a cousin with four kids, and with every single one of them, the day before labor began, she was up all night cleaning. 'Nest building,' she called it."

"Humph. No, I am not even a little bit pregnant, much less nine months gone. Say, what's that light up ahead? Like a glow on the horizon. Is there a big city north of here?" Betsy was leaning forward, looking out the windshield.

Jill immediately pulled over. "No," she said, "it's the northern lights. Sometimes they're like that before your eyes get fully adjusted to the dark, kind of a very faint gold." She turned on the flashers and opened the door. "Come on, let's take a walk."

Betsy climbed eagerly out, and they walked up the shoulder of the road. It was late, dark, bitterly cold. The sky was spattered with stars. The farther they walked away from the flashing lights, the darker it got. As their eyes adjusted, more and more stars appeared. A few minutes later, the strange gold light shifted subtly, and then turned colors and began to dance.

"Listen," whispered Jill, coming to a halt.

Betsy, walking in front, froze and looked around in alarm, fearful a wolf or moose was coming. Then she heard it, the faintest possible crackle, as of someone a mile away wadding up cellophane. "What's that?" she whispered.

"Sometimes you can hear the northern lights."

"Aww—!" scoffed Betsy.

"No, I'm serious. It happens more often if you're up near the Arctic Circle. But it can happen here, too."

Betsy listened some more. "Wow," she breathed. She looked around the sky. "Look," she said, "the Milky Way. And the Big Dipper. And Orion—he's my favorite, I don't know why. I remember the first time I saw Orion from San Diego, and it was strange to be sitting on grass, surrounded by blooming flowers, because he's the winter constellation." She began to walk again, stamping her feet hard because they were getting cold.

"You miss San Diego?"

"Sometimes. But this"—Betsy stopped to gesture at the black shapes of evergreens lining either side of the road, visible in the faint reflection of starlight on snow—"is amazing. It's beautiful, but so harsh, so unforgiving. How did people live up here before furnaces and Thinsulate?"

"Beats me."

"And Naniboujou. I thought that was such a silly name when I first heard it, but now . . . Now I wish he were real, that you could court his goodwill with a pinch of tobacco. I'll never look at wild geese flying in formation the same way again."

They walked a little farther, then Jill said, "We'd better start back. It's late and I'm getting cold."

"You? I don't believe it! You love winter!"

"Yes, I do. But I'm feeling a little blue, thinking about Mr. Owen. He's been living a nightmare, and to escape it he lost both his children."

"Yes," said Betsy, suddenly a little sad herself, and turned to follow Jill back up the road. "Jill, what makes some people turn to murder and others not? You hear people saying, 'No wonder that kid turned to crime, he never knew his father, his mother was a drug addict in a bad neighborhood, he went to a bad school, had nothing but bad companions.' But you hear about another kid from the same neighborhood, same school, no parents, surrounded by the same bad companions, and he somehow turns out great. Why?"

"Beats me."

"Douglas and Elizabeth. Those two had a bad mother, but a good father, and every other advantage. Yet they did a wicked thing. Why?"

"It's not my job to know. It's not your job, either. Not to find them out, or figure out why they did it. I think I'm feeling what you feel after you've solved one of these mysteries, as if you are looking into a terrible, meaningless abyss that swallows the innocent along with the guilty."

"Yes," said Betsy, remembering.

"So if you still want to, call it quits. I won't try to change your mind. I suppose you can knock down that impulse to investigate for good if you keep trying."

They were at the car. They had left it unlocked. They climbed in, Jill started the engine, turned the heater up high, shut off the flashers, and hit the headlights. The road was completely empty and she pulled out. "Shall we start for home in the morning?"

"I suppose so. No, wait a minute. You've still got the whole week off. No need for you to go back. You can run me into Grand Marais and I can catch a bus. Is there bus service from there?"

Jill laughed softly. "A bus ride all the way back to the Cities? That would be a long, serious trip, with a stop at every wide place in the road. It'll take you fourteen hours, probably. No, I'll drive you home."

"But that wouldn't be fair to you. How about I stay on? I want to work on that rose window pattern, and I've got a lot to do. Frogging, then restitching."

"I thought you'd quit working on it."

"Oh, I can give it another chance, I guess. If I give it enough chances, I may get it right."

"Stubborn, aren't you?"

"I prefer to think of it as determined. Just like I prefer to think that I'm curious, not an incorrigible snoop. Nothing wrong with being curious. And maybe, like Carla with her trame, and the geologist Parker, a little obsessed. I start wondering about things, and once I start wondering, I just have to keep going until I have the explanation." She chuckled. "That doesn't sound like nosy Miss Marple, it sounds more like driven Hercule Poirot."

Jill said, "It's neither. Your ability to ferret out crime and make the perps confess is a blessing to the innocent."

And with a rush of something like pleasure, Betsy realized Jill was right. But Betsy was right, too. She had somehow become driven by questions, unable to leave the unexplained alone. But being a blessing to the innocent —she had never seen it from that angle. She smiled to herself, then at Jill, and settled comfortably in her seat. "If I go home, I'll have to start coping with that leak in the roof, and repairing the ceiling of the shop, and finding some part-timers who aren't planning on going away for the summer. I need this break. You need it, too. The stitch-in is over, the stitchers have gone home. We'll have the whole place to ourselves tonight. Maybe all week, unless James gets his wish and the travel editor of the *New York Times* drops in. Tonight we can get what we came here for in the first place—a little peace and quiet, and a good night's sleep."

Denise E. Williams

Design Count: 42w x 42h
Design Size: 3.5 x 3.5 in, 12 Count

Key: ✚ DMC 320   Pistachio Green-MD
     ● DMC 326   Rose-VY DP
     ❑ DMC 725   Topaz
     ★ DMC 740   Tangerine
     ✹ DMC 824   Blue-VY DK

Stich on 12-count canvas using DMC Perle Cotton #3. Design may
be worked in continental stich, or in bargello fashion using long
vertical stitches.

A Murderous Yarn

Acknowledgments

There really is an Antique Car Run from New London to New Brighton in Minnesota every summer, except it's held in August, not June. The members of the club, especially Jim and Dorothy Vergin and Ed Walhof, were incredibly helpful to me, patient with my ignorance, generous with information—even letting me ride in their cars. So if there's an error in this novel, it's my own fault for not listening more carefully. I would also like to thank Gene Grengs for letting me see how to start a Stanley Steamer, Pat Farrel out in Washington State for telling me how to use a Stanley to run down an SUV, and Fred Abbott out in Washington State for letting me "borrow" his magnificent 1912 Renault Sport Touring Car.

The shops Stitchville USA and Needlework Unlimited helped me keep on track with the details of Betsy's Crewel World, and the Internet news group RCTN again proved reliable when I had questions or problems or needed a good idea.

One

Spring came early to Excelsior that year. Everyone remarked that there had been no hard freezes since the fifth of March. The ice on Lake Minnetonka was rotten and great puddles gleamed like quicksilver on it. It was not yet St. Patrick's Day but the robins were back, mourning doves were sobbing, and daffodils budded in south-facing flower beds. Only yesterday, Betsy had been delighted to find a great wash of purple crocuses pushing through the flat layers of dead leaves on the steep, tree-strewn slope behind her apartment building.

She had noticed the rich purple color while taking out the trash. It had been the one good thing about the task. On that same trip, her vision downward blocked by boxes and black plastic bags, she had nearly fallen into one of the yawning potholes that menaced traffic in her small parking lot. And she'd had to put everything down while she struggled with the Dumpster's creaking lid, so rusted around the hinges it resisted being lifted.

How wonderful it would be, she had thought, to bring the trash out to the front sidewalk on Wednesdays for someone else to pick up and carry away. Even better, to dig up the crumbled blacktop parking lot, put in some topsoil, and plant tulips and bleeding hearts and old-fashioned varieties of roses, the kind whose scent lay heavy on the air in summer. And at the back, a row of benches under trellises covered alternately with honeysuckle and morning glories, to draw butterflies and hummingbirds. She'd stood beside the homely Dumpster for a minute, inhaling imaginary sweet-smelling air.

But her tenants' leases promised each a parking space and a container to put their refuse in any day of the week. She had been dismayed to discover how expensive it was to rent the Dumpster, and to have it emptied weekly. And by the estimate for resurfacing the parking lot. Being a landlord wasn't solely about collecting rents.

Now, the next morning, she sighed over her abysmal willingness to leap into things without first learning the consequences. She should have let Joe keep this moldy old building with its leaky roof, potholed parking lot, and rusty Dumpster. It was enough trouble keeping her small needlework shop from bankruptcy.

Her cat interrupted her musings by asking "A-row?" from a place between

Betsy and the door. Was it time to go to work? the cat wanted to know. Sophie liked the needlework shop and yearned to spend even more hours in it. Up here, she got a little scoop of Iams Less Active twice a day. Down in the shop, ah, in the shop were potato chips and fragments of chocolate bars and who knew what other treats. Only this last Saturday, she'd garnered a paw-size hunk of bagel spread with strawberry cream cheese, which she'd sneaked into the back room and eaten to the last crumb—a pleasant victory, since her mistress had a distressing habit of snatching delicacies away before the cat got more than one tooth into them. Sophie weighed twenty-two pounds and was as determined to hang on to every ounce as her mistress was to make her svelte.

Yesterday, Sunday, the shop had been closed. Sophie had not had so much as a corner of dry toast. Now, when Betsy put her empty tea mug into the sink, Sophie hurried ahead to the door.

They went down the stairs to the ground floor, around to an obscure door near the back wall, through it, and down a narrow hallway to the back door into the shop. Sophie waited impatiently for her mistress to unlock the door.

Godwin was already in the shop. To Sophie's delight, he had a greasy, cholesterol-laden bacon and egg McMuffin. He was seated at the library table with it and a mug of coffee. While Betsy put the startup cash in the register, Sophie quietly went to touch him on the left shin to let him know where she was. As quietly, Godwin dropped a small piece of buttered muffin with a bit of egg clinging to it, confident it would never touch the carpet.

"Hey, Goddy!" said Betsy, slamming the drawer shut.

"Hmmm?" he said, startled into a too-perfect look of innocence.

"Remind me to call that blacktop company again this morning, will you?"

"Certainly," he said, and when she began to check an order he'd made out, he dropped another morsel.

An hour later, Betsy was putting together a display of small kits consisting of a square of tan or pale green linen; lengths of green, pink, yellow, wine, dark gold, and brown floss; a pattern of tulips in a basket; and a needle. She had made up the kits herself, putting each into a clear plastic bag with daffodils printed on it, tied shut with curly yellow ribbon. She was arranging the kits, priced at seven dollars, in a pretty white basket beside a pot of real tulips and a finished model of the pattern, still in its little Q-snap holder. A stack of little Q-snaps, which had been selling poorly, waited suggestively close to the basket.

Godwin, meanwhile, had clamped a Dazor magnifying light to the library table in the middle of the shop, and was fastening the electric cord to the carpet with long strips of duct tape.

At home on Sunday, Betsy had put together another little basket with illustrations of various stitches, threaded needles, and an assortment of fabrics, so that customers could try these things before buying, or get Godwin's help in doing an elaborate needlepoint stitch. The Dazor was there to help them see more clearly—and if the customer was delighted at how bright and clear things appeared under the Dazor, Betsy had several of the lights all boxed up in the back room.

Betsy had recently visited Zandy's in Burnsville, where the owner had a similar setup. Zandy had told Betsy that she sold at least one Dazor a month. Betsy had sold two Dazors since she took over Crewel World nine months ago. Even at wholesale, the lights were expensive and a burden on the shop's inventory.

Godwin stood up with a grunt, and brushed a fragment of dust from his beautiful lightweight khaki trousers. "That should keep people from tripping," he said. "What's next?"

"Pat Ingle brought a model to me in church on Sunday," said Betsy. "Here it is. We'll need to find space for it on the wall in back."

"Oh, it's The Finery of Nature!" said Godwin, going to look. "Gosh, look at it! Seeing it for real makes me wish I did counted cross-stitch myself!"

And that was the purpose of models. Crewel World sold all kinds of needlework, but counted cross-stitch patterns needed, more than any other, the impact of the finished product to inspire needleworkers to buy. Betsy had devoted the entire back of her shop to cross-stitch, and the walls there were covered with framed models. But as new patterns arrived and old ones went out of print, a steady trickle of new models was needed.

Betsy used a variety of methods to keep the walls up to date. One was to stitch them herself, but Betsy was still learning the craft and so had to lean heavily on her customers, borrowing finished patterns from them. Sometimes she offered a particularly talented customer free finishing—washing, stretching, and framing, an expensive service—in exchange for the right to display it for a time, or to giving the model maker the materials for a project, plus deep discounts on other patterns and materials, in exchange for doing a particular project.

She had also gained some recent models by a sadder method: Wayzata's Needle Nest had gone out of business, and Pat had sold Betsy some of her models to hang on Crewel World's walls. Fineries of Nature was the last of them.

It was a little after noon when Betsy, looking over a new and complex Terrance Nolan pattern, said, "I wonder if we could get Irene to make a model of this for us."

And as if on cue, the front door went *Bing!* and Irene came in. Irene Potter was one of Betsy's most loyal customers. She was also rude, opinionated, passionate, difficult—and an extraordinarily talented needleworker. A short, thin woman with angry black curls standing up all over her head, she had a narrow face set with very shiny dark eyes. Her clothing came from a Salvation Army store. She wasn't poor, but she put every possible nickel of her income into needlework supplies.

She had a project rolled up under the arm of her shabby winter coat, a faux leopard skin probably thirty years old. "I need your opinion on this," she said without preamble.

"What, on how to finish it?" asked Betsy from behind the big desk that served as a checkout counter.

"No, just an opinion. Yours too," she added over her shoulder, not quite looking at Godwin. This was unusual. Irene had a very accurate notion of Betsy's lack of proficiency but her fear and loathing of Godwin as a gay man normally kept her from acknowledging his expertise in needlework. That most other Crewel World customers thought he had a heightened sense of color and design *because* he was gay cut no ice with Irene.

Godwin, making a comedy of his surprise behind Irene's back, smoothed his face to impassivity as he came to stand beside Betsy. Irene took a deep breath, held it, and unrolled the fabric onto the desk.

Betsy stared; Godwin inhaled sharply. It was an impressionistic painting of a city in a blizzard. The snow blew thickly around the buildings and people, blurring their outlines and the shape of a tall plinth in the center of a square.

But the picture wasn't a painting. It was a highly detailed piece of cross-stitching. "Why, it's wonderful!" exclaimed Betsy. "I've never seen anything like this. Where did you get the pattern, Irene?"

"It's not from a pattern," said Irene. "Martha took me to see the exhibit of American Impressionists at the Art Museum last year. I never could see what was so great about Impressionists; those posters and pictures in magazines look like a mess. But prints are nothing like seeing Impressionist paintings for real."

Betsy nodded. "That's absolutely true, Irene. I didn't get Impressionism either, when all I'd seen were prints. Then I saw my first van Gogh in person and I fell in love. Did you see the Art Museum's exhibit, Goddy?"

"M-hmm." He seemed very absorbed in Irene's piece, moving a step sideways and back, cocking his head at various angles.

Betsy continued, "I don't know why photographs can't tell the truth about Impressionist paintings. Do you, Godwin?"

"It's because they use layers of paint, or lay it on thickly, and use lots of texture, so the light moves across it as you approach. Photographs flatten all that out."

"Yes, I think that's right. This moves with the light, too. It is truly beautiful. Where did you get it, Irene?" Betsy knew she hadn't sold a pattern like this to Irene—she had never seen a pattern like this, in her shop or anywhere.

"I did it myself," Irene said quietly.

Godwin said, "You did? But your work isn't anything like this!"

Irene gave him a freezing glance and said, "I got to thinking about those paintings, and I went back a second time by myself and I borrowed Martha's copy of the exhibit catalog, and I thought some more, and I did this. Is it any good?"

"It's amazing, it's fantastic," said Betsy.

Godwin said, "It really is wonderful, Irene. How did you get those swirls of snow?" They weren't smooth lines, but lumpish streaks, an effect an oil painter gets by using the edge of his palette knife.

"Caron cotton floss," said Irene. "It's got those slubs in it, and I just kept working it over the top until it looked right." A figure in the foreground, walking with the snow pushing her back into a curve, was done in shades of charcoal and light gray, with a touch of wine at the throat and on a package she was struggling not to lose. The curve of her back, done in broken rows of straight stitches, made the viewer feel her strain against the harsh wind.

Betsy leaned closer. It looked to her as if all the figures and images in the work were done with blended stitches. The overall effect was of solid objects seen through a blur of snow.

Godwin, cocking his head at yet a different angle, frowned and said, "I don't think this is an exact copy of the painting in the exhibit, is it?"

"No," said Irene, as if admitting to a fault. "Mr. Wiggins's painting was old; it had old-fashioned cars and wagons pulled by horses. I used modern cars, except for one of those carriages I've seen in movies that get pulled by a horse through the park. I liked the way Mr. Wiggins's horses looked, so that's why I put one in, too. And I found a photograph in the library of Columbus Circle, so I knew what that tall thing really looks like."

"Plinth," said Godwin. "It's called a plinth."

Irene ignored that. She said to Betsy, "I was afraid it was too . . . messy."

Godwin said, "I think all the overstitching is brilliant."

Betsy said, "Yes, that gives it an especially wonderful effect. What are you going to do with it?"

"Well, I don't know," said Irene. "I wanted to know first if it was any good."

"This is beyond good," said Godwin. "This is . . . this is *art*."

This time Irene glanced at him with respect. "You think so?"

"Yes."

"I agree," said Betsy. "Any art gallery would be proud to offer this. Of course, I'd like you to turn it into a pattern. This would be a real challenge for an advanced stitcher, but I'm sure I could sell it. But maybe you should enter it in a competition first. Is there a competition for work like this, Godwin?"

"There are all sorts of needlework competitions," he said. "It would do well in any of them, I think."

Irene said, "Then I'll put it in the State Fair, I guess." Irene had lots of blue ribbons from the Minnesota State Fair's needlework competitions.

"Or CATS," said Godwin. "Hey, they're coming to Minneapolis in October this year, so you could enter it in both." CATS was the Creative Arts and Textile Show, which featured needlework designers, classes, and booths selling the latest patterns and fibers. It had a prestigious competition for needlework.

"This is so different from anything I've done before," said Irene, who had in fact never attempted more than slight changes in someone else's pattern, and who had always selected very literal patterns. "But it felt good doing it. It felt better than almost anything I've done before." She reached for the canvas and began to roll it up.

"Don't you want it finished?" asked Betsy.

"No, not yet," said Irene. "Maybe later. I've got to get back to work." She turned and hurried out.

"Probably can't afford to have it finished," said Godwin. "She came in here on Saturday and bought nine colors of wool, two skeins of metallics, and a fat quarter of twenty-eight Cashel. She counted out the last two dollars in change. Poor thing."

Betsy said, "There are a lot of hobbies that pay enough so the hobbyist can at least break even, but this isn't one of them. Needleworkers can't sell their work for even what the materials cost, much less the hours spent stitching it. That piece she just took out, she'll probably end up giving away rather than be insulted by an offer of forty dollars for it. I just don't understand why fabulously talented people who work with needles and fibers don't get the recognition that people who work in oil or metal do. It isn't fair."

"Would you buy it?" asked Godwin.

Betsy half closed her eyes, picturing it on her living room wall, in a smooth, dark frame . . . "Gosh, yes."

"What would you pay for it? I mean, if it was an auction, and you were bidding on it. How high would you go?"

Again Betsy half closed her eyes, imagining raising her hand with a numbered paddle in it. Fifty dollars, a hundred dollars, two hundred dollars. "Who's bidding against me?" she asked.

"The Getty."

Betsy giggled. "Then I haven't got a chance, have I? But I'd go as high as five hundred, I guess."

Godwin smacked his hand down on the desk. "Sold! Would you really go that high?"

Betsy hesitated, then recalled that figure in the foreground so realistically bent under the wind's constant shove, and the way the snow swirled around the plinth and softened the vertical lines of the buildings. She had worked not far from Columbus Circle many years ago, and had once been out in a city blizzard . . . "Actually, yes, I think I would. But I'd also like to hang it down here as a model for a while, and sell lots of patterns. Oh, darn, I let Irene get away without asking if she'd do that Terry Nolan model for me. Remind me when we're closing up, I need to call her at home."

It was a little after one when the door's *Bing!* brought Alice and Martha in, project bags in hand. It was nearly time for the Monday Bunch to meet. The two went to the library table in the middle of the room, but hesitated when they saw the Dazor light.

"What's this?" asked Alice, a tall woman with mannish shoulders and chin.

"It's a magnifying light, silly," said Martha, who was short and plump, with silver hair.

"I know that. What I meant was, what's it doing here?"

Betsy said, "I've set up a sample basket so people can try out fabrics and fibers and stitches, and I'm going to let them do it under the Dazor if they like, so they can see better."

Alice, who was inclined to blurt out whatever was on her mind, said, "And maybe somehow they'll get the notion they need the lamp, too?"

"Alice!" scolded Martha. A brisk-mannered widow in her late seventies, she was an ardent practitioner of Minnesota Nice.

"That's the idea, certainly," agreed Betsy cheerfully.

The women had barely taken their places at the library table when the door opened again. This time it was Jill Cross, a tall, ash-blond woman with a Gibson girl face. She nodded at Betsy and Godwin and took a seat at the table.

"Not on duty today?" asked Alice in her deep voice.

"No," said Jill, opening her drawstring bag and taking out a needlepoint canvas pinned to a wooden frame. It was a Peter Ashe painting of a Russian church liberally ornamented with fanciful domes. She was using a gold metallic on the one swirled like a Dairy Queen cone.

"That's coming along real nice," noted Alice.

"Uh-huh." Jill was normally taciturn, but this shortness bordered on rudeness.

Betsy said, "Something bothering you?"

"Huh? Oh." She sighed. "All right, yes. I think I told at least some of you that Lars was going to sell his hobby farm."

"You told me," said Martha. "I thought you were pleased. I know you've been wanting him to cut back on the time he spends trying to make a go of that place."

"Yes, that's true. Actually, he's had it for sale for a month now."

"What, you're afraid he isn't going to get his price for it?" asked Alice.

"No, he got his price last week."

"Then what's the problem?" asked Martha.

"I think he's already spent the money."

"On what?" asked Betsy. She knew Lars and Jill had been dating for a long time—two or even three years. They weren't living together, or even officially engaged, but neither dated anyone else so far as Betsy knew.

"That's just it, I don't know. He's been making long-distance calls and reading books about—something. You know Lars, working fifty hours a week isn't enough to keep that man occupied. First it was boats, then it was the hobby farm. I don't know what's next, flying lessons or do-it-yourself dentistry. That's what's bothering me—he never talks to me before he decides what he's going to do."

Godwin said, "Some men are just terrible at sharing their plans. Afraid they'll start an argument, I guess."

"Are you having trouble with John again?" asked Alice, sometimes as perceptive as she was tactless.

"No, not exactly. Well, actually, it's me who doesn't want to start the argument." Godwin lived with a wealthy attorney, an older man who, by Godwin's telling, was kind, generous, and very possessive.

Alice, who had sat down next to the Dazor, made a sudden exclamation.

"What?" asked Betsy.

Alice had casually turned the light on and, instead of using it to light her crochet project, had taken a scrap of twenty-count Jobelan from the basket to look at it through the big magnifying glass. "I can *see* this!" she said.

"So can I," said Godwin, who was at the other end of the table from her.

"No, I mean, I can see the weave, I can actually see the weave!"

Betsy and Godwin exchanged smiles. While Alice was not in a position to afford a Dazor, her reaction was exactly what they'd hoped for. Other customers would sit there and hold a piece of high-count linen under that magnifying light, and the cash register would ring merrily.

Two more Monday Bunch members came in to sit down with projects and soon the table was alive with helpful hints and gossip. Betsy kept the coffee cups filled, served the occasional customer, and brought patterns, fabrics, and fibers to the table to be examined and, often enough, set aside by the cash register.

She came from the back with the newest Mirabilia pattern to hear Martha saying in an amused voice, "Honestly, Emily acts as if hers is the first baby ever born! All she ever talks about anymore is the joy and burden of staying home with an infant."

"All first-time mothers are like that," said Kate McMahon with a little sigh. "My Susan certainly is, and I expect I was, too."

"Have any of you talked to Irene lately?" asked Betsy, anxious on behalf of Alice to change the subject. Alice's only child had died young of a heart ailment.

"No, why?" asked Phil Galvin, a retired railroad engineer. He was working on a counted cross-stitch pattern of a mountain goat.

"She has made the most amazing—"

The door to the shop made its annoying *Bing!* sound, and a very big police officer came in. He was about twenty-five, golden blond, and excited. "Found you at last, Jill!" he exclaimed, his voice as loud as he was big.

"Hi, Lars!" said Jill, getting up and heading toward him. "What's up?"

"Look at this, look what I found!" He had a sheaf of papers in his hand and thrust it at her.

Jill took the papers, glanced at the top one, then more slowly looked at two or three sheets under it. "What is this? Some kind of old car—what, reported stolen?" she asked. "Where'd it turn up?"

"No, no! I finally found this for sale. I can't believe the price. Wait till you see it!"

"See it?" asked Jill, handing back the papers. "What do you mean, what have you bought?"

Lars thrust the papers back at her. "In there, look at the picture of it!"

Betsy, curious, came to look around Jill's shoulder.

"You want to *buy* this?" said Jill, having sifted through the papers until she found the eight-by-ten color photo again. "Why?"

But Betsy, glancing at the printing on the margin of the photo, said, "Oh, my God, it's a Stanley Steamer! Is it for real? Does it run? Where is it?"

"Yes, it's real, a 1911 touring car. It's in Albuquerque. And yes, it runs, or he's pretty sure it will, after it has a little work done on it. He had an accident with it a few years ago and it's been just sitting under a tarp in his backyard. But he says they're harder to kill than a rattlesnake. What I can't believe is the price. Only wants seventeen thousand for it!"

"*Dollars?*" said Jill. "For an old, *old* car that's been in a *wreck* and it will *maybe* run after you've done, oh yeah, a *little* work on it?"

"You're really going to bring it up here?" asked Betsy eagerly.

"Of course he isn't!" barked Jill. "Steam?" she said to Lars. "Like a locomotive?"

"Yeah, just like a locomotive, except it's a car. Isn't that great? It's got the original boiler in it!"

"From *1911*? A ninety-year-old boiler sounds dangerous to me."

"The boiler on a Stanley never blows. Ever. And there are lots of them still out there on the road. There's a whole organization of people who drive them. And there's all kinds of places that make parts for it, tires and windshields and all. The owner is an old guy, a doctor, who can't work on it himself anymore, he's got heart problems." He shifted his ardent gaze to Betsy, whose expression was much more receptive than his girlfriend's. "I found this old book by a guy who got ahold of a Stanley and got it running. He tells some stories in that book that about had me rolling on the floor." Thinking about the stories in the book made his blue eyes twinkle and the corners of his mouth turn up. Lars was a good-looking man, and when amused and enthusiastic, he was irresistible.

Betsy said, "Will you take me for a ride in your Stanley Steamer, Lars?"

Jill turned away and walked back to the table, where she put a great deal of meaning into the way she sat down.

Lars didn't notice. He continued eagerly to Betsy, "Nobody knows how fast the Stanley Steamer can go, 'cause as long as you hold the throttle open, it just keeps on accelerating. In 1906 it set the world land speed record of a hundred and twenty-seven miles an hour. There's a picture of it in this guy's book of the special chassis they put on it, like a canoe. In 1907 they tried again—it was on Daytona Beach in Florida—and this time, at over a hundred and fifty, it hit a bump and the air got under it, and it actually took off, like an airplane!" Lars's hand described a shallow arc. "Of course, it crashed after a few dozen yards, but just think, over a hundred and fifty, and that *still* wasn't its top speed!"

"In 1907? That's amazing!"

Lars continued, "Most cars back then could manage about twenty-five miles an hour going downhill with a tail wind, so it isn't amazing, it's *fantastic*! I wonder if my car can go that fast." His blue eyes turned dreamy.

"But then it crashed," murmured Jill, bowing her head. "Lord, help us not to forget that little part, amen."

Several other members of the Monday Bunch snickered softly.

Lars, aware at last that he had lost Jill, went to her to show her the color photo again. He said in a wheedling voice, "Just look at it. It's beautiful, isn't it? Look at the shape, so beautiful and old and classy. It's got brass trim and wooden wheels, and look at those big old lamps for headlights. Plus, it doesn't have a horn like other cars, but a whistle!" Lars shrilled a creditable imitation of a steam train whistle. "*Wheee-owwwwww!* And it doesn't go brrum, brrum like gasoline engines. It goes *chuff, chuff, chuff, chuff*!" He began to circle the library table, elbows bent and arms working. "*Chuff, chuff, chuff—whee, whee-owwwwwww!*"

Phil and the women laughed.

Jill, her voice sounding strained from her attempt to be reasonable, said, "Listen to me, Lars. This car has got to be dangerous. It's more than ninety years old, and it's been in a wreck. And it's a steam-powered automobile. That's something they tried and gave up on, or why isn't every car on the road today powered by steam? And look at this thing, it hasn't even got a roof! What are you going to do when winter comes?"

"Oh, it's not going to be my main car. I'm just going to drive it for fun!"

Phil, never one to spoil a good argument, said, "I could help you get it going, Lars. I started out in steam-driven locomotives."

"See?" Lars said to Jill.

Phil continued, "And there's an antique car meet every year right here in Minnesota. They drive from New London to New Brighton."

"New Brighton?" echoed Betsy. "You mean *our* New Brighton? The Minneapolis suburb?"

Phil nodded. "They finish up in a park in New Brighton, and the mayor comes to shake every driver's hand. I've gone a couple of times to watch them come in. I remember there's usually a 1901 Oldsmobile, and a 1908 Cadillac, and a spread of Maxwells and Fords. Beautiful old cars—and one year they had those bicycles that have a big wheel up front and a little bitty wheel behind. There's a big club that runs the thing. People come from all over to drive in it."

"Are they the Minnesota Transportation Museum people?" asked Martha. "We've got some of them right here in town."

"No, those folks run the street cars and steamboat and a couple of steam loco-motives," said Phil. "This is a different bunch, they only run horseless carriages."

"An annual meet, huh?" said Lars thoughtfully. "Naw, they probably wouldn't let me in it with my Stanley. I'd be passing them old explosion-engine people right and left." He began to circle the table again. *"Chuff, chuff, chuff, wheee-owwww!"* he crowed, working his elbows back and forth. "Get a horse!" He huffed back to Jill and got onto one knee so he could look up appealingly at her. "Ride with me?"

Jill frowned and looked away—only to encounter Betsy's equally ardent face. "I'll help. In fact, I'll be Lars's sponsor. I'll pay fees and buy coal or wood, or whatever you burn to make steam. Mention the name of the shop and I'll split the cost of restoration. Let me ride along, and it won't cost him a dime. Say yes, Jill, please?"

Jill sighed and looked again at the photo, shaking her head. Betsy looked too, holding her breath, wishing hard. The car was standing on a tarred road against the backdrop of desert scrub and cactus. It gleamed a rich forest green. The wooden wheel spokes were painted yellow, and there appeared to be yellow pinstriping on the body. And Jill was wrong, it did have a top, if that folded hunk of black canvas hanging out over the backseat was any guide.

Something that looked like an old-fashioned vacuum cleaner, complete with hose, was curled up against the passenger's—no, the steering wheel was on the right, so against the driver's side, under the door.

"Strange the photographer didn't notice when he took the picture that there was a vacuum cleaner still on the running board," Betsy remarked. The car was gleaming on the outside, so she assumed the inside had also been cleaned and polished.

"It's not a vacuum cleaner, it's for when you stop to take on water," said Lars, rising to point at the device with a big forefinger. "It just sucks it up out of a well or a pond or even a ditch. But you can pull into someone's yard and use their hose, too."

"Wow!" said Betsy, thinking how thrilling it would be to have a Stanley Steamer chuff up in front of the shop to ask for a bucket of water. How even more marvelous to be riding in a Stanley. What a thrill!

But Jill didn't smile, and Lars, realizing at last how deep in the doghouse he was, knelt again. "I know I should have talked to you before I decided to buy it," he said. "And if you say no, I'll call back and tell him I've changed my mind."

Betsy closed her eyes and crossed her fingers.

She heard Martha say, "I've always wanted to ride in an antique car."

Then Alice said, "We could make costumes. Waists and long skirts, and great big hats with veils."

Godwin said, "We could find boaters and celluloid collars, and make spats and close-fitting trousers! Oh you kid!"

Betsy hadn't thought about costumes. Oh, Jill just couldn't say no!

Phil added, "I could renew my boiler license easy, if it would make you feel better about this."

"Please?" said Betsy.

Jill let out a long breath. "Oh, what the heck. I'm not living dangerously enough already, arresting drunk drivers and the occasional murderer Betsy scares up. So sure, Lars honey, go tell the doctor with the bad heart you'll take his crumpled car off his hands."

Two

A few weeks later, Betsy was preparing to close Crewel World for the night. It was a little after five. The last customer had just left. She ran the cash register, made sure there were no sales slips loose on the desk, took forty dollars out of the register to keep as opening-up money for tomorrow, signed the deposit slip Godwin had made out and sent him off with it and the day's profits.

Then she hurried upstairs to give Sophie her evening meal, put the money into a locked drawer, and change into wool slacks and a heavy sweater. She grabbed her raincoat and a knit hat, dashed back down the stairs and out the back way to her car.

Lars had called in the afternoon to say that he was back with the Stanley, and did she want a ride? She'd been so excited she nearly forgot to ask him for directions to his new place.

It was less than five minutes away, out St. Alban's Bay Road a mile and a half, to Weekend Street, a narrow lane about three houses long. Lars, having concluded the sale of his hobby farm, had rented a very modest cottage at the bottom of the lane. It was surrounded by middle-size trees and a lot of brush, but it had a big yard. A driveway led behind the house to a small red barn.

Beside the barn was a long, low, white trailer, like a multihorse trailer, except this one had no windows. It was hitched to Lars's dirty blue pickup truck, which apparently hadn't gone to the buyer of his farm.

Betsy steered her car onto the weedy lawn, got out, and went through the open double doors of the barn. Close up, the barn was relatively new, sided vertically with aluminum "boards" and floored with cement. The oil stains on the floor and the big electric winch that ran on an overhead rail announced that this shed was no stranger to people who worked on engines. A workbench along one wall had a vise on it and a Peg-Board above it with the outline of numerous tools, though the tools presently on it didn't always match the outlines.

Lars and Jill were both there. Jill, in jeans and Windbreaker, had her hands in her back pockets and a worried look in her eye. Lars was just grinning.

The backside of the old car was higher than their heads, a rich, gleaming green. There was no rear bumper, and the single taillight, near the left fender, was a brass oil lamp with a round red eye.

The tires seemed tall, perhaps because they were narrow. Betsy asked, "What if you get a flat? Do you have a spare?"

Lars said, "No, the spare's on it. I'm going to have to order a new tire. But I hope it never gets a flat. They have inner tubes and they're harder than hell to change. But these are fine, and they last a long time," he added hastily, not wanting to discourage his patron.

He went to wheel a long, narrow, many-drawered steel chest out of the way so Betsy could walk around the car. "He sold me the tool chest, too."

Jill muttered, "*Takes* lots of tools, I see."

"No, it doesn't," retorted Lars. "No more than most old cars, anyhow. It's just that some of them are . . . different."

"How did he wreck it?" asked Betsy, coming to the damaged fender and noting that the big brass headlight was smashed as well. She thought the bulb had been torn out until she saw the other headlight didn't have a bulb, either. They must not make the kind of bulbs it took anymore.

"Last time he had it out, he was run off the road by a gawker. You got to watch for those gawkers, he told me. Anyhow, the wreck triggered a heart attack, so he figured he'd better sell."

"Can you get new headlights, too? I see there aren't any bulbs in these."

"They don't come with bulbs, they're acetylene. But they aren't very bright, so we don't run at night."

"Can you start it?" asked Betsy, coming the rest of the way around it. "I mean, right now? Or is there something wrong with the motor, too?"

"It runs fine," Lars said firmly, glancing at Jill. "Dr. Fine taught me how to start it and had me do it alone a couple of times. It's not hard, but you can't do it fast. His personal record for getting it powered up was seventeen and a half minutes."

Lars got out the owner's manual and consulted it, then checked to make sure there was water and the two kinds of fuel in adequate amounts. The car had several gauges, but not, apparently, a fuel gauge. Lars used a wooden ruler dipped into the tanks to determine fuel levels. "It holds twenty-five gallons of water, seventeen gallons of unleaded gas, and two gallons of Coleman gas, plus a gallon of steam oil, which is a blend of four-hundred-weight oil and tallow."

"Four hund—" began Jill, but was interrupted by Betsy's exclamation: *"Tallow?"*

"Uh-huh." Lars, having produced a handheld propane torch from the toolbox, was twisting the knob. The torch began to hiss and he lit it with a cigarette lighter. "Y'see, this isn't an internal combustion engine, it's a steam engine, so the rules are different. She runs real hot, so you need a lubricant that can take it. He says you get used to the new rules, and they're good ones, and real safe, only different. Dr. Fine says there's people in Wisconsin who own Stanleys, and they can help me. Plus there's a big club I'm gonna join, it's international, so there's a good support group."

Jill remarked to the ceiling, "Unlike AA, these people help you stay with the sickness, not get clean."

"What?" said Lars. Adjusting the flame of his torch, he hadn't been paying attention.

"Nothing, nothing," said Betsy, waving a shushing hand at Jill. "Go on, Lars."

"Anyhow, this club can tell me where I can get the stuff I need to keep her running." He put a big, caressing hand on the intact front fender, then went to the back of the car and turned a flat steel knob on a copper tank. Then he went to the front—Betsy and Jill following—and began playing the torch through a pair of silver-dollar-size holes at the base of the hood, which, Betsy suddenly noticed, was shaped like a fat oval, not flat on the sides like ordinary cars.

"What are you doing?" she asked.

"Getting the pilot light started."

Betsy laughed uncertainly, but Lars said, "I have to get it hot before I can turn on the gasoline."

After a few minutes, satisfied that the pilot light was operating properly, Lars got into the car. He opened another valve, then began to pump a long handle back and forth. "Getting the gasoline started," he explained.

He got out again and showed Betsy the two small, recurved nozzles that came from under the car and ran into the holes he'd been playing the torch into. "Feel," he said, running a finger across one of the nozzles.

Betsy complied, but yanked her hand away from the strong, fine spray. "What's that, water?"

"No, gasoline."

Betsy sniffed her fingertip and was shocked to realize Lars was right. "You mean it just sprays out in the open like that?"

"Sure. It has to mix with the air as it goes into those two holes."

"That can't be safe!" exclaimed Jill. "Spraying gasoline like that, you'll get a vapor that will explode."

"No, you get a vapor that will burn," said Lars.

"Why doesn't it mix in the cylinder—" Betsy stopped.

"Because then it would be an internal combustion engine," Lars confirmed with a grin.

Suddenly a low, eerie *whoooooooooooo* began to sound from the car. Jill grabbed Betsy by the arm and ran her out of the barn. When they looked around and Lars wasn't behind them, Jill shouted, "Get out! Get out! It's going to blow!"

"No, it isn't!" called Lars, his voice filled with laughter. "It's called singing! She sings when she's building a head of steam!"

"Cool!" said Betsy, shrugging her elbow loose from Jill's grip. She would have gone back, but Jill took her by the arm again.

Lars came out to the doorway. "Soon as we get to four hundred and fifty pounds of pressure, we can head on down the road."

"Four hundred and fifty pounds!" Jill exclaimed, then murmured in Betsy's ear, "Don't go, don't go."

But Betsy again shrugged free and this time did go back inside to watch as Lars continued the process of starting up, tapping a gauge on the dashboard, pumping up the gasoline, nodding as he checked his owner's manual; and was reassured by the big man's happy confidence. After all, he'd gone through all this just a couple of days ago, and surely he'd notice if things were going differently. Right?

It took about twenty minutes. The "song" of the boiler slowly rose in tone, then stopped. Lars opened the passenger side door, clambered over into the driver's seat, and said, "All aboard!"

Jill warned, "You are crazy, Betsy, if you get into that contraption with him."

But Betsy stepped up onto the running board, feeling the springiness of the suspension, then up again into the passenger seat of tufted black leather. "This is so high!" she said. She automatically began feeling around for a seat belt, then laughed at herself. "Let's go, Lars!"

"You sure you're not coming?" Lars asked Jill, who in reply backed onto the grass and waved them off.

The car had not made a sound since it left off "singing," and there was not the faintest vibration to show that a motor was running. As Betsy watched, Lars depressed two small pedals crowded together on the floor, and then slowly moved a silver lever up a slice-of-pie metal holder on the steering column.

With a quiet *chuff, chuff* the car moved smoothly backward. Lars steered it to the left, moved the lever downward, and pushed on the third pedal on the floor. The car stopped.

"Yay!" he cheered softly, and Betsy realized he was a little nervous after all. He grinned and waved at Jill then moved the lever up the pie slice, and the car, this time in absolute silence, went down the driveway to Weekend Lane and up to St. Alban's Bay Road. Lars braked nearly to a stop at the road, then turned left. As they moved out, he became bolder and moved the throttle lever up a little more. The car, still making no noise at all, began to gain speed.

"Wow!" cheered Betsy. "Wow!" There was no vibration, no chuff-chuffing, just smooth acceleration.

Lars, his grin broadening, winked at her and pulled a lever under the steering wheel. A very loud whistley racket let loose. Steam roiled up all around them. Betsy would have jumped out of the car, but Lars grabbed her by the shoulder. "Ha, ha!" he cheered, and blew the whistle again.

This time Betsy yelled in delight. It was safe, this was great! Coming to a stop sign, Lars braked, but the car didn't slow. He slammed the throttle down, and tramped hard on the brake, but they were only slowing as they entered the intersection. He pulled the wheel hard right and they leaned very dangerously going around the corner. Despite the narrow tires, the car didn't slide or skid and Betsy grabbed the gasoline pump lever to keep from being thrown out. Once onto the even narrower road, the car righted itself.

"Wow!" exclaimed Betsy yet again, and Lars laughed and reopened the throttle.

There were trees crowding close on either side, the last bits of sun twinkling through the branches. The upright windshield blocked the wind, rapidly cooling as the sun went down, so she felt quite comfortable.

"Yah-hooo!" Lars cheered and blew the whistle as he pushed the lever up a little more. In a smooth, continuing silence the car answered the call, speeding up effortlessly. It was weird, it was surprising, it was wonderful.

Betsy began to laugh; she couldn't help it. It was like the first time she'd gone sailing.

Lars began to experiment with the car, slowing to a crawl, accelerating to about forty—there was no speedometer—slowing again. As he came nearly to a stop, he stomped suddenly on the pair of pedals, and the car jumped instantly backward with a little squeal of rubber. He lifted his foot and the car jumped right into forward again. "Look, Ma!" he said. "No transmission!"

"What—you didn't break something, did you?" asked Betsy.

"No, no, no. The Stanley brothers invented a steam car with a transmission, but sold the rights, so when they wanted to try steam again, they had to figure a way around the patents. They couldn't get around the transmission patent, so they invented a car without a transmission. The motor turns the axle directly, no gears. The engine turns over once, the wheels go around once."

"Uh-huh," said Betsy, not sure if this was brilliant or troublesome.

A hill, not high but fairly steep, was ahead, but the car forged up it with no hesitation. "See? Torque to burn!" cheered Lars.

And Betsy, who happened to know a little about engineering because her father had been an engineer, realized that the lack of gearing was the reason for the torque. Brilliant, she decided.

Around another corner, they were on Excelsior Boulevard, which ran parallel to Highway 7. The highway was crowded with commuters on their way home from work, but several dared to slow down when they saw the Stanley, and two or three honked.

Betsy waved happily at them, and Lars showed off a little bit by blowing the whistle, causing an unaware driver to swerve dangerously. The road was flat and clear along this stretch. They came to Christmas Lake Road, which crossed Highway 7 and joined Excelsior Boulevard. Commuters who lived in Excelsior were backed up on the highway, waiting to make the turn. They crowded onto Excelsior when the light changed. There was only a stop sign for Lars, and he seemed in no hurry to bully his way into the stream of traffic. Waiting for the traffic to clear, he checked his gauges.

"See the winker?" he said, pointing to a small red button light blinking rapidly. "If that stops winking, it means we're running low on oil." Betsy watched it for a while, but it never stopped winking.

Cars coming off the highway slowed for a look, causing others to honk impatiently. One, steering where he looked, swayed toward them, and Lars blew his whistle angrily, nearly hiding the Stanley in the steam and setting off a chorus of honks. Betsy stood and waved her fist at the driver, but was laughing too hard to make her threat worth anything.

Then there came a gap and they went on down the road, past the sudden steep hill of the cemetery, around a curve, and past the police station, then Adele's Ice Cream and the McDonald's. At the next stop sign they turned right and were back on St. Alban's. The circuit, about three miles, had taken less than fifteen minutes.

The view along St. Alban's Bay Road was more open but no less pleasant, with Excelsior Bay on their left and St. Alban's Bay on their right. They went onto a two-lane bridge over the narrow link between them. Some people had already put their boats in the water, though it was a little early for pleasure sailing. Over the bridge was a yacht and boat sales and repair company, then a row of mixed small cottages and bigger houses, some hidden behind hedges, others open, with grass showing green and tulips budding. The trees on either side had leaves almost big enough to hide their branches. Betsy sniffed, testing the spring air, but the car had a strong aroma of its own, an unpleasant combination of gasoline, kerosene, and hot oil. But now, quite suddenly, the scent of gasoline was overwhelming. She turned to ask Lars about it and saw the look of alarm forming on his face.

He shut the throttle down and began to brake. "I hope this isn't what I think it is," he muttered. He reached for a valve knob, pulling onto the narrow, sloping shoulder, fighting the wheel one-handed as the tires gripped hard at the loose gravel.

As they slowed nearly to a stop, he turned to say, "Get—" but was interrupted by an enormous fiery explosion. Betsy flung her arms up and screamed. Smoke, dark flames, and gas fumes filled the air.

The fat oval hood was standing up, and black smoke was pouring out. Betsy was standing in the middle of the road looking at the car, with no memory of climbing down.

And then there were people running toward them.

A car going by swerved sharply to miss Betsy. It pulled onto the shoulder and the man driving it got out and ran toward them, his face alarmed. A passenger got out, cell phone to his ear, gesturing as he spoke.

Betsy suddenly realized she was deaf.

But she felt no pain. She was not scattered in small pieces over the surrounding area. She was not on fire or even burned. Or bleeding.

Lars was standing behind the Stanley cranking down a valve. He was calm, intact, and not on fire.

In fact, the car seemed to be intact, the smoke almost cleared away.

"What the hell happened?" shouted the driver of the stopped car as he came up to them, sounding to Betsy as if he were speaking from under a thick blanket. Lars said something back, which Betsy could not hear at all.

The man repeated his question, and Lars came out from behind the Stanley. "The pilot light went out!" he shouted.

Betsy began to laugh. It was a sick, hysterical laugh, and Lars hurried over to take her by the shoulders and shake her. "Hey!" he said. "Hey! Stop it!"

Betsy managed to stop, and put her hands on Lars's arms to make him quit shaking her. "I—I'm oh-okay," Betsy managed between teeth that were suddenly chattering. Her touch on Lars turned to a grasp, as her knees began to give way.

Several people came close, and one said, "Shall I call 911?"

Everyone's voice was becoming audible, if muffled. Betsy touched one ear with the palm of her hand.

The man with the cell phone said, "I already did!"

"What did you do that for?" demanded Lars angrily.

Betsy heard a sound and turned back toward town. Was that the volunteer fire department siren? By the way the others were looking toward it, it was. She moved her jaw in a kind of yawn, trying to get her hearing the rest of the way back.

Lars said angrily, "Call and cancel! The car's fine, and we're fine!"

That was met with disbelieving silence.

"No, really," said Betsy, "I'm all right. I'm not injured." She looked at the Stanley, which seemed innocent of all wrongdoing, though the hood still stood upright. "But my God, Lars, if that's what happens when the pilot light goes out, what happens when you run out of steam?" And she started laughing again.

"Hey," he began, but she stepped back out of his reach.

"I'm fine," she repeated, and in fact her knees seemed to have regained their strength. "Better see to your car."

"Oh, it's okay, really, it's in perfect condition. We'll let the fumes air out and relight the pilot light, and we're back on our way." He walked over to the front of the car and began looking at the squat white round thing where the engine in an ordinary car would be.

"What the hell kind of a car is that?" asked a stocky young man near the front of the small crowd.

A skinny old man said, "I believe it's a Stanley Steamer."

Betsy said, surprised, "You're absolutely right. How did you know that?"

"My grandfather had one. Kept it in an old shed back of the barn. He used to fire it up and let me drive it over the pastures. It could climb out of the deepest ditch on the place. Ran her on diesel fuel and kerosene, if I remember rightly. But I burned the boiler dry a couple of times and it wouldn't run after that."

He was speaking to the crowd as well as to Betsy. Lars had walked around to the side of the car to lift the front seat and rummage around among what sounded like heavy metal tools.

"What are you going to do?" the man with the cell phone asked him.

Lars came up with a flashlight and a length of stiff wire. "Gonna clean out the pilot light," he said. "If all of you will give me some room!" He spoke with annoyance weighted by the unmistakable authority of a police officer, and everyone decided to give him all the room he wanted.

"I used to use a coat hanger," the old man said, and he was immediately surrounded by people who wanted to hear more about coat hangers and Stanley Steamers.

Betsy went to stand behind Lars, trying to see without interfering in what he was doing. She heard a car horn honking and honking and turned to see a big old Buick roaring up the road. "Here comes Jill," she said.

Lars groaned. "She's gonna make me sell it, I just know she is!" And then he groaned louder at the sound of a siren approaching. Several sirens.

The man who had waved the cell phone said, "I called and canceled! Honest!" Then he hurried into the passenger seat of his car and left.

The Buick slid to a stop across the road and Jill emerged, her face white. "What happened?" she demanded.

"The pilot light went out," said Betsy, shrugging in further ignorance.

"Pilot light—?"

Lars said, slamming down the hood, "When the pilot light goes out, gasoline fumes collect, and if the boiler's hot enough, it sets them off. You get a little bang, the hood flies up, the fumes escape, and you're fine."

Jill said, "I heard that 'little bang' three quarters of a mile from here. I imagine all of Excelsior, most of Shorewood, and half of Deephaven heard it. The 911 switchboard must've lit up like a Christmas tree." She gestured back up the road at the approaching emergency vehicles, their sirens drowning out anything further she might have said.

The fire truck crew listened while Lars explained what was going on, the ambulance crew gave Betsy a cursory examination—Lars refused to let them examine him—and at last they departed. Most of the neighbors by then had gone back into their houses, though the old man hung out at a safe distance to watch Lars work.

Lars spent fifteen minutes clearing the pilot light tube, then reopened the valve to let Coleman gas reach it, lit a long weed stem, and squatted to poke it through one of the holes in the front of the hood. There was a *whump* that shot flame out both holes. Lars fell backward, landing on his hands and bottom, but said, "See? It's fine, she's starting up for me!" He kept his head turned awkwardly away from Jill, and Betsy, in a pretense of going to see if her hat was in the car, saw the reason. The latest explosion had left a blister in place of Lars's right eyebrow. But the burner was hissing happily, and Lars continued the process of rebuilding a head of steam, which took almost no time, as the boiler hadn't cooled much during the breakdown.

Jill insisted Betsy ride with her, that Lars drive very slowly; and she followed behind him, emergency lights blinking, all the way home.

Three

In a Minnesota summer, nights can be gloriously cool. At 4 A.M. Saturday, June 12, in a dead calm, the temperature was sixty-three. By six it had risen to sixty-eight, and as the sun climbed, it continued to rise. A light breeze started flapping the pennants on the sailboats moored at private docks in St. Alban's and Excelsior Bay.

The breeze caused the sailor heading out on Lake Minnetonka to reach for his jacket, but by the time he passed the Big Island, he had taken it off again. By 8 A.M., under a spotless sky, it was seventy-one.

Already the air around The Common, Excelsior's lakeshore park, had begun to smell of grilled pork, hot dogs, cotton candy, smoothies, and deep-fried chicken tenders. Rows of white canvas booths were rising like geometrical mushrooms, filled to bursting with paintings, jewelry, sculpture, Japanese kites, birdhouses shaped like English cottages, and other exotica, as artists prepared for business. Excelsior's annual art fair was hoisting canvas as it prepared to get under way.

The weatherman predicted temperatures in the upper eighties by midafternoon, but added that the continued light breeze off the lake would keep everyone at the fair comfortable.

Betsy came out of her shop around nine. The long block of Lake Street that Crewel World faced was empty of cars, but had a white canvas booth of its own set up in the middle of the street. Betsy headed for it. There were three people in the booth, a man and two women. Above the booth was a plastic banner with ANTIQUE CAR RUN printed on it in rust-brown letters.

The real Antique Car Run, from New London to New Brighton, was next weekend. Today, Saturday, a group of twenty-five drivers were in the Twin Cities on a publicity tour that included a run from the state capitol building in St. Paul to Excelsior and back.

It was rumored the governor would ride in one of the cars, a rumor the club was careful not to extinguish. Minnesota's eccentric governor always drew a crowd.

Both women in the booth were on cell phones, and both were gesturing so wildly that Betsy, approaching, felt a pang of alarm. But the man, a nice-looking fellow about Betsy's age, winked at her and said, "They're always like this just before things get under way."

Betsy said, "Things are going according to plan, then."

"Yes, the first car will leave in about five minutes."

"Where do you want me?"

"Right here. But we don't have anything for you to do until the first ones arrive, which won't be for about two hours. Your tasks will be to note the time of arrival of each vehicle, and to point them at me in the booth so I can direct them to parking places along the curb." He glanced up and down the empty street, which had No Parking signs tied to every pole. "I hear we're not very popular with the committee running the Art Fair."

Betsy turned to look up toward The Common, two blocks away. Starting before dawn, a slow-moving line of vans, SUVs, trucks, and campers bearing artists and their work had clogged this street, the last draining away into the fair only an hour ago. But now the street belonged to the Antique Car Run, so none of the many hundreds of visitors to the fair could park here today. This distressed those running the art fair, because every extra block visitors had to walk to the lakefront meant their feet would give out that much sooner, giving that much less time for the artists to extract money.

No, Deb Hart had *not* been pleased at a meeting of her art fair committee and the Antique Car Run committee.

In vain the Antique Car Run president had argued that people who came to see the horseless carriages would then wander over to the fair so temptingly nearby.

Deb had argued that people who came to look at old cars were not the same kind of people who visited art fairs. She had suggested a parade of old cars up Excelsior's main street, all the way up to the far other end, where there was plenty of room and no competition from fair goers. "Besides," she'd pointed out in a reasonable voice, "there's the car dealership down there, which is probably more in tune with the kind of people who turn out for an event like yours."

But Mayor Jamison had sided with the antique car event planners. "There are all kinds of car people," he had said, "hot rod people, classic car people, new car people. But horseless carriage people are different. They're not interested in tires and cubic-inch measurements of engines, but the history and unique beauty of these early machines. Such people see their antiques as works of art rather than mechanical devices, and so might more properly be classed among the art seekers who come to the fair."

Betsy, who had endured much ear-bending from Lars about main burner jets, valve plungers, and cylinder oil, had not slipped into prevarication by so much as a nod of agreement with the mayor. Instead, she bit her tongue, while Deb Hart, all unknowing, succumbed to the mayor's argument.

Now, on this beautiful June morning, she looked at the empty street and said, "No, the art fair is not happy with us." Then she went back to the shop, unlocked the door, and stood a moment, thinking how she was going to accomplish her next task, which was to get the quilt stand just inside her door out onto the sidewalk.

Last night, a little before closing, an elderly woman named Mildred Feeney had come in asking for Betsy. She said she was associated with the Antique Car Run and asked if she might store a quilt that was to be a prize in a raffle in Betsy's shop "just for tonight," and Betsy had agreed. She had also agreed to bring it out in the morning. But that was before she'd seen the quilt and the stand on which it was to be displayed. She'd been busy in the back while it was brought in, apparently by a big crew of husky men, because now, looking at it, she wondered how on earth she was going to bring it out again all by herself.

The quilt, a queen-size model, was draped over a large wooden frame shaped like an upside down V. The frame was large enough to accommodate the quilt unfolded, holding it several inches clear of the floor on both sides.

And the stand wasn't on wheels. Betsy took one end with both hands, tried to lift it, and decided the wood of the frame was at least oak, if not ironwood. The frame wasn't exactly top-heavy, but without someone to steady it at the other end, it would easily tip over. Betsy's shop was cozy, not spacious, and her front door was of an ordinary size. She hadn't realized there was so sharp a curve from right inside the door to between the white dresser and the counter. How was she to get the long, inflexible frame and its clumsy burden to the door?

By pulling and shifting and, at one point, climbing up onto the counter and down the other side to adjust the angle of the frame.

But the door opened inward, and so the frame had to be moved backward again. And then the door must be propped open—no employee had propitiously turned up, of course—and the struggle begun again.

At last Betsy got the stand most of the way out the door and was beginning to fear there wasn't enough sidewalk. She was pausing to consider this new complication when the quilt suddenly slid away, like a giant snake heading for the underbrush. Betsy grabbed for it, then saw it was being draped over the arms of Mildred Feeney, who was smiling at her. "If we take the quilt off," she said, "the stand folds up and we can carry it to the booth quite easily."

"Oh? Oh, yes, I should have thought of that," said Betsy, blushing at herself for also thinking, even for an instant, that the quilt had made an attempt to escape. Even if the frame didn't fold, which it did (the hinges being clearly visible once the quilt was off), it would have been lighter and easier to manage without all those thick yards of fabric on it.

The naked V, folded, was not hard to manage, especially with Mildred, who was stronger than she looked, helping.

Mildred had already put a cash box and an immense roll of double tickets in the booth. After Betsy helped redrape the quilt, Mildred fixed Betsy with a look. "They're a dollar apiece," she said in her sweet but firm old-woman's voice, "six for five dollars. How many shall I tear off for you?"

Betsy sighed and bought twenty dollars' worth, asking in her own firmest voice for a receipt so she could record the money as a charitable donation. It never occurred to her that she might win—Betsy never won raffles.

Perhaps, she reflected on her way back into the shop, she had been a little too quick to promise her sponsorship of Lars and his Steamer. Between the parts he had had to order—very expensive and one all the way from England—and the strange, also expensive, requirements in cylinder and gear oil and kerosene for the pilot light, and the lousy mileage it got on gasoline—*plus* the entry fee for the Antique Car Run and raffle tickets, this was turning out to be a very expensive sponsorship. She was also beginning to regret that she'd volunteered to help out at the Run. It was taking too much time away from the shop. And since her volunteer assignment on the day of the New London–New Brighton run was to record the names of the drivers as they left on the run, and then to help prepare and serve lunch at the halfway stop, she wasn't even going to get to ride with Lars next Saturday.

She began the opening-up process in her shop. She was going to be in and out today, so Godwin was going to be helped by Shelly Donohue, an elementary school teacher who worked for Betsy during the summer months. Betsy turned on the lights, put the start-up money in the cash register, and tuned the radio to a classical station with the volume barely audible. She was just plugging in the old vacuum cleaner when Shelly came in.

"Did you hear the latest?" asked Shelly breathlessly.

Shelly was an inveterate gossip, and her "latest" was usually exceedingly trivial, but Betsy politely delayed turning on the machine so she could hear whatever the silly tidbit was.

"John threw Godwin out."

Betsy dropped the wand. "Oh, Shelly, are you sure?"

"How sure do you want? Godwin slept at my house last night."

"Is he very upset?"

"We sat up till two this morning, and he never stopped crying for more than five minutes at a time. He's a real mess."

"I suppose that means he won't be in today?" Betsy felt for Godwin, but she really needed two people in the shop on weekends. Especially this weekend, with two attractions bringing lots of visitors to town.

"He said he'd be here, but to tell you he'd be late, because he had to go get his clothes. He got a call from a neighbor that they're in a big pile along the curb outside John's condo."

Betsy sat down. Godwin's clothes were enormously expensive: Armani suits, silk shirts, alpaca sweaters, handmade shoes, all bought by John, of course—Godwin couldn't have bought the sleeve of one suit on the salary Betsy paid him. John loved to ornament his handsome boy toy and had taught Godwin to treat the clothes with respect. If they had been unceremoniously dumped out in the street, this wasn't a mere lover's quarrel; John must be serious about the breakup.

"This is terrible. I feel so sorry for Godwin! And I can't imagine him coming in after having to pick his beautiful clothes up off the ground. How cruel of John!"

"I agree. Goddy is so upset that even if he does turn up, I don't think he'll be much use. So what are we going to do? With you out most of the day, we have to have another person."

"All right, call Caitlin and see if she's available. If she isn't, go down the list. If you get down to Laverne, you'll want a third person." Caitlin, a high school senior, had been stitching since she was six; Laverne, a retired brewery worker, barely knew linen from Aida and was afraid of the cash register. "Meanwhile, I hope he comes before I have to get back out to the booth. I really want to talk to him. Has he got someplace to go? I mean, besides your place?"

"I don't think so. He was crying that John made him give up all his real friends, except me and you. But he can stay with me for as long as he wants. I've got a spare bedroom. And Goddy doesn't mind the dogs."

"Is that what the fight was about, John's jealousy?" asked Betsy.

"Something like that. Goddy says John accused him—falsely, Goddy says—of flirting with Donny DePere at a party. But John is very jealous, he won't let Goddy have any male friends, even straight ones." A smile flickered across Shelly's face. "Goddy says he's so frustrated he caught himself flirting with a girl just to keep his hand in."

"What do you think, was Godwin flirting with another man?"

Shelly hesitated only briefly. "Yes, I think so. But it's still John's fault, don't you think?"

"I don't think I have a right to an opinion. I don't know the rules of that relationship, and I only met John once."

"Yes, well, that snotty attitude you saw at your Christmas party—" Shelly assumed a lofty attitude and sniffed lightly. "'How terribly tedious your friends are, Goddy,'" she murmured, then grimaced. "That's John all over. What a jerk!"

"Yes, but he's a wealthy jerk. That enables Godwin to work here for very low wages, for which I am very grateful," said Betsy heartlessly. "So encourage Goddy to kiss and make up, will you?"

The door went *Bing!* and they turned to see the subject of their conversation come in. Godwin was a handsome young man of barely medium height, slim and blond, wearing tight jeans, a white linen shirt with no collar, and loafers with no socks. Normally ebullient and witty, he was looking very woebegone at the moment.

"Hi, Godwin," said Betsy. "I was afraid we might not see you today. I'm so sorry about you and John."

At this show of sympathy, tears formed in his sky-blue eyes. "What am I going to *do?*"

Shelly went to him. "You're going to stay with me until John comes to his senses," she said, taking him by the arm. "He has to learn that you have feelings, too." She led him to the library table in the middle of the room, and pulled a chair out for him. "Now sit down for a minute and pull yourself together."

"Thank you," murmured Godwin.

"Would you like a cup of coffee? Oh! I haven't made the coffee yet! It'll just take a minute. You just sit and wait, and think happy thoughts."

"All right," he said, but instead he made a little display of his grief, dropping his head and sighing, touching the end of his nose, then wiping under each eye, and sighing again.

Betsy said, pulling the vacuum cleaner over by the door, "Are you going to be able to work today?"

Godwin lifted his head. "Oh, I'll get through it somehow. After all, now I really need the money."

"Shelly says you're staying with her, and can stay as long as you like. That will help."

Godwin smiled sadly. "Shelly is the nicest person in the world. It's *so* lovely having someone coo over you and make you little treats and bring hot cocoa to you in bed. Don't you agree?"

Betsy laughed. "Ever since I was a little child with measles."

Godwin straightened. "Why are you so sure I'm feeling too sorry for myself? John has never gone this far before. My beautiful clothes, all dirty and wrinkled! Does he think I'm going to go crawling back to him after this?"

"If he threw you out, don't you have to wait for an invitation before you go crawling back?"

"Oh," said Godwin, looking disconcerted. "Well, yes, I suppose I do. Well, say, that puts the ball in his court, doesn't it? I don't have to try to think of an excuse to call him, do I? And when he finds out I've got a place to stay, *he'll* be the one getting anxious. Won't he?"

"I sure hope so. But what do I know? What do you think?"

"I think John plays by his own rules," said Godwin, dropping again into gloom.

Shelly came back with a freshly brewed cup of coffee, and Godwin sat sighing over it while Betsy vacuumed and Shelly dusted. Shelly liked to dust; it gave her lots of opportunities to pause and consider a pattern or a new color of wool or floss. She had yet to take home an entire paycheck, spending most of it on things from the shop. Today she picked out a Terrance Nolan butterfly. "I just love his things, but they're really difficult. I saw you have his kingfishers."

Betsy said, "I saw the models at Stitchville USA, and decided to order three kits; they're gorgeous. And I could sell them if I had a model. Would you be willing, Shelly?"

"Not me! His bugs are enough for me; those kingfishers are murder! Maybe you should ask the Turbo Stitcher."

Bitsy Busby had earned that nickname because she could plow through even a large and complex counted pattern in a week or ten days. A chronic insomniac, she sat up most nights watching old movies on cable and stitching. Despite her speed, her patterns were beautifully worked. She was especially fond of linen, particularly coffee-dyed linen. Godwin had once joked that the reason she was an insomniac was because she absorbed caffeine from the yards of fabric that passed through her fingers.

"Well, I'd better go see what's going on out there," said Betsy. "Wish me luck."

"God bless us every one."

Four

The temperature had risen ten degrees in the little while Betsy had been gone. Used to the dry heat of southern California, she was disconcerted by how warm seventy-eight humid degrees could be. Her favorite pant suit, cotton khaki with touches of lace, was too much clothing for this weather even with its short sleeves. She could feel it wilting as she walked to the booth.

One of the women was saying to the man, ". . . a '14 Hupmobile, he wants fifteen thousand for it." She had a phone to her ear, but she was talking to the man.

The man replied, "In running condition?"

"He says it is." She shrugged, showing doubt. "I haven't seen it." The phone made a faint sound, and she replied into it, "Yes, standing by."

Betsy said, "Do you mean there really was a car called a Hupmobile? I've heard that name, but I thought it was a joke."

The man looked at her. "No, it was founded by brothers named Hupp in 1908 and they made cars until 1940. The early ones are collector's items."

The woman said, "It's a Hupmobile on the back of the old ten-dollar bills. Take a look sometime."

"I'll do that," promised Betsy. "Is fifteen thousand dollars a lot of money for a Hupmobile? I mean, I would have thought so a few months ago, until a friend paid seventeen thousand for a Stanley Steamer."

The man said, "Was it Dr. Fine's?"

"How did—" Then Betsy smiled. "Oh, you must have been bidding on it, too."

But he shook his head. "I like rarities, but I wouldn't own a Steamer on a bet. It's just that the world of antique cars, especially the crowd that drives them as opposed to just shows them—is very small. I'm Adam Smith, by the way, and this is Lucille Ziegfield, called Ceil." He bent his head sideways toward the woman standing beside him. Still listening to her cell phone, she nodded at Betsy.

"How do you do?" said Betsy. "This is so interesting and exciting! I had no idea there were people who did this. I'm wondering what makes a person decide to get into these old cars. My friend who bought the Stanley is totally focused on the thing, hardly talks about anything else. That's typical of him, but is that typical of antique car owners?"

Ceil, still listening but apparently to dead air, said, "He has just the one?"
"Well, yes."

"Then he's not typical. Most of the people who get into this hobby wind up with several, sometimes several dozen. It's not a hobby, it's a sickness. My husband owns seven, all Packards. And not all antiques—the latest model he owns is from 1954."

Betsy wasn't sure whether to smile or offer condolences. What would Lars be like with half a dozen Stanleys? "Judging from the time Lars spends working on his one, I don't see where anyone would find the time to build up a collection," Betsy said.

Adam said, "Well, usually one of them is hogging most of the attention. The owner works on it until it's fixed or he can't stand looking at it anymore, and goes on to another."

"A CASITA," nodded Betsy.

" 'Casita'?"

"In needlework, sometimes one project demands all the attention until it turns into a CASITA, you CAn't Stand IT Anymore. So you go on to something else."

Adam nodding, laughed. "Who would have thought antique cars and needlework would have something in common?"

"I never even thought ordinary people could own antique cars," said Betsy. "I mean, I thought they were all in museums. Well, except Jay Leno, I know he owns some. But I certainly didn't know there were clubs of people who drive them."

Ceil said into her phone, "Well, that's politics," folded up her phone, and said to Adam, "The Studebaker the governor was riding in broke down on Selby, so he got out and went home."

"Damn!" muttered Adam, snapping his fingers.

Ceil continued to Betsy, "It's mostly men who get into this. It's not just the money—it takes a working knowledge of machinery, lots of heavy lifting, and a willingness to get really dirty. You'll see some fellow coming out of a shed in the evening with greasy clothes and disgusting fingernails, and only on second look realize he's the richest man in town."

"Who's the richest man in town?" asked a new voice, and Betsy turned to see Joe Mickels standing close behind her, an expression of deep suspicion on his face. A short, bandy-legged man, he had a wide, thin mouth under a great beak of a nose flanked by large white sideburns. He was in, for him, casual summer wear: light blue suit, white canvas shoes, white shirt, light blue necktie. Joe was the richest man in Excelsior, though he didn't want that fact generally known. He had dated Betsy for a short while earlier in the year, and had, in what he considered a tender moment, confided his financial status. Now that the brief romance was over, he constantly suspected her of talking about him, sharing the facts of his wealth with all and sundry.

"I have no idea," replied Betsy coldly. "We were talking about wealthy men who behave like garage mechanics around their antique automobiles."

"How old does a car have to be before it's an antique?" asked Joe.

Adam replied, "Well, for this year's run it's 1912 or earlier."

"Well, then, I've got an antique car."

Betsy had seen Joe's car. It was an immaculate 1969 Lincoln, old but hardly an antique. She frowned at him, and he twinkled at her as if telling her to watch him at work. He said to Adam, "She's seen my Lincoln, but I also have a 1909 McIntyre."

"I didn't know that!" said Betsy.

"There's a lot you don't know about me," said Joe, twinkling more broadly, and continued to Adam, "My grandfather bought it new, then my uncle owned it, then my brother, and now it's mine."

"Does it run?" asked Adam, and Betsy heard a slight change in Adam's voice. Though he was trying to sound casual, it seemed he was very interested in Joe's reply.

"Oh, yes, I started it up last Thursday. It's up on blocks, because it's got these funny big wheels, like wagon wheels, that used to have hard rubber around the rims, but they're worn right down to the metal. But it runs. I cranked her up and ran her for fifteen minutes, then shut her down again. I start her up once a month spring, summer, and fall, run her long enough to circulate the oil and water, then in November I drain the radiator, crankcase, and gas tank, and fill it all up again in the spring, and recharge the battery. That's what my uncle did. I used to help him when I was a boy. I understand some of these old cars are valuable, so I mean to keep her in running order."

"I wish I'd known you had an old car," said Betsy.

"Then I don't see why you didn't ask me," said Joe indifferently, turning a shoulder to her as he focused on Adam. "Of course, I couldn't have taken her for a ride, not without tires, and I don't know where to buy them."

"I could probably give you a source," said Adam. "If you're interested."

"Well, I don't know. The old car's useless, really. I was just keeping her out of sentiment. My Uncle Frank learned to drive with that car, and he used to give me and my cousins rides in it in the summer days of my youth. I think he'd halfway forgotten he had it, and my brother never drove it at all. I found it in an old barn a few years ago and had it moved to a heated shed, because I remembered a magazine article from somewhere that said some of them are valuable to collectors. I don't know if she's of any real value, since she's a McIntyre, and I never heard of that brand, not like the Maxwell, or a Cadillac or a Model T."

"How much of it is original?" asked Adam.

Joe shrugged. "All of it. The engine, chassis, transmission, even the paint job, though it looks a little scabby in places. Original wheels, original seat covers, original glass in the windows. And everything works, except the head-lights. My uncle wouldn't drive it at night because the lights were so weak, and now they won't light at all."

"What kind of headlights?"

"Big 'uns, made of brass. There's no lightbulbs in 'em, but I don't know who took 'em out." He scratched an earnest eyebrow to hide the wink he gave Betsy from under his hand.

Adam said, "If they're original, the lights are acetylene, not electric. That kind doesn't use bulbs."

"Acetylene? You mean like a welding torch?"

Adam nodded. "I'd kind of like to see that car."

"Sure, but it's not for sale."

"Who said anything about buying it? I saw one at a show a few years ago, where they asked me to judge. I didn't like the instruments on the dashboard—they were reproductions—and I'd like to see a set of originals."

Joe produced a business card from an inside pocket. "Give me a call some-time. I'll be glad to show it to you." He walked away.

Ceil snorted softly. "Of course you're not interested in a 1909 McIntyre with all original parts!"

Adam shrugged, eyebrows raised in a show of innocence. "Well, now you mention it, I do know a couple of people who might pay good money to buy that car—from me." He looked at the card, pulled out his wallet, and slid it into a pocket.

"If you manage to pry that vehicle out of Joe Mickels's hands for a nickel less than it's worth, you're a better man than most!" she said, laughing.

Betsy decided not to warn Adam after all that Joe's apparently fortuitous appearance at the booth was, in all likelihood, the first move in a plan to sell his McIntyre for at the very least what it was worth. Joe never parted with any-thing for less than its true value. Moreover, she doubted that sentimental story of it being handed down three generations. Joe? Sentimental? Ha!

There was the sprightly sound of "Für Elise," and Ceil, still smiling, pulled her cell phone from her pocket. "Excelsior," she said into it. "Ah!" She checked her watch. "Thanks!" she added, and disconnected. "The Winton just came onto Minnetonka Boulevard. It should be here in about twenty minutes."

"Not the Stanley?" asked Betsy.

"Why the Stanley?" replied the woman.

"Well, I just thought, because Stanleys are so fast."

The woman laughed. "Yes, for about twenty-five miles. Then they have to stop for water. Every blinking twenty-five miles they have to stop for water.

And of course, if they blow a gasket, or the pilot light goes out, or they run out of steam, then the delays really mount up."

Betsy flashed on Lars laughing as he chuffed around the table in Crewel World, calling "Get a horse!" to imaginary internal combustion cars. Apparently the laugh was not entirely his alone.

She had her clipboard ready when a soft-yellow car with brown fenders came up the street. It didn't look like a car from the teens, but more like something out of an early-thirties movie, with its sleek modeling, long hood, and deeply purring motor. A solidly built, prosperous-looking man in a cream suit was driving, and a very pretty woman wearing a cloche hat sat beside him. They both smiled at Betsy as the car pulled up.

"Number ten," he announced, and Betsy checked off Number Ten, a 1912 Winton, on her list, noting the time beside it.

"Are we the first?" asked the man, though that was obviously the case; there were no other cars in sight.

"Yes, sir, you are," said Betsy. She pointed with her pen at the booth. "Please check in with Adam Smith. He'll tell you where to park."

The Winton had only just moved on down the street when Betsy heard the now-familiar loud and breathy whistle of Lars's Stanley. She looked around and saw it, wreathed in steam, rolling smoothly up Lake toward her. She waited until he pulled up beside her, all smiles, before noting the time. He was one minute, twelve seconds behind the leader.

"Beat 'em all," he announced. "I told you the Stanley was a fast one. I bet number two won't be here for—" He broke off, staring up the street at the Winton pulling up to the curb a little beyond the booth.

"Sorry," said Betsy. But she was smiling.

"Oh, well, like they say, this isn't a race," said Lars, but his smile was now forced.

"How'd she run?" asked Betsy.

"Sweet as milk, and smooth as silk," said Lars. "But I'm thinking I should've looked around for a 1914 model; they have condensers in them, so you don't need to stop every thousand yards to take on water. Someone in St. Paul says he heard there's a guy with one—"

"No, no!" said Betsy. "You don't want to sell this one already! You just got it all restored!"

"Oh, I would never sell this one," Lars replied. "But the 1914, with a condenser . . ." His eyes had gone dreamy. Then he shook himself. "Do I just go up and park behind that yellow car?"

"No, check in at the booth first. Mr. Smith will tell you where to park. And Lars, this time talk to Jill first before you buy another Stanley." But she was talking to his back and he blew his whistle before she'd finished.

There was a half-hour gap before the rest of the cars started trickling in. The trickle grew quickly to a steady stream that as quickly diminished again to a trickle, until Betsy had checked off all but two cars. She was getting very warm standing out in the sun, and suspected her nose was getting sunburned. She wished she'd thought to wear a hat. And sunglasses.

A rust-brown two-seater came up the street, its engine going *diddle-diddle-hick-diddle.* It was a Maxwell with black leather seats and black trim, the top half of its windshield folded down. The car's wax finish shimmered in the bright sunlight as the engine idled unevenly.

The couple driving the car had also dressed in period costumes, he in a big off-white coat called a "duster," a pinch-brim hat in a tiny, dark-check pattern. Goggles with thick rubber edges covered his eyes. There was a dab of grease on his cheek. She wore a duster with lego'-mutton sleeves, a huge hat swathed in veils, and sunglasses.

"We're number twenty, the Birminghams, Bill and Charlotte," said the woman, who was on Betsy's side of the car—like most of these antiques, the steering wheel was on the right. The man stared straight ahead, his gauntleted hands tightly gripping the wheel.

"How long do we have here before we start back?" asked Charlotte, pushing aside her veil so she could wipe her face with a handkerchief. Her face looked pale as well as sweaty—and no wonder, thought Betsy, swathed in fabric like that.

"They're asking the drivers to stay at least an hour," replied Betsy. "And just so you know, there's a reporter from the *Excelsior Bay Times* here, asking to interview some of you."

The driver shook his head and grunted, "No."

The woman apologized. "He's feeling cranky. Something's wrong with the engine, we had trouble the whole trip. He needs to tinker with it, or we'll never make the return. I'm going to get out here," she said to him. "I've got to shed a layer or two or I'll just die. Where do we park?" she asked Betsy.

"First you have to check in—up there, at the booth. Adam Smith will tell you where to park."

The woman hesitated, then sighed. "Oh, all right, I'll ride up with you," she said, replying to an unvoiced complaint from Bill. Betsy smiled. Amusing how people who had been married for a long time could do things like that.

The woman resettled herself, and the little car went *diddle-hick-diddle* up the street to the white booth.

The last car in, a red-orange model, was small and light. It was a real horseless carriage, looking far more like a frail little buggy than a car. It had no hood, just a low dashboard that curved back toward the driver's shins. He was a slim young man in a tight-fitting cream-colored suit, a high-collared white shirt with a small black bow tie, and a straw boater atop his dark auburn hair.

He wasn't behind a steering wheel, but had one hand on a "tiller," a curved silver pipe that ran up from under the dash. The dust-white wheels of his automobile were the right size for bicycles, with wire spokes. The vehicle came to a trembling halt beside Betsy, whose mouth was open in delight. Here, in person, was the car embroidered in the center of Mildred Feeney's quilt, the car that was the very symbol of the Antique Car Club. Before she could check her list to see who was driving it, the driver smiled and said, "Owen Carpenter. Driving a 1902 Oldsmobile, single cylinder."

Betsy made a check mark beside Number Seven on her list, and wrote the time. She directed him to Adam Smith at the booth and stayed in place a minute to watch the Olds toddle down the street. Its little engine, located somewhere on the underside, sounded a very authoritative *"Bap!"* at brief intervals.

Then, her work done, Betsy walked slowly to the booth and past it, looking from side to side at the veterans. That Oldsmobile she had just checked in was the oldest in today's run, having survived its first century, but by definition all the cars here were pioneers, and the oldest ones looked like the buggies and wagons they shared the roads with when they were young. Some had names anyone would recognize: Ford, Oldsmobile, Cadillac. Some were unfamiliar: Everett, Schacht, Brush. Most were brightly painted, orange, yellow, red, blue, brown, green, but some wore basic black. All were surprisingly tall, with a running board to step up on, then another step up to the seats, which themselves were more like upholstered chairs or sofas than modern car seats. They all had brass trim and most featured alertly upright windshields. All but the Olds had wooden spokes on their wheels.

Two men were poking under the hoods and one was on his back doing something to the undercarriage, paying tribute to the experimental nature of these engines and drive mechanisms, but the rest stood in gleaming perfection while people gathered to ask questions or take pictures. The Stanley was leaking steam from several sources, but Lars seemed unconcerned and was boasting to a trio of young men about his trip. He had a bad scald on the back of one hand.

Betsy shook her head, at him and at all the drivers. Seeing these old, *old* cars, and knowing they'd been driven here from St. Paul, was like finding that your great-grandfather was not only still around, but decked out in white flannel trousers and using a wooden racket, capable of the occasional game of tennis.

She gave the clipboard to Adam and went to see how things were going in Crewel World.

It was a huge relief to step out of the glare into the air-conditioned interior. Even better, there were a fair number of customers—a few, by their costumes, from the antique car group.

Godwin wasn't in sight. Betsy raised an inquiring eyebrow at Shelly, who pointed with a sideways nod of her head toward the back of the shop. Betsy went into the little storeroom and heard the sound of weeping coming from the small restroom off it. She tapped lightly on the door. "Godwin?" she called.

"Oh, go away!"

"Why don't you go home?"

"Because I haven't got a home."

"How long have you been in there?"

"I don't know."

"Well, you're not doing us any good holed up like this."

"I won't ask you to pay me for the time."

"Oh, for goodness' sake, Godwin, that's not what I mean! Go over to Shelly's house, you idiot!"

"I know what you mean. I just wish——"

"What do you wish?"

"I wish I could stop feeling sorry for myself."

"Here's an idea. Come out of there and take a walk down Lake Street. You should see these wonderful old cars! They are so beautiful and exotic, just the sort of thing you'd love. And some of the people who ride in them are in period dress." Godwin loved costume parties.

But he only said, "Uh-huh," in a very disinterested voice.

"All right, then go down to the art fair. See if you can find Irene." Irene Potter was sitting with Mark Duggan of Excelsior's Water Street Gallery. Irene's blizzard piece was supposed to be prominently featured, its price a breathtaking six thousand dollars. It was not expected to sell; this was Mr. Duggan's way of introducing the art world to Irene. Irene had done several more pieces and been written up in the *Excelsior Bay Times*, and was behaving badly about being "discovered."

"It's too hot to be walking around in the sun," said Godwin pettishly, though he'd been telling everyone that he was the first to see her potential as a Serious Artist.

"Well, then how about I take you and Shelly out to dinner tonight? It'll probably be late, I don't know how long I'll be in St. Paul, but if you can wait, I'll take you anywhere you want to go."

There was the sound of a nose being blown. "Well," said Godwin in a voice not *quite* so disinterested, "how about Ichiban's, that Japanese restaurant where they juggle choppers and cook your shrimp right in front of you?"

"Fine, if we can get in without a reservation. Because I really don't know what time I'll be back."

"We can call from Shelly's before we leave," suggested Godwin, giving up his struggle to sound sad.

"Fine." Betsy went back out into the shop. Shelly was talking to a man trying to pick something for a birthday present. "All I know is, she pulls the cloth tight in a round wooden thing, and then sews all over it," he was saying.

And Caitlin was helping a woman put together the wools she needed for a needlepoint Christmas stocking.

A woman in an ankle-length white cotton dress trimmed in heavy lace was looking around and not finding whatever she was wanting. "May I help you?" asked Betsy.

The woman turned. "Oh, hello again!" She smiled at Betsy's blank face and said, "You clocked us in just a few minutes ago. The 1910 Maxwell? I was wearing a big hat?"

"Oh!" said Betsy. "Yes, now I remember you! Wow, you went costumed all the way, didn't you? First that big coat and hat, now this wonderful dress! Who do you get to make them for you?"

"The coat is a replica, but this dress and the hat are originals." She did a professional model's turn.

"They *are?*"

"Oh, yes. I collect antique clothes. I like to wear them, so it keeps me on my diet." She laughed and brushed at the tiny bits of floss clinging to her skirts. "I'm also a stitcher, as you can see. Do you know if this store has the Santa of the Forest?"

"We did, but I sold the last one yesterday. I've got more on order, but they won't come in for a week or two, probably."

"'We'? You work here?"

"Yes, ma'am. In fact, this is my shop. I'm Betsy Devonshire."

"Well, how do you do? I'm Charlotte Birmingham. I'd be out there helping Bill with the Maxwell, but I don't know one end of a wrench from another. I see you have knitting yarns as well. I used to knit, but that was a long time ago. Things have changed a great deal since my time." She shook her head as she glanced around at the baskets of knitting yarn. "Back in my teens, there was embroidery floss and there was wool for crewel, and wool or acrylic for knitting." She picked up a skein of silver-gray yarn of grossly varying thickness. "This is different. But what on earth can you make with it?"

"Look up there," said Betsy, gesturing at a shawl suspended on strings from the ceiling. She had nearly broken her neck fastening that up there.

"Why, it's lovely!" Charlotte exclaimed, and it was, all delicate open work, the uneven yarn making it look as if it were knit from fog. She reached up to feel the edge between a thumb and forefinger. "Oooooh, soft!"

"It's surprisingly easy to work with," said Betsy, who had also knit the shawl.

"Really?" said Charlotte. Then she glanced at the price tag on the yarn and hastily put it back in the basket. "Actually, I came in for some DMC 285. It's a metallic, silver. I couldn't find it at Michael's."

"My counted cross-stitch materials are in the back. Come with me, I'll show you." The back third of Betsy's shop was devoted solely to counted. It was set off from the front by a ceiling-high pair of box shelves. Charlotte went to a tall spinner rack of DMC floss, but Betsy said, "No, that metallic comes on a spool. Over here."

A small rack in one of the "boxes" held spools of metallic floss. "Here it is," said Betsy.

"Thank you. So long as we're back here, do you have cashel?"

"Certainly. What color are you looking for?" Betsy didn't have the enormous selection of fabric that Stitchville USA had, but she was proud to have a wide selection, rather than restricting her shop to Aida and linen.

A while later, Betsy rang up a substantial sale—Charlotte was like many stitchers. She couldn't resist poking through the patterns and the rack of stitching accessories, and adding to her initial purchase.

And then, riffling the sale basket of painted needlepoint canvases next to the cash register, Charlotte found a painted canvas of a gray hen that would look "darling" made into a tea cozy, so then Betsy had to help her select the gray, taupe, white, yellow, and red yarns needed to complete the pattern. She added the customary free needle and needle threader to the bag.

"Are you from around here?" asked Betsy after Charlotte had paid for her additional selections. "We have a group that meets every Monday afternoon in the shop to stitch. They do all kinds of needlework so you can bring whatever you're working on."

"Oh, that sounds nice," said Charlotte wistfully. "But we live in Roseville, clear the other side of the Cities, which makes an awfully long drive."

Reminded, Betsy checked her watch and made an exclamation. "We'd better get back out there. It's almost time to start back to St. Paul."

Charlotte said, "I'm not going to ride back in the Maxwell. It's too hot, and the jiggle was making me sick."

"'Jiggle'?"

"It's a two-cylinder and it jiggles all the time. Especially when it's not running well. After a while you begin to think your stomach will never be right again."

"Then how are you going to get home?"

"Oh, I'll ask Ceil or Adam or Nancy if I can ride with them to St. Paul. I can help out in the booth until Bill gets back. Then I'll help him put the Max into the trailer for the trip home."

"Well, I'm supposed to go over there, too. Would you care to ride with me?" After all, Charlotte, who had come in looking for a two-dollar item, had just spent nearly seventy dollars.

"Why, thank you, I'd like that very much. Let me go tell Bill."

They went out together and up the sidewalk to the brown car with a man leaning over the engine revealed by a rooked-up hood. He, too, had removed his duster, and had wrapped a towel around his waist to protect his immaculate white flannel trousers from the grease he was getting on his hands and on his fine linen shirt. Another towel, liberally smeared with grease, was draped over a fender. His head was well under the hood and he was muttering under his breath.

Charlotte came up behind him and said, "Bill, I'm riding to St. Paul with Betsy Devonshire here, one of the volunteers. All right?"

"Okay," grunted Bill. Metal clanged on metal. "Ow."

She bent over to murmur something to him, laughed softly at his unheard reply, touched him lightly on the top of his rump. "See you later," she concluded, and went to open the passenger side door and haul out in one big armload a carpetbag with wooden handles, the duster she'd been wearing, and the big, well-wrapped hat.

"Let's go see if Adam will keep these in the booth for me," she said. "And maybe he has something for me to do."

Adam sighed over the size of Charlotte's bundle, but found a corner for it. And he didn't have anything for her to do, not at the moment. "But say, if you want to assist Betsy in recording the departure times, that would be nice. They are supposed to tie their banners on the left side, but some interpret that to mean the driver's side, and if their steering wheel is on the right, they put it there; and some don't read the instructions at all and put it on the back end or forget to put it on at all."

Betsy said, "That's right. I had to ask a lot of the drivers what their entry number was because it wasn't where I could see it when they drove up." One had had to get out of his car and dig it out of the wicker basket that served as a trunk, remarking he didn't think it mattered until the actual run.

"If you'll stand so the cars run between you," said Adam, "one of you is bound to see the number."

Betsy, remembering the wicker basket, asked, "Why *does* it matter? If it's not a race, and they don't get a medallion for finishing this run, who cares what time they leave here?"

"We need to keep track," replied Adam. "So if someone doesn't show up at the other end, we know to go looking for him."

Ceil said, "They have special trucks that follow the route between New London and New Brighton, but they're not here today. Someone could break down, and if we weren't keeping track, they might not be missed until dark. Most of these cars shouldn't be driven after dark."

Betsy nodded. "I see."

Ceil checked her watch. "The first arrivals can start back in about fifteen minutes. That will be the Winton and the Stanley."

Betsy said, "Not the Steamer."

Ceil asked, "Why not?"

"He lives here, he just wanted to see if the car could make it from St. Paul. Kind of a tryout for the big run."

Adam asked, "His is the Steamer coming to the run, isn't it?"

Betsy nodded, then said, "I haven't seen the whole list of people signed up. Is there only one Steamer?"

Adam nodded. "Yes. Generally we get only one. The steam people have their own clubs. Their requirements and rules are different. Here, why don't you sit inside the booth? It's shade at least."

"Thanks." Betsy and Charlotte came in. The booth was roomy enough, even with the big quilt on its stand taking up most of the center. The booth had a board running around three sides of it that made a counter. Handouts about the Antique Car Club of Minnesota made stacks along it. There were also a few maps of the route stapled to a three-page turn-by-turn printed guide, for drivers who had lost or mislaid theirs. Postcards featuring pictures of antique cars were for sale. Mildred had taken up a post, her cash box on one side and the immense roll of double raffle tickets on the other. By the number of tickets dropped into a big, clear plastic jug, business had not been brisk, but she professed herself satisfied.

"Here, sit beside me," she said to Betsy. "And you, too, of course," she added to Charlotte.

Charlotte sat on Mildred's other side. She picked up a corner of the quilt and said, "Oh, it's embroidery, not appliqué. That's so much more work, isn't it? How many of you worked on that quilt?"

"It varies from year to year. Five of us did it this year. We start right after each run to work on next year's. I hope you noticed that every car on it is a car that has actually been on the run. When we started out, we didn't know much about antique cars. We got a book from the library and made photocopies of cars that we were interested in, and Mabel turned them into transfer patterns and put them on the squares, and we stitched them. The center square is always the emblem of the club—the Merry Oldsmobile."

Betsy said, "Oh, like from the song,

> *'Come away with me, Lucille,*
> *in my merry Oldsmobile'?"*

"Yes, that's the one," said Mildred, with a little smile. "Though I think the theme of the run should be 'Get Out and Get Under.' You know," she started to sing in a cracked soprano,

> " *'A dozen times they'd start to hug and kiss,*
> *and then the darned old engine, it would miss,*
> *and then he'd have to get under,*
> *get out and get under,*
> *and fix up his automobile!'* "

Betsy said, "I remember my grandmother singing that song!" She looked up the street. "Looks as if things haven't changed much with those old machines." The driver who'd been under his car earlier was still under it.

Adam put in, "That's why the run isn't a race. Just getting across the finish line is enough of a challenge, and anyone who makes it has earned his medallion. By the way," he added, holding out a clipboard, "here comes the Winton."

"Oops!" said Betsy, grabbing it. "Come on, Charlotte, time to get to work!"

The cars were spaced about three minutes apart—except when, as sometimes happened, a driver couldn't get his started, and there was a wider gap while another car was waved into its place. This happened with Bill Birmingham's Maxwell. A thin crowd stood on the sidewalks to cheer and clap as the gallant old veterans putt-putted, or whicky-daddled, or pop-humbled their way out of town. Bill finally got his Maxwell started after all the others had left. Charlotte blew kisses at the car, which despite Bill's efforts still went *diddle-diddle-hick-diddle* down the road. "Happy trails, darling!" she called, then turned to Betsy. "Whew, am I glad I'm not going on that ride!"

Five

Betsy checked on Crewel World one last time before leaving for St. Paul. Godwin seemed to have come out of his funk, and was assisting a customer trying out a stitch under the Dazor light. Betsy caught his eye and told him she'd try to be back before closing.

Then it was through the back into the potholed parking lot with Charlotte to Betsy's car.

Betsy's old Tracer had never recovered from a winter incident involving sliding off a snow-covered road into a tree. In seeking a replacement, she considered several high-quality used cars, envied the mayor his amusing cranberry-red Chrysler PT, but had at last bought a new, deep blue Buick Century four-door, fully loaded. It was the nicest new car she'd ever owned and she was very proud of it.

But Charlotte was obviously used to a better variety of cars. She simply laid her duster and big hat in the backseat with her stitchery bag, hiked the bottom of her antique white dress halfway up her shins, and climbed in the front passenger seat.

They took 7 to 494, up it to 394, then skirted downtown Minneapolis on 94 to St. Paul, taking the Capitol exit.

Crossing over the freeway put them on a street leading to a big white building modeled on the U.S. Capitol—except the Minnesota version had a very large golden chariot pulled by four golden horses on top of the portico. There were cars parked in slots in front of the capitol, but no people standing around.

Betsy said, "Looks as if we beat everyone. Even the booth is empty." A twin to the booth in Excelsior stood on the wide street at the foot of the capitol steps. They drove around back and found a parking space. After the air-conditioned interior of Betsy's car, the moist heat was again almost insufferable. Nevertheless, Charlotte donned her hat, draping the veils carefully around her head and shoulders—"It's easier than trying to carry it," she remarked. She did carry her duster and a handful of pamphlets she'd scooped out of the booth in Excelsior. Betsy brought her and Charlotte's stitching. She noticed that by the worn appearance of Charlotte's carpetbag, it was another antique. Its nubby surface was scattered with "orts," what stitchers called the little ends of floss. They walked around the blinding white building and across the broad paved area to the booth, where they collapsed on folding chairs.

"Whew!" said Betsy, fanning herself with a pamphlet. "How did people stand this back before air-conditioning?"

"It's not so hard to bear if you don't keep going in and out of air-conditioned spaces. People survived much worse weather than this before there was air-conditioning. Think of St. Louis—or Savannah—back when what I'm wearing was a marvelous improvement on the much heavier Civil War era clothing."

"Yes, of course, you're right. You know, we didn't have air-conditioning until I was about fourteen, and while I remember how much I loved having it, I don't remember suffering like I am now without it." She looked out across the shimmering heat lake of the parking area to the trees lifting tired arms in the sun. "Hard to believe we had our last snow just two months ago."

"And that in three months we may have another one," said Charlotte. "But that's why we love it here in Minnesota." Her tone was only a little dry. She reached into her carpetbag and pulled out a square of linen tacked onto a wooden frame. On it, in a variety of stitches, was a flowering plant with caterpillars on the leaves and two kinds of bees and a ladybug hovering among the flowers. She saw Betsy's eye on her work and said, "It's from a hanging designed by Grace Christie back in 1909. I'm going to work more of the squares and have them made into pillows."

Betsy said, "Do you know what that plant is? It looks familiar, somehow."

"Someone told me it's borage, an old medicinal herb."

"Oh, of course, 'Borage for Melancholy.'"

Charlotte looked at the nearly finished piece. "Does it work, I wonder?"

"I understand St. John's Wort does. So perhaps borage does, too."

Two tourists in shorts and sunglasses—a man and a woman—came up. Pointing, the woman said, "What a crazy hat!"

Charlotte laughed and said, "You're too kind."

The man said, "We came to see the old cars."

"They're on a round trip to Excelsior," said Charlotte.

"Who drove to Excelsior?" asked the woman, frowning.

"The owners of the antique cars," replied Charlotte.

"So where are the cars?" asked the man.

"The owners drove them to Excelsior." An element of patience had come into Charlotte's voice.

"Why did they do that? The paper said they were going to be here."

"They were here," said Charlotte more patiently. "But they drove to Excelsior to put on a display there."

"But I thought the paper said they'd be on display here!" said the woman.

"They were here, early this morning," said Charlotte, speaking very slowly now. "Then they drove to Excelsior. And now they've started driving back. At"—she consulted her watch—"four-thirty or so, they should be back from Excelsior."

"How come they're driving from Excelsior?" said the man. "The paper said they'd be here."

Betsy started to make a low humming noise, and when the woman looked at her, she coughed noisily, eyes brimming.

"They *were* here," said Charlotte, ignoring Betsy, "and they'll be back here in a couple of hours."

"I don't understand why they aren't here now, when the paper said they would be," said the woman.

Charlotte, speaking as if to a first grader, said, "The paper said they'd be here early this morning, then that they'd be driving from here to Excelsior, then that they'd return here to be on display again."

"Oh," said the woman, looking curiously at Betsy, who, hands cupped over nose and mouth, was trying unsuccessfully to contain that cough. "Thank you. Come on, Lew," she added, taking the man by the arm and leading him away. "I don't remember reading all that stuff about them being here and not being here and being here again."

As they trailed out of sight, Betsy could at last release the laughter. "Why didn't you just give those two a map and suggest they go meet the cars en route?" she asked.

"And have them run someone into a ditch?" retorted Charlotte.

"Never fear," said Betsy. "Those two couldn't possibly follow that map. They would have ended up back across the border in the place of their birth: Iowa."

"A distinct improvement to the gene pool in both places," said Charlotte in a dead-on Hepburn drawl.

Betsy laughed some more and Charlotte joined in. Insulting Iowa is a peculiar Minnesota custom—and while Iowans are happy to reciprocate, their jokes aren't considered half as clever. In Minnesota, anyway.

A woman drove by in a Land Rover, slowing to wave from inside the vehicle at Betsy and Charlotte. Betsy recognized Ceil, one of the women in the Excelsior booth. The Rover went on around to the parking lot in back of the Capitol building.

She came back on foot to say, "What, Adam isn't here yet?"

"Not yet," said Betsy and turned to greet another pair of tourists.

"My uncle once told me his grandfather owned a 1914 Model T Ford," said the man. "But we were here before the cars left on their run, and there was a 1910 Ford the driver said was a Model T. Who was right?"

"I—I don't know," said Betsy, and listened for Charlotte's cough.

Which kindly didn't come. Instead, she stood and said, "The first Model T appeared in 1908, and wasn't replaced by the Model A until around 1928. Of course, Henry Ford made constant changes and improvements as the years went by, but it was always called the Model T."

"Why Model T?" asked the woman.

Ceil came over to join the conversation, "Well, every time he reinvented his car, he gave the model the next letter of the alphabet. By the time Tin Lizzie came along, he was up to T. I don't know why he stuck to T so long; the 1912 model was very different from the 1908 one, and the 1927 Model T was a very different car again. The car that replaced it was the more expensive and sophisticated Model A, which is apparently why he decided to start over."

The couple asked a few more questions, took a brochure on the Antique Car Club, and drifted away. Betsy said, "I didn't know any of that!"

Charlotte smiled. "I only cling to my ignorance when it comes to actually working on restoration and repairs. I prefer to let Bill pack the wheels or replace the transmission bands." She held out her slender, long-fingered, and very clean hands, regarding them complacently.

"Be glad Bill didn't get a Stanley Steamer," said Betsy, "or dirt might not be the worst that can happen. My friend Lars has one, and the places on him that aren't dirty are blistered."

Ceil laughed. "Has he still got both his eyebrows?"

"Well, he has now, since the right one grew back." She sat down beside Charlotte and resumed stitching. Betsy was working on a counted cross-stitch pattern worked on black fabric. It had pale green cats' eyes and the merest hint of paws. In crooked lettering down one side it said, *Sure Dark in Here, Isn't It?* Betsy was adding whiskers in back stitching, counting carefully to make sure they were placed properly.

"Where are you going to hang that?" asked Charlotte.

"Six, seven, eight—in my bathroom," replied Betsy. "The thread glows in the dark."

"Hang it next to the light switch," advised Charlotte. "I'd hate to try to find the . . . er, by the light that thing will give off."

Ceil giggled.

"I don't see Mildred," said Betsy. "Perhaps I should have volunteered to bring the quilt, too."

Charlotte said, "But it wouldn't be any good unless you could sell raffle tickets for it, and Mildred won't let anyone take custody of that roll of tickets or the money jar. That's a job she's very jealous of."

"Speak of the devil," said Ceil, and they looked up to see Mildred, driving a large old Chrysler, pull up beside the booth. She put her car in park, got out, and opened the passenger door. The big heap of quilt engulfed her as she tried to get it out without letting it touch the ground. Betsy and Charlotte hurried to help. The frame was in the backseat, and Betsy wondered how she'd gotten it in there; even with their help, it was a struggle to get it out again. But Mildred again proved stronger than she looked, and was experienced in handling the thing. Under her crisp directions, she and Charlotte set it up in the booth and helped Mildred drape the quilt over it.

Mildred said, "Thank you, Betsy. Now, I'll be right back," and went to park. When she came back, she had the money jar and the big roll of raffle tickets in her arms. Evidently Mildred had hidden them in the trunk.

About twenty minutes later, Ceil said, "Look, here comes Adam at last." Betsy hadn't noticed him drive in, but he was walking from behind the Capitol building, where they—and apparently Adam—had parked.

"What kept you?" demanded Ceil.

"There's an accident in the tunnel," said Adam, meaning a long, curved underpass on 94 in Minneapolis. "It's down to one very slow lane in the eastbound side." He held up a large paper sack. "Plus I stopped for sandwiches." He handed them around.

He'd barely finished his tuna on a whole wheat bun before the first antique car came up, a 1909 Cadillac. Betsy grabbed the board Adam quickly held out, and Charlotte again helped Betsy clock the cars in.

As before, the 1902 Oldsmobile was last—except for Charlotte and Bill's Maxwell.

"Did you see Number Twenty, a rust-brown Maxwell, along the road?" Charlotte asked the driver of the Olds.

"No, when I left Bill was still trying to get it started. And it never caught up with me." Betsy thanked him and waved him through.

"Well, this is a fine thing!" grumbled Charlotte. "I wonder where he broke down?" She went to talk to Adam, Betsy trailing behind her.

"He was having trouble with it, remember?" she said.

"Yes, but he just waved me off when I went to ask him if he wanted to cancel his return trip," replied Adam. "And it seemed to be running only as ragged as it was when he came into Excelsior."

"I know, I know. That darned machine—and he *would* insist on driving it even though he has other cars that don't misbehave!"

Betsy turned to Ceil and Adam. "Didn't you mention a truck that follows the route looking for breakdowns?"

"No follow-up truck for this run," said Adam.

"Anyway," Ceil said, "doesn't Bill have a cell phone?"

"Yes, he does," said Charlotte, frowning. She went to her old-fashioned carpetbag and rummaged in it for her own very modern cell phone. She turned it on and punched in some numbers.

"That's funny," she said a minute later, the frown a little deeper. "He's not answering."

"Maybe he's gone to find someone to help get his car started," said Betsy.

"Wouldn't matter," Charlotte replied. "He carries that thing with him in his pocket." She dialed the number again, listened awhile, and shut her phone off.

Betsy turned to Adam. "Where is that other woman who was with you in the booth in Excelsior?"

"Nancy's gone home, she could only volunteer this morning. Why?"

"I was thinking, if she's still in Excelsior, we could ask her to follow the route the antique cars took, and see if she can find Bill along the way. But I guess not."

"Still," said Adam, "the next step is to go looking along the route. I'm in charge, I'll go." He reached for a map of the route and left the booth.

Ceil called after him, "Let us know right away when you find him!" She turned to Charlotte. "Can you drive the trailer out to pick him up, or are we going to have to find you a driver?"

Charlotte said, "I don't like to, but I can drive it. What I don't understand is why he didn't call me when he broke down, to tell me what was happening, and where he was. I hope he made it most of the way, then Adam won't have so far to drive."

Charlotte seemed more annoyed than angry at this development, but when she came back to sit with her needlework, she didn't pull the needle out to begin. Betsy was moved to ask, "Are you all right?"

"Yes, of course," said Charlotte. After a bit she said, "Only I can't understand why he didn't call."

"Perhaps the battery in his phone has run down," suggested Betsy.

"Yes, that could be the problem. He's forgotten in the past to shut it off after he's used it." She did pick up her needle then, and put a few stitches in the honeybee's wing then said, as if continuing a conversation she'd been having internally, "Well, it just isn't fair!"

"What isn't fair?"

"What?" said Charlotte, staring at Betsy.

"You said it just isn't fair," said Betsy. "What isn't fair?"

"Oh—nothing. I mean, I didn't mean to say it out loud. I'm just a little upset, that's all. I mean, it isn't like Bill to just sit in his broken-down car, when he has a perfectly good cell phone. And even if you're right, and the battery's gone dead, there's always a gas station or even a house he can go to and use their phone. He promised to be better about this sort of thing, not to leave me sitting and worrying. That's why we got the phones, after all."

"Husbands can be the limit, can't they?"

"Beyond the limit." Then Charlotte smoothed the frown from her forehead with what seemed deliberation and said, "But I don't believe he's neglecting me on purpose. I'm sure as anything that he's underneath the hood trying to fix the engine, and has gotten so involved he's forgotten all about the time and that I'm sitting here, tired and dusty and wanting to go home."

Betsy, remembering how he didn't even come out from under to say goodbye back in Excelsior, said, "Whereas we stitchers never get so involved with our needlework that we forget to fix dinner or pick the kids up after soccer or take the cat to the vet."

The frown that had reclenched Charlotte's face relaxed again, and her eyes twinkled. "Well . . . yes," she admitted. "And Bill has been a lot better lately. When he announced his retirement two years ago, I thought we could travel or take up a hobby we'd both be interested in or at least spend more time together. But he didn't quite give up control at the office, and when he wasn't there, he was working on his car collection. We had a couple of serious fights, and at last I went to a therapist—alone, because Bill wouldn't go, of course—but Dr. Halpern helped me start some serious conversations with Bill, and things have been better lately."

"How many cars does Bill have?" asked Betsy.

"Six, all Maxwells but one. I thought it would be fun, riding down the road in these old cars, going to meets and all. And it is. But there are the hours Bill spends in the shed restoring them, and the hours on the Internet talking with other car nuts, and the days he spends traveling all over the country buying parts."

"He should take you along—I thought you said you wanted to travel."

"But he finds these parts in some very out-of-the-way places, never Barbados or San Francisco or London. And since I don't know what the parts are for, I can't help him shop for them, so I have to go off by myself to whatever museum there is or shop for antique clothing. Sometimes I just go to a movie, which I could do just as well at home." Her voice had become so querulous that she became aware of it, so she shut up and with a sigh tucked her needle into the margin of the fabric. "Oh, I admit it's not all his fault. The therapist advised me to change my own ways a bit, too. And when I did, Bill saw I was serious. He said if I was willing to change, then he started to think maybe he could change a little, too. We've been reconnecting—that's my therapist's term, reconnecting—and things have gotten much better. It will take a while to undo old habits, as we've seen today, but Rome wasn't torn down in a day either, I suppose."

"No," agreed Betsy with a smile.

People came up with questions or to pick up a brochure, but in few enough numbers that Ceil could handle most of them. People were far more interested in talking with the owners of the cars than the people sitting in the booth. They went from car to car with their questions, taking lots of photographs. Now and again there was the sound of an old-fashioned horn going *Ahooooo-ga!*—always accompanied by titters and giggles and a little rush of people heading for the source of the sound, a beautiful 1911 Marmon.

It was nearly an hour later that Ceil's cell phone began to play "Für Elise" and she pulled it from a pocket. "St. Paul," she said into it. "Yes?" She glanced at Charlotte. "Oh. Oh, my," she said and quickly turned her back, going as far away as she could without leaving the booth.

Charlotte and Betsy looked at one another, Betsy with concern, Charlotte with the beginnings of fright. Betsy put a hand on Charlotte's.

"I'm sure it's nothing too serious," said Mildred. "He probably ran off the road, broke an axle or something." That she offered this disaster as "nothing too serious" showed how terribly bad she was thinking it might be, too.

Charlotte began putting her stitchery away, making a fuss about it, keeping herself busy while they waited.

"Char?" said Ceil a few minutes later, and Charlotte turned in her chair. Ceil was looking helpless, as if she couldn't think where to begin.

"What is it, tell me what's wrong!" demanded Charlotte.

"It's Bill. Oh, sweetie, I'm so very sorry—" She sobbed twice, but then took hold of herself and said rapidly, "He's dead, Charlotte. When Adam got there, the fire department was already there, the car was on fire, and Bill was underneath it. That's all they know right now."

Charlotte stared speechless at Ceil. She turned wide, horrified eyes on Betsy, then on Mildred. "No," she said very quietly, and fainted.

Six

A dam Smith waited in sick silence as the methodical examination of the scene went on. If someone asked him to list the places on earth he wanted to be, this would be at the bottom or near it. But he couldn't leave. He'd been asked by a police officer to stay. The man had been polite, putting it in the form of a request, but Adam felt it would be put in stronger terms if he refused.

Besides, if he did leave, he'd have to go back to St. Paul, where Charlotte Birmingham waited. And on that list of places to be, going to talk to Charlotte was probably tied for whatever near-bottom place staying here occupied.

Sooner or later they'd let him go, but he had no idea what he could possibly say to Charlotte about what he'd found while driving up County Highway 5.

It was a charming enough section of Minnetonka, a gently hilly area with small, neat cottages on broad lots lining the two-lane road. Just here, there was a white gravel lay-by across the road from a big church, just up from a cemetery. A horribly appropriate location, because here in the lay-by he had found firemen and their truck, and an ambulance, and several squad cars.

And the Maxwell, blackened and blistered.

And Bill, poor dead Bill, lying on the gravel where he'd been dragged out from under the car.

They hadn't covered Bill's body, and Adam's eyes kept wandering to it, sickening him all over again. Medics were standing around him, but in the idle poses that said they had nothing to do, that Bill was far, far beyond anything they could do.

Adam lifted his eyes a little, to watch a uniformed policeman talking to one of the medics and taking notes as he listened to a reply.

The policeman gestured at Bill's body, drawing Adam's attention back to it, so he quickly turned his head to look at Bill's car. There wasn't a crumpled fender, a smashed headlight, even a dent, so there hadn't been an accident. The Maxwell hadn't run into anything, or been run into, or rolled over. It had been driven into this lay-by, which was perhaps an alternate parking lot for the church, now that Adam thought about it. The Maxwell was at the back of the graveled area, shaded by trees. Bill had probably pulled in here when the engine trouble that had plagued him all day got so bad he couldn't continue the run. And Bill had slid under it to check something—no, fix something, because there were tools half visible in the big puddle of dirty water that surrounded the car. The firemen had made that puddle, putting out the fire that had started while Bill was under it.

The car must have exploded into flame, because if it had been just an ordinary fire, Bill would have rolled out from under. And he hadn't, he'd still been under it when the firemen arrived.

Interesting how Bill's upper legs in their white flannel trousers were only a trifle smoky, his lower ones were untouched, and his brown leather shoes were unmarked by anything but a little dust. While the rest of him was so bad . . . *Why can't they cover him decently?* Adam thought again, yanking his eyes away to watch a policewoman on the other end of the lay-by tying yellow plastic ribbon to a tree, pulling a length from a large roll, then walking to a wooden lamppost out near the road, letting the tape unreel on her wrist. Adam frowned at that, then looked at Bill's Maxwell again. *Crime scene tape? Why?* Despite himself, his attention wandered back to Bill, but ricocheted instantly to the burned-out Maxwell.

There was the crime. What had happened to the car was a sorry crime. Despite its lack of dents, the old machine was history, its metal chassis blistered and blackened, the seats and dash and steering wheel all gone into a heap of ash and metal. Leaves on the branches that overhung the car—it was back here because Bill had sought shade, obviously—were withered or burned away, indicating this had been a serious fire. A great fire could be built from an antique car's interior of varnished wood, leather, and straw stuffing, Adam knew.

The fire truck's engine started up. Adam watched it, wondering what kind of horsepower it must pack. Heck of a sound to that engine. The truck was a pumper, the kind with a blocky back end, parked at an oblique angle beyond the Maxwell. The last few yards of hose were being neatly stowed into the back by two volunteer firemen who had taken off their hats in the heat.

Beyond the fire truck, two squad cars from the Minnetonka Police Department were side by side, and another squad from the Sheriff's Department beside them, with a severely plain official automobile behind them. An ambulance-sized van with HENNEPIN COUNTY MEDICAL EXAMINER painted on its door and rear end had parked between the body and the road, blocking the view of passersby. Cars on the road slowed to see what the fuss was about, naturally, but were being encouraged to move along by a cop who had put on soft white gloves to make his hands more visible. The last vehicle in the lay-by was Adam's, a midnight blue sedan. He was standing outside it, leaning against the door because he was tired of standing. He considered opening his car door and sitting down, but decided against it.

Two men in civilian dark slacks and shirts were examining the Maxwell. One was standing on the far-side running board, getting black streaks on his white shirt; the other, in a light blue shirt and dark tie, gesturing while he asked a question. He then turned to gesture at a young woman in khaki slacks and green T-shirt who was taking photographs of the back end of the car. As Adam watched, the woman climbed up on the near running board, leaning forward to take a photograph and garner her own sooty streaks, which she brushed at with a weary, used-to-it sigh.

Meanwhile, one of the men went to stoop for a closer look at the nightmare ruin of Bill, to reach out and touch—Adam turned away again.

After a minute a voice said, "Mr. Smith?"

"Yes?" asked Adam, straightening.

"I'm Dr. Phillip Pascuzzi, with the Medical Examiner's Office. May I ask you a few questions?" The man wore a white shirt and had a notebook in one hand.

"Certainly."

"Was Mr. Birmingham a friend or relation?"

"He was a member of the Minnesota Antique Car Club, of which I am President. And he was a friend."

Writing, "And you're quite sure the body over there is, in fact, Mr. Birmingham?"

"Yes." Adam swallowed. Having to go look closely at what had been Bill Birmingham was the worst thing he'd had to do in his entire life.

"The body is badly burned, especially around the upper body. What made you sure?"

"Well, he's Bill's size, and he's wearing what Bill was wearing today, and the car is Bill's. Nobody else driving in the Run is missing. I don't see who else it could be."

"Did you talk to Mr. Birmingham today?"

"Yes, briefly."

"Where and when was this?"

"In Excelsior, this morning. He was having trouble with the car, and I said something about it, and he agreed it was running rough. As soon as he got parked along the curb, he opened the hood and began working on it. Didn't quit until it was time to start back for St. Paul. He was the last to leave because his car didn't want to start. After he left, we tore down in Excelsior and went to St. Paul to greet the cars as they came back and help them set up an exhibit over there. And when Bill didn't turn up in St. Paul, I started driving back, following the route, looking for where he broke down."

"I take it you didn't follow the route the old cars took when you went to St. Paul."

"No, we went out 7 and caught the freeway at 494."

"So Mr. Birmingham was the last to leave Excelsior on this route. Everyone else was either ahead of him or went by another way."

"Yes, that's right." The Antique Car Club had notified law enforcement agencies of the twisting route the antique cars would follow so they could come out and direct traffic or practice a little crowd control or at least be aware if there was a report of trouble involving an antique car, their choice.

"You didn't suggest that perhaps he shouldn't make the return trip?"

"No, our members usually have a pretty good idea whether or not their cars are able to continue a run. You have to realize, these cars are valuable, so most drivers are very reluctant to push a car even up to its limits. And Bill was proud of his Maxwells. I don't think he'd get stupid about making a trip when a car wasn't up to it. He tinkered with this one, and got it started and set off, so we assumed he'd be okay."

"There's a cell phone on the body. Why do you suppose he didn't call for help when he broke down?"

"We were wondering why we hadn't heard from him when he didn't come in. Probably he got to working on it and time got away from him."

"Is that also normal behavior for him?"

"Absolutely. It's a common trait among car collectors. Bill's wife complained more than once how he'd forget to come in to supper when he was out working on his cars. It's very likely the trouble he was having today got bad enough to make him pull in here, where he tried to fix it or at least get the car able to finish the run. Then he got all wrapped up in what he was doing, and somewhere in there . . . this happened."

"Have you any idea what kind of trouble he was having with the car?"

"The engine was running ragged when he drove up to the booth in Excelsior. I didn't ask him what he thought it was, I was busy. He went right to work on it, but he still had a hard time getting it started again. He finally did, though he was the last car to leave for the trip back. His wife said she was getting an upset stomach from riding in it, and she opted not to ride back with him. She rode over to St. Paul with one of my volunteers and is in St. Paul now. I don't look forward to going back there and trying to talk to her about this. We've never lost a driver during a run before."

"Not even in an accident?"

"No, never. We had a close call with a rollover, and a few other injuries—sprained wrists from hand cranking, for example, and Dick Pellow's Overland caught fire a few years ago, but he's fine. What I don't understand is, why didn't Bill get out from under when she caught on fire? Unless it blew up—I mean like parts scattered to hell and gone—which it didn't, he should've been able to at least roll away, I'd've thought."

"I'm inclined to agree with you, Mr. Smith. And there are some other oddities about this situation."

"Like what?"

"I don't want to start speculating, not without further investigation. We are going to impound the car and there will be an autopsy on Mr. Birmingham. Perhaps you could inform Mrs. Birmingham? She can contact me at my office for further information. Do you have her phone number? I'll want to get in touch with her."

Adam read it to him off the card. Dr. Pascuzzi gave him a card with his name, the notation that he was Hennepin County's Assistant Medical Examiner, and a couple of phone and fax numbers.

"Thank you," said Adam. "Am I free to go now?"

"Yes, sir, and thank you for your cooperation."

Charlotte recovered from her faint puzzled at what had caused it, so Ceil had to tell her all over again that Bill was dead. She shrieked loudly, causing heads all over the area to turn toward her, then clapped both hands over her mouth to keep from shrieking some more. Her eyes were wide and terrified.

Betsy sat down on the blacktop beside her and pulled her head onto her shoulder. "There, there," she murmured as Charlotte began to weep noisily.

"Oh, my God," mourned Charlotte between sobs. "Oh, my God, my poor Bill! Oh, Broward will be just devastated, he and Bill worked so closely together! Oh, all my children, how can I bear to tell my children? Oh, I can't bear this!"

It was a minute or two before she felt the discomfort of her twisted position and began to pull back from it. Betsy helped her sit up straight, and took the proffered handkerchief from Mildred so Charlotte could mop her face. Her eyes were puffy and bewildered.

"Did . . . did you say it was a fire?" she asked Ceil. "He caught on *fire?*"

"Yes," nodded Ceil. "Adam said there was a fire engine there putting it out."

"A fire," repeated Charlotte, frowning. "Then why didn't he just pull over and jump out?"

"I don't know," said Betsy.

"Perhaps he meant there was an accident, and it caught fire after," said Mildred.

"Oh, yes, that must be it," said Charlotte. "Maybe a tire blew out, and he ran off the road and into a tree or telephone pole. Or did someone run into him? People do that, you know, they see the funny-looking car and steer right for it. Was there another car involved?"

Ceil said, "Adam didn't mention that."

"That stupid Maxwell! It was misbehaving all the way out there, he should never have tried to drive back. If it wasn't a tire, then I suppose something went wrong with the steering or brakes, and he ran into a ditch. And the car caught on fire, and Bill was hurt, unconscious . . . Yes, that must be it, don't you think?" She looked around at the other women for confirmation, as if figuring out what had happened would make it less dreadful.

But realization still clouded her eyes, and she began to weep again, saying over and over, "No, no, no, it's too awful, too awful."

A crowd had gathered, drawn by Charlotte's distress. Among them were members of the Antique Car Club. Ceil caught the eye of the largest of them, and semaphored a message with her eyebrows. He began to move between the onlookers and the booth, facing outward. "Drivers, go back to your cars!" he ordered in a big, loud voice. "We've still got a crowd here with questions, cameras, and sticky fingers, so move it, move it!" He raised his hands in a backing motion. "As for the rest of you, this isn't any of your business. Please give this woman a little privacy."

The crowd broke up, and the big man leaned over the booth's counter to say to Charlotte, "I just heard. I can't tell you how sorry I am, Char. Bill was a good man, he'll be missed."

"Oh, Marcus, what am I going to *do*?" wept Charlotte.

"You relax, we'll take care of whatever needs taking care of," promised Marcus. "Do you need someone to drive you home?"

"I—I suppose so. I don't know, I can't think!"

"Never mind, you just sit here awhile, until you calm down and this show is over. I'll stay around until you decide what you want." The man strode over to a Cadillac touring car of immense size and, when he turned and saw Betsy watching him, gave a wave and a gesture of support.

"How long should I stay?" asked Charlotte of no one in particular. "Adam's been gone so long, why hasn't he come back? Why doesn't he call? Should I call him?" She seemed to be working herself into another fit of hysterics.

Betsy said, "Come on, Charlotte, let's go someplace cool and private." She helped Charlotte to her feet and said to Mildred and Ceil, "I'll sit with her in my car awhile." She repeated that to Marcus, who nodded understanding, then went on to the parking lot around the back of the capitol.

Betsy started her engine, and the Buick's inside quickly cooled. The purring of the engine was a soothing sound, and Charlotte began to regain control of herself. "I made a fool of myself back there," she murmured, using another Kleenex from the supply Betsy kept handing her from the box she always kept in her car.

"No you didn't," said Betsy firmly. "I'm sure this has been a terrible shock to you, and I think you're taking it very well."

Charlotte made a sound halfway toward a giggle. "If this is taking it well, I wonder what taking it badly might be."

"Oh, screaming and running in circles, tearing your clothing, and throwing dirt on top of your head."

"Oh, if only it were correct in our culture to do that, what a relief it would be!" sighed Charlotte. "I really yearn to scream and kick dents into the trailer that dreadful car came in, set fire to the shed he keeps the other cars in." She amended in a small voice, "*Kept* the other cars in. Oh, dear!"

"I shouldn't go setting fire to anything until I made sure the insurance was up to date," said Betsy in a mock-practical tone.

"Oh, no fear of that," grumbled Charlotte, blowing her nose again. Her tone moderated and she became reflective. "I remember when we were first married, Bill put me in charge of the checkbook, paying bills and such. When the baby came, I was a very nervous mother and I made several long-distance calls to my mother. This was back when long-distance charges were actually scary, not like today, and my mother lived in Oregon. And when the bill came, I couldn't pay it. When Bill saw the overdue notice we got from the phone company, he hit the ceiling. He said he didn't care if we lived on day-old bread and baloney, I was not to let a bill go unpaid ever again. And I never did. Of course, as Bill's company began to thrive, that became less of a problem." She smiled just a little. "He was a good provider. We were looking forward to a long, comfortable retirement."

"He wasn't retired, then?" asked Betsy.

"Not quite. He had turned over most of the day-to-day management to Broward—he's our oldest son—but went in to the office three mornings a week, just to keep an eye on things. People like Bill never really retire, I suppose. He was thinking of organizing a new company, one that would centralize the ordering of parts for Maxwells, and perhaps do some restoration work as well. He really liked working on those cars." She sighed and sniffed—then stirred herself to take a new tack. "Your husband, what does he think of you owning your own business?"

"I'm divorced," said Betsy. "I inherited the shop after the divorce. My sister founded it. And her husband was proud of her, though at first he didn't take her seriously. You know how men are, or how they used to be, anyway. He thought of it like a hobby, a way of keeping the little woman busy."

"Yes, I know," said Charlotte, with some feeling.

"Did you help your husband in his business?"

"I was in sales for several years at the start, until I got pregnant with Broward. I was pretty good at sales, and I liked it. But he wanted me to stay at home, and before I knew it, there I was with four children, and no time for anything outside the home. Not that I minded too terribly. Our children were a great pleasure always, reasonably good kids, very bright. Lisa won several scholarships and is a pediatrician in St. Louis. Tommy owns a car dealership in St. Paul, and David is working on his masters in education at the U. But after the youngest left home, I wanted to do something more, get a job, but Bill was too used to me being home. Do you have children?"

"No, it turned out I couldn't get pregnant."

"I'm sorry."

"It turned out I couldn't pick a good man to father them either, so it's just as well. Are you close to your children?"

"Oh, yes, of course. It's going to be hard on them, losing their father all of a sudden like this. Broward and Bill were especially close, working together like they did."

"What sort of company is it?"

"It's called Birmingham Metal Fabrication. We make doors, metal doors, for houses and apartments, garages, and businesses. We sell to builders mostly. Broward's been wanting to expand into window frames and maybe even siding. He's very ambitious."

"Perhaps you could get back into sales, working for your son."

"Perhaps." Charlotte let her head fall back on the headrest. "All that crying has given me a terrible headache."

Someone knocked on the window and Charlotte jumped. "What, what?"

she cried. "Oh, it's Adam!" She began to fumble with the door. "How do I roll the window down?" she demanded.

Betsy pushed a button on her side, and the window slid down about eight inches. Adam's anxious face peered in at them.

"Hello, Betsy," he said. "Charlotte, may I talk to you a minute?"

"Is something else wrong?"

"Well, I'm not sure."

"What do you mean, you're not sure? What's wrong, what's happened?"

Adam said uncomfortably, "Well, the medical examiner was there, he and the police looked at the scene, and they seem to think there's something funny about what happened. Here—" Adam handed her a business card. "This is the medical examiner's name and phone number. You can call him when you feel up to it, though he said he would be in touch anyway. He's going to do an autopsy, and they've impounded the Maxwell."

"Something funny?" echoed Charlotte. "What could that mean?"

"I have no idea, they wouldn't tell me what they're thinking."

"What could be funny about Bill's dying in his car?" Charlotte turned to look at Betsy. "What do you think?"

"I don't know," said Betsy, afraid to say the word that was big in all their minds: Murder.

Seven

Monday morning, Betsy was preparing an order of stitched items to be sent to Heidi, her finisher. A Christmas stocking done on needlepoint canvas, stiff with metallic threads and beads, needed to be washed, stretched and shaped, cut out, lined, and sewn to a heavy fabric so it would be a proper stocking. A highly detailed counted cross-stitch pattern of a Queen Anne house needed washing, stretching, and attachment to a stretcher before being matted and framed. There were five other items needing finishing, two to be made into pillows. Some needleworkers finished their own projects, but many turned to a professional. It was expensive, but gave a proper finish to a needlework project that its proud owner hoped would become an heirloom.

Last on the list of items to be finished was an original Irene Potter. Name of owner: Betsy Devonshire. Betsy had gone to the art fair on Sunday—and been disappointed to find the amazing Columbus Circle Blizzard piece Irene had brought half-shyly to Crewel World had been sold. However, there were three other pieces on display, and Betsy, wincing only slightly, had written a check for a piece called Walled Garden, a riot of color and stitches about sixteen by sixteen inches, done in brightly colored wool, silk, ribbon, cotton, and metallics on stiff congress cloth. There was a pond in the center, worked in irregular half-stitches of blue silk and silver metallic floss. A single orange stitch suggested a goldfish in its depths. A rustic wooden bridge crossed the pond, leading to a winding path among daisies, azaleas, daffodils, lilies, and many other varieties of flowers, some invented, done with no regard to season or proportion or perspective. In the upper background, the waving limbs of mighty trees threatened to crush or climb the wall, which was braced here and there by slender young poplars. Outside the wall a hurricane raged. Within was a hot, strangely lit, tense silence.

The work made Betsy feel she was looking into Irene's mind, or perhaps Irene's notion of the world. Whichever, it was a place both beautiful and frightening.

"Oh, my *God*, what is *that*?" demanded Godwin, reaching for the piece.

Betsy started to explain, then changed her mind. "What do you think?" she asked.

"It's wonderful, it's . . . what a garden must seem like to the plants. Who stitched this—no, who *designed* it?"

"It's another Irene Potter," said Betsy. "I bought it at the art fair."

Godwin tenderly fingered the stitching of the garden wall, done in shades of red, garnet, and brown in a herringbone stitch that looked like bricks laid in Tudor fashion. The formal wall formed an orderly base for the tree branches tossing in bullion and wildly irregular continental stitches. In front of the wall were stiffly formal blooming shrubs worked in—what? He looked closer. Fancy cross? No, a variety of half-buttonhole.

"I am humbled," he said sincerely. "This is totally amazing." He handed it back. "You're having it framed, I assume."

"Yes, but in something severe, I think. Narrow cream mat, thin black frame? Because the work is so hot and wild."

"Sounds good." Godwin looked around. "Where are you going to hang it?"

"Upstairs. This isn't a model. Irene says she can't turn these pieces into patterns."

"Bosh," retorted Godwin. "If she can stitch it, she or someone can make a pattern of it. They'd be difficult patterns, but not impossible ones. She just doesn't want to share. I don't blame her, I guess. Do you realize this confirms she's turning into an artist with a capital A?"

"Oh, yes. And so does she. You should have seen her at the fair, preening and talking with vast condescension to anyone who stopped to look at her work. But she's earned the right, her work is wonderful. She brought nine

pieces to the fair and sold all of them. Mr. Feldman is now taking her very seriously indeed; he was asking three or four thousand apiece."

"You paid how much?"

"Thirty-five hundred for this. I know that's a lot—"

"She should have given you a discount."

"No, she shouldn't. We've laughed too often at her expense. Besides, this is
really wonderful. I think it's worth the price. Plus, it's only going to increase in
value. Irene said the Walker Art Museum bought one, and a reporter from the
Strib wants to interview her. If this keeps up, a local employer is going to lose
the head of its shipping department very soon."

"Maybe I should bring them my résumé."

"Why would you do that?"

"Because I am going to need a job with benefits. Betsy, I talked with John
yesterday. He started shouting at me, right there in the restaurant—" Godwin
sobbed once, gulped it back, and continued, "And I got hysterical and ran out.
And . . . and he didn't come after me. He just let me *go*!"

"Oh, Goddy," sighed Betsy, putting an arm around his shoulder.

He suddenly twisted around to embrace her, soaking her shoulder with
hot tears. "Betsy, what am I to *do*? I don't know how I'm going to live without
our darling house, and having wonderful clothes and traveling, and him taking care of me . . ." His voice trailed away, and then he pushed himself away to
stare at Betsy aghast, his eyes still shining with tears. "Oh, my *God*! It's happened. Donny told me it would happen, and it *has*!"

"What's happened?" asked Betsy.

"The *Golden Handcuffs*! I don't miss *John*, I miss all the *things*! John got
me used to nice things, and now I'm upset because I'm losing the things, not
because I'm losing *John*!"

If Godwin hadn't been so sincere, Betsy would have laughed at him. As it
was, she couldn't withhold a smile. "Oh, Goddy," she sighed.

"What?" he said, and when she didn't answer at once, he demanded,
"What? Tell me!"

"Well . . . I'm afraid I always thought what you and John had was an
arrangement, not a relationship. Now I've only met John once, but he didn't
impress me as a very nice person. And I've never met anyone who seemed to
actually like John. So I guess—" She broke off, afraid she was getting into
dangerous waters. "Let's not go there."

"No, no," said Godwin, suddenly very serious, more serious than she'd ever
seen him. "Tell me."

"I don't know how to say it, or even whether I should say anything at all."

Godwin's eyes gleamed, though his expression remained serious. "I think
it's important that you try to tell me anyway."

"Well, I've always known gay people, and some were friends. But I've never met a gay person before who was as much like the old stereotype of the gay man as you are. I'd gotten to thinking no real gay person was like that, until you came along. So . . . well, I sometimes wonder if it's really you, either. I mean, I wonder if maybe I've never really met the real Godwin. I've wondered if this is a put-on, that you only pretend to be this person who is solely interested in clothes and parties and startling straight people. Now I like that fun and funny persona, and it's extremely valuable here in the shop. But is this surface Godwin . . . perhaps too frivolous to be real? I sometimes wonder what you're like when it's late at night and you're tired. Or what you might be like when the party comes to an end. I've never tried to dig into your personality, because I like the surface Godwin very much, and because that Goddy has been so useful to me. I wonder if that was wrong of me, because I think of you as a friend."

"And because maybe you were afraid that's the only me there is?" asked Godwin with a little smile.

"Not afraid, just wondering. You know me, I can't help wondering if things are as they seem. But I don't want you to feel you have to act serious just to make me think you're deep."

Godwin shrugged. "I suppose there is another me down inside somewhere, but he's not nearly as much fun as this upper me. Being the fun Goddy *is* fun. And it's taken me a long way. Being serious is . . . *serious*. And not much fun. See how my vocabulary suffers when I try to be serious?" He grinned. "So that's enough depth plumbing for today. Why didn't you buy the Columbus Circle Blizzard piece?"

"I couldn't, it was the first thing sold on Saturday." Betsy took Walled Garden back and held it in both hands. "But I like this one, too."

"Speaking of Saturday—" began Godwin, but was interrupted by the electronic *Bing!* that announced the door to the shop opening.

They looked up and saw a tall, very slender man standing just inside the door. He wore a lightweight gray suit, white shirt, and dark blue tie. He looked to be close to sixty, with thin silver hair, a bit of a stoop, and a diffident, thoughtful expression somewhat at odds with his stuck-out ears and humorous narrow jaw.

He glanced at Godwin, and took in his whole life story in a single intelligent look. His smile was friendly, with a hint of amusement in it.

Godwin, not sure whether to be affronted, stood fast.

Then the man looked at Betsy and the smile broadened into a sideways grin. "I bet you own this place," he said in a reedy voice too young for his years, gesturing around with a large, thin hand.

"That's right," said Betsy, wondering why alarms were sounding in her head. He certainly looked harmless enough. "Is there something I can help you with?"

"I certainly hope so." He came to the big desk, fumbling in an inside pocket for a slim wallet. Only it wasn't a wallet, it was an identification holder. Opened, it told Betsy he was Detective Morrie Steffans, Minnetonka Police. "I've been talking with Mrs. Charlotte Birmingham, and she says you can confirm that she was with you most of Saturday."

Alarms now sounding loud indeed, Betsy said, "Why do you need that confirmed?"

"Weren't you with her when she was told there were unanswered questions about the death of her husband and the burning of his car?" He put the wallet away and brought out a thick, palm-size notebook and a ballpoint pen.

"Yes—I take it some of the questions have been answered?"

He grinned. He had very light blue eyes and good teeth. "I take it she hasn't contacted you since she talked with me?"

"Why should she contact me?" asked Betsy. "Will you tell me what this is about?"

"Certainly, as soon as I get some basic information from you." He took Betsy's name, address, and phone number, then said, "It seems that the late Mr. Birmingham was shot in the chest before being put under that old car of his."

"Oh, my," murmured Betsy. "How terrible."

"Shot?" echoed Godwin. "You mean he was *murdered*?" He said accusingly to Betsy, "You didn't say there was anything funny about his death!"

"I didn't know there was, not for certain," replied Betsy. "None of us did." To Detective Steffans, she said, "So I take it the car didn't catch fire by itself, either."

"That's right, it was torched. A clumsy attempt was made to make it look like an accident, but this was clearly homicide."

"Or suicide," suggested Godwin.

Detective Steffans frowned at Godwin. "Why would someone crawl under a car, set it on fire, and then shoot himself?"

"Oh," said Godwin.

Detective Steffans said to Betsy, "You talked with Mr. Birmingham?"

"Yes, we exchanged a few words," replied Betsy. "I was a volunteer for the Antique Car Club, and they assigned me the task of logging the arrival of the antique cars in Excelsior. I wrote down their number and time of arrival, and instructed the drivers to report to the booth. Mr. Birmingham didn't say much, but I could see he was upset because his car was running badly, so I talked mostly with his wife, Charlotte. I did tell him reporters were here and might want to interview him, and he said he didn't want to answer questions."

"Had you met Mr. Birmingham before?"

"No."

"But you're sure it was him."

"Well, Charlotte seemed sure, and she was his wife."

Steffans chuckled and made a note. "You've never met Charlotte before, have you?"

"No. Are you going to tell me you don't think the woman was Mrs. Birmingham?"

"No, of course not. I'm at that stage of my investigation where I check everything. However, I am satisfied that it was Mr. and Mrs. Birmingham in the car. And I'm asking if it was during the halt in Excelsior that you and Mrs. Birmingham struck up an acquaintance."

Betsy nodded. "Yes, she came into my shop and spent a nice amount of money, and helped me log the drivers out of town when they left. Adam Smith asked her to assist me. She didn't want to ride in the Maxwell anymore, because the engine running so rough made it jiggle, which upset her stomach."

Steffans nodded. "Leaf springs."

"I beg your pardon?"

"Leaf springs, from before shock absorbers. Smooth out the bumps, but can't dampen the jiggle."

Betsy nodded. "All right. Anyway, Charlotte rode with me to St. Paul, and helped me again when we logged in the drivers on the return leg. Bill Birmingham's Maxwell didn't come in, and we didn't hear from him, so after a while Adam left to drive the route looking for him. Charlotte sat with me in the booth in St. Paul until Adam called Ceil—that's Lucille Ziegfield, a member of the club—and Ceil told Charlotte that Bill was dead. Charlotte was very upset, of course. I took her to my car—"

"Why?" interrupted Steffans.

"Because she was crying and people were staring. And we both were hot. She was wearing an old-fashioned dress and a big antique hat, so she was more uncomfortable than I was. So I took her to my car, started it, and turned on the air-conditioning, and we sat and talked until Adam Smith arrived to tell us that Bill's body was taken for an autopsy because the police weren't satisfied it was an accident. She left about half an hour later. Her son Broward came and picked her up."

"And you stayed with her that whole time?"

"Yes, she was in no state to be left alone. Broward came with his wife, who seems like a very nice woman. She kind of gathered poor Charlotte in and Broward drove them away."

"What was your impression of Charlotte Birmingham?"

"I liked her. She seemed to be a nice person. Interesting company. Good needleworker. She's really into this period thing; she not only wore the correct clothes for her ride, even the needlework pattern she was working was period."

"Did she seem to be upset or distressed in any way before you learned of Mr. Birmingham's death?"

"No. Well, she got worried when his car didn't come in. And annoyed that he didn't call on his cell phone to say where he was and what the problem was."

"You saw the two of them together, however briefly. What was her attitude toward her husband?"

"Affectionate. Indulgent."

"'Indulgent.' That's an interesting choice of word." Steffans's blue eyes searched her face, but not unkindly.

"Is it? Well, maybe it is. I was just thinking of how she said something to him that showed she understood he was feeling grumpy and was willing to do her bit to make him feel better."

"What was that?"

"When they first arrived in Excelsior, they stopped beside me. He was holding the steering wheel like grim death, jaw sort of set, because the car was misbehaving. And she said she was going to get out of the car and take off a layer of clothing— she was wearing an old-fashioned long white dress with a long coat over it—"

"A duster, I think they're called."

"Yes, that's right, a duster. Well, she looked very hot in it, so it wasn't surprising that she wanted to shed a few layers. He didn't say a word, but then she didn't get out, she said she'd ride with him up to the booth where Adam would tell them where to park. You know how people who have been married awhile can tell what the other one wants without him having to say a word? It was like that. He didn't want to talk to anyone, so she agreed she'd stay with him and talk to Adam and anyone else. Even though he didn't ask her to. She wasn't grumpy herself about it, but kind of cheerful. So I guess that's where 'indulgent' comes from."

Steffans smiled at her. "Very perceptive. You paint a very clear picture of what happened. Thank you." He consulted his notebook and asked, "You're sure that Charlotte was with you the entire time between her and her husband's arrival in Excelsior and the time you got word that he was dead?"

Betsy thought. "Well, there was that time between her and Bill's arrival and the time I clocked in the last car, turned in my clipboard, and went into my shop, where we introduced ourselves again. I didn't recognize her out of that hat and duster. But we saw Bill again after that. She went to tell him she wasn't riding back with him, and I went with her. He was working on the car, and was still unhappy. She took her duster, hat, and carpetbag out of the backseat of the car and we went to the booth. From then on she was with me."

"You saw Bill Birmingham leave Excelsior?"

"Yes, Charlotte was helping me log departure times. He was the last one to leave, because he had a lot of trouble getting the car started. He'd go to the driver's side and make some kind of adjustment then come back to the front end and yank the crank around, then make another adjustment, and crank again."

"Retarding the spark, I think it's called."

"Yes, that's right, advancing and retarding the spark. Not that it helped much. I'm surprised he didn't fall down from heat exhaustion, bundled up as he was."

"He wore a duster, too?"

"Oh, yes, and a hat—what's it called, pinch-brim? The soft kind where the crown is high in back and comes down over the bill in front. And goggles, great big old-fashioned goggles. About all you could see of his head was his mouth and chin and a bit of dark hair around the edges. He looked very authentic, and very warm. He'd open the hood and do something under there, then start in again, advancing the spark and cranking. Someone passing him on his way out of town yelled, 'You need to get a bigger hammer, Bill!' and laughed. Charlotte said that's the usual joke, get a bigger hammer."

"I thought it was 'Get a horse!' "

"No, that was what people who didn't drive back in the old days would say. Or so Charlotte told me. She knew a lot about the old cars and that time period. Her dress and hat weren't reproductions, but the real thing. She said she collected antique clothes."

"But she didn't try to help Mr. Birmingham fix the car."

"No, she said she deliberately didn't learn much about the engines and—and transmission bands, that's one term she used. She didn't want to ruin her hands working on the cars."

"All right, thank you. You've been very helpful."

After Steffans had left, Godwin said, "You didn't tell me you were mixed up in another murder."

"I didn't know until just now that I was. And anyway, you might be right about the suicide."

Godwin's eyebrows lifted in surprise. "You think so?"

Betsy nodded. "I was thinking about the insurance. You know, the suicide clause, the company won't pay off if you kill yourself?"

"Oh, of course," said Godwin. "So you're thinking he might have committed suicide and tried to make it look like an accident. Or how about he just shoots himself, and someone found his body and put it under the car and set the fire so it would look like an accident, so his widow could get the insurance."

Betsy said, "The problem with that is, who would do such a thing? And he was seen in St. Paul that morning, he was seen in Excelsior, and he was the last driver to leave on the return run. So it must have happened while he was on that return run. Except everyone involved in the run was either driving in it ahead of him or took the freeway to St. Paul after he left. So it would have to be a stranger who came along and found him—and why would a stranger do that?"

"Yeah, that would be the question, all right."

A customer came in at that point, and Godwin went to help her, leaving Betsy to think some more. She and Charlotte had waited quite a while in St. Paul for Adam and the others to arrive. Could one of them have gone after Bill? Or could someone ahead of Bill in the run have pulled into that lay-by and waited for Bill to come along?

It looked as if the only person with a solid alibi was Charlotte. Interesting.

Eight

❖

At two, the Monday Bunch gathered. There were five members present, which surprised Martha. "I guess they haven't been watching the news," she said. Normally all twelve members turned out when there was a crime to discuss.

"Why, what did we miss?" asked Phil Galvin, retired railroad engineer. He was short and gray, with a round face and eyes, small, work-thickened hands, and a loud, rough voice. He was working on a counted cross-stitch pattern of Native Americans in war paint riding bareback alongside an old steam locomotive.

Martha explained, "During that antique car race on Saturday, a car caught on fire in Minnetonka, killed the driver. His name was William Birmingham."

Phil nodded. "Birmingham. Yeah, I heard about that. Too bad they ain't makin' any more of those old cars."

Betsy frowned at Phil. Though the old man prided himself on his tough-guy attitude, she felt this was going too far.

Martha said, "Well, it turns out the driver was shot, not burned to death. It's a murder case. The police came and talked to Betsy, because she was the alibi for the man's wife. The wife was with Betsy all the time between when the man left here and when he was found dead."

Phil exclaimed, "No! I didn't hear about that!" He grimaced and mumbled, "Well, that makes a difference, I guess."

Martha said, surprised, "Betsy, you were on the news?"

Betsy smiled. "No, that part was spread locally." She looked at Godwin, who had the grace to blush.

Alice said, "So what do you think, Betsy? Who would shoot Bill Birmingham?"

Betsy answered with a question. "Did you know him?"

"Not personally, but I know about him. He grew up over in Wildwood, so there are probably locals who do." Wildwood was one of those Hennepin County "cities" on Lake Minnetonka that was really barely a village. It was only seven miles from Excelsior.

"I'm from Wildwood," said Phil. "I knew the whole family. In fact, I went to school with his older brother."

"What were they like?" asked Betsy.

Phil began emphatically, "Their father was the biggest—uh-ah!" He skidded to a halt, recalling who his audience was. "That is, he was one of those men thinks he was born to be boss. Couldn't stand to be disagreed with. Every kid in town, including his own, was scared of him. But both his sons grew up to be a lot like him. The older one got a double dose of it. He thought he was smarter than his teachers or anyone else who tried to teach him anything. Dropped out of high school, got fired from six jobs in seven months. He tried to kill a man he thought was after his wife, got sent to Stillwater, where he wound up knifed to death by a fellow inmate. He was twenty-six when it happened, and left a widow with a baby girl.

"Now Bill, he was different. He was a hard worker like his dad, but he was smart, and he didn't have a bad temper like his brother. He graduated from Cal Tech, and soon after invented an improved metal-stamping machine. He started a business stamping out all kinds of small metal parts, and eventually settled down to make metal doors. But he was also like his dad in that once he figured out how to do something, then that was the best way to do it, and the only way it could be done. His oldest son majored in engineering with a minor in business, but when the boy came back to go into business with his dad, the old man wouldn't listen to any of his ideas. So Broward went off to another company, bigger than his father's, and became a vice president in charge of production."

Betsy said, "But Charlotte told me Broward was working for his father, and was at the point of taking over Bill's company, since Bill was about to retire."

Phil nodded. "Yes, about two years ago, Bill's doctor warned him for the fourth or fifth time to retire or die in harness, and this time Bill believed him. He asked Bro to please come and take over. And Bro did. Quit his job and came home. Only Bill couldn't let go; he'd go to the office and make some decisions without consulting Bro—or even undo some of what Bro was doing. Drove Bro nuts, not least because Bro is a chip off the old block, and doesn't take kindly to having his decisions trifled with." Phil picked up his Wild West cross-stitch piece. "It'll be interesting now to see if Bro really does have some better ideas."

Alice asked in her blunt way, "So what do you think, Betsy—Broward Birmingham murdered his father?"

Betsy said, "I don't know. Phil, does Broward share his father's interest in antique cars?"

Phil shook his head. "All he'll be interested in is how much they'll bring at auction. He knows something about them, the whole family does, but he's not interested in owning one. Charlotte knows a lot because she believes in sharing her husband's interests, plus she likes dressing up in those old-fashioned clothes, but she's strictly a passenger. Her offspring would likely be more interested if Bill had let them drive once in a while, or shared the restoration work instead of only letting them hand him the tools, but as it is, the cars will probably be sold."

"What are they worth, I wonder?" said Alice.

"I understand the Maxwells were a very popular car, and a lot of them are still around," said Betsy. "So not as much as something rarer. Still, Charlotte said there are six of them, so that's got to amount to money. I suppose they're from different years. I wonder when they went out of business."

"They didn't," said Phil. "Walter P. Chrysler bought the company in 1923 and didn't change the name until 1926."

"Oh," said Martha, amused, "then the mayor's cute PT Cruiser is really a . . . Maxwell?" They all laughed.

Except Kate. "What's so funny?" asked Kate, the youngest member.

"Rochester used to drive Jack Benny around in an old Maxwell," chortled Godwin. "Mel Blanc had all kinds of fun making the noises of that car on a radio show. Mr. Mayor will be pleased to hear that, I *don't* think!"

"Who's Jack Benny?"

After an initial astonished pause, everyone took turns talking about Jack Benny, his awful violin playing, his comic miserliness, his futile aggravation, but it was Godwin who got to imitate Mr. Benny's most famous bit, when the robber stuck out a gun and gave him the traditional choice: "Your money or your life!" And Godwin put one hand on his cheek and fell silent while the giggles grew and grew, finally blurting, "I'm thinking, I'm thinking!"

Kate, laughing, said, "That'd be even funnier if Joe Mickels were driving one!" Joe's authentic miserliness was well known.

"Well, he does own an antique car," said Betsy.

"Is it a Maxwell?" asked Godwin, prepared to laugh.

"No, it's a . . ." Betsy thought. "A McIntyre."

Godwin said in a hurt voice, "Betsy, you've taken to keeping things from me."

"I'd forgotten all about it," said Betsy, and she related the tale of Adam Smith and Joe Mickels maneuvering around one another over the possible sale of Joe's McIntyre. "Adam collects rare cars, and this is very rare."

"Must be," said Phil. "I never heard of that brand. It'll be interesting to see who skins who in that deal."

Forty minutes later, the Bunch started picking up and putting away. The door went *Bing!* and everyone turned to see Charlotte Birmingham in the doorway, her sewing bag in her hand and a shy look on her face. She was dressed in darkness, black shoes, dark stockings, a severely plain black dress. There were even dark shadows under her eyes.

Betsy stood. "Hello, Mrs. Birmingham," she said. "Is there something I can do for you?"

"It looks as if your meeting is breaking up," replied Charlotte, coming toward the table. "I was hoping to join you." She looked the very opposite of the friendly woman in white Betsy had met on Saturday, more ravaged than the shocked and bewildered woman who had sat in her car later that same day.

"I'm afraid you're a little late," said Betsy, shaking herself out of her stare. "We meet at two, and it's nearly three-thirty."

"Oh, I thought you met at three," said Charlotte. "How stupid of me not to have phoned to check that!"

"Well, since you drove all that distance, why don't you stay at least for a little while," said Betsy. "Perhaps Godwin can sit with you for a while."

"I don't have to leave right now," said Phil, who was retired.

"Me, either," said Alice, sitting back down.

The other women left—reluctantly, because they were going to miss something to gossip about. Charlotte got out a counted cross-stitch pattern of her son's name done in an alphabet by Lois Winston. It had little engineer's tools worked into the letters: a compass, a T square, a level. Betsy remembered seeing the pattern in *The Cross Stitcher* magazine.

"It's for Broward's office door," said Charlotte.

While Charlotte talked quietly with Godwin, Phil, and Alice, Betsy began the task of pulling the wool needed for a needlepoint canvas a woman had called to say she wanted after all. The canvas was a Constance Coleman rendition of a Scottish terrier looking out a big window at a winter scene that included a stag. Betsy enjoyed the task of finding just the right colors and textures to suit the painting—Very Velvet for the deer, Wisper for the terrier, shades of maroon wool for the chintz curtains. She considered the problem of the windowsill. Something vaguely shiny, maybe, to echo the lacquer finish of the paint?

Bing! went the front door, and Betsy looked around to see Phil and Alice heading up the street. She looked over and saw Charlotte bent over her needle-work and Godwin signalling Betsy by raising and lowering his eyebrows.

"Goddy," said Betsy obediently, "could you come look at this? I can't decide what would do for the woodwork, and we need something creative for the snow. You know how Mrs. Hampton is." And in fact, she would complain if the fibers weren't clever enough.

"Certainly," said Godwin just as if he hadn't been desperate for her to summon him. He came over and, under cover of looking at the canvas, murmured, "She wants to talk to you about something. She keeps looking around for you and sighing."

"All right. But do finish getting this ready. Mrs. Hampton will be by to pick it up soon."

"All right."

Betsy went to sit down across from Charlotte. "I hope you aren't finding all the terrible details of your husband's death too much for you," she said.

"No, I'm lucky to have my children all rallying around to help," Charlotte said. "Lisa has been a great comfort to me, and Broward has taken over most of the work. All I do is sign where he tells me to sign, and try to decide where we are going to ask contributions to be sent in lieu of flowers." She smiled sadly. "But still I feel all off balance, like half of me is gone."

"That's what happens when a good marriage ends, I'm told," said Betsy. "It will pass, and you'll have some wonderful memories."

"So my children tell me. The sad part is, we were building some new wonderful memories, going to a much better place in our marriage, but we never got a chance to finish the journey." She bowed her head. "I am *so angry* about that! This should be a time of mourning, and instead I am angry. And I am angry about being made angry." Her upside-down smile reappeared. "And isn't that ridiculous? Being angry because I've been left angry."

"I'm so sorry," said Betsy, not knowing what else to say.

"But I didn't come here to talk about my sorrows. In fact, I was looking for a little time away from all that, and here I sit talking and talking about it. But I do want to thank you for taking me under your wing on Saturday. As it turned out, it was more than kind. The police were looking rather sideways at me until they found out you were with me all through the . . . important hours."

"I'm glad I could be of service," said Betsy. "It was shocking to hear that your husband was killed. I remember how angry I was when my sister was murdered, too, so your anger is very understandable to me."

Charlotte put down her needlework to confide, "The worst part is learning that someone hated Bill so much he felt the only way to handle it was to kill him. I know Bill could be difficult, but lots of people are difficult. *I'm* difficult at times. That's no reason to kill! I can't figure out what Bill might have done to make someone hate him enough to shoot him. It makes me feel as if my whole world is constructed of very thin boards over a very deep hole."

"There is no need for you to feel like that. In fact, it's just as well you don't know why. If you knew why, perhaps the murderer would come after you."

Charlotte stared at Betsy. "Are you trying to frighten me?"

"No, of course not!" said Betsy hastily. "On the contrary! The fact that you can't think of anyone angry enough at Bill to shoot him means it doesn't involve you at all. It's probably about his work, or something from his past."

"Not his work, not his work," protested Charlotte.

"Why not?"

"Because that might involve my son Broward. And he can't have anything to do with this, he just can't."

"All right," said Betsy, deciding Charlotte was not in any condition to seriously consider who might have done this terrible deed, if she was willing to let desire overwhelm fact. "I'm sorry you missed the Monday Bunch. Perhaps you can come again next Monday? I'd love to have you join us." Betsy stood. She had a lot of work to do.

"Wait a minute," said Charlotte, gesturing at her to sit down again. "Betsy, is it true that you have a talent for solving crimes?"

Obediently, Betsy sat. "Yes. But you don't want me to look into this."

"I don't?"

"No, because you are already afraid of what might be found out."

"No, I'm not." But Charlotte's face was afraid—and suddenly she seemed to realize that, and smiled. "Well, perhaps I am, a little. I suppose it can't be helped that the police will find out things that are better hidden. That's why I'm here, really. When the police find things out, it gets into the newspapers. But you can find things out and maybe only tell the police things that will lead to the murderer."

"My looking into this case won't stop the police looking as well. And anyway, what if it turns out the murderer is someone you don't want found out?"

Charlotte said very firmly, "I am perfectly sure that won't happen."

Godwin, who had been lurking with intent to eavesdrop, could no longer resist. "There are some people in prison right now who were perfectly sure an amateur sleuth couldn't possibly figure out what they'd done."

Charlotte looked around indignantly, but Godwin smiled and said gently, "I think that if you have a secret you don't want revealed, whether about yourself or someone else, you should either tell her right now what it is, or change your mind about asking her to look into things. She will find it out."

"Yes, but it won't become part of an official file, or turn up in the newspaper." She looked at Betsy. "Please, please help me. Help preserve the reputation of my family."

"Is there something bad about your family the police can find out about?"

"No!" said Charlotte, too sharply. Then, "Well, yes. Do I have to tell you what it is?"

"Might it have given someone a motive to murder your husband?"

"No," said Charlotte.

"Then I don't need to know."

After she had left, Godwin said, "So you're going to look into this."

"Looks like it."

"I wonder what the big secret is."

"I suspect it has something to do with her son. And remember what Phil said, about Bro and his father struggling for control of the steel door company. Do you know anything about the company?"

"It's Birmingham Metal Fabrication of Roseville, I know that. Our back door was made by them. Our decorator recommended them, but he always wants us to buy local."

"So you don't know if it's in good financial condition."

"No. But I'd think a quarrel in the uppermost management couldn't be a good thing."

"Yes, that's true. But was the quarrel serious enough to lead to murder? That's the real question."

Nine

First thing Tuesday morning a man in a handsome three-piece business suit came into Crewel World. Despite the vest, and though his shirt had long sleeves with French cuffs held together with heavy gold links, and his bright blue silk tie was tight against his collar, he did not look the least wilted in the early-morning warmth and humidity. The big American sedan he'd climbed out of in front of the shop was a variety that came with heavy air-conditioning.

He was tall, with dark brown hair and blue eyes, square-jawed and handsome, moving with athletic grace. The fit of the suit bespoke wealth. Betsy could almost hear Godwin's engine start to race.

But the man ignored Godwin's flutter of inquiring eyelashes and came to the desk to ask Betsy, "Are you Ms. Devonshire?"

"Yes, that's right."

"I'm Broward Birmingham." He didn't hold out his hand, and his tone was that of an executive seriously thinking that order could be restored only by firing someone. Betsy suddenly realized that his jaw was so prominent because the underlying muscles were clenched.

"How do you do?" said Betsy.

"My mother came here yesterday and talked with you." It was not a question.

"Yes, she did."

"She asked you to do some unofficial investigating of the murder of my father."

"That's correct."

"I am here to ask you not to do that."

"Why not?"

"Because this isn't any of your business. I see no reason to ask an amateur to second-guess the police."

"Actually, I wouldn't be second-guessing them. I don't have any idea what they might be doing. I will just talk to people, listen to their stories, and draw my own conclusions."

"And who knows what conclusions an amateur might draw? This isn't something you've been trained to do."

"That's true. But I seem to have a talent for it. Also, I am unhampered by the rules—of evidence and so forth—that the police must follow."

"That is exactly why I am asking you to stay out of this. I don't want you screwing up an official investigation."

"I wouldn't dream of doing that!"

"I'm sure you wouldn't, not on purpose. On the other hand, if you come across evidence and handle it or move it or take it away, that can compromise the rules that must be followed for the evidence to be used in a court of law."

"Oh, I see what you're getting at. But, you see, I wouldn't do something like that. I have a friend who is a police officer, and she advises me about particulars like that. I don't usually pick up things, mostly I just talk with people. It can't hurt to talk."

"I'm not just concerned about you moving evidence. I don't want you to investigate, period. Let me tell you as plainly as I know how: Stay out of this."

Betsy nearly continued arguing with him. Then she saw that the muscles in his jaw were even more prominent, and she recalled what Phil had said yesterday about the Birmingham men: They don't like people to disagree with them.

Broward had no legal authority over Betsy, but something her mother used to say rolled across the front of her mind on those letters made of dots: *Those who fight and run away, live to fight another day.*

"I understand," she said as meekly as she could, and dropped her eyes.

"Thank you," he said tightly, turned on his heel, and walked out.

Godwin withheld his snigger until Broward slammed himself into his big car and drove away. "Good for you," he said. Because Betsy had not said she was going to obey Broward's order, only that she understood it.

"I wonder how long I'll be able to poke around before he finds out?"

Godwin's amused smile faded as he thought that over. "I think you ought to be even more concerned about what he'll do when he *does* find out."

Adam Smith sat at the head of the old wooden table, his six steering committee members arranged down either side. Five were, like him, white males in their sixties. The sixth was Ceil Ziegfield, married to a white male in his sixties. Every one of them owned at least one antique car; every one had made the New London to New Brighton run at least three times.

Adam had tried it fourteen times in six different cars, and had finished it only nine. He liked the rarer makes, which tended to be more delicate, eccentric, and cranky than the ones which had proved their worth by becoming numerous. But he always had chosen the road less traveled.

"Have we got all the pretour routes printed?" Drivers would gather in New London early, and would drive to nearby towns: Paynesville on Wednesday, Spicer on Thursday, and Litchfield on Friday, following complicated routes on back roads, trying to keep off busy highways as much as possible.

"All set," said Ceil. She was secretary of the committee, naturally; it never occurred to the men to think a woman wouldn't be pleased to take minutes and do the endless paperwork connected with this project. Ceil wasn't pleased. On the other hand, the men who had done the job in previous years—this was the first year a woman had been honored by being chosen to sit on the steering committee—had managed all right, and so she supposed she could, too.

"Who's going out ahead to put up arrows?" asked Ed.

"Me, I guess," said Adam. Small squares of paper with bold black arrows printed on them were to be stapled on fence posts at intersections to aid drivers. This had been the late Bill Birmingham's job, as he had been in charge of laying out this year's routes.

But after a discussion about possible problems Adam might have to be on site to resolve, it was decided that Jerry, who had laid out the routes last year, should put up the arrows. Ceil handed over the shoebox full of them and a staple gun.

"What else?" asked Adam. "What have we forgotten?" There was always something forgotten, something that was thought to have been taken care of that wasn't, some glitch in the planning. This would be the Sixteenth Annual New London to New Brighton Antique Car Run, but he was sure that even now, after sixteen years, there was a screwup somewhere.

But everyone turned confident smiles on him, and Ceil even said aloud, "Nothing. Everything's fine."

"We have enough banners," Adam prompted, meaning the heavy plastic squares with a soft drink logo and a number on them—a past president of the club owned a soft drink bottling company, and supplied the banners for free, complete with logo.

"We have fifty-three drivers signed up as of yesterday evening, and expect perhaps twelve more by Saturday," said Ed, consulting his notes. People were allowed to sign up as late as the day of the run. "We've never had more than seventy, and we have banners numbered up to eighty-five."

"Have we got enough volunteers at Buffalo High for lunch?" Buffalo wasn't a big city, but the high school was one of those massive consolidated ones, with a huge parking lot. Drivers came in for a hot lunch of hamburgers and hot dogs, with cole slaw and watermelon on the side. The Antique Car Club had to rent the cafeteria from the school district, and then find volunteers to buy supplies and prepare the meal. The soft drink bottler would provide drinks at cost.

"I think we're okay," said Ed, "though I'm hoping to scare up another server on the lunch line."

"Get two," advised Adam. "You'll always have a no-show, and if another one gets sick, you're in big trouble. How's the program coming?"

"Fine," said Ceil. "The layout's done, the printer's been warned it'll be a rush job, and I'm just waiting another day because Milt said he's FedExing his photo to me." The program was printed as late as possible in order to include as many entries as possible. It came in the form of a magazine, and each entry was to supply a color photograph of his or her vehicle. Onlookers enjoyed being able to look up and identify a car they had seen and liked.

"Did we take Bill Birmingham's name off the program?" Adam asked, and there was an awkward shuffle.

Ceil said, "That's something we should discuss. Some of us think we should leave it, maybe put a black border around it." Bill's photo showed him at last year's run, the first one he and Charlotte drove in the 1910 Maxwell. The photo had been taken in New London, with the two of them aboard looking happy and confident. The look had vanished by the halfway point, when they'd staggered into Buffalo two hours late. Their car had not been able to continue.

"What will Charlotte think when she sees it?" Adam asked.

"She's not coming," Ceil said. "I talked with her this morning and she told me to tell you not to expect her."

"When's the funeral?" asked Henry.

Ceil replied, "They don't know yet. The medical examiner hasn't released the body."

There was a moment's silence, then Ed remarked, "This whole business sucks. I don't know which aspect sucks the worst, but there isn't an aspect that doesn't."

"I call the question," said Henry, who was familiar with Robert's Rules of Order.

"What does that mean?" asked Adam, who wasn't.

"That means, let's vote on the motion."

"Nobody made a motion," noted Ceil.

"All right, I move we leave Bill's name and photo in the program, with a black border."

"Second," said Mike.

The motion carried five to two, Henry and Adam being the two dissenters.

Henry thought they should either make a big fuss, dedicate the run to Bill, ask for a moment of silence and put a big picture on the first page of the program— or drop the photo out of the program and say nothing at all. Though no one wanted to say so now, Bill hadn't been popular enough for the first to have any meaning, so Henry voted for the second. Adam thought it would make people who knew the ugly details of Bill's death uncomfortable to find him beaming out at them from the program, even with a black border. He knew it would him. So he voted against it.

Early in the afternoon a woman came into Crewel World. Betsy didn't recognize her. She was in her late twenties, too thin, with fine-grained skin lightly touched with freckles, dark blond hair pulled carelessly back into a scrunchie, and a sleeveless, pale pink dress a size too large. She looked around with an experienced eye, then went to the racks of counted patterns. After a few minutes, she picked up a black-on-white pattern called A Twinkling of Trees and brought it to the desk.

"What do you recommend for the fabric for this?" she asked. Her light blue eyes would have been her best feature if she had thought to use a touch of mascara on her very pale eyelashes.

"I'm doing it on Aida," said Betsy. "I should warn you it's almost all backstitching," she added, because many stitchers become very cross about backstitching.

"I can see that, but there's something primal about trees standing in snow, don't you think? Plus it reminds me of where I grew up. We don't get a lot of snow where I live now."

"Are you from Minnesota?"

"Oh, yes, I'm Lisa Birmingham." But not for long, to judge by the three-carat engagement diamond on a long, slender finger. Well, unless she decided to keep her name, thought Betsy. Which she might, because this was *Dr.* Lisa Birmingham, the pediatrician.

"How do you do?" said Betsy. "I'm Betsy Devonshire. I'm so sorry about your father."

"Yes, well, that's the real reason I'm here. You spoke with my mother yesterday. Has my brother been to see you as well?"

"Yes, a little while ago."

"Well, I'm sure he tried to warn you off."

"Yes, he did."

She leaned forward and said with quiet intensity, "Ignore him. Help my mother. She's going crazy, and the police won't leave her alone."

"You don't think the police suspect her?"

"Yes, I do, though I don't see how. But I want as many people as possible working on solving this. The more people trying, the better, don't you agree?"

"Possibly. Your brother seems to think I'll do something that will spoil the investigation."

"Will you?"

"Not if I can help it."

"Well, then. Do your darndest to help us, won't you?"

"All right. Have you got a few minutes to talk with me?"

"What for, what about?"

"Your father, your brother, anything you think might help."

"All right. But I live in St. Louis, and have for three years. I don't get home very often. So I don't know if I'll be much help."

Betsy led her to the back of the shop, where two cozy upholstered chairs faced one another across a small, round table. "Here, have a seat," she invited the woman. "Would you like a cup of coffee, or tea?"

"Coffee, black, thanks."

Betsy brought her the coffee in a small, pretty porcelain cup, and for herself a cup of green tea. Each took a polite sip. Betsy said, "How much older than you is Broward?"

"Three years. Bro is the oldest, then there's me, then Tommy is not quite three years younger, and David is two years younger than Tommy. I assume Mother bragged about us?"

"Yes, of course. She said Broward quit an excellent job to go into business with his father, that you are a pediatrician, Tommy owns a car dealership, and David is going for an advanced degree in education."

Lisa nodded, smiling. "I see she's still prouder of my M.D. license than my engagement to Mark. You have a good memory."

"I was interested. Your mother has good reason to be proud of her children. But tell me, how did your father persuade Broward to give up a position with a bigger company and come to work for him?"

"That wasn't the way it was supposed to be. My father was supposed to retire and let Bro take over the business. Father's doctor warned him years ago that he had to retire and start taking it easy. Father chose not to believe him. His blood pressure was high and he said medications prescribed for him weren't working, though what I think was, he wasn't taking them. They make you sleepy, you know, and he couldn't stand that. So he'd take them for a couple of days before he was supposed to go have his pressure checked, and that wasn't always long enough. Drove his doctor crazy until he finally figured out what Dad was doing. And meanwhile Father refused to work fewer hours.

"Then he had a ministroke, and that scared him. He phoned Bro and told him he was ready to retire, and did Bro want to take over the company. Bro said sure—he wasn't moving up fast enough in the company he was working for.

"But Father couldn't quit, not completely. At first he said he had to show Bro the ropes, then he said he wanted to see how Bro was doing, and finally he said he just couldn't trust Bro to run the company the way it should be run."

"Bill's way," said Betsy.

"That's right. Bro had his own ideas, and Father couldn't allow that."

Betsy took another sip of her tea and said, "How angry was Bro at his father?"

Lisa thought a moment and said, "Not murderously angry, of course. He could have quit, gone back to being a production manager at his former company—they want him back, they write him letters asking him to come back—and he told me he was thinking about going back to wait for Father to die."

"Was that likely to have happened soon? I mean, do you know how dangerously ill your father was?"

"Last time I talked to Mother, before all this happened, she said the doctor told her that Father would have a serious stroke within six months if he didn't slow down."

"Did Bro know this?"

"I don't know. I think so. If Mother told me, she probably told Bro, Tommy, and David, too."

"Was your father supposed to give up the cars, too?"

"Oh, no. They were a hobby. I'm reasonably sure it never occurred to anyone to tell the doctor that he worked as hard on those cars as he did at running his company."

"Did you know he was thinking about starting a company to supply parts to antique car collectors?"

Lisa sighed. "No, but that sounds a lot like Father."

"Do you have any idea how valuable his antique cars are?"

"The Maxwells are fairly common. Mother will probably get the best price for the Fuller. That's a really rare car."

"Fuller? I thought all your father collected were Maxwells."

"He did, except he bought this one Fuller. It's a Nebraska Fuller, not a Michigan, a high wheeler from 1910."

Betsy hadn't been this confused since she first worked in Crewel World and someone asked her if DMC 312 could be substituted for Paternayan 552. Betsy hadn't even known the customer was talking about embroidery floss. "High wheeler?" she repeated now, in the same tone that she'd echoed, "Paternayan?"

"Oh!" said Lisa. "I thought since you volunteered to work on the Antique Car Run that you knew something about these old cars."

"Well, I don't. What's a high wheeler?"

"The wheels are bigger in circumference, like buggy wheels. Automobile wheels are smaller. I think Father bought the Fuller because Adam wanted it."

"Do you mean Adam Smith?"

"Yes. He and Father were kind of rivals. You know how they keep saying, 'This isn't a race, the run isn't a race'?"

Betsy nodded.

"Well, not everyone believes that. And whenever Adam beat one of Father's Maxwells in one of his frail old rarities, Father was fit to be tied. Adam collects rarities and he wanted that Fuller very badly. Father bought it mostly to annoy him."

"And partly because—?"

"Oh, once Father was sure Adam had given up trying to get it, he was going to sell it at a profit. He'd already had a couple of bids on it from other collectors."

"So this wasn't a friendly rivalry."

Lisa hesitated, then decided candor was necessary. "At first it was. Then Adam bought a 1910 Maxwell that Father wanted badly. His plan was to resell it to Father at a nice profit. But Father, just to spite him, bought a different 1910 Maxwell—and it turned out to be a cantankerous machine, always something wrong with it. So Father was doubly angry with Adam. I think Adam was feeling guilty about the trick, but then Father bought the Fuller and wouldn't sell it to Adam at any price. Adam was furious."

"Couldn't they have gotten together on some kind of trade, maybe with cash added to make it even? I assume the Fuller was worth quite a bit more than the Maxwell."

"Yes, quite a bit, but neither was willing to talk to the other. In fact, Mother told me that the last time Adam and Father's paths crossed, Adam told Father that he was looking forward to Father's death, so he could come to the estate sale and buy that Fuller." She looked at her watch and jumped to her feet. "I'm supposed to take Mother to the lawyer's office, and I'll be late if I don't leave right now." She plunged her hand into her small white purse and pulled out a card. "Are you on the Internet?"

"Yes."

"Good. This has my e-mail address on it, contact me that way if you have any more questions. If Bro finds out I'm talking to you, he'll be angry, so I'd better not come out here anymore. And you can't call me. With everyone at home, e-mail's the only way to guarantee a private conversation. Bye." She grabbed up her purchases and left. Since they had been put into a Crewel World plastic drawstring bag, it was likely at least some of the family knew where she had been. This would serve as a reason why. But the metro area was scattered with needlework shops, most of them closer to Roseville than Crewel World, so most would quickly figure out why Lisa found it necessary to travel all the way out here to buy a cross-stitch pattern.

Betsy rinsed the cups and went out front to assist a customer who came in to buy the threads for a pattern she'd found at a garage sale. Betsy managed to find all but one, which had been given the unhelpful name "Dawn's Favorite." But by consulting the pattern and locating where the unknown color was to be used, then looking at the colors around it, she realized it must be a shade of pink not already selected. She pulled three related shades from a spinner rack and, by giving the customer her choice, made her a collaborator and less likely to decide later she was unsatisfied with the color.

"Did Lisa help you decide Broward is a murderer?" asked Godwin when the customer was gone.

"No. In fact, she gave me a new suspect, Adam Smith."

"I thought you liked Adam Smith."

"I do. But it's a shame how many nice people commit murder."

Ten

The shop was closed, but Betsy remained, restoring order to the sale bins, restocking spinner racks, washing coffee cups. Saving the best for last, she opened a box containing an order of twelve clear glass Christmas tree ornaments. She was making a small display of them on a shelf in the back area when someone knocked on the front door.

It was Jill, bent over so the night light fell on her face as she peered around the needlepointed Closed sign. She was wearing a very pale yellow blouse and tan capri pants.

Betsy unlocked the door, and Jill said, "I rang the bell to your apartment but there was no answer so I decided to see if you were in here."

"Is something wrong?" asked Betsy.

"No, I have the night off, Lars is doing something strange to his Stanley, and I just wanted to talk. Mind?"

"Not at all. Come in," said Betsy. "I'm working in back." Jill went on through the opening between the high stacks of box shelves, into the counted cross-stitch section, while Betsy relocked the door and reset the alarm.

Betsy had turned off the ceiling lights in back, turning the many models hung on the walls into angled shadows.

"Whatcha doin' with those?" Jill asked when she saw the ornaments. "Isn't it kind of early for Christmas?"

Betsy said, "RCTN gave me the idea. You take these plain ornaments and fill them with orts." *Ort* is a crossword-puzzle word whose dictionary meaning is "morsel, as of food." But RCTN, the Internet news group of needleworkers, had adapted it to mean the little ends of floss or thread left over from stitching. Most threw orts away, but some collected them, filling old glass jars with the tiny fragments and displaying them. Betsy had seen the ornaments at an after-Christmas sale, and had bought one to fill with her own orts. Long before it was filled, she saw how beautiful it was going to be, and was sorry she hadn't bought more to sell in the shop. Then a few weeks ago she'd seen the ornaments in a catalog and ordered a dozen.

Now, she picked up her ort-filled ornament and handed it to Jill. "What do you think?"

"Say, this is *nice*! What a great idea! How much is one?"

"Empty, three dollars. I haven't set a price for filled yet."

"Who wants one full of someone else's leavings? It'll be fun filling it with my own. In fact, I'll take two."

Pleased at this early evidence of a success, Betsy said, "I'll put them aside for you—my cash register's closed for the night. Have you had supper yet?"

"No, I was going to ask if you wanted to go halves on a pizza."

"I'd rather have Chinese."

"But I was thinking of eating at home—yours or mine. Like I said, I want to talk to you."

"Is this about Lars thinking of buying another Stanley Steamer?"

Jill stared at Betsy.

"I take it he didn't tell you."

"No." Jill could be very terse when annoyed.

"He said the later models had condensers on them so he wouldn't have to stop every twenty-five miles to take on water."

"I see."

"I told him to consult you before he bought one."

"Thank you."

"Chinese take-out, then?"

"Fine."

"I'll buy if you'll fly."

"Okay."

Excelsior had its own Chinese restaurant, the Ming Wok, just a few blocks away. By the time Jill came back with the warm, white paper sack emitting delectable smells, Betsy had finished in the shop and was up in her apartment.

And Jill was over her mad.

They sat down to feast on Mongolian beef and chicken with pea pods.

Jill, feeling the cat Sophie's gentle pressure on her foot, dropped one hand carelessly downward, an ort of chicken even more carelessly hanging from her fingers. Sophie deftly removed it and Jill brought her hand back up to the table to wipe it on a napkin.

"If you leave your hand down there, she'll lick it clean and I'll be less likely to notice you wiping your fingers and guess what you're up to," said Betsy.

Jill laughed. "I'll remember that. But since you didn't jump up and shout at Sophie, or me, I take it you no longer disapprove. So why don't you just give up and feed her, too?"

"I do feed her. She gets Iams Less Active morning and evening. She gets enough to maintain a cat at sixteen pounds, which is what she'd weigh pretty soon if everyone else would just stop sneaking her little treats."

"I mean—"

"I know what you mean. Jill, you stayed here last December, and you saw what she's like when feeding time approaches, whining and pacing and driving me crazy. That's what she'd be like every time I sat down at this table if she thought I allowed her to have something from my plate. So long as she thinks I forbid it, she's content to be slipped a treat on the sly by someone else, and she's very quiet about it. So I do my part, scolding her—and you and everyone else—when it gets too blatant. Look at her."

Jill looked down then around and saw Sophie all the way across the living room, curled into her cushioned basket. She looked back with mild, innocent surprise at their regard. "See that smirk? She thinks she's got me fooled. Help me maintain the fiction, all right?"

Jill raised a solemn right hand. "I promise," She opened her fortune cookie. "Mine says, *Tomorrow is your lucky day.* Always tomorrow, never today. What does yours say?"

Betsy opened hers. *"The solution lies within your grasp,"* she read. "To what, I wonder?"

Jill said, with a little smile, "How about the Birmingham murder? How's that coming?"

"Not very well. I don't know the people, I don't know enough about antique cars, I don't know as much about the actual scene of the crime. And you can't really help this time because the Excelsior police aren't investigating."

"Well," drawled Jill, "it just so happens I have prints of photos taken at the Highway 5 lay-by."

Betsy said, "That's what you came to talk about, isn't it? You came here meaning to show them to me."

"Only if the subject came up. Which it was going to. Where's my purse?" She looked around, saw it in the living room, and stood. "Come on, have a look."

But a minute later, pulling a brown envelope out, she hesitated. "Um, these aren't pretty."

Betsy hesitated, too. She was not fond of the uglier details. "Well, let's see how bad they are."

They were awful. Betsy hastily took several close-ups of the head of the victim off the top of the stack, putting them facedown on the coffee table. The next one was of the horribly burned upper body, and she pulled it off, too. "How do the people who deal with this sort of thing stand it?" she asked.

"By making horrible jokes." Betsy looked up at Jill, who was standing beside the upholstered chair Betsy was sitting on. "I'm serious," she continued. "They call burn victims crispy critters, for example. They have to; otherwise, they'd be so sick they couldn't conduct a proper investigation." She shrugged at Betsy's appalled expression. "You asked."

Betsy returned her attention to the photographs. The next few were of the burned-out Maxwell. "The whole inside seems to be gone," she noted.

"Yes, and it smelled of accelerant."

"Accelerant?"

"Something combustible, like gasoline or kerosene. Which at first wasn't suspicious, because after all a car uses gasoline. But some of the ash they collected from the backseat contained gasoline."

Betsy looked at the photo again. "How could there be any accelerant left in something this thoroughly burned?"

"Because it isn't liquid gasoline that burns, it's the vapor. You can actually put a match out by sticking it into a bucket of gasoline—unless it's been sitting long enough for fumes to gather, in which case the fumes will explode as your lit match enters the cloud. Arsonists who spend too long splashing accelerant around are arrested when they go to the emergency room with burns."

"You know the doggondest things."

"I know. Look at the rest of the photos, and see if there's anything to see." She had taken out a notebook and pen, prepared to write down anything interesting Betsy might notice.

Betsy obediently looked. Since she knew very little about automobiles and even less about antique ones, the photos of the burnt-out car told her nothing. She noted the hammer in the puddle of dirty water around the car and remembered the joke hollered by a fellow driver last Saturday: Get a bigger hammer!

She asked Jill, "Do you know if they found evidence Bill was struck on the head before being shot?"

"Not that I know of. Why would someone do that?"

"Maybe it was a quarrel he had with someone and he got hit in the head with that hammer. Or maybe he swung it at someone, who pulled a gun and shot him. I understand he was a very aggressive type."

"Hmmm," said Jill, writing that down.

Farther down were more photos of the corpse. Again Betsy hurried past them, but she slowed at several taken of just the lower portion of the body, which was barely damaged. The white flannel trousers were barely smudged, and then only above the knees. Except . . .

"What?" asked Jill.

Betsy looked closer, frowning. "That's funny, that smudge right there looks more like someone wiped his dirty fingers than smoke or fire damage."

"Let me see." Jill took the photo and peered at it closely. "Where's your Dazor?"

"In the guest bedroom."

"Bring it here, will you?" She spoke peremptorily, slipping into cop mode without thinking.

Betsy went into the bedroom her sister had used and opened the closet to pull out the wheeled stand with the gooseneck lamp on it. She wheeled it out into the living room and plugged it in.

Jill turned on the full-spectrum fluorescent light that encircled the rectangular magnifying glass and bent the gooseneck to a convenient angle to view the photo. "Huh," she said after half a minute. "It does look like someone wiped dust off his fingers, it's so faint . . ."

Betsy took the photo and held it under the magnifier. "Maybe it's an old stain that didn't wash out. Funny I didn't notice it Saturday."

"Why funny?"

"Well, I do remember noticing how immaculately white they were. No, wait, he had a towel tucked into his belt to keep the grease off, so it would have covered these old stains up. Oh, and here's—no."

"No, what?"

"Not flecks of dirt, orts."

"Where?"

"On his trousers, near the cuffs. Charlotte really could use one of those glass ornaments, she sprinkles orts wherever she goes. Her daughter Lisa came into the shop on Monday and I said I knew she was a stitcher when I saw the orts on her dress and she said they were her mother's—though I was right about Lisa being a stitcher. Her mother is a nice, nice woman, but even I came home Saturday with some of her orts on my clothes. She kind of flicks them off the ends of her fingers." Betsy looked again at the photo. She could not have said why she found the few tiny ends of floss clinging to Bill's trousers so touching.

She gave the photos back to Jill and said, "I assume the police have the same two suspects I have. Do you know if they have more than two?"

"Our department is only marginally involved, so I'm not sure how many suspects Steffans at Minnetonka PD has. I hear he'd love Charlotte for this, but you gave her a terrific alibi."

"He'd love her why, because they always look at the spouse?"

"That's part of it. The other part is, they're getting reports that the couple weren't getting along, hadn't been getting along for the past several years."

Betsy said, "Charlotte told me they were in counseling, and things were starting to turn around. Certainly she seemed affectionate toward Bill when I saw them."

"Seriously affectionate or polite affectionate?"

"She patted him on the rump when she went to tell him she was riding with me to St. Paul."

"If she was feeling so chummy, why didn't she ride with him?"

"Because he was having trouble with the car, and she said it was jiggling so unevenly it was making her sick." Betsy frowned. "Is that likely? I've never ridden in an old car other than Lars's, and that old steamer has a very smooth way of going."

"Lars told me that was a selling point, that the internal combustion cars of that period did jiggle. He says it was a combination of too few cylinders and no shock absorbers."

Betsy nodded. "In Charlotte's case, there may also have been the prospect of having to sit in the hot sun wearing all those clothes while Bill worked on it after it broke down on the road—I mean, he had trouble starting it, and when he did, it was still idling rough, so she probably guessed it was going to break down. Which apparently it did. He spent the whole time they were in Excelsior with his head under the hood."

"So if not Charlotte, who are your suspects?"

"I hardly dare say they're actual suspects, but the two I'd like to know more about are Bill's son Broward and Adam Smith."

"Who's Adam Smith?"

"He was in charge of Saturday's run," Betsy said. She explained about the ongoing quarrel between him and Bill, concluding, "I don't know how powerful a motive that is, but I do know Charlotte and I waited quite a long time for Adam to show up in St. Paul."

"Who could you ask, do you know?"

"Not offhand, not anyone who wouldn't go right to Adam and tell him I'm asking questions. He's president of the Antique Car Club, and from the little I've seen, he seems to be very popular." Betsy had gone to exactly one meeting of the Antique Car Club with Lars, just to see if it was something she wanted to get more deeply involved with. It had been interesting—but also obvious that this was one of those organizations that ate up all a member's spare time, and Betsy didn't feel she wanted to spend what little spare time she had on this organization.

After all, she was not going to buy an antique car of her own. She told Lars on the way home that she would volunteer for this year's run, because Lars was a part of it and she was Lars's sponsor, but after that, he was on his own.

"Are you afraid that if he did it and thinks you're closing in on him, he might come after you?"

"Oh, nothing like that," Betsy said. "I don't want to get people all stirred up about my thinking it might be Adam, when I really think he's only a possibility. Being suspected of murder can ruin someone, even if it turns out he didn't do it. If I knew more about antique car owners or the Antique Car Club, I might form a real opinion. Why do people collect them and how fanatical do they get about them? Adam would have to be totally invested in getting that Fuller to consider murdering Bill."

Jill said, "They're probably like every other set of hobbyists. Some are casual, some are intent, some are fanatical. You talked with Adam, which kind is he?"

Betsy remembered Ceil's jeer at Adam's remark that he might be willing to find a buyer for Joe Mickels's McIntyre. "As if you'd let anyone else get their hands on it!" she'd said, or words to that effect.

But Betsy was unwilling to say anything out loud, even to Jill.

Godwin was in Shelly's kitchen, doing the dishes, when the phone rang. "I'll get it!" he caroled, wiping his hands on his apron. He lifted the receiver on the wall near the back door. "Hello?"

"Goddy?" said a man's voice in a near-whisper.

"Who is this?" said Godwin, though he knew.

"Don't be stupid, for heaven's sake!"

"Why, hello, John," drawled Godwin in as dry a voice as he could manage, though his heart was already singing.

"I'm concerned that I haven't heard from you."

"Well, you made it pretty clear—twice—that you didn't want anything to do with me ever again."

"I was angry. You made me very angry. Sometimes, Goddy, when you act like you don't care about me, I just can't stand it."

"You suspected I didn't care about you, so you stopped caring about me."

"I have never stopped caring about you. Ever. Even when I'm angry—even in a jealous rage. Goddy, sometimes you exasperate me beyond endurance. You know you do. You know you're doing it when it happens."

"I wasn't doing anything you could get mad about."

"Goddy, I *saw* you talking to—"

Godwin hung up at that point with a satisfied little smile.

Eleven

Wednesday morning Betsy's alarm went off at 5:15. Sophie, who had been rescued from the street many years ago, retained a fear of abandonment. She became very much underfoot and vocal at this change in routine. Betsy reassured her, "Come on, I've been doing this for a week," though it had been only three days a week, not enough to have sunk into Sophie's unsophisticated brain.

Betsy put on an old swimsuit, over which she put a good linen-blend dress in a shade of pale rose and matching sandals, her going-to-work outfit. She packed underwear, shampoo, soap, and a towel in a light zippered bag and, ignoring Sophie's anxious inquiries about breakfast, went down to the back door and out. She was going exercising.

Betsy had been meaning to take up horseback riding or maybe power walking, but with running her shop, trying to learn enough about roof repair to choose a roofer for her building, dealing with her tenants, volunteering with the Antique Car Run, and keeping up with household chores, she just hadn't managed to add an exercise program.

She did manage a couple of hours for a physical a few weeks ago, and her doctor said she would have more energy if she would stop writing IOUs to her body and find some kind of exercise she would actually do. So Betsy investigated and found an early-bird water aerobics program that met three mornings a week. Betsy chose it partly because of all forms of exercise this was the least distasteful, but mostly because she didn't have to carve a couple of hours out of her working day, an impossible task. This flock of early birds met at 6:30 A.M. for an hour. Betsy would be back in her apartment by 8:30, showered, dressed, and on time for her pre-exercise routine: her and Sophie's breakfast, e-mail, a bit of bookkeeping or bill paying, and down in the shop by 10:00.

But first she had to get there. Oddly enough, at 5:45 in the morning, the rush hour into the Cities was swift enough to deserve the name. Betsy drove toward Minneapolis, but only as far as Golden Valley. She exited onto Highway 100, then took Golden Valley Drive to The Courage Center, a brick building in its own small valley, parked in the nearly empty lot, and went in. All three women behind the big reception counter were in wheelchairs. The Courage Center's primary aim was to restore injured bodies to health and bring handicapped bodies to their full potential—hence its name, and the status of its employees—but it also offered pool exercise to all comers.

In the women's locker room four other women greeted Betsy with that muted cheer found before 6:30 A.M. All were at least middle-aged. More women came in until they were eight and they all, after perfunctory showers, trailed down a short hallway to a large room nearly full of an enormous swimming pool. Between pillars on the far wall large panes of glass were hung, with stained glass sections making a thinly traced and almost abstract map showing a confluence of rivers.

The water was warm. The pool, instead of sloping from shallow to deep, had four large flat areas, each a foot or so deeper than the one before. The shallowest area was three and a half feet deep, and Betsy went there with three of the other women to start walking back and forth. Two men joined them. Disco music began to play. A cheerful and energetic young woman in a professional swimsuit came to stand in the water and direct the movements.

"Good morning, Jodie," said several of the more-awake women. This did not include Betsy, who could not even remember Jodie's name, though it had been Jodie who had interviewed Betsy just last week while signing up for this program.

"Let's keep walking, knees high," called Jodie, standing waist deep in the pool. She was taller than Betsy, on whom the water came nearly to her armpits.

After a few minutes of this, Betsy's brain sputtered to life. "Hi, Florence, hi, Ruth, hi, Barbara," she said, pushing her way through the water past them, knees high and glutes tight. She had a lot of catching up to do.

A few minutes later, they were sidestepping, bending sideways, and reaching with the lead arm, when Florence, at eighty the most senior person present, said as Betsy flowed past her, "Look, Betsy, we have a new person here today." Florence nodded toward one of the deeper areas, and Betsy looked over. And stopped dead in the water.

"Why, I know her, that's Charlotte Birmingham!"

"No, not Charlotte," said Florence impatiently. "She's been coming for a long time. I mean the man."

"But I don't remember seeing Charlotte here before," said Betsy.

"She sometimes stops coming for a week or so. She travels, I think."

"Oh." Of course. Charlotte had been getting ready for last week's run. Betsy thought about going deeper to say hello, then decided against it. She was getting into this sidestepping business, feeling the push of water against her legs and *reeeeaching*, feeling the good stretch. In a while everyone would climb aboard a foam "noodle" and go paddling out into the deepest water. She'd say hello then.

"Jumping jacks with elbow kisses, side to side!" called Jodie, and everyone continued moving sideways but now in jumping jack motions, bringing elbows together in front and out again. There was no way Betsy could have done this for this long on dry land, but with the lift and support of the water, it was fun and not too difficult.

She looked again at the man, who was out beyond Charlotte, in the second-deepest area. He was taller than Charlotte, but not by a lot. He was trim and muscular, though he wasn't young. His hair, a light brown, showed no trace of gray—Grecian Formula, concluded Betsy. He had a pleasant face, presently lit with laughter as he struggled with the unfamiliar movement. Charlotte, facing him and moving well, said something to him and his head went back as his laughter intensified.

"Find a place to cross-country ski!" called Jodie, and the swimmers settled into stationary places where they could swing their arms and move their legs without bumping or splashing one another. The man looked around to see how it was done, and set a rapid pace, churning the water with arm movements, grinning. Charlotte turned to face him, her expression a mirror of his.

Betsy was surprised, then surprised at her surprise. The man was enjoying himself, why shouldn't Charlotte? Then she realized Charlotte's face held the same warm, open look of amused affection she'd had last Saturday. Only then it had been directed at her husband.

So she was having a good time," said Godwin when Betsy told him about it. "I've heard it's possible for people to enjoy doing more than one thing. Who is he, anyone we know?"

Betsy was going through her half-price-floss basket, pulling out items that were starting to look shopworn. She'd use them to make up more kits. "I don't think so. I wonder if he's another antique car buff. I talked to Charlotte in the locker room, but only briefly because we both had to get going. She said the man's name is Marvin Pierce, a business associate of Bill's who became friends with both of them, and now he's rallied round the whole family, running errands and being a general help."

"So what's the problem?"

"I'm probably making something out of nothing, but she seemed so . . . cheerful with him. She wasn't acting like a new widow and he wasn't acting like a comfort to the bereaved. It was startling to see her laughing and having a good time."

"Well, you can't cry twenty-four hours a day, can you? And she told you this guy's been really helping out. So she laughed for an hour because he made her forget." A thought struck. "You say she didn't introduce you in the pool. You think that was on purpose?"

"No. I went over to Charlotte and we exchanged hellos, and she said I was going to love this program, she's been doing it for years. Then Barbara noodled over to ask me where my shop was, and when I finished telling her and looked around, Charlotte was over talking with Ruth and Leah." Betsy frowned, trying to be sure there'd been nothing suspicious about her not getting introduced to Marvin. She would have introduced herself, but Marvin had gone to share a joke with Joe and she hadn't wanted to intrude.

"You can't be thinking she did it," said Godwin.

"No, of course not, I know that's impossible. But I'm thinking how she told me that she'd been going to a counselor and things had been improving between her and her husband. But she said he wouldn't go with her, and I've heard that both have to go before you can turn a marriage around. So suppose things weren't actually improving? And suppose she turned to an old friend for advice and comfort?"

"You mean this Marvin fellow."

"Yes. And suppose that old friend and she decided the best form of help involved killing Bill? Maybe it was a plot the two of them cooked up, because then, you see, she would have a very good reason to get close to someone on that Saturday, and stick with that someone, who could give her an unbreakable alibi."

"Does this Marvin fellow drive an antique car?"

"I don't know. But he didn't need to, really. All he had to do was sabotage the Maxwell's engine and watch for Bill to pull over."

Godwin said admiringly, "How your mind works! That's a wickedly clever plot—too bad for whoever did it that you're even cleverer! But how can you prove it? I mean you can't find out if the Maxwell was sabotaged, because it's all burned up. And who did it?"

"I don't know, but he took an awful chance, burning the Maxwell. The police are very clever nowadays proving arson. Or is it the fire department that investigates suspicious fires? Whichever, they thought the fire was suspicious from the start."

"Not so clever, then."

"And you know, I may be wrong about all this. It's just one of several possibilities." Betsy remembered again that look of affection Charlotte had given her husband, the gentle caress she gave as she left him to his frantic car repairing on Saturday. It had seemed spontaneous, authentic. She said, "I haven't had a chance to look into Adam Smith's drive from Excelsior to St. Paul, for example." She checked her watch. "Time to open up," she said.

Godwin went to turn the needlepoint sign so OPEN faced outward, and realized someone was waiting for the door to be unlocked.

It was Irene. "Hello, hello, hello!" she caroled, striding into the shop with a broad, happy smile. Betsy and Godwin exchanged a surprised glance. Neither had ever seen her wholly joyous like this, without a hint of anxiety or arrogance. "Have you got a shopping basket?" she asked.

Godwin grasped the situation faster than Betsy. "Big or small?" he asked, reaching for a two-gallon size currently holding yarn and nodding at the pint-size one Betsy was taking floss out of.

"Oh, the big one," said Irene, and Godwin happily spilled its yarn onto the library table, then handed it to her.

Godwin said to Betsy, "Some people go to Disney World, Irene comes here."

Irene chortled in agreement and began to fill the basket. Never in her life had she been able to buy as much as she wanted of ribbon, floss, wool yarn, silk yarn, alpaca yarn, and fabric, in every desirable color, all at one time, with no thought of the cost. Irene filled the basket three times. Betsy, eyeing the heap, estimated there was over a thousand dollars' worth, and Irene had not bought a single painted canvas—the most expensive single item a needleworker can buy.

"Have you quit your job yet?" teased Godwin, helping Betsy start to write up the order.

Irene said, "No, but I'm thinking about it. What do you think, Betsy?"

Betsy said, "I think you shouldn't, not yet. You'll lose your benefits when you do, and I know from experience how expensive buying your own medical insurance is. Right now you need to talk to a financial advisor, which all by itself is going to cost you something."

"Oh," said Irene, the light in her eyes dimming just a little.

"I'm sorry to let more air out of your balloon," said Betsy, "and much as I would like to encourage you to continue buying one or two of everything in my shop, I think you should be aware that you are going to have to share any money you received with the state and federal government."

"Maybe I should put some of this back," said Irene, now definitely looking alarmed.

But Godwin said, "Oh, come on, it's not as bad as all that. How much did you take in last weekend?" asked Godwin.

She turned to him. "Twenty-seven thousand."

Godwin whistled.

"But I had to give fifteen percent of that to the gallery. On the other hand, I have orders for two more pieces, and Mark—Mr. Duggan—wants me to bring in three more by the end of the month. That's why I was thinking of quitting, because I can't think how I can do all that in so short a time. These pieces take a lot of planning, and they're complicated to stitch. Also, a reporter from the *Star Tribune* interviewed me and they took pictures. After that appears in next week's *Variety* section, there's likely to be even more orders."

"Then for heaven's sake, don't worry about spending a single thousand here! What are you charging for these orders?"

"Depends. The most expensive is five thousand. One of the orders is for a small piece, and I'm asking twenty-two hundred for it. It's only six inches by six inches. Is that too much?"

"On the contrary. Raise your prices."

"But I'm already charging so much—"

"You can't fill the orders you're getting now. Raise your prices until you have only as many orders as you can fill. I bet you could charge twenty or thirty thousand apiece and still have enough work to keep you busy." He glanced at Betsy. "*And* buy medical insurance. What you'll have left over even after you pay those nasty taxes will keep you very comfortably."

Involuntarily, Irene's hand reached out as if to touch Godwin on his hand, but stopped before she made contact. She turned to Betsy. "Could he possibly be right?"

"He might be. He knows a lot about things like this. Maybe you also need to hire an agent."

"Oh my, oh my, oh my," Irene murmured. The glow had come back. "An *agent.*"

Godwin said, in a darker voice, "So long as you're listening to me, hear this: Art is the strangest thing. What you're doing may grow and grow, or it may vanish entirely overnight. It's like, one year the museums can't get enough big piles of penny candy, the next year it's Lent."

"What I do isn't silly like those piles of candy!" flared Irene. "What I do is real work!"

"Oh, I agree," said Godwin quickly. "It's a form of Impressionism, which has been around for a long time and is a very respected art form. But the quote real unquote Impressionists use paint on canvas. It may be the critics will decide you're just as real in this different medium. Or they may decide it's a weird offshoot, a cute fad, but not really valid."

Irene glared at him, panting, yearning to fight, but she was weaponless.

"Do you have some vacation time coming?" asked Betsy, anxious to sooth her savage breast.

"What? Oh, yes, I haven't taken any yet this year, and I get three weeks."

"You might see if you can take some now to get a running start on these commissioned pieces."

"Now that's a good idea! And I will also seek professional advice." She smiled. "I am so glad I came in here to buy my materials!"

"So are we," said Godwin, smiling as he added his sales slips to the stack Betsy was adding up on her little calculator. "So are we."

Twelve

On Wednesday, her hair still damp despite riding home from
Courage Center with the windows down—she would never get used to the
humidity around here—Betsy sat down at her computer to download her
e-mail, going to make a second cup of tea while RCTN downloaded. There
were always lots and lots of messages from the newsgroup, and there was generally a useful nugget or two among them. Betsy quickly arrowed down the
subject lines, read several, replied to a few, then deleted the download.

Among her e-mail messages was one from Susan Greening Davis about
window displays, a response to a question from Betsy—and another from Lisa
Birmingham in reply to Betsy's e-mail of yesterday evening.

Lisa said she had long suspected her parents' marriage was "under a strain,"
but hadn't known about the counseling sessions. She was not surprised her
father had refused to go. *My father never thought anyone else's opinion was superior
to his own*, she wrote.

*Did you get to talk with Marvin at The Courage Center pool? Isn't he a dear?
I know it's far too early, but maybe in a year or two, Mother will stop seeing
Marvin as the family's good friend and develop a romantic interest. I think
he's in love with her. I think he's been in love with her for years. But he never
even flirted with her, so far as I know. I remember when he came with my
family to see me get my baccalaureate degree. Mother and Father were simply
beaming at me, and a little off to the side I saw Marvin. He was looking at
Mother. There was just that something in his eyes, you know what I mean.
And I saw him look at her that way again when I was home last Christmas
and she was opening his gift. He gave her an inexpensive piece of antique jet
jewelry. She gave him a gag gift, a pair of socks in a shocking fuchsia color I
think she knit herself. I mean, where on earth would you find socks that color
in a man's size? He actually wore them to a New Year's Eve party at the Her-
bert Manleys the next week. He didn't care who saw the socks, and if that's
not love, what is? But I asked Mother what she thought of Marvin not long
ago and she said, "I'm so glad he's a friend of this family." She's a bit of an
actress, but I'm sure she has no idea.*

Betsy clicked on Reply and typed, *You are very observant. Thank you. Now, can you find out where Broward and Marvin were on the day your father was murdered?*

Lars never did anything by halves. Now that his new hobby consisted of an old car, he researched it thoroughly, reading books and looking for web sites on the Internet devoted to Stanley Steamers, and downloaded diagrams of Stanley Steamer plumbing to study. He joined an international organization of Stanley Steamer owners. Once a Steamer came to live with him, he contacted two Steamer owners in Wisconsin with questions, and drove to Eau Claire to watch and learn how to maintain his vehicle.

Lars's Stanley was built in 1912, an era when twenty-five miles an hour on the road was remarkable. But F. E. and F. O. Stanley, identical twin speed demons, looked ahead to a period when forty miles an hour sustained road speed would be desirable, and built their car for that foreseen time. And just as they refused to consider the assembly line, they refused to acknowledge planned obsolescence. When someone ordered a Steamer from their factory, he had to wait for it to be built by hand—and then was expected never to replace it. That's why, as late as the mid-1950s, pioneer Stanley boilers were still in outdoor use, lifting, cutting and grinding stone in a New England gravel pit.

Currently, having acquired some understanding of his Stanley, Lars was in a mood to manipulate it. While he wouldn't dream of taking his Stanley on the Interstate, he did sometimes get out on the state and county highways, where forty miles an hour was slow. He wondered if there was some way to adjust the flame under the boiler so fifty or even fifty-five miles per hour could be attained without having to stop even more often for water.

So when Betsy stopped in to see him around midday on Thursday, he had the burner disassembled and was consulting his owner's manual for advice.

"Oh, no!" she said, and he looked around to see her standing dismayed in the doorway to his barn.

"What's the matter?" he asked, putting down the vaporizing coil and reaching for a towel to wipe his hands.

"That's what I was about to ask you," said Betsy. "How bad is it?"

"How bad is what?"

"Are you going to be able to repair it by Saturday?"

He grinned. "It doesn't need repair," he said, to her obvious relief. "I was trying to figure out how to get a bigger head of steam without having to stop even more often for water."

Betsy began to giggle. "You sound like Tim Taylor on *Home Improvement*: 'More power!'"

"No, I sound like the Stanley twins that morning on Daytona Beach in 1907."

"Just be careful you don't become airborne. The run this weekend isn't a race, remember."

"I'll remember," he promised, without a hint that his fingers were crossed behind his back.

"So when are you going down to New London—tonight or Friday?"

"If I can figure out this burner business fast enough—or decide I can't figure it out soon enough—I thought I'd take 'er down this evening. Otherwise I'll leave here early in the morning. What, are you looking for a ride?"

"Oh, no, I'm leaving this evening after we close. I'm driving down. You do know a lot of drivers are already there, terrorizing the countryside with their infernal machines?"

Lars grinned. "I hear the populace turns out to wave as they go by. But I had to work yesterday."

"Do you have a motel reservation?"

"Naw, there's room for a bunk in the trailer, so I thought I'd camp out with it. It's only two nights. You?"

"I let it go too late. Every room in New London is taken, so I'm staying at the Lakeside Motel in Willmar, and commuting. But it's not far. So, I'll see you there. Oh, here's your sponsor's banner." Betsy handed over a twenty-four-by-ten-inch rectangle of plastic-coated canvas with the logo of her shop printed on it: CREWEL WORLD worked in X's as if it were cross-stitched. On the corners were pockets holding powerful magnets, so Lars could put the banner anywhere on the vehicle he chose.

He took it, looked at it, then smiled shyly at her. "I want to thank you—" he began.

"It's all right, really," she interrupted hastily. "I was glad to do it." *Golly*, she thought on her way back to her shop, *I'm really turning into a Minnesotan, embarrassed to be thanked.*

The door went *Bing!* and Betsy came out from the back of her shop.

Charlotte stopped short when she saw Betsy. There was a tall man with her—Betsy suddenly realized it was Marvin Pierce, AKA Friend of the Family. "Oh, I thought you were in New London already," said Charlotte.

"No, I'm going up as soon as I close this evening. I had hoped to see you up there."

"No, no, I'm not going. The funeral has to be planned, though we still don't know which day that will be, the medical examiner hasn't, er, released

Bill's body. Anyway, I couldn't face . . . those people. Not right now." Once the surprise drained away, her face showed the stress and sorrow of a new widow.

Marvin put a sympathetic hand on Charlotte's shoulder, and Betsy said, "Yes, of course, I understand. So what brings you out here?"

"I understand you have a very competent finisher."

"Yes, Heidi's wonderful. Do you have that Christie piece ready?"

"Yes." Charlotte came to the checkout desk and put a plastic bag on it. She opened it and lifted out a square wrapped in tissue paper.

Betsy came to unwrap it, saying, "You take such good care of your work. I had someone come in last week with a piece that looked as if she'd washed the car with it."

Marvin snorted his amused surprise. Charlotte said, "My regular finisher won't take a piece that's dirty."

"I can't afford to be very picky. I even have a woman who will go over pieces and fill in missing stitches, or repair torn or moth-eaten pieces. Sandy has rescued lots of heirloom pieces. But this looks perfect."

"It's as good as I can make it, and if there's some mistake in it, I don't want it fixed. This work is all mine. I found the original, photographed it, scanned it and made the pattern, and stitched it all by myself." She glanced up from it to meet Betsy's eyes and said, "Oh, all right, Grace Christie designed it, so it's essentially a copy. But I made some changes to her original pattern, worked some areas in different stitches from the original, and even altered the colors a little."

Marvin said, "She won't admit it, but I think what she does is equivalent to real art."

"Oh, tosh, Marvin," said Charlotte with a little frown.

Betsy's smile appeared. "Have you heard about Irene Potter?"

Charlotte said, "I read an article about her in one of our little weekly papers, yes. She stitches Impressionistic patterns, right?"

"Yes, but her first piece was almost a copy of a painting she admired. She did just about what you did, altered the pattern a little, changed some of the colors. So don't apologize."

Charlotte's spine straightened. "All right, I won't. I think this piece is great, and I'm proud of it."

"So you should be," said Marvin.

Betsy said, "I believe you wanted this made into a pillow?"

"Yes, that's right. But—well, can you give me an estimate of the cost?"

"Oh, never mind the cost," said Marvin. "If it's something you want, then go ahead and buy it."

"And who's going to pay for it?"

He looked at her, confused, and she looked away with a pained expression.

Betsy said, "Speaking from experience, it takes a long time to settle an estate. Things can get tight during that interim."

"Plus there are taxes and fees and all kinds of expenses," said Charlotte.

Marvin said, his voice showing he was still a little puzzled, "I understand all that. But how much can it cost to get someone to sew this into a pillow? Twenty-five or thirty dollars?"

Betsy said to Charlotte, "He's not familiar with finishers, is he?"

Charlotte smiled. "No."

Betsy said to him, "I'm estimating this at about a hundred and fifty, minimum."

Marvin's eyebrows went high. He turned and looked around at the fibers, fabrics, and esoterica of needlework. "I had no idea. Cute little hobby you picked, Char." He turned back to show a very charming grin. "Of course, it isn't as pricey as antique cars."

Betsy said, "Do you own an antique car?"

"Whoa! Not me!" Marvin raised both hands. "I'd like to acquire some champagne tastes despite my beer budget, but not that one. What I like is for my cars to be as up to date as possible, with all the bells and whistles, thank you very much."

While Charlotte and Betsy became deeply involved in fabric selection, kinds of trim available, size, filler, and other considerations, Marvin went wandering around the shop. About twenty minutes later he was back at the desk.

Charlotte wrapped things up with Betsy, saying, "Use your best judgment, Betsy, but try to keep it under two hundred, all right?"

"Of course. How about I call you with Heidi's estimate before I tell her to go ahead?"

"Thank you." She turned and her eye was caught by a spinner rack of the newest in Watercolor flosses. She made as if to go to it, but instead said, "All right, all right, we can leave now," to Marvin, although he hadn't said a word.

Betsy's parting smile faded once the door closed behind them. Interesting how Charlotte could read Marvin's mind, too.

At five, Betsy hurried Godwin through the closing-up process, wrote up a deposit slip for the day's slim profits, and went upstairs to finish packing for the trip to New London.

She was debating whether to pack a light nightie or her pajamas when her doorbell rang. Thinking it was probably Jill, she went to buzz her in and left the door to her apartment ajar while she went back to her packing.

"Hello?" asked a strange voice. Male. She picked up the cell phone she'd been about to put in the big purse she was taking on this trip, and went to peer out the door.

Two men were standing at the end of the little hallway to her living room. They were looking awkward, half prepared to retreat.

"Hello," said Betsy.

"Are you Ms. Devonshire?" asked the taller of the pair. He was also the more robust, and likely older, his dark hair thinning and gray at the temples. He was wearing a short-sleeved tan shirt, brown trousers, and dressy shoes.

"Yes. Who are you?"

The shorter one offered a shy smile. He was wearing gold-rimmed glasses, a faded blue shirt, old blue jeans, and thick black sandals. "I'm David Birmingham, and this is my brother Tom. Our sister Lisa seems to think you might want to talk to us."

"I'd love to talk with you, but I don't have much time. I'm leaving for New London."

"Oh, are you involved with the run this weekend?" asked Tom.

"Yes, I'm a volunteer and I'm sponsoring the Stanley Steamer that Lars Larson is driving."

"Love those Steamers," said Tom with a smile, and Betsy recalled that he owned a car dealership.

"Why is that? Do you sell antique cars?" asked Betsy. "Come in, sit down. May I get you a soft drink?"

"Not for me, thanks," said David.

"Not me, either," said Tom. They came and sat side by side on the love seat, which was just barely long enough to contain them. He continued, "I sell new and used cars, but not *that* used. The Steamer was a remarkable car for its time, and many people are fascinated at the notion of a steam-powered car. But they never had a chance against the internal combustion engine."

"Why was that?" asked Betsy, taking the upholstered chair at right angles to the love seat. "Because it had to stop to take on water so often? I understand the later models had condensers."

Tom nodded. "That's right. But steam was inefficient, because it adds a step between the fuel and the wheels. The fuel heats the water to produce steam, which drives the motor, which turns the wheels. An internal combustion engine uses the fuel to drive the motor which turns the wheels. You lose energy every step you take away from the fuel. Those Stanleys got terrible mileage per gallon. On the other hand, I *love* that whistle." He smiled. There was something both slick and charming about him, which, Betsy considered, figured.

"So you've seen Lars's Stanley?"

He shook his head. "No, but one generally turns up at the run, and I've been to a lot of runs."

"Are you going this year?" asked Betsy.

"No." He suddenly looked sad. "Probably won't go again, now that Dad's not gonna be there."

David said, "Lisa said you're investigating our father's death?"

"Yes, informally. I'm not a police investigator or even a private eye. I'm involved because your mother and I spent most of the day together."

The phone in Betsy's hand rang, startling her. She punched the Talk button, said "Excuse me" to the brothers and "Hello?" into the phone.

"Betsy, it's Jill. Are you on the road?"

"No, I'm still at home."

"Oh, well, I was starting to worry about you. I called the motel in Willmar, and you weren't there yet."

Betsy didn't know whether to be grateful for Jill's concern or annoyed at it. "I'll be leaving soon. The two younger Birmingham brothers are here. Tom and David."

"I hope you have something to ask them. And listen to this: We got a report from the medical examiner on time of death and guess what? Time of death could be as long ago as Friday afternoon."

"But we know it can't be that long ago. I saw the man Saturday around eleven."

"Yes, I know. Lars says it's because the body was burned. The ME does say he might have died as late as Saturday morning. But it wasn't well into Saturday afternoon."

Betsy said, "That still fits, doesn't it? He only went as far as Minnetonka, and that was before noon. Listen, I've got to take care of my company. I'll see you tomorrow, okay?" Betsy hung up.

David said, a little too brightly, "Funny how the phone knows to ring when you have company, isn't it?"

"Yes. Why did you two come to see me?"

Tom said, "We told you, Lisa said you wanted to talk to us."

"I never told her that."

Tom said, "You didn't? Funny, because she said—"

David interrupted, gently but firmly, "All right. Bro said he told you not to poke into this mess we're in, and we decided to talk to you ourselves, to ask you to continue. Independently, actually. Tom called me to see if I knew where you lived. I didn't, but I'd found out you own this building. We came over to see if one of your tenants had your address and we saw your name on one of the mailboxes."

Tom said, "So we rang the doorbell and here we are," putting a chipper face on it.

David said, "Mother told Lisa you investigate crimes. Are you a licensed private investigator as well as a businesswoman? We're prepared to pay you a fee."

"I'm not licensed," Betsy said. "I do this nonprofessionally, strictly as an amateur. I'm actually out to protect the innocent, rather than find evidence of who committed a crime. Of course, that often means finding out who really did it."

"Then this should be right up your alley," said Tom. "Our mother didn't kill our father—you know that, but the way the cops are sniffing around, it looks like they'll try to find a way to charge her."

"I don't see how that could possibly happen," said Betsy. Then a light went on inside her head. "Oh, this isn't about her, is it? It's about Marvin."

Tom said, "How could it be about Marvin?"

But David said, a little too eagerly, "What have you found out?"

"Your sister is wrong, isn't she? This isn't a one-way love affair, Marvin worshiping your mother from afar. Your mother is as much in love with Marvin as he is with her—and you know it."

Tom said, "Maybe. But they never did anything. There wasn't an affair or something."

But David, leaning back out of his brother's line of sight, grimaced at Betsy in disagreement.

Tom went on, "We think Sergeant Steffans suspects Marv and our mother were, er, having an affair." He hesitated, trying to decide if he should deny it again.

David leaped into the breach. "So, you see, that gives Marv a motive, big-time. Mother would never cheat on Father, but she would never leave him for his best friend, either. So Steffans thinks maybe Marv got impatient."

Betsy asked, "What do you think?"

"He's wrong."

Tom said, "I agree. Not Marv Pierce. Not in a million years."

Betsy said, "Is Marvin as wealthy as Bill was?"

Tom said, "What's that got to do with it?"

"Older women may love as ardently as the young, but they've generally developed a pragmatic streak and are less likely to surrender financial security in the name of love."

David nodded. "Otherwise, Mother would have divorced Father years ago."

Tom said indignantly, "She would not!"

David said, "But Mother isn't as rich as she would have been if Father had died before Bro came home."

"I don't understand," said Betsy.

"Father had to give half the company to Bro in order to get him to agree to take over. His will left quote half his property unquote to Mother, and wills mean what they say, not what the testator meant, so that means she gets a quarter of the company instead of half. Most of her and Father's income was the profit from Birmingham Metal, so she's going to have to cut back on her spending big-time."

Betsy said, "Does Sergeant Steffans know this?"

Tom nodded. "He was asking me questions about it. I told him the profits would be less even if Father hadn't died, because Bro is putting the profits into an expansion program. He thinks he can double the company's business."

Betsy said, "Charlotte told me Bill was countermanding some of your brother's orders. I take it there was a power struggle going on."

David said, "Yes. Father liked the company where it was. Very stable, profits very reliable."

Betsy said, "I hope you see that puts Bro very high on the list of suspects."

Tom stared at her. "No. This was another reason to suspect Mother—but she's got an airtight alibi, thanks to you."

David said, "Tommy, maybe you don't know how mad Bro was about Father not letting go of the company like he promised."

Tommy waved that notion away. "Bro? Not a chance. Bro's too square to murder anyone, much less Father. He's a bigger square than you are."

That set off a mild argument about the merits of being square that Betsy finally interrupted with an announcement that she wanted to be in New London at a reasonable hour. They apologized and left.

Betsy went back to her packing, and as she put her pajamas into the suitcase, she remembered Broward's sincere anger in warning her off—and Lisa's assessment that Bro was a chip off a very aggressive block. Tom and David were wrong. Bro was near if not at the top of Betsy's list of suspects.

Looking around to make sure she'd left nothing behind, Betsy saw her unread copy of the *Excelsior Bay Times* weekly newspaper. Remembering the reporter and photographer at last Saturday's event, she picked it up and put it in her stitchery project bag. Maybe there was a picture of Lars with his Steamer in there.

Thirteen

Despite the delay in getting out of town, Betsy took Highway 55 west rather than 12. Twelve was almost a direct line to Willmar, but she wanted a look at both Buffalo and New London, which lay on the other two sides of a triangle formed by the Twin Cities, Willmar, and Paynesville.

Still, she was surprised at how long a drive it was. She knew, on the one hand, that the route the antique cars would drive from New London to the

Cities suburb of New Brighton was a trifle over a hundred miles—but the route wandered and meandered to avoid main highways and their traffic. On the other hand, apparently there was only so much meandering a route could do.

The early-evening air was cool, and she rolled down all the windows. Out past Rockford, some farmer had been cutting hay and the sweet scent was paradise. The sun was below the horizon but the sky was still blue when the speed limit dropped and signs announced Buffalo, where the antique cars would pause for lunch on Saturday. Betsy noted the turnoff for the high school was on the eastern side of the town, and marked by a gas station. She'd be coming here to help prepare and serve lunch on Saturday. The highway skirted Buffalo's downtown, so she couldn't tell if it was a brisk little city on the move, or a dying country town full of sad, boarded-up commercial buildings.

At Paynesville she turned south on Highway 23, which went past New London on its way to Willmar. By the time she got there, it had been completely dark for a long while, and she didn't get even a vague impression of what New London was like.

By then she was tired, and Willmar was twenty long minutes away. She turned on the radio and found a talk show with a very aggravating host. Being annoyed got her adrenaline flowing, and she came into Willmar bright with anger.

In Minnesota it's hard to find a city, town, or village that isn't wrapped around, alongside, or divided by a lake. Willmar was no exception. Highway 23 joined a divided highway as it ran along the water. A frontage road appeared on the other side of the highway, and soon after Betsy saw the sign for her motel. She pulled into the graveled parking area with a sigh of relief, signed in, called Jill to report her safe arrival, and went to bed.

But she was still too annoyed to sleep. She got into her project bag and found she'd left her knitting in Excelsior—another annoyance. She'd been working on an infant's sweater for a homeless program, and forgot she'd brought it down to the shop to show a customer. The counted pattern she had brought along was too complex to tackle for relaxation, so she picked up the *Bay Times*. There was no story about the antique cars on the front page, or the second page, or the fourth page—there it was, a two-page spread in the very center, with lots of photographs. One was of Lars, standing in streamers of steam like a character in a Gothic movie, his expression serious and his pose dramatic. Jill might like a print of that. Betsy made a note in the margin to call the paper and ask if prints were for sale. There were more than a dozen photos surrounding a short article in the middle of the spread. In an upper corner was the 1902 Oldsmobile, and there was the Winton, its cloche-hatted rider standing with one foot on the running board, needing only a machine gun to look a lot like Clyde's girlfriend, Bonnie. In a lower corner was a white-flannel rump sticking out from under the hood of a Maxwell. "Getting to the seat of the problem," read the caption, "an unidentified driver works on his Maxwell." Bill Birmingham had said he didn't want to be interviewed, Betsy remembered, and apparently hadn't paused in his labors even long enough to give his name. Cute photo, in a way, and an even cuter caption—but too bad the last photograph of Bill had to be this ridiculous pose. Such a contrast to the noble look the photographer had somehow found in Lars.

Betsy yawned. Amusement had washed away her annoyance, and suddenly she was very tired. She folded the paper and put it on the nightstand, turned out the light, and in less than five minutes was sound asleep in her rented bed.

A loud noise startled her out of a dreamless sleep. For a moment she couldn't think what the noise was or why the bed felt unfamiliar. Oh, Willmar, sure. And it was the phone, which made its harsh noise again, and she fumbled the receiver to her ear.

"H'lo?" she mumbled.

"Aren't you up yet?" asked a chipper voice she recognized as Jill's. "I was going to buy you breakfast if you were about ready to go."

Up? Was it morning already? Yes, that seemed to be sunshine shining around the edges of the heavy curtain pulled across the window. Wow.

"Are you here in Willmar?" asked Betsy, blinking to get her vision going. She'd had laser surgery on her eyes a few months ago and was still pleased and a little surprised, once she pried them open, to be able to read the little bedside alarm clock without help. Six A.M. Wow.

"No, I'm in New London. There's a nice little café on the main street that knows how to fry an egg just like you want it."

"Poached," said Betsy. "Can they fry it poached?"

"I wouldn't be surprised. In forty-five minutes then?"

"What's the name of the place?"

"I can't remember, but it's the café on the main street, you can't miss it," said Jill. "Lars and I will meet you there."

Must be a really small town, thought Betsy, hanging up and tossing back the covers.

Soon after, she drove into New London across a beautiful curving bridge over a big old millpond. It dropped her off in downtown, which was two blocks long and did not in any way resemble its namesake. There was a needlework shop, Betsy noticed as she got out of her car, and a gift shop, a restaurant, a gas station, and a café. The café was full of people, and the air was heavy with the old-fashioned, pre-cholesterol-scare smells of bacon, sausage, fried eggs, toast, hash browns, pancakes, and hot, maple-flavored syrup. There was a counter, whose seven stools were made of red plastic and stainless steel, and pale,

Formica-topped tables along the other walls. Pictures of wildlife adorned the smokey blue walls.

At a table along the wall were Jill, Lars, and Adam. Lars and Adam were facing the door, and so raised their hands when Betsy came in to show her where they were.

Betsy sat beside Jill, who handed her a menu. "They can poach you an egg if you like," she said. "I already asked."

Lars and Adam were digging into platters laden with Canadian bacon, fried eggs, and hash browns, with toast on the side.

Betsy ordered a poached egg on a slice of whole wheat toast, and coffee. Jill had a gigantic sweet roll with pecans glued to it with melted brown sugar.

Adam smiled at Betsy. "Ready to go for a ride?"

"What, you mean with Lars?"

"Okay, if you like. But there are other cars making the short trip to Litchfield today. You can hitch a ride with one of them, if you like, maybe on the way out or back."

"Gosh, thanks!" said Betsy, glancing at Lars to see if he minded.

He shrugged and smiled around a mouthful of potato.

"Do I have some duties to perform today?" Betsy asked Adam.

"Not really. We're not logging people out for Litchfield, it's an informal trip."

"Are you driving to Litchfield?" she asked.

"Yes. You want to ride with me? I'm driving my 1911 Renault sport touring car. You won't see another like it in your life."

Betsy asked, "Do you mean because it's restored so beautifully, or because it's rare?"

Adam grinned. "Both."

"Well, how can I turn down a double once-in-a-lifetime opportunity? Though I probably won't appreciate it like I should. I'm so ignorant about this car-collecting business."

Adam's grin broadened. "Just watch the envious eyes on us, and you'll know all you need to know."

Lars said, "You want to make the return trip with Jill and me?"

Betsy looked at Jill. "You're finally coming to terms with that car, aren't you?"

"I suppose so. I went for a ride in it a few days ago, and I have to admit, it's slick."

"Next year, in costume!" announced Betsy happily. To Lars she said, "Yes, I'll be glad to ride with you."

Jill asked Adam, "Is there a layover in Litchfield, or do we just go there and come right back?"

"Whatever you like. Since we don't note departure times for these little practice runs, you're entirely on your own. But if you're interested in staying awhile, Litchfield has a nice Civil War museum, and some antique shops."

Betsy wondered what sort of Civil War museum there could be in a place so far removed from the battle sites—and decided she'd take a look and see. She looked at Jill and thought she detected the same notion.

Lars did, too. He sighed. "All right, we'll take a look at the museum."

Betsy smiled at yet another instance of someone knowing someone else's mind very well. "What time are you leaving, Adam?" she asked.

"About ten, if things are running all right at the Boy Scout building. That's our headquarters here in New London." He checked his watch. "I'd better get over there. See you at ten." He smiled at Jill and Lars. "You, too," he said, rose, and departed.

As soon as he was out of earshot, Lars said, "So what have you found out so far?"

"About what?" asked Betsy.

"About this murder," he said impatiently.

"Nothing."

His light blue eyes widened. "I don't believe that," he said.

"Why not?"

"You're too clever to have gone around asking questions like you do and not found out *something*."

Jill said, mock-proudly, "And you thought he was just another dumb blond, didn't you?"

Lars guffawed, but his eyes remained expectantly on Betsy.

"All right. I have been told by two of her children that a friend of the Birmingham family was hopelessly in love with Charlotte. I think she returned that love, and may have been having a long-term affair with him. His name is Marvin Pierce, and I have a sad feeling that since Charlotte wouldn't divorce her husband for him, he may have found another way to set her free."

"If they were mutually in love, why wouldn't Charlotte divorce her husband?" asked Jill. "From what I've heard, Bill Birmingham was a workaholic, and when he did come home, he was a tyrant. Why not leave him? Divorce is easy enough nowadays."

Lars said, "Maybe she was afraid of Bill's reaction. If he was bad-tempered, was he also abusive?"

"I don't know," said Betsy. "I haven't heard anything on that order."

"Well, what else do you know?" asked Lars.

Betsy said, "Bill Birmingham was a very wealthy man, wealthier than Marvin. If it wasn't me supplying the alibi, I'd certainly be trying to poke a hole in it, because Charlotte is the obvious suspect. On the other hand, Bill's

death came at a bad time. It seems a substantial part of his income was the
profits from his company. When Bill had a ministroke, he invited his son Broward to come home and take over the business. Bro has all kinds of ideas for
expanding the company, and he'd been plowing the profits back into it. Bill
was trying to stop him, but not only had Bill turned the management over to
Bro, he had to give half the company to Bro to get him to agree to come home.
Bill was taking steps to stop or at least slow Bro down when he was killed."

"Where does that leave the grieving widow?" asked Lars.

"Not as well off as she'd have been if she'd killed Bill before Bro came into
the picture."

"Ah," nodded Jill.

Lars asked, "Where was Bro Saturday morning?"

"I don't know. Is there a way to find out, maybe from Sergeant Steffans? I don't want to ask Bro myself—he has his father and grandfather's bad
temper."

Jill pulled a notebook from her shirt pocket—Betsy was amused to notice
that even out of uniform Jill carried one—and made a note. Writing, she said,
"I wonder if Marvin is as eager a lover now that Charlotte's not rich?"

"Well, I'm not sure how not-rich she is. I'd like to find out the situation
with Bill's estate. Surely there's more to it than the business and a set of antique
cars."

Jill made another note. "Looks like I'll have to take Sergeant Steffans to
lunch next week." She was so busy writing she missed the massive frown that
slowly formed on Lars's broad forehead.

Sergeant Steffans ran his thumb and long, knobby fingers down
either side of his narrow jaw. He was standing in Marvin's small office in
the Lutheran Brotherhood Building downtown. Lutheran Brotherhood was
a large insurance company with headquarters in a bloodred building with
copper-coated windows, one of a set of buildings apparently colored by a
comic-book artist on the south end of downtown Minneapolis. Steffans grew
up in St. Paul, whose sedate old skyscrapers and narrow streets show plainly
why it considers itself at best a fraternal twin to Minneapolis's broad avenues
and sci-fi buildings.

Marvin Pierce was about five-nine, with light brown hair in a very retro
crew cut. He was trim and athletic in build, dressed Friday casual in Dockers,
sport coat, and blue dress shirt without a tie. His face couldn't carry the build
or the hair, being very ordinary and middle-aged. His blue eyes were wary.

"It's just routine," Steffans said. "We have to check and double-check every possibility." He could see Marvin didn't believe that, but it was true—most cases were broken by following a well-marked routine.

"I didn't see her Saturday morning," Marvin said, "so I don't know what time she left her house. I know she was home by five-thirty, because that's what time it was when I checked my watch when I was in her kitchen heating water to make her a cup of tea. I'd been there about, oh, I'm not sure, twenty minutes? But of course, by then, Bill'd been dead for hours." He bit his lip and stroked the top of his head, yanking his hand away when he encountered the bristly haircut. New style then. Was that important? Steffans wrote a very brief note—he was a thorough note taker—while Marvin mused, "God, what a mess! I still can't believe he's gone."

"How long had you known him?"

"Years." When Steffans held his pen ready and looked inquiring, Marvin calculated and said, "Twenty-six, twenty-seven years. Maybe twenty-eight. I worked for him for a while, foreman in the plant."

"Why'd you quit?"

"Got a better offer, which wasn't difficult. Bill Birmingham hated to pay a man what he was worth. Not a bad boss, a little hard, and tight. Good businessman and better friend. Liked him, liked his kids, liked his wife."

"You married?"

"Twice, once right out of high school, lasted ten months, no kids; then nine years to Alice. Three kids, all girls, all doing fine, turned out nice. 'Course, a lot of that is due to Alice's second husband, a good man, walked the second two down the aisle when they got married." Marvin was looking inward, a half smile on his lips, and half of that was pained.

Steffans made another note. "Did you murder Bill Birmingham?"

That directness surprised Marvin; he looked up, mouth half open, eyes wide. "No," he said.

"Do you know who did?"

"No!" This came out a bit sharply, and he grimaced. "No way I could know that," he said. "I wasn't there when it happened."

"Where were you?"

"At home."

"Alone?"

Now he was amused. "Yes, as it happens. I had some friends over the night before and we sat up late, playing poker, shooting the bull, drinking beer. I got up Saturday, but I was feeling so bad I had to call Buddy Anderson, who I was supposed to meet for golf, and beg off. I don't know if it was the beer or the sandwiches, but I was pretty sick all day Saturday. I stayed home with the TV, so I was there when Char's son Bro called me late in the afternoon with the news, and asked me to come over. Char was taking it hard, he said, and asking for me."

"Were you surprised?"

"Hell, yes! I thought that when old Bill went, it would be a stroke, him having high blood pressure and all."

"No, I mean that Charlotte Birmingham would ask for you."

"Oh. No, not at all. I've sat up with her and one or another of the children many a time. Been there for the good times, too. Done it so much people are surprised to learn I'm not a member of the family."

As she drove behind Jill and Lars around the millpond, Betsy noted small houses of the post–World War II variety, then a wide, grassy field full of motor homes, closed trailers, and antique cars. Jill turned there, and a little farther along were some enormous, modern sheds on one side of the narrow street and on the other an old cemetery. At least some of the enormous sheds were bus barns, their big open doors showing that inside were not city buses, but the luxury kind that are rented to groups making jaunts. Except one of the barns had antique cars inside and in front of it.

There were more antique cars parked on a sandy verge along the narrow lane.

Betsy was so busy looking around that she almost failed to notice that Jill, on making another turn, had immediately pulled onto that scrubby verge. She slammed on her brakes as she went past Jill's car, and pulled in at the far end of the row, beside a sky-blue vehicle the size of a Conestoga wagon. It had blue and white striped awning material for a roof. The hood was small for a car that size, and the radiator sloped backward from its base. Like most of the antique cars, its wheels were wagon size, with thick, wooden spokes. When she got out, she could hear that the car's engine was running, but in a very peculiar manner. Every antique car she had met so far had its own motor sound, but this one had to be the strangest. *Brum*-sniff, *brum*-sniff, *brum*-sniff, it went.

Jill and Lars were walking up to an old, white clapboard house. There was a big sign, BOY SCOUTS OF AMERICA, over a screen door marked only by a small concrete slab. Betsy took two steps to follow, then turned to listen some more to the huge car's motor. Yes, it was inhaling sharply between short engine sounds, *brum*-sniff, *brum*-sniff, *brum*-sniff. A man in jeans and blue checked shirt who had ducked around Lars on the walk now came angling toward Betsy.

"Whaddaya think?" he asked as he stopped beside her.

"What is it?" asked Betsy.

"A 1901 Winton. Single cylinder. This is the car that made a transcontinental crossing of the United States, New York to San Francisco, before there were paved roads or gas stations."

"Wow," said Betsy. "The pioneering spirit was still alive then, I guess."

That remark pleased him. "And I own a hunk of it." The man got in and put his machine into reverse. Whining and tilting dangerously, it backed onto the lane, but then rolled smoothly on down toward the bus barns. Apparently it only sniffed while idling.

Must be a heck of a big cylinder, thought Betsy, *if you can hear it sucking wind like that. Of course, to move something that big, it would have to be one heck of a cylinder.*

She went up the walk and through the screen door—which made a very nostalgic creak when opened and a satisfactory slap when it closed. But this wasn't a home. The floor was faded linoleum tile; the walls were dotted with Boy Scout posters and an old black bearskin.

They had come in through the long side of a rectangular room. Tables of assorted sizes and styles were scattered around it. Behind a long one made of plywood, under the bearskin, stood three women and two household-moving-size cardboard boxes. On a nearby table was a stack of the banners drivers were to put on their cars, canvas squares with ANTIQUE CAR RUN, the soft drink symbol, and big black numbers printed on them. Ties ran off each corner.

The women behind the table were all wearing big green T-shirts with the logo of the Antique Car Run printed on their fronts. Half a dozen men and four women waited patiently in two lines in front of the table. Lars and Jill were among them.

One man at the head of the line was laughing at some jest he'd already made, and as the woman handed him a shirt and a clear plastic bag of materials, he asked, "What's the difference between roast beef and pea soup?"

"What?" asked the woman.

"Anyone can roast beef!" he said. She made a "get away with you" gesture at him, and he turned to leave, laughing heartily. *I bet he started out as a traveling salesman,* thought Betsy.

On the long table was a big computer printout listing each driver's name, hometown, kind of car, and number of passengers. When it was his turn, Lars announced, "I'm Lars Larson, number sixty-three," and one of the women ran a finger down the list. When she found it, she ran a highlighter mark through it.

"Welcome to New London, Lars," she said. "Are these your two riders?" she added, smiling at Betsy and Jill.

Jill nodded, and Betsy said, "No, but I'm a volunteer. I'll be logging departures tomorrow."

Another woman, very brisk and tiny, asked Lars, "What size T-shirt do you wear, dear?"

"Two-X," he replied, and she asked the same question of Jill and Betsy, then turned to one of the enormous boxes, which came up to her armpits, to dig around until she found examples in the right sizes.

"We've got to get these sorted out," she remarked to the woman with the marker. "Or I'll fall in reaching for one and never be seen again. Here you go, dears." Then she turned to lift out a clear plastic bag from the other box. It held maps and instructions.

The other woman said to Lars, "Tie your banner on the left side of your car. That's where the monitors will be standing, and they'll want to be able to find your number quickly if you come in with several other cars."

Lars grinned. "I won't be among several other cars, I'll be way out in front."

The woman frowned severely at him. "Remember, this is *not* a race."

Jill snorted faintly and Betsy smiled. Not officially, no. But the cars were mostly being driven by men used to overcoming competition, and who did not like losing.

Fourteen

As they went down the walk out of the Boy Scout building, Betsy checked her watch. It was not quite quarter to ten, so she continued across the narrow lane and through an opening in a tall hedge into the cemetery.

"What's up?" asked Jill, hurrying to join her.

"Nothing, we have a few minutes, so I thought I'd look around."

"In here?" asked Lars. "This is a cemetery," he added, in case she hadn't noticed the headstones.

"I know. I just like cemeteries." Betsy said it somewhat shamefacedly.

"So do I," said Jill.

"You do?"

"I thought you'd got over that!" groaned Lars. "I don't get it, what's the attraction?"

Betsy said, "I like the epitaphs. They're coming back, you know. For a long while it was too costly to put more than names and a date on a tombstone, but with laser cutters, you can have drawings and sayings all over your stone. Every so often I try to think up one for myself. I like really old ones best. 'Behold O man, as you pass by—'"

Jill joined in, "'As you are now, so once was I. As I am now, you soon must be. Repent, prepare to follow me.'" Jill and Betsy laughed quietly, pleased to find another thing in common.

Lars said, "I'm going to go start my car," and walked away.

"He's a little sensitive," apologized Jill. "Or are we a little mad?"

"There's something peaceful about cemeteries," said Betsy. "I think long, easy thoughts in these places. Oh, look at that stone with the bus on it!"

"Someone in the Boy Scout building said the man who owned the bus company was buried here so he could keep watch over his company."

A large monument near where they came in had lettering on every side. They paused to read it and found an account of an Indian massacre, noting, the remains of the victims were buried here. "Say, you don't see many of these," said Jill.

"I know. From the cowboy movies you'd think they'd be common, but they're not."

They heard a quiet voice, and moved sideways just enough to see a woman on the other side, talking to a man taking photographs of the monument. She was saying—not reading from the monument, which had the usual sentiments about savages and innocent settlers, ". . . and the local Indian agent told them that the money promised from the federal government in payment for their land was not coming and they could try surviving that winter by eating grass. So of course, they got upset."

"Uh-huh," said the man. "Here, come point at the writing so I can show in the picture how big this sucker is."

"Come on," murmured Jill, and Betsy followed her back through the hedge.

They went the short distance down the lane and then crossed the faded blacktop street to the bus barn. Drivers, some wearing the big white dusters of the period, were standing beside their machines, or tinkering with them, or running a chamois or soft cloth over them, or talking with others about adventures on the road.

It was indicative of the determined goodwill these people had for one another that they said nothing when Lars began the lengthy process of firing up his Stanley. Steamers make internal combustion people nervous. Lars did his part by rolling his machine out of the shed first. Betsy came to help push and was surprised to find the car light and easy to move. "No transmission to weigh things down," Lars reminded her.

While Lars worked with his blowtorch, Betsy went to look at the other cars preparing for departure. Some she had seen in Excelsior last Saturday.

Trembling like Don Knotts was the rickety, topless, curved-dash Oldsmobile. Near it was an ancient green Sears, whose tiller came up from the side and made a ninety-degree turn to lay across the driver's lap. The International Harvester farm wagon with hard rubber tires came rolling by.

Here also was the immense Winton's younger sibling, the soft-yellow car with brown fenders that could have passed as a car from the twenties, that had beat Lars to Excelsior. And there was another, brighter yellow car of very dashing design. It had wide tires, a very long hood, two seats, and a big oval gas tank on top of the trunk, right behind the seats. On the back bumper was a spare tire with a black canvas cover on which was printed MARMON, 1911. Like the Winton, it looked very competent, and she began to feel a little better about being here with the super-capable Stanley.

Falling somewhere in between the Olds and the Marmon were a black 1910 Maxwell two-seater and an immense dark blue Cadillac touring car from 1911. There was also a beautiful, snub-nosed two-seater Buick, bright red, with its name spelled in brass on its radiator and *1907* in smaller figures.

An early REO pickup truck, also red, with hard rubber wheels, *buck-whuddled* by, an enormous American flag flying from the bin. "John!" called someone as he went by, "you're not allowed to use a sail!"

John, laughing, answered, "That's *my* line, Vern!"

A little yellow Brush with its top up puttered along behind the REO, driven by a man who looked a great deal like Oliver Hardy. Behind it *dick-dicked* a red Yale whose driver and passenger were wearing white knickers and jackets, pinch-brim hats, and goggles. The car, Betsy noticed, had a back door one could use to get into the backseat. "What year?" she called to the driver.

"Ought five!" he replied and waved as he continued up the road.

There came an eerie sound, a low howling slowly climbing the scale as it grew louder. Heads turned in alarm toward it, then just as Betsy recognized it as the Stanley building a head of steam, someone said, "By God, you'll never get me up in one of those things!" and there was laughter.

"Hey, Betsy!" called Lars. "Com'ere!" She waved and went over.

Jill said, "We're going to leave now. Have you met up with Adam?"

"No." Betsy looked around, but didn't see him. "You go ahead, I'll find him."

Jill followed Lars into the car, the route papers in her hand. "We go south, which is the way we're headed," she said, looking at the directions. She waved at Betsy. "See you in Litchfield!"

Lars politely waited until he was well away from the bus barn before blowing his whistle, but still some people waved impolitely at him.

When all but one of the cars going on the jaunt had departed, Betsy was still standing there. The driver of that last car, a tall, slim man with nice blue eyes said, "Miss your ride?"

"I don't see how," Betsy replied. "I was supposed to go with Adam Smith in his Renault."

"Last I saw him, he was in the Boy Scout building," said the man, climbing down. "That was just a few minutes ago, but he looked all tied up."

Betsy's face fell and he said, "Why don't you ride with us? Plenty of room." He gestured at his car, a big Model T. A woman sitting in the passenger seat waved invitingly.

Betsy hesitated. She wanted to talk to Adam. On the other hand, if he was really tied up, she was not only not going to talk to him in any case, she wasn't going to get to ride in one of these pioneers. "All right. I have a ride back, which I won't get if I can't get to Litchfield. I'm Betsy Devonshire."

"Mike Jimson. That's my wife Dorothy. Climb aboard. Spark retarded?" he asked his wife.

"Yes, love," she said.

Betsy opened the door and climbed into the spacious backseat, which was black leather and deeply comfortable. Mike cranked once, then again, and the Model T shook itself to life. He came around and got in, as his wife said, "South on Oak to the Stop sign at County Road Forty."

Used to the incredible smoothness of the Stanley, and the very faint vibration of her own modern car, she was a little surprised at the steady jiggle of the Model T, and suddenly empathetic of Charlotte's complaint last weekend of an upset stomach.

There was a line of six antiques waiting to cross Highway 23. The old cars were slow getting into motion, and so needed the road to be clear a considerable distance in both directions. Looking up the line, Betsy was amused to see how it was sort of like looking at a movie slightly out of focus, as each car vibrated to its own rhythm.

When the Model T's turn came, they waited only a couple of minutes before Mike raced his engine, and, the gearbox groaning loudly, they went slowly, slowly up the slight incline and out onto the highway. They were only up to walking speed as they started down the other side, and a modern car whizzing by on the highway tooted its horn derisively.

But now there was a clear stretch, and Mike, relaxing, suddenly burst into song. Dorothy immediately joined in:

> *"Let me call you Lizzie, I'm in love with you;*
> *Let me hear you rattle down the av-e-nue;*
> *Keep your headlights glowing, and your taillight, too;*
> *Let me call you Lizzie, I'm in debt for you!"*

Betsy laughed. "Who wrote that?" she asked.

"Who knows?" Dorothy replied. "It was a schoolyard song when I was young, though it might have been a vaudeville number about the time the first Model T came out. The Model T was called Tin Lizzie, you know."

"Yes, that's one thing I knew about them. So I guess that song is as old as the joke that you could have a Model T in any color you wanted, so long as it was black."

"Do you know why all Fords were black?" asked Mike.

"Why?" asked Betsy, expecting another joke.

But Mike was serious. "Two reasons: first, because black paint dried quicker than any other color; and second, because it made supplying spare parts a snap. No need to try to figure out how many green fenders or blue doors or brown hood covers to stock when everything came in black. And all the parts were interchangeable, thanks to the assembly line method. People forget what a huge innovator Henry Ford was. He once said he could give his Model T's away and make money just selling parts."

When they got onto County Road 2, which was a busy two-lane highway, the old cars had to run on the shoulder. Cars rushed past, some honking in greeting, others in warning, one or two in anger. Mike summoned the Ford's best speed, which came with even more noise and so much vibration Betsy wondered why parts weren't shaken free.

"How fast are we going?" she asked, her voice sounding flat against the racket.

Mike checked his primitive instrument panel. "Twenty-eight mind-blowing miles an hour. What's next?" he asked Dorothy.

"We're on this for six miles," she replied, "until we come to a Stop sign where Route Ten joins us and we turn left."

"Okay," he nodded.

Betsy tried to relax in the capacious backseat, stretching her arms out on either side. *Seize the day*, she told herself. The breeze made her light dress flutter against her legs, and kept her cool. She had wisely dabbed sunblock on her face and arms this morning, so no fear of sunburn. She decided she liked riding up high and having her feet flat on the floor instead of resting on their heels. And in the open like this, and at this slow a speed, there was plenty of time to look around and enjoy the sights and smells of the countryside. Unlike in the Stanley, with its low sides, in the Model T she felt very much "inside" and safe, and so didn't mind the lack of a seat belt very much.

But the noise was such that she soon gave up trying to talk with Mike and Dorothy.

In a little over an hour they came into Pine Grove and pulled over behind a row of antique cars for a pit stop at the Home Town Café. Betsy climbed out, dusty, windblown, and a little deaf from the noise of the engine. She crossed the highway, surprised at her unsteady pace. That jiggle was really something, especially when it stopped.

Pine Grove was a hamlet strung along one side of the highway, the other side marked by a well-maintained railroad line. She looked around, at the dusty buildings, the flat landscape, the old cars. She'd admired the people who made the movie *Paper Moon* for traveling around the Midwest in a search for authentic dirt roads and small towns, thinking then it must have been hard to find them; but they'd traveled down a dirt road a while back, and here was an authentically shabby little town, right on a highway, not hard to find at all.

Betsy felt as if her brain had shaken loose during the ride. She had gone into some strange, reflective mode—not the kind that comes from actual meditation, but the kind that comes from heavy-duty pain pills. Everything had become a tinge unreal. She saw an elderly man sitting very erect on a bench in front of the café, and wanted to go ask him if he'd fought in the Civil War, just to see if he'd cackle and tell her a story about Gettysburg. Of course, another part of her knew that question was better asked of the old man's great-grandfather, that she was caught up in the pseudo-reality of a moving picture. This was the early twenty-first century, not the early twentieth. Right? She began to look for an anachronism to prove it. Like in the movie *Gladiator*, spoiled for her when the ancient Romans handed out hastily printed leaflets. The movie makers had apparently forgotten the printing press was at least ten centuries forward from ancient Rome.

And now, here came a good anachronism in the form of a train rumbling down the tracks behind the row of cars. The engines pulling the train were diesels, which didn't replace steam engines until the fifties. She waved gratefully at it, and watched the whole train rumble by. It was long, mostly grain cars. There was no little red caboose at the end, which made her feel sad.

She went into the café and bought a Diet Coke, which came in an aluminum can. Aluminum, she knew, was once an extremely rare metal, so rare that the builders of the Washington Monument paid huge sums for enough to cap the point, forgoing the far less expensive gold or platinum.

Times change in unexpected ways, she reflected, and no period movie ever gets it exactly right. Especially when it came to women's hairdos; no matter how authentic the costumes, you could always tell when a movie was made by the way the lead actress wore her hair.

The people were sitting at tables talking about cars and the trip, but also about other things: "It's not the size of the boat, but its ability to stay in port until all the passengers have disembarked," said a man in a low voice with a hint of a snigger in it. He was the same man who earlier couldn't "pea" soup.

A woman was saying to another woman, "And then, darling, when the judge called for a trot, that woman behind me went into a *rack*, I am not kidding, a *rack*! *And* the judge gave her the blue ribbon! I nearly fell off my horse, but decided instead I'd had enough of showing Arabians, and I sold Sheik's Desire the next week and bought the Yale that Tom had been panting after."

A man boasted with a hint of regret, "I had her up to forty last week, on that downhill slope on County Five, but she was shaking so hard I thought a wheel had come loose. She hasn't been the same since. I think she scared herself. I know she scared me."

Betsy didn't see Lars and Jill, but that didn't surprise her; she hadn't seen the Stanley outside, either. They must have already stopped and gone on, or not stopped at all, more likely. After having been beaten last Saturday, Lars was probably determined to arrive first in Litchfield.

Although this was not, of course, a race.

What was a bit more problematic was that Mike and Dorothy weren't there, either.

Betsy took her Coke outside, to be reassured by the sight of the Model T still parked across the street. *They must be in the restrooms*, she thought. Two drivers came out and started cranking their cars. The driver of the REO had to adjust his magneto twice before the engine caught. *Grunge, grunge, grunge*, it complained, before he pulled out well behind the other and *putt, putt, putt-putt-putt*, started up the road.

She watched him diminish to a heat-waved mirage then heard a sound—not quite like a modern car, but not like the rickety sound of an old one, either. She turned and saw something spectacular coming up the road, to pull off behind the Model T.

It was a gorgeous antique limousine, tall and long, a rich, royal blue with inlaid brass stripes on the hood and along the back door. The backseat was under a black leather roof, but the front seat wasn't. There was a kind of second windshield behind the front seat, with hinged wings to further enclose the rear passenger compartment, which appeared to be empty. The very distinctive hood sloped downward to the nose, then sloped very steeply down and forward to the front bumper. The radiator was *behind* the hood, sticking out around the edges. The tires were fat, the heavy wooden spokes of the wheels painted creamy white. The engine, ticking gently over, stopped, and a man shifted over to the passenger side and climbed out. He was slim, broad-shouldered, and extremely elegant in royal blue riding pants, the old-fashioned kind with wings, and black leather gaiters with buckles. He wasn't wearing a coat or jacket, but an immaculate white shirt whose upper sleeves were encircled by royal blue garters, and as he got out, he took off a royal blue cap with a narrow black bill and wiped his brow with the back of his hand.

Betsy suddenly recognized him. "Adam!" she called.

He looked over at her and smiled and waved his cap.

Betsy looked both ways and hurried across. "Oh my, oh my, oh my!" she said. "Is *this* the Renault? Golly, what a car! Was it made by the same people who make Renaults today? I've never seen anything so elegant!"

"Yes and yes," said Adam, pleased at her enthusiasm. "And I agree, it's about as elegant as a car can get. Body and chassis by Renault, who of course still make cars, running board boxes by Louis Vuitton, who still make luggage, headlamps by Ducellier and ignition by Bosch, both of whom are still in the automotive business."

"What is that half-a-top called, a landau?"

"No, a Victoria."

Betsy swept her eyes down its length. "Gosh, it must be twenty feet long! I didn't know they made limos this far back!"

He laughed. "It's not really a limo, but a sport touring car. It's seventeen feet long, seven and a half feet tall with the top up."

"Does it have a speaking tube? You know"—she mimed holding something between thumb and two fingers—"home, James," she said in plummy accents.

"As a matter of fact, it does."

"The engine compartment doesn't look very big—how fast does it go?"

"It has four cylinders, which for 1911, the year it was built, is pretty good. She'll do about fifty on a level stretch, if it's long enough. She's heavy, so it takes a couple of miles to get to her top speed. She has a big muffler, so the ride is both smooth and very quiet."

"Wow, I can't get over it, this is so beautiful! I'm so glad you were able to catch up. Mike Jimson told me you got busy just about the time we were supposed to leave, so I rode with him and his wife in their Model T." Betsy gestured toward the car parked ahead of the Renault.

"I'm glad I caught up before you left Pine Grove. But come on, I need something cold to drink before we head out."

They waited for a truck and two cars to pass, all honking at them, one swerving while the driver and his passengers waved madly. While Adam got his can of root beer, Betsy found Mike and Dorothy at a table in the back and explained that she was going to continue the trip in Adam Smith's Renault.

"So Adam got here after all," said Mike. "Good for him. And you're gonna love riding in that thing."

As they went back across the road, Adam asked, "Front or back?"

"Oh, front, so we can talk."

"Wait till I get her started, then." He went to the front of the car, Betsy following, to push a short lever by its brass knob with his left hand, and began to crank with his right. The engine went *fffut-fffut*, he released the lever, and the car started.

"What is that, some kind of spring windup mechanism?" she asked.

"No, the lever is a compression release. It opens the exhaust valves a little so it's easier to crank. Here—" He pointed to a small silver knob on the front— "this is what retards or advances the spark on the magneto, so the car won't backfire and break your cranking arm." He went to climb in, Betsy following.

She looked across the road and saw a small crowd gathered on the side-walk, some of them fellow antique car drivers.

"You'd think they'd be used to seeing this," said Betsy.

"No, I don't bring this one out very often. It's really rare and it would be a pity if it got in an accident."

The notion of an accident made her reach for her seat belt, which of course wasn't there. "Do you ever think of having seat belts installed?"

"Nope. I only put back what once was there," he said with a smile.

"Do you want me to navigate?"

"No need. I helped lay out this route, so I know it pretty well."

They rode in silence for a bit. The Renault had the weighty, comfortable feel of a big sixties convertible, but the inside wasn't much like a modern car—especially the blank dashboard.

"How do you know how fast you're going?" Betsy asked.

"Look down on the floor near my feet." Sure enough, the speedometer was on the floor. "And the key to turn on the ignition is on the seat, behind my legs. This car has many unique features. You notice there's plenty of room up here."

"Yes?" said Betsy.

"Makers of chauffeur-driven cars wanted to give as much room as possible to the passengers, so the driver's compartment was very small. That's one reason there was a fad for Asian chauffeurs, who, generally being smaller, weren't as cramped."

"That's the kind of trivia that could win someone a lot of money," said Betsy laughing. "All right, why was the driver of this car given more room?"

"Because this wasn't really a limo, and the buyer needed a driver who could double as a bodyguard, someone big enough to need extra space."

"What was this, a gangster's car?"

Adam laughed. "No, not at all."

Betsy was pleased to have put Adam in a good mood, but a little silence fell while she tried to think how to phrase her next question. At last she simply began, "Adam, what do you think happened to Bill Birmingham?"

"What do you mean, what do I think happened? Someone shot him and set his car on fire."

"Who?"

He frowned at her briefly, then returned his eyes to the road. "How should I know?"

"Well, who would want to do such a thing?"

"I don't want to say," he said. "It's hard to think it might be someone I know." His attitude was so sincere, Betsy began to worry she was on the wrong track entirely. She thought again how to continue, but before she could say anything, he went on. "His son Bro, obviously."

She said, "Because he wanted the business?"

"Because his father wouldn't quit the business like he was supposed to. That was Bill all over, couldn't let go. He just couldn't let go."

"Is that why he wouldn't sell you the Fuller?"

"What?" He glanced at her, frowning deeply. "What are you getting at?"

"He bought that Fuller because you wanted it, right? His original intention was to sell it to you at a profit. But maybe once he got hold of it, he just couldn't let it go."

Adam considered this. "Maybe. But it's more likely he hung on to it in order to make me as mad at him as he was at me. Stick your arm out."

"What?"

"I want to pass the Sears, stick your arm out."

Betsy glanced at the road behind, saw it was clear, and extended her left arm. Adam pulled smoothly out onto the highway, went around the Sears with a wave, and pulled back onto the shoulder again. The Sears sounded its bulb horn and Adam replied with a beautiful French horn note.

They rode in silence for a bit, then Betsy said, "Bill was mad at you because you bought that Maxwell he wanted, right?"

"Partly. But mostly because I ran against him for president of the Antique Car Club. And I beat him. He would have made a lousy president because he didn't know the meaning of compromise, and everyone knew it. He thought he lost because I was spreading ugly rumors about him."

"What kind of rumors?"

"That he rarely listened to what anyone else said, and if he did happen to hear a good idea, he'd take it as his own without giving credit. Which weren't rumors, they were facts, and I said as much in the course of a free and open campaign."

This time Betsy held her tongue on purpose, and after a minute, Adam said, "And because he heard that if he got elected, Charlie and Mack and I would quit and start our own club. And that after six months ours would be the only antique car club in Minnesota."

"Did you say those things, too?"

"Well, yes. But I was only repeating what Mack said first. Besides, it was God's truth."

"I imagine he was pretty angry with you."

"I imagine he was. The truth can hurt."

"Are you going to buy the Fuller from Charlotte?"

"Yes, if she offers it for sale. And if I'm not in prison, convicted of murdering Bill."

"You think that's possible?"

"Ms. Devonshire, anything's possible. I've been reading about those convicts on death row they're finding didn't do it after all, and let me tell you, it's keeping me up at night."

"Minnesota doesn't have the death penalty."

"If they did, I'd've moved to Costa Rica by now."

Soon they turned onto County 11 and a few miles later entered Litchfield. It was a small city with a really wide main street which put Betsy in mind of some New England towns she'd visited long ago. They'd passed a few of the slower antique cars along the way, but Lars's Stanley was already parked at the top of the street that bordered a pretty little park. He was making some arcane adjustment to the valves when Betsy came up to him.

"Were you the first to arrive?" she asked.

"Of course," he replied, a little too carelessly.

"Where's Jill?"

"Over in the museum." He nodded his head sideways and Betsy looked over at a modest building with a Civil War era cannon in front of it. "I went in with her, but it's just some old pictures and stuff, so I got bored after a while and decided to check my pilot light. If I leave the pilot light on, it keeps a head of steam on and I can start 'er right up."

Betsy said, "How long before you want to start back?"

"Oh, anytime you two are ready. I proved my point today already, and I'll take her easy on the trip back, so she'll be in good trim for tomorrow." And a big, confident grin spread all over his face.

Fifteen

The main room on the first floor of the museum was devoted mostly to enlarged photographs of every Litchfield man who had served in the Civil War. There were about twenty, most of them with names like Svenson and Larson and Pedersen. Brief bios under the oval frames indicated some had been in America only a year or two before marching off to war. Betsy found herself touching the frame around the solemn face of a young man who hadn't been in Minnesota long enough to learn English, but had died at Bull Run, age twenty.

Elsewhere on the ground floor was a small collection of dresses from the 1890s. The pride of the collection was made of light green silk, all ruffles and gathers and ruching, worn by a bride at her wedding. It must have been put away carefully, since it showed few signs of wear or fading. But the dress was on a mannequin from the midtwentieth century, when notions of what made a woman's form beautiful were quite different. The dress wasn't designed for a cantilevered bosom, and the mannequin, despite a look of cool indifference, looked as if she would have preferred a pair of pedal pushers and a sleeveless shirt, maybe with a Peter Pan collar.

Betsy went upstairs and found Jill wandering among a large collection of toys. There were electric trains and windup cars and dolls in great variety. "I used to have a doll just like that," said Betsy, pointing to a doll with a composition head and cloth body. "It makes me feel old to see it in a museum."

"Maybe you are old," said Jill, deadpan.

"Oh, yeah? Look over there," retorted Betsy, pointing at a Barbie doll. "I bet you had one of those."

"You want to know the truth? I didn't. My mother didn't like dolls that looked like miniature grown-ups, and anyway, I preferred baby dolls or little kid dolls. My favorite doll was Poor Pitiful Pearl—remember her?"

"Gosh, yes! She made me think of Wednesday Addams. Remember the old television show? *Biddle-dee-boop!*" She snapped her fingers twice. *"Biddle-dee-boop!"* Snap, snap.

Jill smiled. "Did you get to ride with Adam Smith?"

"Yes, from Pine Grove to here. Jill, you should see his car, it's a 1911 Renault sport touring car seventeen feet long. Gorgeous, gorgeous car, rides like a limo. It's right out front, he parked behind the Stanley."

"How fast does it go?"

"Around fifty."

"Rats, we'd better get back to Lars." Jill started for the stairs.

"Why?" asked Betsy, hurrying to keep up.

"Because when he finds out how fast that car is, he'll go nuts waiting for us. Let's go!"

Sure enough, Lars was in a fever to be gone. "Smith already left in his blue yacht. That Renault's hot, and he doesn't have to stop for water."

"You got steam?" asked Jill.

"Yes, yes, yes, let's go!"

Betsy grumbled, climbing into the backseat, "This is not a race, you know."

"Well, of course it isn't!" said Lars. "Otherwise we'd be lined up at a starting line so's everyone would leave at the same time. Which way out of town?"

"We're not going out of town, we're supposed to go someplace around here for lunch."

"Jill, we don't have time for lunch!"

Betsy said, "But I'm hungry."

Jill said, "Me, too. And anyway, it's included in the entry fee."

Jill was not a little woman, but Lars was very large, and when he turned toward her, his expression angry, he seemed very intimidating. But she had that special look of her own, one that simply absorbed his anger and frustration, giving nothing back and leaving him deflated. He sighed, "Oh, well, what the hell. Which way?"

"Go to the corner and turn right. Go one block and turn left on Sibley."

"Right," said Lars, settling himself in the driver's seat. He opened the throttle about a third of the way, and the Stanley obediently pulled smoothly away. Lars appeared resigned to lunch, but as they rounded the corner at the end of the block, the car let loose a loud and angry *Whooooo, whoo-whoo!*, making pedestrians jump and stare. Some waved, laughing at their own surprise. One exception was a young man standing in the dark, wet ruins of a two-liter bottle of Coke. His gesture was unkind.

Jill read instructions until they were safely parked at Peters on the Lake. " 'Please remember to order from the Antique Car menu,' " she concluded.

"Hey, Smith is here, too," said Lars, nodding at the long and beautiful Renault parked in a distant and shady corner.

"Wow," said Jill, pausing to stare.

"Come on," said Lars. "Let's order sandwiches to go."

"We will sit at a table and eat like civilized persons," said Jill.

Lars sighed, but said nothing, not even when Jill asked for soup and a salad.

They joined Adam Smith, who greeted Betsy warmly and shook hands with Lars and Jill. Betsy said, "Are you giving someone a ride back?"

Adam said, "No, but if you'd care to join me again, that would be great."

Jill gave Betsy an encouraging look, but Betsy said, "No, I think I'll stay with the Stanley." The fact that he was unafraid to answer more of her questions meant either that he had no guilty knowledge or was very confident of his answers.

In another few minutes more people joined them, and the talk became strictly about the cars. Betsy listened anyway, hoping to pick up something useful.

Mike Jimson grumped to Adam, "I took your advice and resleeved the number two cylinder. I thought the rod was rapping, but you were right, it was the piston slapping. The clearance was great. I don't know why it was doing that."

The man beside Mike was saying, "That damn foot brake locks. I use it and I got to stop and release it by hand, so I was taking my foot off the gas and yanking on the hand brake, and be dipped if it don't work like a charm, finished the run, and got my fourth medallion."

The woman beside him said, "I told Frank he ought to soak that Caddy in LokTite and see if that won't keep parts from falling off. Sometimes I think I spend half our time on the road stopping to run back and pick something up. Today it was the license plate and one of the bolts off a fender."

Adam told Jill, "It was Leland and Falkner got Henry Ford's second failure at car making to run, you know."

Betsy had taken only a few bites of her sandwich when Lars stood. "Come on," he said, dropping a heavy damask napkin on his empty plate, having inhaled the roast beef sandwich that ornamented it only minutes before. "See you in New London," he said to the table, a wicked glint in his eye.

"This isn't a race, Mr. Larson," said a woman, glinting back.

"No, it sure isn't," agreed Lars. "But I left the pilot light burning, so I should get back out there. Come on, you two."

Betsy brought the uneaten portion of her sandwich with her.

Jill got them out onto Meeker County 31, where there was a straight run of several miles, before turning to Betsy to ask something about Adam Smith. Betsy couldn't understand half the words, even though Jill was shouting. Once Lars got out on the highway, he had opened the throttle, and there was a mad tumble of wind over the upright windshield that tangled Jill's ash-blond hair and lifted Betsy's dress indecently.

Betsy, trying to eat her tuna fish sandwich with one hand and hold her dress down with the other, said, "I can't hear you," mouthing the words elaborately.

Jill turned to shout at Lars, "Slow down, for heaven's sake!"

"And let that lah-dee-dah French car pass me?" Lars replied, tightening his grip on the steering wheel.

So Jill sat down again. Betsy gave up on her sandwich to exalt in the smooth, fast run, and waved at the occasional car or pedestrian or bicyclist as the Steamer rushed past them.

Lars pulled into a gas station at the intersection with Tri-County Road. "We're just over twenty-one miles from Litchfield, so this is placed perfect for us to stop and take on water."

He steered over to the side of the building and this time ignored the instant crowd his car attracted. Jill got out so he could get out. "Have you got a water hose I can use?" he asked the man who came out of the station to stare.

Jill climbed into the backseat and said to Betsy, "Talk fast."

"Adam said Bill was angry with him over the car, but even angrier because Adam beat him in a race to be president of the Antique Car Club."

"What do you think?"

"Well, Adam didn't seem angry himself, but of course he wouldn't, he knows he's a suspect. And he hasn't got an alibi. What I don't like is that he was late getting to St. Paul, arriving way behind Mildred Feeney, who is very elderly and therefore hardly a speed demon."

"So you think he's the one?"

"I don't know. He said if Minnesota had the death penalty, he'd be living in Costa Rica right now."

"Let's go!" said Lars, and Jill got out to follow Lars back into the front seat. "Got the route sheet?" he asked, checking his gauges.

"Right here," said Jill. "We need to get an odometer on this thing. The directions keep telling us how many miles to turnoffs and I can't estimate mileage. And another thing, we made that twenty-one miles in something less than twenty minutes. The speed limit out here is fifty-five. If you don't drive slower, we're going to get a speeding ticket, and think how that poor schnook of a trooper is going to feel testifying how he wrote up a 1912 automobile?"

"He won't have to testify, I'll plead guilty!" said Lars proudly, and Jill sighed.

But he did slow down a bit. Still, they arrived at the American Legion building in New London well ahead of the others. The downstairs of the new-looking building was mostly a wide and low bar room, the decor heavily patriotic. It was well lit and deliciously cool. Betsy went to the restroom to find a comb and spend several minutes wrenching it through her hair. Those long veils women wore when riding in these cars seemed a lot less ridiculous now, especially considering that they wore their hair long. She went back out and ordered a Diet Coke at the bar.

It was fifteen minutes before Adam Smith came in, and forty minutes before the Winton's owner and his wife showed up. Adam smiled at Lars and greeted him, but said nothing about coming in second, nor did the Winton's owners say anything about finishing third. Then again, only the first-place driver had a mayonnaise stain on his shirt from hurtling through his lunch.

Betsy allowed Mike to buy her a refill and sat down at a little round table with a big bowl of pretzels on it to talk with him and Dorothy.

"I understand Bill Birmingham ran against Adam for the presidency of your club," she said after pleasantries had been exchanged.

Dorothy nodded, but said, "It was more like Adam ran against Bill, wasn't it, Mike?"

Mike said, "Sort of. Our outgoing president was moving to Arizona as soon as his term was up, and Bill, who was vice president, kind of thought the office was his by right. He was an effective VP, and since he'd cut back to half-time at his company, he had the time. Adam was route manager, you know, getting out maps and driving the back roads, laying out the runs. Important, but not management. And no one knew at the time he was about to retire, not even him, we think."

Dorothy put in, "Also right about then, their youngest went off to college and Adam's wife, who probably had been waiting for that to happen, divorced him. That was last fall, and he suddenly had all the time in the world to devote to his cars and the club."

"What did he do for a living?"

"Upper management," said Mike. "CEO, in fact. Only been there six or seven years."

Dorothy said with a significant eyebrow lift, "But they gave him one heck of a golden parachute, and he'd been given stock options in lieu of cash bonuses the whole time he'd been there, so he is simply *rolling* in it. So it doesn't matter that he can't find another job in his field." Again the eyebrow lifted and she nodded weightily.

Mike said, "He didn't do anything dishonest. From what I've heard, he had a theory of management that made him a lot of enemies. Plus the last company he was with . . . Well, it's going to take them a few years to get back on course." He looked at his wife. "He's like Bill was, in some respects. When he thinks he's right, he goes full out for it, and hang the consequences."

They talked awhile longer, then Betsy went back to Jill. The place had filled up with antique car owners, their spouses and even some children, other friends and passengers, and townsfolk wanting to meet the owners of those strange old cars. "Where's Lars?" asked Betsy, unable to spot him in the crowd.

"He's here, making the rounds, talking cars and engines and the run tomorrow."

"Jill, are you okay with this new interest of his?"

Jill sighed. "I guess so. The cars are beautiful, and the people who own them seem nice enough. And now that I'm more confident that Lars knows what he's doing with the Stanley, I enjoy riding around in it. On the other hand, this is a very expensive hobby he's gotten into. It's a comfort to know that while Lars can get very crazy about something, it never lasts forever."

"Except you?" asked Betsy with a smile.

"Okay, except me."

Lars circulated for a while, finished his third beer, and came back to ask Jill, "Are we staying here for dinner? They're setting up a big grill outside, and I hear their burgers are great."

Betsy said, "How about I take you and Jill to the Blue Heron in Willmar? It's supposed to be very nice. I left my copy of the *Excelsior Bay Times* at the motel, and it has a nice picture of you and your Steamer in it."

"Really? Well, sure, I wouldn't mind having a look at it. How about you, Jill?"

"Fine. We can't talk here, anyhow. How about we follow you in my car, Betsy, so you don't have to drive us back."

The Blue Heron was a Frank Lloyd Wright—style building on top of a hill overlooking Lake Willmar. It was the clubhouse of a private golf course, but the restaurant on the second floor was open to the public. The far wall and the long adjacent wall were made of panes of thermal glass and overlooked a putting green and the lake.

The hostess at first said there would be a wait, but when Betsy gave her name, she said, "Oh, there's someone from your party here already, holding a table for you."

Betsy followed her to a table by the longer wall, where Sergeant Morrie Steffans rose to his considerable height as they approached. He looked pleased, or perhaps amused, at her surprise.

"How did you know we'd be coming here?" asked Betsy as he came around to hold her chair for her.

"I'm a detective, remember?"

She frowned at him, so he elaborated. "One of your employees told me where you were staying. I drove out here and had a talk with the manager. He told me he always recommended the Blue Heron to those guests who like poached salmon and the Ramble Inn to those who like deep-fried perch. Somehow you struck me as a salmon person so, like the salmon, I swam upstream to here." He smiled at Betsy, who, rather to her surprise, found herself smiling back.

She introduced Jill and Lars, and he said, "What, you collect cops as a hobby?"

"No, Jill was my sister's best friend and I guess I sort of inherited her. Lars is Jill's steady. He's the reason we're here for the run. He owns a Stanley Steamer."

"Yes, I guessed that by the scorch marks," said Steffans.

Lars put the hand with the scald into his lap. "These things happen until you learn the tricks of the boiler," he said.

"There must be compensations, then," said Steffans and he listened with apparent interest while Lars rode his hobby horse for a while. When the waitress arrived with the menus, Steffans said, "I understand you do a beautiful poached salmon here."

"We do," she said, "but we had a big crowd at lunch and they all ordered it, so we're out until Sunday," and looked confused when this amused everyone at the table. "We have some very nice lamb chops," she offered and was reassured when this didn't set off another round of laughter.

Betsy and Steffans had the lamb, Lars ordered a porterhouse steak, and Jill decided to try the stuffed chicken breast, another specialty of the house. No one wanted a predinner drink, so the waitress went to fetch their salads.

Marvin and Charlotte watched Betsy go into the restaurant from the bar. "Who are those two with her?" asked Marvin.

"I don't know—wait, that man was driving the Stanley last Saturday, and Betsy told me she was sponsoring the Stanley. I don't remember his name. He's new to the Antique Car Club."

"So he's not a cop."

"I don't know what he does, she didn't say."

"Who's the other woman?"

"I don't know. But it doesn't matter. What matters is they didn't stay for the barbecue in New London, so we can talk to them about Adam without anyone else in the club seeing us and telling him about it."

They gave Betsy and her friends a few minutes, then strolled casually into the dining room. They were halfway across when they saw Betsy and then the fourth person at her table. "Oh, my God, it's that Minnetonka detective!" murmured Charlotte, gripping Marvin's arm to bring him to a halt. She would have turned around except the detective had already seen her. His look of surprise brought the attention of the others.

Betsy lifted a hand and said, "Well, hello, what are you doing here?"

Charlotte led Marvin to the table. "I was feeling caged," she said, "and I just wanted to go for a long drive. Marvin has a convertible, and the night was warm, and before we realized it, we were nearly to Willmar. Then I remembered this as a nice place, and we decided to stop in."

Steffans, with old-fashioned manners, had risen to his feet as Charlotte came to them, and after a puzzled moment, so did Lars. Betsy performed the introductions. Charlotte said, a trifle dryly, "Yes, Sergeant Steffans and I have already met. And he's talked with Marvin Pierce, too." To Lars: "That's a beautiful Stanley you bought. I hope you have many happy miles in her." To Jill: "I think Betsy mentioned you to me. It's needlepoint you do? I'm a counted cross-stitcher."

"Won't you join us?" said Steffans. "We just placed our order, but we can get the waitress back, I'm sure."

"No, no," said Marvin, beginning to turn away. "We don't want to interrupt your conversation."

Charlotte added, "Besides, there's no room."

But Steffans was already moving his chair to one side so he could bring the small table behind him up. "See how easy it is to fix that? Now, Mrs. Birmingham, you sit right here, and Marvin, you sit there, and I'll just go find our waitress." He gave a sort of bow, and was halfway across the room in a couple of long-legged strides.

Charlotte looked around the table with an uncomfortable smile. "Goodness, isn't he the managing kind? He must have been terrific at directing traffic!"

Betsy, laughing with the others, said, "I hope you don't mind. By the way, have you seen this week's *Excelsior Bay Times*? I brought it along because there's a a a beautiful photograph of Lars with his Stanley. But there's a photograph of Bill, too, working on his Maxwell."

"There is?" said Charlotte. "Well, isn't that interesting. I remember you saying there was a reporter in Excelsior covering the run, but I didn't see him. May I see it?"

Betsy handed it across to her. "It's in the middle, lots of pictures."

Charlotte opened the paper and ran her eyes quickly over the photographs. She gave a little scream when she saw the Maxwell with a white flannel rump hiding most of the hood and engine, "Oh, my God, Bill would have hated to see that!" she said, and handed it to Marvin. "Isn't that just awful?" she said, and laughed. But she felt her lips twist and her eyes began to sting. "Excuse me, I'm sorry," she said and fished in her purse for a handkerchief. "I had to dig this old thing out," she said, waving it in her hand before dabbing her eyes. "My mother always carried one, but I never did until this happened to Bill. The oddest things set me off crying, and I just hate those wads of Kleenex." She touched her nose but didn't blow it. "I'm sorry," she said again.

"We understand," said Jill.

Marvin, shaking his head, said, "It's a shame this had to be the last picture taken of Bill. Not exactly his best side."

"Oh, stop it, Marvin!" said Charlotte, trying not to laugh, and dabbing at more tears.

Marvin said to Betsy, "Charlotte told me you investigate crimes, is that true?"

Betsy nodded. "Yes, as an amateur. I seem to have a knack for it."

"I also hear you're looking into Bill's death. What have you found out?"

"A number of things. Broward, for example, was unhappy with his father's continuing interference in Birmingham Metal Fabrication, as you undoubtedly know."

Charlotte felt a cold hand grip her heart. "You can't possibly think my son would murder his own father!" she said in a quiet voice she hardly recognized as her own.

Betsy's look did nothing to warm the grip. "I'm sorry, but I do," she said. "Unless you can think of a better candidate?"

Charlotte exchanged a look with Marvin. "Well, as a matter of fact, I can. We can, Marvin and I."

Sixteen

Detective Sergeant Morrie Steffans, one of those people who pays attention, didn't have to ask who the waitress was for his table. He quickly picked her out from the quartet serving the room, and went to waylay her on her way from another table to tell her there were two new people at Betsy Devonshire's.

But he didn't go immediately back to his table. He stood a minute or two, watching Charlotte Birmingham and Marvin Pierce talking to Betsy, Jill, and Lars.

Lars, he knew, was an excellent patrol cop, very happy at his work, and therefore likely to stay on patrol until his back or his legs gave out. Which might be never—he looked built on the lines of the Stanley boiler he admired so much.

Jill, on the other hand, was on a different track. She had the quiet tenacity and wholesome integrity that would probably put her in a command position someday. She might even wind up Chief of Police.

And then there was Ms. Devonshire. Wholly amateur, not at all disciplined or even learned in the field of investigation. Yet she'd broken several cases, most of them locally. She claimed, according to Sergeant Mike Malloy of the Excelsior Police Department, to be merely lucky, a sentiment he heartily endorsed. But luck was a genuine gift, a wonderful thing to be blessed with. Really legendary investigators had it, held on to it with both hands, and were deeply grateful for it. Malloy disliked Betsy, said she was an interfering civilian of the worst sort, by which he meant she was better than he was at solving crimes—at least the sort of crimes ordinary people got mixed up in, not the sort done by professional criminals. The ordinary crook could probably run rings around Ms. Devonshire, just as the pair at the table right now could run rings around Mike Malloy.

Steffans's eyes narrowed as he watched them work Betsy over. He didn't think for a minute they were fooling her. He began to walk slowly back to the table, his stuck-out ears already picking up the threads of the conversation.

Charlotte was here to protect her son Broward. To do that, she would see anyone else, *anyone*, indicted, convicted, and sentenced to life in prison. The best candidate she could find was Adam Smith, so here she was—and she didn't care if her story about just driving around aimlessly and just happening to stop at the Blue Heron was a little thin. It hadn't been hard to find Betsy Devonshire. A few phone calls and here she was. Sergeant Steffans thought he was clever finding Betsy, but here was Charlotte, just as clever.

But Betsy's face showed only keen interest. "What have you found out about Adam Smith?" she asked.

Clever Charlotte let Marvin help dig the hole into which she hoped to push Adam.

Marvin said, "It's about the rivalry between Adam and Bill. I'm sure you know Bill bought a 1910 Fuller that Adam wanted, and wouldn't sell it to him. But that was only one round of an ongoing fight. Adam had previously bought a 1910 Maxwell that Bill wanted, even though Adam collects only rarities and Maxwells are about the most common pioneers around."

Jill said, "I thought you weren't an antique car owner, Marvin."

He said, surprised, "I'm not."

"But you know a lot about them."

He shrugged. "Heck, I've been friends with the Birminghams for a lot of years. You can't help picking up the language."

The police investigator's chair suddenly moved, and Sergeant Steffans sat down. "The waitress will be here in a minute," he said.

Charlotte said, "We were talking about how Adam Smith did things that showed he hated Bill. I think the worst was when Adam decided to run against Bill for president of the Minnesota Antique Car Club. Adam is route manager, that's what he does best, and he's always liked laying out the runs. Then Wesley Sweet decided to retire to Arizona. He was president for the past four terms. Bill was vice president for two, and he was very efficient, he did a lot of good work, so naturally he decided he had the best chance to be president. And like from out of left field"—Charlotte made a sharp gesture—"here comes Adam, hot to be president himself. And he runs the dirtiest, the hardest, the nastiest—"

"Now, Char, you're getting excited," interrupted Marvin quietly.

Charlotte's breath caught in her throat, but she stopped herself from saying something rude to Marvin. Because he was probably right, she had gotten carried away before. "Do you think so?" she said instead, making her voice sweetly humble. Marvin's smile of admiration made the sweetness genuine. "Well, maybe I am a little excited. But"—she turned her focus onto Betsy—"it was a very ugly campaign. Adam told lies about Bill, said he was incompetent, uncooperative, high-handed. It was just terrible, the things he said. I told Bill not to reply in kind, and I think that was a mistake, because Adam won by a very clear margin."

"But then why, if Adam won, would he murder Bill?"

"Oh, I'm not saying Adam murdered Bill because of the election. That would be ridiculous. I'm just telling you about it to show how deep the animosity went, that Adam really hated Bill."

"Because of the car thing," guessed Lars.

"No, the car thing was just another symptom. You know Adam was forced out of his position as CEO of General Steel?"

Betsy said, "I know he was given a golden parachute when he was asked to retire. I didn't know it was from General Steel."

"Well, Adam's method of improving a bottom line was to diversify. He was among the first practitioners of that. He wanted General Steel to get into manufacturing steel products as well as mining and smelting. He'd been expanding into a rolling mill already."

Steffans nodded. "I remember reading about that. The mill's in Gary,

Indiana, I believe." He said to Betsy, who was giving him a surprised look, "One of my mutual funds is into metals."

Charlotte said, "Yes, well, a lot of the processing of taconite is done overseas nowadays, because it's cheaper. But instead of expanding into overseas processing, Adam decided to broaden his base, and he started looking at Birmingham Metal Fabrication." Charlotte smacked a hand onto the table to underline the enlightenment she saw in Betsy's eyes. "That's right, that's why Bill brought Broward into the company, to fight off Adam's attempt to buy us out. I was never so proud of both of them, the way they worked together to keep the company ours."

Lars said, frowning, "You mean General Steel wanted to do a hostile take-over?"

"No," said Charlotte, "you can only do a hostile takeover by buying up the stock of a publicly held company. We are family-owned. But Adam saw a clean, profitable, well-run company, and he started making offers."

"All you had to do was just say no, surely," said Betsy.

"You'd think so, wouldn't you? But Adam sent men in to talk to our employees, about a rival company that had better benefits, and hinting we were in financial trouble—lies, just like the lies he told about Bill during the election. That's how he works, not by showing he's better, but that the alternative is worse, getting everyone stirred up. Production was falling off and some of the men threatened to quit."

"So what did Bill and Broward do?" asked Lars.

"They sicced a lawyer on Adam's company. I don't know what the lawyer said, but a few months later Adam was out on his keester, and General Steel never bothered us again. They won't tell you so, of course, they have strict rules about privacy. But that's what happened." She saw belief on their faces and smiled.

The waitress took Charlotte's and Marvin's orders. Betsy made sure the waitress understood that she, Lars, and Jill were on one ticket.

The food, when it came, was delicious. Charlotte became intelligent and witty. Marvin, while more low key, was charming and funny. Betsy could see why Lisa Birmingham hoped one day the two would pair off.

It was Steffans who most surprised Betsy. He was relaxed, intelligent on a number of issues, nice without the least bit of condescension.

Toward the end of the meal, Charlotte asked Steffans point-blank, "Are you close to arresting someone for the murder of my husband?"

To Betsy's surprise, Steffans nodded. "As a matter of fact, I am. If I can get a few more answers, I might make an arrest tomorrow."

"Here at the run?" she asked, her attention almost painful in its intensity.

"Yes," he replied, and she relaxed all over. Betsy nodded to herself. *Broward's not coming to the run.* She thought, *Charlotte's glad he's safe.*

"But you're out of your jurisdiction," said Jill, faintly scandalized.

"Oh, I've been in touch with the Meeker County Sheriff, and I can get a warrant like that," he said, snapping his fingers.

"If you need backup, I'll be there tomorrow," said Lars.

"Me, too," said Jill, and there was a subtle shift in them, the way they sat, that linked them in a new way to Steffans. Betsy suddenly felt like an outsider.

"If you're handy, sure," said Steffans. Seeing the amazed look on Charlotte's face, he said, "I see you weren't properly introduced. These are Officers Jill Cross and Lars Larson, Excelsior PD."

Charlotte said angrily to Betsy, "You didn't tell me!"

Betsy replied mildly, "I didn't think it mattered. They aren't here in their official capacity, or at least they weren't until just now. Lars came as owner and driver of a car I'm sponsoring, and Jill really is his girl and my best friend."

"We understand," said Marvin, placatingly, speaking as much to Charlotte as to Betsy. "We're just a little surprised—which is understandable, considering the circumstances."

"And it's all right," said Steffans. "We're all still friends, right?"

"Right," agreed Marvin.

But it was a moment before Charlotte nodded agreement.

Still, the convivial mood was gone and the party began to break up. Soon Betsy found herself down in the small parking lot in front of the building, waving as Jill and Lars in one car, Charlotte and Marvin in another, pulled out and away.

Steffans stood beside Betsy until the cars' taillights disappeared around a bend.

Betsy asked, "Are you really going to arrest Adam Smith tomorrow?"

"No."

"Why did you say you would?"

"I said I might make an arrest tomorrow. But not Mr. Smith. He has an ironclad alibi."

"Then who? Broward isn't here—is he?"

"Not as far as I know."

Charlotte had an ironclad alibi of her own. *"Marvin?"*

"Come on, Ms. Devonshire. You've been dancing around the truth all evening. I could see it in your eyes. Let's go someplace and talk. Do you still have that copy of the *Excelsior Bay Times* with you? I want you to show me what you saw that none of the others did."

* * *

Saturday dawned cool and cloudy. Drivers listened to weather reports and studied the sky. Putting up the tops on the old cars that had them was a lengthy, difficult chore. They didn't like their bars being fitted into their slots, resisted having their braces tightened, and at every opportunity pinched blood blisters on fingers. Once they were up, they blocked vision, the wind roared under them loud enough to deafen a driver to other road hazards and they caught enough wind to slow travel. The only thing worse than struggling to put the top up before starting was stopping alongside the road in the rain to do it.

Most caved in and put tops up, swearing and complaining. The few who didn't claimed that since most did, it now certainly wasn't going to rain. "It's the opposite of washing your car," one said.

Lars shrugged off Betsy's suggestion that he put his top up. "I'm gonna go so fast I'll run between any raindrops," he boasted, then went back to recheck against his directions his list of places where water could be obtained, making sure he hadn't made a slip somewhere. Running his boiler dry would damage the hundreds of copper tubes inside it, a very expensive error.

Because the Steamer was so fast, it was put near the back of the pack that gathered in a large church's parking lot the other side of the cemetery. Despite the threat of rain, a large crowd gathered to watch the old cars set off on their hundred-mile-plus run. Five church ladies had set up a table near the church hall's entrance, from which they dispensed cookies and coffee: free to drivers, a dollar a hit for onlookers. Beside the table was the car-run quilt, on its stand. Mildred Feeney, in a big flowered hat at least as old as she was, worked the crowd, selling last-chance raffle tickets. Two men from the American Legion, in uniform and with rifles, guarded the starting line, which had a tiny red-striped building beside it meant to look like a Cold Stream Guard's shelter. The mayor of New Brighton was on hand, in top hat and tails. *Talk about mixed messages*, thought Betsy, standing on the other side of the line from the mayor and the Cold Stream Guard shelter, clipboard in hand. She was herself wearing slacks, a blue-checked shirt, and sneakers—yet another fashion statement.

Off at the back of the parking lot a group of men with walkie-talkies and cell phones consulted under a big ham radio antenna. The leader of the pack was a heavyset man leaning on a huge four-wheel-drive vehicle. Not police officers, these were the crew charged with finding and rescuing old cars that faltered on the journey.

The mayor, red-faced and sweating—his suit was made of heavy wool, and it wasn't *that* cool—made a brief speech honoring the people who found and restored these venerable ancestors of road travel. He said he'd be on hand again in New Brighton to greet in person every driver who completed the journey. He held up a dull gold medallion the size of his palm and said this was what the run was about, this was the prize to be given to every car that finished the run. "Good luck and Godspeed!" he concluded.

He stepped back and a man with a big green flag came out from behind the guard shelter. The two American Legion veterans crossed to Betsy's side of the starting line, and Betsy checked the time on the big old pocket watch Adam Smith had fastened to the top of her clipboard. She looked at the 1902 Oldsmobile standing in quivering eagerness behind the line painted on the blacktop. The man twirled his flag, and on dropping it, the Legionnaires fired their rifles. The Oldsmobile tottered across the line and rolled past the crowd cheering him on. Betsy put a checkmark next to the Oldsmobile's banner number and wrote the time down: 7:12 A.M.

By 8:30, most of the veterans had departed, and so had perhaps half the crowd. Some were headed for Buffalo to watch the cars arrive for lunch, while others had seen what they came to see and were headed somewhere else. Betsy could see Charlotte and Marvin now, making their way closer to the starting line, looking for Sergeant Steffans—who was closing in from behind. They did, however, see the deputy sheriff off to their right, moving toward them. Assuming he was heading off Adam Smith, they altered course, toward the starting line.

There was a roar of big engines as the follow-up trucks started up, preparing to follow the line of antique cars.

Betsy looked down the short line of cars still waiting to begin their run. Lars was at the very end, behind Adam in his Renault.

Charlotte and Marvin came close to the guard shelter to watch two deputies and Jill approach as a 1908 Buick in a bright shade of orange came up to the starting line. A fast *pipe-pipe-pipe* started coming from the car, but it slowed in tempo as the driver came to a stop, waiting for the green flag. The piping was obviously connected to the motor somehow, and by the grin of the driver, something intentional. The flag dropped and the car scuttled past the spectators, who made up in noise what they lacked in numbers. The piping, which had increased to a warble as he raced his engine, cut off as he turned out of the parking lot onto the street.

Next was the 1912 Winton, a woman behind the wheel wearing a pinch-brim cap turned rakishly backward and her male passenger, in shirtsleeves, waving grandly; then the 1911 Marmon, whose driver sounded its *ooooooo-gah!* over and over as he raced out of the lot. Betsy noted the time of each, then turned to watch Adam pull up in his huge and beautiful Renault touring sports car. *He should have someone wearing Erte clothing in the backseat, perhaps with an Afghan hound*, thought Betsy, smiling at him. While she would never give up the right to wear trousers, a car like Adam's called for old-fashioned elegance.

The deputy stepped out into the starting lane behind the Renault.

Adam waved to the flagman, who raised his flag. The flag fell and the Renault pulled away and was gone, to the astonishment of Charlotte and Marvin.

Steffans, now immediately behind them, said something, and it was Charlotte who realized first what was about to happen—and she helped Marvin get away. She raised a bloodcurdling scream and flew into Steffans, knocking him down. She fell on him, clawing and scratching and still screaming. People behind them hastily backed away.

Marvin hot-footed it across the starting line, brushing past Betsy—who was stupidly frozen to the spot—to the huge four-wheel-drive SUV, where he did a very credible stiff-arm block on the heavyset man who tried to get in his way.

The heavyset man fell, Marvin jumped in the vehicle, and the man did a spectacular leap from the ground, much like a freshly landed fish, landing out of the way as the SUV bolted forward.

Betsy found her voice and yelled, "Stop him!" as Marvin roared out of the lot.

One of the deputies trying to untangle Steffans and Charlotte looked up and raced off, bound for his patrol car at the far end of the lot.

Jill stepped in to grab Charlotte by the hair with one hand and her arm with another. "That's enough!" she said.

Betsy ran to the Stanley, wrenched open the door, and said, "Let's go!" (Though she later remembered it as, "Follow that car!")

Lars shoved the throttle all the way open, the steamer's tires screamed, and Betsy was flung back into her seat. By the time she got herself untangled, the Stanley was flying up the street, actually gaining on the SUV. Lars grabbed a brass-headed knob and the Stanley's whistle gave a long blast, causing innocent cars to swerve out of their way.

Marvin slewed crazily making the turn onto the highway, but the SUV was surefooted enough to cling to the road. Marvin got back into the right lane and floored it, and the big gas engine responded with a will.

So he must have been horrified a few seconds later to look in his rearview mirror and see an antique car still gaining on him.

Betsy, hanging on to the gas lever, was yelling encouragement at Lars, who had a fierce grin on his face.

But as they closed the gap, Betsy began to worry. How would they make Marvin stop? Was Lars going to try to pass him and cut him off? What if Marvin just crashed into them? Suddenly the Stanley's rooflessness, its lack of seat belts, made it a very dangerous place to be.

The SUV's brake lights came on, and the gap closed swiftly.

"He's giving up!" said Betsy, vastly relieved. Lars shut down his throttle, and Betsy remembered how weak the primitive brakes were. They were going to overshoot. Lars would have to stop down the road and turn around. No cars oncoming, good. She looked behind. No flashing lights and sirens, just a single private car, well back.

But Marvin wasn't finished yet. There was a grassy lane across the broad ditch that ran alongside the highway, an access lane for a farmer to get into his field. The SUV swerved onto it and crashed through the pipe-and-wire gate into the pasture. Grazing cows, startled, began to move.

Lars braked, but the Stanley was already past the lane.

"Hang on!" yelled Lars and the Stanley bounced off the highway, *down* into the wide ditch, and t-W-i-S-t-e-D its way up out of the ditch. Chuffing under the load, it nevertheless went through the barbed wire fence as if it wasn't there.

The SUV was ahead of them, climbing a steepish slope, bouncing and skidding, flinging sod, mud and worse in all directions. Cows, only as alarmed as calm and stupid animals can get, scattered slowly.

The Stanley might have been on a country road, climbing the hill smoothly and effortlessly.

On the other side of the slope were the remains of a woodlot: stumps and fallen logs, heaps of brush, mudholes. The SUV swerved and slid between the obstacles, bottoming here and there. A hubcap flew off. Marvin tried to dodge back toward the highway and snagged his exhaust on a stump. It tore loose and suddenly his engine was very loud.

The Stanley went over everything. This was common terrain when it was on the design board, and its big wheels kept the underside clear of obstructions. Lars, after years of hard driving, with special law-enforcement training and the amazing Stanley to ride, kept thwarting Marvin and his SUV's every attempt to regain the highway.

Betsy, hanging on like grim death, watched the SUV finally dodge wildly around the last heap of brush, then crush another barbed wire fence. They were still on downhill terrain, and the SUV gained speed as it roared into a field that some hopeful farmer had plowed, harrowed, and planted with corn that had sprouted into neat rows of green about eight inches high. "Got 'im now!" Lars crowed, though Betsy couldn't see how.

The SUV destroyed the sprouting plants in their hundreds as it veered down the gray-black field. It started up another slope, this one steeper than the last, slowing as it went, fishtailing madly, earth and small green plants flying in all directions. The big whip aerial on the back was flailing as if wielded by a mad driver and the horses under the hood were real and needed beating to greater effort.

Lars was by now close enough that some clods struck his windshield. By the time they reached the top, the SUV, despite its roaring engine and whipping aerial, was barely making any progress at all—and blocking its passage was a white board fence. On the other side; a dozen flesh and blood horses stood, heads raised in amazement.

The SUV lacked momentum to break this fence down. By twisting the wheel hard, Marvin managed to turn and start along it, Lars close behind.

"He's going to get away, isn't he?" said Betsy, as the SUV started again to build speed.

"Nah, there's another fence up ahead. I'll corner him there."

And he did. Marvin tried to turn, but Lars was crowding him in his outer rear quarter, and Marvin ended up hard against the fence, too close to open his door. Lars shut the throttle down and leaped out of his car all in one movement. Before Betsy could even think what to do, Lars was sprawled across the hood of the SUV, pointing a gun at Marvin through the windshield, yelling at him to shut the engine off.

Marvin shut the engine off and raised his hands.

Lars called, "Betsy, blow the whistle until you see some backup coming."

Betsy pulled the brass-headed knob on the dash, sending the horses in the meadow into wild flight. She blew a long and then a row of shorts, then a long again. She kept doing it.

It seemed like a long time before a farmer drove up on an immense tractor, curious to know what these people were doing in his field. He had a cell phone in a pocket.

So it was Marvin after all?" said Godwin from a stool in the corner. He was wearing immaculate white shoes, socks, and trousers, and not anxious to get anything greasy on them. His pearl-gray silk shirt was also vulnerable and he hitched the stool just a little bit farther from the wall where, he was sure, spiders lurked. Godwin was not afraid of spiders, but surely their little feet were dirty from crawling up and down that dusty wall. If one got on him, it might leave a *trail*. He had a date with John for dinner, and John had sounded very quiet and gentle when he'd called yesterday. Things were going to be all right, probably, but Godwin always felt more confident when he was dressed especially well.

"No, it was both of them," said Betsy.

She was sitting on a low rolling chest designed to be sat upon, made of plastic, used by gardeners who didn't like stooping or kneeling but who had a long row to plant or weed. She was wearing denim shorts and a sleeveless pink blouse, although she was getting too old to be going sleeveless, except among friends.

But everyone present was a friend. Jill was there, sitting on the workbench, her bruises from the fight with Charlotte making bold purple comments on her smooth complexion.

And Lars, of course, since this was his barn. He was in his grubbiest, jeans and T-shirt, under the Stanley, "swaging the boiler"—banging a shaped metal plug up the numberless copper tubes, making them round again. It was a long, long job. He'd divided the tubes into areas, and worked on one area at a time; otherwise, he'd fall into despair at the large number there were to swage.

During the wait for backup to arrive, the boiler had run itself dry. Lars should have told Betsy to shut it down, close off the valves, but he'd been concentrating on keeping Marvin from doing something stupid.

Betsy took most of the blame. She should have thought of it, paid attention to the gauges. But the Stanley had sat there in silence and she had fallen into her internal combustion habit of thinking a silent car was a car shut off, and so the boiler was scorched.

"How do you know it was both of them?" asked Godwin.

"Because that was the only way everything fit. She was the one who pulled the trigger. She shot him early in the morning of the Excelsior run, as they were getting ready to leave the house for St. Paul. Then she called Marvin, and he came over and took Bill's body over to the lay-by in the trunk of his car. Charlotte followed with the trailer they hauled the Maxwell in. It was Marvin who drove the Maxwell in the run, not Bill."

"But surely people talked to Bill," objected Godwin. "How could they mistake Marvin for him?"

"Actually they didn't really talk to him. Charlotte stayed with Marvin until he was parked. She talked to Adam and to anyone who came by, until Marvin was well under the hood and able just to grunt at anyone who tried to talk to him."

"Why would Marvin help her like that?" asked Godwin.

"Because they were lovers, had been for years. Everything was okay until Bill started spending more time at home. Then he got suspicious. Marvin wanted Charlotte to divorce Bill, but Marvin wasn't a wealthy man. And while Bill wasn't taking care of his high blood pressure, he may have had his suspicions about Marvin confirmed before he had that fatal stroke everyone was anticipating."

"Golden handcuffs," said Godwin sadly.

"Yes, at least in part. But also, tyrants don't make loving husbands."

"What do you think, she just decided she'd had enough and shot him?" asked Jill.

"I don't think so. She's a very intelligent person, she would have had a better plan set up in advance. I think she told the truth in her confession; they had a quarrel, he got violent, which he'd done before, and she went for the gun and shot him."

"Self-defense, then?" asked Godwin.

"Detective Steffans says no. She had to go into another room, unlock a drawer, and then go back with it. She could have left the house instead. On the other hand, one reason she wore those enveloping dresses was because sometimes she had to hide bruises. Bill struck her often, but was careful to hit her in places she could cover up with clothing."

"The monster!" said Godwin, with a shiver.

"So what put you on to them?" asked Jill.

"Orts," said Betsy.

That had been said into a break in the hammering from Lars, and he wheeled himself out from under his car long enough to inquire, "Orts?"

"Those little pieces of floss you cut off the end of a row of stitching. When you run it down so short you can't take another stitch. The end you cut off is an ort."

"Oh," he said and went back to hammering.

"What about orts?" persisted Jill.

"The photographs of the crime scene you brought me, remember? There were orts on Bill's trousers, just like they were on Charlotte's dress. She said she left them wherever she stitched. Anyone who lay on the floor of her sewing room—where the shooting took place—would come away with orts all over his clothes. But the man who drove into Excelsior and dove under the hood of his car to repair it, had no orts on his trousers. That photograph of him in the *Excelsior Bay Times* showed them immaculately clean, as clean as Godwin over there."

Godwin looked down at himself, then smiled at Betsy. "Thank you," he said.

"That's it?" said Jill. "Just because of some orts?"

"Well, there were some other things. The way she knew what Marvin was thinking when they came into my shop without his saying a word was exactly the way she knew what 'Bill' was thinking when he was sitting beside her in the Maxwell. I thought she did that with everyone she knew well, but she didn't do it with anyone else. The smile she gave Marvin at the Courage Center pool was the same she gave the person we all thought was her husband. When I found out what kind of a tyrant Bill was, I wondered how Charlotte could feel so affectionate toward him. The answer was, she couldn't."

Godwin said, "So you just put it all together in your usual clever way."

Betsy frowned. "I tried to think of other explanations, but none worked. Broward acted badly about my investigating because he thought he was the only one who knew about Marvin and Charlotte's affair and was trying to prevent my finding out and telling his sister and brothers. Charlotte lied when she said Bro and Bill teamed up to keep Adam from taking Birmingham Metal."

"How'd you find that out?" asked Jill.

"I didn't. Steffans did. Bro told him the reason he came home was because he heard from Bill's doctor that if Bill didn't retire, he'd be dead in six months.

Since Bro knew Steffans was looking for motives, Bro had every reason to point at Adam—and he did tell him about the Fuller and the race for president of the car club.

"And there was an accident in the tunnel that Saturday, just as Adam said, so his alibi checked out. So it wasn't Broward and it wasn't Adam."

She turned to Jill. "Another thing that bothered me was the medical examiner's statement about time of death." She turned to Jill. "You know what I mean. The estimate was, he died between late Friday night and noon on Saturday. That makes the window curiously lopsided, if he'd been killed in that lay-by around noon. But if he was killed early in the morning, that was right in the middle of the window."

Jill nodded. "I see what you mean."

"I thought for a long while it was Marvin who did the whole thing, shot Bill and hid his body in the lay-by. But when? The night before? Marvin had an alibi for the night before; he was playing poker with some friends. Maybe late at night, after the poker game, or the day of the run, early in the morning. I thought about Bill going to confront Marvin over the affair he was having with Charlotte. I thought perhaps Marvin shot him when Bill got violent, and then, to cover the time of the murder, he took Bill's place, driving the Maxwell in the run. But why bring Charlotte into it? He could just bury the body somewhere, or make it look like a robbery. Surely Marvin would never ask the woman he loved to be an accessory to murder. But if Marvin drove the Maxwell, Charlotte *was* right in the middle of the cover-up, deeply involved.

"So I thought she must be the one who shot him—only not at the lay-by, she was with me all day Saturday. Then I thought, well, what if she shot him early Saturday morning, when they were getting ready for the run? Then, okay, it still was Marvin doing the driving. She called Marvin to help her, and they came up with this hasty scheme. And there it was, all the pieces in place."

"Clever of her to get you to provide her with an alibi," said Godwin.

"No, it wasn't," said Jill. "She didn't know about Betsy's sleuthing skills or she would never have involved her. Once she found out Betsy has a nose for crime, she had to pretend she wanted Betsy to investigate, which was really the last thing on earth she wanted."

Betsy nodded. "And because she was scared of what I might find out, she kept coming around to check on me. That was another thing that made me look at her. She couldn't wait for me to come to her, she just had to find out if I was getting close. When she turned up in Willmar to shove Adam under my nose, I knew I was right."

"That's two police investigators you've gotten in ahead of," said Godwin. "Sergeant Mike Malloy and now Detective Steffans."

But Betsy shook her head. "No, he was onto her as well. He followed her out to Willmar because he was afraid she might try to murder me. While she was out there, he had a forensics team picking up all kinds of evidence in her house."

Godwin cocked his head at her. "You like him, don't you?"

"Heavens no!" said Betsy. "For one thing, he's too tall and gawky. For another, his ears stick out. For another . . ." She tried to think of a personality trait to complain about, but once she started thinking about his shy smile, his charming wit, the way he looked at her with admiring eyes, she had to stop, because she couldn't think of anything else.

Fabric: Aida, White, or Black
Design Count: 73w x 79h
Design Size: 7.3 x 7.9 in, 10 Count

Key: ● DMC 928   Grey Green-VY LT
     □ DMC 931   Antique Blue-MD
     ◉ DMC 932   Antique Blue-LT
     ✂ DMC 3727   Antique Mauve-LT
     ■ DMC 3787   Brown Grey-DK

The designer, Denise E. Williams, stitched this design on black 14-count Aida. On any other color fabric, stitch the design first, and then fill in the blank stitch spaces using DMC Black.

HINTS

1. Take the pattern to a copy shop and enlarge it so the markings in the squares are easy to read.

2. Find and mark the center of the pattern, and the center of your fabric.

3. If you use black fabric, put a white cloth behind it to make the weave easier to see.

4. This pattern is trickier than it looks. Count twice so you only have to stitch once.

Hanging by a Thread

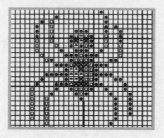

Acknowledgments

Some of the ghost stories told here are at least based on actual accounts made by real people. A Thursday knitting group is helping me improve my knitting skills or at least talk a better game. Mia McDavid read an early version of this novel and made some very helpful suggestions. And, of course, the Internet newsgroup RCTN continues to be a valuable resource.

One

It was just after one on a dreary late-October day. Betsy had enjoyed September with its crisp, apple-scented air, and early October when the trees formed immense bouquets of bright autumn colors. She even liked it now, when her little town of Excelsior was seen through a waving crosshatch of bare tree limbs, as a strong wind ripped low-hanging clouds to tatters. It made her feel daring to go out in it, and grateful to come into a dry, heated place of her own.

Though Halloween was still a week away, last night it had snowed. The snow had turned to sleet and then rain. Autumn, stripped of its gaudy garments, was being hustled off the stage as Puritan winter entered stage north.

Today was Monday, and the Monday Bunch was in session around the library table in the middle of the floor of Betsy's needlework shop, Crewel World. An informal club of stitchers and gossips, there were five present this afternoon: Alice Skoglund, Martha Winters, young Emily Hame, newcomer Bershada Reynolds, and Comfort Leckie.

Chief clerk Godwin was presiding and shamelessly encouraging the gossip. He was a slender, handsome young man with bright blond hair cropped short and a carefully nurtured golden tan. "Arne Thorson should be *ashamed* of himself," he said. "That girl is young enough to be his *granddaughter*!"

Comfort, a widow in her late seventies who didn't look a day over sixty, said, "She seems happy enough." She peered closer at her work, a cross-stitch pattern of flowers. "Doggone, it takes me about three tries to get a really nice French knot." She began picking apart the one she'd just done.

Bershada offered, "On high-count linen like what you're using, I just put the needle through an adjoining space instead of back through the same hole." Bershada was a slim black woman, a freshly retired librarian who wore magnifying glasses halfway down her nose.

Betsy yearned to join them; she had a very fancy needlepoint Christmas stocking under way that she hoped to have finished in time to display in the shop. But there was a shipment of the new DMC colors to sort and put out, a phone call to be made to her supplier to find out why her order of padded-board easels hadn't come, and a reservation form to be filled out and check written for the Nashville Market next March.

She was nearly finished comparing the shipment of floss to the packing slip and her original order form when the front door went *Bing!* She looked up as it opened to admit a man in a yellow rain slicker. It was Foster Johns, her general contractor. He was tall and well built, in his late thirties; not handsome but with a pleasant face.

"Hello, Mr. Johns," she said with a smile, and then noticed with surprise the chilly silence that had fallen on the group around the table.

When the patch Joe Mickles had put on her building's roof just before signing the title over to her proved even less than temporary, she did what she should have done in the first place: hired an independent inspector. He told her she needed not a better patch but a whole new roof. She had tried and failed to get Joe to share in the expense. "It's your building now, kid," he'd said.

It was then she discovered there were roofs and roofs. What kind of insulation, and how much? Tar or membrane sealer? Local roofer or national chain? She didn't have time for all this!

So she got out her phone book and found a general contractor right here in Excelsior. She'd made an appointment and found a quiet man in an orderly office who had listened carefully to her description of her building and asked what sounded like intelligent questions. His last three clients spoke highly of his work. Relieved, she'd hired him to find the people it would take to get the work done.

And his early promise had been fulfilled; he'd been businesslike but not distant, knowledgeable without being overbearing, friendly but never familiar, always perfectly correct.

As the stink of tar finally faded from the neighborhood, he'd hired the same independent inspector to ensure the job was well finished before she wrote that final check. He said he'd bring him over sometime today.

Now she was surprised at the unfriendly silence that fell at his entry. The group at the table turned with almost military precision to follow his walk across the room. It was impossible he was unaware of the stony faces, but he ignored them. It was as if he were used to such a reception.

"The inspector is here to take a look at the roof, Ms. Devonshire," he said in his usual polite voice, stopping at the desk. "I'm sure he'll find everything in good order."

"I sure hope so," said Betsy. "How long will it take?"

"About an hour, unless he discovers a problem. I don't think he will; I've never had trouble with this roofer before. But I assume you want to wait for his report before making that final payment?"

"I think I should, don't you? Do you want to wait here while he does his thing?"

He turned briefly toward the people at the table. Alice Skoglund, her expression that of someone about to do something brave, nodded at him almost imperceptibly. He didn't return her tiny sign of recognition, but turned back to

Betsy. "No, I've got some errands to run." He checked his watch. "I'll be back in ninety minutes, all right?"

"I hope to have that check waiting for you."

A look of pain crossed his face so swiftly, it was gone almost before she recognized it. "Me, too."

After he left, Betsy walked to the library table and asked, "Okay, what is it? I am about to give that man a large check. If you know of any reason why I shouldn't, please say so now."

Godwin said, "Oh, no, I'm *sure* he did a good job for you!" He glanced at the women. "We all are! But honestly, Betsy, I wish you'd told me you were thinking of hiring him before you did."

"You know I ask you about anything to do with the shop. I didn't think that extended all the way to the roof," she said sharply. "Besides, you didn't leave the phone number of your hotel in Cancún."

Godwin blushed and said, "All the same, I wish you'd said something to me."

"Or to any of us," said Martha angrily. She was a short, plump woman in her mid-seventies, normally laughing and pleasant. Seeing her indignant like this was a warning Betsy didn't like.

Betsy frowned at her. "Why? If he isn't a crook, what's the problem?"

"Foster Johns is a murderer."

"I don't believe it!"

Godwin said, "It's true. I'd have warned you, Betsy, if I'd known you were thinking of hiring him. I thought you hired the roofer yourself."

"I told you I was having trouble deciding who to hire; that's why I went to a general contractor. Mr. Johns seemed very competent."

Martha said, "Competence has nothing to do with it. No one in town will have anything to do with Foster Johns since it happened five years ago."

"The accusation was never proven," said Alice in a low, firm voice. She was about Martha's age, a tall woman with big hands, broad shoulders, and a mannish jaw, currently set hard.

"Only because Mike Malloy is a stupid, incompetent investigator," said Martha, still pink with indignation.

"Even so," said Betsy, "if it was never proved, why are you all so sure he's guilty?"

"Because he's the only one who could have done it," said Godwin.

Comfort added, "Certainly he was the only one with a motive." She had a very pleasant, quiet voice.

"Who did he murder, his wife?" asked Betsy.

Comfort finished another French knot using Bershada's suggestion and nodded with satisfaction. Without looking up, she said, "He murdered his mistress one night and a few nights later murdered her husband."

"He killed *two* people?"

Young Emily, nodding, said, "I can't believe no one warned you about him."

Betsy said, "Maybe because it's not a question that occurs to me when asking around about a contractor: 'By the way, has he ever murdered anyone?' I called him and he seemed to know his business, and his fee was reasonable. Not one of the references I called said don't hire him, he's a killer. And I like working with him, he seems very competent."

"No customers were from Excelsior, right?" said Godwin.

"Well, as a matter of fact, no," agreed Betsy.

"He has to go out of town for customers," said Martha. "No one from right around here will hire him, because we all know what he did."

Alice unset her heavy jaw to say, "Because it's everyone's *opinion* that he murdered those people. There was never any proof."

Godwin said, "All right, it's true Malloy couldn't find the kind of evidence it would take to convict him before a jury of his peers. That's why he had to let him go. But it's not because it wasn't *there*, it's because he didn't look *hard* enough, or in the right *places*. I heard he nearly lost his job because he bungled the investigation."

"I've often said he should be busted back to patrol," offered Bershada, a trifle diffidently, as she was still feeling her way into this group.

Betsy nodded; she knew Investigator Malloy. "I'll grant that Mike's not the sharpest knife in the drawer," she said. "Still, it must have taken a depressingly large amount of incompetence to allow a man who has murdered twice to walk free." Free so that innocent shopowners could hire him to arrange repairs, restorations, and/or renovations of commercial properties. Betsy looked out the rain-spattered front window, but Foster Johns was already out of sight. It was almost an equally shattering thought that she, with a talent for uncovering amateur criminals, had found this alleged murderer to be an honest, trustworthy sort, with an attractive personality. Betsy tended to trust her feelings about people. How could she be so wrong?

Two

What can you tell me about these people he murdered?" asked Betsy, sitting down at the table, her work forgotten.

Martha said, "They were Paul and Angela Schmitt. It was the old, old story. Angela was married to Paul but having an affair with Foster."

Alice said quietly, "I remember how shocked and sad Foster was the day Angela was found dead. I know everyone thinks he did it"—she looked at Martha—"but there is someone sitting right here at this table who knows the value of 'everyone thinks.'"

Martha, who had once been popularly suspected of a double homicide, said in a shocked voice, "That's different!"

"No, it isn't." Alice looked at Betsy. "You told me that one reason you look into crime is not so much to discover the guilty as to rescue the innocent. If Foster Johns is innocent, he certainly could use rescuing. His life has been extremely difficult since those murders."

Godwin said, "Don't even think about it, Betsy."

"Never fear, it's about to become the busiest time of year for me. I don't have time for distractions." Reminded, she stood and went back to the desk.

"All he had to do was move away—" began Emily.

Alice said, "Do you think if he had gone away, he wouldn't have lived in fear the rest of his life that someone from his old hometown would show up and tell that story to his new friends? Anyway, he has a business here that took him years to build! If he tried to sell it, who'd give him a good price? No one!"

"Well, if he's guilty," said Bershada, "that would be about what he deserves!"

"That's *right*," declared Godwin. "Are you saying he should be treated nicely, Alice? He should be *in jail*! And since that hasn't happened, the least we can do is cut him right out of our lives! It was *horrible* that a man Angela Schmitt loved and trusted *murdered* her!" He turned to Betsy. "She was the *sweetest* little thing," he said, "like a timid child, and Paul loved her for it—he was very protective of her."

Emily said, "I remember him. He had that kind of face that's always smiling. He'd see you coming and he'd always say hello. He loved Angela and bought her anything she wanted."

"'A man may smile and smile and be a villain,' Shakespeare wrote," said Alice.

"So what?" said Godwin. "It wasn't true in this case. He even took that second job in the gift shop so he could be near her."

"She couldn't have been afraid of him," said Martha, "if she started an affair with another man."

Betsy put down the packing list to ask, "Why did she start an affair with Foster if Paul was such a wonderful husband?"

Godwin said, "The lure of the new and exciting, I suppose." He made a sad-comical face. "Of course, I'm no expert in heterosexual affairs of the heart, but are they all that different from my own?" Godwin was gay, and his flirtatious ways sometimes infuriated his partner. "But she found out the hardest way that the grass isn't always greener on the wrong side of the fence."

"Possibly Foster didn't want her to leave her husband," suggested Bershada. "This way, Paul bought the cake and Foster got the icing."

"Well, that brings up another question," said Betsy. "Suppose she was going to leave him. That's a common pattern: The husband finds out that his wife wants a divorce, so he murders her and then himself. Couldn't that have happened here?"

"No," said Emily. "Paul's death was a murder, all right. There was some kind of fight in his house the night he was shot."

Martha said, "And the gun was never found."

Emily said, "*I* think Angela came to her senses and told Foster she wanted to break it off. There was a quarrel, and he murdered her. And he was so mad at Paul, he murdered him, too."

Comfort said thoughtfully, "There are women who, for whatever reason, pick domineering men. She married one, and when he made her unhappy, she chose another one as a lover."

Betsy said, "But Foster doesn't strike me as domineering. Maybe it's more that she was the kind of woman who liked to make her man jealous. Maybe she was making Paul angry by taking up with Foster."

Alice said, "I never, ever saw her do anything that would make me think she was a flirt or a tease. She was quiet and a little standoffish."

"How sure are you that she really was having an affair?" asked Betsy. "If it was all a tease—"

Godwin said, "Oh, Foster admitted it! It was on the news and everything. He probably seduced the poor thing."

Betsy said, "While my relationship with Foster is strictly business—"

"Yes, how *is* Morrie?" asked Godwin sweetly. He'd been delighted and amused to learn Betsy had a beau. Morrie Stephens was a police investigator with the Minnetonka Police Department. He had met Betsy last summer and admired her sleuthing ways. They were seeing a lot of each other and he was already hinting he wanted her to sell Crewel World and move to Fort Myers with him, after he retired this winter. Betsy hadn't told Godwin this not-so-amusing detail.

"Hush," she said, blushing lightly. "I'm about to make a point here. Am I so wrong about Foster, is he the sort who goes about seducing shy married women for sport?"

"Well, no, he didn't impress me that way," said Alice. "I was surprised to find out about him and Angela. But when I was married to a pastor, I found out things that happen between men and women you wouldn't believe."

"The thing is, there isn't any other explanation," said Comfort. "No one else was close to Angela, no one else had any reason at all to murder her."

"Except Paul, if he had found out his wife was making a fool of him with Foster Johns," said Betsy. "Any husband—or wife, for that matter—is apt to be very angry when they learn something like that." Betsy had divorced her husband when she found that he had been repeatedly unfaithful. "So it's logical to suppose that if Paul found out about Foster, he murdered Angela. Then perhaps Foster, in a rage, murdered Paul. That would make sense."

Martha said, "But the police said the same gun was used to kill both of them."

They looked at Betsy to explain that, if she could. So of course she tried. "Well, okay, still say Paul murdered his wife. Foster, in a rage, went to see Paul, who naturally became frightened and pulled out his gun. They fought over it, and Foster got it and shot Paul."

That made sense, and the challenging looks faded.

"But then why didn't Foster call the police?" asked Emily. "Isn't that self-defense?"

Betsy, remembering the cool, competent way Foster had handled the complex details of getting the building permits, hiring a roofer and the company to haul away the remains of the old roof, and while he was about it someone to replace the gutters, frowned. The Foster she thought she had come to know would certainly call the police if he had shot someone in self-defense. She thought a bit, then asked, "Why suspect only Foster Johns in this case? Couldn't someone else have murdered Paul Schmitt? Doesn't Angela have family in the area who might have avenged her murder?"

"Her father lives in Florida most of the year. He was down there when she was murdered, and was just about to fly back when Paul was killed," said Godwin. "She has two brothers, but one lives in California, and the other was overseas with the Army. So, you see, there really isn't anyone else. Paul wasn't the kind to blow his cool. He wasn't as sweet as Emily thinks, but who is?"

Emily blushed but said, "He was too!"

"He managed that Scandinavian gift shop really well," Godwin continued, "expanded their reach into British and Irish stock, which improved their bottom line—he was bragging about it at a party. I can't think of a single enemy he had. And, of course, no one in his right mind had any reason to hate Angela."

"Maybe a robbery?" suggested Betsy.

Martha said, "Well, I think that's what the police thought, right at first. Angela was alone when she was shot there, she was closing up that night. But she wouldn't have resisted if someone came in with a gun, she wasn't the least brave. Anyway, nothing was taken."

Alice said, "That's because the gun being fired brought people's attention, so whoever it was had to leave or be caught."

Martha said, "That's right, a bullet broke a window, and the bookstore's right on Water Street, so there were a lot of people who came rushing to see what was going on. And of course everyone thought it was a robbery. But then Paul was shot, and at home. So then everyone thought what you suggested, Betsy, that Paul shot her and then himself. But when we heard about the fight, and that the police couldn't find the gun, we knew it was something else."

Godwin said, "And that time it wasn't Malloy doing the investigating. Paul lived in Navarre, that's where he was shot."

Martha said, "But Mike was over there because they thought there might be a link between Paul's and Angela's murders. And there was: The same gun was used in both murders."

Comfort said, "I remember hearing on the news the morning after it happened that a neighbor heard shooting at the Schmitt house and called the police."

"You meant there was a gunfight?" asked Betsy.

"No, no, there was just one gun involved, but there were several shots fired."

"That's right, I remember reading that in the Minneapolis newspaper," said Godwin. "The neighbors were too scared to look out their windows, or there might have been a description of Foster running away or a license plate number or something. But there wasn't. And that's one reason he wasn't arrested. Which is too bad; Paul Schmitt was shot two or three times, so it wasn't an easy death."

"Dreadful," murmured Emily, and there was a little silence.

Betsy said, "Wait, it doesn't make sense that Foster would murder Angela and then Paul. In fact . . ." Her frown deepened. "I suppose I can see Foster going to Paul to tell him he was in love with Angela and demanding Paul divorce her, then getting in a fight and killing Paul. And I suppose it could happen that his mistress was so upset about it, she threatened to turn him in, so he killed her, too. But that's not the order this happened in. I suppose it's possible a man might be so exasperated and infuriated with his mistress that he murders her. But then, having done that, why round it off by murdering her husband? I mean, he's so handy as a suspect, isn't he?"

"But maybe Paul knew Foster did it, maybe he even had some kind of proof, so Foster had to kill him," suggested Bershada.

"There you go," said Godwin, his eyes lighting up.

"No, no, there was just one gun involved, but there were several shots fired."

"That's right, I remember reading that in the Minneapolis newspaper," said Godwin. "The neighbors were too scared to look out their windows, or there might have been a description of Foster running away or a license plate number or something. But there wasn't. And that's one reason he wasn't arrested. Which is too bad; Paul Schmitt was shot two or three times, so it wasn't an easy death."

"Dreadful," murmured Emily, and there was a little silence.

Betsy said, "Wait, it doesn't make sense that Foster would murder Angela and then Paul. In fact . . ." Her frown deepened. "I suppose I can see Foster going to Paul to tell him he was in love with Angela and demanding Paul divorce her, then getting in a fight and killing Paul. And I suppose it could happen that his mistress was so upset about it, she threatened to turn him in, so he killed her, too. But that's not the order this happened in. I suppose it's possible a man might be so exasperated and infuriated with his mistress that he murders her. But then, having done that, why round it off by murdering her husband? I mean, he's so handy as a suspect, isn't he?"

"But maybe Paul knew Foster did it, maybe he even had some kind of proof, so Foster had to kill him," suggested Bershada.

"There you go," said Godwin, his eyes lighting up at this evidence of clever thinking. He smiled at Bershada.

"Instead of going to the police?" asked Betsy.

"Well, maybe he wanted to protect his wife's reputation," said Comfort.

"Oh, that's so old-fashioned!" scoffed Godwin. "People nowadays don't care a rat's right ear for things like that."

"Only Foster knows why it happened in that order," said Martha darkly. "And he's not telling."

Alice squared her shoulders and asked Betsy, "Could it be that Foster didn't commit any murder at all?"

"Why are you so eager to defend him, anyhow?" demanded Godwin.

"Because . . . because I was paying attention before all this happened," said Alice. "I think Paul might not have been a good husband. And I saw the way Foster behaved after Angela was murdered. He didn't act the least bit guilty."

"That's because he has nerves of steel and a heart of ice," said Comfort.

"I mean he was sad and upset, not calm and cool," said Alice.

Bershada said, "Well, if I murdered someone, I'd be sad and upset, too. Anyway, if he didn't do it, who did?"

Alice said, "I don't know. You all think you know Foster did it, but the police couldn't find enough evidence to charge him, much less convict him. That has to mean something, doesn't it?"

"Not with Mike involved in the investigations," said Martha pointedly.

"Well, we're not the clever ones when it comes to solving mysteries, Betsy is. Think for a minute, Betsy. Who do you think did it?"

"Thinking wouldn't help," said Betsy frankly. "There's not enough information for me—"

She was interrupted by the annoying *Bing!* of the front door. Foster Johns, his back to them while he closed the door, turned and saw the faces turned toward him. But his voice was calm when he said, "The inspector finished quicker than he thought he would and came looking for me. He seems to think everything is fine. What are you going to do about it?"

Three

I'll write you a check after I talk to the inspector," said Betsy.

The relief in Johns's eyes was palpable. "He's outside," Johns said, and turned and opened the door. Its *Bing!* sounded loud in the rigid silence of the shop, and Betsy noted irrelevantly that she'd forgotten to turn on the radio when she opened up that morning. She glanced around at the table and Alice caught her eye with a tiny, encouraging nod.

At Johns's gesture, a short man in heavy blue coveralls came in. "Ms. Devonshire," he said with a little nod, removing his red hunter's hat to reveal a bald head surrounded by white hair.

"Mr. Jurgens." Betsy nodded back.

He frowned at the silent group at the table. "Is there a problem?"

"I don't think so," said Betsy. "Unless you found something else wrong with my roof." Betsy had thought the job done two weeks ago, but the inspector had discovered a pair of flaws, necessitating a removal of part of the new tarred covering, replacement of some of the insulation, and then fresh hot tar being applied to the patches. This, Foster Johns assured Betsy, was not really unusual, and the patch would be as sound as if it were original to the roof.

"The repair is fine. They did a good job—that roof should do well for prob'ly twenty years, if not more." He unbuttoned the top of his coveralls, revealing a red plaid shirt, and fumbled in a pocket for a thin sheaf of papers folded lengthwise. "Here's my report."

Betsy took the papers and glanced them over. Computer printouts, they included a copy of his first report saying she needed a new roof, then the one describing the flaws he'd found, and on top the newest report indicating the roof was now properly done and resealed. He had signed this one in thick, soft pencil and dated it today.

"These look fine," said Betsy. "Thank you." The inspector put his hat back on, glanced again at the people around the table, and departed.

"If you can wait here a minute, Mr. Johns," said Betsy, "I'll go upstairs and get my checkbook."

"May I come with you? I'd like a word with you, in private."

"Sure—no, wait a minute." Betsy glanced at her watch. It was nearly two, and she hadn't had lunch yet. "How about I go get my checkbook and then we both go to Antiquity Rose for a bowl of soup? Or have you had lunch?"

He hesitated, then nodded. "Not yet."

Antiquity Rose was a house converted to a tea and antique shop. It had an excellent kitchen, which was currently featuring a hearty potato-cheese soup. Betsy had hers with a bran muffin. Foster chose the fat, warm breadstick.

After a few spoonfuls, Betsy said, "Did you bring your bill with you?"

"Yes, but that's not the problem I wanted to talk to you about."

"No? What's the problem?"

Foster looked across the little table, his face a mix of desperation and hope. "I heard you do private investigations for people falsely charged with crimes."

"That's approximately true. Who's in trouble?"

His smile was wry. "Don't tell me they didn't give you an earful while I was gone. Because of people like them, I've been living in hell for five years and eleven days."

"Ah," said Betsy. "Yes, they told me about Paul and Angela Schmitt."

"I was hoping that if I could get just one person in town to give me a chance, then they'd start to come around. But I guess now you're sorry I took advantage of your ignorance."

Betsy's lips tightened. "That's not true."

"Of course, if I murdered two people, nothing could be bad enough to be worse than I deserve. But I didn't. I've done everything I can think of to show people I'm an honest citizen, but nothing's worked. Then someone told me about you—"

"Who?" interrupted Betsy. "Who told you?"

"Jurgens, the inspector. He told me you solved your sister's murder and another murder up on the North Shore. 'She's real slick,' is how Jurgens put it. I hope he's right and this is something you're willing to do for me." Indeed, he looked so hopeful, Betsy's heart was again wrenched, and all her promises about this being too busy a time of year for sleuthing began to crumble. Still, she held herself to a mere nod, and he continued, "I don't know what you charge, but if you can clear my name, any amount is worth it. How much do you want as a retainer?"

"Nothing. I don't have a private investigator's license, and I wouldn't dream of taking money from you."

He tossed his spoon into his bowl and sat back. "I'm sorry you feel like that."

"Wait a minute, I didn't say I wouldn't try to help. I am willing to look into your problem, but it will be strictly as an amateur." Hope flared on his face—here was no heart of ice or nerve of steel—and she added, "I just hope you aren't in a big rush. It will probably be after the first of the year before I can give your case the attention it deserves. All I can do now is try to gather some basic information."

He nodded. "I've waited this long, I can be patient awhile longer. What do you want to know?"

She asked, "First, have you thought about hiring a real private investigator?"

"I did that. He charged me three thousand dollars and all he could tell me was that Paul Schmitt probably abused Angela. I already knew that to be a fact."

Betsy said, "It's been five years. If I start asking questions, people are going to recall some sordid details. Are you sure you want me bringing the whole mess up again?"

"What again? It's never gone away. I'll tell you anything I can. What do you need from me to begin with?"

Betsy thought. "Let's start with Angela. Tell me about her."

Foster leaned forward and a slow smile formed as he cast his mind back. "I didn't mean to fall in love with her," he said. "I don't even know exactly when it happened. I do know that it started when I said something to her on the steps after church one Sunday about it finally getting warm enough to do some work outdoors, and she thought I meant gardening. I said, 'No, I own a construction company,' which I did back then, and we were making a joke about the misunderstanding when her husband came from out of nowhere and yanked her away so hard, she dropped her purse. The look on his face surprised me, it was so full of anger. But I thought I was mistaken. I mean, I thought I knew Paul, we'd ushered together a few times, and I'd had a few conversations with him about roofing—he was a good amateur carpenter. He was one of those guys who almost always has a grin on his face, like he's got the point of a joke the rest of us don't. So that look that day was surprising. I actually remember trying to decide if it was the angle of the sun putting a funny shadow on his face. You see, he was always willing to lend a hand, jump-start a car, bring groceries to a shut-in, like that.

"But while I was surprised by him, I was surprised even more by the look on her face as she went off with him, like she was scared to death of what would happen when he got her home. Even weirder, when he noticed it, he shook her arm and she all of a sudden looked fine." He shrugged.

"At the time, of course, I didn't think of it that way, that he was ordering her to wipe that look off her face. It was only later I learned what a son of a bitch he was, excuse my French. That she was right to be scared.

"We were born the same year, Angela and me, and Paul was two years older. I went to high school with them both, though I never dated her—I was into big, cushy blondes back then, so I didn't see her as my type. She was just a bit of a thing, and dark-haired. But she was pretty enough, and I think could have been popular if she put herself out some more. But she was shy, hardly said anything to anyone in school. I went on to get my degree in architectural engineering, but she dropped out of college to marry Paul.

"Anyhow, the Sunday after I talked to Angela about the weather, Alice Skoglund said it was sad how Angela seemed so unhappy nowadays, and something about the way she said it made me think of that scared look. So I kind of kept my eye on her for the next few weeks, and once I paid attention, I could see Angela wasn't just unhappy, she was scared. So I took to talking to her when Paul wasn't around, which was like a minute here and a minute there—he was generally right with her. But I kept trying to find out what was going on. Pretty soon she trusted me enough to really talk to me. And soon after I got the hint from her that he was abusing her. I got mad on her behalf, and told her to walk out, just leave him, go down to Florida to stay with her parents; but she said she was afraid of what he might do.

"By then I wasn't just out to rescue a fellow Lutheran; it was getting personal. So I paid attention, I got to know her schedule, and we'd meet while she was grocery shopping or on her way to and from work, friends' houses, like that. He was always checking up on her, phoning her, making her account for her time, so it was tricky." He smiled. "But I'm an efficient scheduler, and we got pretty good at it. Then I started pressuring her to leave him for me. I said I'd send her to live with my parents in North Carolina, or my sister in Las Vegas, until he gave up looking for her, but she said he'd never give up, and when he found her, he'd kill her *and* whoever was giving her shelter, so she just couldn't do that. I was even looking into those ways of giving someone a new identity when it happened." His face tightened.

"You're saying he's the one who killed her," said Betsy.

"Of course. There was no one else, how could there be? He never let her get close enough to anyone, so there was no one else to love her or hate her enough to do that."

"You managed."

"And he found out."

"How do you know?"

"Because she phoned me from work the day it happened, to warn me to keep away from her, that Paul had gone from suspecting she was fooling around to being sure she was, and that I was involved. He'd actually started writing down the mileage on her car, and it didn't match the driving she was supposed to be doing, so he figured she was going somewhere she shouldn't. Which she was, of course. He'd seen me going into the bookstore and talking to her, and she smiled at me in a way that, he said, told him all he needed to know. That night it was her turn to stay and close up the shop, and normally we would have a few minutes together. But this time I walked up Water Street a little after five, just to look in the window and see her. It was pouring rain and when I waved at her, I got water up my sleeve—funny the things you remember. She waved back and I went on up the street. I wish I'd gone in, I wish . . ." He twisted his head, dismissing that futile thought. "He worked just two doors down from her, did you know that?"

Betsy said, "Yes, in the Heritage gift shop on the corner." Betsy could see it in her mind's eye, it was light red brick and went around the corner in a curve just broad enough to accommodate a door. Its big windows were generally full of imported dishes, sweaters or dresses, and glassware.

"He took that job to spy on her. He did freelance computer programming in an office in their house for very respectable pay; and he did some freelance home repairs, carpentry mostly, for which he got paid under the table. Not paying taxes made up for not getting union wages. He didn't need that job at the gift shop."

"How long did Angela work at the bookstore?"

"Not quite two years. She'd begged and pleaded with him and he finally said she could get a part-time job. It wasn't for the money, not entirely, she just wanted out of the house. But he couldn't stand the thought of her meeting strange men all day long, so right after she started, he got that job so he could watch her." Foster smiled. "He wanted to work in the pet shop right next door, but she was allergic to cat hair, and he'd've come home with it on him. And he couldn't work in the place on the other side of the bookstore, it's a beauty parlor." He ripped his bread stick into three pieces. "There's the proof he was some kind of nut, taking that job just to spy on her. She was never, ever unfaithful to him."

Betsy's eyebrows went up at that, and he said, "I mean it. We wanted to— God, how we wanted to! But he made her carry a cell phone and he called her about every fifteen minutes when she wasn't home or in the bookstore, where was she, what was she doing, who was there with her. He said he loved her, but it was a crazy love. He was crazy, insane."

He looked up at Betsy. "So you see, when she was shot, I knew it was him. It had to be. It wasn't me, and there wasn't anyone else. The police thought so, too, when they figured out it wasn't a robbery. But he'd rigged some kind of alibi, so when Gloria in the bookstore told them about me coming in to buy more books in six months than I'd bought in five years, and talking like a friend to someone I ignored when her husband was around . . ." He made a pained face. "Funny how there's always a slip somewhere, isn't it? Gloria knew me because her husband hired me to remodel their house back when I was just starting out, and she's a member of my church, which is where she saw me not speaking to Angela in front of Paul. We tried so hard to be cool in front of Paul that she noticed.

"Anyhow, Mike Malloy came to talk to me. I told him that I was very fond of Angela, that she'd told me her husband was crazy jealous and beat her up every time the mood took him. I told him Paul had just found out about me and Angela, so it had to be Paul who shot her."

Betsy said, "But then Paul was shot."

Johns nudged a fragment of breadstick with a forefinger. "Turned everything on its head. Now they were looking for someone with a motive to shoot both of them. And the closest they can come is me."

"So why didn't they arrest you?"

"They did. But they had to let me go, because while I was near the bookstore that night, I had an alibi for the night Paul was shot."

"An *alibi*?"

"Paul and my cleaning lady provided it between them. Damnedest thing. He phoned me at my office and said he wanted to see me. Well, I didn't want to see him, but he said he had evidence of who murdered Angela. He said the cops would think he cooked it up, but if I was the one who brought it to the cops, they'd believe me. He said, 'It'll help you, too, Foster, because the cops are sure that if it isn't me, then it's probably you.' I asked him, 'Who did it?'—not believing him, of course—and he said, 'It's someone who's after me. He killed Angela because he knows how much I loved her and he wants me to suffer before he kills me.' And I asked him again, 'Who is it?' and he said I wouldn't believe it, he had to show me, and that's why he wanted to talk to me in person about it.

"Well, I didn't know whether he had anything or not, but I didn't want him in my house, so I said, 'Come to my office with your proof.' And we set a time of nine o'clock that night. Yes, it occurred to me that he might do something really stupid, like shoot me, too. But what if he really had something? I owned a little tape recorder, it had a switch position for sound activation; it stops when it's quiet, then starts when people start talking. I put it in a desk drawer I left a little bit open, figuring that if he admits he did it, or if he pulls something, there will be a recording.

"You know my place, it started life as a little gas station up on Third and Water back in the thirties." Betsy nodded—the design of the little stucco building with its steep tile roof announced its origins. "I've got a reception area in front, and in back a room for the guy who helps me do estimates and supervises the crews at work and my own office, which I also use for meetings. I went out for supper at Hilltop about six-thirty, and since I had nothing else to do, I went back to my office. We have a cleaning lady but she was already done when I got back, and that saved my hide."

"How was that?" asked Betsy

"Well, we'd been asked to take a look at the old Ace Hardware store— this was before the fire, and the owner wanted to upgrade the apartments over the store. He wanted my ideas and an estimate on remodeling. I hadn't had a chance to look at the specs yet, so I got out the notes I'd taken when we talked, and the plans and my calculator, and did some work while I waited for Paul Schmitt to come by. Which he didn't. At nine-twenty I phoned his house, and when there was no answer, I assumed he was on his way over. But he wasn't. I finally went home a little after ten, and the police came and woke me up around eleven. They wanted to know where I was between nine and nine forty-five and I said I was in my office. Alone, of course."

Betsy asked, "So how did your cleaning lady help give you an alibi?"

"She told the cops that when she left my building at seven forty-five, my desk was clear and my office was perfectly clean, but when I took the cops back over there, the wastebasket but was half full of wadded-up notes, and the top of my desk and a table were covered with plans and blueprints and estimates, and there were a couple of drawings pinned up on my bulletin board that weren't there before. I'm a messy worker, and when I'm working on a job, I tend to leave things out, for which I thank God—and for not staying until I finished, because I would've put things away. I mean, it's not the greatest alibi in the world, but it was good enough. That and the fact that there wasn't a mark on me or any blood on my clothes, because there had been a knock-down, drag-out at Paul's house."

"Did the police find the evidence Paul said he had about who murdered Angela?"

"The detective never mentioned that they found anything. Not that he would have, but I don't know that anyone else was ever questioned about it. And they never arrested anyone else, damn it to hell."

"Do you think Paul ever had any evidence of who really murdered Angela?"

"I don't know. My first thought was that Paul set it up somehow, trashed his living room and ran into things until he was all beat up, then shot himself."

"Now wait a minute," objected Betsy, "surely the police could tell the difference between someone running into something and the marks of a fist!"

"Maybe he punched himself in the face." Seeing her doubtful expression, he said earnestly, "Angela convinced me Paul was crazy," said Foster. "Seriously crazy, as in mentally ill. He liked to get mad at her, she said, so he'd have an excuse to beat her. He'd set her up so no matter what she said he could convince himself he had a right to be angry. He'd come home in some kind of weird mood and she'd know that before bedtime, he'd find a reason to hit her. He never let anyone else see how things would get to him, so when he was angry about something, he'd still be nice and smiling to other people, but he'd come home and take it out on Angela. And he didn't feel pain like normal people. She said one time he cut his knuckle on her tooth and wouldn't even put a Band-Aid on it until she complained he was getting blood all over the sheets."

"All right, buying for a minute your theory that Paul was capable of beating himself up, where did the gun that shot him go?"

"Yes, that's what throws it all in the toilet, doesn't it? The damn gun is gone. So maybe Paul was right, he had an enemy who really hated him, who murdered Angela to torture him and then beat him up before shooting him."

"Have you any idea who that might be?" asked Betsy.

"Not an inkling. But"—he leaned forward to point a knobby index finger at Betsy—"don't let the people you talk to make a saint of him, talking about his good deeds and that smile he always had on his face. Angela told me that his smile was like the smile of a dolphin. His face was just made that way, a kind of birth defect, it didn't mean a thing. He had to make an effort to not smile. He would smile in his sleep and he would smile while he was punching her."

Four

Betsy gently rubbed the surface of a Christmas tree ornament done in shades of antique gold and deep red. Very Velvet was a narrow, ribbonlike fiber with a short, dense nap, luxurious to the touch. Her stocking design was painted on canvas by an artist named Marcy, and depicted a branch of long-needled pine hung with very elaborate ornaments and tinsel. She should be doing her books, but she was in a race with the calendar to get this stocking done in time to be "finished," cut from its surrounding of blank canvas, lined, and sewn to a backing that would turn it into a real Christmas stocking.

Not that she would ever put anything in the stocking, of course. Such a beautiful and labor-intensive object would be strictly for display. She had other painted canvases by Marcy, and would hang this in her shop among them to show customers how lovely the finished project could be.

Jill said, "Don't rub the fuzz off," but not with any rancor. Jill was a police officer, a young woman whose Scandinavian heritage showed both in her ash-blond coloring and the low emotional content of her speech. She loved subtle jokes, cross-country skiing, and needlepoint, and was pleased to see Betsy doing something elaborate in the last area.

Betsy held the stocking at arm's length by its scroll bars so she could admire it. The colors and pattern of this piece were already so complex that she'd decided to do all of it in basic basketweave, and add interest by using different fibers: overdyed silks, perle cotton, metallics, wool, a difficult tubular ribbon called Crystal Rays, and Very Velvet. Each fiber caught the light differently, adding depth and interest to the work.

Jill, working on her own needlepoint canvas of a Siamese cat looking at itself in a mirror, asked, "Are you going to try to help Foster Johns?"

Betsy replied, "I'm going to look into it a bit." She cut a length of black wool and threaded her needle—there being no other color she hadn't used, she was doing the background of the stocking in black. "I don't have time to do a really intensive investigation, it's about to become very busy in the shop—I hope."

"So you don't think he did it?"

"I don't know what to think. What do you know about the night it happened?"

"Which murder?"

"Angela's."

"I wasn't on duty, so I wasn't one of the first responders, but I got called in to stand guard at the back door of the bookshop."

Excelsior was a small town, with a small police department. All sworn officers had to be prepared to respond to a call to duty at any time. Fortunately, in law-abiding Excelsior, this was a rare occurance. Jill tilted her canvas back and forth under the light to see if the next few stitches were in the same shade of cream she was using or a lighter one. "I was new to the force at the time," she continued, "so I didn't dare say what I thought—that Malloy should call in the BCA. Those state fellows run a lot of crime scenes, while murder is a rare event around here."

"Did you get to see the crime scene?" Betsy ran her needle through some completed stitches on the back to anchor the yarn, then poked her needle through.

"No, but I got an earful, then and later. No sign of a struggle. Apparently two shots were fired, but Angela was shot just once, from behind, and the bullet went through her chest and out the front window of the bookstore."

Betsy frowned. Someone had mentioned a broken window, but not this horrible detail. "Out the window—is that possible?"

"Sure, with a magnum-style bullet. It punched a big hole in Angela, and a bigger hole in the glass."

"Oh, gah!" said Betsy, never fond of gory details. "You said two shots were fired. Could someone have shot Angela and then fired out the window?"

"Why would someone do that?"

"I don't know. Maybe he shot out the window and then shot Angela?"

"Again, why?"

"I don't know. But why two shots?"

"Oh, I thought you meant on purpose. I think he shot at Angela twice, missed the first time and got her the second. But they never found either slug," Jill said.

"That's odd."

"Yes, it is. Of course, Mike didn't find the second shell casing, either. His report says one shot, it went through Angela and out the window. One of the store employees found the second shell casing months later, when they were replacing some bookshelves."

"So you don't think the murderer shot out the window on purpose?" Betsy asked.

"Why would he do that? It called attention to the bookstore. The 911 operators reported three calls in less than two minutes. One said it was a bomb, one said it was a drive-by, one said it was a robbery in progress. Like most first calls, they were all mistaken. It wasn't a bomb, the bullet came from inside the store, and nothing was stolen. Mike suspected for a while that it was an attempted robbery, and when the window blew out, the would-be robber ran out the back before alarmed passersby could catch him."

"Does he still think that's a valid theory?" Betsy put a single angled stitch beside the teardrop-shaped ornament.

"Not really. Not since Paul was killed so soon after. But he still thinks Angela must have let the person in, because both doors were locked when the police arrived."

"So how did the murderer get out?"

"The back door didn't have the dead bolt keyed shut, just the Yale, which you can open by hand from inside and which locks itself when you close the door."

"Fingerprints?"

"The only ones found were hers and the owner's. Gloves, probably."

"Did she ordinarily let people into the store after it closed?"

"I wouldn't think so. You don't let people in after you close, do you? Unless it's an emergency."

"True. And more people think it's an emergency that they need another skein of DMC 758 than that they need a copy of *The Ten Stupid Things Women Do to Mess Up Their Lives*," said Betsy.

"Malloy might agree, except for the part about needing an emergency skein of DMC floss. But you can see why, when Malloy and his partner went to tell Paul about his wife, they had some hope of arresting him for her murder."

"You mean Paul wasn't standing outside the bookstore demanding to know what was going on?"

"No, they found him doing paperwork in the gift shop."

"Hmmm."

"Why hmmm?" asked Jill.

"Because he is alleged to have taken that job just so he could keep an eye on Angela. Presumably a fuss of any sort would have him right out there taking a look. There were sirens, right?"

"Oh, yes, lots of sirens."

"So why didn't he come running to see what was going on?"

"I don't know. Maybe he was hard of hearing. Oh, wait a minute. It was pouring rain that evening, with lots of thunder and lightning. It's possible the racket covered up what was going on. I remember that night, it had snowed once, so seemed weird to be having a thunderstorm instead of a blizzard. I remember that because I was worried about standing outside in the storm—but also because that storm gave Paul his alibi."

"It did? How?"

"Well, if he'd gone from the gift shop to the bookstore and back, he'd've gotten soaked, even though it's only two doors down. But he was bone dry, hair, clothes, and shoes. He'd brought a raincoat with him to work, because the forecast was for thunderstorms, but it was dry, too. He was looking good for that murder, so they really searched for wet clothes he might have changed out of, for a hair dryer, plastic garbage bags with head and arm holes, any evidence he'd been out in that rain, and didn't find a thing. And no one saw him outside the gift shop. Despite the rain, there were people on the street, and some of them knew Paul by sight."

"So if it wasn't Paul, and it wasn't a robber . . ." said Betsy.

"Yes. And Foster was seen on Water Street right about the time it happened."

They stitched in silence for a while, then Betsy said, "Did you get called to the scene again when Paul was murdered?"

"No. He and Angela lived in Navarre. The police force out there called in Malloy, of course, when they identified Paul, because of Angela; so some of what happened got back to us. I heard there was clear evidence of a fight, a broken mirror, overturned furniture, blood spatters. Paul was shot twice, once in the leg and again in the head. The same gun was used in both murders, and it was never found." Jill put her stitching down to frown in thought for a few moments.

"What?" asked Betsy.

"What I think is, it's a shame that no one saw Foster in Navarre the night Paul was killed, the way people here saw him on Water Street."

"Maybe they didn't see him because he wasn't there. Foster told me he was in his office, waiting for a meeting with Paul that never happened."

Jill said, "I don't think I ever heard that."

"Foster says Paul called him and said he had evidence that would clear both of them of Angela's murder. Paul said he had proof of who really murdered his wife."

"Who did he say it was?"

"He told Foster he had to see the proof to believe it, that it was someone no one thought it could be."

Jill asked, "And you believe that story?"

"I don't know what to believe. Foster said Angela told him that Paul was a very strange person. It's a weird alibi Foster has, too. But Foster says the police found evidence he was in his office after the cleaning lady left. On the other hand, it's hard to imagine that Foster would agree to meet the man he cuckolded, a man he described as a crazy wife-beater."

"Did he tell anyone he was meeting Paul?"

"That's a good question, I'll ask him that next time I see him. Jill, did you ever hear or see anything that would make you think Paul was insane?"

"That's a funny question."

"I know. But Foster said Angela was afraid of what he might do if she left him, that Paul was dangerous. He said Paul was always grinning, even when he was sad or angry."

Jill stopped stitching to close her eyes and think. "I remember that smile," she said at last. "But I didn't think it was crazy, I just thought he was a happy person. It wasn't one of those grins that don't reach the eyes, like you see sometimes. Paul's eyes squinched up, too." She considered a bit more. "He seemed like a happy, friendly person to me."

"That's two very different pictures. How well did you know him?"

"Not all that well."

"Who was Paul's best friend?"

"I don't know."

"Who does know?"

Jill smiled faintly. "Well, I'm sure the Bureau of Criminal Apprehension looked into his past pretty thoroughly, but I don't know how you could access their records."

"Do you have a connection in the BCA who might look for me?"

"Nope. Now you see, if you were a real police investigator, you could just call the BCA and ask to take a look at their files on the case."

"If I were really a police investigator, then Crewel World would be owned by someone who wouldn't let you return unused needlepoint wool."

Jill said with every appearance of deadpan sincerity, "There's a downside to everything, I guess."

The next day, Betsy phoned Alice Skoglund. "Hello, Betsy," she said in her deep voice. "What may I do for you?"

"I want to ask you a question about Paul Schmitt."

A bit warily she asked, "What about Mr. Schmitt?"

"He was a long-time member of your church, wasn't he?"

"Well . . . yes, why?"

"I was wondering if you knew someone who was a good friend of his."

Alice didn't reply at once. Then she said, "I don't think I know of any."

"Think hard, Alice. This is important."

Alice had the curious trait of falling into what seemed like a noisy, deep-breathing coma when thinking, and suddenly the sounds of that were carried through the receiver at Betsy's ear. After a minute it stopped, and Alice said, "Well, he used to go hunting with Vern Miller and his sons, Jory and Alex. Paul and Jory are about the same age, and they were in the same Sunday-school class for several years. Paul and Alex were friends until Paul married Angela, but as far as I know, Vern and Jory stayed friends with Paul right up until Paul's death. Jory works for his father in that garage he runs over on Third. They'll probably be able to tell you who was Paul's best friend—if he had one."

Betsy had been to that garage, a scabrous place converted from a livery stable. It didn't sell gasoline, just did repairs on older vehicles, the kind without computer chips or built-in VCRs. Though she had heard he was very talented, Betsy would not allow Vern, who was built on the approximate lines of a shell for a large naval gun, and was about as intelligent, to touch her old Mercury Tracer. And of course her new Buick was outside his expertise.

So he watched her walk into his little office with a frown of puzzlement.

"Help you?" he offered in his deep, gruff voice. He was an old man, his face deeply creased, his white hair both overgrown and thinning. But his sloping shoulders were heavy, and his filthy overalls and black fingernails indicated he was still a working man.

"Is Jory here?" she asked. "I'd like to talk to both of you for a few minutes, if you can spare them, about Paul Schmitt."

Without rising he threw his head back and roared, *"Jory!"* His office was built into a corner of the workshop with old boards and chicken wire, he could have called his son with far less effort than that.

"What?!?" came the reply, equally loud, equally needlessly.

"C'mere!" He sat back in his ancient, battered chair behind a dirty, cluttered desk and smiled at her. "He'll be right in."

A minute later a man in his mid-thirties came in. He was slimmer than Vern, but not by much, and not much taller. Though he resembled his father, there was an Asian cast to his features, and Betsy suddenly recalled that Vern had brought a bride home from the Korean War. "What's up?" he asked, glancing at Betsy suspiciously.

"I dunno. This lady wants to ask me and you some questions." He asked Betsy, "Are you doing another investigation?"

Jory said, "Oh, she's *that* lady!" He looked at her curiously, apparently having been told the story of the time Betsy had suspected Vern of murdering a vanished high-school sweetheart.

Vern said, "Yeah. I bet she's out to prove once and for all it was suicide, Paul killed his wife then hisself."

Jory retorted, "Or maybe she can prove it was Foster Johns murdered both of 'em." He smiled and leaned against the doorframe of the tiny office. "Sure, I'll answer any questions you have."

"Thank you. I understand you and your brother Alex were good friends with Paul."

"Sure. And with Foster Johns, too, back then. We all kind of hung out together."

"I never liked Paul Schmitt," growled Vern.

"Ah, you did too! You used to take us hunting and fishing."

"Maybe I did. But Paul was a strange kid, mean as a snake even with all his jokes."

Jory chuckled. "Remember that time he got hold of a little propane torch and would heat up a quarter and drop it on the sidewalk? Ow, ow, ow!" Jory laughed and shook his fingers as if they were burned.

Despite himself, Vern grinned, then drew up his sloping shoulders. "Yeah, but that time he scalded our cat, that wasn't funny."

Jory frowned. "That was an accident, he told you that, I told you that."

"I didn't think so. Neither did Alex."

"Aw, Alex! Who cares what he thinks?"

Vern shrugged. "Not me."

Betsy asked Jory, "How long have you known Paul Schmitt?"

"Since high school. He was a great guy, the funniest person I ever knew. He liked every kind of joke, and liked to play jokes on people."

"What can you tell me about his wife Angela?"

"I can tell you he murdered her," Vern cut in.

"You don't know that!" Jory said sharply. To Betsy he added, "He was nuts about her, totally nuts. He bought two cell phones and he was callin' her up all the time, asking her what she was doin'. An' he was always buying her things, a new dress, jewelry, flowers, fancy nightgowns. Then he'd call her three or four times to ask how she liked 'em, just so he could hear her thank him one more time. He'd say, 'Gotta keep 'em happy.' " Jory's smile faded. "He was real upset when she got shot. He looked so bad that when he was killed, the first thing I thought was that he killed himself. I said, 'I bet he killed himself,' didn't I?" He looked at his father.

Vern nodded, rugged face pulled into a heavy frown. "He took it hard, all right, but I don't agree that somebody else killing his wife would make him kill his own self. He wasn't the type. He was the type to kill her, and then kill hisself."

Jory shook his head, "It was proved he was beat up and shot by someone else."

Vern waved a thick, dirty hand dismissivly. "Yeah, but who proved it? Mike Malloy, who couldn't prove corn flakes taste better with milk. Nah, I say he killed hisself and Malloy bungled it somehow. Maybe the gun fell behind the couch and Malloy couldn't find it, or it's even possible he had it and mislaid it, so he just said it was murder."

Betsy said, "Malloy isn't as stupid as all that—"

"Sure he is," said Vern. "Dumber than a box of rocks."

Jory said, "So what? It couldn't've been Paul, it had to be someone else; the same gun killed both of them. Paul wouldn't murder Angela, he was crazy about her."

Vern shifted his weight in his chair, settling in for an argument. "Same gun, sure—but it could've been Paul's gun. He had one, you know that."

"Then where is it?"

"I told you, Malloy lost it. And crazy is the right word. You said it yourself, he called her every five minutes when she wasn't at home, checking up on her. He liked her to stay at home, and he worked at home so he could be right there with her. He hated it when she took that job at the bookstore, so he took a job right down the street. They didn't need the money she brought in; I think she wanted out of the house because he was smothering her. Ten, eleven years they was married, and was like they'd gotten married last week. It wasn't love, it was more like he was obsessed. And he was getting worse, not better. He was always thinking she was having an affair, which it turned out she was, though where she found the time I don't know. But I don't blame her. So okay, he found out, and he shot her. I thought from the start he done it."

By the unheated tones of the argument, Betsy was sure this was an old, often-rehashed one.

Jory said, "Nope, you're wrong. Once Foster Johns admitted he and Angela were messing around, I knew it was Foster who killed her. Why the hell our police couldn't prove something as open and shut as that, I don't know."

Vern shook his head. "If Foster was in love with Angela, why in hell would he kill her?"

"Lover's quarrel. Or because she wanted to break it off. One or the other, plain as the nose on your face."

"The only thing plain—" began Vern.

Betsy intervened. "All right, all right. I understand you two don't agree. But suppose it wasn't suicide, and it wasn't Foster who killed Paul, either. Do you have any idea who else might have wanted him dead?"

"Don't you say it!" Vern said suddenly to his son, who had opened his mouth.

Jory obediently didn't say it. Instead he said, faux innocently, "What were you thinking I'd say, Dad?"

"You know what I'm talking about, and I won't have it said in my presence, I don't care if you are my son." His glare intensified. "Blood's thicker than water, no matter what he's done."

"Are you talking about Alex?" she asked.

"I never said a word, and I won't," said Jory, his expression truculent. "Anyhow, it was Foster. I knew all along it was Foster."

"Please don't say things like that when I'm in the same room with you," said Vern. "One of these days you'll say that and the roof will fall in on you, an' it might take me along, too. You told me yourself right after Angela's murder that you thought Paul did it, and you even predicted Paul would either be arrested or kill hisself in the next couple days. You said it happens all the time, men killing their women, then themselves."

"I did not—"

"Dammit, yes, you did!"

"Well, all right, maybe I did, but just at first. Then we found out what really happened, only the cops couldn't prove it, and we end up living in a town where a murderer walks the streets!" Jory threw a disgusted look at his father, a half-shamed look at Betsy, and walked out.

Five

The Monday Bunch was again in session. The weather had warmed enough to rain, but gale-force winds made it rattle against the front window of Crewel World like hail. "Raincoats and umbrellas for the trick-or-treaters this year," noted Martha.

"If they go out trick-or-treating at all," said Bershada. "My grandkids haven't since they were toddlers, and then it was just going around inside the apartment building they lived in."

It was Halloween. In honor of the holiday, Betsy had made a five-gallon urn of hot spiced cider for her customers, and all five members present had a steaming cup in front of them. Despite the holiday—or perhaps because of it—every one of them was working on a Christmas project. But the talk was of Halloweens past, when children in homemade costumes went door-to-door soliciting candy. "I remember one year when my brother, who always dressed as a tramp, came home with a pillowcase nearly full of candy," said Comfort. "Mother made him take most of it to the children's hospital in St. Paul, and he

still had enough left to give himself three or four stomachaches." She was knitting a child's sweater dappled with snowmen, a gift for a great-grandchild.

"My father used to say that when he was a boy, they pulled awful pranks,
soaping windows and tipping over outhouses," said Martha, who was working
on Holiday House, a complex work in two pieces. One, lying finished on the
table, was the front of a two-story house done in Hardanger and other fancy
white-on-white stitches. The second had an elaborately-decorated Christmas
tree down low and a lit candle up high; when the first piece was laid over it,
the tree appeared in the living room window and the candle in an upstairs
bedroom. She was working on the tree, using silks, metallics, and tiny beads.
"Once, they dismantled a neighbor's Model A and reassembled it in the hayloft
of his barn."

Alice said, "My brothers never thought up anything more imaginative
than stealing the mayor's front gate."

Godwin, fashionable in a blue-and-maroon argyle sweater that set off his
golden hair beautifully, said, "I always *loved* dressing up on Halloween." He
was knitting a red-and-green scarf without looking, his fingers moving swiftly
and economically. A tiny smile formed. "*Never* as a tramp, however."

Emily, her dark eyes focused on the Cold Hands, Warm Heart sampler she
was cross-stitching, said, "Oh, I wish there were fancy dress balls nowadays,
the really elaborate kind, where people come as Harlequin and Marie Antoi-
nette and go dancing in a gigantic ballroom all lit with candles." She paused
to complete a stitch. "But I've never even heard of someone holding one, much
less been invited."

"You just don't move in the right circles, my dear," said Godwin. The
ladies laughed. Godwin loved to hint at scandalous gay parties, but they were
almost sure he'd never been to one in his life.

As on last Monday, Betsy yearned to sit down with them, but today she
was stuck at her desk designing a new seasonal display. As soon as the store
closed this evening, the cross-stitched black cats and jack-o'-lanterns would be
cleared away to make room for a framed counted cross-stitch cornucopia, and a
stand-up pillow shaped like a turkey. But there would be only a very few other
acknowledgments of Thanksgiving—not with the retailers' most important
holiday on the horizon: Christmas.

Her window and the major components of her seasonal display were due to
go up tonight. Already she was behind other retailers, whose Christmas lights
had begun to twinkle right after school started.

She glanced at the soft fabric sack under the table, three steps but many
hours away. It held her Christmas stocking and a Ziploc bag of floss. If she was
to get it to her finisher, she would have to work on it every night after the shop
closed—and starting this weekend, the shop would be open all day Saturday

and Sunday. That meant she couldn't go to Orchestra Hall Saturday night. She took a sip of hot spiced cider and sighed. She enjoyed stitching, and she enjoyed owning a needlework shop, but there never seemed to be enough time left over for anything else.

She looked down at her barely-started plan for the front window. Betsy kept a few needlepoint Christmas stockings out year-round and, of course, Marilyn Leavitt Imblum's Celtic Christmas hung with the counted cross-stitch models year-round. But there were other big, complex Christmas patterns it took cross-stitchers months to finish. They needed prodding to remind them to buy these projects in March, when everyone else was thinking about tulips and Easter bunnies. Betsy envied Cross Stitch Corner in Chicago, a shop with enough floor space to have a big, year-round Christmas display. As it was, her customers who bought the big ones now would display them next Christmas.

She studied her list of Christmas patterns in stock, her list of finished models, and her floor plan. She hadn't owned Crewel World very long, and while she was more sophisticated than when she began, she was still feeling her way into the retail stitchery business. Learning on this job was a dangerous undertaking; if it weren't for her other sources of income, Crewel World would have gone under months ago. And she knew she'd be much further along if she hadn't also encumbered herself with ownership of the building her shop was in, with its own numerous demands.

And weren't so often sidetracked by crime.

Interesting at this stage of her life—Betsy was in her middle fifties—to discover a heretofore latent talent for sleuthing. But once uncovered, it proved a powerful draw, eating up time she would otherwise have devoted to ordering stock, paying bills, record keeping, tax planning, salesmanship, and home improvement.

And designing her displays.

She looked over the assortment of patterns and models, and was satisfied with the plentitude and variety. Now, which was to go in the big front window to catch the eye of potential customers? She had already used a ruler to make a rectangle scaled to her window's dimensions, and had cut some blue scrap paper into rough shapes scaled to represent the items she thought should go in the window—too many, of course.

This scrap represented a spectacular, hand-painted needlepoint Christmas stocking, very eye-catching—but there was only the one, so if it sold at once, it would make a hole in the display. She put its paper shape aside. Maybe she should put up one of the knitted stockings instead? But which, the one knitted in bright Christmas colors? Or the one knitted in Scandinavian blue and white? Or the buff one knitted in fancy stitches, like an aran sweater? Not all three, that might make passersby think this was primarily a knitting supplies

shop, which it wasn't, and also wouldn't leave room for the beautiful and complicated Teresa Wentzler Holly and Ivy sampler Sherry had begun for Betsy's
predecessor and only finished a week ago. Betsy also had a nice collection of
counted cross-stitch stockings. Maybe her window could be all stockings, knit,
cross-stitched and needlepointed. Yes!

No. She'd already decided there must be a place for Just Nan's Liberty
Angel, the one done in red, white and blue with a star-spangled banner.

There was the large and magnificent Marbek Nativity, but that would go
in the back, on a low table against the wall, looking out through the opening
between the tall set of box shelves that divided the counted cross-stitch area
from the front of the shop. She would arrange one of the ceiling spots to shine
directly on the big, glittery figures, so customers in front would feel as if they
were looking into the Stable.

She pulled her attention from the back of the shop to the window. She'd
put some of those small, adorable, *affordable* needlepoint canvases of Santas
and rocking horses and alphabet blocks that could be finished quickly even
by beginning stitchers. And she'd better save a corner for an announcement of
January classes that needlepoint and knitting customers should sign up for.

And, of course, there were the fairy lights that would frame the window—
she sketched some loops to indicate the space they'd take.

Already the window was looking overcrowded. Hmmm, if she took out
two of the inexpensive canvases, and moved this stocking over here, and then
this counted piece could go . . .

Her sketching was interrupted by the *Bing!* of the front door. Betsy looked
up to see Mrs. Chesterfield coming in, and went at once to greet her. Mrs.
Chesterfield was a good customer, but she could not pick a skein of wool from
a basket without spilling all the contents, or pull a pattern from a rack without
tipping it over. Equally bad, she often stepped on whatever fell near her feet.

"May I help you find something, Mrs. Chesterfield?" Betsy had decided
that the next time Mrs. Chesterfield came in, she would follow her around, trying to keep her from bumping into racks and picking things up she knocked
over before they got stepped on.

"I'm looking for a sampler pattern. But I don't know who it's by."

Mrs. Chesterfield went into the back room of the shop, where the counted
cross-stitch patterns lived, and was reaching for a book on samplers when
the rack behind her tipped over. Betsy was almost sure the woman's hip had
bumped it and sent it rolling crookedly across the floor, shedding Water Colors
floss as it went.

"I'll get it, it's all right," said Betsy. "You go ahead with your selection."
She stooped to gather the beautiful pastel skeins.

Perhaps because she was concentrating on that task, she didn't see how

Mrs. Chesterfield managed to pull a book from the middle shelf and at the same time cause half of the pretty display of clear glass "ort collectors" on an upper shelf to tumble to the floor. She must have reached up to brace herself—Mrs. Chesterfield was a bit arthritic.

"Watch where you're stepping!" said Betsy more sharply than she meant to, as one of the ornaments crumbled under Mrs. Chesterfield's heel.

"Well, where did those come from?" asked Mrs. Chesterfield, looking about her as she moved away from the shelves. "Honestly, Betsy, you should be more careful how you set up your displays. Every time I come in here, something gets broken."

"I know, it's awful," said Betsy, frowning because that was true. "I'll try to do better in future," she promised. "Here, why don't you sit at this table and look at your book. I'll bring you some more so you can see which one you like best. And would you like a cup of hot cider?"

"Why, thank you, Betsy, that would be lovely. Do you still have that tea-dyed linen in thirty-six-thirty-eight count? The pattern I'm looking for is an old one. I think it has a Tree of Life on it." Women who did samplers often found that to do an exact replica of very old patterns, they needed linen woven, like the antique original, with fewer strands per inch in one direction than the other. Thank God for Norden Crafts, which not only had such linen, but could supply it in a number of colors and counts.

Betsy said, "Yes, I have that. What size piece will you need?" Betsy selected three books on samplers and brought them to Mrs. Chesterfield. "Here you are."

"I won't know until I find the pattern. I know it's in one of these books, Margaret told me about it."

Betsy didn't do samplers, so she couldn't help look. She brought a cup of cider to Mrs. Chesterfield, and on seeing she was securely seated in the chair, went back to her desk.

She had barely taken her seat when there was a soft crash from the back, its exact location hidden by one of the twin walls of box shelves that made a separate room of the back of the shop. Before Betsy could move, Godwin, winking and grinning at Betsy, was through the opening. Mrs. Chesterfield was heard to say, "How did that happen?"

And Godwin to reply, "It's just a few magazines, Mrs. Chesterfield. Nothing to worry about." His tone was very dry, pitched to reach Betsy's ears.

"I told you so," said Martha to Alice, and to Comfort, "What's she doing?"

"Told her what?" asked Betsy.

"Godwin says Mrs. Chesterfield has a poltergeist," said Comfort. "And Martha agrees with him." She was leaning back in her seat, trying to see what was going on. "Looks to me like she's sitting down."

"If Godwin is as bright as he seems, he'll make sure she stays in that chair."

Emily giggled. "Do you all really believe Mrs. Chesterfield is haunted?"

"I don't," said Alice, but quietly. Last Monday she had disagreed that Foster Johns was a murderer; she didn't like being the one who always disagreed. "No such thing," she added, and checked the count on the bright blue mitten she was knitting with an air indicating she would say no more, and continued working down the palm.

There was another crash, this one louder. Emily stood and went to the entryway between the box shelves.

"Oh, my goodness, look at that!" she said.

"What?" asked Betsy, standing and leaning forward for a look. "Oh, no, that rack of scissors!"

"I've got it, you all stay out of here," said Godwin. He could be heard adding to Mrs. Chesterfield, "Please sit down again; I'll bring you whatever you want."

Emily and Betsy went back to their respective seats, too, and Emily said in a low voice, "Did you see how Mrs. Chesterfield was nowhere near that rack?"

"She never is," said Martha, rolling her gaze around the table.

"She moved away when it fell, of course," said Alice in a barely audible voice.

"Of course she did," agreed Betsy firmly, hoping to quash the gossip, and annoyed with Godwin for spreading it.

"Well, this is interesting," said Comfort, looking around the table, her knitting forgotten. "Do you mean to tell me that some of you believe in ghosts?"

"I don't," said Alice.

"Anyway, it's not a ghost, it's a poltergeist," said young Emily. She picked up her sampler. "And whether or not anyone believes it, Mrs. Chesterfield is haunted."

"What's a poltergeist?" asked Comfort.

"It's a mischievous spirit that throws things and breaks things and moves things," explained Martha. "It tends to hang around a particular individual, usually an adolescent."

"Mrs. Chesterfield is hardly an adolescent," noted Alice.

"Only *usually* an adolescent," underlined Martha. "And usually these things happen only in their homes. But Mrs. Chesterfield's poltergeist isn't active in her home at all; instead, it follows her everywhere. It doesn't always 'act out,' but obviously today it is very active."

"Why, because it's Halloween?" asked Comfort.

"Could be," agreed Martha. "But I remember one Fourth of July when all the fireworks went off at once, scaring the men getting ready to fire them half to death, and there she was, sitting on the beach watching."

"How can you think that was her fault?" asked Alice with a snort. "My dear friend Mary Kuhfeld was in Philadelphia for the weeklong bicentennial celebration in 1976, and the night of July third all the fireworks on a pier went off at once, some coming right at the people standing on the shore. Do you think Mary is haunted by a poltergeist? Of course not. It was an accident. A worker dropped his flare, which started a fire and that's what set them all off. The same thing happened here that Fourth."

"Wouldn't surprise me to learn Mrs. Chesterfield was in Philadelphia that night, watching while her poltergeist tripped fireworks technicians," said Martha, but not seriously. The others chuckled.

Alice said, "You shouldn't say things like that. Some people will take you seriously, and they'll start thinking there's no such thing as accident or even coincidence." She raised a defiant hand and snapped her fingers. "Poltergeists—hah!"

A huge black web fell out of the ceiling, wrapping her hand, her head, her shoulders.

Bershada screamed, Emily shrieked. Struggling to get free, Alice fell backward out of her chair.

"Here, here, here!" Betsy yelled, running around the table to stoop beside Alice. "Stop pulling at it, please!"

"Get it off me!" shouted Alice.

"What, what?" called Godwin, rushing out from behind the shelves.

"It's all right, it's all right!" cried Betsy, trying to hold Alice's hands still through the webbing. "Lie still, please, Alice!"

"What *is* it?" cried Alice, trying to obey and at the same time shrink from the horrible thing.

"It's a shawl," said Betsy.

"Why, of course!" said Comfort. "It was hanging from the ceiling," she explained from her place well away from the table, holding the tiny, half-knitted sweater to her breast like a shield. She took a step forward, her expression swiftly changing from frightened to amused.

"Oh? Oh!" Alice suddenly relaxed. "That's all it is?"

"Are you hurt, Alice?" asked Martha, coming out from behind a spinner rack of knitting accessories.

"I—I don't think so. But I'm afraid I may have torn this, Betsy."

"Yes, it is torn, a little." Betsy's face was twisted with dismay. There was a substantial tear near one edge.

"Well, what was it doing up on the ceiling, anyway?" demanded Bershada, lifting her glasses and looking up.

"It's a display method, that's all," said Godwin. The other women also looked up at the several shawls hanging on the ceiling.

"Oh, why, so it is," said Bershada. "Clever."

"Not *that* clever," said Betsy sadly. Seeking more display space, she had taken to hanging some of her lighter models from slender threads attached to the soft tiles of her shop's ceiling with pins. None had ever broken loose before. On the other hand, this was the largest item she had ever attempted to suspend.

"Three Kittens uses plastic hooks that fasten to the metal strips of their acoustic ceiling," said Martha, naming a yarn shop in St. Paul.

"Where do they get them, I wonder?" said Betsy. "No, don't try to get up yet, Alice."

"Here, let me help," said Godwin, stooping across from Betsy.

"What's going on?" asked a new voice, and Mrs. Chesterfield came out from the back. "Is someone hurt?"

"No, but that beautiful Russian-lace shawl Betsy had hanging from the ceiling fell onto Alice's head," said Martha.

"Well, how on earth did that happen?" asked Mrs. Chesterfield.

"I think it was your polter—" said Godwin.

"Don't you say it!" she said, turning on him. "I won't listen to any more talk of me and a poltergeist!"

"No, of course not," said Betsy. "Goddy's just being silly. Aren't you, Godwin?"

"All right," he agreed, but with a smirk.

Mrs. Chesterfield looked at him suspiciously, but he instantly switched to his famous faux innocent look, complete with batting eyelashes and, barely mollified, she went back to the sampler books.

Godwin and Betsy continued disentangling Alice from the large black shawl, and in the silence there came a muffled choking sound. It was Emily, trying to stifle a giggle.

"Hush, Emily," said Martha. "Alice has received a terrible fright."

"Th-that's true," giggled Emily. "It scared all of us. Did you see the way we all shot out of our chairs when that shawl fell?" She giggled some more.

Bershada said with a significant smile, "That will teach Alice to say 'hah' to poltergeists."

"Come on, both of you!" said Betsy. "Didn't you ever hear of coincidence?"

Bershada said, "Coincidence? Mmmmm-hmmmm!"

Emily giggled from behind both hands held over her nose and mouth.

Godwin asked Alice, "Well, if it wasn't the you-know-what, how in the world did it manage to tear loose?" He glanced up at the ceiling, which was about nine feet high. Alice was a tall woman, but her reach wasn't *that* high.

"I didn't touch the thing!" said Alice crossly, trying to hold still as the last strands of fine black yarn were unwound from her earrings. "Ouch, please be careful! I was just sitting there when it fell on me with no warning! Now help me—Oof!" She grunted as Godwin helped her to her feet.

"Are you all right?" asked Betsy.

"I think so. But oh, all my joints are shaken loose! Thank you, Godwin."

"Is it repairable?" asked Comfort, watching Betsy look at the tear. The shawl was a fragile, very difficult pattern of knit lace, a large but gossamer article Betsy had borrowed from a customer to interest advanced knitters in a book of patterns and the expensive wool it called for.

Betsy began to fold the shawl. "I'll see if Sandy can repair it." Sandy Mattson had more than once saved important pieces with her ability to invisibly repair them. At a price, of course. Betsy sighed, and took the shawl to the desk.

Godwin winked at the table and went between the box shelves to ask Mrs. Chesterfield in a high voice, "Have you decided which book you want, Mrs. Chesterfield?"

"Goddy," warned Betsy.

"We're fine, aren't we, Mrs. Chesterfield? Of course we are. Now, how about this one?" His tone was obediently subdued, and only lightly cordial.

"Yes, I think so. Thank you, Godwin. And I want a fat quarter of the uneven weave linen. If you don't have it in tea-dyed, then unbleached."

"Yes, ma'am."

The women stitched in silence until Mrs. Chesterfield paid for her book and linen, and left.

Alice said, "I feel sorry for that poor woman."

"What's this?" said Martha. "I thought you didn't believe in poltergeists."

"I don't," she replied, lifting her strong chin in a stubborn gesture. "But her life in the last few years has become a series of sad coincidences. I wonder if she has come to believe in the poltergeist herself—and how sad for her if she has."

Six

Let's talk about something else," said Martha. "Something more cheerful."

Godwin, coming to sit down, said, "Well, it's Halloween, so let's tell ghost stories."

Comfort laughed. "Ghost stories are cheerful?"

Bershada said, "I just love ghost stories—the scarier, the better."

"Maybe we shouldn't go there," said Emily. "I think we just met a ghost.

Alice, I know I was laughing, but when that shawl fell on you, that was authentically scary."

Alice said, "Even I was foolish, panicking like that. Why, you'd think I changed my mind about poltergeists, when of course I haven't. I was just startled."

"Mmmmmmm-hmmmmh," said Bershada. "Still, something like that is enough to turn all of us into medieval peasants, hanging wolfsbane on the door and wearing garlic around our necks, scared of every bump in the night."

"It's not night," said Emily, "it's broad daylight." She looked out the window at the rain-dark street. "Well, cloudy daylight. Look, someone's coming."

The door to the shop went *Bing!* and with an effort a woman in a wheelchair pushed herself over the threshold. She was an attractive woman of about thirty with short blond hair—currently plastered against one side of her face by rain—and brown eyes. She wore a red sweater and blue jeans under a yellow rain cape, which she pulled off and dropped on the floor near the door.

"Hi, Carol," said Betsy, coming to close the door for her. "Glad you could brave such terrible weather."

"Oh, wheeling around in the wind blows the cobwebs out of my head. I miss going to an office where there are live human beings and coffee breaks and football pools. Of course, one pleasure of working at home is that weekends become moveable feasts. I worked yesterday so I've declared today a Sunday." She stopped at the other end of the library table. "What are we talking about?"

"Ghost stories," said Alice, disapproval in her deep voice.

"Of course, what else on Halloween? Have I missed any juicy ones?"

"Not yet," said Bershada. "But we did have a little scare a few minutes ago." She explained about the shawl's fall onto Alice's head.

"Have mercy!" exclaimed Carol. "That must have scared you out of ten years' growth, Alice."

"Not to mention the rest of us," said Godwin, "But Mrs. Chesterfield is gone, taking her poltergeist with her."

"Do you believe in poltergeists, Godwin?" asked Carol.

"No, of course not," he said, pretending to spit lightly to the left and right and making fake cabalistic signs with his right hand. "Do you?"

"No," she said, laughing, "but I have to believe in ghosts, since we have one living with us."

"Does he follow you around like Mrs. Chesterfield's poltergeist?" asked Bershada, looking past Carol for traces of ectoplasm.

"No, he stays at home." Carol made a little ceremony of getting out her project, a half-completed cross-stitch pattern of Santa standing sideways in a froth of fur and beard: Marilyn Leavitt-Imblum's Spirit of Christmas. These were all delaying tactics that allowed the tension to grow.

"Oh, all right, I'll break down and beg: Please, tell us all about it," said Godwin.

"She doesn't have to if she doesn't want to," objected Alice, still shaken from the episode of the shawl.

Emily seconded her. "Anyway, how can we be interested in ghost stories when we're all working on Christmas projects?"

Carol said, "Christmas is a very traditional time for ghost stories. Dickens's *A Christmas Carol* is a ghost story."

"Why, so it is," said Martha. "I never thought of that. So tell us about your ghost, Carol. "What does it do? Go bump in the night?"

"Once in a while, though it's more usually a sound like a marble rolling across the floor. But he's mostly a friendly ghost, except to carpenters and plumbers and electricians."

Betsy chuckled and asked from across the room, "What has he got against them? Their prices?"

"No, he doesn't want any changes made to the house. He's the original owner, my housemate's grandfather. His name is Cecil, he was a dentist. He and his wife bought the house back in the early 1920s as a summer vacation home—their other house was in Minneapolis."

Godwin jested, "How do you know that's who it is? Does he come into your bedroom and try to pull your teeth?"

Carol laughed back, but persisted, "I'm serious. Let me tell you the story. Cecil, his wife, and their four daughters all moved out to that house every summer to get away from the heat of the city."

Emily nodded. "My great-grandparents did the same thing, moved out here in the summer. Great-grandpop commuted every day on the streetcar steamboats."

Carol said, "This was a bit later, Cecil drove a car into town. But in the summer of 1935, when he was only forty-seven, Cecil had a heart attack. He survived it, but he became very worried about leaving his family without a man to take care of them. He tried to get well, but two years later he had another heart attack and died. The next summer, his widow and her daughters moved out of the city as usual, but started experiencing strange noises in the house. At first they didn't know what it was, but then they started getting an occasional whiff of pipe smoke. Cecil had loved his pipe."

"Ooooooooh," said Bershada, smiling.

"Go on, go on," urged Comfort.

Carol smiled. "Well, one by one the daughters married and moved away. The youngest daughter inherited the house when their mother died; and she and her husband decided to live there year round. She was Susan's mother. All this time, there were still these noises and sometimes the smell of pipe smoke.

Nothing was ever broken, but she did notice the noises were worse when they'd do spring-cleaning, especially if they hung new drapes or painted. Like I said, he didn't like changes. Cecil would slam doors and stomp around upstairs until they were finished.

"Susan says she was aware of a presence in the house from her early childhood, and just accepted it as part of what it was like to live there. A few years ago her mother needed money, so Susan bought the house from her, but her mother still lives with us. She's an invalid now, the last of the four sisters. Susan says Grandfather Cecil is still watching over his last daughter, and will likely go when she dies."

"So this ghost story is only hearsay," said Alice. "You've never seen or heard anything."

"Oh, no, I've experienced him, too, door closings, footsteps, marble rollings, pipe tobacco, and all. In fact, I am the cause of a really serious outbreak. You see, when Susan invited me to move in with her and her mother, they had to make some changes, real changes, building ramps and widening doorways and installing an elevator to the second floor. When things got under way, Cecil really went to work. Doors wouldn't stay closed—or open, footsteps went up and down the stairs all day long, and marbles rolled all night. Then the carpenter began complaining he'd misplaced a hammer or screwdriver, and the electrician couldn't keep track of his wires and switches. This was something new and we just thought they were careless. But then Cecil started to sabotage their cars. The carpenter knocked off work one day, and his car wouldn't start. He checked under the hood and fooled around with it, and finally he called a tow truck. And once the car arrived at the garage, it worked just fine. The first time this happened, we were thinking he ought to get a tune-up, but after it happened a few times, we knew: It was Cecil. We discussed it and finally agreed to tell the workmen what it was. The way they stared at us, I thought we'd have to find a new construction firm. I've never seen five pairs of eyes that big."

"Did they quit?"

"Oddly enough, no. They kind of dared each other, and it turned into one of those macho games. But it worked, they stuck with it, and finally got it done. I think they were even more relieved than we were by the time they finished up."

Bershada said, "Funny he doesn't aim any of that stuff at you. I mean, doesn't Cecil realize you were the reason for all those big changes to 'his' house?"

"Well, I *am* grateful he didn't think I was an intruder and try to run me off," said Carol. "I wonder if perhaps he understands there's a bond between Susan and me. For example, just the other night we were finishing supper and I heard music coming from upstairs. 'What's that?' I asked, 'Do you hear that music?' Susan's mother got the funniest look on her face, and Susan went up to see what it was. It was a big old music box, the kind that plays when you open the lid. She brought it down to show us." Carol moved her hands to describe a box about fourteen by eight inches. "No one had touched it in years, but she walked into the kitchen with it still playing. You know the song, 'Two Sleepy People'?"

"*Sleepless in Seattle!*" exclaimed Emily. "That was one of the old songs from that movie."

"Yes, and that's what was playing on the music box. Susan's mother said Cecil loved that song and bought the music box as a present for his wife."

"Awwwww," said Emily. "That's kind of nice."

Martha agreed, "For a ghost story, it wasn't very scary."

"It scared the carpenters and the plumber. But I'm glad Cecil's only concern is that his remaining daughter is all right. He loved Susan's mother the best of his girls, and he's still concerned about her."

There was a little silence, then Comfort said, "I saw a ghost once."

"Tell us about it!" said Bershada.

"Well, remember when Paul and Angela Schmitt were murdered?"

"Oh, not that again!" said Martha. "We talked that to death last week, remember?"

"Did you?" said Carol. "I'm sorry I missed it. I would have told you how Angela and my sister Gretchen were best friends in high school."

"Did you know Angela?" asked Betsy alertly.

"Not really. But the day she was killed, Gretchen came over and cried for hours in our mother's kitchen. She was sure Paul had done it; that is, until he was shot two nights later."

Comfort said, "It was Paul's ghost I saw, and on the night he was shot."

"Really!?" exclaimed Carol. "What was he doing? Did he know you? Did he tell you who murdered him?"

"No, it wasn't like that, not as if he came especially to speak to me. You see, I was walking up Water Street from the Minnehaha ticket office—I volunteer there four days a week when the boat is running," she explained. "Anyway, it was near the end of the season and I'd stayed late to do some bookkeeping and restock the racks of sweatshirts, so it was after dark. The weather was pretty much like it is right now, wind and all, and there wasn't another soul on the street. I stopped in front of the bookstore to turn my umbrella right side out, and noticed they had replaced the broken front window. I stood there a minute because my eye was caught by the display of Jim Ogland's *Postcard History of Lake Minnetonka*. That book has such a nice cover. And then I saw someone in the store. A man."

"Was he all bloody and awful?" asked Bershada hopefully.

"No. Or at least it was so dark, I couldn't see much detail. The wind died down suddenly and my umbrella came to its senses, and then I saw someone move. At first I just thought someone was in the store, an employee. But then I realized there was only that dim light burning at the back, the one they turn on as they leave for the night, so then I wondered if I was seeing a burglary in progress."

"That would have been enough for me," declared Emily. "There are lots of things just as scary as ghosts, and burglars are one of them."

"You're right, and I should have run away, but I was so surprised, I just stood there, gaping. Suddenly, the man stooped down, and I thought he'd seen me, but then he straightened up again. I couldn't imagine what he was doing. It was dark in the store, and I wasn't even sure I was seeing someone. He was over beside the checkout counter, near the wall and halfway behind that rack where they keep the finger puppets, or used to. He moved, kind of glided, away from there and went behind that couch they have for browsers. He was standing sideways, and I could see his silhouette against the light, and suddenly I recognized Paul Schmitt. He was standing still, head down, like he was praying, or waiting for something. Then he turned away—and all of a sudden he was gone, like he melted into the shelves. I couldn't think what he was doing in there. I had been thinking, it's a burglar, I should go call the police, but I couldn't get my feet to move. Now I recognized Paul Schmitt, that nice man from church, not some unknown burglar. Then I thought about Angela, and I was embarrassed, like you get when you see someone doing something and he thinks no one is looking. I wondered if he wasn't paying a private visit to the scene of his wife's death.

"That made me feel embarrassed to stand there staring, so I got my feet back under control and walked away."

"You should have called the police," said Alice.

"And told them what? Any story I tried to tell them would sound ridiculous. I went on to the Lucky Wok and had some of their moo shi pork for dinner and then walked home."

"Weren't you scared to go home?" asked Godwin. "I mean, you live alone and all."

"No, not at all, because I didn't know it was a ghost I'd seen. I was tired and went to bed before the news, so it wasn't till the next morning I heard that he'd been found murdered in his house. And when I thought about it, it seemed to me that I saw him in the store right about the time that someone shot him."

"Ooooooooh," breathed Bershada, and they all looked thrilled down to their toes—except Alice, but she didn't say anything.

Emily said, "I suppose he went there to gather up his wife's spirit and take her with him to the afterlife."

"Well, I don't recall hearing any reports that Angela's ghost was seen in the bookstore," said Comfort. "Do you?"

"Well . . . no," said Emily. "But that doesn't mean she wasn't there. Maybe she knew he was going to follow her into the spirit world and kind of hung around waiting for him."

"If I were Angela's ghost, I certainly wouldn't hang around hoping the ghost of my husband, who I doubt was going to heaven, would come and take me with him," declared Alice.

"Why wouldn't he go to heaven?" asked Godwin.

"Anyway, she certainly did," declared Martha. "She was such a sweet and good woman. Maybe he hoped she would put in a good word for him."

"That doesn't explain why she waited for him," said Bershada. "How did she know he was coming so soon?"

"We don't know everything about the afterlife," said Emily. "Maybe she did know."

That brought a little pause while they reflected on the mysteries of love and the afterlife.

"He did love her very much," said Godwin softly.

"I don't think he did," said Alice. "I think it was more like an obsession."

"I'd like someone to be obsessed with me," said Bershada. "Someone whose every thought is about my happiness."

"No, you don't," said Alice firmly. "It's not about your happiness, and it isn't nearly as pleasant as true love. And when someone dies, my understanding is that such things as human relationships are abandoned."

"Oh, I don't believe that!" said Godwin. "Surely true love would last through eternity! There are all kinds of stories about a ghost coming to the bedside of a husband or wife."

"Yes, Alice, how can you doubt such serious things as love and ghosts and the afterlife?" said Bershada.

"I'm not doubting the afterlife, which I believe in most firmly," said Alice. "But ghosts are stuff and nonsense."

"But all those stories!" reiterated Godwin. "There are fictional ghost stories, I know that, but there are true ghost stories, too. And Comfort is only telling you what she actually saw!"

"I think that when it's late at night and you're tired or hungry and already nervous because you're out in a thunderstorm, or you are all alone in an old house and perhaps have been reading spooky stories, naturally you may conclude an unusual noise, or a dance of headlights on the ceiling, or even your own reflection is a ghost."

Martha said, "You're right, of course, Alice. But how to explain what happened to me back when I was about eleven or twelve? It was the dead of winter and the middle of the night. My father used to turn the furnace down at night to save fuel, so it was very cold in the house. I had a thick quilt on the bed and was sound in a cozy sleep—until something bumped into the bed and woke me up. I thought it was the cat jumping up, and I waited for him to come up to the pillow purring like he usually did." She smiled. "There's nothing quite as friendly as a cat with cold feet. But it wasn't the cat, or at least he didn't come up to ask to be let under the covers. Then I heard a voice say, plain as day, 'Her eyes are open.' It was pitch dark in that room, there's no way anyone could have seen whether my eyes were open or closed."

"Cool!" said Carol. "Then what happened?"

"Nothing, I burrowed under the covers and didn't come up till morning."

There was a reflective pause. "It was probably your mother," said Alice, "checking to see if you were all right in the cold."

"No. It was a woman's voice, but definitely not my mother's. Anyway, like I said, no one could have seen if my eyes were open or not."

"Were they?" asked Emily.

"Of course, I told you, I woke up when something bumped my bed."

"Who do you think it was?" asked Carol.

"I have no idea. And I never heard them again."

"'Them'?" said Betsy. "How do you know there was more than one?"

"Well, she wasn't talking *to* me, she was talking *about* me. So that meant at least one other . . . person was present."

"Oooooooooh," said Bershada, moving her shoulders to dislodge a delicious shiver.

Godwin said maliciously, "How do you explain that, Alice?"

Alice shrugged. "A dream, obviously."

"It wasn't a dream," said Martha. "I was wide awake, I'd been wakened by the bump. But there also weren't any weird lights or footsteps or a chill breeze, or any of the usual stuff of ghost stories. And it wasn't my father, either," she said with a little sniff, forestalling Godwin's next sly suggestion.

So instead Godwin said, "How about you, Bershada? Do you have a ghost story?"

"Well, actually, I do. Only mine's different from Martha's, I didn't know it was a ghost. I thought it was an usher."

"At a *wedding*?" said Martha, scandalized.

"No, no," said Bershada, laughing. "At the Guthrie!"

"Oh, *him*!" said Godwin. "You saw Richard Miller!"

"Yes, that's the name. Have you seen him, too?"

"No, but I've heard about him. When did you see him?"

"Oh, this was years ago. My husband's parents took Mac and me to see *Amadeus*, and this usher kept walking up and down the aisle, blocking our view. The ushers are supposed to go out to the lobby during a performance, so it was annoying. He didn't seem to be looking for someone in particular, like you'd expect if it was an emergency or something. And he didn't seem interested in the play, either. He was just kind of observing the audience. I could see he was young, maybe only in his late teens, and he had a big mole on one cheek, very noticeable. I knew he was an usher because he had the sports coat they wear, with the insignia on the pocket?" She made a gesture over her left breast. "So during the intermission we complained to one of the other ushers, and he laughed and said we'd seen Richard Miller, who was an usher back in the sixties who committed suicide."

"How did this usher kill himself?" asked Betsy. "Hang himself from a balcony rail?"

"*Betsy*!" said Emily.

"He didn't kill himself in the theater at all," said Godwin. "He did it in the Sears parking lot on Lake Street."

"That old place?" said Bershada. She explained to Betsy, "It's closed now, has been for a long, long time, but the building is still there, and the parking lot. It's a big building, very nice-looking in that art-deco way. They keep talking about doing something with it, but haven't so far. Anyway, you'd think he'd haunt that building."

"Maybe he does," said Martha. "Only there's nobody around to see him."

"Or he haunts the parking lot," said Comfort. "I can just hear the warnings: 'Don't park in row three, slot nineteen, or you'll come back to find a see-through stranger in your backseat.'"

Emily giggled uncomfortably, but Alice cleared her throat in a disparaging way.

Godwin said, "Instead, for some reason, he came back to the Guthrie and he gets in the way of customers." He frowned and said, "Maybe that's what Paul Schmitt was doing, not haunting the house he died in, but a place where something sad happened."

"Or a place where he did something wicked," said Carol.

"What do you mean?" asked Martha.

"Well, suppose he found out about Angela and Foster and murdered Angela. True love can turn to hate in a wink of an eye, you know. I remember wondering right after Angela was murdered if maybe Paul hadn't done it."

Godwin objected, "Well, if that's a cause for haunting, you'd think Paul would haunt Foster Johns's office. After all, Foster murdered Paul."

Alice said, "Nobody knows that for sure. Everyone's been saying how nice Paul was. Well, suppose he wasn't nice, despite his smiles. Suppose someone were to get serious about looking into his and Angela's deaths." She raised an eyebrow at Betsy. "I think it's possible there might be other suspects."

"You shouldn't speak ill of the dead," said Bershada with a frown.

"You shouldn't make saints of people who don't deserve it!" said Alice. "If Martha is right and Paul was a jealous man, and it is not at all uncommon for that emotion to accompany obsession—or 'true love,' as you will have it—then he would have been upset about any man who talked with his wife. So you can imagine how painful it was for him to think of her in that bookstore, where men came in every day. I think he was a brother to those dreadful Taliban people who made their women cover themselves with—what was it called? That sack thing. He would have loved it if America adopted Taliban customs for women, and made Angela wear that sack thing and never go anywhere without him along."

Emily said, "I'd like to see them try to put the women of America into burkas!"

Martha snickered. "And how could they get American men back to the twelfth century? Make them all ride donkeys to work?"

The mental picture of a big herd of donkeys laden with men in business suits trekking down 35W and 394 into Minneapolis, talking on their cell phones and batting their unfortunate mounts on the rumps with their brief-cases, caused everyone to stop and smile for a few moments.

Then Godwin said, "I've never seen a ghost, but my grandmother heard one. She was baking Thanksgiving pies one morning when she heard, plain as day, her sister Frankie saying, 'Milly, call an ambulance! I fell and broke my ankle! Help, Milly!' What was weird is that Great-aunt Frances was in Columbus, Ohio, at the time, and Grandmama lived in St. Paul. Grandmama was so sure she'd heard her sister asking for help that she called the police in Columbus and insisted they go to Frankie's house. Sure enough, she'd fallen on a patch of ice in the backyard and would have laid there until her husband came home from work, and as it wasn't even noon yet, likely he'd have found her frozen to death."

Martha said, "That's not a ghost story. Your great-aunt wasn't dead."

"Well, okay, I guess it isn't. But it's a paranormal story." He looked at Alice. "Explain that, if you can."

Alice obediently tried. "I suppose she was thinking about her sister and imagined she heard her voice. Or perhaps . . . perhaps Frankie prayed very hard for rescue and a miracle happened. God allowed her cry for help to reach Milly's ears."

"He works in mysterious ways," agreed Bershada. "Or perhaps Godwin had just made that up, another way to pick on Alice. Shame on you, Goddy!"

"This *is* a true story," said Godwin, hurt. "It was written up in the *Columbus Dispatch*. You *have* to believe it, Bershada, I believed *you* about Richard Miller. I've been there *lots* of times, and I know *all about* him, but I've never *seen* him.

Now they're tearing down the old theater, I probably never will. Unless—do you think he'll go haunt the new building?"

Bershada said, "Can they do that sort of thing?"

Carol said, "There is supposed to be a family in the United States who are direct descendants of a duke, and they had a family ghost from the twelfth century follow them over here. One of those kind that when she appears, there's a death in the family."

Emily said, "I know a story like that."

"What, about someone who saw Richard Miller's ghost and died?" asked Godwin.

"No, mine is about the Wendigo."

Everyone at the table smiled but Betsy. "What's the Wendigo?" she asked.

"He's a really old spirit, the Indians told the white settlers about him," said Godwin.

"Oh, no, it isn't a spirit," said Carol, surprised at him. "The Wendigo is a big, hairy creature, sort of like Bigfoot, who finds Indians alone in the forest and eats them."

"Ish!" said Bershada.

Godwin said, *"Eats them? Like a cannibal? I didn't know that."*

Betsy said, "It's not cannibalism to eat something other than your own kind."

"Anyway," said Emily, to regather their attention. "The Wendigo is like nine or ten feet tall, and covered with gray fur. And it has a bright light shining in its forehead. Early settlers saw it, and pretty soon they realized there was a death in the family of whoever saw it, that's why what Carol said about the duke's ghost reminded me. It's still around, people still see the Wendigo, only now mostly just up north. And when they do, someone dies."

Godwin said, *"That's your scary story?"*

Emily said, "No, that's just the explaining part. My great-grandmother saw it. She and her second husband were up on the Iron Range, on the road between Eveleth and Virginia—he was a surveyor, and she was his assistant— and she told my mother, who told me, that they were walking back from a job. It was getting dark, and there were trees along one side of the road, and she saw this light-colored thing back in there, and first she thought it was the trunk of a birch growing alone among the pines, and then that it was a light-colored bear standing on its hind legs. Only it was too tall to be a bear. It turned toward them, and she saw it had a light shining out of its forehead, and she knew what it was. She screamed 'Wendigo!' and they both ran all the way back into Eveleth. Almost two miles it was, and they never stopped once. And Ralph—that was her second husband—he died two days later of a heart attack."

"And we mustn't think that perhaps running scared in near-darkness for two miles might have been the cause of that," said Alice very dryly.

"Did her husband know about the legend of the Wendigo, that it means a death?" asked Betsy.

"Oh, yes, they both did, and they wondered who it was going to be. Great-grandmother called all her children the next day to see if they were all right, and they were, so she was starting to think it was a mistake when Ralph collapsed at the supper table and died. Great-grandmother had thought it might be she herself who was doomed, but it never occurred to her it would be her husband, because he was five years younger than her, and he didn't have any medical problems."

Betsy asked, "Do all of you believe in the Wendigo?"

"I don't, of course," said Alice.

Godwin said, "I understand you don't have to believe in the Wendigo for him to appear to you." There was a blank silence, then everyone laughed, even Alice.

Seven

When Betsy climbed the stairs to her apartment that night, she was exhausted. Sophie, anxious and whining, trotted ahead and led the way into the kitchen. Betsy opened the cabinet under the sink and gave her cat the little scoop of Iams Less Active that was dinner. It was not possible the vastly overweight animal was hungry—Sophie snacked all day long: potato chips, fragments of cookies and the occasional mayonnaise-soaked corner of lettuce, all cadged from customers down in the shop.

Betsy had tried to institute a policy of no food or drink in the shop, and failing that, of not feeding samples of it to the cat. When that also failed, she pretended it wasn't happening. Sophie held up her end by pretending to be famished in the evenings. So not just in the morning but also in the evening the cat was served a small low-calorie, high-protein meal that at least filled in the vitamin gaps her otherwise poor diet offered.

Betsy was too tired to even think of cooking for herself. She was searching her larder for a can of tuna when the phone rang. She thought about letting her machine catch it, but the receiver was in easy reach, so she picked it up.

"Hello," she said.

"Oh, my dear, are you as tired as you sound?" drawled a friendly voice.

"Gosh, yes, totally bushed. Hi, Morrie, I'm glad to hear your voice, but I hope you aren't thinking to take me somewhere tonight."

"When you check your machine, you'll find I've been calling you all evening. But it's too late now to go trick-or-treating, we've missed the start of the special showing of *Abbott and Costello Meet the Wolfman,* and the costume party has reached the stage where only people with at least three drinks under their belts are having any fun. Where have you been?"

"Down in the shop. We did our Christmas window tonight."

"Ah, you're one of those merchants who starts in right after Halloween."

"That's right, I'm very conservative, unlike those who begin in September. Still, by the time Christmas Eve rolls around, I'm going to be totally sick of Christmas patterns, Christmas wrap, yarn in Christmas colors, and angels with wings done in Wisper and gold metallic. But by gum, the shop is going to be in the black."

Morrie laughed. He had a good laugh, frequently used, and she could picture him, head thrown back and mouth wide open. He was a tall, thin man in his early sixties, with not quite enough silver hair, a lantern jaw, and ears that stuck out. But he had the kindest eyes and sweetest demeanor Betsy had encountered in a long, long while. He was wonderful to have around, because with quiet ardor he had taken charge of making her life enjoyable. "Have you had supper yet?" he asked.

"I was about to open a can of tuna. I can make it into a salad if you want a share."

"Put that can opener away right now. I'll be there in half an hour with—what shall I bring, a pizza?"

"Bless you. Thanks."

Ninety minutes later, over the last slices of now cold pizza, they were talking about—what else?—ghost stories.

"Do you believe in ghosts?" he asked.

"Well, I saw a ghost once, so I guess I have to."

He was amused. "Where did you see a ghost?"

"In that most traditional of places: a cemetery. I was standing in one of those little country ones, the kind a family would put up for itself back in the pioneer days. I was reading epitaphs—don't you just love old epitaphs?"

" 'A coffin, sheet, and grave's my earthly store; 'tis all I want, and kings can have no more,' " he recited in an oratorical voice.

"Oh, that's a nice one! Did you read that on a tombstone?"

"No, in a book I got as a Christmas present a long time ago. It's called *Over Their Dead Bodies,* which has to be one of the cleverest titles ever dreamed up. But you were in this cemetery at midnight and a ghost swirled up out of a grave and said to you . . ." he prompted.

"No, it wasn't anything like that. I was in this little cemetery, but it was a sunny afternoon, and my sister Margot said, 'Hey, look at this one!' and I turned to look, and as my eyes went past the woodlot that was the border of the cemetery, suddenly it wasn't a woodlot, but an open field of grass and a woman in a long white dress was standing there with a child in a shorter white dress and one or the other of them had a parasol. I was just so surprised, I looked again and it was the woodlot again."

"Can it be a ghost if it's a whole landscape?" Morrie asked.

"I don't know. I only know what I saw, for just an instant."

"What were they doing, the woman and child? Did they see you?"

"No, they were looking down at something in the grass. It wasn't scary or anything, it was just a glimpse of a long-ago time, that piece of ground reciting a lesson it had learned. Or that's my theory, anyhow."

"Are you sure you didn't imagine it?"

"Yes, because I was about twelve and if I ever thought of the parade of fashion, which I didn't very much, I would have assumed that somehow we jumped from huge skirts, like during the Civil War, to the flapper's fringed little dress, like during the Roaring Twenties. But this woman was wearing something long and soft with no hoops. Her dress was like gauze, several layers of gauze. I found out later that material is called 'lawn.' She had a ruffle somewhere on the bodice, I think. And not leg-o'-mutton sleeves, but long ones."

"What was her hairstyle?"

"I don't remember. She was holding the child's hand. They were happy, I think."

She took a sip of wine, and let it rest on her tongue a moment before swallowing it. Morrie's taste in adult beverages was much like hers, not highly sophisticated—the bottle had a picture of a toad in a vest on it—but well beyond soda-sweet stuff.

"Do you know what the temperature was in Fort Myers today?" he asked.

"No, what?"

"Seventy-eight. You'll love it down there. How much vacation do you get every year?"

"None. I'm the owner, I don't get a vacation."

"Nonsense. You have to take at least a week off in, say, February or March."

Morrie was being forced to retire—well, not entirely forced, he knew it was coming and in fact was ready for it. He had bought a house in a Fort Myers gated community five years ago, furnished it, spent two weeks there every winter and rented it out the rest of the year. He was planning to move down there permanently when he retired early next year.

Then he'd met Betsy. It was during a course of a homicide investigation—

where else?—and there had been an immediate attraction. He'd found her clever and lucky, and she thought him charming and intelligent. But while in a few months he was ready to commit to a relationship, she was unwilling to relocate to Florida.

He thought she was crazy to want to stay in the frigid north; she thought he was crazy to abandon a lifetime's worth of friends. Neither was seeing anyone else, but he couldn't persuade her to sell the shop and she couldn't persuade him to stay in Minnesota.

"Why do you think I should take a vacation in March?" she asked now.

"Because by then you'll be really sick of winter—and I'll really be missing you." He lifted her pepperoni-scented fingers and kissed them.

Betsy came down to the shop a little heavy-eyed the next morning. She had let Morrie stay a little later than she should have, and her only satisfaction was that he had to be at work by nine, while her shop didn't open until ten. She went down around quarter to, Sophie happily trundling ahead of her.

In the shop, Betsy looked around with satisfaction. There was a little artificial Christmas tree on the checkout desk, waiting for customers to decorate it with stitched ornaments. Her own ornament, a white cat with a wreath around its neck, stitched on maroon Aida cloth from a Bucilla kit, already hung on a branch. The tree would be given to someone in town who otherwise wouldn't have one. Betsy's sister, who had founded Crewel World, had begun the custom, and Betsy was pleased to keep it up.

The Marbek Nativity glowed under the track light, and on the wall behind it were three counted cross stitch stockings, Marilyn Leavitt-Imblum's Angel of the Morning, Dennis P. Lewan's scene of snow-covered Victorian houses at sunset, a Christmas sampler from Homespun Elegance, and a cross-stitch pattern of Santa aloft in his sleigh with an American flag flying off the back of it.

For the less sentimental, there was an amusing model of Linda Connors's black cat destroying a Christmas tree.

For the curmudgeons, there was Santa sitting on a chimney, pants down, a satisfied scowl on his face, and under it the legend, "For Those Who Have Been *Really* Naughty . . ."

But Betsy was most concerned about the front window. She went out to take a look at it in the daylight. Last night she had thrown out her plan for a Christmas theme, having been overcome by a wonderful, exciting *Idea*. But what if the Idea had been a bad one? After all, she'd been tired. Or if it had been a good one, perhaps she'd done it too fast, and now, in the chill light of morning it looked slipshod. She hadn't sat down and drawn up a plan, after all. She and Godwin, laughing with excitement, had just pulled patterns and models and stuck them up quickly, like children drawing on a wall. (How great it was to have an employee like Godwin!) But what if the window was just a muddle?

She stood a moment, eyes closed, outdoors in front of the window. Then opened them.

It wasn't awful, or slipshod. It was good. The theme was the onset of winter, which every culture that ever lived in four seasons has marked. The layout was terrific—not too cluttered, not too regimented. The eye moved naturally from place to place.

There was a knit stocking with its pattern of Christmas tree lights, and Just Nan's Liberty Angel, and the needlepoint rocking horse, but there was also a canvas that, when finished and cut out, could be sewn up into a set of Hanukkah dreidels. And there was a Wiccan pattern of Bertcha, goddess of the winter solstice. There was the Kwanzaa kinora with its black, red, and green candles, stitched in silks. There was a canvas of Arabic calligraphy, to be covered with gold and silver stitches, a verse from the Koran admonishing the believer to study nature in order to understand the mind of God. There was an American Indian in a blanket huddled close to an evening fire, the Hunger Moon glowing in the background to illuminate subtle patterns of wildlife among the naked trees all around him. There was even a deep blue cloth covered with elaborate patterns of silver snowflakes, for the atheists.

Betsy had these models on her walls, the patterns in stock, but it hadn't occurred to her to pull them together in a single display, until last night. She looked long at it, deeply satisfied. She had left two not obvious blank spaces in case customers came in with suggestions for other winter celebrations— and the name of a pattern she could order. There were growing populations of Hmong and Somali in the cities. Betsy wanted them to know they were welcome, too. Excelsior itself was mostly white Christian, but her shop drew customers from all over the area.

The sky was clear this morning, but the thermometer had fallen into the teens overnight. Any more precipitation between now and April would be snow. Betsy suddenly realized she was cold, and came back into her shop shivering and chaffing her arms. She went on through the back to start the coffee perking and the electric teakettle heating. She'd had a cup of strong English tea with her breakfast bagel, but she'd need at least another to get her brain fired up.

She went behind the desk to put the start-up money in the cash register, check order slips and billing statements (the price of fuel oil was up again; thank God the new roof was deeply insulated). There was a note to remind her to phone Jimmy Jones, the man she'd hired last winter to plow the parking lot in back, to make sure he was on again for this winter; and another to say her accountant would be in on Friday to balance her books.

The door made its annoying *Bing!* (another note: replace that ugly noise!), and in came a tall woman in her late fifties, her full face marked with an emphatic pug nose: She had a lot of makeup on for this early in the morning. Betsy frowned—she was sure she didn't recognize her, but the woman looked familiar. Her brown hair was done in complicated curls and her gray winter coat had a beautiful silver fox collar. The woman glanced at Betsy, hesitated, then took a breath and approached the desk as if afraid she'd be sent away. Betsy hastily turned the frown into a smile of welcome.

"Good morning, may I help you find something?"

"I hope so," said the woman in a low, husky voice. "I'm thinking of taking up needlework. I did factory work all my life, and it ruined my hands." She held them out, and they were indeed work-thickened, though clean, and the nails carefully polished. "I'm retired now, and hoping to regain some fine motor skills by taking up a hobby. I first thought about music, but I was told I have no talent, so my brother recommended your shop."

"Oh!" said Betsy, recognition setting in. "You must be Mr. DeRosa's sister! You look a lot like him."

"Yes, everyone says that. We're twins, in fact. I'm Doris Valentine. Mick has said some nice things about you."

"Well, that was kind of him." Michael DeRosa lived alone in the smallest apartment upstairs and kept very much to himself. Betsy couldn't imagine what nice things he might have said about her; she couldn't have said anything at all about him, except that he always paid his rent on time. When the couple who rented the other apartment waylaid Betsy in the upstairs hall to complain about the smell of tar last month, he had stood shyly in his doorway, and only nodded in agreement when she looked at him.

"How long are you going to be visiting?" asked Betsy.

"Oh, just this week. But I've moved into the area, and will stop by often, I hope. Mick is my only surviving relative, and I want to spend as much time as I can with him." She looked around the shop and asked timidly, "Where do you suggest I start?"

"Have you ever done embroidery or knitting?"

"No, I'm afraid not. I can turn up a hem and sew buttons on, but that's all. My mother knitted, but she never taught me how. Not that I was very interested—I liked outdoor activities, horseback riding and softball."

Still ashamed of her frown, Betsy reached out with, "Me, too. In fact, I used to ride all the time. I keep making plans to take it up again, but never find the time."

"Did you ever try jumping?"

"Not in competition; to do that, you need a good horse, and we couldn't afford one. You?"

"I won a blue ribbon at our state fair the year I turned fifteen. But we had to sell the horse when Daddy lost his job, so that was the end of that."

"Too bad. Well, let me show you some of the things involved in stitchery. We also offer classes, if you don't live too far away to come in once a week."

"You know, I think I could manage that, if it turns out I have an aptitude for this stuff."

Betsy recommended Stoney Creek's wonderful and extremely basic *The ABC's of Cross-Stitch*, which Doris took, along with a book of simple patterns for beginners, a skein each of Anchor 403, 46, 305, and 266—black, red, yellow, and green—a roll of fourteen-count Vinyl-Weave, and an inexpensive pair of scissors. Betsy threw in a needle and a needle threader, told her about the Monday Bunch, and gave her a schedule of classes.

"Now, I tell you what," said Betsy. "Why don't you sit down in back for a while and try out some things from the book? Just shout if you get stuck, and I'll be glad to show you how to go on."

"Why . . . thank you," said Doris, a little overwhelmed at all this kindness. Betsy wondered where she'd gone to be told she had no musical talent. Funny how some shop owners seemed determined to put themselves out of business. Which of course just left more for those willing to go a little distance.

Betsy showed her how to use the needle threader, and then the door went *Bing!* and she went out to see who it was.

Godwin was taking off his gorgeous Versace leather trench coat to reveal a silk shirt in a heavenly shade of lilac under a purple vest. He said, "That window looks good, boss lady."

"Thanks for not complaining when I had my flash of inspiration and made you tear down the original."

"Aw, shucks, ma'am," he began in a teasing voice, then saw there was someone in back.

"Who's that?"

"Doris Valentine, my tenant Mr. DeRosa's twin sister. She's visiting for a week, and decided to try her hand at counted cross-stitch. Very much a beginner."

Godwin went back to introduce himself and soon had her trying out French knots and the satin stitch. When she'd finally had enough, she thanked them both profusely and departed, all smiles.

Godwin, amused by something, said, "Kind of fun to watch someone take those first steps down the road."

"Do you remember your first steps?"

"Depends on which road you mean." He waggled his eyebrows, grinned, and sashayed away.

"Give me strength," Betsy sighed and went to brew another cup of black tea. When she'd finished it, she called Alice Skoglund. "Would you care to have lunch with me?" she asked. "I want to talk with you,"

"All right. Where? The Waterfront Café?"

"No, too many eavesdroppers. How about the sandwich shop right next door to me? He's featuring a tomato-basil soup that's very good."

"All right. Twelve-thirty okay? I'll meet you there."

Eight

❖

There were two other shops in Betsy's building, a used-book store called Isbn's on her right and Sol's Delicatessen (though the owner's name was Jack Knutson) on her left. Betsy went into the deli. It looked as if it were original to the building and never redecorated, with a potted palm partly blocking the front window, large black-and-white tiles on the floor, and a long, white-enamel case faced with slanted panes of glass behind which were displayed cold cuts, cheeses, smoked salmon, salads, and a tray of enormous dill pickles. The stamped-tin ceiling was high.

The deli was mostly a carry-out place—there was a line of customers waiting to buy Sol's (or Jack's) wonderful thick sandwiches—but the owner had set up a couple of small, round, marble-topped tables and wire-backed chairs for the few who chose to eat in.

Betsy picked a chair that faced the door. She had barely sat down when the door opened and Alice came in. Tall for a woman in her sixties, and broad-shouldered, Alice wore a man's raincoat and sensible lace-up oxfords. Her eyeglasses had unstylish plastic rims. Her face was set with grim determination, an expression that did not change when she saw Betsy and came to her table.

She sat down stiffly and said, "I know what you want to ask me. And I'm glad to tell you, get it off my chest. This is all my fault."

"What is?" asked Betsy.

But Alice's answer was forestalled by Jack's appearance at their table. He was a tall, bald man with tired eyes and a paunch that sagged into his white apron. His hands were covered with clear plastic gloves. "What can I get you ladies?" he asked, with a special nod to Betsy, his landlady.

"I'd like a mixed green salad with strips of smoked turkey on top, ranch dressing on the side," said Betsy. "Water to drink."

Alice consulted the menu handwritten on a whiteboard behind the white enamel case and said, "A cup of coffee, black, and a mixed meat sandwich with mayonnaise on an onion roll, please." Mixed meat meant ham, smoked turkey, thuringer, salami, and roast beef, sliced thin but piled high. Alice was not afraid of cholesterol.

When the man had walked away, Alice said to Betsy, in a low, shamed voice, "It's my fault Foster is suspected of murder."

"How can that be? You were saying he was innocent only yesterday."

Alice replied, "I mean it's my fault he's suspected, not my fault he did it— which I'm not convinced he did."

"I still don't understand."

Alice frowned and shifted around on her chair. "Maybe I should start at the beginning, which was when I realized Angela was afraid of her husband."

"What?"

"I said, when I realized Angela was afraid of her husband. Paul was a bully and a brute. And she wasn't timid, she was *intimidated*. I told her once that if she wanted to get away, she could come hide in my house. But she didn't even thank me, much less take me up on the offer."

"I don't understand. Why—how did you get involved?"

"My late husband was a pastor, you know that. Well, we both heard a lot of sad stories. After a while, you learn to look at people, and I could very plainly see that Angela lived in fear of her husband."

"If that was true, why didn't she leave him? After all, she had Foster to go to."

"True. But women stay in abusive relationships for a number of reasons. Fear of what he might do if she leaves is near the top of the list."

"So he really didn't love her."

"What he felt was nothing like love, it had nothing to do with wanting the best for the beloved, it had everything to do with control."

"How long were you aware of this situation?"

"I first saw it about eight or ten months before her murder. But Paul's smile had never fooled me, ever; more than once I saw him smiling when there was nothing funny or happy going on. But as I said, I saw Angela looking unhappy when she thought no one was noticing. That worried me, and I offered to help her any way I could, but I wasn't the pastor's wife anymore, and anyway, I don't know how to be subtle, so I only scared her more. Then one Sunday I saw her talking to Foster after church. It seemed an innocent conversation, but friendly." Alice made a sudden curved gesture with a large hand, startling Betsy. She nodded. "Like that, Paul swooped in and just yanked her away. He was smiling, but for just a second there was a look on Angela's face that frightened me, she looked terrified. I phoned her at home that evening, pretending I wanted a recipe, and she seemed almost all right, you know what I mean?"

"Not exactly."

"I mean she wasn't crying, but she seemed anxious to get off the phone. Then all of a sudden I was talking to Paul, as if he'd snuck up and yanked the receiver out of her hand. I think he thought he'd caught her talking to a man, and when I said, 'Hello? Hello?' he said something like, 'Oh, it's you.' It was then I knew I had to do something."

"Why?" asked Betsy. "I mean, I understand completely how you could believe she was in danger, but why did you feel responsible for rescuing Angela?"

"Because I was the only one who thought she was in danger. I had talked to our pastor that Sunday, but he was a young man and—well, he was sure Paul was a good man and I was an interfering old woman. I couldn't call the police, they won't go over unless there's a loud fight going on that minute. And that organization that protects battered women won't take someone else's word there's a problem. There was no one else to tell; when people looked at Paul Schmitt, all they could see was that smile, all they noticed about him was how helpful he was to their neighbors."

"But you were sure he was a thoroughly evil man."

"Not thoroughly evil. He was like a lot of people, he put different parts of his life into different boxes. There was the Paul who programmed computers, the Paul who built cabinets for money under the table, the Paul who drove people home from the hospital. But I believe that at home there was a Paul who made his wife's life a living hell."

"Do you know why he did that? Not that she provoked him, nothing should provoke a man to behave like that, but what was it about him?"

"I don't know. Abusers happen for different reasons. In Paul's case, it may be because he needed to live up to that smile, he needed to make people think he was a good and happy man. And all the while, inside, he was afraid he wasn't good at all. Or that he wasn't good enough for Angela, who was a very sweet and gentle person—too sweet and gentle for her own good in this wicked world. Perhaps he was afraid someone would take her away from him. Do you know what I mean?"

Betsy nodded. "It's what used to be called an inferiority complex and today is called low self-esteem. Some people are sure that if people saw what they really are, they'd despise them."

Alice nodded back. "And he was sure Angela couldn't really love him, or that one day she'd meet someone truly good, and begin to see him for his real self. When my husband was pastor of our church, he dealt with abusive husbands surprisingly often. And even once an abusive wife, a dreadful person who terrorized her children and nearly killed her husband one night with a frying pan full of hot grease. I learned that you don't look only at someone's face, you look at the spouse's face as well. Paul was a smiler, but what I saw in Angela's face told me that she needed to leave him, or find someone to protect her from him."

"Did you ever see any bruises?" asked Betsy.

"Only once, the very next Sunday. She had finger marks around her wrist. She saw me looking and the shame in her eyes about broke my heart, but she hurried away when I tried to talk to her, and didn't come to church for two Sundays after that. So that's when I decided to put Foster in her way."

"Why Foster?"

"Because he seemed to be a good man, a nice man—and he had a way of paying attention to people. He was an usher back then, and he could spot a child about to get sick or a woman about to faint or a man starting to nod off, and get them away before they disrupted the service—and so they wouldn't embarrass themselves. And he was discreet, he never said a word to them or to anyone else afterward."

"Your church won't let people nap during the sermon?" asked Betsy, amused and diverted.

Alice smiled. "Oh, we don't mind the napping, it's the snoring that gets on people's nerves. Especially during the sermon."

Betsy laughed, then sobered. "All right, you knew Foster had an eye for trouble and a talent for averting it. He told me how you did it, by mentioning to him that Angela seemed unhappy, What did you think he would do?"

"The old-fashioned thing—throw a scare into Paul. Foster was taller than Paul, and he worked in construction, so he was strong. I wanted him to say something to Paul that would let him know we suspected he was cruel to Angela, and that he was prepared to take action if he wasn't nicer. That might have been enough, if I was right that Paul cared very much what people thought of him. But . . ." She sighed. "I had no idea Foster would fall in love with the girl. I feel very bad about that. And worse for what happened after." She lifted her head toward the ceiling and the lights blanked her glasses, hiding the pain in her eyes. "I wish with all my heart I never, ever said anything to Foster."

"So you think Paul murdered Angela."

Her head came down. She was surprised at the question. "Yes, I think that's most likely what happened. Abusive husbands, if they aren't stopped, go further and further until at last they go all the way to murder. I have heard he has an alibi, but Mike Malloy was the investigator, and I'm afraid Mike is not always good at his job."

"Did you tell Foster what you suspected?"

"No, of course not!"

"But you do think Foster murdered Paul?"

"I'm afraid that's possible. That beating Paid was given before he was shot, that's the kind of thing an angry man would do. I can well understand that anger, I was angry myself when I heard Angela was dead." She was silent for a few seconds, then said bravely, because she was a good Christian and this went against her beliefs, "Betsy, if you find evidence that Foster killed Paul for murdering Angela, can I persuade you not to tell anyone? No matter how awful it is for Foster now, it would be far worse if he went to prison for murdering a man who badly needed to be killed."

Betsy said, as gently as she could, "I'm not sure it could be worse than what he's dealing with now. Nor am I convinced he did it."

Alice's homely face, lit up. "Have you found something out?"

"No, nothing concrete. But don't you see? That's why I have to keep looking. If he didn't do it, the agony he's been going through for these past years is a gross injustice. And it's been hurting you as well, because you're blaming yourself for being an accessory. Just ask yourself: How would you feel if you found out for certain Foster was innocent?"

Alice blinked slowly, then nodded. "If you really could do that . . . Oh my, what a tremendous relief to have that burden lifted! Yes, then I hope you will continue your investigation. And may God guide you in your efforts."

Betsy went back to her shop to find no customers, and Godwin in an interesting mood, cheeks pink and his movements somewhere between preening and strutting, as if he'd won a fight.

"Guess who was here," he said as soon as she hung up her coat.

"Who?"

"Foster Johns. Said he wanted to talk to you. But I sent him packing." He snorted. "Don't look at me like that! You've paid him for his services, and it's not as if he was actually going to buy something!"

"Goddy, he needed to talk to me—and I needed to talk to him!"

"Say, you don't believe that stuff Alice was putting out, that he didn't murder anyone? No way, boss lady! Why, I'm sure that when you get to the real facts of this business, you'll prove once and for all that he did murder Angela and Paul!"

"That may be true," retorted Betsy, "but I'm not setting out with that in mind! I don't investigate with an eye to proving anything. I want to find out the truth. But that means, Goddy, that I need to talk to Foster Johns and anyone else I think can help. Which means you don't run him, or anyone else you happen not to like, out of the shop!" Betsy, her own cheeks flaming, went to the back room to fix herself a cup of raspberry tea. She sat down at the little table in the rear of the shop to drink it and allow her blood to cool. She shouldn't have snapped at him like that. Saying that was over the line, and she was ashamed of herself. But she wanted to talk to Foster and was annoyed Godwin had prevented that.

And besides, Godwin had gone over his own line more than once lately. It was part of his attraction in the shop to be catty. His "gay bitchy" riff was amusing, and customers liked it; it made them feel sophisticated to realize he didn't mean anything by it. And he had never been really cruel—though there had been a slightly unpleasant edge to his remarks lately. He was going through a bad patch—again—with his lover, she knew. That was enough to make anyone moody, but Godwin was in special circumstances.

She thought about that. Godwin had begun as John's "boy toy," and played the sweet young thing to John's mature protective instincts. The relationship had lasted far longer than was usual with these arrangements. John had seemed honestly in love with Godwin, and certainly Godwin loved him back. But Godwin's growing signs of maturity were stressing the relationship.

It was John's continued support of Godwin that enabled him to work for minimum wages and no benefits at Crewel World, so these signs of strain bothered her. Godwin had been around long enough to know better than to put off customers, and—her own stress notwithstanding—she had to find a way to remind him of that without reducing him to tears or making him angry enough to quit. Godwin at his best was a tremendous asset, and his knowledge of needlework was too important to her to risk losing him.

She heard the door signal go as someone came in, but Godwin, his voice only slightly too cheerful, took care of it.

She had nearly finished her tea when he came and sat down across from her, a study in shame and gloom. "You don't like me anymore," he murmured.

"Of course I like you!" she replied at once, and was unhappy to note the edge in her own voice.

"Not really. You don't talk to me anymore."

"But I do, I talk to you all the time!"

"Not about important things. You didn't tell me you were thinking of hiring a general contractor instead of finding a roofer yourself, for example. I could have warned you about Foster if you'd said something. And you haven't been talking about Morrie. I have no idea how serious you two are. Are you perhaps thinking of selling the shop and moving to Florida with him?"

"No. He wants me to, but I'm not giving up this business. I enjoy the independence too much."

He smiled in bright relief, and she suddenly realized that here was another source of his distress. "Oh, Goddy, I should have said something, shouldn't I?

Don't worry about your job here. This job is yours as long as I'm here, and I have no intention of leaving."

He smiled. "That's super! I'm relieved about that. Sad for Morrie, of course."

"Don't be. He can continue to use that house in Fort Myers as a winter getaway, I'm sure."

"Well, at least in the winter then you'll talk to me." His eyes turned serious. "That's what it is, right? You've got him to talk to, and that's why you don't talk to me anymore."

Betsy took a breath to deny that, found she was going to put it a trifle indignantly, and paused while she reconsidered her answer.

"See? I *knew* it! You tell *him* things you don't tell me!"

Betsy began to laugh. "Well, of course I do! I imagine you tell John things you don't tell me."

Godwin hesitated, then blushed deeply. "That's not quite fair," he remarked.

"Neither of us is fighting fair," agreed Betsy. "On the other hand, you have a point, I do confide in Morrie, and it's made me confide less in my friends, particularly you and Jill."

"Are you going to marry Morrie?"

"Not right now. That's a question for the future, the *distant* future." Godwin grinned in relief. "Anything else on your mind?"

"Do you really think Foster Johns is innocent?"

"It's possible."

"How *can* you think that?"

"Well, I talked with him. He *wants* me to investigate, Goddy. He's heard that I'm good at sleuthing, and he offered me money to look into his case. Would a guilty man do that?"

"Oh-kaaay," Godwin drawled, not willing to concede she had a point.

"Besides, Paul Schmitt really may have murdered Angela. He was very abusive to her."

"I don't believe it!"

Betsy told him what both Foster and Alice had said about Angela being afraid, and what Foster had said Angela told him about Paul's abuse.

"Strewth!" said Godwin, taking it all in. "That's incredible! Why didn't anyone else notice it?"

"Do you know, I think some may have. But Paul and Angela are dead and all anyone wants to remember is what a devoted couple they were."

"Yes, there is that tendency, isn't there? But think, suppose Paul murdered Angela. Doesn't that give Foster a super motive for murdering Paul?"

"Yes, it does. But he has an alibi for Paul's murder," said Betsy. "Confirmed by the police."

Godwin stared. "I didn't know that." Then he scoffed, "A half-assed one, I bet."

"Well . . ." conceded Betsy, and added, over his rising look of triumph, "But it was given to him by Paul Schmitt!"

That quashed him properly, but after she explained, he said, "Half the credit has to go to that cleaning woman—do you know who she is?"

"No, why? Do you?"

"No, but it would be interesting to know if she bought a car, or even a house, after the police let him go."

Betsy said, "Hmmmm. The thing to find out would be if he talked to her before the police did."

"Betsy, is it possible Paul was telling the truth, and he had evidence of who really murdered Angela? And then someone killed him to stop him showing it to anyone?"

"The police didn't find anything in his house. But then, if the killer came after him, he would have taken it away, wouldn't he?"

"Do you have any idea who this other suspect might be?"

"Not the remotest." But she was thinking of Vern Miller's warning to his son not to speak his brother's name.

Nine

Hello, Carol? It's Betsy at Crewel World. It's hard to know when to call someone who works at home, so if I'm taking you away from your work, just tell me when would be a better time to call."

"This is a good time, in fact; I'm rolling around the kitchen waiting for the water to boil for a cup of tea. What's up? More ghost stories?"

"No. I wanted to tell you that the new DMC colors are in, but also ask you if you'd be interested in stitching another model for the shop." Betsy sometimes asked experienced customers to stitch a pattern to hang on Crewel World's wall. A color photograph could not always do a cross-stitched pattern justice; it took an actual model to entice customers.

After some discussion, they came to terms for the stitching of Janlynn's complex Once Upon A Time, which was of a rearing unicorn about to be mounted by a medieval lady holding a spear with banners. "I'm sure it's lovely, but it sounds so incredibly Freudian, I'm surprised you dare to hang it in your shop!" said Carol with an amused gurgle.

The deal concluded, Betsy said, "You were saying the other day that your sister and Angela Schmitt were best friends. Is she a stitcher, by chance?"

"You want to talk to Gretchen about Angela, don't you?"

"Yes, I do. But I don't know her, and so I'm not sure how to approach her. I was hoping to do it through the shop."

"Well, she doesn't stitch." Carol paused in a pregnant way. "But she knits."

"Ah," said Betsy. "What level, beginner?"

"Just about. She's looking to try a sweater."

"Perhaps I should tell her that Rosemary is going to teach a sweater class in February. It's one of her most popular."

Carol made that gurgling sound that meant she was amused. "So not only are you going to pick her brain, you're going to pick her pocket. How much is the class?"

"Forty-five dollars, not including materials. Can she afford that?"

"From her change purse, probably. She married really well this time, and they go to New York City at least once a year to buy a bauble at Tiffany's and catch a Broadway show."

"Great. May I have her phone number? Or her e-mail address?"

Carol gave her both and they hung up.

Betsy was too busy to go upstairs and log on, so after she sold Mrs. Peters a winter solstice pattern and the floss she didn't already have to complete it, she picked the phone up again and dialed the number Carol had given her.

The voice that answered sounded so much like Carol's that for an instant Betsy thought she'd had a senior moment and dialed Carol's number again. But she glanced down at the number Carol had given her and her fingers recognized it, so she said, "This must be Carol's sister Gretchen. I'm Betsy Devonshire, of the needlework shop Crewel World."

"How do you do? Yes, I'm Gretchen Tallman. What can I do for you?"

Something in Gretchen's impatient voice made Betsy discard her round-about ploy. She said directly, "I'm looking into Angela and Paul Schmitt's murders, and I'd like to talk to you."

"What do you mean, you're looking into their murders? Isn't Crewel World a stitchery store? Are you also a private investigator?"

"No, I'm working as an amateur. Foster Johns wants me to look into the case."

Now the voice was distinctly frosty. "Foster Johns? Isn't he the man who did it?"

"I'm looking for more information to see if I can figure out just who did it."

"But of course it was him!"

"He was never charged with the crime. Can you tell me something that can be used as evidence, so he can be arrested and brought to trial?"

"Wait a minute. If you're working for him, why would you tell the police anything I might tell you?"

"I'm not working for him, or for the police. What I'm looking for is some new evidence I can bring to the attention of the police."

"And they'll listen to you because . . . ?"

"Because I have discovered evidence in other cases. I have . . . connections in two police departments."

"Hey, do you know Jill Cross?"

"Yes, I do. Why?"

"What's your phone number there?" Betsy gave it to her, and Carol said, "I'll call you back," and hung up.

Ten minutes later the phone rang. Betsy picked up the receiver and said, "Crewel World, Betsy speaking, may I help you?"

"Okay, let's meet somewhere."

"Gretchen?"

"Who did you think?"

"Well, you sound a lot like Carol."

"So they tell me. Jill says you're all right, that I should trust you. So when and where can we meet?"

Betsy smiled, relieved Gretchen had called Jill and not Mike Malloy. "I'm working today, so you can come to the shop. Or we can meet for lunch, or after we close. We're open till five tonight."

"Lunch at Maynard's. One too late?"

"No. How will I know you?"

"They tell me I look like Carol, too. See you at one." ~~Carol~~ Gretchen rang off.

Betsy was prompt, but a woman who looked a lot like Carol, except she wasn't in a wheelchair, was waiting, a highball in one hand. Maynard's was a waterfront restaurant, slightly upscale, with a large wooden dock running around two sides of the dining room. In the summer, the dock nearly doubled the seating area. This time of year it was bare of tables, and today the water beyond was gray and choppy. A windsurfer made rooster tails across the bay, as sleek and anonymous as a seal in his black wet suit.

"You ever try that?" Gretchen asked Betsy as they sat down at their table, beside a big window.

"Not I," said Betsy. "I swim and I sail, but not at the same time. How about you?"

"Not for a while." Gretchen watched the surfer for a minute, giving Betsy a chance to study her. Gretchen could be either Carol's older or younger sister, it was hard to tell. There was a strong family resemblance, but she had that careless arrogance of a woman with a lot of money, which Carol lacked. Gretchen was lightly tanned and very fit, her blond hair streaked and cut in that expensive way that falls back into place with a shake of the head. Her hands were knobbier than Carol's, possibly because she was thinner, possibly because she was older. She wore pleated black trousers and a black cashmere sweater. Her Burberry was draped over the back of her chair. Her eyes came back to Betsy. They were large and a blue so dazzling that Betsy deduced tinted contacts.

"So why don't you think Foster Johns murdered a very dear friend of mine?" asked Gretchen.

"Because the same person who murdered her also murdered her husband, and Foster has an alibi for that crime."

"An ironclad one, no doubt. It's those watertight alibis that are so often carefully planned for, don't you think?"

"Sometimes," agreed Betsy. "But this isn't ironclad. Paul called Foster and asked for a meeting. Paul said he had evidence of who really killed Angela, but that if he presented it to the police, they'd think he contrived it. But he said perhaps Foster would be believed. Foster agreed to meet Paul in his office on Water Street, but Paul never showed. Foster got out some paperwork while he waited, plans and figures, but he finally went home. His cleaning lady told the police the office was perfectly clean when she left, and Foster said he couldn't possibly have had time to both drive to Navarre to murder Paul and get his office that entangled in paper."

"If I were Foster, and I thought Paul murdered Angela because she was having an affair with me, I'd be damned if I'd agree to meet him alone. If Paul killed Angela for messing around with me, he might kill me, too. No way would I have agreed to meet him alone." She took a swallow of her drink and made a wry mouth. "Actually, I did meet him alone one time when I was me, and wouldn't do that again." She frowned. "I mean, I *am* me, and Paul's not meeting anyone again. But when he was alive I wouldn't have met him again at the Mall of America on the day after Thanksgiving surrounded by a platoon of cops on horseback." She made a big, sloppy circle in the air with her glass.

After a pause while Betsy made sense of that, she said, "How did you happen to meet him alone?"

"It was down at the docks. I'd been sailing with some friends and got in after dark. I'd had some vodka gimlets and was thoroughly shellacked. This was pretty soon after Angela said we shouldn't see each other anymore, so I never told her about it. Another thing I'm sorry about, because that might have been enough to pry her loose from that bastard. Anyhow, I came up the dock all by myself and I stopped by that kiosk thing on the shore, where they have announcements and historical information and like that inside it?"

Betsy nodded. She'd made a contribution to the Excelsior Chamber of Commerce and been rewarded with a paving stone outside the kiosk that came with the name of her shop cut into it. Most of the stones had names of individuals or companies on them; a few were still blank.

"The strap of my sandal was twisted so I was leaning against the wall of the kiosk trying to straighten it with a finger when all of a sudden he was there. I could see his teeth gleaming in the streetlight—he was always smiling, did I tell you that?" She blinked a little owlishly and Betsy wondered if the drink in her hand wasn't her third or even fourth.

"Yes, you did."

"'Need a hand?'" he asked, all nice. 'Nope,' says I, 'I'm just fine.' And he kind of grabs me around the waist, only lower, and I slither away and say something like, 'How dare you?' only I put it stronger, and all of a sudden he's on me like paint on a fence, and I have this thing I do, where I stomp on an instep and it will make just about anyone alive yip like a dog and back off. Only all he says is, 'Hey, quit that,' and keeps on coming, so I send my elbow hard into his midriff, and he had to let go then, because he couldn't breathe anymore." She widened her eyes and shaped her mouth like a fish out of water, gulped a few times in imitation of a man with the wind knocked out of him, then chuckled maliciously. "That was the only time I ever saw him without that damn grin." She lifted her glass and drained the liquid, tonguing the ice to shake loose the last of it.

"Good for you," said Betsy as Gretchen put the glass down with a victorious thump. "Nice to be able to take care of yourself like that."

"Well," said Gretchen, tossing her head to make her hair shift and fall back, "when you start moving in the upper class, you either learn or go under." She snickered.

"When you heard about Angela, did you think right away that Foster Johns murdered her?"

"Of course not. I was sure Paul did it." She stared out the window, those amazing eyes filled with tears. "He pretended to be a nice person, but he didn't have many friends, though lots of people are saying now how much they liked him. I went to high school with Paul, and even back then I thought there was something wrong with him. It was like a glass wall between him and you. He was always smiling and doing favors, but you couldn't get close to him. And it didn't change after he married Angela. He was nice to me, but all he'd talk about was sports or fishing or hunting—never about anything deep or important. I sometimes wondered if he didn't have any deep thoughts. There was just this weirdly happy guy, with a smile a yard wide—and an inch deep."

"How long had you known Angela?"

"Since middle school. She was like the opposite of Paul. She was really shy, but when you got to know her, she was deep. I remember when she was twelve, she had worked out what it must be like after you died. She said time was a river and we rode down the river all our lives, seeing the shoreline in sequence; and then when we died, we were like flying over the river and could see where it started and all the places it went and where it ended. And everything that ever happened or was going to happen was all happening on the river, so that's why God knew what we were going to do before we did it. I mean, she was *twelve,* and she had this all worked out. I was the only person she told. She was good with books and tests, but her grades suffered because she almost never talked in class. There were some boys she liked in high school, but she never went out with them because she was too shy to let them know she liked them. I was the wild and crazy one, dances and parties and midnight movies, and people used to ask me why I liked Awkward Angie, and I'd say, 'But she's so *deep!*'" Gretchen laughed self-deprecatingly.

"So why did she marry Paul?" asked Betsy.

"I asked her that once and she said, 'Because he asked me.' I think she had a real self-esteem problem, she could have done *so* much better if she knew what a great person she was."

Their waitperson brought the big menus at this point and there was a pause while choices were made. Gretchen ordered another Manhattan, Betsy a sparkling water; Gretchen ordered a big salad, no dressing; Betsy a salmon steak that came with fresh fruit and a frozen yogurt dessert for fewer than a thousand calories.

"What did Angela tell you about Paul?" asked Betsy when the menus were taken away.

'That he was wonderful, outgoing, and always cheerful, with lots of friends. That was at first. Then she said less and less and finally didn't say anything. Then it got hard to get hold of her, and she finally said Paul didn't like her to spend so much time out with her friends, he wanted her at home with him. Well, I was working on wrecking my first marriage about then, so what the hey, we didn't move in the same circles anymore and it was easy to let things slide." Gretchen shrugged, but her mouth was weighted down by regret. She rattled the ice in her empty glass, looked around and brightened. "Here come our drinks, about time."

When their entrees arrived, Betsy said, "If Paul was such a nasty piece of work, he must have had enemies. Any idea who they might be?"

"Not a clue. Angela never said anything about him having trouble with anyone, and I don't remember anyone else saying they hated his guts. You really believe Foster Johns didn't whack him, don't you?"

"I don't know anything for sure right now. I do believe the only way to prove whether or not he did it is to find out who had a motive to kill both of them."

"Well, don't look at me. After that encounter at the docks, I could have cheerfully shot him, but there's no way on earth I would have killed Angela." Her voice broke. "Oh, Angie, my sweet angel!" She snatched up her napkin and held it to her nose and mouth. "I hope you find out who it was, with proof and everything. I want to hire the worst lawyer on earth to defend him."

Back in the shop, Godwin said, "I hear you're moving up in the world, lunching at Maynard's with Gretchen Goldberg-Tallman?" He walked in a circle, nose in the air, arm lifted and bent at the wrist. "How *do* you do?"

"The FBI and CIA should come and study the grapevine in this town," declared Betsy. "They could throw away their wiretaps and bitty cameras and position-locating satellites. The frozen yogurt hasn't even melted in my stomach, and you have a full report. Is Gretchen all that high in society?"

"Ooooh, first-name basis and *everything*!" said Godwin.

"Goddy . . ."

The young man knew that tone, and sobered. "Yes, she moves in the upper circles, dinner with the Daytons, weekends with the Humphreys and the Wellstones. Len Tallman's name turns up on the lists of Minnesota's most wealthy—plus his father's grandmother was Teddy Roosevelt's granddaughter. Gretchen's a trophy wife, his third; he's her second husband."

"Carol didn't strike me as someone who moves in those kinds of circles."

"She doesn't. Len says Carol makes him uncomfortable, so Gretchen doesn't see much of her sister."

"Len dislikes Carol because she's a lesbian?"

"No, because she's in a wheelchair. He has a 'thing' about handicapped people. He'll give a million to charity or a research hospital, but he can't bring himself to touch a person with any kind of handicap."

"How do you know this?"

"Well, rich people need lawyers, and who is my beloved John but one of the best? John is also something of a gossip."

"Has John ever said anything about Foster?"

"Only that he must be pretty slick to get away with murder. Foster's not a client; John gossips mostly about his clients."

Betsy's eyes narrowed. "I wonder what would happen if Len Tallman were ever injured so severely he'd need special aids to get along."

"Can't happen," said Godwin, "He's got living wills on file around the world, saying let him go if it's worse than a bad chest cold. I heard he's even got

DNR tattooed on his chest. Oh, by the way, the *Bay Times* called. Number's on your desk."

The *Excelsior Bay Times* was a weekly newspaper given away free but widely read. Expecting to be connected with somebody trying to persuade her to buy a bigger ad, Betsy dialed the number and found herself talking to a reporter.

Someone had told him about Betsy's "Winter Window," and he thought it would make a nice little article. He proposed to stop by with a photographer at Betsy's convenience. About an hour later, she was posed beside her window, smiling broadly, and the reporter took at face value her comment that she liked diversity and hoped her window would bring a diverse collection of customers to her business.

That evening, Betsy had Foster Johns to dinner. It was supposed to be Morrie's dinner, but by the time she'd gotten hold of Foster, it was too late to have him come back to the shop. So she'd called Morrie to explain that she needed to talk to Foster, and Morrie had been fine with that.

Foster arrived at her apartment looking tired. He seemed to have lost ten pounds—and also that controlled air she had noted about him. "How are you doing?" she asked, taking his jacket. He was wearing Dockers and an old gray sweatshirt.

"Could be better, could be worse. I lost a client in Chanhassen today; apparently some idiot here in Excelsior phoned him. If I find out who did that, I'll sue his ass. Maybe some of the gossips in this town lose their house for slandering me, they'll think twice before they spread lies. But on the other hand, two women in the Excello Bakery smiled at me yesterday. One of them was Alice Skoglund, but I don't know who the other one was."

"Alice is definitely on your side, she's hoping I'll find proof of your innocence," said Betsy. "Wine?" He nodded, and she filled his glass. "She's been feeling guilty because she wanted you to threaten Paul Schmitt with a poke in the nose if he wasn't nicer to his wife, and instead you ended up falling in love with her and then suspected of her murder. Here, come and sit down; the chicken will take a few minutes more to bake."

Once he was comfortable, she asked, "Why did you agree to meet Paul the night he was murdered?" she asked.

"Because I wanted to know who really murdered Angela," Foster replied.

"You believed he had the evidence?"

"I didn't know what he had. He said he had something, and he said the police might not believe it if it came from him."

"Weren't you afraid to meet him alone?"

"Hell, yes! But this was three days after Angela's murder, and the police

hadn't arrested anyone. I was going crazy. I was sure as I could be that Paul
did it, but when he called, he sounded so sincere, it kind of threw me. But I'm
no fool, I also figured maybe he was thinking to round things off by killing
me, too. But I thought, well, what if he really has something? So I told him
to come to my office. I set up the recorder in the top drawer of my desk, and
I left the drawer open about an inch. I walked around the office saying 'Testing, testing,' and adjusting the volume so it would pick up his voice no matter
where he was. And a lot of good it did me. I'm sure I bored some unfortunate
cop out of his mind when he had to sit and write down everything he heard
on that recorder, which was me saying 'Testing, testing' about twenty times,
then fragments of me wadding up paper, scratching lines and figures on paper,
swearing, and whistling through my teeth. But because it only came on when
it heard a noise, it didn't help much with the alibi because it didn't record the
long periods of silence."

"And you didn't phone someone to tell him you were meeting Paul, in case
they found your body the next day?"

"No. It was supposed to be a secret, him turning the evidence over to me.
If he really had something, then I was more than willing to be his cat's paw in
getting it to the police."

"Do you remember who your cleaning lady was back then, the one who
helped give you an alibi?"

He smiled. "Sure. She's the same one I have right now. Her name's
Mrs. Nelson. Treeny Nelson. You want to talk to her?"

"Well, yes, I think I do."

He said, "Call me tomorrow and I'll give you her phone number. Or come
by at five and wait for her."

Ten

The next day Betsy was busy unpacking and putting out items
from Dale of Norway's Trunk Show. The boxes came from Needlework
Unlimited in Edina. Betsy was pleased to see that not only was everything
there, it had been carefully packed. Dale of Norway sold beautiful sweaters at
Hoigaard's and The Nordic Shop and at upscale stores at the Mall of America.
But they also sold patterns and wool. Betsy mooned over the authentic Norwegian sweaters that served as models—she put one pattern aside for herself, a

typical snowflake-on-sky blue one—but there were also some lively and beautiful nontraditional patterns. She was particularly taken by a dark gray scarf
with pockets at either end, whose orange edging was finished with little picots.
It was worked with two strands of wool, making it thick and heavy, but also
quick to work. Perhaps Jill would like it for Christmas, if it were worked in
shades of blue. (Betsy sometimes thought Jill became a police officer because
she could wear blue to work every day with nobody thinking anything of it.)
She put one of those patterns aside as well.

She removed the small paper sign announcing the show from her
glass-fronted door and replaced it with a much bigger one, which also offered
fifteen percent off all knitting materials. The trunk show would be here for a
week and then move on to Duluth.

She had no more than hung the new poster up when three women marched
into the shop, one an adolescent twelve, the next old enough to be her mother, and
the third old enough to be her grandmother. Betsy didn't recognize any of them
as regular customers. The girl had dark brown eyes and the dark auburn hair that
sometimes accompanies them. She said, "I need a kippah for my bat mitzvah, and
they"—she tossed her head in the direction of the other two women—"didn't like
any of the ones for sale at Brochin's." Which was a store in St. Louis Park.

In a heavy Russian accent the grandmother said, "What did she say?
What's a kippah? We are here for a yarmulke. I want to stitch a yarmulke for
my granddaughter. Bad enough they do this bat mitzvah for girls, but if they
do, I want something nice in blue and white. You have such a thing?" She
looked around doubtfully.

The girl said, "Kippah is the correct term for it, I learned that in
Talmud-Torah school."

The mother said, "It doesn't matter." And to Betsy, "My mother-in-law
said she would sew one if you had a yarmulke pattern or even just a circular
pattern we liked in the right size." She made a round shape about six inches
across with her thumbs and fingers. Her English came from Brooklyn with just
a trace of Russia in it.

The daughter said firmly, "I want something pretty, with horses on it. Or
soccer."

The grandmother said something in angry Russian, the mother replied in
kind, and the daughter shouted, "Speak English!"

"You hush!" said her mother. "Your grandmother wants to make you a gift,
and so what if she calls it a yarmulke and you call it a kippah? It comes to the
same thing, so why do you always want to make trouble?" She turned to Betsy,
and, her voice suddenly sweet, she asked, "So, what do you have?"

Betsy had spent some years in New York City, and this was so much a taste
of there, she could not stop smiling.

"I have some needlepoint yarmulkes, but only a few. Let me show them to you." She pulled four canvases from a drawer in the white dresser near the front door, and the child immediately picked a pink one with black silhouettes of dancing children around its edge.

But the grandmother wanted the blue one with white Stars of David. The child refused to even consider putting such a lame article on her head, which scandalized her grandmother no end. "What are they teaching you at shul, how to be rude?" she demanded.

Another shouting match began, into which Godwin walked, his arms full of boxes picked up from the post office. He was so startled at the racket that he dropped them, which in turn startled them into silence.

"What's going on?" he asked.

"A little disagreement over what pattern of yarmulke the young woman is going to wear for her bat mitzvah," said Betsy.

The fight started in again and faintly, in the background, Betsy heard the phone ringing. At this point she'd had enough of New York and withdrew gratefully to answer it, taking the cordless phone into the back of the shop.

It was Alice. "Is today the start of the trunk show?" she asked in her deep voice. On being assured that it was, she asked Betsy to not sell the last of any mitten patterns until she had a chance to come by "probably tomorrow" and take a look at them.

Betsy promised and then said, "You seem to have disliked Paul Schmitt for a long time. Surely you weren't the only person who didn't like him. Alice, I'm trying to find someone who hated him, perhaps someone he hurt badly. Can you think of anyone like that?"

Betsy had to wait while Alice sank into her noisy coma for a minute, thinking. The sound cut off.

"Alex Miller, maybe," she said.

"Jory's brother?"

"That's him."

"Why?"

"Because Alex and Jory were supposed to go into partnership with their father in that auto repair shop Vern founded. Then there was a family fight that kept getting worse and now Alex isn't speaking to either his father or his brother, nor they to him. His mother told me that Alex blames Paul, but even now, with Paul dead all these years, the quarrel hasn't been made up. Alex's wife, Danielle, talked to Alex's mother about it, but she can't get them to make peace. Alex is the one most hurt, he was really close to his brother and wanted to go into business with him so his father could retire, but that's not possible anymore. Jory can't do it all alone, so Vern has to keep working. Vern's wife is worried about him. She and I work on several committees together and we talk."

Betsy recalled the angry way Vern Miller and his son Jory had talked about Alex. "What does Alex do?"

"He works at the Ford plant in St. Paul."

"Do you know where he lives?"

"No, you'll have to ask Mrs. Miller. Vern won't speak to Alex, but I'm pretty sure Jin stays in touch, for the sake of the grandchildren."

Betsy hung up, then realized the quarrel out in front had stopped. She went out for a look and found Godwin alone in the shop. "What happened?" she asked.

"I sold them that round needlepoint canvas with the ocean theme. The grandmother is going to stitch the ocean in a solid blue and the fish in very pale shades of gray and white, so she gets her Israeli flag colors and the daughter gets sharks, dolphins, and a beluga on her yarmulke."

Betsy heartily approved of this clever solution. "I wish you'd been here instead of me when they came in," she said and immediately changed her mind. "No, it was fun to hear the accents again. Do they have a Jewish neighborhood in the cities?"

"There's a suburb called St. Louis Park that has so many, they call it St. Jewish Park."

Betsy was startled. "I didn't think there was anti-Semitism in Minnesota!"

"Why not? We're just like everyone else. There's even a small KKK chapter. Every time they parade, the onlookers argue over whether the Klansmen are stupider than they are ugly or uglier than they are stupid. But St. Jewish Park isn't a slur, the nickname was given by the Jews who live there."

"Oh," said Betsy, and went to call Vern Miller's wife.

Jin Miller spoke unaccented English, but in a soft and gentle voice without the flat tones common in middle America. "Why do you want to talk to Alex?" she asked.

"I'm hoping he can tell me something about Paul Schmitt."

There was a little silence. "He will not say anything good about that man," Jin said.

"That's all right, I'm not looking for only good things."

"You are the woman who investigates murders, am I right?"

"Yes."

"And you are looking for the name of the person who murdered Paul and Angela?" Jin asked.

"Yes."

"I can tell you that. It was Foster Johns. He was in love with Angela, and when she told him she would stay with her husband, he killed both of them. The police didn't have enough proof to arrest Mr. Johns."

"Perhaps I can find the proof, one way or the other."

"Oh, I see." A little pause. "All right, if you think Alex can help, I will give you his number."

At a little before five, Betsy left Godwin in charge and hurried the few blocks up to Foster Johns' s little office building. His receptionist said Foster had already left on a consultation, but that Betsy was welcome to wait; she wanted to speak to their cleaning lady, right?

"Thank you," said Betsy, and sat down in the little reception area to look at a copy of *Architectural Digest.* She was studying an ad featuring a sumptuous easy chair, when the door opened and a short, stout woman with a snub nose and blond hair well mixed with gray came in. She wore a puffy winter jacket of sky blue with big yellow patches, and heavy mittens, which she pulled off after closing the door. She greeted the receptionist in a quiet, dour voice, then saw her nod toward Betsy and turned to look.

"How do you do," said Betsy. "Are you Mrs. Nelson?"

"Yah, that's me. What can I do for you? I warn you right now, I'm not taking on any new customers."

"No, this isn't about that, I just have some questions for you, if you don't mind."

Mrs. Nelson looked at the receptionist, who said, "Mr. Johns said she'd be by. It's all right. Why don't you use his office?"

"Yah, okay," said Mrs. Nelson. "It's back this way."

She went around the big desk that stood in front of a paneled oak door, Betsy following. It opened into a room with tilted tables and big windows and, when Mrs. Nelson threw the switch, merciless fluorescent lighting. To the right was another paneled door, and this led into a very comfortable office with a modern leather couch, an antique desk, and a big, plain table. One wall was made of corkboard. A single blueprint was tacked to it; otherwise the table and desk were empty. There were framed architectural drawings on the other walls.

Mrs. Nelson went to the couch but didn't sit down. "What did you want to ask me?"

"Do you remember the night Paul Schmitt was killed?"

"Do I? Ha! You bet I do! The police come and get me out of bed in the middle of the night—no, *past* the middle of the night, it was like three A.M.! Want to know if I cleaned Mr. Johns's office. Of course I cleaned it. I give it a once-over every night and a heavy cleaning once a week, more often if it needs it. They said did I clean it that night and I say sure, and they ask me what did it look like when I got there. They couldn't wait till a decent hour of the morning? I asked them."

"You understand how important it was to get the answer to their questions, don't you?" asked Betsy.

"Yah, sure I did, but only later. What they wanted was to know if Mr. Johns murdered Mr. Schmitt. They didn't tell me that then, so I was cross with them, like anyone would be, waked out of a sound sleep."

"So what did you tell them?"

"That the big workroom was kinda messy, but the office was neat, only the wastebaskets was full. So they took me back to look, and what a mess! Paper and blueprints and drawings and all, everywhere."

Betsy asked, "Had you ever seen it like that before?"

"Yah, sure. Whenever he's workin' on something, he hasta get everything out and he sticks some of it up on the wall with thumbtacks and lays other stuff on the table and his desk, sometimes on the couch even."

As if reminded, she unzipped her jacket and sat down. "And he leaves it out, spreads it around, rearranges it, whatever, until he knows how the project's gonna go, then he cleans it up."

"He never asks you to put it away?"

"Oh, no, no, I know better than to touch any of that there stuff. I dust and I vacuum and I empty wastebaskets and I scrub the toilet and every once in a while I do the windows."

"What's he like to work for?"

"Well, I used to hardly ever see him, y'know. That was good, because when he would stay after special, it was so he could complain about something. He was a real shouter, and he went through receptionists like they was Kleenex. I'm surprised I stuck with him, and maybe I wouldn't've, but the place is easy to clean, no grease or mud. Then after this murder thing he calmed down a lot. He used to give me a Christmas bonus, but now I get another one, on my birthday."

"Mrs. Nelson, do you think he murdered those people?"

She looked at Betsy, surprised. "Yah, I do. Everyone knows he did it. I think it made him sad and that's why he's nicer than he was. It was almost good for him, in an awful way. He's suffered and he's still suffering, worse maybe than bein' put in jail. I hope they never prove he did it." She looked at her hands, small but red and thickened. "Surprised me, it did, coming into that office and seein' all that paper out, because when I left it, there wasn't so much as one sheet of paper showing."

"But you don't think that proves he was here at work rather than over in Navarre shooting Mr. Schmitt?"

"No, I don't. It'd take maybe ten minutes to pull out papers and drape 'em all over everything, wouldn't it? Didn't prove a thing to me."

Betsy thanked her and went back to the shop to find Godwin selling her tenant's twin, Doris Valentine, a set of Christmas tree ornament patterns and floss.

"Hi, Betsy," she said in her husky voice. "Godwin says, can I make an ornament to put on the tree." She beamed at Godwin. "*Such* a nice young man!"

Godwin said, "I wouldn't usually ask someone so new to cross-stitch to commit to doing that, but Doris is an unusually hard worker, and she's doing really well."

Doris simpered a bit. "Well, I have such a good teacher. He was just showing me how to grid." She held up a scrap of evenweave fabric basted in rows five threads apart.

Betsy smiled at both of them. "I remember how great it was when someone showed me about gridding. All of a sudden counted cross-stitch became actually possible for me. I'm glad Godwin has taken the time to show you; he's a good teacher. This isn't a difficult craft to master, but it helps to have someone show you the steps to take."

Eleven

Alex Miller worked second shift over at Ford Motor Company, where he was a line supervisor. He was suspicious and reluctant, but at last said that if Betsy wanted to talk to him, he'd meet her at the gate to the plant at 11:00 P.M. tonight, when he was on break.

Betsy called Morrie and he agreed to drive her over after she closed, and watch from the car while she talked to Alex.

She spent the next several hours, between customers, going over her stock, straightening, sorting, removing anything worn or frazzled, putting things back where they belonged. Keeping up with tasks like this made inventory less of a chore.

When she first inherited Crewel World, she'd often found a pattern or painted canvas tucked out of sight under or behind other items—a flower canvas pushed in among the Christmas ones, for example. At first she attributed it to absentmindedness, or the stress of trying to learn how to run a small business with a large and varied inventory. But now, settled in and comfortable with the work, it was still happening. A Laura Doyle Sea Images cross-stitch kit was hanging near the back of the Marc Saastad flower kits. "Look at this, Goddy," she said, exasperated. "Am I getting senile? Already?"

"What's the matter?" asked Godwin, and came for a look. "No, it's not you," he said, amused. "When customers want something and don't have the money at hand, or when a sale is coming up, they'll hide what they want so they're sure it will still be there when the sale starts. I've done that at Macy's, put a sweater I want in among the extra-extra large sizes, so it will be there when I come back with my credit card."

Betsy began to laugh, her relief so great that she forgot to be annoyed at her sneaky customers.

But between trying to restore order and serve customers, who were turning out in great numbers now that office hours were over, there was little time to worry, or even sit down. Betsy was beyond tired when she finally turned the needlepoint sign around to "Closed." She made three mistakes on the deposit slip and had to do it over twice before it was right. She sent Godwin yawning off with the money and slip, turned the lights off, punched the code for the alarm system, and went out the front door, yanking it shut and pushing it hard to make sure it locked.

Morrie was already waiting outside, engine running. She clambered into his Jeep Wagoneer for the forty-minute ride, and fell asleep before they were halfway to Minneapolis.

Morrie began to shake her gently as they crossed the short bridge into St. Paul at Minnehaha Falls Park. "Hello? Hey, sugar, wake up!"

"What?" said Betsy sleepily. She looked out the window as he pulled to the curb beside a very large, single-story brick building across a wide sidewalk. A familiar logo said "Ford." "Oh, are we there already?" She thrust her fingers into her hair and pulled hard to wake herself up. "Why'd you let me fall asleep? Now I'm all groggy!"

"What do you mean, 'let' you fall asleep? I talked to you, I played the radio, I whistled—loud and badly—to the music, and you fell asleep anyway. Maybe we should call this off for now and try again later."

"No, no, it was hard enough to get him to meet me the first time. What time is it?"

"Ten fifty-eight."

"No time to go scrounge up a Coke then. Well, here's luck." Betsy climbed wearily out of the Wagoneer. The rain had stopped, but the temperature had dropped, and the icy wind whipped her coat around her legs and tousled her hair as she walked up to the high chain-link fence that surrounded the plant. A stocky man in a dark leather jacket and wool cap was just coming to a halt by the truck-size gate.

As Betsy got closer, she could see that he looked very like his brother. "Alex Miller?" she said, closing the distance, and he nodded. "I'm glad you agreed to see me."

"What's this all about?" he demanded gruffly.

"Paul Schmitt," she said.

"That son of a bitch? I suppose you're another one of those who wants to canonize him!" He turned to walk away.

"I think you may be right to hate him!" she called, and he turned around, one eyebrow lifted in surprise. "I'm here to find out the truth!" she declared.

"If I told you the truth about him, your ears would burn for a month!" he declared.

"I used to be in the Navy, where I dated a bosun's mate. I doubt if you could surprise me."

He came back to grab hold of the fence with all his fingers and describe in ugly, graphic terms what he thought of Paul Schmitt's mind, heart, and organs of generation, the various perversions he practiced on victims of many species, and the likely entertainment his soul was giving the devil at present.

"Mr. Miller," Betsy interrupted firmly when he paused to regroup his imagination, "this is all very interesting, but you gave me only ten minutes, and I have some questions to ask."

He snorted, then relaxed and put his hands back in his pockets. "All right, ask away."

"Do you consider Paul Schmitt somehow responsible for the breach between you and your brother Jory and your father?"

Alex's eyebrows rose high on his forehead, then came down again. "Well, how did you figure . . . ? Yes, I do. He played all three of us, one against the other, until now neither Dad nor Jory will speak to me."

"Why would he do something like that?"

"For the fun of it, I guess."

"Why would he think it was fun to do that?"

"Because he was a low-down, filthy, sneaky, grinning snake, who—"

"Seriously," said Betsy, cutting him off before he could get all wound up again.

Alex rubbed his jaw, then his face, then the back of his neck. "My wife got onto me the same way you are," he said. "Saying there had to be a reason. And what we finally came up with is, because he saw me kiss his wife on the cheek. Before God, that's all I can figure."

"When did you kiss his wife on the cheek?"

"About the time her mother died. I went to the funeral and when we were shaking hands after, I leaned over and kissed her. She was looking sad, and just shaking her hand didn't seem like enough. But she kind of jumped back like I did something wrong, and looked around kind of nervous, and there was ol' Paul, looking at me like a lightbulb had gone on over his head."

"Did you know he was a very jealous husband?" asked Betsy.

"Oh, yeah, he was always suspecting her of playing him for a fool. But we were friends, Paul and me, or I thought we were, and he didn't say anything to me about it, so I thought she explained it to him, and he was all right with it. But right about then I started having trouble with Dad and Jory. I never connected Paul to that, they never mentioned him, so it never occurred to me. And then Danielle, that's my wife, started acting suspicious toward me, accusing me of playing around. It was getting to the point we were talking divorce when Paul was shot dead—and damned if things didn't start coming around right again with Danielle. I was just grateful that things were straightening out, again I never thought about Paul. But Danielle noticed it, too, and she sat me down and made me talk about it. I told her I didn't know why things were better, I wasn't doing anything different. But she said that wasn't so, that before I'd been acting like the biggest jerk in the world, and now I wasn't. And I repeated I wasn't doing anything different now than I was before. And after she quit shouting at me about how I'd been fooling around on her—which I wasn't, and where did she get that idea, and why was she trying to have a baby behind my back, and we fought over that for a while, and then she said stop shouting and listen to me. And we figured it out. I didn't even know she'd been talking to Paul, and all along it was Paul's doing. At first I couldn't believe it, and then I did, and it was like the sun coming up. And after a couple of days I started thinking of the fights with my brother and Dad. I wanted to ask them about it, but they wouldn't talk to me, so Danielle went to Mom, and the two of them figured it was the same thing between me and Jory and Dad, pretty much. Only it's too late to do anything about that, I guess."

He heaved a big sigh, lifted his arms in an exaggerated shrug, then pointed a thick forefinger at Betsy. "You can't imagine how grateful I am to Foster Johns for shooting that bastard. It was too late for Jory and Dad, but at least he saved my marriage for me."

"I don't understand," said Betsy, wondering if she was so tired she was missing something obvious. "How did Paul Schmitt work it so you quarreled with people?"

"Well, suppose someone your husband thinks of as a good friend tells your husband he better start using a condom because you want another baby and you've quit taking your little daily pill? And then this 'friend' comes to you acting all concerned and says he thinks you ought to know that he and your husband went to this whorehouse together and your husband now has a social disease. So you think your husband's using a condom because he's got the clap, and your husband thinks he better use one if he doesn't want another mouth to feed, which he can't afford. And this 'friend' tells your husband to tell you that he's using condoms because he heard that the brand of birth control pills you're using isn't always effective, and then he tells you that he heard your husband say the lie he's gonna tell you is that he's using condoms because he heard there's a bad batch of birth control pills out there."

Betsy, trying to keep track of who she was supposed to be and fuddled by all the pronouns, said, "You mean this was happening to you? I'm not sure I understand what Paul was up to with all this running back and forth."

"He was causing serious trouble between Danielle and me. I mean, pretty soon I was ruining my back trying to sleep on the couch and Danielle was dropping ninety-pound hints about rent-a-slut, which I didn't understand. And the kids were looking like refugees from a war zone, which it just about was at our house. I will never, ever forget the day my wife made me sit down for a talk and there it came to us, we figured the whole thing out. It wasn't me, it wasn't her, it was Paul, him carrying lies back and forth to the both of us. That was the biggest relief I ever felt, it was like I'd been drowning and got saved at the last minute. I actually thought I was going crazy there for a while, my whole life was coming apart and I couldn't figure out why. And all the while it's this bastard who's pretending to be my friend—and all I can figure for a reason is because he saw me kiss his wife!"

"You also think he played that same kind of game to ruin the relationship with your brother and father?"

"I don't think, I know it. Jory and me was tight like Siamese twins all our life, but Paul played him and my dad first, just like he played me and Danielle later. He convinced me Jory wanted Dad's business all for himself, and told Jory I wanted him out, and told Dad we both wanted to give him the shove. I never even heard of someone doing what he did, not in real life. While it was happening it was like a combination *Twilight Zone* and one of those spy novels where everything's a double cross." He held his watch up to catch the light and said, "I can't talk anymore, I got to get back to the line."

"Thank you, Mr. Miller," she said, but it was to his back, because he'd already turned to walk away.

Betsy was shivering with more than cold on her way back to the Wagoneer.

"What'd he say?" asked Morrie as she climbed in.

"He's either totally paranoid or Paul Schmitt was a dreadful, cunning person." She repeated Alex's story.

"What do you think?" asked Morrie.

"He's sure he's telling the truth. And I'm halfway to believing him. I've already gathered that Paul was a jealous, suspicious man, always prepared to believe someone was making a play for Angela. And back in junior high he had a talent for getting other people in trouble."

Morrie asked, "Did you ask Alex where he was the night Paul was killed?"

"No, why?"

"You *are* tired, Kukla. If Alex figured this out while Paul Schmitt was still alive, he had one hell of a motive."

"But he said he didn't start figuring it out until things started to straighten out on their own."

"And that may even be true."

Betsy rode in a thoughtful silence all the way home.

It was nearly midnight before they got back, which meant a second night Betsy did not get enough sleep; and this time not even the thought that Morrie had to be at work an hour before she did comforted her.

The story of her window would not appear in the newspaper for another week, but word apparently was spreading anyway, because the next morning there were two customers Betsy had not seen before waiting at the door. They wanted the dreidel canvases.

Four more followed soon after, one wanting a knitted Christmas stocking pattern, the bright-colored wool, the bobbins, and a pair of knitting needles. She said she hadn't knitted in years, but the window had inspired her to knit one for her grandson. The others were regulars, but they, too, remarked that the window was exciting to see, and one signed up for Rosemary's January knitting class.

Jill, currently working nights, came in yawning, saying she was shopping before going to bed. She bought some Kreinik gold cord and stayed to look at a new shipment of hand-painted canvases. She lingered over an M. Shirley canvas, a big tree in winter with small birds or animals on every branch. It was complex, beautiful—and four hundred dollars. Phil, a retired railroad engineer, came in to pick up a kit he'd ordered, and sat down at the library table to open it and make sure all the colors were there in the right quantity. He soon had that dreamy look all fiber fondlers get as he sorted, smoothed, and straightened the flosses, knotting them onto a floss stick, plotting his angle of attack on the pattern. Jill sat down to talk with him.

Two more women came in to buy the snowflake pattern, and another wanted the Hunger Moon pattern. Betsy was making a note to order more copies of both when the door made its annoying *Bing!* sound. Betsy looked around to see who was coming in, and didn't even notice the little silence that fell, because she was herself immediately focused on the tall, handsome stranger standing right inside the door. He was somewhere in his thirties, dressed in a fleece-lined leather jacket that was either old or expensively "distressed," a white turtleneck sweater, and Dockers pants. His hair was dark, falling casually over a broad forehead. His eyes were dark, too, with early signs of laugh lines around them. His firm jaw was marked with a trace of beard shadow. His mouth was wide with a hint of sensuality, his shoulders filled the jacket, and his stomach hinted at six-pack perfection under the sweater.

In Los Angeles or New York, he'd be an actor or a model trying to become an actor. Here in Excelsior, Minnesota, he had to be someone's husband.

Betsy looked around to see which of her female customers was looking at him possessively. Everyone, of course. Even Godwin. Especially Godwin, who was the first to move, heading toward him, lips eagerly parted. But the man brushed past him to stop at the desk and say, "I'm looking for a counted cross-stitch pattern of a dog, just the head, preferably." His voice was slightly rough-edged, perfectly designed to tickle in private places. "I saw in the Spring preview of *The Stitchery* magazine that Stephanie Hedgepath does any breed to order, but I accidentally threw my copy away, and don't know how to contact her."

Betsy almost said, "Huh?" just to get him to talk some more, but got a grip and said, "I keep the more popular patterns in stock, including Hedge-path's. Which breed are you looking for?"

He smiled, happy to reply, "A golden." Because about every third purebred in America is a golden lab.

"I'm sure we have several patterns you could use."

She went into the back to help him sort through the rack of cross-stitch animal patterns. His hands were broad with slightly knobby fingers, and without a wedding band. *He can't be married,* thought Betsy; *no wife would let a husband who looks like this wander around with a naked third finger.* Several of her customers decided they were interested in animal patterns, too, and came to look. Interestingly, one of them was Jill, whose only usual foray into counted was small Christmas tree ornaments.

Godwin hovered, making helpful noises. Even Sophie, the fat shop cat, came to rub gently around the man's calves—but perhaps she thought there was a sandwich in his pocket.

The man selected a pattern of the head of a golden lab, a piece of green evenweave to do it on, a set of stretcher bars, and a needle threader—"I'm into rotation, so I keep a threader on each project." The only sign he gave he was aware of the stir he was causing was the wink he gave her as he paid for his purchases. He strode to the front door and was gone.

"Strewth!" exclaimed Godwin, one hand splayed across his chest. "Who was *that*?"

"I never saw him before," said Betsy.

"He paid with a check," said Jill. "Read his name off it, will you?"

"Oh, he's got to be Elmo Slurp or something equally awful," said Godwin. "There has to be *something* imperfect about him."

"I don't think so," said Betsy, putting it in her cash drawer and shutting it firmly. "The imperfection here is that each of us has a perfectly nice boyfriend."

"Oh, yeah," sighed Godwin. And Jill gave a little nod, as if waking from a pleasant dream.

"I'm available," announced Phil, who had gone to the window to watch him drive off. "Not that I'm gay, but did the rest of you notice he drove off in a Porsche? Hell, *I* might consider converting for a rich man who does counted cross-stitch."

Laughter broke the mood satisfactorily. But Betsy said, "Goddy, can you come back and show me that trick with the coffee urn?"

There was no trick with the coffee urn, it was what Betsy said when she wanted to talk to Godwin out of range of eavesdroppers.

"Sure," said Godwin, following her back.

Betsy shut the door. "Are you all right?" she asked.

Surprised, he replied, "Yes, I'm fine." He felt his forehead worriedly. "Why, do I look sick?"

"No, not sick, but your reaction to that handsome customer made me wonder just how bad things are between you and John. You've told me before he gets upset if he thinks you're flirting with someone else. If this is how you behave around good-looking men, maybe John is right to feel threatened."

"Oh for heaven's sake, there's no rule that says a man can't *look*! Anyway, there's nothing seriously wrong between John and me right now. Well, nothing newly serious. Not *that* serious."

"Goddy. . ." Betsy was pulled between compassion and annoyance.

"There's nothing you can do about it. There's nothing *I* can do about it, either. He's so cruel and suspicious right now, he *drives* me to behaving badly! He'll get over it, he always does. It's just that when he's like this, I get to thinking what it might be like with someone else. Someone like—"

"Mr. Lightfoot?"

"Is that his name? Too *dreamy*! What's his first name? Where's he from?"

"His first name is Rik, spelled *R-i-k*, and he's not from Minnesota." This wasn't exactly true. His check had been printed with a Montana address, but lines had been drawn through it and a Minneapolis one handwritten beside it. His bank was a national chain with local branch offices.

"Where, then? Iowa? Wisconsin?" Betsy put on her best poker face. "Oh, not farther? Where, then? I don't remember an accent. Don't tell me he's from Atlanta!"

"I'm not going to tell you, or anyone else."

"*Wait* a minute." Godwin's blue eyes narrowed. "I thought you didn't take out-of-state checks."

"Perhaps in his case, I made an exception." But her cheeks burned, and Godwin grinned.

"He *is* local, isn't he? Well, well, well, I wonder who's in line to have his heart broken, John, Lars—or Morrie?" He fluttered out.

Betsy followed more slowly, thinking. How deep was her affection for Morrie when a pretty face—all right, a truly gorgeous face, not to mention body—could turn her head like that?

The shop remained busy until a little after one, when it abruptly became empty. Betsy had had a cup of coffee and a slice of untoasted raisin bread for breakfast and her stomach began making nonnegotiable demands for lunch. She said to Godwin, "I'm going to run down to the Waterfront Café for a sandwich, then to the pet shop to get some cat food. Can I bring you a sandwich or something?"

Godwin said, "If the café has a nice-looking apple, buy me one, otherwise I'll take three ounces of bunny kibble." He pinched at his waist. "I'm up two pounds and the holiday season is on the horizon." He flexed his upper right arm, squeezing it tenderly with his fingers. "I'd better rejoin my health club, too. This pretty boy doesn't want to get all flabby."

Godwin, barely but still in his twenties, was engaged in a struggle to stay seventeen, which meant slim but not skinny, athletic but not muscular.

Betsy went out into the chill and walked briskly down Lake to Water Street, then up half a block to the small café on the other side of the movie house. She went in and was greeted by name by the young woman behind the counter and two late-lunch customers. Two women sitting in a booth raised their hands in a tentative wave. Betsy sat in the single booth under the front window.

The Waterfront Café's feature that day was their hearty but not very spicy chili. Betsy had a big bowl further thickened with crackers—she was a cracker crumbler from way back—and a small milk.

She had only taken a few bites, when someone sat down across from her. She looked up and saw a slender man with light blue eyes and a thin mouth set in a face dusted all over with freckles: Detective Sergeant Mike Malloy.

"Well, well, Sergeant Malloy," she said. "What brings you in here?"

"You do. I went to your place and Mr. DuLac said you were here." He leaned forward. "What's this I hear about you?" he asked in a low voice—the Waterfront Café was Gossip Central in Excelsior, and he was obviously unhappy being seen even talking to her. Two customers sitting at the counter had swiveled their seats around to look.

Betsy replied equally softly, "What have you heard about me?"

"That you're poking around in the old Schmitt double murder."

"Do you object to that?"

Surprisingly, he grinned. "If you can prove once and for all who it was who killed Angela Schmitt and her husband, I'll be the happiest cop in the state."

"So it's all right with you if I continue to look into things?"

He sighed. "I'm not empowered to stop you. But I do want to warn you, this involves someone who has murdered twice. Someone who apparently still has the gun he used on Angela and then on Paul. You haven't got the training or the experience to deal with the kind of person who would do something like that."

"Thank you for being concerned—no, I really mean that. I know you think I'm a silly, interfering amateur, and in a way you're right. There are times I wonder what on earth makes me think I can do this. But it keeps happening, and I keep getting it right. If I do find things out, or have questions, may I come to you?"

He made a face and seemed about to say no, but changed his mind. After all, she had solved a couple of baffling cases. "What kind of questions?"

"Did you think at first, when Angela was shot, that Paul had done it?"

He shrugged. "You always look at the husband. He seemed nice enough, and he'd never been arrested for anything, but I never liked that smirk of his."

"What about his alibi?"

"Aw, it was okay, but I would've liked it better if someone had come into the gift store and seen him. There were some other oddities, too, but not enough to make an arrest. Then someone beat the crap out of him and then shot him with the same weapon . . ." He tugged a freckled ear. "That put paid to any idea he did it. Except . . ." He held out one hand, palm down, and waggled it slightly.

"What?" asked Betsy.

"If you weren't a damn civilian . . ." he said, and stopped yet again.

She decided not to argue with him. After all, she *was* just a damn civilian, with no badge or private eye license. She straightened in her seat and took a deliberate bite of her chili. It reminded her of her mother's chili; it even had elbow macaroni in it. She took a sip of milk, then dipped her spoon into the chili again.

"All right, all right," he grumbled as if she had been arguing with him. "There were powder burns on his trousers where he was shot, on his head, and on his hands. This means the gun went off very close up. This tends to mean self-inflicted wounds."

"But the beating wasn't self-inflicted, surely."

Malloy nodded. "I know. I thought maybe someone came and beat him up for killing his wife, and Schmitt shot himself after that person left, maybe with an eye to framing whoever beat him up. But who? And then where's the weapon? It's gone. It's never been found."

Betsy leaned forward to ask quietly, "Is it possible he could have thrown it out the door or out a window before he died?"

Malloy shook his head. "With a bullet in his brain? Not a chance. He was dead before he hit the floor." He shrugged. "Anyway we went over the whole property with a fine-tooth comb. The only possible conclusion is that someone shot him, and took the gun away with him."

"The same gun that shot Angela."

"Very probably. We never recovered the slug that killed her. It went out the window and, for all I know, fell into the back of a passing pickup and was carried away."

Betsy smiled incredulously. "Is that possible?"

He shrugged. "All I know for sure is, six of us looking damn hard couldn't find it. But we recovered the shell casings and they're all the same caliber and the mark of the firing pin on all of them is identical." He glanced around the café, but the men on the stools had turned away again.

"How conclusive is that?"

"Pretty good. Not as good as the marks the rifling of the gun barrel would've left on the slug, but pretty indicative."

Betsy took another bite of chili. "So what did you decide about the gunpowder burns?"

"That it was close-in fighting. A struggle for the gun."

"Did Paul Schmitt own a gun?"

"Yeah." He looked uncomfortable, and added, "See what I mean? This whole case has screwy parts to it. The gun was registered, and it's the same kind of gun that was used in the murders. And it's gone, too."

"Did Paul Schmitt report it missing before the murders?"

"No. He told us he had a gun when we first talked to him, but when we went to his house for a look at it, he couldn't find it. He said he had no idea how long it had been missing. I thought he'd tossed it away after using it on his wife, and I wanted to arrest him right then, but there just wasn't enough evidence."

She asked, "How sure are you that Foster Johns did it?"

For the first time, Malloy spoke in full voice. "Damn sure! He was on the scene of Angela's murder at the time it happened. We've got three or four witnesses to that. He has a half-assed alibi for Paul's murder, but I think he could have rigged that. I hauled him in and grilled him good, but he wouldn't break. So I had to let him go. I wish he'd leave town—just seeing him walking around free grates me hard."

There was a little murmur that ran around the café, and one of the men sitting at the counter grinned at the other.

Malloy left, Betsy hastily finished her chili and went to the checkout counter. There was a bowl of apples and pears sitting by the cash register, so she chose the biggest apple and paid for it with her bill. As she stuffed it into a pocket, she looked around the little café, and there in a back booth she saw Foster Johns looking like a man waiting to be hanged.

Twelve

Betsy went out into the chill air and up the street, past the beauty parlor and the bookstore. She paused a minute to look in the pet shop window. A lop-eared rabbit nosed about its low, wide cage, and two white kittens with blue eyes and just a hint of darkening on their ears and tails were tangled into a shifting, complex ball in their big cage. One was trying to chew the ear off the other. A bearded lizard in an adjacent aquarium was watching them with a beady eye.

She went in. The shop was warm, the air moist and redolent of small animals and pet foods. Canary and parakeet noises filled the air. The aisles were crowded with items—it was a small shop, but tried to meet the needs of a large variety of pet owners. Betsy went down the aisle that catered to cat owners, then to the front counter, where a curly-headed blonde was allowing a man in a raincoat to hold a friendly parrot on the edge of his hand. The bird was gray with a red tail.

". . . two thousand," the shop owner was explaining.

"Does that include the cage?"

"No, a good cage will run you another thousand. Plus you'll want some toys. African grays get bored easily, and they have a poor response to boredom."

"Hmmm," said the man.

"I looove you," crooned the parrot in the blonde's voice, and bent its head, asking to be tickled on the neck. The man complied and the bird made a low chuckling sound of pleasure.

"He's nearly two and already has a vocabulary of about a dozen words," said the shop owner. "We call him Gray Goose, but you can change that."

Betsy, thinking of Godwin being unhappy in front of customers back in her shop, and Foster being desperately sad in the café, said impatiently, "I can't find the Iams Less Active."

"It should be right beside the Science Diet Hairball."

"The Science Diet is there, but no Iams."

"I'll clip those for you if you like," said the shop owner to the man, who was now lifting the compliant bird's wing. She went back for a look and agreed there was no Iams Less Active on the shelf. "I've got some down the basement, can you wait a minute?"

"Sure," said Betsy. She went back to watch the man ask the parrot to step from hand to hand as if on a Stairmaster, which it did obediently.

But when four minutes had passed and the woman hadn't come back, Betsy went to the open basement door for a look. The steps were thick old wooden boards. There was only silence coming from down there.

Cautiously, Betsy started down. There were shelves and stacks of crates forming crooked aisles on the floor. The lighting was of the harsh fluorescent kind, but too widely spaced, so the place was full of sharp shadows.

Betsy heard a rustling and dragging sound from halfway down a dark aisle and started toward it. Then she stopped and stared. "Hey!" she said.

"What?" said the shop owner, turning around. She had two seven-pound bags of dry cat food in her hands.

"The basement of this place is *huge*!" Betsy could see through the backless shelf the pet food had come off of. There was a wall made of rough old boards, but the boards were badly warped, and the ceiling light shone through them into a big space beyond. And judging by where the basement stairs were, the board corresponded to the wall of the pet shop above.

"Oh, sure," said the shop owner. "My store is the middle of three in the Tonka Building."

"Tonka Building?" Like most people, Betsy went around gawking upward at buildings only on vacation. The buildings on this block formed a single solid row, and the entrances to each store were different in design, so she hadn't realized three were in a single building. Betsy's own building had three shops in it, but the building had open space on either side, making the arrangement obvious. Here, the Tonka Building was up against the next building, which was a beauty shop, which was next to the Waterfront Café. Were the beauty shop and café in a single building? Betsy had no idea.

This was for a moment merely interesting.

But if the pet shop was the *middle* of three, why, "Then Heritage II on the corner, your Noah's Ark, and Excelsior Bay books next door are all in the Tonka Building."

"Sure. And a CPA, a dentist, and a chiropractor have offices on the second floor."

"Are you saying it's possible to go from one of the three stores to another without going out in the rain?"

"Not through the shops themselves."

"Not now . . ." agreed Betsy, pausing hopefully.

"Not ever, there never were any doors," said the shop owner, handing Betsy a bag of cat food and picking up a third. She headed for the stairs. "Of course, there used to be gates between the board walls down here, but they were nailed shut years and years ago."

"Gates? There are *gates*? Are these walls original? Were there always gates in them? How long ago were they nailed shut, do you know?"

The woman stopped on the third step and turned to look at Betsy, surprised at her interest. Then she looked around the basement, thinking. "Well, it was divided like this when I started Noah's Ark, and that was nine years ago. I'm pretty sure the walls between the basements went up shortly after the auto dealership moved out of the corner store, and that happened in the early sixties, I think. The building itself dates to the forties."

"But when were the gates nailed shut?"

"They wouldn't open when I moved in, so longer ago than nine years."

"Oh." Betsy looked back along the shelves. They were sets of shelves rather than one long shelf, but were put right up against one another. They were made of dark gray metal with X bracing at the ends. They ran the parallel to the walls and formed two aisles. They were sturdy, which was good, because the one against the wall was crowded with bags and cans of pet food. That would, however, complicate the life of someone trying to come through from the gift shop. He would not only have to pry out the nails in the gate, he'd have to unload a shelf and crawl across it, then put it all back together again on his way back.

"Hold on a second, okay?" said Betsy. She went quickly to the other side of the basement and found the situation even worse for a potential crawler-through; the shelves were laden with heavy and frangible glass aquariums and goldfish bowls, big boxes of filtering kits and lights, and weighty bags of gravel.

"Come on, Betsy, if Goose hasn't bitten Mr. Winters, I think I've got a book-balancing sale waiting for me."

"All right," sighed Betsy.

But upstairs, watching Mr. Winters write out a very large check while his new friend chewed the buttons off the epaulets of his raincoat, she had another idea and said, "Excuse me, Nancy, but may I ask you something?"

"Certainly, in a minute. That's right, Mr. Winters, with tax that comes to two thousand, two hundred thirty-six dollars and fifty cents."

"Those shelves down in your basement. They're very nice. Where did you get them?"

"At Ace Hardware, right across the street."

Betsy nodded. Ace Hardware's building had suffered a fire and the store had pulled out of the building two years ago, but people talked about the hardware store as if it were still there.

Nancy continued, "I'm sure they're a standard item, so if you want to drive over to Highway Seven and 101, you'll probably find them at the Ace there. They're nice, because they're strong, easy to set up, and on sale. I can't remember how much they were, not that remembering would help, I've had them for about three years. Before that I only had a single row of wooden shelves down the middle of the room."

"Really?" said Betsy, and Nancy looked up from writing the sales slip, surprised that Betsy was pleased. "Listen, would you mind terribly if I went down for another look? Thanks, Nancy!"

Before Nancy could object, Betsy went back down the stairs. Over on the side with the aquariums—"Why didn't she put these in the middle?" grumped Betsy—she began very carefully lifting items off the shelf where the gate was. The shelves blocked access to the gate, but Betsy leaned into the shelf opening where the gate's handle would be. There were about two inches of space between the gate and the back of the shelf. Betsy grasped the handle—a thick wooden C that didn't operate a latch—and pulled gently. The gate didn't give. She pulled harder. Still no give. The reason why was right there, too; she could see the slotted backs of rusty metal screws that held the edge of the gate against its frame. Just like Nancy had said: nailed shut. Well, screwed shut.

Betsy backed out and carefully put things back where she'd found them.

She went back upstairs, where Nancy was explaining to a new customer that the black-and-yellow canaries were a wild variety whose song was prettier and more varied than the domesticated solid yellow.

She waved at Nancy as she went by, put seven dollars and change on the counter for the cat food, and hurried out. She went next door, to the bookstore.

"Hi, Ellie-Ann, I'm in a hurry, but I need you to do me a really large favor."

"Certainly, if I can."

"Let me go down in your basement and poke around a bit. I'll try not to move anything, and if I do, I'll put it back."

Ellie-Ann looked doubtful, but Betsy said, "It's about Angela Schmitt's murder."

"Oh, my God, really? Then go ahead, go ahead. Here, let me show you where the light switch is."

The entrance to the basement was through the far end of a storage closet behind the checkout counter, which was near the center of the north wall of the store. The stairs were concrete, and the basement was clean but cluttered, like a storage place not open to the public tends to get. There was a wooden plank table with a microwave and small office refrigerator on it, and in boxes all around were surprisingly few books, some bright book posters, a supply of stuffed animals and puppets (a feature of the Excelsior Bay Bookstore), props for their display window—Betsy recognized four slender, whiter-barked birch trees from last spring—and the teapots and coffee urns brought out for author appearances.

There was a clear space along the boards that divided the bookstore's basement from the pet shop's. Betsy found the gate to the pet shop near one end of the clear space. It didn't open to a push from this side, either, though there were no screws in evidence here. She looked across the pet shop space—Betsy had neglected to turn the lights off—and wondered if, in the gate on the opposite wall, there were screws on the gift shop side or the pet store side.

A voice behind her said, "What are you looking for?"

Betsy jumped and came down facing Ellie-Ann. "Mercy, you scared me!"

"Sorry. Is that what you were looking for? Yes, it's a door; no, you can't open it, it's been nailed shut since before I took over the store; yes, there's another one on the other side of the pet shop; no, it hasn't been tampered with, either." Ellie-Ann was obviously repeating replies to questions she'd been asked before. She smiled and explained, "Mike Malloy looked at it after Angela was killed upstairs."

"Ellie-Ann, what did you think of the investigation? Were they really thorough? Could they have missed something?"

"I'm no judge, of course. But actually, they did miss something. They had to come back and do a better search before they found it."

"Was it something to do with the gate?"

"How could it be something about the gate? It's there, it doesn't open. No, it was a shell casing. When Mike didn't find one the first time, he said the gun was a revolver. But they found shell casings at Paul's house after he was shot, so they came back and they searched some more, and they found one."

"That's interesting."

"Is it? It made me wonder if they didn't miss something else. I was pretty sure Paul shot Angela, y'see. That is, until I saw in the paper that Paul was murdered; and with the same gun, which they couldn't find. So I guess it wasn't another of those dreadful murder-suicide things."

"Did you know Angela was having an affair?"

"No. I suspected she and Foster Johns were attracted to each other. He developed an interest in books he hadn't shown before Angela started to work here, and she always seemed especially pleased to see him. But I had no idea it was a real affair. I don't know how they managed it. Paul kept such careful track of her, it was ridiculous." She added, almost irrelevantly, "Paul did some good things in that gift shop, but he was rude to browsers. Once he insulted a man dressed in dirty jeans, who turned out to be the mayor's brother, visiting from Arizona, and a very wealthy man. He'd been helping Odell paint his boat when he suddenly remembered it was his wife's birthday." She chuckled. "He came in here instead and bought a copy of every book about Minnesota I had in stock and asked if there was a jewelry store and a flower shop in town, and left at a fast trot."

Betsy tugged at the wooden handle of the gate, which still refused to move. "Why were there gates here in the first place?"

"I don't know," said Ellie-Ann. "Maybe in case of fire?" She shrugged. "The man I bought the bookstore from said the doors were nailed shut when he moved in, and that was eleven years before I took over, and that was six years ago. So it's at least seventeen years since you could go from one basement to the next."

Discouraged, Betsy went upstairs to retrieve her bag of Iams Less Active. As she went out the door, Ellie-Ann called, "Betsy?"

"Yes?"

"Please, solve this one, will you? Angela was a sweet person, and she didn't deserve to die."

Thirteen

The next morning Betsy, feeling much fresher after a good night's sleep, came down to find another new customer waiting in the doorway. She was an elderly woman in a long, dark blue coat, a red knit hat pulled down over her ears. She huddled close to the door because, while the sun was shining painfully bright, there was a cutting wind blowing and the temperature was in the mid-twenties.

Betsy hastily unlocked the door and let her in. "Good morning," she said. "Come on, sit down. If you can be patient a few minutes, I'll finish getting open for business. There will be hot coffee or tea soon, too."

"Thank you," said the woman, easing herself gratefully into a chair at the library table and pulling off her red mittens. Sophie jumped up onto "her" chair, the one with a powder-blue cushion, and looked the customer up and down briefly before deciding this was not a Person With Goodies. The cat settled down for a nap.

Betsy busied herself with lights and cash register, then went into the back, and soon the warm smell of coffee brewing wafted into the shop.

"Now," said Betsy, coming back to the library table, "what can I do for you?"

The woman said, "My name is Florence Huddleston, and I am a retired schoolteacher. Alice Skoglund said I should come and talk to you, because Paul Schmitt was a student in my seventh-grade English class many years ago."

Betsy pulled out the chair next to Ms. Huddleston, turning it so it angled toward the woman, and sat. "What can you tell me about Paul?"

"Nothing as an adult. But I remember him quite well as a seventh grader. He was a bright boy but an average to poor student, because he was lazy. I once told him he should grow up to run a charm school, because he could be very charming when it suited him, and he was forgiven too often. But his real talent was in laying the blame for his misdeeds onto others, and for getting others to behave badly while maintaining his own—what is the modern word? Deniability. I'm certain these traits continued into adulthood, as many do. Certainly they seemed innate in Paul. And another thing: He wasn't really brave, of course; people like him never are. But he had a curious ability to ignore pain that made him seem brave. He once broke his left wrist in a lunchtime wrestling match, but on his way to the nurse's office he stopped in my classroom to say why he wasn't coming back this afternoon. He pulled that horrible arm out of the front of his shirt and displayed it like a trophy to the two girls I was tutoring. There was no doubt it was broken, it was swollen and the fingers were purple. But he so enjoyed shocking and frightening me and the girls, he couldn't resist the opportunity."

"He doesn't sound like a very charming boy to me, if he could do things like that."

"Surprisingly, even I sometimes found him charming. He was very popular among many of the students and even some teachers. He was generally helpful, taking half of a load, opening doors, picking up after people, and he was always smiling and polite. That charm was as real as his deviousness. But I remember he used to fascinate a certain set of boys and even some girls with a gruesome collection of true crime stories."

Betsy, blushing faintly because of her own helpless fascination with crime, sat back to absorb this for a moment, then asked, "You didn't by chance know Angela Schmitt—well, she wasn't a Schmitt back then—the girl who married Paul?"

"Angela Larson. I know she was in my class, but I can't remember her at all. She came into the classroom on time, did her homework, scored well on tests, but never volunteered anything in class. Teachers love students like her, the invisible ones, because they make the larger classrooms bearable. I only know about her because I looked her name up in my class records after she was murdered. According to my diary, she was a B-plus student who wrote a rather good paper on *The Mill on the Floss*."

"How about Foster Johns? Was he also a student of yours?"

"Yes, he was." The old woman touched her mouth with slender fingers, picking her words carefully. "He was a very bright young man, but aggressive, impatient, and hotheaded, a dangerous combination. He was a very competent artist, but he wasted that talent drawing cartoons of, er, scantily-clad women with extraordinary physical endowments. He was funny and popular, but with that streak of wildness, I often wondered how he would turn out. I was pleased to learn he'd tamed his creative talent by going into architecture, but sadly disappointed to discover his impetuous affair with a married woman, and worse, that his temper led him to murder both his mistress and her husband."

"So you think Foster Johns murdered Paul Schmitt?"

"Yes, of course, and Angela as well. Isn't that what you have set out to do, prove it once and for all?"

"I'm trying to discover the truth, and I'm not convinced Mr. Johns is guilty."

"Whom else do you suspect?"

"Well, did you have the Miller brothers, Jory and Alex, in your class?"

"Not Jory. He heard I was very demanding about grammar and he signed up with Mrs. Jurgens, who allowed vernacular and even ungrammatical language and phonetic spelling. Alex was forced to take my English class because Mrs. Jurgens's class conflicted with a shop class he wanted."

"What an extraordinary memory you have!" Betsy said.

Ms. Huddleston laughed gently. "I do have a good memory, but most of what I'm telling you came from the diaries I spoke of. I went back through the years pertinent to your investigation before coming to talk with you."

"I'm pleased you kept them, then," said Betsy.

"Oh, they are often useful to me. Whenever I hear about a person's success, it is a special joy to me to look in my diaries and find I not only gave him high marks in my class, I predicted his future success. And when someone does something shocking, I will look to see if I predicted that, as well. I'm not always right, but more often than mere chance would have it. I think character is formed early."

"So what did you write about Alex Miller?"

"That he was not nearly as interested in the mechanics of good writing as he was in auto mechanics. That he was touchingly loyal to his friends and family, and would probably go into some kind of partnership with his brother when he came to adulthood."

"Yes, too bad about that," said Betsy.

"Well, as I said, these predictions of mine don't always come true."

"It nearly did; he wanted to join Jory with his father in his auto service company, but someone instigated a quarrel between him and them."

"Do you know who the instigator was?"

"Alex says it was Paul Schmitt."

"But Paul and Alex were close friends when they were my students! I remember that because I thought no good would come of it."

"And that's probably what happened. There was a breach when they were in their twenties, and Alex now blames Paul for setting his brother against him, and causing his plans to go into the family business to fall apart. The quarrel was very serious."

"So you think it's Alex rather than Foster who might have murdered Paul?"

"He was still murderously angry at Paul when I spoke to him two days ago, and Paul has been dead for five years."

"Oh, dear. That's so dreadful. Do you think it possible that Paul was in fact responsible for the breach?"

"I'm afraid I do."

"Oh, my. Oh, if you are right, that is truly dreadful." She stared at the surface of the library table. "I knew Paul was a troubled child, and I was afraid he'd have an unhappy life. But I didn't know it was to be so short. It was bad enough to think that two flawed youngsters such as Foster and Paul crossed paths to the deadly injury of one of them, but to think that Paul is responsible for an essentially decent fellow to go so terribly wrong, that is indeed a tragedy."

She stood. "I had intended to buy a kit of Christmas ornaments from you," she said. "But I no longer have the heart to work on them. I'm sorry."

"I'm sorry, too," said Betsy. "Perhaps at a later date. Christmas is still nearly two months off. Meanwhile, won't you have a cup of coffee or tea before you go? It's so cold outside."

"No, thank you. I think I'll just go on home now."

Betsy watched her going up the street seemingly unaware of both the cheerful sunlight and the cold wind that whipped around her.

Godwin had the day off and the part-timer scheduled to come in had the flu, so Betsy had to work alone that day. Her customers seemed more impatient than usual, and more inclined to take things off the racks or shelves and put them down anywhere (even into their pockets and purses). They didn't like her herbal tea, the coffee was too weak (never mind that it was free), and why didn't she have the Mirabilia pattern the customer had driven all the way from Anoka to buy?

The talk with retired teacher Ms. Huddleston colored her morning. On the one hand, it saddened her, because it reminded her the people she was investigating had once been children full of promise, who were hotheaded and impetuous, malicious and manipulative, loyal and unscholarly, rambunctious and impatient. Character forms early, Mrs. Huddleston had said. So on the other hand, trying to see the hopeful child that still lived behind the eyes of her demanding customers helped Betsy stay friendly.

Toward noon she went into the back to get down a new package of foam cups from a high shelf—only special customers got the fancy porcelain ones—when the step stool wobbled and she grabbed at a lower shelf to steady herself. The shelf, which held the aforesaid porcelain cups, as well as containers of imitation and real sugar, cans of coffee and tea, stir sticks, and creamer, broke loose. Down came Betsy, the shelf, and its contents—and the three-gallon coffeemaker, which was half full of very hot coffee.

Betsy yelled in fright and pain, and the tiny back room was immediately jammed with all five customers present, who got in one another's way and shouted contradictory orders at her and one another.

Betsy managed to get her feet under her and with a faint cry of, "Hot! Hot! Water!" pushed through the little mob into the restroom where, sobbing, she turned on the cold water and tried to cool her burning arm.

Once that was taken care of, she looked down at her red knit dress, bought new barely a week ago. Coffee and wet grounds had made huge dark patches all over it. Unless it went into cold water immediately, it was ruined. She'd have to go upstairs and change.

But how, with a shop full of customers?

Wait a minute, hadn't one of the customers been Bershada? Bershada, the retired librarian, who therefore knew how to deal with the public.

She opened the door a few inches to peer out, looking for a dark face wearing glasses. And found it.

"Bershada, could you do me a big favor?"

"I hope so," said Bershada. "What is it?"

"I have to go change clothes. Could you possibly watch the shop for just five minutes? You don't have to collect any money, just answer questions until I come back down. And maybe keep anyone from leaving with merchandise they haven't paid for yet."

"Sure, I can do that."

Betsy slipped out the back door and down a short corridor to another door that let into the entrance hall of the apartment stairs. She hurried up.

Her keys were in her pocket, and in two minutes she was in her bedroom, stripped to her underwear. Which also had to be changed. She put her dress into the bathtub and turned on the cold water while she went to get dressed.

But there was no time to rinse out her hair, which was damp on the back and right side. "There must be no coffee on the floor down there, I think I soaked it *all* up!" muttered Betsy.

Four minutes later, resplendent in jeans, chambray shirt, and head scarf, she went through the back door into her shop.

Where she was met with applause and laughter.

"Well, I know I've got a heavy clean-up job ahead of me," she announced. "I might as well dress for it."

The rest of the day was as if every customer present at her accident went home and phoned her friends, who all decided they had to come and laugh at Betsy looking awful and stinking of coffee. Bershada, apparently lonesome, hung around and answered needleworkers' questions.

But of course, having come in, the curious had to buy something. Business was brisk, which almost made it worthwhile.

It got to be quarter to three. Betsy still hadn't had a chance to clean the mess in back, and she was getting really hungry. She was about to phone the deli next door to ask Jack to bring her a sandwich, when Jill came in with an aromatic paper bag. "Tomato rice soup from the Waterfront Café, which is rocking with stories of your fall from grace," she announced.

With it came half a grilled cheese sandwich, which Betsy ate first, for an immediate dose of fat and carbs. The soup came in a large round carton. Betsy declined a spoon, electing to drink it straight.

"Ah," she sighed after three big gulps. "That's better. Jill, have you met Bershada Reynolds? She's going to be coming to Monday Bunch gatherings now she's retired. Bershada, this is Jill Cross."

"Officer Cross," said Bershada in greeting, adding to Betsy, "She's given me a traffic ticket or two."

"Around the station house we call her Miss Leadfoot," said Jill gravely.

"Well, it's hard for me to decide which of you is my brightest star," said Betsy. "One kept customers from walking off with my shop and the other kept me from dying of hunger. Thank you both."

Bershada was still laughing when she left the shop with her purchases. Jill said, "How bad was it?"

"Was? Still is. Take a look, I can't find a minute to even start picking up. It's all the fault of that one stupid shelf. It broke as soon as I took hold of it."

Betsy drank more soup while adding up the purchases of another customer. Jill came to report, "That shelf can go back up. And the urn doesn't appear to be broken. You'll need to buy more supplies, though."

"I'm glad about the urn, but I think I'll replace the shelf with something sturdier."

"No need to, really. Just use heavier nails—or better, wood screws. You can even use the same holes if you use wood screws thicker than the original nails. That way you won't have to get in there with that imitation-wood paste."

Betsy stared at her.

Jill smiled. "What? You don't know about wood paste? Or wood screws?"

"Sure I do. But Jill, you are a genius, you showed me the way!" Betsy was so excited, she lost the thin veneer of Minnesota restraint she'd grown the past year and gave Jill a big hug.

Jill politely allowed it for a short while, then disentangled herself. "I don't understand," she said.

Betsy caught the eye of a customer over Jill's shoulder and said, "That's a DMC skein of floss you're holding, Mrs. McLean, please don't put it in with the Anchor colors." Then she leaned forward and said quietly, "Both Nancy and Ellie-Ann used the word 'nailed' when talking about the gates leading from her basement to the pet shop basement—the bookstore and pet store and gift shop are all in one building, did you know that?"

Jill nodded.

"And that there are gates between the barriers set up between the basements?"

"No, I didn't know that."

"The gates were nailed shut years and years ago, so while Paul Schmitt could have gotten into the basement of the gift shop, everybody decided he couldn't get through the pet shop basement into the bookstore basement."

"Okay."

Betsy continued, "But when I looked at the door to Ellie-Ann's basement, it's not nailed shut, it's screwed shut. And when you just now said you could put bigger screws into the nail holes, it struck me." A customer came up with a cross-stitch pattern and a fistful of DMC floss, so there was a pause while Betsy wrote up the sales slip and collected the money. Then she said, "Don't you see? That's why Paul was 'bone dry' when Mike went to talk to him about Angela. He didn't have to go out in the rain to get to the bookstore, he went through the basement. Back then Ace Hardware was selling wood screws right across the street."

"But surely even Mike would have noticed that the screws were new."

"Oh," said Betsy, frowning. "Well, the screws I saw were rusty, but of course this happened five years ago, so they would be."

"Unless . . ." said Jill.

"Unless what?"

"If Paul was a handyman, one of those people with a shop in his basement or garage, he probably had a tin can full of old screws and nails. Lars does, and my dad did, anyone who does work around his house does."

"Paul did carpentry work well enough to get paid for it," said Betsy. "So, see? That could explain it, couldn't it? Of course it would have taken time to put those screws in. Did Mike go down in the bookstore basement right away?"

"I don't know. I wouldn't think so."

"How soon after he got to the crime scene did they go looking for Paul?"

"Not right away, I wouldn't think. In fact, I know they didn't. They still hadn't when I got there. I was called in to guard the back door, as I told you, and arrived about fifteen minutes after I was called, which was probably half an hour after Mike got there, which was probably twenty minutes after the patrol officer arrived."

Betsy nodded. "Plenty of time for him to screw those doors shut before they came looking for him."

Jill said, "But he wouldn't know he had that much time."

"He wouldn't need that much time. I'll bet he didn't do both doors, you know, just the one between the bookstore and the pet shop."

"You're right, that's the one Mike would go to, and if it wouldn't open, he wouldn't try the other—why should he?"

"Especially if the screws holding it shut were old and rusty. I'll bet he did the one door and hurried back upstairs. He wouldn't want to be found missing at the gift shop when they came looking for him. There was plenty of time later to go down and screw the second gate, between the pet store and the gift shop, shut. Is this enough to take to Mike, Jill?"

"He likes corroborative evidence, not just theory."

"Like what, after five years? If only there was a way to find out if he had a can of rusty screws around the place!"

Jill smiled and said, "I used to know the couple who bought his house. The man is Jack Searles and I went to college with his sister. Even better, the wife is Paul's cousin, or second cousin. She may be able to tell you something useful."

"So the house is still standing?"

"Oh, heck, yes. Or at least it was a couple of years ago."

"Do you know them well enough to visit them and bring me along?"

"I think so. When do you want to go?"

"How about tonight, after I close up at five? When do you have to be at work?"

Jill moved out of the way so Mrs. McLean could buy her mix of DMC and Anchor floss, saying, "I'm doing the graveyard, so not until midnight. All right, I'll phone them as soon as I think up a reason."

After Mrs. McLean was out of earshot, Jill said, "So you're thinking Paul murdered Angela."

"Yes."

"So who murdered Paul?"

"I'm not sure yet," said Betsy.

Jill said, "If Foster Johns thought Paul murdered the woman he loved, he had a powerful motive to kill Paul."

"Yes, but you weren't here when we were telling ghost stories on Halloween. Comfort Leckie said she saw Paul Schmitt's ghost in the bookstore the night he was killed. She said it bent down, straightened, then disappeared. I don't think it was a ghost, I think it was Paul planting the shell casing Mike found only after a second search—after Paul was shot."

"Why would Paul go back two days later to plant a shell casing?"

"To frame someone else for the murder."

"Who?"

"Foster Johns. He made sure Foster was out of sight while he planted the casing and then set the other part of his plan in motion. I think he planned to shoot this other person and blame Foster. But after Paul lured him to his house, the person took his gun away from him and killed him instead."

"And you think you know who that person was?"

"I think it was Alex Miller."

"Why on earth would Paul want to kill Alex Miller?"

"Because he caught him kissing Angela. It was perfectly innocent, but Paul didn't think so. He went to an enormous amount of trouble destroying Alex's relationships with his father and brother, and was working on breaking up Alex and his wife when this happened. I think he hated Alex—and Alex didn't even know it until long after. I think when Paul needed another victim to complete his frame-up of Foster, he naturally thought of Alex Miller."

Fourteen

Just before closing, Morrie called. "What's this I hear?"

"Did Jill call you?" Betsy asked indignantly.

"Call me about what?"

Betsy hesitated. "Why did you call?"

"Because I heard you tried a crash landing in the back of Crewel World—which is a very appropriate name, I think—and ruined your nice red dress."

"It's not ruined. Or at least I hope not. It's soaking in cold water and Orvus. I'll wring it out later and see."

"That's good. Now, what would Jill have told me if she'd called?"

"How should I know?"

"If I may be so bold as to quote Ricky Ricardo, 'Looooo-see, what are you up to?'" Morrie did a pretty good Cuban accent.

"All right, I'm going out to visit the people who live in what was once Paul and Angela Schmitt's house. Jill's taking me."

"What do you think you'll find out there after a lapse of five years?"

"I'm not sure. Why did you call?"

"I wanted to take you out to dinner."

"Not tonight."

"Tomorrow?"

"Yes, all right. About six-thirty?"

"See you then, sweetcakes."

"God, he's nice," said Betsy, climbing into Jill's big old Buick Roadmaster an hour later.

"Who?"

"Morrie. He's taking me out to dinner tomorrow."

"Where to?"

"I didn't ask. We did Italian last time, so probably to a steakhouse."

"Has he ever cooked for you?"

"Once." Betsy chuckled. "That's when I learned why he's so thin."

They went up Water Street, away from the Excelsior Bay of Lake Minnetonka, turned right at the top onto County 19 and followed it back around until the lake came into view again.

Lake Minnetonka isn't exactly one lake. It's more an awkward sprawl of seven lakes all run together, and the little towns that once dotted its border have nowadays pretty much run together to form a single town four hundred miles long and a quarter of a mile wide.

Navarre begins a little before County Road 19 joins County Road 15. Coming up 19, a big gray board sign reads "Navarre" and under it "City of Orono." Spring Lake is around the corner on 15, with its own smaller sign (though it's actually a bigger town) announcing that it, too, is both Spring Lake and City of Orono, and at the other end of Spring Lake is Mound, City of Orono. Orono is a small city that has done on a small scale what many of its big sisters have done: grown until it engulfed its neighbors.

The streets of all three towns followed the meandering lakeshore, and were a maze of curves and dead ends. Betsy was glad Jill was driving, because in the early dark she was hopelessly confused a minute after they turned off the highway. But Jill went confidently down this street, up that street, turned onto this lane, and pulled into an asphalt driveway, up to a two-bay garage.

Peering into the dimness, Betsy saw an ordinary gray clapboard house, probably built in the 1950s as a little summer cottage. A partial second floor had been added, and a new-looking mud or utility room now connected the garage and the house. The nearest house was at least fifty yards away, and a number of mature trees obscured its shape.

"Handyman's special," remarked Jill as they went up a newly-laid brick walk and up two cement steps to the little porch, whose roof was held up by two raw timber beams.

The door frame looked new, but the window beside it had its original and inadequate shutters. The clapboards were also original, made of wood. Jill rang the bell, which pealed in three impressive notes.

The door was opened by a very fair girl about nine years old. "Hi, Ms. Cross," she said. "Won't you come in?" She saw Betsy and added hastily, "And your friend, too."

"Is your daddy home yet?" asked Jill as she and Betsy shed coats in the small entrance hall. A narrow stairway with white balusters rose ahead of them. To their right was an open doorway leading into a sparely furnished living room.

"Yes, he's in the kitchen with Mommy making hors d'oeuvres. That's what he calls 'em, but I think they're just crackers and funny-tasting cheese." She led the way into the living room, which, Betsy saw, had a brick fireplace with a raised hearth surrounding it on three sides. A small fire was burning merrily—a gas fire, Betsy noted, licking around a pair of imitation logs.

Jill and Betsy sat on a couch facing the fireplace, and the child went to sit on the raised hearth.

"What's your name?" asked Betsy.

"Kaitlyn Marie Searles."

"How old are you?"

"I'll be ten on December fourteenth."

"How long have you lived in this house?"

Kaitlyn had to think about that. "When we moved here, I was in second grade."

"So about three years."

"I guess so."

"Do you like this house?"

"Oh, yes, it's got lots more room than our apartment. And we have a great big yard, and we have a boat and everything."

"Do you know who lived here before you?"

The child turned solemn, and nodded. She nodded toward the floor in front of the fireplace. "That's where it happened."

"What happened?" asked Jill.

Her voice fell to a very soft whisper, which she aided with elaborate mouth movements. "The murder."

"Who was murdered?" asked Jill in an interested voice, leaning forward to make a friendly conspiracy of the conversation.

"A man named Paul Schmitt. He was my mommy's cousin. This used to be his house. Someone shot him with a gun, right here in this room. Everything was washed and they even painted it before we came here, but . . ." She leaned sideways and put her finger into a big chip taken from a brick in the top row of the hearth. "See that?"

Jill and Betsy craned their necks. Jill said, "Yes, I do. Can you see it, Betsy?"

"Yes. What is it?"

'That's from a bullet."

"It is?' Jill looked very impressed.

Betsy went for a closer look. The chip was substantial. She said, "Who told you that?"

"No one," said the child. "Daddy said it is not from a bullet, but Mommy said that chip wasn't there *before*."

"Before what?"

"Just before. I think before Paul Schmitt was . . . *murdered*. Mommy used to come here to visit Paul Schmitt."

Testing, Jill asked, "Did Paul Schmitt have a wife?"

"Yes. I think she was murdered, too, only not in this house."

The child was beginning to look nervous, so Betsy said, "This looks like a nice house for pets. Do you have any?"

"Yes, we have a cat and a dog."

"Do you? I have a cat, too. I bet my cat's bigger than yours. My cat Sophie weighs twenty-three pounds." Betsy formed a shape with her hands to show the immense dimensions of Sophie.

Kaitlyn came back stoutly. "Okay, but I bet our dog is bigger than your cat. He's a chocolate Lab, except he's not real chocolate, he's just the same color as chocolate."

"If you have a grown-up Lab, he probably weighs as much as three Sophies."

That tickled Kaitlyn, and she was still laughing when her parents came into the room.

"What's so funny?" asked Mr. Searles.

"Toby weighs as much as three cats!"

"He weighs as much as six cats, you mean."

Betsy said, "I have a cat that weighs twenty-three pounds."

Mr. Searles stared at her. He was an average-size man with light brown hair surrounding a bald spot. His face was long, his eyes blue and kind. He wore relaxed-fit jeans and a green sweater. "In that case, it only takes a cat and a half that size to make one Toby."

The notion of half a cat tickled Kaitlyn even more. Her father put a tray of crackers with dollops of a melted cheese mixture on the coffee table. "Kaitlyn, go help your mother bring in the drinks."

"You're being too kind," said Betsy. "We weren't expecting to be treated like company."

He raised an eyebrow at them, meaning they should wait until Kaitlyn left the room before continuing.

Once the child was gone, he said, "She doesn't know."

Betsy said, surprised, "Doesn't know what?"

"That my wife's cousin was murdered in this house."

Betsy looked to Jill for guidance. Jill said, "Kaitlyn was showing us the chip taken out of the hearth of your fireplace the night Paul Schmitt was murdered in this room."

"Oh, jeez," he said, and dropped into an easy chair at right angles to the couch. "How much does she know?"

Betsy said, "She knows that Paul was shot to death in this room, and that his wife was murdered elsewhere. She didn't seem troubled by the murder of Paul, but instead rather thrilled by it. She does seem a bit bothered by Angela's murder."

Jill said, "That may be because she doesn't know as much about it. She may think there is something especially awful about her death, or something somehow threatening to you or Mrs. Searles."

Betsy asked, "Where are your other children?"

"Alan's at a Cub Scout meeting. Jessica is staying overnight at a neighbor's. They don't know . . ." He grimaced. "I *thought* they didn't know anything about this. But if Kaitlyn knows—she's the second oldest, and a blabbermouth—then I suspect they all know."

"How did you come to move into this house?" asked Betsy.

"My wife's mother and Paul's mother were sisters, their parents' only children. Paul's parents are divorced, and his mother is remarried and living in Ohio. We'd been trying to save for a house, but with three children, it was slow going. This house was notorious and they were having trouble finding a buyer. We put in a very low bid, they offered a contract for deed, and so far, so good."

"It looks as if you're making improvements, too," noted Jill.

"Some." Searles nodded and looked around the room. "Some were done by Paul. He tore down half a wall to put a built-in china closet in the dining room, remodeled the kitchen at least once, enlarged the garage, and installed the gas log. That last one I really appreciate. We all love a fire, but I hate chopping wood."

"About that chip on the hearth," began Betsy.

"Yes, I keep saying I'm going to replace it, but it's pretty low on the list right now. It's not a functional defect. We don't know what it's from."

"Kaitlyn said your wife said it wasn't there, quote, before, close quote."

"It wasn't there when she visited the house, or at least she doesn't remember it," said Searles. "But she hadn't visited here for months before it happened. There wasn't any, er, that is, the place was all cleaned up when we moved in. No bloodstains, no broken furniture, nothing to show what happened here."

"No ghosts?" asked Betsy.

He gave her a funny look, but shook his head. "No one's reported anything."

"Here we are!" caroled a woman's voice, and Kaitlyn came skipping sideways ahead of her mother through a swinging door. Mrs. Searles carried a tray on which were four mugs and a steaming pitcher. The air warmed with the scent of apples, cinnamon, and cloves.

The mugs were filled and handed around. "What were you talking about before we came in?" asked Mrs. Searles.

"Little pitchers," said Searles.

"Little pictures of what?"

"The kind that have big ears," said Searles.

"Oh. Kaitlyn, Mommy and Daddy want to have some grown-up talk with these two ladies. Do you think you could give Toby a walk in the yard for a little while?"

"Okay, Mommy."

Searles made sure he heard the back door close before he explained to his wife that Kaitlyn, and probably the rest of the children, knew about Paul Schmitt's murder. "She told Jill and her friend that the chip taken out of the hearth was probably done by a stray bullet."

Jill had risen while Searles was talking and gone to look into the fireplace. Now she stooped for a closer look at the chip.

Mrs. Searles said, "I never said anything like that to her, of course. Anyway, I thought it was done during the fight, Paul's head striking it, maybe."

Jill said, "If a man's head hit this brick hard enough to break it, there would have been no need to shoot him. I'm no expert, but this doesn't look like it was done by a bullet. There's no trace of lead, for example. And no other mark of a ricochet—were these doors new when you moved in?" Jill indicated the brass-framed glass doors of the fireplace.

"No," said Mrs. Searles. "I remember them from way back."

"Then I'd say this is from a hammer or other tool, maybe done when the gas fire was being installed."

"Really?" said Mrs. Searles. "Well, then, Bob, you're off the hook." She explained to Jill, "I've been nagging him to replace that brick, it bothered me to look at it."

Betsy said, "Do you remember visiting Paul's workshop on a visit out here?"

The woman nodded and took a sip from her mug. "Mmmmm, this came out really good! But I couldn't tell you much about his shop, I really don't know much about tools."

"What I was wondering was, did you notice that he kept old nails and screws? A lot of carpenter types do."

She frowned and took another drink while she thought. "Oh, you mean in jars? He did this clever thing where he nailed the lids to the underside of a shelf and screwed the jars onto the lids. That way he could have glass jars he could see into but without the danger of knocking one over and getting broken glass all over the floor. He had nuts and bolts and nails and screws all separated in them. He was a very neat person, and clever, too."

Betsy asked, "Were the nails and screws bright and new or old and rusty?

"Both. Some were new, some were rusty."

Betsy smiled and took a deep draught of her cider. "Ummm, this *is* good!" she said.

Mrs. Searles said, "I just remembered, that chip couldn't have happened when the gas log was put in. The last time I was here, it had just been installed, and there wasn't that chip out of the brick. Angela really liked that gas log, she said something about not having to sweep the bricks anymore since they didn't have shaggy logs on the hearth, and I distinctly remember noticing how clean and smooth the hearth was. She was *such* a good housekeeper!"

On the way home, Betsy asked, "Did you mean it about that brick being chipped by a hammer, not Paul's head or a bullet?"

Jill nodded. "Yes. Or a piece of flying furniture. You know, I looked around, but didn't see any other evidence of a violent man. Maybe they patched the walls and replaced the windows."

"Was he the sort who broke things?"

"Mike Malloy said he was. They thought at first the murderer had broken down the back door to get in the house, then realized the door had been broken well before the murder. Very typical. Paul being a handyman kept rumors from being spread by a steady stream of repairmen."

"It's a good thing the Searles aren't the kind inclined to see ghosts. I think that place would give a sensitive person nightmares."

Jill smiled. "Do you believe in ghosts?"

"Sure. Don't you?"

Fifteen

❊

Around nine the next morning Betsy was pouring a second cup of English Breakfast tea when her phone rang.

It was Foster Johns. "Have you found out anything?" he asked, hope painful in his voice.

"A few things," she replied. "For one, Paul's alibi for Angela's murder is no good anymore."

She explained and he fairly exploded with pleasure. "There! There it is! I was hoping against hope, and by God you've done it! I knew that bastard killed Angela, and now you've proved it!"

"I haven't proven anything, yet. All I've done is poke a hole in Paul Schmitt's alibi."

"Have you talked to the police about this?"

"Not yet. Sergeant Malloy isn't fond of amateur sleuths, though he hasn't ordered me not to investigate. He's even hoping I'll prove you did it."

"Let him hope," growled Foster. "What next?"

"I want to ask you something. Do you know Alex Miller? You went to school with him."

"Well, I remember him. Haven't seen him in a long time. Years. He has a brother who last I heard works with his father in his auto shop; his name's Jory."

"Yes, that's right, I talked with Jory and his father, and I've talked with Alex. Did you know both brothers?"

"You bet. They're a year apart, Alex and Jory, but they hung out together so much, people thought they were twins. They each bought a beater car in high school, and they were always swapping parts, trying to keep them running. After a while, I don't think they knew which car was whose, there were so many parts from each car on the other." Foster was chuckling at the memory.

"Do you remember that Paul Schmitt was also friends with Alex and Jory?"

That put an end to the laughter. Betsy could hear Foster drawing a long, be-patient breath. "Yes, I do remember that. Actually, we were all friends back then, Paul, Alex, Jory, and me. And three other guys, Max, Mark and Mike,

the 3M Company, they hung out with us sometimes, too. We played softball,
went to Twins games, pulled practical jokes on each other, talked about cars
and girls."

"Did Paul strike you back then as the jealous kind?"

"No, not particularly. But we didn't pair off like the kids do today, getting serious in sixth grade. Dating was casual for most of us; in fact, I don't
remember that Paul had a real girlfriend at all, until he met Angela. And that
was in college."

"Do you remember Paul getting angry with any of you?"

"Well, yes. Not viciously angry, not enough to quit hanging out with us
altogether. He'd be sore for a day, then pull some kind of prank, you know, a
practical joke, and we'd all laugh at the poor sucker he'd done it to, and we'd
be friends again. Well, except one time he really set up the 3M boys. I don't
remember all the details, it was kind of complicated, but Mike ended up on
suspension and Max actually transferred to another school. Mike blamed Max,
but Paul told us later he rigged the whole thing—whatever it was. I thought
at the time Paul started something that turned into more than he meant it to.
I do know he ran quiet the rest of the semester."

When Betsy went down to open up, there was yet again a figure
standing in the doorway, this time a Minnesota-style Valkyrie, a tall, sturdy
guardian of lives and property. But this one wore her armor under her shirt and
carried her weapon in a holster. In other words, Jill.

Betsy hurried to unlock the door. "Did you talk to Malloy? What did you
find out?" she asked.

"Mike says he checked the gate in the bookstore basement. He says it was
fastened shut and so he didn't feel a need to check the other gate. He recalls
being told by the owner of the building that the gates were nailed shut in 1973.
Note once again the use of the word 'nailed.' But he says it's possible that Paul's
alibi can be considered broken."

Betsy said, 'That's good, that's great! Anything else?"

"Not much. I read the report on Paul Schmitt's murder."

"What time did it happen?"

"The 911 call came in at nine twenty-seven."

"Okay, Alex works second shift now, but maybe he was working graveyard
or first shift back then. Can you find out?"

"If I call up there, they'll want to know who I am. When I say Officer Jill
Cross, they'll want to know why I'm asking, and what can I say? I'm not an
investigator, I'm not doing it because a supervisor asked me to."

"Jill—"

"No. You want to know, you ask." Jill wasn't speaking sharply, she didn't even look annoyed. But her cool, Gibson-girl face gave Betsy no hope at all.

"Turn the radio on for me, will you?" Betsy asked, and went to the checkout desk to haul a phone book out of a bottom drawer. She found the number of the Ford plant and dialed it. She said to the person who answered using her most brisk and impersonal tone, "Personnel, please." When a man from personnel got on the wire, Betsy said in the same voice, "I need a confirmation of employment for one Alexander Miller, please." This was the term credit card people used when they asked Betsy about her employees.

There was a pause while computer keys rattled faintly. "Yes, he's our second shift engine assembly line supervisor," reported the man in personnel.

"How long has he worked for you?" asked Betsy.

"Hmmm, twelve years."

"Always second shift?"

"Why do you ask?"

Betsy allowed her voice to soften. "Well, I've got a cousin who's working first shift and he has an idea he'd like to try second, now he and his wife have a baby. This way, they don't have to put him in day care. But I was wondering if people who work second shift stay with it. I mean, the hours are screwy, you're trying to sleep when everyone else is up, and so on."

She looked over and saw Jill staring at her with raised eyebrows, and looked away again, lest she start laughing.

The personnel manager said, "Well, I've never worked second shift, but Mr. Miller has been on it for seven years."

"Is he late a lot, or taking a lot of sick leave? I mean, Will is very reliable and all, but I'm wondering if that might change."

"I don't think checking just one record is going to help you much, you know."

"You know, you're right. I shouldn't be asking you all this, anyhow. His wife asked me for advice and I don't know what to tell her. He says the pay is better if he'll move to second shift, and they could really use the money."

The manager sighed. "Tell me about it. And for what it's worth, Miller takes all his vacation in one lump every December and he hasn't been late or off sick since he started that shift."

"Say, that's very encouraging." Betsy resumed her brisk voice. "Thank you very much. Good-bye and have a nice day." She hung up.

Jill, leaning against the box shelves that divided the counted cross-stitch back of the shop from the knitting and needlepoint front, said, "Girl, I had no idea you were such a con artist."

"Well, what else could I do? You wouldn't help me!"

"I take it the news is bad."

"Not for him. He was at work the night Paul was murdered."

"Ah. Too bad."

"Yeah."

"You're back to Foster, then."

"Yeah." Betsy opened the cash register and began to put the opening-up paper and silver into the drawer. "Alex did tell me he didn't know what Paul was doing to him until after Paul had been dead awhile. I was hoping he was lying." She mulled that setback over while the soft airs of something classical played on the radio. Then she asked, "Do you know where Comfort Leckie lives?"

"No, why?"

"I want to ask her something."

Jill murmured, "Bulldog, bulldog, rah, rah, rah."

"What?"

"Just glad you're not quitting. I'm sure she's in the phone book, why don't you call her?"

"All right, in a while."

Jill, smiling, said, "How about I buy you lunch in a couple of hours? You can tell me all about it."

Betsy laughed. "All right. But it's my turn to buy."

Comfort, it's Betsy Devonshire."

"Hello, Betsy. What's up?"

"I was thinking about your story of seeing Paul's ghost in the bookstore. Do you know about what time of the evening that was?"

"Let me think. It was such a long time ago . . ."

Betsy waited patiently, and at last Comfort said, "Near as I can remember, it was after six-thirty. It was dark—real dark, not the dark you get when the weather is bad, but I don't think it was as late as seven. It was windy, the wind turned my umbrella inside out. It was sleeting hard and had been for a while, there was slush on the streets and sidewalks. Is that what you wanted to know?"

"Yes, that's it. Thanks, Comfort."

"I take it you'll explain that question one of these days."

"I sure hope so. Bye."

May I special-order the linen?" Mrs. Hubert asked Godwin. She had just paid for several Marc Saastad iris patterns—she grew varieties of iris in her beautiful front yard, and the Saastad patterns were very accurate about varieties—and the expensive silks to stitch them. But Crewel World didn't have the high-count linen in the shade of green she wanted.

Godwin considered that. Special orders were a special pain for a small business. It cost twice as much per yard to order a small piece as it did to order five or more yards, plus there was the rapid-delivery cost, and of course the customer grudged the difference—and only too often found the fabric at another store before the special order arrived, or changed her mind altogether about the project.

"Can you pay in advance?" asked Godwin.

Now it was the customer's turn to consider the problems with that. "How much?" she asked after a pause. Godwin had already calculated the add-on charges, and named a price that included a small profit.

"I'll write you a check—can you get it before the fifteenth of November? We're leaving for Florida the twentieth."

"Certainly. I'll call Norden Crafts today." Godwin wrote up the order and phoned it in as soon as Mrs. Hubert left. He bantered a bit with salesman/owner Dave Stott and, so long as he had him on the line, placed another order for three more Kwanzaa patterns. Stott reported the linen was in stock, and said he might be able to get it in the mail yet today.

The door went *Bing!* a few minutes later, and so did Godwin's heart when he saw the incredibly handsome Rik Lightfoot come in.

"Hi," said Rik in his rich voice.

"Hi," said Godwin, batting his eyelashes furiously. "May I help you, I really, really hope?"

Rik laughed. "Down, boy, I'm heterosexual. I thought I had enough Anchor 308 for that lab pattern, but it turns out I don't." He went to the wooden cabinet and ran a forefinger down the sets of shallow drawers until he found the deep golden brown he was looking for. He bought two skeins and said, "Where's the lady who was behind the counter last time I came in?"

"She's at lunch. She's heterosexual, too."

Rik laughed and Godwin thought he'd melt right into his penny loafers.

"Is it true that the best bass fishing in the state is right here in Lake Minnetonka?" asked Rik.

"I've heard that," hazarded Godwin, who didn't know one of the biggest bass fishing tournaments in the country was held on the lake every year.

"Can people fish off the docks here?"

"Sure," said Godwin, who had no idea at all if that were true.

"I want to see if a technique I learned in Montana works here. You see, you skip your jig sideways so it goes under the dock, where fish hang out in the shadow of the boards, just like they hide around sunken logs or under water lilies." Rik made a sideways casting gesture and Godwin melted all over again at the display of shoulder and back.

"You make it sound really interesting," said Godwin fervently, leaning on the desk to get just a little closer to the man.

"Well, Minnesota makes a lot of famous lures, and with all those lakes, I should think just about everyone here likes to fish."

"Oh, I agree with that," nodded Godwin without mentioning he was an exception.

"It must be nice, living right on the shore of such a great lake."

"I love to go out on the water," said Godwin. "I get out there whenever I can in the summer."

"Of course, Mille Lacs is good, too," continued Rik.

"That's what I hear," said Godwin, whose only trip to that lake was to visit an Indian casino.

"Nothing like a fresh walleye. The best I ever had I caught in a Canadian lake that didn't even have a road to it, we had to fly in. Caught my limit in less than an hour. Used a spoon. Dropped it . . ." Again Rik made a casting gesture, this time forward, toward the door. "I barely started to reel it in when all of a sudden, *bam*, he hit that line and took off with it. I thought I was gonna lose him, he ran right up along the shore, wound himself around tree roots, practically buried himself in some big rocks. But I just set the reel and let him go, and pretty soon he came right back at me, and five minutes later he came alongside the boat, tame as a kitten, practically asking me to take him out of the water."

"How . . . interesting," said Godwin, a little desperately.

"I tell you, after eating those fillets, I just about swore off fishing back in the States. But it's the sport that draws me, I do a lot of catch and release now."

"I suppose that happens a lot," said Godwin. "I mean to people who have eaten walleye fillets, er, caught with a spoon in Canada."

Rik, enlightened, laughed. "Yes, you're right. Well, thanks for an interesting conversation—what's your name?"

"Godwin DuLac. Nice to meet you. Come back again when you need anything in the needle arts line."

He watched Rik go with a little sigh, and when Betsy came back from lunch, he announced that he had saved her from a terrible fate: having to listen to fish talk. "I tell you, I thought that man was perfect, he is *so* handsome and he does needlework and he drives a *Porsche*, for heaven's sake. But he not only fishes, he *loves* to talk about it. Do you know what he told me? He said he fishes with a spoon! Is that possible? Or did he see my eyes glazing over and start to spoof me?"

"There's a kind of fishing lure called a spoon," said Betsy, laughing at his woebegone expression. "So I take it he is gay?"

"Oh. Well, no, he said he was heterosexual when he heard me panting at his approach. But if you are wise, Betsy, when he comes in again, run for the back room or he'll start teaching you how to cast under a dock."

"All right," lied Betsy, who used to love to fish. "Anything else interesting happen while I was gone?"

"Well, I sold a set of Kwanzaa patterns, that's the third set, so I told Dave to send us three more. And—I hope you aren't angry about this, but I took a special order. I know you don't like them, but it's for Mrs. Hubert, and she bought all the silks as well as the patterns for three Saastad irises, plus she paid in advance." He held out the order.

"And she agreed to pay a premium for the fabric, so it's all right," said Betsy, looking at it. "But before it happens again, I want to try something Susan Greening Davis suggested, and call some other shops to see if we can't order some of this less popular stuff together. If I can get three others to go in with me, the order will be big enough to get a price break."

"But you don't have room for more fabric on your shelves," warned Godwin. "And you're already storing stock in the bathroom."

"I know. Goddy, do you think it would be a good idea to set up some storage shelves in the basement? I was thinking of moving all the household stuff out of there and putting the stock in that back room into the basement. I nearly broke my neck yesterday trying to reach that top shelf."

"I know. But if you start thinking you've got lots of storage room, next thing you know, you'll have way too much money tied up in stock."

"Hmmm." That was a good point. The temptation was to carry items no one else did. What fun it would be placing an order for some of the real exotica! But the intelligent way to offer a wider range of products was to expand, to move the deli or the bookstore out and take over the space, so the stock could be out on shelves for her customers to see and be tempted by. On the other hand, she was barely making ends meet in the needlework shop right now, while Jack and Fort were paying their rent every single month. Could she afford to take a big hit while her expanded store got on its feet? Not really. Maybe she should work harder on getting the present Crewel World farther into the black before considering expansion.

Of course, having made that decision, the next two customers each wanted uncommon patterns Betsy didn't carry. The idea of expansion remained a flickering hope in the recesses of her heart.

* * *

Where are we going?" asked Betsy that evening, as Morrie handed her up into his big Wagoneer.

"A place called Thanh Do."

"Vietnamese food." Betsy nodded, pleased. She had changed into a royal blue dress he liked on her because, he said, it showed how blue her eyes were. She carried a delicate shawl a shade lighter than the dress in case of drafts, but wore her heavy winter coat for the journey because the forecast was for temperatures to drop below thirty.

He got in on his side and said, "Not just Vietnamese, they do all kinds of Asian food. It's becoming very popular, and I think you'll like it." A true Minnesotan, he just wore a sweater-vest under a wool sports coat.

They drove up Highway 7 to just past Knollwood Mall in St. Louis Park, turned left on Texas and went to Minnetonka, left again and almost immediately turned into a parking lot beside a dry cleaners. The parking lot was narrow but deep and behind the dry cleaners was a two-window storefront with a modest green sign. "Thanh Do," it read, the A formed by a pair of red chopsticks. A red hibiscus bloomed in one window.

Morrie had made it sound fancier than this, but she didn't say anything—he was very reliable about restaurants.

They alighted and went in. A significant portion of the floor space was taken up by a life-size gray stone statue of Buddha as a slim young man surrounded by plants and bamboo. A table or altar with lit candles stood in front of the statue and a fat sitting Buddha was on it. The air was fragrant not only with the usual "Chinese restaurant" smells of hot sugar, garlic, ginger and meat, but also of herbs.

A waiter with blond hair and delicate metal earrings took them to a black Naugahyde booth in back. He left them with big ivory-colored menus that noted that all meals were cooked from scratch with fresh ingredients, so customers were asked to be patient.

"What do you recommend?" asked Betsy.

"Well, do you like seafood?"

"Yes, but only on the coasts, where it's fresh. Why?"

"Never mind."

Betsy looked and found the item he was hinting about, a teriyaki dish for two called Pacific Blue, containing shrimp, scallops, squid, salmon, and yellow-fin tuna on a bed of steamed vegetables and wood mushrooms. A pair of asterisks warned it was spicy. She was tempted, but the herb-scented air made her decide on single-asterisk Vietnamese basil chicken. Morrie chose a triple-asterisk curry dish and asked them to bump it up to four stars. She ordered a Chinese beer, Morrie a Beck's Dark.

"So how's the sleuthing coming along?" Morrie asked while they waited for their food.

"Paul murdered Angela, and I think I've figured out how."

"Tell me."

"You know he worked in that gift shop called Heritage II, on the corner of Second and Water?"

Morrie nodded.

"Well, Heritage and the pet shop next door and the bookstore next to that are all in one building, with a single basement."

Morrie's eyebrows rose. "You don't mean Sergeant Malloy doesn't know that."

"No, he knows it, he even checked on it right away. But there are board walls dividing the basement space according to the shop space overhead, and while there used to be gates between them, they were nailed shut years before the murder took place."

"Ah," nodded Morrie. "But you think . . . ?"

"Well, first of all, I thought it was odd he didn't come out to see what the commotion was about when the window of the bookstore was broken. After all, he took that job to keep an eye on Angela, so he'd be sensitive to anything happening outside and nearby. Even a thunderstorm doesn't make a racket every minute, and he should have at least heard the sirens. I think he didn't come out because he had to stay dry, so his alibi would work.

"You think he came through the basement spaces?"

"Yes. It's true, people will tell you, that these gates were nailed shut many years ago. However, if you go look at them, they are *screwed* shut."

"Screwed, nailed, what's the difference?"

"I think Paul concluded some while before the murder that Angela and Foster were in love, and that's why he decided to murder her. Then he waited for several things to come together. One was the storm. Rain or snow, it didn't matter, but it had to be wet out. I think he pulled the nails on those gates so he could get through to the bookstore, so he'd be bone dry when Mike Malloy went to talk to him after Angela was shot. It's possible he put the screws in, just in case someone tugged on the gates, but when conditions were right, he unscrewed them. It was Angela's night to close up, she was alone in the store. Foster had come by to wave at her. Paul went down through the basements, up into the bookstore, and shot Angela. On his way back, Paul screwed the bookstore gate shut—no sound of hammering, by the way—then went down late that night or the next day and screwed the gate between the pet shop and the gift shop closed. He used rusty screws he brought from home—I have a witness who saw the jars of screws in his workshop. His cousin, who now lives in his house, described how he kept a very neat shop, with new and rusty old screws and nails and such kept in separate jars."

The waiter brought their beer and frosty glasses and Morrie poured his professionally, down the inside of the glass, so it wouldn't form a big head. "I take it you've looked at the gates?"

"I looked in the pet store basement and in the bookstore basement. They are screws, not nails; they have that slot in the head. They're on the pet store side of the gate to the bookstore."

Morrie looked interested. "And are there, by chance, nail holes beside the screws?"

"No."

He winced with regret at scoring a point and looked away.

"But," said Betsy, "I had a shelf fall down in my shop the other day, and Jill told me to use wood screws a size bigger and put them in the nail holes when I put it back up. Paul Schmitt was a good amateur carpenter, he would surely think of that. And, since he used old screws, they weren't shiny new when Mike went to take a look at the gate. This isn't proof he murdered his wife, but you see how his alibi isn't worth spit anymore."

Morrie thought that over for a few moments. "Well, all right, you're right," he said. "How did you get the idea to go exploring in the basement, anyhow?"

She told him about the search for Iams, adding, "If you go down there today, you'll see the pet store has lined both walls with metal shelves crowded with stock—but that happened *after* the murder of Angela. But I'm not sure if I should go to Mike yet. What do you think?"

"Do you think he'll listen to you?"

"Maybe. I don't know. Maybe not. I wish I could convince him I'm just another informant. I'm sure he has informants."

Morrie grinned. "If you want to be an informant, you'll have to make him pay you for your information."

She laughed. "That's what my problem is, I've been giving him information for nothing, and he values it accordingly."

"What else have you found out?"

"I thought I had come up with an alternative to Foster for Paul's murder, but it turned out he has a really good alibi, given by a time clock." She told the story of Alex Miller's claim of a plot by Paul to ruin his life, and how she'd found out he was at work at the critical time. "So I guess Alex is in the clear, his alibi seems solid."

Morrie said, "But was Alex right about Paul's sabotage? That sounds a little elaborate for someone who isn't operating in a James Bond novel."

"Well, his middle school teacher remembers that Paul was a born genius at setting others up to take the blame for something he'd done, or getting them to do something against the rules; and Jory remembers Paul loving practical jokes, one of which involved injuring a cat. So that's why I'm thinking that Paul was killed while trying to frame someone else for Angela's murder."

"How?"

"Comfort Leckie saw his ghost in the bookstore the night he was murdered."

He stared at her. "Ghost? You're not going to tell me you believe in ghosts!"

"Of course I do, I've seen them myself. But listen to this." She repeated the story Comfort had told of seeing Paul's ghost in the bookstore.

"You think Paul's *ghost* planted evidence of some sort?"

"No, no. I think the living Paul did, and Comfort saw him doing it."

Distracted, Morrie asked, "What kind of a name is Comfort, anyhow?"

"It's an old pilgrim name, handed down since the seventeenth century to every other generation of women in her family. She's miffed none of her daughters gave it to one of their daughters. But that's beside the point. Comfort saw Paul *before* he was murdered, and what he was doing was planting the second shell casing. Mike didn't find the first one, you know. It went behind a shelf and wasn't found until they took the shelf down to replace it."

"Maybe she didn't see Paul at all, maybe she saw her own reflection in the window. People do that, and call 911 to report prowlers."

"That isn't what happened here. He turned sideways and she recognized him. The Monday Bunch thinks it's a ghost, and they're all moonstruck about it, saying Paul must have been very deeply in love with Angela."

"But you think . . . ?"

"Can you be married to someone you're stalking? He tracked her every movement, he even took that job at the gift shop so he could keep an eye on her at work in the bookstore."

"I see."

Betsy took a drink of beer and went on, "Mike Malloy searched the bookstore after Angela's murder and concluded she'd been shot with a revolver because he didn't find a shell casing. But there were shell casings in Paul's living room, and the bullets were the same caliber, so Mike went back to search the bookstore again, and this time he found a casing. Obviously, Paul planted it. Comfort saw him doing it."

He hid a smile behind a big, thin hand. "Hon, you don't even know it was him in the shop."

"Yes, I do. Comfort didn't think she was seeing a ghost, remember. She recognized Paul and wondered what he was doing in the bookstore. It was only later, when she heard about the murder, that she decided it was his ghost. And I'll tell you something else: I talked with Mike the other day and he said both casings came from the same kind of gun and they all have marks on them that make him pretty sure they were shot out of the same gun."

He sat back, defeated but still smiling. "All right, *mo chroíde.*" Morrie called Betsy by different endearments, trying to find one they both liked. "But why did Paul Schmitt want the cops to know the same gun was used in both murders?"

"Because he was going to frame Foster Johns for the murder of his wife."

"How?"

"I think he was going to shoot someone else with the gun he used to kill Angela, and since the bullet from Angela's murder had gone flying out the window, he needed the shell casing for them to compare. But Mike couldn't find the bookstore shell casing. So he fired the gun and went to plant a new shell casing."

"But he didn't shoot someone else, someone else shot him."

"Come on," said Betsy, "he didn't know he was going to end up dead! I think he arranged for Foster to be alone in his office that night so he'd have no alibi. Then he invited another person to come over to his house. I think the plan was to take that person to Foster's building, murder him there, and leave the gun for the police to find."

"Or her," corrected Morrie gently. "Maybe he planned to murder another woman."

"No, only a man could win a knock-down battle with Paul. Because that's what happened. He got into a fight and the person took his gun, shot him, and ran away."

"Who was this person?"

Betsy grimaced. "Since it's not Alex Miller, I don't know."

"Well, consider this. Maybe the person Paul planned to murder was Foster. Maybe Foster's lying about Paul telling him to wait in Foster's office. It's not a very good alibi, you know. I'm sure Foster could have faked it."

"I know." She lifted and set down her beer bottle on the white paper table covering, making a series of overlapping circles. "I've been thinking the person who fought with Paul was Foster Johns. Except . . ."

"Except what?"

"I just don't think he did it."

This time he didn't bother to hide his smile.

"Don't laugh at me," she protested, but she was making a rueful, amused face herself.

"I wouldn't dream of laughing at you, not with your record," he said. "But I was thinking what my boss would say if I came to him and said I didn't want to press an investigation because I had a feeling the suspect didn't do it."

"But surely you get feelings about suspects!"

"Sure I do. Often. Sometimes I'm sure a suspect did it, and sometimes I'm equally sure a suspect didn't. Sometimes I'm right. But those feelings are more than instinct, they come from experience. You haven't been at this long enough to learn if your feelings are always right."

"I know," she sighed, sitting back in her padded seat. "But Foster Johns was so careful and, and *scrupulous* over putting that new roof on my building. I talked with the city inspector about him, and he said Foster Johns has a reputation all over the state for honest dealings. He follows the rules, he said, he insists on an independent inspector, and he only hires sub-contractors who agree to do things over if they aren't perfect. How could someone as honest as that be a murderer?"

"Well," said Morrie, leaning back in his own seat, "if I did something horribly against the law and wanted to get away with it, I'd obey the laws and follow the rules and mind even Miss Manners forever after."

"Hmmmm," conceded Betsy, turning her beer bottle around by the neck to draw a wavy line through her circles. "A middle school teacher, now retired, came to the shop the other day and told me about Paul, Jory, and Foster, all of whom she taught English. She kept diaries of her classroom days and recalled Foster as an impatient, aggressive seventh grader. He certainly is none of those things today."

Her expression was troubled, and he said, "Look, dear heart, your interest in crime is not so much to discover the culprit as to see justice done, right?"

Betsy nodded.

"Well, perhaps it already has. If Paul Schmitt murdered Angela and tried to frame Foster Johns for it, and Foster killed him, then the scales are in balance. Perhaps you should withdraw from this one. If justice is your game, then Mum should be your name. Go home and tell no one what you've found out." He made a little motion in front of his mouth, as if turning a key. "Tick-a-lock!" he said. "Look, here comes our dinner."

Sixteen

Thanh Do's Vietnamese basil chicken was so fabulously delicious that Betsy couldn't do anything but make delighted little humming noises for a while. There were big pieces of fresh Asian basil strewn among the chicken tenders, and pineapple chunks and streamers of sweet onions in a delectable brown teriyaki sauce.

Morrie had to stop and blow his nose after every three bites of his fiery curry, which was making Betsy's eyes water clear across the table.

"Where did you learn to like food that hot?" Betsy asked when she was able to form a thought that didn't have the word "basil" in it. "Certainly not here in Minnesota, which thinks a dash of fresh-ground pepper is going wild."

Morrie nodded. "My first wife and I used to vacation in Texas every winter for about ten years. Their Tex-Mex food is wonderful, but hot enough to melt horseshoes. I actually tried to wrangle a job down there, with Houston PD, but didn't succeed."

"I'm glad," said Betsy.

"Me, too, now." He smiled at her in a way that made her heart turn over.

"Do you always fall in love this easy?" she asked.

"No. You?"

"Oh, gosh, yes."

He stopped eating to stare at her, and very slowly his face began to change, from surprise to disappointment, to sorrow, to deep, deep sorrow.

At first embarrassed, she soon began to giggle. He heaved a despairing sigh, incandescent with curry, and she became helpless with laughter.

When he pulled a handkerchief from his pocket to touch his eyes, she lay down sideways on the seat, and there, unable to see his brokenhearted face, she regained control. "Are you finished?" she asked from that position.

"Yes," he replied in a voice with a sad catch in it. "Sit up, people are staring."

She came up to see him eating his dinner with a satisfied smirk. "Idiot," she said.

"Tell me a ghost story," he said.

She told the one about Cecil's ghost haunting the house his granddaughter owns. "When the house was being remodeled to accommodate a wheelchair, Cecil would steal tools, slam doors, and wreak some kind of breakdown on the man's pickup . . ." She stopped suddenly to think.

"What?"

"I wonder how long ago it was that that happened."

"Why, is that important?"

"Probably not, but wouldn't it be strange if the carpenter was Foster Johns? He started out as a carpenter, then got into construction, and is now a general contractor."

"Are you thinking that these women played a trick on Foster?"

"No, no, nothing like that. This is a small town, and so there are lots of connections among people. Carol and Sue have been living together for sixteen years. Carol didn't say the carpenter's name. That's kind of sad, isn't it? She has this wonderful story, but she can't say it involves Foster Johns without spoiling it."

"Tell me another ghost story."

"Just let me finish this little bit here first," said Betsy, and ate some more. She was disobeying the rule slender women follow: Eat only until you're not hungry anymore. But she wasn't slender—and obviously the maker of that rule had never eaten Thanh Do's Vietnamese basil chicken. "Is everything here as good as this?"

"I haven't been disappointed yet."

"Your turn, tell me a ghost story now," she said.

"I don't know any ghost stories. But you said you've actually seen a ghost, so tell me about that."

"The bright and good one, or the scary one?"

He considered. "The scary one."

"We were camping, my parents and my sister and I. I think I was eight or nine years old. I don't know where we went, it wasn't a campground with a building that sold ice and soft drinks and charcoal starter, but a forest with no road into it, or even trails. We drove for hours, it seemed like, and arrived near sundown, and had to walk back in for a long time, carrying things. We came to a clearing in the woods and put up the tents by lamplight. I remember there were owls, two owls, hooting back and forth. Dad dug a shallow hole and we built a wood fire in it and we roasted weenies and marshmallows. He and Mama talked about themselves as children, and what school was like and what they did for fun. Mama said a favorite thing was to take an old wallet and put green paper in it so it looked nice and fat with money, and put a rubber band around it and tie a length of button thread to it and put it on the sidewalk, and when someone would reach for it, yank it back, then laugh like anything. She laughed again when she told us about it." Betsy shrugged.

"Every generation has its own sense of humor. Have you noticed that cartoons aren't funny anymore?"

Betsy said, "Boy, are you right! If I want to enjoy a cartoon, I have to wait for the Bugs and Daffy Hour."

"That wasn't much of a ghost story," said Morrie.

"I hadn't gotten to the ghost part yet. Let's see, oh, yes, parents' stories about their childhood. Well, Dad told about a brown-and-white pinto pony his father had as a boy that would rear up and strike at anyone who came near with a saddle. Only Granddad could ride it, and he had to ride bareback. It was a menace in the barn, sneaking a bite if someone got within reach of it. Except it loved Granddad and never bit him. That night I went to bed simply wild to have a pony of my own that no one but me could ride."

"Still no ghost," noted Morrie.

"Be patient, my dear. We had two tents, one for our parents, one for Margot and me. I woke up very early the next morning, convinced I'd heard a pony neighing not far away. I was absolutely positive that pony was white with big brown patches and that it would let me ride it. So I got out of my sleeping bag, put on jeans, T-shirt, and sandals, and went out looking for it. I listened and heard it neigh again, and started for it. Every time I'd get discouraged, I'd hear it again, and pretty soon I was a long way from the camp. I kept thinking about how much fun it would be to come back to the camp riding my spotted pony, which I felt I pretty much had to do, because I remembered my parents had warned me not to leave the camp alone, so I needed a spectacular excuse.

"At last I came to a meadow, but it wasn't the one we'd parked the car in the night before. And there wasn't a beautiful brown-and-white pony grazing in it, either.

"It was about then it stopped neighing, so I decided it had been a ghost pony, haunting the meadow and crying for its old owner to come play with it again.

"But I'd been wandering the woods for so long, I didn't know where I was or which way back to the camp. I started walking aimlessly, got into some brambles, and fell a few times. Some mosquitoes found me, and invited all their friends and relations to come and feast. The woods seemed dark after the sunny meadow, and I started to feel afraid. I couldn't find the tents. I just kept walking and crying and even praying. Then I saw a big box turtle. I loved turtles, so I knelt down and stroked it and cried some more, because I was really scared and getting very hungry. And so long as I was down there, I prayed really hard, and when I stood up, there was the camp on the other side of some bushes, not twenty yards away.

"I came running into camp bawling and woke everyone up. It was only about seven-thirty, I must have gotten up before six. My mother wanted to know why on earth I went off into the woods like that, and I told them about the pony, and Dad said there wasn't a horse or a pony for miles."

"How did he know?"

"He didn't say, but I'm sure we didn't just pull off the road and go camping in some stranger's woods," said Betsy. "He must have known the area."

"Still . . ." Morrie looked skeptical.

Betsy sniffed loftily. "I told the story of that ghost pony at camp, and it was very well received."

Morrie laughed. "You made that up! Well done!"

"The getting lost part wasn't made up," said Betsy. "Once when we went camping, I went out for an early-morning walk and got lost and stooped to play with a box turtle, and when I stood up, there were the tents. When I told that story in camp, I added the ghost pony and said I went out later looking for proof of the pony and guess what I found?"

Morrie said solemnly, "Horsefeathers!"

That set Betsy off into another peal of laughter. "I wish I'd thought of that when I told that story!" she said when she was able to speak again. "The best I could do was to say I found an old, rusty horseshoe just the right size for a pony's hoof."

The waiter came by. "Do you want to take that home in a box?" he asked, looking at the platter, which was still nearly half full.

"All right, thank you," said Betsy.

She was quiet on the ride home.

"A penny for that thought," Morrie said at last.

"Something . . . I said something, or you said something that triggered something, only I can't think what it is."

"Sleep on it. If you're like me, it'll come to you in a dream."

Betsy didn't know who the grinning bad man was, but he had a gun and he was going to shoot her if she didn't give him forty thousand dollars. She didn't have any money and went out on the street to look for some. And there on the sidewalk was a fat billfold full of money, but every time she stooped to reach for it, it leaped away. She finally threw herself down and grabbed it with both hands, but it resisted and finally worked itself loose from her fingers, as if it were attached to something by a rubber band.

She woke up to find herself sleeping on her belly, crosswise on the bed, one arm reaching out. "Maybe I should have tried the curry instead of eating all that basil," she muttered, straightening herself around, pulling the sheet and blanket back into place. She pushed the little button on her watch, whose face obediently lit up. Four o'clock. She had another hour and a half to sleep—today was early-bird water aerobics day. She rubbed her forehead and composed herself for sleep.

No good. She got up, grumbling.

The stupid dream had her wide awake.

Sophie, wondering what she was doing awake at such an hour, came to ask if, so long as they were up, perhaps Betsy could give her loyal, loving cat a little snack? "Not a chance," Betsy told the cat. "If I feed you now at"—she checked her watch—"four-ten A.M., my God, then when I do get up at five-thirty because it's Friday and I have early-bird water aerobics, you'll have very conveniently forgotten all about this, and want your breakfast. Again. It may also cause you to decide this is customary, rising at four to feed the cat. But it isn't, so I won't. Now, go to your basket and take a nap. Shoo."

Having after countless lessons learned that Betsy could not be cajoled away from *no* when it came to food, the animal did as she was told; except she didn't take a nap, but leaned on one elbow to stare at Betsy with her yellow eyes at half mast, thinking resentful, self-pitying thoughts.

Betsy ignored her and sat down in an easy chair, turned on the standard lamp that stood behind it, and reached for her knitting, which lived in a big, bowl-shaped basket beside the chair. She had three projects under way and, considering the tired state of her mind, picked the easiest one, a thin blanket meant to be sent to Africa, part of a program her church was sponsoring. She was using an inexpensive acrylic yarn, not because she was cheap but because it could stand repeated washing, even in very hot water. There was no complexity to the stitchery, just knit and knit and knit—though she was changing colors every eight inches. But that was more to keep herself from being totally bored than to provide something a little less plain for the unfortunate individual who would sleep under it.

It took a great many stitches to get a width sufficient for even a narrow blanket, and even the promise of a change from mint green to tangerine in another three inches didn't help all that much. Betsy could knit much faster now than she could a year ago, but she was not yet up to a speed that would impress anyone but a beginner. The blanket was growing very slowly.

But after a few minutes she stopped noticing how slowly the work was progressing and fell into a state that was almost like meditation. Giving her hands something to do stopped that little voice that recited a list of things she should be doing: cleaning the bathroom, dusting, updating the books, reviewing her investments—she had an appointment with Mr. Penberthy next week, and he could always tell when she had merely glanced at them. That little voice was silent now because she *was* doing something.

On the other hand, what she was doing took about seven of her brain cells, which freed the rest to wander around and inspect the newest information she had logged into her head.

Funny how everyone had thought Paul killed himself when they first heard about his death. Jory had said Paul looked sick with sorrow over his wife's murder. Even if Paul had been obsessed rather than in love, it must have been terrible for him to have lost her.

And that would be true even if he had murdered her. Because if he had murdered her, it was because he thought he had already lost her, to another man.

So it would make sense for him to have committed suicide.

That was the ugly pattern in so many cases, a man kills his estranged wife, and then himself. Betsy thrust the needles angrily for a few stitches. What a stupid thing, that "take her with me" syndrome! Where did they think they were going? Were they suddenly some kind of pagan, thinking that in the afterlife she would be a loving spouse again?

But in Paul's case the evidence was clear, it wasn't murder-suicide. Paul may have murdered Angela, but someone else had killed him. Who? Some-one he had planned to kill, who turned the tables and killed him? Then why not come forward? Fear of arrest? People didn't go to jail for killing in self-defense.

Suppose Paul had been planning to murder Foster, and make it look like suicide. Had it been Foster at the Schmitt house? Was Treeny Larson right when she said it took only a few minutes to pull out those blueprints and papers to make it look as if Foster had been working for hours? Had Malloy gone over the papers, or had someone who really understood them looked them over, to see if they were merely random papers?

Foster Johns was happy because Betsy had broken Paul Schmitt's alibi. Betsy wondered if it was possible to prove that Paul had replaced the nails with screws. Perhaps, if the nails had been significantly longer than the screws. There would be a telltale hole that went past the end of the screw. She would have to tell Jill about that.

Rik Lightfoot was a bore about fishing, Godwin said. Betsy hadn't been fishing since—wow, was it really twenty years? More like twenty-five, actually. Anyway, he was much, much too young for her. When she had last gone fish-ing, he wasn't even a teenager yet. How strange it was, to be that much older than a grown man, and still feel the juices rise. She remembered something her mother said once, about looking in a mirror and wondering who that old woman was. "The heart stays young, Betsy," she'd said. And so it did.

Was Morrie surprised at the silver-haired man who looked back at him during the morning shave?

How nice it would be, to hear that faint scraping sound of a man shaving again, and smell the sweet-sharp scent of aftershave newly applied! Funny the things one missed when there wasn't a man in the house.

Rats, she'd dropped a stitch. She'd only gone two stitches past it, so she unknitted two and picked it up.

She thought about her dream, about the resistant wallet. Where had that come from? Of course, from telling Morrie the story of the practical joke her mother had played when a child. People must have been awfully dumb not to have seen that string. Just as she was, in her dream, not seeing the big rubber band that yanked the wallet out of her feeble fingers.

She was getting sleepy again. She folded the needles beside each other and stuck them into the ball of yarn. Yawning, she stood and stretched a kink out of her shoulders.

"A-row?" asked Sophie.

"Back to bed, Sophie," said Betsy. "Let's hope I don't go running after any more wallets in my dreams."

She massaged her scalp vigorously as she started back to her bedroom. Then she stopped.

Could it be?

"Ra-arow?" asked Sophie.

Betsy needed to talk to someone who spoke English. But who, at four forty-five?

"Jill!" Betsy said. Jill was still on nights at present, a thankless job in a sedate and orderly town like Excelsior; perhaps she might welcome an interruption. Jill carried a personal cell phone, which she could turn off while giving someone a ticket or taking part in an arrest. Betsy dialed the number and was pleased when she got a gruff, "Yeah?"

"Jill, it's me, Betsy. Have you got a minute?"

"What on earth are you doing up at this hour?"

"I think I know what happened to Paul. It all depends on where the gun is."

"What gun?"

"The gun Paul used to shoot Angela, and which was used on him."

"I thought no one knew where it is."

"I think I do. But you'll need to get a search warrant."

"I can't ask for a search warrant; I'm not an investigator. Anyway I'm not assigned to the case."

"Who is?"

"Mike for Angela's murder, someone in Orono for Paul's. What happened, what did you find out?"

"I went out to dinner with Morrie last night and then I had this dream about a wallet."

"Betsy, why don't you go back to bed and get some more sleep?" Jill could remember another time when Betsy got all excited about a conclusion she'd reached based mostly on wishful thinking and exhaustion.

"No, it's almost time for me to get up anyway, I have water aerobics this morning."

"Then tell me what it is you think you've figured out."

And Betsy did.

Jill, a patient listener, didn't interrupt. When Betsy was done, Jill said, "What if the gun isn't there?"

"Well, then, it's all snow on my boots. Gone with the first breath of hot air." For some reason that tickled Betsy a bit and she giggled.

"I don't know if we can get a search warrant based on just that theory."

"Then let's just go out there and ask if we can look."

"Not at this hour. No one with any brains is going to allow people to tramp all over their living room at five o'clock in the morning. Let me talk to

Mike in the morning, and if he's not game, I'll call Orono PD." Orono supplied law enforcement for its three suburbs, including Navarre.

Jill must have used all her powers of persuasion—more even than Betsy used in persuading herself to follow her morning routine and drive to Golden Valley for her exercise—because when Betsy came home, there was a phone message for her from Jill. And when she and Jill drove up to Paul Schmitt's old house about nine, there were three official-looking dark cars and a squad car waiting.

Mike Malloy was beside one dark car, looking uncomfortable and grumpy. He cast a skittish eye on Betsy, then went over to say something to the blue-jowled man in an open overcoat standing nearby. The blue-jowled man looked as if he'd been sent by central casting to play the role of a police detective. As Malloy looked at Betsy and laughed, the blue-jowled man rolled his eyes and lifted his arms a little in a tired shrug. Betsy felt a twinge of doubt and wished she was as sure she was right as she'd been a few hours ago. This immediately turned into a stab of anger. Of course she was right!

Jill, still in uniform, walked over to the pair, motioning Betsy to follow. She introduced Betsy to Sergeant Fulk Graham, Orono PD, in a respectful voice, but merely nodded at Malloy.

Then Betsy saw the real reason for this turnout: Morrie Steffans, looking nonchalant until he sneaked a wink at her. A senior investigator, he had the pull to convince these people to come around. Jill must have called him. Jill went next to talk to him, and her smile had a subtle element of triumph to it when she glanced toward Betsy.

Please, please, let me be right, thought Betsy. For the first time she realized that being wrong would not only reflect badly on her, it could put a major kink in Jill's career. But she took a steadying breath and went up to Jill.

"Has anyone knocked yet?" she asked.

"No, we were waiting for you," said Mike brusquely.

"Let's get this show on the road, can we?" said the Orono detective.

Betsy went up on the porch and rang the doorbell. She had phoned the house early this morning and caught Mrs. Searles in the confusion of trying to get her children out in time to catch their bus, and her husband off to work. Yes, she would be at home today, and yes, Betsy could come out and if Kaitlyn didn't stop feeding her toast to Toby, there would be no toast for her in this house ever again.

The kids had departed, as had the husband. The house was warm and smelled of bread rising and Lemon Pledge. Mrs. Searles had left the fireplace alone, as instructed. Morrie had a flashlight, but so did Betsy, and Mike, and Jill, and the Orono cop.

It was Morrie, being slim and having long arms, who got to twist himself between the glass doors and shine a flashlight up the chimney. He grunted and came back out, soot marring the snowy white of his shirtsleeves.

"There's something up there, all right," he said. "Looks like a cord of some sort. But no gun."

Mike frowned, but didn't say anything. He'd been wrong about the gates and just the presence of the cord was a point in Betsy's favor.

"Isn't there a ledge up there?" asked Jill. "You know, where the chimney narrows."

Morrie put the flashlight down on the hearth and twisted himself back into the firebox, one long arm reaching upward. There was a scrabbling, scraping sound as he fumbled for the ledge—and a surprised grunt when he found something.

He came back out with a large and very dirty semi-automatic pistol in a filthy hand. "Heck of a hiding place," he noted. "Might've gone off and hurt someone."

"Son of a bitch!" said Malloy.

"The one place we didn't think to look," said Fulk, staring hard at Malloy.

The slide was very resistant, but at last yielded and showed the gun to be empty.

"He used the last bullet on himself, because he didn't want it to go off and show people where it went," said Betsy.

"Who didn't?" asked Mrs. Searles, staring at the weapon.

"Paul Schmitt," said Betsy.

Seventeen

I will work here forever," promised Godwin, right hand raised, "but only if you tell us *everything*." He was sitting at the library table, his lunch of a chef's salad—dressing on the side—forgotten in the excitement. Beside him was Shelly, a schoolteacher who worked part-time during the school year—she was supposed to be at a teacher's conference today but called in sick when Betsy phoned to ask her to work.

Shelly had planned to miss just the morning sessions, but when Betsy came in all cock-a-hoop with news of a resolution, she decided the heck with it.

Jill was also present, tired but smiling, as were Alice and Martha. Betsy had called Alice on her way back from Navarre, asking her to come in for a "vindication." Alice had phoned Martha, who drove them both over.

And Foster Johns, sitting very still in a chair at the other end of the table from Betsy—but his stillness was that of a bottle of beer shaken hard and its open top covered with a thumb.

"It was Paul who murdered Angela," began Betsy. "He went through the basement from the gift shop to the bookstore."

"Wait a minute, wait a minute," said Martha. "I don't understand about Paul going through the basement. If it was that simple, how did Mike miss it?"

"The gift shop, the pet store, and the bookstore are all in one building," said Betsy.

"Yes, I know, it's the Tonka Building," said Martha. "That corner store started life as a Ford dealership, back in the late forties, early fifties."

"Anyway," said Betsy, "there's one basement under all three stores. Then some owner decided each store should have its own storage area, and put up board walls. But they cut gates through them, probably in case of fire, or so that if someone later joined two stores together, he could use all the space without having to come upstairs to get from one part to the next. But after that, someone nailed the gates shut, possibly to prevent theft."

"But if the gates were nailed shut, how did Paul get from the gift shop to the bookstore?" asked Shelly.

"Paul pulled the nails," said Betsy.

"And no one noticed?" asked Martha.

"No, because on his way back to his shop after he shot Angela, he put screws in the same holes, using rusty screws from his collection in his home woodworking shop so they'd look like they'd been in place for years. I noticed there were screws holding the gates shut even though everyone kept saying the gates were nailed shut. That didn't prove he killed her, but it broke his alibi."

"That's better than Mike could do," said Godwin.

"That's right," said Alice.

Betsy continued, "And when Mike Malloy searched the bookstore for clues, he missed another one, the shell casing that flew out of the pistol when Paul fired it. Paul needed that casing found to complete his frame-up of Foster Johns."

"Why?" asked Martha.

"Because when he shot Angela, the bullet went out the window and disappeared. The police can compare slugs, and Paul wanted it understood that the same gun that killed Angela was used in another murder. But shell casings are almost as good, and Mike didn't find the casing that flew out of Paul's gun when he shot Angela."

"But they did find a casing," objected Shelly. "In fact, they found two of them."

"No, at first Mike couldn't find any. Then after Paul was shot, and shell casings were found, he went back and looked again. This time he found one. The second one was found when the bookstore replaced some shelving. But only one bullet was fired in the shop."

"I don't understand," said Alice.

"Remember when Comfort said she saw Paul's ghost? That wasn't a ghost, that was Paul, planting a shell casing. Mike hadn't found the first one and Paul needed it found so he could frame Foster for the murder."

"Foster was *framed*?" exclaimed Martha. "You mean, he didn't murder Paul, either?"

"No, he didn't."

"*Hah!*" exclaimed Alice, smacking the surface of the table with a large hand.

"It was just what everyone thought it was when they heard Paul was dead," said Betsy. "A murder-suicide. Paul shot Angela and then himself. But he decided to play one last vicious practical joke by framing someone else for both deaths."

"Oh, are you *sure*?" asked Martha in a terrible voice.

"Yes," said both Betsy and Jill together.

"Oh, but . . . Oh, that's terrible, because . . ." She bit her underlip and fell silent.

Betsy continued, "I think Paul first intended the police to think Angela was killed in a robbery, but when he shot her, the bullet went out through the front window, drawing immediate attention, so he fled down the stairs, pausing only long enough to drive a wood screw into the nail hole on the pet store side, so when Mike went down there, the gate was fastened shut. If Paul had taken time to break the lock on the back door, the notion of a robbery gone wrong might still have been a logical theory. But the back door *is* all the way at the back, and the stairs to the basement are behind the checkout counter, right where he was standing, and people were running toward the store.

"So Mike was left assuming Angela let someone in, which meant she was shot by someone she knew. The logical suspect was the husband, Paul. But Paul had a bone-dry alibi—which would hold only until Mike figured out the business with the screws. Paul was sure Mike would figure it out and come to arrest him. And he *deserved* to be arrested, he'd murdered the one woman he'd loved in all his life. His solution to his dilemma was to take his own life and frame someone he hated for both deaths."

"But the murder weapon disappeared—" began Martha.

"It's been found," said Jill. "But let her tell the story in her own way."

Betsy said, "Now to Paul, the real cause of Angela's murder was her adultery with the man who'd made a fool of him, the man who had stolen the love of his life: Foster Johns.

"Another obsessed man might have simply gone over and shot Foster before going home to shoot himself. But Paul was different. Once before, he'd caught a man kissing his wife. Just a consoling kiss, on the occasion of his mother-in-law's funeral. But Paul couldn't handle even that slight threat to his possessive pride. And while this perhaps wasn't a killing offense, the man needed to be taught a lesson."

"God knows what he did to Angela for it," remarked Foster, speaking for the first time.

"Yes," said Betsy, and there was a small, dark pause. Then she continued, "Paul began telling the man lies about his father's offer to bring the man and his brother into his business. He told the father lies, he told the brothers lies, egging each on. When the quarrels started, he suggested to the father and brother what to say in explanation, and then told the man what lies of explanation would be told. When the man was totally estranged from his brother and father, he began to play the same game with the man and his wife. Paul was murdered before the man and his wife divorced, and things started coming around right for him. The man talked to his wife and began to understand what a filthy trick had been played on him—and by whom. He told me he would never cease being grateful to the person who murdered Paul. The man, who was by nature a loyal person, watched his whole life wrench apart in a series of betrayals, and had actually begun to feel he was going insane."

"Who was the man?" asked Martha.

"It's not important, he had nothing to do with Paul's death."

"Does he live here in Excelsior?" asked Shelly.

"Not anymore."

Alice sighed and looked away. "Is there no end to the pain he caused?" she murmured.

Martha said, "Is there anything we can do to help?"

"I don't think so," said Betsy.

Shelly said, "Go on, Betsy, tell us the rest."

"There are four things about Paul that helped me figure this out. First, he had an unusual capacity for pain. Gretchen Tallman stomped hard on his instep when he put unwelcome hands on her, and it didn't deter him, the way it would any normally-wired man. And back when he was in middle school, he broke his arm and detoured from the nurse's office to frighten his teacher by waving the injury under her nose."

"Why would he do that?" asked Shelly.

"For the pleasure of seeing her shocked face. He knew the arm looked horrible, but it didn't hurt enough to make him hurry to get it taken care of."

"Ick," said Shelly.

"Second," continued Betsy, "he was very fond of true crime stories. Third, he loved cruel practical jokes. And fourth, he was clever at laying the blame for his misdoings at the feet of others."

Jill said, "The first explains how he came to be so beat up, right? Most people couldn't endure hurting themselves enough to cause bruises, at least after the first one."

"But he was shot more than once," Martha pointed out. "I understand being shot is extraordinarily painful."

"He was very angry," said Betsy, "very determined."

"Okay, what's the true crime angle?" asked Alice.

Betsy said, with an air of confession, "I read a lot of true crime stories myself when I was in high school, and I don't think I've ever lost my taste for them."

"So I guess I'm not the only person here who loves the forensics shows on the Learning Channel," said Martha.

"Hush," said Godwin. "She's getting to the good part now, I bet."

Betsy continued, "Last night I went out to dinner with Morrie and somehow we got to talking about a very old-fashioned prank involving a wallet and a length of button thread. And when I went to bed, I kept dreaming of a wallet that jumped out of my hands whenever I tried to pick it up. And that finally reminded me of one of those old true crime stories. There was a man who was determined to commit suicide, but he'd recently taken out a large life insurance policy that had a suicide clause. So he bought a long and thick elastic band and fastened one end up a chimney and the other end to his gun. After he shot himself, the gun was pulled from his hand up the chimney. It wasn't until the house was torn down years later that the gun was found, and the truth discovered."

Godwin said, "Is that what Paul did?"

Betsy nodded. "He used a bungee cord. The gun broke a chunk of brick off the hearth as it rushed by on its way up the chimney. The fireplace had been converted to gas, but there was still enough heat to eventually rot the cord. But the gun fell onto a ledge. Morrie found it there a few hours ago. The police are satisfied with my explanation, and will mark Angela's and Paul's deaths as a murder-suicide and close the case."

Foster said, very quietly, "Thank you, Ms. Devonshire." The thumb had come off to find the beer cool and calm.

Betsy said, "When Morrie crawled up inside that chimney, we all held our breath. He was there long enough that I thought he couldn't find anything. He came out covered in soot with a piece of crumbly bungee cord and a rusty old gun."

Jill said, "It was a .45 semi-automatic. The serial number on it matches the number on the gun registration made by Paul Schmitt."

Godwin jumped to his feet and spread his arms wide. "I have said it before, and I say it again, you are the very *cleverest* person I know! I wish we had a rare wine in the place, but we don't. May I bring you a cup of tea instead, my lady?" He executed an elaborate bow.

"Yes, please," said Betsy, suddenly aware her throat was parched.

Alice said, "We will have to do something extremely nice for you, Mr. Johns. We have to make sure everyone knows you are innocent of the murders of Angela and Paul Schmitt."

"How about we start right now," said Martha. "Alice, Shelly, let's go have a cup of coffee and a sandwich at the Waterfront Café. My treat. We can talk over what we just heard, nice and loud."

Jill yawned hugely and said she had to go home to bed.

Foster said he had work to do. He wrung Betsy's hand for a time longer than courtesy demanded, then left without another word.

Betsy, smiling, watched him go. Excelsior was a gossipy town, and Gossip Central was the Waterfront Café. Before the sun went down, the word would have spread all over town. Foster Johns's long nightmare was over.

Denise E. Williams

Fabric: *Aida*, Fiddler Lt, or Antique White

Design Count: 43w x 92h

Design Size: 3.1 x 6.6 in, 14 Count

Key: ✖ DMC 321

  ◓ DMC 3859

  ☐ DMC 3858

  ● DMC 3031

Stitch the spider's web using DMC 3031. For a glitzier web effect, I used one strand of DMC 5283 metallic in place of one of the strands of DMC 3031.